AS LONG AS I CLING

A PROMISES OF GOD NOVEL

KIM CASH TATE

AS LONG AS I CLING

A Promises of God Novel

Kim Cash Tate

Cover Design: Jenny Zemanek at Seedlings Design Studio

Scripture quotations are taken from the NEW AMERICAN STANDARD BIBLE ®, Copyright © 1960, 1962, 1963,

1968, 1971, 1972, 1973, 1975, 1977, 1995 by The Lockman Foundation. Used by permission. (www.Lockman.org)

Tate, Kimberly Cash.

As Long As I Cling / Kim Cash Tate.

ISBN 978-1-946336-05-7

1. African American women—Fiction. 2. Christian fiction.

ALSO BY KIM CASH TATE

You shall follow the LORD your God and fear Him; and you shall keep His commandments, listen to His voice, serve Him, and cling to Him.

DEUTERONOMY 13:4

My soul clings to You;
Your right hand upholds me.

PSALM 63:8

In Your presence is fullness of joy;
In Your right hand there are pleasures forever.

PSALM 16:11

DEDICATION

To My *Promises* Fam,

This special deluxe volume is dedicated to you. Thank you for patiently awaiting this next book in the series. I didn't plan to take this long. I started writing this book the same month I released *When I'm Tempted*. But two months later, the Lord flipped my plans and took me down an unexpected path to creating and writing a web series (*Cling The Series*) and—even more unexpected—becoming a singer/songwriter. I know. Who would've thought? Only God.

Throughout that journey, I'd try to work on this manuscript, but one thing I've always known—if the grace isn't there, I can't write. The Lord reminds me time and again, especially at my laptop, that apart from Him I can do nothing (John 15:5). I said, *But Lord, I'm in the middle of a series. I can't just leave my readers hanging.* Sigh.

I kept praying and waiting and during the quarantine of 2020 He poured out grace. I pray my way through every book, always surprised by the way the story unfolds. This time, I was also surprised by how lengthy the book was getting. Still, I was moved to take my time and tell the story without regard to artificial word limits. When I got to the end, I couldn't believe it was double the normal word count!

And I had to thank God. He knew my heart's desire, that I wanted to get you this book long before now—and He made it two in one!

I pray the Lord meets you in these pages. Praying His richest blessings upon you as you cling to Him.

With Love,
Kim

DOWNLOAD OR STREAM THE "PROMISES" THEME SONG!

Watch the lyric video at YouTube.com/kimcashtate

DOWNLOAD OR STREAM "AS LONG AS I CLING"

Watch the lyric video at YouTube.com/kimcashtate

CHAPTER 1

F̶reshman Year

      Jillian waved her hand, beaming as her sister made her way across the crowded Roy Rogers cafeteria in the Student Union. In dark slacks and a cobalt blue sweater, hair framing her face and dusting her shoulders, flawless makeup on flawless skin, Treva could just as well have been gliding down a runway.

Jillian got out of the booth and hugged her big sister when she approached. "Heyyy, I've missed you."

The irritation showed in Treva's brow. "Jill, why are we meeting in Roy's?" She glanced around at students congregating at tables, her tone hushed despite the noisy chatter.

"What do you mean?" Jillian got back in the wooden booth. "What's wrong with Roy's?"

"The greasy food, for one," Treva said, still standing. "I prefer What's Your Beef but I don't have time to order from a menu. How about the sandwich shop downstairs?"

"I need to stay here," Jillian said. "You only had a few minutes, so I set up a writing tutorial right after. He's meeting me here." She took money from the front pocket of her backpack. "I was waiting to see what you wanted. I can go stand in line."

"I'll just grab a sandwich downstairs on the way out." Treva moved into the booth, wiping the table with a napkin before placing her bag there.

"Okay," Jillian said. "I'll get something after you leave."

"I love your hair like that," Treva said, taking her in now.

"This?" Jillian fluffed sandy-colored ringlets that fell past her shoulders. "It's just my lazy wash and go."

Treva shook her head. "You literally get out of bed, shower, throw on jeans and a sweatshirt you probably wore the day before, skip the makeup—and you're drop-dead gorgeous. It's so ridiculous."

"And who was the one turning heads just now?" Jillian said. "You're always stunning."

"Yeah, okay."

"I can't wait for the day when you get Mama's junk out of your head and start seeing yourself as you really are."

"You sound like Hezekiah," Treva said. "That's what he's been telling me."

"Uh, no, Hezekiah sounds like me," Jillian said. "I've been telling you that for years."

"True," Treva said. "But you're my little sister, so it didn't count."

"So how are you?" Jillian leaned in with a smile. "What have you been up to? And how do we stay on the same campus and never see each other?"

"Because you're in freshman world, and it's crunch time for me," Treva said. "My transcript needs to be impeccable. I'm also studying to take the LSATs again."

"Why?" Jillian said. "Didn't you get a great score the first time?"

"Not great enough," Treva said. "I need to be perfectly positioned to get into a top law school. Lots of stress right now." She glanced to her right, distracted by the chatter. "That's what's keeping me so busy."

"Mm-hm. Hezekiah has nothing to do with it?"

Treva allowed a faint smile. "Maybe a little. But I'm keeping a level head. I doubt anything will come of it."

"I'll hope *for* you then," Jillian said. "From what I could tell the couple of times I've seen him, Hezekiah's a great guy. I'm looking forward to being home for Christmas break so I can see more of you, and maybe him too since he's from around here."

"I'm hoping this is the last time I ever have to go back home," Treva said. "I should be in my own apartment for law school next year."

"Or married to Hezekiah." Jillian waggled her eyebrows.

"Since when did you start embracing fairytales?"

"I embrace facts, unlike some people."

Treva's gaze fell for a moment. "Hezekiah wants our families to meet over the break—a challenge under any circumstances, since his family isn't Mother's 'style' as far as status and all that. But also, Hezekiah and his family are churchgoers."

"I don't think that would be a problem," Jillian said. "We were never churchgoers, but Mama had friends who were."

"But it sounds like his mom and dad are serious Christians," Treva said. "Hezekiah said he shouldn't even be dating me. I think he strayed from his faith a little when he went to college. He says he's praying for me."

"Praying for what?" Jillian said.

Treva shrugged. "Something about seeing myself like God sees me, and to believe like he does."

"I don't know," Jillian said. "*That* could be a problem. Do you think he'll try to force his beliefs on you?"

"Do you think he even could?" Treva said. "He knows I'm my own person."

"I just hope it doesn't become an issue down the road."

"If we even get down the road." Treva checked her watch. "I'd better go. I want to catch my professor before class to see what I can do to increase my average."

"Don't kill yourself, Treva," Jillian said. "You don't have to prove anything to Mama."

"I'm doing this for me," Treva said. "But you know I won't hear the end of it if I don't get into the right schools."

"Once again," Jillian said. "Mama's junk. Who cares—"

"Oh, good, I thought I was late."

Jillian looked behind her. "You are. Always," she said. "Treva, this is Tommy Porter. Tommy, my sister Treva."

Treva extended her hand. "Good to meet you, Tommy."

Tommy shook it. "Good to meet you too."

"Tommy's the one I've been tutoring," Jillian said.

"This girl can write," Tommy said, clad in jeans and a sweatshirt himself. "I just need a fraction of it to rub off."

"Hey, Tommy, come here real quick," a guy called from another table.

Tommy went to see what it was about, and Treva looked at Jillian. "Tutoring, huh?"

"What do you mean?" Jillian said.

"He's really cute, Jill," Treva said. "You don't have to tell me it's tutoring if it's something more."

"And if it's something more, why wouldn't I tell you?"

Jillian took a glance back at him to see what Treva saw. No doubt he was cute. About six-one, average built, his chestnut skin and easy smile had been the first things she'd noticed about him. Something about his eyes too, and the thick brows. But for whatever reason, Jillian never focused on his looks.

Tommy returned and Treva moved out of the booth.

"I'll leave you two to it." Treva shouldered her bag. "Oh, Jill, can I stop by this evening and get that Gucci bag Mother gave you? I need a new look for an event this weekend, and I know you don't use it."

Jillian nodded. "I'll be in my room after six."

"LaPlata, fifth floor, right?" Treva said.

"Really?" Jillian said. "I lived in LaPlata all of two weeks and moved to Elkton over two months ago. Just call when you get there. I'll bring it to the lobby."

"Perfect," Treva said, starting off.

"Is she a model or something?" Tommy dropped his backpack in the booth. "Your sister is beautiful."

"I can't wait to tell her you said that."

Tommy sat opposite her, the easy smile on his face. "So what's new, Jilli-Jill?"

"Every time you say that, I think of Treva," Jillian said. "She called me 'Jilli' growing up. My mom hated it."

"Why?"

"It wasn't proper enough. She would say, 'We named her *Jill-i-an*.'"

Tommy donned a look of importance. "So should I call you *Jill-i-an*?"

"Nope," Jillian said. "Not unless you want to."

"Does anybody else call you 'Jilli-Jill'?"

"No one on earth."

"Then that's what I'm calling you." Tommy took out a binder. "Did you eat yet?"

"Heyyy, Tommy." A young woman smiled at him as she walked by with her friend.

"What's up, Debbie?" Tommy said.

Jillian looked at him. "How is it that every time we meet, two or three women need to get your attention? This despite the fact that you have an actual girlfriend."

"Oh, it's nothing," Tommy said. "Just . . . situations."

"Situations?"

"I'd try to explain if I wasn't starving," Tommy said. "Do I have time to go grab something?"

"I'm hungry too," Jillian said. "If you order for us both, I'll watch our things." She handed him a bill. "Here you go."

"I got it," Tommy said. "Cheeseburger, small Coke?"

"Yeah, but you don't have to pay for me," Jillian said.

"You help me with my writing every week, no charge," Tommy said. "Let me do *something* for you."

Jillian watched as Tommy stopped at about four tables before he made it to the serving line. First semester freshman and he seemed to know everybody.

Moments later he returned, sliding the tray in the middle of the table, steam coming off the piping hot chicken.

"That smells really good," Jillian said.

"You say that all the time." Tommy tore into his straw. "Take a piece."

"I would feel too weird," Jillian said. "My mom gave lectures as to why we needed to avoid fried foods. Only baking, roasting, and grilling in our house."

Tommy sipped his soda. "You're not saying you've *never* had fried foods, are you?"

"I'm sure I have," Jillian said. "I just can't remember."

"And you haven't been wilding out in the dining hall?" Tommy said. "I woulda been eating fried chicken, fried eggs, fried hot dogs, fried okra—"

"Fried okra?" Jillian said.

"I hate okra, but if I were you, I would eat it just because it's fried," Tommy said. "Over there talking 'bout it smells good. You better eat some of this chicken. Here"—he tore off part of the wing and gave it to her—"live a little."

Jillian held it, the aroma enticing her even more. She brought it closer and took a bite.

"Look at you, living on the edge." Tommy gave her a hand-clap. "How is it?"

Jillian took another bite. "So good." She finished it and placed the bone on a napkin.

Tommy smiled at her. "Want some more?"

Jillian unwrapped her burger. "I would get addicted to that. I'm already fighting the 'freshman fifteen.' How do you stay in shape eating that all the time?"

"If you're fighting the 'freshman fifteen,'" Tommy said, "you must've been a toothpick when you started." He tore white meat from the breast. "And I don't eat this *all* the time. But I play ball at the gym."

Jillian got her red pen from her backpack. "So what are we looking at today?"

"Not the red pen," Tommy said. "I'm just saying—blue and black are kinder."

"They don't show up as well," Jillian said. "You need to be able to see my marks."

"It feels like life is all wrong when I see red torture marks every-where," Tommy said. "Okay, so"—he wiped his hands with a napkin and took his essay from the binder—"I spent the most time ever on this so if you tell me—"

A young woman moved into the booth next to him with a tray of food.

Tommy stared at her as she sprinkled salt on her fries. "Candice, what are you doing?"

"Eating my lunch." Candice glanced at his tray. "Same thing you're doing."

"I'm not just eating lunch," Tommy said. "I'm here for tutoring—you remember Jill, right?"

"Mm-hm." Candice looked at Jillian. "Hey."

"How are you, Candice?" Jillian ate some of her burger.

"Doing really well."

"Candice, you can't be doing stuff like this." Tommy spoke in a low tone, his head next to hers.

"Stuff like what? Lunch with my boyfriend—who I've been with since high school?" Candice gave Jillian a look. "We're in here at the same time, and I can't sit with you?"

"Slide out so we can talk." Tommy waited as she moved out of the booth then led her a few feet away.

Jillian focused on eating her food until they returned moments later.

Candice picked up her tray. "I'll see you this evening." She kissed him then joined a table full of women across the cafeteria, all of whom were staring at Jillian.

Tommy heaved a sigh as he sat down. "Sorry. She's jealous of anyone I'm talking to. You especially."

"Why?" Jillian said.

"She hates that we meet for tutorials *and* we've got two classes together." Tommy ate more of his breast. "She's always saying, 'I know you think she's pretty.' So last time, I said, '*Yeah*, she *is* pretty. She can only help me if she's butt ugly?'"

"Probably not the right response, Tommy."

"Whatever, man." Tommy ate some fries. "This is why I've got situations, because that's probably not lasting much longer. Anyway, *this essay . . ."* He pushed it toward her. "We got this wide open assignment in my sociology class to write about how a cultural phenomenon has impacted and shaped us. I *could not wait* to dive into it."

"I've never seen you this excited about a paper," Jillian said. "What did you write about?"

A smile spread across Tommy's face. "Music. Spent two whole evenings doing research. As in—listening to my favorite songs and thinking about how I'd been impacted and shaped by them."

"Ooh, I would get excited about that too," Jillian said. "I can't imagine an assignment where I *have* to listen to my favorite songs."

Tommy gave her a wary look. "What kind of favorite songs *you* got? For somebody who's never had soul food, I'm thinking you're about to shout out some country music."

"I said I never had *fried* food."

"So your momma cooked soul food with baked chicken or ribs or something?"

"No. She didn't cook soul food either, but—"

"Okay, stop." Tommy held up a hand, chuckling hard. "I'm sorry. I've just never in my life . . . No fried food. No . . ." He was looking at her, incredulous. "No soul food?—*what does that even mean?* Have you never had mac-n-cheese? Collard greens? A piece of corn bread?" He spoke through the chuckles. "Girl, you're a sociological specimen all by yourself."

"I can't believe you're laughing at me," Jillian said.

"I'm sorry, I'm trying to . . . Wait—what about Kool-Aid?" Tommy lost it when she shook her head no. "Don't be mad," he said, trying to contain himself. "I'm not laughing *at* you."

"You *are* laughing at me." Jillian chuckled herself. "If you think *that's* surprising, I could keep you entertained for hours with stories about my upbringing." She picked up her burger. "But you have to let me redeem myself by sharing my favorite songs."

"I don't know what you might say. I think I need to brace myself." A soft chuckle eked out still. "Answer this first, since you're from here—what was your favorite radio station growing up? I just need some kind of clue."

"WKYS during the day," Jillian said. "WHUR Quiet Storm in the evening."

"Okay, okay," Tommy said, nodding. "Since you said Quiet Storm, let's make it fun. If you had to pick your top five favorite slow jams—just slow jams—what would you pick?"

"That's way too hard," Jillian said. "Only slow jams? Top five? I need to really think about that." She sipped her Coke. "You've been on this for a couple nights now. You go first."

"I didn't think through my top five slow jams, though," Tommy said. "It's definitely hard. I've got current faves, all-time faves . . ."

"You're the one who came up with this," Jillian said. "So go."

"Other than my number one, these are in no particular order," Tommy said. "But I should've said top ten because five through seven are basically interchangeable—"

"Go."

"Okay, my clear number one—'Voyage to Atlantis.'"

"Ohhhh, I can't believe you said that." Jillian could hear it in her head. "Definitely in my top five."

"Come onnnn," Tommy said. "Don't play with me."

"Seriously," Jillian said. "It came to mind right away. The first few seconds with that electric piano and electric guitar, and the way the drums come in . . . *Crazy*. And that's before you even get to Ronnie's voice."

"Done." Tommy high-fived her. "You redeemed yourself. I don't care if you never eat another chicken wing. You are all right with me."

Jillian shook her head at him. "What's your next fave?"

"Again, no order," Tommy said. "I'd probably have to say 'A House Is Not a Home' for classic, slow jam brilliance."

"Oh, most definitely," Jillian said. "That's my number one."

Tommy cocked his head at her. "You would put it ahead of 'Voyage'?"

"Luther?" Jillian said. "Absolutely. I'd probably put 'If This World Were Mine' ahead of it too, and 'Voyage' at number three. I could listen to Luther and Cheryl Lynn on repeat all day."

"See, now we got a problem," Tommy said. "I'll give Luther his props, but he ain't got nothing on Ronnie. And from a musicality standpoint, 'Voyage' blows both those Luther songs out the water. It's like *miles* apart."

"Excuse me," Jillian said. "Did you ask about *my* favorites? Or did you just want to tell me what they *should* be?"

"Sorry, that shook me," Tommy said. "So for my last three—I'm not as attached to these—I'd say 'Zoom,' 'Love's Train,' and 'Love Ballad.'"

"I know exactly what I'm doing this evening," Jillian said. "Studying to all these songs. And I've got the cassettes. I *love* the ones you just named. I don't know if they're in my top five, but they're close." She thought a moment. "I'd probably say 'Am I Dreaming' and then a toss-up between 'Stay' and 'Very Special.'"

"Whaat?" Tommy said, staring at her. "Chaka and Debra Laws?"

"You're objecting again?"

"No, I just wouldn't have expected it," Tommy said. "Those are my jams."

Jillian checked her watch. "We're about to be late for class, and we haven't even gotten to the paper. Knowing you, it's due tomorrow."

"I started this one early," Tommy said. "Not due for two more days."

"I'll look at it tonight then," Jillian said, tucking it into her bag, "and we can go over it tomorrow."

"Same time?" Tommy put his binder in his backpack.

"That works," Jillian said, moving out of the booth.

Tommy got up and threw away their trash. "And while you're taking your red pen to my paper"—he shouldered his backpack as they walked out—"I need you to listen to 'Voyage to Atlantis' and make the proper adjustment to your top five."

"I see you're gonna keep harassing me about it." Jillian pushed the door and walked outside. "I said it's my number *three*. What if I didn't like the song at all?"

"Oh"—Tommy gave her a side-eye—"I would've had to fire you."

"You're not paying me."

"I might need to start," Tommy said. "I feel like you're underprivileged with your non-Kool-Aid drinking, no soul-food-having self."

Jillian took the crosswalk with him and started the path to South Hill. "Don't be surprised if you see more red than usual on your paper tomorrow."

"You would do that?" Tommy said. "Pay me back with additional torture marks?"

"You kill me calling them torture marks." Jillian looked at him. "If it's torture, why do you keep coming back for more?"

"Good question." Tommy walked in silence a ways. "I don't know. If I'm honest, you just . . . make me better."

CHAPTER 2

January
Minutes till airtime Tommy Porter took his spot at the KTVI anchor desk, ready to run down the latest in St. Louis's entertainment news. A breaking story from overseas had producers scrambling, while Tommy waited to see if he'd have news to break himself. With time running out, he checked his phone once more—and saw a text from his sister Adrienne.

Just saw this on fb. Thought you'd want to know.

She'd attached a picture—Allison and her newborn. He exhaled a little. *She had the baby.* Tommy stared at the picture a moment, Allison looking into the eyes of a baby wrapped in a blue blanket. It was what he'd envisioned when they'd gotten married less than two years ago. Except, he thought she'd be holding *their* baby.

"Tommy, standby," a producer said. "We're going with this breaking story first."

The commercial break wound down and the camera crew moved into place, focusing on Rita Farley, the early evening news anchor.

Tommy's eyes went to the picture again, to the woman he'd vowed to be with for the rest of his life. How could he have gotten it so wrong?

A second text came from Adrienne. **I debated whether to send this one . . .**

Tommy scrolled to the new picture. Same scene except a guy stood with Allison, holding the baby. Was he the father? Looked like the two of them—

His phone vibrated with a call—Alonzo. Tommy slipped out of his chair and moved quietly off the set to hear the news he'd been awaiting.

"I'm hoping it's a go," Tommy said.

"Not the vision I had," Alonzo said, "but it's a go."

"So the love story?" Tommy said.

"Right," Alonzo said. "The new investor pushed for it, thinking the film could be marketed better that way. Shooting starts next month."

"Seriously?"

"Also, we knew Shane would have a conflict when we put everything on hold in the fall," Alonzo said. "But God *keeps* showing up. I can tell you now that Mariah Pendleton's on board as director."

"I can't believe that," Tommy said. "She's amazing."

"I'll hit you later, though," Alonzo said. "About to head into another meeting."

"So you know I'm at the station, about to go on-air," Tommy said.

"Go for it," Alonzo said. "It'll be on the blogs by tonight anyway."

Tommy moved back into place and tucked his phone away, moments later getting the cue that they were ready to roll.

"It's Friday," Rita said, "and that means Tommy Porter from the *St. Louis Post Dispatch* is here to tell us about the hot acts heading our way and other happenings in the city." She turned to him. "Good to see you, Tommy. I hear we've got a big concert coming."

"Good to see you too, Rita. And yes"—Tommy turned to the camera—"Justin Timberlake just added St. Louis to his national tour—he'll be here December 11th at the Scottrade Center. Also just announced—John Legend will be the headliner at Variety's Dinner With the Stars. A different move for them this year, featuring someone younger and more relevant. That's April 28th at the Peabody Opera House." He looked at Rita. "That was the big entertainment news until moments ago. I just received word that the movie about local pastor Lance Alexander will begin filming here next month."

"This is indeed big news," Rita said. "The last report was that much of the funding had fallen through. So next month, Hollywood is coming to St. Louis?"

Tommy nodded. "And we know that much of the excitement around this movie had to do with the story of Lance and Kendra—"

"The 'Amazing Love' story," Rita said. "That's what it was dubbed at the time."

"Exactly," Tommy said. "People were hoping the movie would spotlight that part of Lance's story. Turns out, the love story *is* the movie now, so excitement will only increase."

"And as usual," Rita said, "we anticipate a compelling performance by Academy Award winner Alonzo Coles."

"Also big—Mariah Pendleton is directing," Tommy said. "And keep an eye on relative newcomer Brooke Shelley, who's been cast in the role of Kendra Alexander. You can be sure we'll be following this story as cast and crew descend on St. Louis." Tommy turned to a different camera. "But we don't want you to miss what's happening this weekend, plus summer concert dates are already in full swing . . ."

Tommy left the news studio and headed to his car, his phone vibrating. He looked at it and answered. "Jilli-Jill, what's good?"

"Hey, Big Time," Jillian said. "That's what the kids just called you."

"You've got to be kidding." Tommy clicked the remote to his Lexus.

"They think it's cool what you do," Jillian said. "David wants to know if he can shadow you sometime. He's thinking about journalism as a career."

"Tell him no problem," Tommy said.

"I told him he has to ask you himself," Jillian said. "I'm calling because we've been talking about dinner the past two weeks but we've both been busy. I thought today might be a good day."

"Why?" Tommy threw his gym bag into the trunk.

"Because the kids have plans tonight," Jillian said, "and I don't know, just saw you on the news and thought about it."

"Try again."

"Stop acting like you know me."

Tommy got into the car and started it, waiting.

"Fine," Jillian said. "I was worried about you. Faith told me Allison had the baby."

"I'm not going to dinner," Tommy said, "to hear you ask, 'Are you *sure* you're all right?' fifty times."

"But are you free for dinner?" Jillian said.

"Yup."

"Just come get me then," Jillian said. "I'll only ask once if you're all right."

"You're ready right now?" Tommy said.

"I'll be ready when you get here."

"'Ready' doesn't mean dressed but 'I need to do my makeup real quick.'"

"That only happened one time," Jillian said.

"And make sure you do your hair."

"Boy, bye."

Tommy held his phone a moment then went to his sister's text messages, taking in the pictures once more. Allison looked happy. But then, he'd thought so on their wedding day. He'd thought many things back then. Many happy, hopeful things.

He pressed delete on the pictures.

Tommy held the door for Jillian as they walked into Cantina Laredo, a Mexican restaurant in downtown Clayton.

The hostess smiled at them. "Good evening, you two, and you're in luck." She grabbed two menus. "A family just vacated your booth."

Jillian looked at Tommy. "Do we come here that often?"

"I can't get you to go anywhere else," Tommy said.

The hostess escorted them to the booth and they slid in, opposite sides.

"So finish telling me about your car," Tommy said.

"I don't know what's going on." Jillian shrugged off her coat, her hair falling to just above her shoulders. "The starter's giving me problems and yesterday it cut off at a red light."

"Did you get a winter maintenance check?" Tommy said.

"It's hard enough trying to make time for doctor and dentist appointments for everybody now that I'm working," Jillian said.

"When was the last time you had the oil changed?"

Jillian thought a moment. "No idea."

Tommy shook his head. "Make an appointment for next week, early morning. I'll drop you off at work and take it in."

"You would do that?" Jillian said.

"You know I got you."

"Hey, guys, good to see you this evening." The server approached with a smile. "I saw you over here, so I brought water with lemon for you"—she set a glass in front of Jillian—"and one without for you." She took more items from a tray. "And tortilla chips with the hot and mild salsa."

"Thank you, Emily," Jillian said. "This is why I come back"—she gave Tommy a glance—"because you're always so on it."

"My pleasure," Emily said. "Do you want a little time or are you ready to order?"

Tommy looked at Jillian. "You're going with the usual?"

Jillian nodded. "Combo fajitas, but if you could put the guacamole in a separate container—"

"And give it to him," Emily said. "Gotcha. And you want the corn tortillas, extra cheese, and lettuce."

"Perfect," Jillian said. "Thanks."

"And I'll take the chicken fajitas," Tommy said.

"And you want your pico on the side to give to her." Emily wrote it down. "And flour tortillas and extra sour cream."

"You got it," Tommy said. "Thank you."

Emily collected their menus and stopped at another table.

Jillian took a chip and dunked it in the mild. "So your latest movie review . . ."

Tommy crunched into his. "I can tell—you're about to rip it."

"Why would I rip it?" Jillian said. "You're a gifted writer." She ate the chip and dunked another. "But you said you wanted me to see where you could improve."

"And you've been giving good tips," Tommy said. "I was just hoping you'd covered everything and every piece was perfect now." He chuckled a little. "What'd you see?"

"Your opening analogy," Jillian said. "You actually referred to the lead actor as being 'busy as a bee' lately." She spread her hands as if to say—really? "I'm guessing you were under deadline, rushing to get it done, and wrote the first thing that came to mind. I've seen you do that more than once."

"Do you know how long it takes to come up with a pithy analogy?" Tommy said.

"You didn't even need an analogy," Jillian said. "But if you want to use one, take the time to shoot for excellence. You've got a column that gets great traffic in the city and online. There are no throwaways. Dig deeper until you get an analogy that sings. Do you pray over your pieces?"

Tommy crunched into another chip. "Hate to admit it, but . . . not really."

"Oh, you're about to go to a whole new level then," Jillian said. "Ask God to help you, Tommy. Everything you write. 'Lord, I need the perfect analogy right here. Show me what that is.'"

Tommy gave a slow nod. "All these years later, and you're still helping me step up my writing game."

"I'm just reminding you who can *really* help you," Jillian said. "The One who's given you the grace to write."

Tommy focused on Jillian, thoughts bubbling in his heart.

"What?" Jillian said.

He shook his head. "Nothing."

"Here we go," Emily said, "sizzling hot, so don't touch." She set their entrees before them along with the fixings.

"Looks delicious, thank you," Jillian said.

"I'll be back to check on you guys shortly."

Tommy reached across and took Jillian's hand. "Bless our food, Lord, we thank You for it. And Lord, I just want to thank You for friendship." He paused a moment. "For *this* friendship that has endured—and I can't even believe I used that word because You know that's Jill's, not mine. But I can't think of a better one. Because of Your grace, mercy, and everything else—it has *endured*."

"Thank You, Lord," Jillian murmured.

Tommy kept his head bowed, his mind filling with more. But he said simply—"in Jesus' name, amen."

"Amen," Jillian said. "So." She got a warm tortilla from the covered dish. "How are you?"

"I was waiting for it." Tommy added chicken to his. "I'm good."

Jillian gave him a look.

"For real. I'm good." He shrugged lightly. "I can't say it *felt* good to see my ex-wife with her baby and boyfriend or whoever."

"'I can't say it felt good,'" Jillian repeated. "Maybe use two words instead of six—'it hurt.'"

"Now you're editing my conversation?" Tommy took a piece of her steak.

"I'm just saying—be real with yourself," Jillian said. "And I keep telling you to order the combo."

"I only want a little bit of steak," Tommy said. "And I'm sticking with my six words. I can't say it felt good, but it didn't *hurt* either." He picked up the fajita. "I remember what the hurt felt like. Thank God I'm not there anymore." He took a bite.

"It may not hurt as much, but I don't think you can say you're not there anymore." Jillian took a bite of hers as well.

"It's been about a year since she left," Tommy said. "I'm supposed to act like God can't heal?"

"Okay," Jillian said. "If you're not there, where are you?"

Tommy thought a moment. "Just . . . adjusting. To a new season, a new outlook."

"The 'no relationship' outlook."

"It's not *no* relationship." Tommy sipped his water. "Friends and family are relationships."

"You know what I mean," Jillian said. "No *relationship*."

"Yeah, nah, I'm done," Tommy said, "despite what everyone wants to tell me. Suddenly it's wrong to value being single. My Bible says differently."

"Is it that you value being single," Jillian said, "or that you've made a sweeping life decision from a place of pain?"

"Fair to say it's both," Tommy said. "Because of the pain, I can better see the value in singleness."

"For the rest of your life."

"Didn't you say you couldn't see yourself marrying again? How is that any different?" Tommy scooped up some refried beans.

"I said that months ago," Jillian said. "And I said I couldn't see it. I didn't make grand pronouncements of 'never.' We have to leave room for God to work. He might cause you to see what you couldn't see before."

"So where are you right now with all that?" Tommy said.

Jillian lowered her fork, thinking. "Next month will be a year since Cecil went to be with the Lord." She sank into her thoughts again. "The grief is still real. I don't know if or when I'll ever be ready to date, let alone marry." She paused. "But I'm going out for coffee Sunday afternoon."

The words hit Tommy's gut. "Who are you going for coffee with?"

Jillian stirred her Mexican rice. "Silas Keys."

"How did you and Silas connect?"

"I work at Living Water, Tommy," Jillian said, "and he's on the pastoral staff. So of course I see him during the week, and on Sundays obviously. And dinner at Lance and Treva's a couple times."

"And what?" Tommy said. "He let you know he was interested?"

"He's only been in town a few months," Jillian said. "I think he just wants to get to know people."

"I doubt he's asking 'people' on a date," Tommy said.

"It's not a date."

"It's a date."

"I specifically told him I wasn't ready to date," Jillian said. "And he's widowed himself, so he understood."

"Are you guys doing okay over here?" Emily said.

Jillian glanced at Tommy. "I think we're good. Well, maybe more water."

"Sure thing," Emily said, trotting off.

Tommy got another tortilla and filled it with chicken, adding cheese, lettuce, and a dollop of guacamole. He took a bite as Emily returned and refilled their water glasses.

Jillian looked at him once she'd walked away. "I meant to ask if you'll be at Zoe's birthday party tomorrow."

"I live there," Tommy said.

"It doesn't mean you'll be at the party."

"I'll be there."

"What's going on with you right now?" Jillian said.

He added more guac. "Nothing's going on with me."

"Tommy, I know you."

He drank some water, the ache palpable. "I just didn't know that's where you were."

"It's only coffee, Tommy, but I'm confused," Jillian said. "What difference does it make?"

His jaw tightened as he stared downward a moment. "You're right. None."

Tommy could feel Jillian's gaze resting on him. He returned it, looking into her hazel eyes, but only for a moment.

A moment was all he could bear.

CHAPTER 3

Faith Porter took a creamy chicken and rice casserole from the oven, setting it on a trivet as her phone rang. Either Reggie or Cinda, she guessed. She moved to the kitchen table to get it.

"Finally," Faith said. "I got the text updates, but I've been waiting to get some details."

"Sorry it took a while," Cinda said. "Once we got the green light, everything ramped up really fast. I'd get ready to call you, and my phone would ring again."

"You know I know how it is," Faith said, checking the casserole. "That's why I love working for you and Alonzo. You never know what the next moment will hold." She turned off the oven. "So first—it's super exciting that the movie is on again. But shooting next month? I know that means we've got a million things to do—*now*."

"The good thing is since we were supposed to start filming last November, a lot of the pre-production work is done," Cinda said. "So thank God for that. Some of the crew will start arriving in St. Louis next week, so one of the first things we need to do is secure accommodations."

"I'll check with the hotel we booked in the fall." Faith grabbed a notepad and pen and took notes. "Hopefully they've got enough rooms. I'll also call Steph. I know you want to put Mariah Pendleton and Brooke Shelley there."

"Yes, I'm so hoping Steph's not booked," Cinda said. "Let's reserve the third room too, if possible, for whoever's playing Kendra's brother, Trey."

"I thought you wanted the B and B for core cast plus the director," Faith said. "Trey's role is minor."

"Not anymore," Cinda said. "Now that the focus is Lance and Kendra, they're beefing up Trey's role and casting someone with a higher profile to play him."

"Oh, wow, okay," Faith said. "When are you and Alonzo getting back from LA?"

"Sunday or Monday," Cinda said. "So here's a list of things that really need to get done ASAP . . ."

Faith heard the front door open and close. "Hey, Reggie just got home. Can you email or text it to me? Or I can call you back?"

"I guess I did tell you about 'what's first,' didn't I?" Cinda said.

Reggie walked in and did a double take.

"Yes, ma'am, you did," Faith said. "And Reggie loves it."

"I'll email it," Cinda said. "Then call me back later to talk about it."

"Will do," Faith said.

She clicked off and looked at Reggie. "That was Cinda. Can you believe filming starts next month and—"

"Cinda who?" Reggie pulled Faith to himself. "I don't even know what film you're talking about. Everything is cloudy right now except my wife in this—what is this?"

Faith glanced down at it. "Sort of a lingerie romper thing. I found a really good sale—"

Reggie kissed her and let it linger. "You lied to me."

"What did I lie about?"

"You said it wouldn't be like this when we got married—home cooked meal, you wearing something that drives me out of my mind."

"Well, it's not. Typically," Faith said. "I've only done it maybe three times."

Reggie held her. "Why tonight?"

"Tommy had dinner plans," Faith said, "Zoe's with Jesse, and I'm still a little awkward when it comes to feeling sexy, so I thought I'd practice."

"Whether you feel it or not, it's a fact, baby." Reggie kissed her neck. "You are *sexy*. But I ain't mad if you want to practice."

"I had heels on, but it felt too silly."

"I love that you're the same best friend who tells me exactly what's on your mind."

Faith kissed him. "And you're the same best friend who's patient with me. I know I've got a lot to learn as far as, you know . . . being spontaneous and initiating things."

"If you've got a lot to learn, I can't wait to see where we go from here," Reggie said. "Seriously, baby. I don't know what measuring stick you're using, but we are *good*." He glanced at the casserole. "I just need to know what I'm supposed to do. I see a delicious meal over there, but I've got this irresistible woman in my arms."

"That's why I made a casserole," Faith said. "Easy to warm up. After."

"That's all I needed to hear." Reggie took her hand and led her up the stairs. "And by the way, I think we need to get our own spot so you can 'practice' same time every evening."

The doorbell rang when they got to the top of the stairs.

"We're ignoring it," Reggie said, moving to their bedroom.

It sounded again.

"Might be Jesse and Zoe," Faith said.

"I thought he wasn't bringing Zoe back till tomorrow," Reggie said, "so we can get ready for the party. And he always lets you know when he's coming."

It rang a third time.

"You have to go see," Faith said.

Reggie sighed as he walked back down to open the door. Faith listened from the top of the stairs.

"Told you they were home—both cars are outside. Hey, Reg."

"Joy, what are you doing here?" Faith called.

"Sophie and I are headed to the movies," Joy said. "But we wanted to run an idea by you first."

"I just left you two a couple hours ago," Faith said. "And I have a phone."

"Just come down," Joy said. "What're you doing?"

Faith went to the room and covered up, then found her sister and cousin in the kitchen.

Joy eyed her as she drank some juice. "Why are you in a robe?"

"Why are you all done up just to go to the movies?" Faith noted her sister's hair was down, long and wavy, and she'd put on makeup. "Who are you meeting there?"

"I know you think you're our mom," Joy said. "But we've already answered questions from our actual moms."

"Baby, this is really good." Reggie held up a plate. "Only got a little, just to taste." He looked at Joy and Sophia. "I'm telling y'all—you need to get with this."

"We already ate," Joy said.

Faith tightened her robe. "So what's this idea that couldn't wait?"

"Sophie came up with it, after Mom told us they're gearing up to film the movie." Joy looked to her cousin to continue.

"So we think it would be awesome," Sophia said, "if we could intern on the set. Since we're homeschooling, we've got the perfect schedule."

"In theory," Faith said. "But both of you are always talking about how you're swamped with school work. Even if an internship were possible, I don't see how you'd have time."

"But this is a once-in-a-lifetime opportunity," Joy said. "Our own stepdad's got a movie being made about him. And we actually know the people making the movie. If we can only intern for a couple hours every afternoon or twice a week—whatever—it would be *dope*."

"I have to agree it would be pretty dope to get that kind of experience in high school," Reggie said.

"But that's just it," Faith said. "I doubt they'll be taking on interns. And if they did, the interns would be college students pursuing a career in film, not high schoolers."

"Can't you just ask Alonzo and Cinda?" Joy said. "If they say no—fine. But just being around a camera crew and seeing what they do would be everything for me."

"And I'd love to work in wardrobe with Cinda," Sophia said. "I'd literally just carry garment bags if that's what she needed, just to get a glimpse of what it's like."

Faith looked from one to the other. "If you're serious about wanting experience and being willing to help—and not just trying to hang out—I'll ask." She nodded to herself. "I do think it could be a good opportunity for you, and production only lasts a few weeks. If you have to grind it out between your studies and coming to set, it'd be worth it."

"Yes!" they said, high-fiving one another.

"Don't celebrate yet," Faith said. "I'll let you know what they say. And keep in mind you wouldn't get to choose the work you want to do. We're a small, independent production company. It's all hands-on-deck to do whatever."

"We are *so* down," Sophia said.

"Okay, we'd better go," Joy said, leading Sophia to the door.

Faith followed. "Hey." She hugged them at the door. "Be careful."

"What's that about?" Sophia said.

"I'm not trying to be 'mom'," Faith said. "But I love you both, and I won't apologize for looking out for you." She kept her voice low. "You've seen the wrong choices I made, and Courtenay was heart-broken sharing hers over Christmas. We told you—we're praying you learn from our experiences and don't test the boundaries with guys and sex."

"We're going to the movies," Joy said. "How did you jump to guys and sex?"

"I haven't forgotten our wedding weekend," Faith said. "You were flirting with Reggie's groomsmen and letting them think you were twenty-something. Who knows what else you're up to. I'm just saying —don't flirt with mischief. Now's the time to press in and walk out a real relationship with Jesus."

Joy and Sophia gave a vague nod as they glanced at one another and left. Faith found Reggie in the family room in front of the television watching ESPN.

"Sorry," Faith said. "I think Joy has a sensor when it comes to interrupting us."

"Not a problem," Reggie said.

Faith waited a moment, looking at him. "What are you doing?"

"I'm waiting to see this score."

"Really?"

Reggie glanced at her. "What?"

"I'll be upstairs when you're ready."

Faith dropped the robe at his feet and walked off.

"Oh, you know that wasn't right," Reggie said.

She quickened her steps as Reggie came after her, overtaking her on the stairs.

"I thought your football days were over." Her back pinned, Faith looked up at him. "You can't be tackling me like this."

Reggie kissed her and let it linger so long she thought she'd lose it —then he sat up. "So no tackling, you said?"

"You can't just stop like that."

"Why not?"

"Stop playing."

"That was sexy, what you did back there." Reggie nodded at her. "You're getting all kinds of practice tonight."

"And how is it you're still fully dressed?"

"Did you really just say that?"

"I said that."

Reggie leaned on an elbow. "I'm not sure I can handle *this* Mrs. Porter. I remember the one who said she was nervous and—where are you going?"

"To the room." Faith moved up the stairs. "You can join me when you're ready."

"I know you didn't—did you just drop that romper thing?"

Faith smiled as she walked into the bedroom, Reggie coming after her.

CHAPTER 4

Stephanie London reclined in her bathtub, water nice and warm, eyes closed as she thought about the morning and everything she had to do. Breakfast was the main thing, since the B and B currently had guests, four cousins spending a weekend away, enjoying the simplicity of long conversation, food, and an endless pot of coffee. They'd spent hours at it yesterday, moving from the dining room to a sitting room, to their guest rooms. The laughter had been endless as well. She'd get breakfast going and visit with them a bit, then—

She groaned and sat up, the sensation of a spasm moving across her belly. Leaning over now, she held herself and breathed in and out as it heightened to a strong cramp.

"Babe, check these shirts out." Lindell walked in, holding them up. "Cute, right? I thought we'd wear them to Zoe's party."

Stephanie looked over at him. "Babe, nothing looks cute . . ." She blew out a breath, her stomach tightening. ". . . when I'm in the middle of one of these stupid contractions."

"It started up again?" Lindell came closer. "That's the reason you took a bath, because it usually helps."

"It stopped for a little while," Stephanie said, "then started up again *in* the tub."

"I'll get you some tea," Lindell said, walking out. He turned. "The bath water's not too hot, is it?"

"No, Dr. London, not too hot." Stephanie breathed out. "Are you going to ask that every time I take a bath?"

"Can't help it," Lindell said. "I have to make sure you and the baby are in good health."

Stephanie nodded, breathing out again as the tightening started to subside. "And I'm thankful, babe. You take good care of us."

She rested her hands on her belly as Lindell closed the door. At thirty-two weeks, she'd had a mostly uneventful pregnancy, except for consistent nausea in the beginning. But now, Braxton Hicks contractions had shown up. Looked like they were working to be consistent too.

She smiled, feeling the baby kick. "Good morning, little one. You in there stretching, getting yourself ready to come out? Only a few more weeks to go."

Stephanie got out of the tub, toweled off, and put on her terry robe. She walked into the room as Lindell brought her tea. "Thank you, babe," she said, taking it from him. She sat on the edge of the bed. "Okay, show me those shirts again."

Lindell got the dark gray tees and lifted them up—one with "Mommy," the other, "Daddy."

"Those are really cute," Stephanie said. "I love the lettering. But babe, you don't think it's a little over the top? Do we really need 'Mommy' and 'Daddy' on our chests? I'm having a hard enough time trying to find cute maternity-wear."

"I just thought it would be fun to wear to a two-year-old's party," Lindell said. "Why not be over the top? We're having a baby. It's the happiest time in our lives."

Stephanie took a sip of tea. "Fine, babe. We'll wear the shirts."

"Why do you sound like that?" Lindell said.

"Nothing," Stephanie said.

"No, say it."

"It's just . . . that part about 'happiest time in our lives' might be over the top as well." Stephanie set her tea on the nightstand. "I just don't want us to gloss over the fact that things could be better."

Lindell sighed. "Do you enjoy dwelling on the negative? I think you *look* for issues in our marriage."

"I'm not looking for issues," Stephanie said. "They're just there."

"Like what, Steph?"

"There's no time to get into it." Stephanie got up to get dressed. "I need to get downstairs and make breakfast."

"Which is probably our number one issue," Lindell said. "We hardly ever get moments to talk because the B and B's got your attention from early morning till late at night."

"Wow." Stephanie turned to him. "The B and B is our number one problem?"

"I don't even see you at night," Lindell said. "You're dealing with guests, handling B and B matters on the computer, doing laundry . . . By the time you get upstairs, it's late and I'm asleep."

"And what would be the point of rushing upstairs?" Stephanie stepped into a pair of leggings. "It's not like we'll be having sex, so I'd just end up frustrated."

"That's your only reason for coming upstairs early?" Lindell said. "We can't just generally enjoy each other's company?"

"Of course," Stephanie said, slipping on a white top. "But shouldn't a love life come into play at some point?"

"That's not even a fair statement," Lindell said. "You wouldn't know because you're never up here."

"I know from the many nights I *have* come up here and all I hear is what a long day you had and how tired you are." Stephanie added a long, mocha-colored kimono over her top. "Honestly, it's a wonder I'm even pregnant." She paused. "And I'm not trying to argue, babe. It's just been on my mind because it'll only get worse when the baby's here."

"Well, since you only want to look at the downside," Lindell said, "I guess everything's about to get worse. Between the B and B and the baby taking your attention, I'll have to make an appointment to see you."

"So what are you saying?" Stephanie looked at him. "You think it's time to transition out of the B and B?"

"I didn't say that," Lindell said.

"I'm asking."

Lindell thought a moment. "It would probably make life a lot easier," he said. "But I know you love what you do here. It's a ministry to you."

"But we have two huge issues affecting our marriage, and the B and B is yours." Stephanie sighed. "I can't just ignore that." She sat on the bed again. "Maybe I need to talk to Mrs. Cartwright, give her a heads-up that we might make some changes with the baby coming. We never said we'd do this forever. And she'd need to start looking for another caretaker."

"Before you do all of that," Lindell said, "what if we just took some time to get away? Maybe that would help. Our last trip was Hawaii for Lance and Treva's wedding."

"Two years ago," Stephanie said. "And we've never been anywhere with just the two of us. Didn't even have a honeymoon."

"Yeah, and why was that?" Lindell said.

"Definitely don't need to go there," Stephanie said. "Forget I mentioned it."

"Let's do it then," Lindell said. "Let's plan a trip. And we would need to do it now, given where you are in your pregnancy."

"But filming's about to start," Stephanie said. "People will be arriving as early as next week. They've booked all three of our rooms for weeks."

"You just said we've got two huge problems in our marriage," Lindell said, "but you don't want to take the time to work on it? Once again, the B and B is more important to you?"

"That's not fair," Stephanie said. "You know I would love a getaway. The timing just stinks. Who would take care of the B and B and our guests?"

"It would only be for a few days," Lindell said. "There has to be somebody who would fill in for you."

"Right," Stephanie said. "Hey, can you do us a favor? Move in for a few days and work 'round the clock?'"

"At least you're acknowledging how much work this place requires."

"I know it's way more than a full-time job," Stephanie said. "It just doesn't *feel* like work to me. But it would to someone else." She slipped her feet into her slides. "We'll see everyone today at the party. Let's pray for favor."

"See, that's another reason why we need to wear these shirts," Lindell said. "Remind people that our mode of life is about to change, and we've got one last shot at a long overdue honeymoon. Then hit them with the request."

"I'm thinking we don't need the shirts to remind people, babe." Stephanie rubbed her stomach. "But I'll rock it today. I love that you're excited about the baby." She started for the door. "I'd better get down there."

"Steph . . ." Lindell walked toward her. "I heard what you said about our love life." He paused a moment. "I know we don't have the same sex drive. I know I'm just . . . wired differently. Always have been. It was obvious when Cedric was the one who always attracted the ladies and knew exactly what to do once he got them. I was just his awkward, pudgy little brother."

"Lindell—"

"I'm just saying, I understand," Lindell said. "It's not been easy for *me*. So I know it's not easy for you. I just want you to know it's something I've prayed about." He paused again. "Don't give up on me—on us. God has brought us a long way, and I know He's still working."

Stephanie leaned in and kissed him. "I'm not giving up. I only brought it up because I'm praying things get better. And look what happened—we might finally get our island honeymoon."

CHAPTER 5

*T*ommy lay in bed staring at a half composed text. He wasn't sure when it started, but he and Jillian began each day this way. One or the other would send a text, and dialogue would ebb and flow all day and into the evening. Neither had sent one after dinner last night. And dinner itself had ended with little conversation. His fault. He knew that. He just couldn't get past what he was feeling—even as he grappled to understand it.

Now he was trying again to get past it. He read what he'd typed thus far:

Hey, still in your quiet time? I know I was weird last night. I don't know it just felt like

He didn't know where to go with that. He could unpack it *with* her. That's what they did, helped each other understand what was happening down deep. But it usually involved other people and other things. Plus Jillian had been right. What did it matter how he felt? He just needed to suck it up and—

He sat up as a text came from her.

Morning, Tommy-Tom. Up praying for you. About to type it up and send it.

It had been a while since either of them had done a prayer text.

He'd sent the last one, a couple of weeks before, as Jillian edited a Living Water Bible study. She'd gotten to a section on marriage and family, and grief wouldn't let her get through it. She'd asked Tommy to pray, and since the need was ongoing, he'd typed it up for her.

Tommy erased the text he'd started and began another. **Thank u for praying, Jilli-Jill. But it wasn't that serious. It's a new day. I'm good. It was just**

"Aye, Tommy!" Reggie called from the other side of the bedroom door. "I thought you were helping with this balloon arch." He'd texted a half hour ago to see if Tommy was up and able to help.

"Yup, be there shortly," he said.

Tommy's phone dinged as Jillian's next text came.

Lord, I'm lifting up my best friend to You . . .

He took a breath and opened the text to read it in full.

He's been through so much, Lord, even now with Allison having another man's baby. That's hard, Lord. I know You've been answering prayer and healing Tommy. But I feel like there's so much there still, maybe that he doesn't even realize. Heal the deep places, Lord. Let your balm soothe every hurt. Flood his soul with the light of hope. Let Your love cast out every fear.

Tommy paused, reading those words again before he continued.

Lord, it's my continued prayer for Tommy, whether he likes it or not—give him grace to wait on You, to believe that you're working everything he's been through for good. And give him grace to endure this healing process. Build him back up, Lord, and let him run like never before.

Tommy wanted to argue with the prayer. Jillian clearly felt much of his existence was being filtered through pain, but even seeing that picture of Allison and her baby didn't affect him as he might've thought. He *did* believe God was working everything for good.

But he wondered . . . What would it be like if God soothed *every* hurt? If his soul filled with hope? If *every* fear were cast out? Was that even possible in this life?

Tommy got up with a sigh and headed to the bathroom. He'd reply to Jillian as soon as he landed on what to say. Problem was—she had a knack for honing in on what he *wasn't* saying. He could finesse it at least a little in text messages. But he'd see her again in just a few hours.

~

"It's the same thing every year." Tommy stood on a ladder, hanging hooks above the fireplace. "Reggie moaning about the Redskins not making the Super Bowl."

"I get it, though." Jesse threaded a needle through the knot of an inflated balloon and slid the balloon down the fishing line. "They get these flashes of momentum and you're like *maybe this year*. Then it falls apart." He glanced up at Reggie. "We've got a lot of fuchsia right here. I need a light pink and a white."

Reggie passed the colors to him. "Tommy doesn't know what it means to be a diehard fan. This is the dude who *actually* rooted for the Cowboys this season. That's that unthinkable type stuff."

"Say it ain't so, man." Jesse gave Tommy the eye. "You went to the dark side?" He added the light pink and started on the white one.

"First of all," Tommy said, "there's a difference between diehard and delusional. The Skins haven't made a Super Bowl once *in your lifetime*"—he gave Reggie a look—"but every fall you think it's their year." He hung another hook. "And I was rooting for Dak Prescott, not the Cowboys."

"Whatever," Reggie said. "Traitor." He passed Jesse more balloons.

Tommy moved to the other side of the fireplace. "Yeah, but you don't have a rebuttal for the delusional part."

"Hey, every year at playoff time, *I* think I might be delusional." Reggie chuckled.

"I'm just glad I'm not alone," Jesse said. "I've been known to wear burgundy and gold on Super Bowl Sunday." He cut the end of the fishing line and knotted it.

"That's what I'm talking about." Reggie fist-bumped him. "Be proud in your delusions."

Tommy shook his head as they put up the string of balloons over the hooks he'd put in place.

Faith walked into the family room. "Ohh, that looks so pretty. Even better than the picture—Jesse, I didn't know you were still here."

"Yeah," Jesse said, "the plan was to drop Zoe off and head back home till the party."

"You wouldn't have had your Pinterest moment without him," Reggie said. "I was about to tell you the balloon arch idea wasn't working. Jesse looked at what we were trying to do and went to Home Depot to get what we needed to make it work."

"We found out that engineering degree was real," Tommy said.

"What's that you're doing now?" Faith moved closer.

Jesse glanced back at her. "Using a glue gun to fill in the arch with smaller balloons. You blew up a ton, which is good. It'll be nice and full."

"I can't wait till Zoe sees it," Faith said. "I'm trying to get her to take a nap before the party but she's up there playing in her crib."

Reggie stood near Jesse, passing balloons as he glued them. "She said she's two and doesn't need naps anymore."

"Ha," Faith said. "Not hardly." She looked at Jesse. "Jordyn's coming, right?"

"She'll be here," Jesse said. "Plus she's got my gift in her car."

"That fancy doll's house you were talking about?" Faith said.

"It's not *fancy*."

"You know you spoil that girl," Faith said. "But I can't wait for her to see that too." She turned to Reggie. "The food's ready, but I need to pick up the cake, snacks, and drinks. You coming?"

"Let's do it," Reggie said.

"Faith, wait." Jesse put down the glue gun, reached into his pocket, and pulled out his wallet. "It's for Zoe's party. And don't tell me you've got it"—he handed her a few bills—"just take it."

"Okay, thanks, Jesse," Faith said. "And can you guys listen for Zoe? I'm hoping she falls asleep, but . . ."

"We got her covered," Jesse said.

Tommy took Reggie's place, passing the last balloons. "Hey, we're having people over for the Super Bowl next Sunday. You should come hang out. Jordyn's welcome too, of course."

"Sounds like fun, thanks." Jesse glued two more. "So, I've been wondering . . . have you considered leading a life group?"

"You mean here at the house?" Tommy said.

"I know some meet in people's homes and others meet at the church," Jesse said. "I wasn't so much thinking about the place, but whether you'd thought about it."

"Nah, it's not something I would start," Tommy said. "Why do you ask?"

"A couple of reasons," Jesse said. "I keep thinking about that time we met for the temptation study. I liked that dynamic of studying in a small group setting, talking about our walk with God, encouraging one another." He glued the last ones. "But also, I think it would be dope to get to know you better and glean from you. I'm still young in the faith with lots to learn."

"Glean from me?" Tommy said. "Don't you and Lance get together?"

"Not so much anymore, now that he's at Living Word," Jesse said. "He's stretched for time."

"True," Tommy said. "Cedric would be good, though. He actually leads a group at church on Sunday mornings, which you should check out, if you haven't already."

Jesse nodded, setting down the glue gun. "I figured you might not be up for it. Things didn't exactly start out on the right foot with Reggie and me."

"Man, that's old and buried," Tommy said, leading him to the kitchen. "You're my bro, and real talk—I've got big respect for you as a father. I just don't see what you could glean from me." He opened the fridge. "Help yourself to whatever you want to drink. And if you ask me, Faith made way too much food. I say we go ahead and get an appetizer."

Jesse got a bottled water. "I haven't eaten today so enough said." He took the plate Tommy handed him. "About what I could glean . . . If I'm honest, I'm always thinking about myself first and what I need.

36

I'm not that way with Zoe, but only because she's my daughter." He started adding food on his plate. "You've got one of the biggest servant hearts I know. Always helping with this and that. And little things, like making a point to talk to elderly people at church, and not just a quick convo." He took a seat at the kitchen table. "Somebody even mentioned you shopping for groceries for an older gentleman. Come on, man—you're wondering what I could glean?"

"Who would even be talking about that?" Tommy said, getting his own food. "That was only while he recuperated from surgery." He joined Jesse at the table, saying a quick prayer for the food. "Listen, you heard some of my story when we met for that temptation study. You know about Jillian and me. And the two failed marriages. I'm just being real—I'm not the one you want to glean from."

"So tell me what that means," Jesse said. "I'm supposed to find a perfect person? And I remember what you shared. You said you were working like crazy, trying to make it as an entertainment reporter, and your first wife left you for another man. That was before you knew Jesus, right?"

Tommy nodded. "I was in my twenties."

"And Allison left and was living with another man, and got pregnant by him. What does that have to do with gleaning from *you*?" Jesse drank some water. "And before you bring up Jillian again, if you want to know the truth, that's a big reason why I'm asking you."

Tommy looked at him, waiting.

"The part of your story that spoke most was the confession and repentance," Jesse said. "Lance said you didn't hesitate to confess your sin. Cedric said you went to see him as well, broken. And you got right back with Jesus, to an even deeper walk." He looked at Tommy. "You know my story too. I'm nowhere near perfect. *That's* what I want to glean from. If you lead a group, I'm *there*."

"That's the other thing," Tommy said. "I don't lead stuff like that. I'm a deacon, director of operations. Totally different." He paused. "But I'm with you—that study was special. It would be really nice to have that on an ongoing basis."

"Mommmmmyyyy."

Jesse shook his head, chuckling. "That little girl is wide awake."

"And heading into this party with no nap," Tommy said. "You already know."

"Mommy! Mommmmyyyyy!"

"She'll be surprised to see Daddy coming to get her," Tommy said.

Jesse looked at him. "You want me to get her?"

"Well," Tommy said, "at the very least, we can start hanging more. So you might as well make yourself at home. Go on up and get your daughter."

CHAPTER 6

*J*ordyn Rogers put on a fleece jacket and grabbed her keys. "You should just come on and go."

Jade took a plate from the microwave. "Why would I tag along with you two to a toddler's birthday party?—no offense, Jesse."

"Why would I take offense?" Jesse sat on a stool at the kitchen counter. "That's what it is."

"But it's more than that," Jordyn said. "It's always fun just getting together. And you forget—these were Dad's friends. They see us as family. It's a chance for you to get to know them better."

"I think you think because you knew them first, you have to bring me along and make sure I'm part of the circle." Jade took Italian bread from the oven. "It's cool. For real. We don't have to run in the same circles."

"Jade, you don't run in *any* circle," Jordyn said. "It won't kill you to do something different, put some people in your world."

"I'm putting some of this lasagna in my world," Jade said. "And some video editing. I need to finish the one on flexi rods."

"All right, then." Jordyn looked at Jesse. "You ready?"

"Umm, I was about to ask my sis over here if I could taste that lasagna." Jesse eyed her plate. "It's looking *too* good."

"I thought they had food at the party," Jordyn said. "But yeah, you might want to taste it. I don't know what Jade did, but it's better than Mom's."

Jade put her plate in front of Jesse. "Help yourself."

"I can have it?" Jesse said.

"You don't even know if you like it yet," Jade said. "But if so, go for it. I can warm up some more."

"Hold up," Jordyn said. "I thought the rest was for me."

"Not anymore," Jesse said, a bite in his mouth. "I'm about to take this out." He looked at Jade. "For real? You can burn like this?"

"I didn't know either," Jordyn said. "But she's been in the kitchen more, and I'm loving the results."

Jesse looked at Jordyn. "So, uh, have you been, you know, watching and learning?"

Jade looked amused. "In other words, Jesse wants to know if you're planning to step up your culinary skills." She put another plate in the microwave.

"Do I have a reason to step up my culinary skills?" Jordyn said.

"Aren't you always saying you need to learn to cook more dishes?" Jesse said.

"But it sounded like *you* wanted me to learn," Jordyn said.

Jesse shrugged. "Be nice if one of us knew how, don't you think?"

"Why?" Jordyn said.

Jade got another piece of bread. "She's going to make you say it, Jesse."

"Just thinking in terms of the future," Jesse said, "and specifically, the two of us in the future . . . you know, possibly . . . but my imagination might run wild sometimes."

"Wow," Jade said. "You actually went there. Sort of. I'm impressed." She took her plate from the microwave. "I'm about to get to this editing. Y'all have fun at the party." She went to her room and closed the door.

Jesse finished the lasagna and took his plate to the sink, rinsing it.

"So that was interesting," Jordyn said.

"What was?" Jesse put the plate in the dishwasher.

"You talking about the future," Jordyn said, "since you don't say a whole lot about how you feel in the present."

"I don't?" Jesse said. "When I'm not at work, I spend most of my free time either talking to you or with you. That's not telling you how I feel?"

"I mean, yeah, I guess," Jordyn said.

"I know you didn't really know the old me," Jesse said, "but I never gave a woman this much of my time. Never included anybody in this much of my life. Even Brandy, who I was living with for a minute, didn't know where I was or what I was doing half the time." He put his jacket on. "You know everything. I'm committed to you, Jordyn."

"I know you are." Jordyn sighed. "I think I just want you to say certain things that you haven't said. And since you haven't, I wonder if it's because you don't feel it, which is fine. But I just wonder—"

"You want me to tell you I love you."

"It's like you said, Jesse, we've spent so much time together over the past several months," Jordyn said. "And I just wonder what it means, whether it's leading anywhere. Or are we just kicking it? I'm sure the fact that we don't do anything physical is part of it too. It's hard to tell if you're feeling anything."

"So you think if this was physical, you could tell what I'm feeling?" Jesse said. "The fact that we're *not* physical should tell you what I'm feeling, Jordyn. I'm focused on *you*. Getting to know you. Trying to build something that's lasting." He moved closer to her. "I really want you to understand something about me. It was nothing for me to tell a woman I loved her. I would say it just to get her in bed. With you, I want to *show* you how I feel. I've changed up everything with you, because you mean that much to me." He shook his head. "I can't believe you've even got me talking about the future."

Jordyn put her arms around him. "I needed all of that."

"I need you to know how much you mean to me," Jesse said, embracing her.

"I think this should be our moment," Jordyn said.

41

"On our way out the door for a toddler birthday party?"

"I want to kiss you."

"I want to kiss you too," Jesse said. "But does that make it a special moment?"

Jordyn sighed. "You're right. We've waited this long, and I do want it to be a *moment*."

"And we're supposed to both agree that it's a moment," Jesse said. "Maybe it'll be the moment you cook some lasagna."

"Ha. Ha." Jordyn started for the door.

Jesse followed. "But it has to be lasagna *like that*."

CHAPTER 7

"**Z**oe, turn this way, sweetie." Jillian aimed her phone at the birthday girl, recording the moment. "Your Grandma Patsy wants to see you opening her gift."

Zoe lifted the lid off of the box, tore into the tissue paper, and started tossing clothes aside.

"Little girl," Faith said, shaking her head. "She's thinking, there has to be a toy in here somewhere."

"Zoe, you don't appreciate it yet"—Treva picked up one of the sweaters and folded it—"but Grandma Patsy will keep you looking fly."

"Grandma Patsy?" Faith said. "Who got her these rose gold Mary Jane's?"

"Okay?" Stephanie said. "And Treva knows shoes are my thing. Those are fly *and* flat, which is what I need these days."

"You've always got the look, Steph," Treva said. "Those Converse with the 'Mommy' shirt and jeans are too cute."

"Could you say that again, Treva?" Lindell said.

The doorbell rang, and Jillian glanced at Tommy as he went to get it. They'd hardly spoken since she got there.

"Got held up in a meeting at church," Lance said, walking in. "I didn't miss singing 'Happy Birthday,' did I?"

"Yup," Treva said. "And the lovely cake smash. I've got it on video, babe."

Lance picked up Zoe from beside Faith. "Look at you, big girl, looking so pretty." He gave her a hug.

"Granddaddy, toys." Zoe pointed at her new collection.

"You've got some nice new toys," Lance said. "Nice new *noisy* toys." He chuckled. "Okay, sweetie, I'll let you rip open the next one." He gave her back to Faith and took a floor spot next to Treva and Wes.

"No ripping on this one," Jesse said. "Let me get it." He went to the hall closet and returned with a big doll's house. "Happy Birthday, Princess."

"Daddy, Daddy, Daddy!" Zoe motored over to him, excited for him to set it down. "Ooh, look!" She took a frying pan from the stove. "And look—look, Mommy!" She showed her a bed in her other hand.

"I see that," Faith said, smiling. "You're going to have a blast with this."

Jordyn handed her another gift. "Zoe, you want to open this next? It goes with the doll's house."

"Jordy!" Zoe did a little dance as she took it. She ripped into the gift and squealed at the additional food and furniture items. She dumped them from the container and began setting them up in the doll's house.

"I don't think we're doing all that right now, Princess," Jesse said.

Faith nodded, redirecting her. "Zoe, let's finish opening your other gifts, then we've got—"

"No, Mommy!" Zoe pointed behind her. "House!" She marched back over to it.

"Zoe, we'll play with that later." Faith picked up another package. "Look at this pretty gift. Don't you want to open this one?"

Zoe folded her arms and stomped a foot. "No! House!"

"So that was a major tactical mistake," Jesse said. "Sorry. I should've saved it for last." He took the next gift and looked at Zoe. "Come on, Princess, I'll open it with you. Let's see what's inside."

"No want it!" Zoe said. "House!" She grabbed some of the food and threw it into her play kitchen.

"Okay, little girl," Faith said, picking her up. "I see what this is about. I wish you'd taken a nap."

Zoe let out a wail, kicking as Faith carted her upstairs.

David looked at Sophia. "Which means we don't get to see Zoe open that lame plush bowling set you picked out."

Lance stood. "Which also means we can switch gears and get a game going."

"I'm way ahead of you," Tommy said. "Already took the cards out." He started moving the cake and food off of the dining room table. "Hey, Jesse," he called over his shoulder. "Partners?"

"Absolutely." Jesse moved to a seat at the table.

Lance and Cedric followed and moments later Tommy was shuffling cards at the table.

"It's been so long," Tommy said. "I'm thinking Pastor Lance has forgotten how to play."

"In your dreams," Lance said. "But if you need to brush up with a couple of hands, Cedric and I are all for charity work."

"Hey, put us in the rotation." Jillian called from the circle of women in the family room. "Pam and I are up next."

Tommy looked over at her. "This is for serious players, Jill."

"You're just gonna clown me like that?" Jillian nodded. "Okay."

Pamela winked at Jillian. "Don't say another word."

"Uh, brothers, before you embarrass yourselves," Lance said, "Mom is a for-real player, and I think she's been schooling a couple people."

"Oh, I believe it," Tommy said. "Momma Pam is no joke on many levels." He looked at her. "I might need some of your tips and tricks myself."

"That's not a might," Lance said.

"Momma Pam"—Tommy dealt the cards—"how attached are you to your son?"

David came over to Jillian. "Mom, we're leaving for the movies in a few minutes."

"You're taking Hope and Trevor?" Jillian said.

"Yes, Mom," David said. "It's a cousin outing."

"Somehow they got left behind on a 'cousin outing' last month," Jillian said.

"That was a miscommunication," David said.

Music boomed suddenly through speakers in the room and everyone looked around.

"Sorry, didn't know it was so loud." Reggie fiddled with the music player. "Trying to find a playlist."

Different songs played as he scrolled—

"Ayyyee!" sounded from Joy and Sophia as they launched into a similar dance move.

"I guess y'all want to hear this one," Reggie said.

"Don't be hiding over there, girls," Stephanie said. "Let me see the latest dance."

Joy and Sophia looked at each other, one goading the other to go show her.

"Oh, we're shy now?" Reggie said.

He pulled them both to the middle of the family room floor and started dancing with them. Joy and Sophia fell back into their dance.

"Look at y'all," Stephanie said, smiling. "That's really cute. All three of you can go."

Treva came closer. "Joy, when did you learn to dance like that? I was watching you at Faith and Reggie's wedding too and remembering when you didn't have much rhythm."

Sophia chuckled. "That's true, Aunt Treva. I guess she grew into it."

"That's not fair," Faith said. "I never grew into it."

"That's okay, baby." Reggie kissed her as the song faded. "But if you want, we can add dancing to the practice schedule."

"What practice schedule?" Joy said.

"Never you mind," Faith said.

The teens prepared to leave as Reggie went back to scrolling playlists.

"Ohhh," sounded seconds later as Tommy started bobbing his head.

Jillian didn't realize she was bobbing hers until Sophia brought David back into the family room to look at her.

"Check you out, Mom," Sophia said.

"This was one of those jams that got everybody on the floor in college," Jillian said.

"Yup," Reggie said. "Old school playlist. Doug E. Fresh."

Sophia gave her a look. "You're telling me you could dance?"

"You've seen me dance, Soph," Jillian said.

"Not *dance* dance," Sophia said.

"Jill and Tommy," Stephanie said. "Stop grooving in your seats and come to the floor. Show us the back-in-the-day dances."

Jillian tossed Stephanie a look. "There is no way—"

Sophia pulled Jillian to her feet. Faith pulled Tommy to his and pushed him to the middle of the floor.

Jillian and Tommy looked at one another.

"Are we doing this?" Jillian said.

"If we are," Tommy said, "then do it for real. No half-stepping."

"Start with the prep?" Jillian said.

"Let's go."

Side by side, they started moving in synchronized fashion, remembering the dance like it was yesterday. The teens gathered next to Stephanie and Faith, then Treva and Cyd came.

Jillian moved in front of him, and they started the snake. Seconds later they switched to the Reebok.

Sophia beamed. "Okay, Mom, I see you."

"And look at Tommy with the old school swag," Faith said.

They switched it up again, moving around one another.

"Y'all are taking me back." Cedric got out of his seat. "I totally remember the Wop." He brought Cyd to the floor. "And what about the Roger Rabbit?" He started it and the other three joined in.

David stood watching. "I had no idea."

Jesse got up next. "Y'all know about Doug E. Fresh, but can you teach me how to Dougie, teach me how to Dougie . . ."

"Oh, you going there?" Reggie said.

"Let's do it, Reg," Jesse said.

The two guys took the floor and everyone backed up, watching.

"I have to get this on video." Joy aimed her phone at them. "This is so lit."

Sophia nodded. "Look how they're taking it low. Crazy swag."

Stephanie waved a hand in the air. "Go, Jesse! Go, Reggie!"

"I never learned that one." Cyd moved beside the guys. "So you can really teach me."

"Me too," Treva said, joining them.

Lindell took Stephanie's hand and led her to the floor.

Stephanie laughed. "We done turned a toddler birthday party into a house party, *with* the pastor present."

"And I better see every one of you at the early service tomorrow," Lance called out.

Sophia turned to Jillian. "Mom, we're leaving, but looks like you guys will be having more fun than we will."

Jillian smiled. "Drive safely, sweetheart. Text when you're on your way home." She saw them out then went to the kitchen, opening the fridge to get water.

"Can you pass me one?" Tommy walked in behind her.

Jillian gave him a bottle then uncapped hers and took a sip. "You've been acting funny all afternoon."

"Not really," Tommy said.

"Towards me you have."

Tommy took a gulp. "Just giving you your space."

"What does that mean?"

He gave a slight shrug. "For your new pursuits."

"Why are you talking around the issue?" Jillian said. "Just say what's on your mind. You didn't even respond to my prayer text."

"That wasn't intentional," Tommy said. "I just . . . wasn't sure what to say."

Jillian looked at him. "Let's talk, at the park."

"I'm in the middle of a card game," Tommy said.

"Reggie or Pam can take your place."

"And it's freezing outside."

"It's in the forties."

"Why the park?" Tommy said.

Jillian leveled a gaze at him, and Tommy met it, letting it linger a moment.

He gave a vague nod. "All right."

Tommy got a replacement, Jillian told Treva they'd be back, and they got their coats. Riding mostly in silence to Forest Park, they maintained it as they walked the first few yards along a tree-lined path under a dusky sky.

"You excited about your date tomorrow?" Tommy said finally.

Jillian gave him a glance. "Say what's on your mind, Tommy."

"Why can't that be what's on my mind?"

"So this is like college," Jillian said, "when you'd ask if I was excited about a date, and you'd sincerely want to know?" She nodded. "Okay, so after coffee with Silas, you and I will talk about it, just like in college. I'll tell you what I thought, you'll ask if I like him, give me advice on what to do from there . . ." She looked at him. "Is that what we're doing, Tommy?"

He stared at the pathway ahead.

"Everything flipped the moment I mentioned coffee with Silas," Jillian said. "Just say it—you don't like the fact that I'm going."

"I don't have the right to tell you that," Tommy said.

"The right?" Jillian said. "I just want to know what you're thinking. Talk to me."

Tommy stared vaguely. "At Faith and Reggie's wedding we said we'd be friends, and I wasn't sure what that would look like. But these past few months, we found this rhythm. We hang out, talk on the phone, send texts with prayers and silly stuff . . ." He took several seconds to continue. "And I don't know, I guess I thought it would just *be* like that, for a while at least. I thought our friendship would be something I could hang onto. But when you said you had a date—or whatever you're calling it—I knew things were about to change."

Jillian walked in silence a while, focused on trees with bare limbs, trying to find words, then wondering if she should say the words she'd found. "I didn't know what it would be like either. But the friendship went deeper." She paused. "The love went deeper."

49

"Jill . . ."

"I know we don't talk about it," Jillian said. "It's this unspoken rule between us—steer clear of feelings. But I have to say it, Tommy." She looked into his eyes. "I love you more than I did a few months ago."

Tommy looked away, his steps slowed.

"Is it just me?" Jillian said. "What are you feeling?"

He looked at her. "I love you so much it hurts. You're on my mind when I wake up, before I fall asleep, and too many minutes in between."

"Well why does it hurt?" Jillian said.

"Because there's nowhere to go with it."

"Why isn't there?"

"I meant it when I said I'm done with relationships, Jill. I can't go down that road." He paused, waiting for a guy and his dog to pass. "Even you said last night you don't know if or when you'll be ready. And you're asking why there's nowhere to go?"

"But that didn't apply to you," Jillian said.

"What didn't?"

"I may never be ready when it comes to any other man on the planet." Jillian took a breath. "But then there's you."

Tommy stared into her eyes long seconds. "To try to go down that road with you—and fail—would hurt more than anything else." He glanced away for a moment. "I just have to deal with the inevitable— you will move on with your life, without me."

Tears brimmed in Jillian's eyes. "But we can keep doing what we've been doing. Why does it feel like you're pushing me away?"

"I'm not pushing you away," Tommy said. "I'm falling back."

"It's the same thing."

"You said you're open to where God might take you, and you should be," Tommy said. "I can't stand in the way, and you sure don't need to complicate things with feelings for me. Whether it's Silas or another man—somebody will sweep you off your feet because you have a beautiful spirit, you love the Lord, you happen to be gorgeous, and you can even dance a little bit."

Jillian couldn't hold it in anymore. She looked away as tears fell from her eyes.

Tommy took her into his arms and the tears fell all the more.

"So what now?" Jillian's face nestled against him. "We're cutting this off again?"

"No," Tommy said. "The way you treat that car of yours, I'd be afraid for your life."

Jillian gave him a look, though he couldn't see.

"So I'm doing what I said—taking your car to the shop next week." Tommy took a step back and looked into her eyes. "And I'll be here, Jill. There's nothing I wouldn't do for you, and I hope you wouldn't hesitate to ask. We'll still see each other around and catch up. We'll just cut back on everything else."

"It still sounds like we're cutting it off," Jillian said. "I feel the sadness."

"I know." Tommy wiped a streak of tears from her face. "It'll pass. You just . . . might have to wait and endure for a little while."

"You actually think it's a time for jokes."

"How am I joking? Are you joking when you tell me to wait and endure—fifty million times?"

Jillian sighed, moving away. "Let's just head back."

Tommy walked beside her across a bridge with a stream running underneath, silence reigning again.

He looked over at her. "So what are you thinking now?"

"Nothing," Jillian said.

"Wow," Tommy said. "It was a crime when I wouldn't say what was on my mind."

"I said everything that was on my mind."

"We both know that's not true."

"Well, once again, Tommy"—Jillian glanced at him—"what difference does it make?"

She continued on to the car.

CHAPTER 8

"*I*t's like a dream, being here in your home."

Cinda Coles passed the Kung Pao Chicken to their dinner guest, Brooke Shelley. "We're just glad you could make it," Cinda said. "Sorry again that it was so last minute."

"Are you kidding?" Brooke said. "I would've dropped everything if I had to." She tucked her hair behind an ear as she added the chicken to her plate and passed it. "If you had told me two months ago that I'd be dining at the home of Alonzo Coles, I would've said no way. God just *keeps* showing me how amazing He is."

"That's what we're saying right now." Alonzo tasted the Wonton soup. "We had no idea you were a believer before tonight. I'm still shaking my head." He looked at Cinda. "Wait till we tell Pam."

"Who's Pam?" Brooke said.

"Pamela Alexander," Cinda said.

"Oh, *the* Pam, from the movie," Brooke said, smiling. "I should've known." She passed the beef and broccoli to Alonzo.

"She's been praying about every facet of this project," Alonzo said, adding to his plate, "but she was *really* praying over the selection of cast and crew."

"And especially *your* part," Cinda said. "They had to get Kendra right."

"That's the thing." Brooke cut into the beef. "When I went to audition, I was sure I *wasn't* right for the part. I had seen the wedding video and had come up with every reason why I couldn't be Kendra. I knew my hair didn't have to look like hers—"

"Which is funny," Cinda said, "because it totally does. I was looking at pictures she took before her diagnosis, and she had those sleek, bouncy curls like yours."

"I did see that when I googled her," Brooke said, "but in the wedding video, she has on a head wrap. And all I could see was that my complexion was a little darker, and my facial features were different. I said, oh, well, it'll be another role I don't get." She paused, taking a bite. "I knew I needed to stop focusing on myself and have faith, but it's hard when you're measured all the time based on appearance. When I got the call, all I could do was praise God."

"We had a couple of people in mind for the role from the beginning," Alonzo said. "And someone else auditioned who looked promising. Then I heard about this woman who showed up and killed it. When they brought me in to read with you, I said, 'I don't know where she came from, but that's Kendra.'"

"Oh, man, I didn't even know you were coming," Brooke said. "And when you walked in, I got so nervous." She ate a bite of chicken with steamed rice. "I'm not trying to weird you out, but I would watch your movies over and over and study your craft. So to be face-to-face with you, reading a script? I could feel myself shaking. I thought I did terribly."

"It was all in your head," Alonzo said. "You went there—the fear and dread from learning that the chemo wasn't working, and the fear of allowing Lance to love you. But you didn't overplay it, which would've been easy to do. You brought me into the emotion of the scene."

Brooke looked at him, shaking her head. "None of this has sunk in yet."

"It'll sink in real soon," Alonzo said, smiling, "because you'll be in

St. Louis in about a week." He spooned up more of the soup. "With everything ramping up quickly, we wanted to have you over and get to know you a little better, also answer any questions you might have."

"So, St. Louis," Brooke said. "You two have a home there, don't you?"

"We're back and forth," Cinda said, "in St. Louis mostly, though."

"What made you do that?" Brooke said. "If you don't mind my asking."

"St. Louis is a big part of our story," Alonzo said. "It's where we met, where we got grounded in the faith and with a family of believers." He drank some water. "We knew that was where we wanted to spend a large part of our time."

"And obviously," Brooke said, "that's where you met Lance Alexander and got inspired to do this film."

"Exactly," Alonzo said.

"Will Lance be around during the shoot?" Brooke said. "How involved is he in the project?"

"He started pastoring a larger church a few months ago," Alonzo said, "so we may not see him as much as we'd like. But he's meeting with us during rehearsals. And just a side note . . . we're planning to take people to service on Sundays, as many as want to go."

"Wow," Brooke said. "Okay." She focused on her food a moment. "So I should tell you . . . You got excited that I'm a believer, but I didn't try out for this part because it was a Christian movie. I just wanted to work. But more and more I'm seeing that God has a lot more in mind for me than the work." She sighed a little. "I'm not where I need to be."

"I think we can all say that," Alonzo said.

"Well, I'm living with my boyfriend," Brooke said. "I moved out here after college and met him—he's in the business as well. And you know how it is when you're struggling, trying to get a break. It was easy to pool our resources and move in together. But God convicted me about it from the beginning."

Cinda and Alonzo focused on her, listening.

"And what did I do?" Brooke said. "Drifted from Him, stopped going to church . . ." She sighed again. "So now I'm blessed with this role, and God is totally shaking up my life in the process. My first big break, and it's a Christian movie with field trips to church on Sunday?"

"A team of people has been praying for every person who's part of this project," Alonzo said. "So I'm not surprised that God is shaking things up."

Cinda looked at Alonzo. "That's what happened with you on the *Bonds of Time* movie."

He nodded. "That's exactly what happened."

"So on one hand I'm excited about this project," Brooke said, "and on the other, I'm nervous because I know God is telling me to get my life together—and I'm afraid of what that'll look like."

"Well, you'll be in St. Louis for a few weeks," Cinda said, "so you'll have time to pray and seek God about what He's doing in your life— and what He wants you to do."

"True," Brooke said. "The schedule will be hectic, but I'll be removed from normal life. And I definitely want to attend Lance's church, so this is about to be way more than I thought." She sighed. "And you totally didn't ask me over to hear my problems. I apologize."

"Girl, that's exactly why we had you over," Cinda said. "I mean, not that we were trying to get in your business." She smiled. "But like Alonzo said, we wanted to get to know you, and you get to know us. We've been saying this is so much more than a movie. Now we know how we can be praying for you."

"My boyfriend is a big fan of yours as well, Alonzo. He was wondering if all the Christian talk was real." Brooke forked up more Kung Pao Chicken. "I'll have to tell him—absolutely." She paused as she ate her food. "So, Alonzo, I know you're working on changes to the script. Will they be extensive?"

"You'll have a lot more lines," Alonzo said. "We're going deeper into Kendra and Lance's story. So more Kendra/Lance scenes, and also more from her brother, since he was a big part of their lives. Also doing more with the scenes we already had. The wedding will be amazing."

"Oh, it has to be," Brooke said. "I pulled it up on YouTube the other day and it's got over three million views. One comment with tons of likes said, 'Is it just me? I couldn't marry someone if I knew she'd be gone soon.'"

"I think that's what captures people," Alonzo said. "You wonder—who would do that? What kind of love is this?"

"Especially since Kendra's fiancé *couldn't* do it, and left her," Cinda said.

"I think about her all the time now," Brooke said. "Wondering what she must have been thinking when she got the diagnosis, when her fiancé left, when she was feeling so alone . . ." She reached for the carton of potstickers. "That's why I wondered if Lance would be around. I'd love to be able to ask questions about her."

"He would welcome that," Alonzo said. "He wants the portrayal to be true to who Kendra was."

"Do you think this is hard for him?" Brooke said. "I don't know if I could relive all of that."

Cinda and Alonzo glanced at one another.

"It's certainly not easy," Alonzo said.

Brooke nodded soberly. "I can't imagine. Okay and since I'm new to all of this and really anxious, I have to ask—if you could go back, what advice would you give to yourself as you were preparing for your first big role?"

Cinda sat in bed twisting her hair, watching as Alonzo did pushups on the floor. "Since when do you exercise right before bed?"

"Didn't get a chance earlier," Alonzo said, winded. He'd done a couple dozen so far.

She added styling cream to the next section of hair, fingered it through, and started the two-strand twist. "Or maybe you're alleviating stress?"

Alonzo did three more, his body a straight line from shoulders to feet. "I'm not stressed."

Cinda continued with the next section as Alonzo did at least ten more. He got up and took a swig of water from a bottle on the dresser.

"I know this is hard for you too," Cinda said. "Did you talk to Lance today?"

"I didn't expect to," Alonzo said. "I knew he had meetings then Zoe's birthday party."

"I think he was just reacting in the moment," Cinda said. "You shouldn't take it to heart."

Alonzo leaned against the dresser with a sigh. "Cin, he said he wished he'd never agreed to this. And I get it. When we were focused on the bigger picture—his life story—you couldn't help but also focus on Christ and redemption. When you narrow it to Lance and Kendra, it's a love story."

Cinda worked her way to the end of a twist. "But that's all about Christ and redemption as well."

"Yeah, but it won't ring as loudly." Alonzo sat on the bed. "Plus we have to take out everything related to current life, including Treva. Lance would've had to deal with a focus on him and Kendra anyway, but now, that's *all* people will talk about. He doesn't want to relive that season. Definitely doesn't want it overshadowing this one." He sighed again. "I thought I'd heard from God in this. But the way things have turned out, I don't know . . ."

"They haven't 'turned out' yet," Cinda said. "You haven't even filmed it."

"We know what the focus is," Alonzo said.

"Zee . . ." Cinda let a section of hair fall. "As much as you love and respect Lance, you have to remember that you were praying and felt persuaded that this was what God was calling you to do."

"Yeah, I was persuaded," Alonzo said, "about the *other* vision."

"You were moved to do a movie about Lance's life," Cinda said, "one that would glorify God. And that's what you're doing." She continued with her hair. "Do any of the changes require you to water down the Christian elements?"

"No," Alonzo said. "It's all in there. It's a for-real Christian movie."

"And the whole thing almost fell through. You should be rejoicing right now."

"But look at this." Alonzo opened the Instagram app on his phone. "All these 'black romance' and 'black love' hashtags on posts about the movie. I love the excitement, but I don't want people to miss Jesus in this."

"Zee, it *is* a romance, and a beautiful one," Cinda said, finishing the last twist. "I love that people are excited about that." She got up to wash her hands. "And there's no way they'll watch the film and miss Jesus. You can't worry about what's out there or even about Lance. Just make the movie. God will use it."

Alonzo looked at her as she returned. "So you still believe in this project?"

"I'm working my butt off for this project—I better believe in it." Cinda sat next to him. "Better yet, I believe in the man who's been seeking God about this project from the beginning."

"But what if people walk away from the movie still not getting what we tried to—"

"Okay, I'm calling it." Cinda turned out the light and got into bed.

"You only called it because you're done with your hair."

"I called it because you're stressing."

"Baby, I'm not stressing." Alonzo climbed into bed with her. "It's just a very real probability—"

Cinda put her lips to his, kissing him softly. "Not another word," she whispered.

Alonzo looked into her eyes. "About the movie or in general?"

"Not another word. Period."

"So we're going to sleep?"

Cinda narrowed her eyes at him.

Alonzo smiled. "I was just checking."

CHAPTER 9

"**Y**our son was not happy with me at all." Treva looked over at her husband as he drove. "He had that indignant cry. Like, 'How dare you leave for church without me?'"

"I'm not sure how to take that." Lance glanced at her. "He's never upset to see me leave."

Treva chuckled. "That boy is a creature of habit. Somehow he knows that on Sunday morning, he rolls with Mommy." She checked a notification on her phone. "And once we get to church, he's fine when I leave him in the nursery. But I know Pam calmed him down."

"I still say you didn't have to do this," Lance said. "I had no idea reporters would start calling you for interviews about the movie."

"Well, this is the one who tried to interview you first, remember?"

"I can't believe she even thought I'd have time," Lance said. "It's *Sunday*. You don't have time yourself." He looked at her. "Babe, please don't feel that you have to indulge this stuff. Filming hasn't even started, and it's out of control already. Do you know how many interview requests are in my inbox?"

"The story just broke," Treva said. "And it's a big deal locally. But you know it'll die down."

"And meanwhile what?" Lance said. "I'm supposed to make time to answer everybody's questions about Kendra and me? Even if I had time, I wouldn't want to. Do people think it's easy to just chat about walking with your wife through cancer and watching her die?" He tapped the brakes as a car in front of him slowed down. "And if I hear 'Kendra and Lance's love story' one more time . . ."

"Babe, it's a beautiful story," Treva said. "It's what first moved my heart toward you, hearing your heart for Kendra."

"But people have made it larger than life," Lance said, "and romanticized it. Almost every day was hard in some respect, and painful. I don't think people get that." He looked over at her. "And now I'm married to you. The only love story I want to focus on is Treva and Lance. The last thing I want is for you to feel that the two of us are taking a backseat to all the 'Kendra and Lance' talk."

"Babe, you love me too well for me to feel that way." Treva focused on him. "And I think you've got the wrong attitude about this. We've been praying from the beginning, and when funding fell through and it looked like there wouldn't be a movie. And this is what we got—the 'Kendra and Lance' story." She held his gaze at a red light. "My pastor once said answers to prayer can be unexpected and even unwanted."

"There should be a law against throwing my sermons back at me."

Treva smiled. "God clearly has a purpose in all of this. Look how you switched up your sermon for today."

"Yeah, that was all God," Lance said, taking off at the green light. "I went to bed frustrated about the movie news Friday night, and He woke me up *early* Saturday to work on a new message." He glanced at her. "Thank you. I needed that perspective."

"Just reminding you of God's promise to hear and answer prayer."

"Which is what our focus should be this morning anyway." Lance looked at her. "How are you feeling, now that the *Promises* study is about to release?"

"I can't believe it's finally here," Treva said. "I had no idea how long the publishing process would take. But I think Cyd and her team are more excited than I am. They've been updating me on the plans for next Tuesday's book launch."

"I want you to take a moment to soak it in," Lance said.

"Remember when you couldn't see yourself as a Bible teacher? Now you're head of Living Word's women's ministry and you've got a Bible study coming out."

"It'll never soak in, which is fine," Treva said. "It just means I keep reminding myself that it's all God's grace. If I went by how I see myself, I wouldn't be doing any—wait, what is Joy talking about?" She read the text that came. "Why is she asking us to invite Silas and Lucas to dinner?"

Lance looked over at her. "You know she's got a crush on Lucas. Hope's been teasing her about it."

"And now she's scheming—and using us—to get close to him?" Treva dialed her daughter.

"Mom, we just came up with the best idea ever," Joy said.

"We who?" Treva said.

"Sophie and I," Joy said. "So you know a lot of us from youth group went to the movies Friday night. Well, Lucas was there, and he looked really cute, so now even more girls like him. But Sophie just reminded me that I have an inside edge, with y'all being close to his dad. So since it's been a few weeks since they've been here for dinner, can you invite them again?"

"Joy, you cannot be serious," Treva said. "We need to talk about this preoccupation you seem to be having with boys lately."

"Mom, I'm not preoccupied with boys," Joy said. "Just Lucas. I mean—not *preoccupied* with him. But Mom, he's cute and smart and he totally loves God. Isn't that the kind of boy you *want* me to like?"

"Again, we'll have that conversation later," Treva said. "As far as your request, I'm sure we'll invite Silas and Lucas to dinner again, but it won't be because you're trying to manipulate the situation. It might even be a night when I know you've got other plans."

Lance chuckled to himself.

"Mom, you wouldn't," Joy said.

"Wouldn't I?"

"I would die if you did that."

"I appreciate your letting me know," Treva said. "I'll see you later this morning, my dramatic daughter." She hung up and looked over at

Lance. "Can you imagine Joy and Lucas setting their sights on one another? As soon as it went left, it would be awkward for you and Silas."

"Babe, it's just a crush on Joy's part," Lance said. "We don't even know how Lucas feels. Don't jump the gun."

"The Jill and Silas thing is awkward enough," Treva said. "Now we've got Joy liking his son?" She skimmed another text. "I still can't believe Jill agreed to go out with Silas. He's clearly smitten with her, but—"

"We're staying out of it, babe."

"I can't stay out of it," Treva said. "She's my sister."

Lance shook his head as he drove onto the Living Word complex. He navigated past a number of cars that had gotten there early and pulled into a parking spot.

"Deneen stays on top of that hospitality ministry." Treva watched the woman walk across the parking lot with grocery bags in hand. "She's gonna make sure there's fresh fruit, fresh pastries, juice, and whatever else for visitors."

"Absolutely," Lance said. "The hospitality ministry is always on point, especially since they make sure I get some of that fresh fruit." He chuckled. "Still, I can't help it. I'm partial to the women's ministry." He cut the engine and leaned over. "The leader is pretty hot." He kissed her.

"And I hear she's got a thing for the pastor," Treva said. "Members are starting to talk." She kissed him again, and they heard a rap on the window.

Lance rolled it down.

"It never ends with you two." Tommy looked at Lance. "Your phone must be off."

Lance took it from his coat pocket. "I forgot I silenced it. You called twice? What's up?"

"Carload full of women road-tripped to see you and Momma Pam." Tommy leaned down to the window. "Said they signed up to get prayer requests for the movie and been praying for months. When they got the praise report Friday night that it was back on, they decided to drive from Oklahoma City to celebrate and meet you two."

"Are you serious?" Lance said.

"I told them your schedule is full, meetings before and after service," Tommy said. "They're in the entryway. Just tell me what you want me to do."

"Nothing to do but head inside and meet them," Lance said.

"I'm letting Pam know." Treva texted as they walked. "Maybe she can get here earlier. She takes that prayer team seriously. She'd want to thank them."

They walked into the main building, and five young women got up from a seating area and came towards them.

"Oh, my goodness," one of them said. "I can't believe we're meeting you after all these years." She focused on Lance. "You have no idea. My friends and I fell in love with you and Kendra from the time we heard your story. We couldn't get enough of the wedding video—especially that moment when Kendra nearly collapses during the ceremony and you carry her to a seat."

"If you could've seen our reaction when we first heard there'd be a movie," another woman said. She nudged the first one. "I wish we could show him all of our group text messages."

"Then we found out there was a website for the movie and that your mom was posting prayer requests," another chimed in. "We kept up with every request and update, even fasted when the funding fell through. And when we heard that God had answered—and it would be about the love story—we said we've *got* to drive to St. Louis and finally meet them."

"We understand how busy you are," the first woman said. "But to be able to meet you and hear you preach in person—trust me, well worth it. And I'm sorry, we're talking nonstop."

"And it's not a problem because I'm kind of speechless," Lance said. "Let me introduce my wife"—he brought her closer—"this is Treva and we're glad to welcome you to Living Word. And please—tell us your names."

Each of the women spoke up, and Lance and Treva shook their hands.

The first woman held up her phone. "Would you mind if we got a picture with you?"

"I can take it," Treva said, reaching for the phone. She snapped a few of Lance with the women.

"Could we take one with my phone?" another woman said, extending it.

Tommy stepped forward. "Ladies, our apologies. I need to make sure Pastor Lance gets to where he needs to go."

"Oh, definitely, we understand," one of the women said. "Thank you so much. Maybe we can catch you again after service. And we're hoping to meet Pamela Alexander as well."

"I'm sure you will," Treva said. "I've already let her know."

Lance took Treva's hand as the three of them moved on.

"So you're a rock star now?" Tommy said.

"Don't even start," Lance said.

"I'm heading to the ministry building," Tommy said. "They're getting press inquiries about the film, and we need to coordinate a unified response."

"Sounds good," Lance said, pushing the elevator button. "But you're coming to the logistics meeting?"

"This won't take long," Tommy said. "I'll be there."

Treva moved into the elevator with Lance. "So, wow, hearing those women, I see what you mean about it being larger than life. It's like the wedding video made it a fairytale or something. They said they couldn't get enough of it."

"And I can't watch because all I remember is how much pain Kendra was in." Lance said. "Again, it's a lot, babe. I want to do what I need to do at home and at church. Alonzo can handle the movie stuff."

"The filming and everything that goes with it will come and go quickly," Treva said, walking off. "We just have to stay mindful that God is working—hey, Silas."

"Treva, hey, congrats on the upcoming launch," Silas said, coming toward them.

"Thanks, Silas," Treva said. "I love that you're preaching next week as part of the launch. I'm looking forward to hearing you for the first time. Well, first time at Living Word."

"Silas is a gifted preacher," Lance said. "I'm looking forward to the message as well."

"Appreciate you both," Silas said. "Oh, and Lance, we're meeting in twenty, right?"

"Right," Lance said. "In my office."

They continued toward the offices and saw a woman waiting just outside. She got up to greet them.

"Treva?" The woman, roughly in her forties with dark blonde hair, extended a hand. "Hello. Sally Turner with the *St. Louis Courier*. I'm a little early. Hope that isn't a problem."

"It's no problem at all, Sally," Treva said. "Great to meet you."

"And Pastor Lance Alexander"—Sally extended a hand his way —"pleasure to meet you."

"You as well," Lance said, shaking her hand.

"Sally, we can go right into my office," Treva said, leading the way.

Sally paused, turning to Lance. "Lance, I know you don't have time for a full interview this morning. But I wonder if you might do ten minutes with your wife. Most coverage I've seen focuses on you and Kendra. I'd love to give our readers a glimpse into the current love of your life."

"Ten minutes is about all I have," Lance said. "But I appreciate that focus. I need to stop in my office then I'll be in."

Treva went into her office, taking off her shawl. She hung it on a hook behind the door.

"Sally, I can hang your coat," Treva said.

"Oh, thank you," Sally said, handing it to her. "This is quite a property you all have here. I'm not really the churchgoing type, but my family went now and then when I was growing up." She glanced out of a window. "It was a far cry from this. This is impressive."

"It didn't start out this way, as you can imagine—please, have a seat." Treva sat behind her desk. "When Pastor Mason Lyles founded the church, they were a small group that met in a junior high school."

"Yes, as I prepared for the interview, I read about the transition of leadership from Pastor Lyles to Lance," Sally said, "which also included a history of the church. Again, quite impressive in terms of growth, not just at this location but the global ministry."

"It's a ministry that benefitted me personally," Treva said, "long before I moved to St. Louis." She looked as Lance walked in and sat beside Sally. "I'm grateful to be able to serve here."

"Well, we should get to it. I'll be using the voice recorder on my phone, if that's okay." Sally took out a pen and notepad as well. "Thank you so much, Lance, for a moment of your time. Treva, if you don't mind, I'll circle back to introductory questions with you. I'd like to first hit questions that involve the two of you, given Lance's time constraints."

"Of course," Treva said. "No problem."

"Lance, as you know"—Sally turned toward him—"we received news two days ago that the movie about your life has been given a green light. Except it's not so much about your life but your *love* life, with your former wife Kendra. Can I get your reaction to that change in focus?"

Treva shifted in her seat. *Lord, I prayed about this interview before I knew Lance would be part of it. But You knew. Please give us both wisdom as we answer these questions.*

"So, right," Lance said, "initially, Alonzo's vision was to show the span of my life—"

"And for the record," Sally said, "when you say 'Alonzo,' you're referring to Academy Award winner Alonzo Coles?"

"That's correct," Lance said. "He wanted to show my life from childhood with an addicted mom, to getting expelled from high school, becoming a drug dealer, and spending time in prison—and how Jesus radically transformed all of that. I was excited about that particular vision." He took a moment. "But from the beginning, a lot of prayer has gone into this movie, including an online prayer team my mom started. So I'm trusting that God's in control of all of this. I'm thankful the movie is going forward."

"In the minds of many," Sally said, "you're fixed in a moment in time in this love story with Kendra. But people may not know that you've moved on to a different love story, if you will, with your current wife. Tell us how you met."

"Treva came to a Living Word women's conference," Lance said. "She was scheduled to give a personal testimony about her life."

"Yes, I found that on YouTube and watched it," Sally said.

"Right before the conference," Lance continued, "one of the workshop speakers had to drop out at the last minute. It happened to be a workshop on grief. Since Treva and I had both lost our spouses, we stepped in and did the workshop together, and bonded through that."

"That's quite a story in itself," Sally said. "You fell in love as you worked through your grief?"

"Well, there was more to it, of course," Treva said. "And we didn't fall in love that very weekend—"

"Speak for yourself," Lance said, eyeing his wife.

"I absolutely love this," Sally said. "Lance, you certainly have a knack for finding yourself in unorthodox romances."

"What was unorthodox about Treva and me?" Lance said.

"Oh," Sally said, "just thinking in terms of . . . well, I saw an interview you did after Kendra died, and you said you looked forward to marrying again and having a house full of children. Which would be the normal, expected course. Yet you fell in love with Treva, whom I believe is older than you, with older kids from a late husband, and she's even a grandmother."

Lance took a moment to respond. "I guess you could call it unorthodox. But Treva is more beautiful, more intelligent, and more in love with Jesus than any woman I could've ever imagined as my wife. And on top of that, I still got the house full of children. I'm a blessed man."

"Oh, absolutely," Sally said. "I wouldn't suggest otherwise."

Treva said another prayer as Sally took a moment with her notes.

"Treva," Sally said, looking at her, "when you met Lance, had you heard about this 'amazing love story' between him and Kendra? Had you seen it in the news?"

"I actually hadn't," Treva said. "My sister told me about it, though.

And interestingly, when Lance told me the story himself, that was the thing that moved my heart toward him, the way he loved Kendra."

"Now that's fascinating," Sally said. "I would think that hearing how he loved Kendra and cared for her—the sacrifices and all of that —might cause some trepidation about getting into a relationship with him. Did you wonder if his love for you would measure up?"

Treva could see Lance shifting in his chair.

"I can't say that was a concern," Treva said. "It was the love of God that fueled Lance's love for Kendra. And that's what fuels his love for me. That's why I'm so passionate about this movie—it's the love of Christ that's on display."

"Now before you have to go, Lance," Sally said, "I would love to get a comment from you on the video released by Desiree Riley. It's getting a lot of buzz."

Treva looked at Lance, brow raised.

"I don't know anything about it," Lance said, "so I can't comment."

"I can give you the gist," Sally said. "As you may know, Desiree has a large following on YouTube chronicling her travels around the world. But part of her appeal is that she chronicles her personal journey as well." She clicked around on her phone then turned it toward them. "In this video posted yesterday, she says she's never spoken publicly about the fact that she was once engaged to you. And she relates rather tearfully that one of the biggest mistakes of her life was walking away from that engagement."

Treva looked at Lance again. Lance looked at Sally, his jaw set.

"Desiree said that people need to understand that true love may only come once, and you have to grab hold of it," Sally said. "Given that, can I get a comment from you?"

"My only comment," Lance said, "is that I don't think you were genuine about the focus of this interview. You said you wanted to give readers a glimpse of the current love of my life. But that's not what this is about." Lance stood. "With respect, this interview is over."

"I'm just a reporter doing my job," Sally said.

"And I can appreciate that," Lance said. "But this went beyond the scope of what was agreed to."

Sally nodded, rising. "Understood. My apologies for any misunderstanding."

Treva got Sally's coat. "Thank you for your time, Sally. And we would love for you to join us for service this morning."

"I appreciate that, thank you."

Sally walked out, and Treva turned to her husband.

"Why did I just get blindsided in that interview?" Treva said. "You had a whole fiancée that you've never told me about?"

"Because there's nothing to tell—"

"Were you in love with this woman, Desiree?"

"Yes, but—"

"So much so that you asked her to marry you?"

"Yes, but—"

"And there's nothing to tell? How have you never mentioned her?"

"The engagement only lasted two months," Lance said. "I dumped it from my mind a long time ago."

"Lance, we're not talking about an old girlfriend," Treva said. "How do you dump from your mind someone you wanted to spend the rest of your life with? When was this?"

"*Years* ago," Lance said. "Like, maybe ten? Treva, I'm sorry I didn't tell you, but it's because it's not important. *She's* not important. It literally didn't come up in my mind as something we needed to talk about."

"So what happened?" Treva said. "Why didn't it work out?"

Silas stuck his head in. "Hey, Lance, you ready?"

"On my way." He looked at Treva.

"Go," Treva said. "We'll talk later."

Lance took her hand and pulled her close. "I'm sorry, babe. I just didn't—"

"We'll talk later, Lance."

She walked to her desk and sat down, opening her laptop. Lance watched her for a moment then left out and closed the door.

CHAPTER 10

Stephanie hurried through one of the doors to Living Word, glad she wasn't *too* late. The cousins checked out of the B and B this morning, but not until they'd enjoyed a leisurely breakfast and taken several pictures, some of them with Stephanie, which held her up. She was still amazed sometimes at the bond that could develop in a short period of time with guests. They were already planning to do another cousin reunion same place, same time next year.

Stephanie could hear the praise and worship through the speakers in the building, which meant the second service was already underway. She moved through pockets of people congregating, looking for Jillian who was supposed to meet her. She'd probably gone back to the women's ministry table, where she was serving. Checking her phone, she saw a text from two minutes ago, but—

"Hey, there you are," Jillian said, approaching.

Stephanie took a step back, eyeing her. "Okay, with the mocha brown sweater dress and boots. Aren't you looking cute today." She hugged her. "And I've been meaning to tell you—I loved your hair shorter, but this look is bomb too." She flicked Jillian's curls. "Love that you're letting it grow."

"Thanks so much, girl," Jillian said, "and ahh, thank you for *that.*"

She took the watch Stephanie dangled in front of her. "You don't know how relieved I was when you said you had it. I thought it might've fallen off at the park." She put it on.

"I was wondering what was up with you and Tommy mysteriously disappearing," Stephanie said. "The park, huh? Then he came back and you didn't."

"Long story," Jillian said. "And we're long overdue for one of our talk and pray sessions."

"*Long* overdue," Stephanie said. "And believe me—I need it. But let me get in here. Hey, how was service?"

"So good," Jillian said. "Lance changed it up today. Instead of the next chapter in the series, he talked about—well, I'll just let you hear it for yourself."

"Okay, and just so you know," Stephanie said, "Lindell and I started looking at destination spots, possibly leaving as soon as next Monday."

Jillian smiled. "So you're moving forward with booking the trip."

"Girl, I guess," Stephanie said. "I still can't believe you said you'd help with the B and B."

"And I can't believe you didn't want to ask," Jillian said. "Like it's a huge burden to stay at that mansion."

"You won't be 'staying' at the mansion," Stephanie said. "You'll be *working*. You have no idea. But I won't tell you too much or you'll back out."

Jillian chuckled. "When my kids found out that people from the cast and crew would be there, they wanted to stay the entire shoot. I'm excited for you and Lindell. You definitely need this."

"Well, be praying," Stephanie said. "We won't have anything to do but focus on one another. The warts might only get bigger."

"They can't get bigger than God," Jillian said.

Stephanie headed for the sanctuary then thought again and veered to the ladies' room. If pregnancy had taught her anything, it was that her bladder was no longer her own. This way, maybe she'd make it through the sermon. On her way out, she texted Lindell. He'd left earlier to attend Cedric's class during first service, and she wanted to make sure he was in their usual—

Stephanie stopped cold, heart thumping. *It couldn't be.* She watched the gait from behind, noted the build, the hair. It was unmistakable.

Lord, no. Here? No.

She continued to hang back, letting the distance grow between them. If she could just—

"Hey! Bro, is this your phone?"

Someone came from the men's room, calling after him. And he turned. And saw her.

The guy gave him his phone and continued on. And she and Warren stood fixed for a moment, eyes locked on the other.

"What are you doing here?" Stephanie said. The words came of their own accord.

Warren came toward her, and Stephanie was sure he'd never looked better. What was he doing, hitting the gym *every* day? Hair trimmed shorter, but there was no way to miss those curls. And those eyes that once searched her soul were still locked on her.

"Wow," Warren said. "Congratulations on the baby."

"Warren, what are you doing here?"

"Crazy, right?" Warren said. "Remember how many times you tried to get me to come to Living Word?"

"Yeah, years ago." Why was his beard situation everything? "You can't decide to come *now.*"

"I'm not trying to make you uncomfortable," Warren said. "Since you go to third service, I went to first. And thousands of people go here. I didn't think you'd even see me."

"I usually go to second service now," Stephanie said. "But come on, there are hundreds, maybe thousands, of churches in St. Louis. You suddenly decide to go and pick *this* one?"

"If you want to know the truth," Warren said, "when you reached out a few months ago, I took it as a sign. I had been feeling like God was moving me to go to church, but my excuse was I didn't know where to go. Then you called, and it became clear."

Stephanie moved closer and lowered her voice. "I told you right after that that I shouldn't have called."

"And I get that," Warren said. "Still, I think God used it to get me here. I've been coming for about a month now." He shook his head. "Never heard a pastor who keeps it real like that. I'm actually taking notes and thinking about the sermons during the week. By the way, I met him at the visitors' reception, and he remembered me."

"Remembered you from where?" Stephanie said.

"Your birthday party," Warren said. "I think it was your twenty-fifth."

"I can't believe this," Stephanie muttered.

"But Steph, I need to run," Warren said. "My fiancée's in the car waiting for me."

"Your fiancée?" Stephanie said.

"Yeah, got engaged on Christmas." Warren was suddenly beaming. "I feel like God is moving in my life." He turned and headed out.

Stephanie exhaled, taking a moment to gather herself before continuing to the sanctuary. She checked her phone, saw Lindell's confirmation, and eased in, now so late that Lance had begun his sermon. She moved to the row and squeezed past two women who made room for her to sit beside Lindell.

"What took you so long after you texted me?" he whispered.

"Ran into somebody," she whispered back.

"But since Friday all I've heard are the words 'love story,'" Lance was saying. "And even way before that, when the wedding video went viral—'love story.' And there's always this dreamy tone to it. Look at this quote from an article about Kendra and me." He turned as it came on the screen. "'Sometimes you get that sweet spot of falling in love with someone, and that person falling in love with you, and together you've got this amazing love story. That's really the ultimate situation.'" He turned back to the congregation. "How many of you think that's the ultimate situation?"

A good smattering of hands went up around the sanctuary along with chatter all around, giving Stephanie a moment to exhale. Her heartbeat was erratic still from the run-in with Warren. *At Living*

Word. Did he really say God used her to get him there? She groaned inside. How could she have opened that door?

"I see some hands," Lance said. "But based on what you all tell me privately, I'm thinking there's more." He started toward the other side of the platform. "Let me ask again—how many think that's the ultimate situation?"

The number of hands more than doubled, including those of the women next to Stephanie.

"Okay, here's my next question," Lance said. "If that's the ultimate situation, and you don't have it, where does that leave you? Do you have a second-class life?" He moved closer. "Because listen—I've talked to people whose hearts are aching because they don't have that. They're praying for that, and they feel as if God's not blessing them, that He's not answering their prayers."

Chatter started up again, and Stephanie glanced around, wondering what Lance had said. The replay of the dialogue between her and Warren was louder than everything else.

"And what if you do have that—the 'ultimate situation,'" Lance said, "and you lose it? Do you know how long my marriage to Kendra lasted? One year." He let that settle. "Does that mean I went from ultimate situation to hopeless situation?"

Stephanie's mind raced with more thoughts. What if she'd been with Lindell when she ran into Warren?

"Or what about this?" Lance said. "What if you have the ultimate and mess it up? Stick with me because I'm headed somewhere." He moved across the platform. "Listen, if there's such a thing as an ultimate situation, it won't be ultimate for long because we're flawed people." He paused and looked out at them. "How many of you were here a few years ago when Scott Elliott came before the congregation to confess sexual sin?"

Stephanie looked up. Did Lance just say something about Scott's confession? Lindell's hand went up, along with many others. Stephanie raised hers as well. That was a weekend she'd never forget, her wedding weekend.

"I woke up early yesterday morning with Scott's confession on my mind," Lance said. "I couldn't shake it. The Lord moved me to listen to it again. And Scott, if you're in here for second service, thank you for giving me your blessing to talk about it this morning."

Stephanie took a quick glance around but didn't see him.

"For those who don't know," Lance said, "Scott and his wife Dana had the 'ultimate situation,' so ultimate that they served as co-leaders of Living Word's marriage ministry. As a younger believer, I'd see them and think, 'I want a marriage like that one day. I want that type of love and commitment.'" He paused. "Then one Sunday Scott publicly confessed to cheating on his wife."

The chatter rose again. Stephanie thought back to when she'd initially heard that news. Given that she'd been close friends of the couple, it had indeed been shocking.

Lance walked the platform. "In hindsight I don't think I heard much of what Scott said, because I was so rocked by the headline— that he'd had an affair. So when I listened yesterday, something jumped out at me." He pointed toward the media room. "Let's play the first clip."

Stephanie looked as video of Scott's confession came on the screen.

"You might be thinking, I would never, and I don't blame you. I thought the same thing. Thought I'd never do something like this to my wife, my marriage. But temptation comes." Scott spoke slowly, clearly shaken. "And it can come stronger than anything you've experienced, in ways you hadn't anticipated. If you're not constantly praying, constantly clinging to God, constantly avoiding improper situations, you just might fall."

Lance's eyes stayed on the screen. "And now the second clip."

"I love my wife more than life itself," Scott said. "Yet I've dealt her enormous pain. I don't know how she'll ever forgive me. I don't deserve it." His voice cracked with emotion. "But I'm begging God for a second chance, and I'm begging you"—he paused, looking out at them—"Please. Cling to God. Cling to your spouses. And . . . if you have a mind to, I'm asking you to please pray for my wife and me."

The screen went black, and Lance turned to them. "Did you hear that? Twice he mentioned clinging to God. I knew that's why the Lord wanted me to listen to it. I knew the message I needed to bring today. Because I need everyone to get this—there is no 'ultimate situation' apart from Christ." He paused. "No, let me put it this way—Jesus *is* your ultimate situation. Your greatest love story. And your heart doesn't have to ache if you don't have *this* ultimate situation—you can receive Him today. You can and will mess up but don't worry—He's not going anywhere. Not even death can separate you—it only gets better because you'll be in His presence."

"Glory to you, Jesus." A woman in front of Stephanie raised a hand in praise.

"But to make the most of this ultimate situation?" Lance said. "You need to cling to Him. Not because Scott said so. Because the Bible says so. And we're about to look at that. We're focusing today on *the* relationship. Because if you're not clinging to Him, you might find yourself idolizing romance and even marriage."

"I don't know if I'm ready for this today," the woman next to Stephanie muttered.

"But if you're clinging," Lance continued, "you'll have an intimacy with God that impacts everything else. You'll have that ultimate situation. Turn to Deuteronomy 13:4 and let's get into this word 'cling'."

"I need to listen to that again." Lindell stood, lingering in the pew. "Intimacy with God isn't something I think about. You know?" He sighed. "Kind of depressing, though, if I'm struggling with intimacy with you *and* God."

Stephanie swished around in her bag, looking for her bag of mixed nuts. "I think 'intimacy with God' is one of those things that sounds good in theory, but do you ever really get there? What is it supposed to look like?" She found it and popped a couple of almonds in her mouth.

Lindell looked at her. "Isn't that what he spent the past thirty minutes breaking down?"

"I guess I need to listen again myself." If she'd heard one-third of the message, she'd be surprised. "You know how it is with this pregnancy brain. I feel like I have ADD." She saw Cyd and Cedric coming up the aisle toward them.

"I already know what you're about to say," Stephanie said. "Lance took us *back*."

"Talk about an avalanche of memories," Cyd said. "Everything happened that weekend." She hooked an arm inside Cedric's. "That's the weekend I met this guy."

"And that's why I didn't remember much of Scott's confession either," Cedric said. "I only came to church that day to try to get with Cyd." He shook his head. "Which was Lance's point. I could pursue a woman with *all* the fire. But how much do I pursue intimacy with the Lord?"

Cyd nodded. "Such a powerful message." She looked at Stephanie as they started up the aisle. "How are you and my niece or nephew doing?"

"Doing good," Stephanie said. "I love how active the baby is now." She rubbed her stomach as she leaned closer to Cyd. "You won't believe who I saw at church today."

"Who?" Cyd said.

The aisle filled with more people and they weaved through bodies, moving a little ahead of Lindell and Cedric. Stephanie leaned even closer to Cyd. "Warren."

"*Warren?*" Cyd looked at her. "Why would he show up here?"

"We'll have to talk later," Stephanie said.

"So there's a story?" Cyd said.

"*Obviously*," Stephanie whispered.

Cyd leaned in. "Have you been talking to him?"

"Just once," Stephanie said. "Months ago. But can you believe he's been coming for a month now?"

"I've got so many thoughts swirling I can't even think straight."

"Well, here's one more," Stephanie said. "He's engaged."

"Oh," Cyd said. "Seriously?"

"Why did your whole countenance change?"

77

"Hey, you two must be deep in conversation," Cedric said. "We asked if you want to go to brunch."

"Oh," Stephanie said. "You know I'm down. I stay hungry."

The four of them walked toward the exit.

"Cedric and I will go get Chase and meet you guys," Cyd said.

"Sounds good," Stephanie said.

"You okay, Steph?" Lindell said. "Seems like you've been somewhere else entirely."

"Oh, yeah, I'm okay," Stephanie said. "Just a lot on my mind."

Stephanie continued to the car. All she could think was that at any moment on any given Sunday, Lindell could run into Warren, the one person he'd never been able to stomach.

Church had now become a powder keg.

CHAPTER 11

*J*illian felt a range of emotions as she made her way to Silas's office. All week she'd told herself *it's just coffee.* But all morning—during service, as she worked the women's ministry table, when the final service let out—she'd felt the anxiousness building. She'd be spending one-on-one time with Silas. They'd be getting to know one another, sharing about their lives, knowing they wouldn't be there unless there was *something*, even if only a surface something. As much as she'd tried to think otherwise, it was a date. Something she hadn't done in well over twenty years. Her heart beat an irregular rhythm at the thought of it.

Lord, we just heard the sermon, and that's the desire of my heart—to cling to You. Whatever Your will, Lord, let it be done. I don't want to get ahead of You or lag behind. I just want to cling.

Jillian paused at Silas's opened door and gave a knock. "Hey, if you need some time I can wait downstairs."

"Hey, no, I'm good." Silas looked up from his laptop. "Just finishing an email." A couple more clicks of the keyboard and he rose, packing up the laptop, then walked toward her. "I realized this morning that timing this for after church may not have worked well for you. You had to stay through three services."

"That's my norm," Jillian said, walking with him toward the elevator. "I'm on staff with Living Water and serve with Living Word's women's ministry. And they both have busy resource tables that need volunteers."

"So the better comment was—I hope you're not too tired," Silas said, smiling.

Jillian moved into the elevator and pushed the button for the main level. Standing so close, she couldn't help but take note of him. Tallish frame, on the slender side, cashew colored skin, and without a doubt, kind eyes.

"By the way," she said, "I figured I'd just follow you since you know where we're going."

"Or I could drive us," Silas said, "and bring you back. It's not that far. I love this spot. The coffee's really good."

"So you move to a new city and scope out the best coffee spots, huh?"

Silas smiled a little. "I do that on vacation too."

They stepped out of the elevator and Jillian paused to slip on her coat, Silas moving to help. She felt her phone vibrate as they continued on and answered when she saw her son's name.

"Mom, where are you?" David said. "I'm in the building looking for you."

"I thought you left with Sophie and Trevor," Jillian said. "I'm near the entryway."

"Oh, I'm headed that way," David said. "You didn't get my message?"

"No, sweetheart, when did you—" Her heart lodged in her throat as David rounded the corner with Tommy. She'd gotten through the morning seeing him only at a distance. Of course she'd run into him now.

Their eyes met and for a moment, everything else dimmed.

"Hey," Jillian said.

Tommy gave her a light hug. "Hey, Jill." His words grazed her ear, and he moved on to Silas, chatting.

"Mom, where are you going?" David spoke in a low tone, glancing toward Silas.

Jillian sighed inside. She hadn't told her kids about the outing with Silas. She didn't want them to think she was now "dating." They knew she and Tommy went out from time to time. He'd even stayed for dinner after doing work around the duplex. But that wasn't a big deal in their eyes. It was only Tommy.

"Just going for a cup of coffee," Jillian said. "Why were you looking for me?"

"I'm going with Tommy," David said. "I didn't think you'd mind."

"Going with Tommy where?"

"Remember you said if I wanted to shadow him, I had to ask him myself?" David said. "Well, I asked this morning. And he told me what was coming up on his schedule. You know I was hype when he mentioned the Majestic Road concert today."

"I told David he had to make sure it was all right with you." Tommy moved closer. "Concert's at six. He said he could hang at the house with Reg and me until then, and we'll get something to eat. I'll bring him home right after the concert."

"Mom, seriously," David said. "It's cool, right?"

"I thought this was supposed to be educational," Jillian said. "Learning about life as an entertainment reporter. Sounds like you just want to hear one of your favorite bands. I think you should write a review of the concert tomorrow for school."

Tommy slipped her a look. She knew what he was thinking. She was being a killjoy.

"*Okay*, Mom," David said. "I'll do a review."

"Let me get you some money for dinner." Jillian reached into her purse.

"Jill, you know I got it."

"Tommy, I told you, you don't have to . . ." Jillian took a breath. "Fine. Thank you for doing this for David."

"It'll be fun," Tommy said, ushering him out.

"Thanks, Mom," David called over his shoulder.

Jillian took another breath and looked at Silas. "Ready?"

～

"Okay, I wasn't sure about trying a burnt orange latte, but this is delicious." Jillian took another sip.

Silas sat across from her at the two-top table. "I told you I couldn't explain the flavor. You just had to try it." He took a sip of his own. "Glad you like it."

"The vibe here is nice too." Jillian glanced around. "Artsy. Cozy."

"So I get points for taste?" Silas said. "No pun intended."

Jillian nodded with a faint smile. "You get points for taste."

Silas set his coffee mug down. "I know we said this isn't a date. I don't know about you, but I'm still feeling that first date awkwardness, which I haven't felt in decades. So if I seem a little weird . . ."

Jillian raised a hand. "I guess we'll be weird together."

"At least it's not completely awkward," Silas said, "since we've done the small talk thing at Lance and Treva's. I know you grew up in DC, you and your husband Cecil were married over twenty years, and you've got four beautiful children—the oldest at Spelman, right?"

"That's right," Jillian said. "And you grew up in the Denver area, married your college sweetheart Audrey, your oldest son is a junior at Baylor and Lucas is a high school senior. And for college . . . don't tell me . . . Michigan State?"

"Good memory," Silas said. "And I know you and Treva both went to Maryland. Wait, didn't Tommy go there?"

Jillian nodded, sipping her latte. "Tommy and I were best friends in college. He was like a brother."

"I had never been around the two of you," Silas said, "but just now leaving church . . . I can definitely see that."

"So how did you and Audrey meet?" Jillian said.

"I was a year ahead of her," Silas said. "Spring of sophomore year she showed up with a mutual friend at this eatery near campus that had *the* best wings—"

"So it's a coffee and wings thing with you."

"Ha. True." Silas smiled. "So I met her and we all hung out. By the time we were walking back to campus, Audrey and I had paired off,

82

just talking. Found out she was a believer, and we started going to this campus Bible study together."

Jillian smiled. "Love at first sight?"

"I can't really say that," Silas said. "We grew as friends for a few months. But the following year we became inseparable. Married in March of my senior year."

"Wow," Jillian said. "I'm curious why you didn't wait until you graduated."

"Honest answer?" Silas looked amused. "We were committed to celibacy, and 'it's better to marry than to burn' became our favorite verse."

Jillian chuckled. "I love it, though. Sounds like you were a strong believer in college. What's your story?"

"Actually, I didn't know the Lord till college," Silas said. "My room-mate freshman year was a serious believer. Wasn't into a lot of stuff the rest of us were into, read his Bible and all that—and he was a really cool guy. We'd play ball at the gym, talk about life, and I'd ask him a ton of questions because he was just intriguing to me." He paused, looking at her. "He led me to the Lord over a plate of wings."

Jillian gave him a look.

"I'm so serious," Silas said.

"So how long have you been in ministry full time?" Jillian said.

Silas thought about it. "About six years," he said. "I served as a lay elder for a while before that. Audrey and I prayed long and hard about whether I would leave my corporate job, and I eventually did. Joined the pastoral staff full time then two years later, our lead pastor announced his retirement. I was on track to replace him." His gaze fell a little. "Soon after we found out Audrey was sick."

"I can't even fathom," Jillian said. "When you told me about the illness and what she went through, my heart hurt for your family. So incredibly painful."

Silas nodded soberly. "It was a blessing that I had time to care for her," he said. "The church was very supportive. But as we walked through that, naturally I didn't have the energy or the inclination to pursue a lead pastor position. Plus Lucas was having a really hard time with everything. It was a season to focus the bulk of my energy on home."

"Definitely a blessing that you could do that," Jillian said, "and that you had a heart to do it." She paused. "I don't think I ever asked what led you to move to St. Louis."

"It's funny," Silas said. "As a young believer I used to eat up Living Word Bible studies. Felt like I knew Pastor Lyles."

"Oh, goodness, same," Jillian said.

"About four years ago I connected with Lance at a pastor's conference." Silas drank more of his coffee. "We kept in touch and when my wife got sick, he was the only person who really got what I was going through. And he was there, reaching out at just the right time." He seemed to ponder it even now. "I came to Pastor Lyles's home going, and Lance told me about the process to replace the pastor. I said, 'Hey, man, you would be an excellent choice. And if it happens, I'd love to talk.'"

"That's so interesting," Jillian said.

"God had been moving in my heart to make a change," Silas said, "and the thought of serving at Living Word—it just resonated. It all fell into place." He focused on her. "So how have you and the kids adjusted to life in St. Louis?"

Jillian thought a moment. "It's hard to say because life itself is one big adjustment."

"True," Silas said.

"But it's been a blessing for them to be near their cousins," Jillian said. "And I don't know what I would've done without my sister. Actually, it's been a blessing to have a whole circle of sisters here."

"And you've got your brother too," Silas said. "Tommy. It's a blessing to have such a lasting friendship."

Jillian nodded. "The other thing is, we're still not fully settled. Our house in Maryland sold pretty fast, and Cecil and I had been looking for a house here when . . ." She took a moment, staring downward. "Everything happened so quickly. I rented a duplex as a temporary measure and haven't begun the process of finding something permanent. It's starting to weigh on me."

"We're in a similar situation," Silas said. "Rented a condo thinking I'd have more time once I got here to look for a house. Then you get busy with work."

"Exactly," Jillian said. "I haven't had time to take my car to the shop, let alone go house hunting."

"Your car's giving you trouble?" Silas said.

"A bit," Jillian said. "I've got an appointment this week."

"Let me know if I can do anything to help," Silas said.

"That's nice of you, thank you."

"I used to think about what life would be like for Audrey if something happened to me," Silas said. "I knew our sons would be there, but still . . . I just want you to know I do mean it. If you ever need anything."

"And I do appreciate it," Jillian said.

Silas held his mug. "So, I have to admit I didn't think you'd say yes to coffee. You're always kind, easy to talk to. But at the same time you can seem a million miles away—understandably. I expected a gracious no."

"Well, I did have to think about it," Jillian said. "And I was toying with different versions of no." She smiled a little. "But we'd had a few conversations, good ones. And I knew you weren't crazy"—she gave a shrug—"plus it helped that we were in the same place. The fact that you said coffee and not dinner was huge."

"Does that mean I can't say dinner next time?"

Jillian's gaze shifted as she finished her coffee.

"I'm sorry," Silas said. "I didn't mean to make you uncomfortable."

"It's just . . . somehow that's more of an affirmative step in my mind. I'm not ready for that."

"I understand," Silas said. "I don't know that I'm ready either." He looked at her. "But this was easier than I anticipated. I hope it's okay to say I enjoy your company."

"You're interesting, Silas Keys." Jillian looked at him. "I would've called you understated. But I see you don't have a problem saying what's on your mind."

"No, you're right," Silas said. "I lean toward less. I'm not saying everything that's on my mind."

"Hmm maybe you *are* crazy," Jillian said. "I just haven't heard it yet."

Silas chuckled a little. "Nothing crazy. Just thoughts like—it's almost disarming, how beautiful you are. But see, I would've never said that."

"And you don't get to say anything else," Jillian said. "I'm speechless enough."

Silas tipped his mug, finishing his coffee. "I guess it's time to head back then—in silence."

Jillian rose and put on her coat. "It has to be an awkward silence, though, given the quasi-first-date thing."

"Agreed," Silas said, heading for the door. "We need to end this right. Awkward and weird." He held the door for her.

Jillian shook her head as she passed. "It was easier than I anticipated as well, Mr. Keys."

Silas followed. "You just messed it up, though. That wasn't weird."

CHAPTER 12

reva brushed her teeth quickly, eager to make her next point. "So now"—she spat into the sink—"this thing has blown up so much that even though Alonzo just got back into town last night—he's showing up here *Monday morning* to talk about your ex-fiancée?"

"Will you stop calling her my ex-fiancée?" Lance replied from the bedroom.

"That's what she is," Treva said. "Everybody's calling her that. Google it." She put her toothbrush up and gargled with mouthwash.

"Alonzo was coming anyway," Lance said, "to talk about the change in the movie focus."

Treva walked into the bedroom. "I thought you said he wants to talk about the situation with Desiree too."

"I don't know why, but yes." Lance was typing on his phone. "He wants to talk about Rae—"

"Oh. Yes, I forgot. It's *Rae*." She threw on jeans she didn't care about.

"Treva, I thought we talked about this last night," Lance said. "I keep telling you it wasn't important. Why do you still have an attitude?"

"Oh, sorry I can't 'dump' things as quickly as you can," Treva said. "I have an attitude because there's a whole part of your life I didn't know about, a significant part." She pulled a shirt over her head. "And if you could dump that from your mind, what else did you dump? Do you have kids somewhere?"

"Treva, come on," Lance said. "We never sat down and had a conversation about people from our past. Don't act like you've told me about every guy in your life."

"There's *one* besides you," Treva said. "Hezekiah. And no, I don't need to know about every woman in your life. Just the ones you were so deeply in love with that you asked to *marry* you." She put on a hoop earring. "And I can't believe you're calling that a talk we had last night. All you wanted to tell me was how unimportant it all was."

"Because I don't want to spend any energy on her," Lance said. "But fine. What else do you want to know?"

Treva put on the other earring. "How did you meet?"

"I told you we met at the camera shop," Lance said.

"But how?"

Lance put down his phone. "She came in to buy a camera but didn't know what she wanted or needed. I happened to be the one to wait on her, so I was telling her about the different models, options, all that."

"So how did you jump from that to dating?" Treva said.

"We didn't jump to anything," Lance said. "I taught classes at the shop, and she signed up to learn how to use the camera she bought. Then she signed up for private tutoring." He sat on the bed. "We'd go to different places to practice what she was learning, and one day church came up. She was skeptical based on her experiences, so I invited her to Living Word. From there we started talking about the Bible during our outings. It was more like a discipleship situation at first."

"Until you fell in love," Treva said.

"Which is when the problems started," Lance said. "I became more and more aware that I wasn't good enough for her."

Treva sat next to him. "Yeah, but you always battle those 'I'm not good enough' thoughts."

"It wasn't in my head. Her parents told her—'You need someone on your level.'" Lance gave a slight shrug. "She fought them on it for a while, but bottom line . . . She was working on a graduate degree. I had no degree, not even high school. I *wasn't* on her level. I could tell it started to bother her."

"How could you tell?"

"She'd say things like—'You need aspirations beyond working at that camera shop.'"

"But you were a youth pastor also," Treva said.

"Not yet," Lance said. "I hadn't even launched my photography business. All of that came after the breakup."

"So you propose," Treva said, "you're planning a wedding, everything's great for two months. Then what? What did she say?"

"Everything wasn't great," Lance said. "Once we got engaged, she became more critical. She knew I was close to Pastor Lyles, so she said I should see about joining the pastoral staff. Then I'd have a more well-respected position."

"Wow."

"We got engaged around the time she graduated with her Master's," Lance said, "and her parents gave her a graduation gift to travel overseas. She left maybe two weeks after we got engaged. A two-week trip stretched to three weeks, then a month."

"Don't tell me she broke off the engagement over the phone," Treva said.

"Letter," Lance said. "She was brutally honest, I'll give her that. Said it was always her dream to travel the world, and now that she was living it, she couldn't go back. She felt trapped in St. Louis. She said she loved me and loved every moment she spent with me, but she couldn't give up her dreams for a dead end life."

"She didn't put it like that, did she?"

"Her very words," Lance said. "Funny. I gave her the tools she needed to make a living out of traveling the world, the thing that took her from me."

"Did you talk to her at all after that?"

"Never." Lance checked his phone. "Mom says Alonzo and Cinda are downstairs."

Treva looked at him. "So how do you feel about her making this video with all the regrets? She said she'll always love you."

Lance got up and started walking with her downstairs. "You watched it?"

"Of course I watched it," Treva said.

"I don't feel anything," Lance said. "Why would I care?"

Treva led the way to the kitchen. Alonzo and Cinda stood talking to Pamela, Alonzo holding Wes.

"Hey, you two, welcome back," Treva said. She and Lance hugged them both. "Seems like you've been gone forever."

"I know," Cinda said. "Only a little over a week, but so much has happened."

"For sure," Treva said.

"Again!" Wes kicked his legs, looking at Alonzo. "Again!"

Alonzo gave Treva a sheepish look. "We may or may not have been doing the thing where I throw him in the air."

"You mean that thing that almost gives me a heart attack?" Treva said.

"Again!" Wes said, laughing in anticipation.

"We have to wait, little guy," Alonzo said. "We need conditions to be just right." He chuckled.

"Have a seat, you all," Treva said. "Can we get you anything?"

"Momma Pam already got us something to drink." Alonzo moved to the table and sat with Wes in his lap.

"And we ate before we came." Cinda sat next to him. "So we're good, thanks."

"Alonzo said the team was up half the night working," Pamela said.

"So now you have to actually make the movie, huh?" Lance said. "And you know how to do that?"

"Somebody better," Alonzo said, smiling. "We've got a great team. They're excited to get here in a couple days and get rolling."

"So, Alonzo"—Pamela joined them at the table—"since you were up half the night, I'm surprised you're over here so early."

"I wanted to come first thing to convey everything in person." Alonzo turned to Lance. "First, I really did fight for the initial vision. I even prayed about whether to walk away from negotiations." He dodged Wes's hands as he poked him in the face. "I felt God was saying to move forward, especially since we can still tell the story of your early years through flashbacks. But I can't blame you for having second thoughts."

"You told Alonzo you were having second thoughts?" Pamela looked at her son. "About the movie?"

"I can't help but have second thoughts." Lance leaned against the counter. "If Alonzo had come to me in the beginning and said he wanted to do a movie about Kendra and me, I would've said no." He moved to get Wes, who was reaching for him. "I never liked that the wedding video got uploaded to YouTube. I didn't marry Kendra thinking it would be some love story. And I definitely don't want people calling me a knight in shining armor—a reporter actually said that in an interview request."

"Lance, why are you worried about all of that?" Pamela said. "You can't control how people spin stuff."

"I get what he's saying, though," Alonzo said. "The original script focused on the two of you for the first part of the movie, mother and son struggling through addiction and poverty. Then an entire section focused on Lance's downward spiral, culminating in a prison sentence. And what I really loved was showing Pastor Lyles ministering at the prison, how the two of you connected, and the moment you gave your life to Jesus behind bars." He sighed. "Now it begins and ends with Kendra and Lance. I'm hoping the main message of the power of Christ isn't lost."

"Alonzo," Pamela said, "you told me that after you won the Academy Award, you prayed specifically about your next project." She shifted more toward him. "And you said you heard from God about turning down that other project, the one people thought was a perfect fit where you would've played the pastor's son. And instead, you felt strongly that this was what God was calling you to do." She cast a glance at her son. "Don't let Lance's second thoughts give you second thoughts."

Cinda took Alonzo's hand. "He's already having second thoughts, thinking maybe God didn't really move him to do this."

"Okay, listen"—Pamela leaned in now—"just because Lance is a pastor and has been walking with God a little longer doesn't mean he hears from God any better than you do."

"Mom, of course it doesn't," Lance said, sitting beside her with Wes. "Alonzo knows that."

"I'm making sure he knows," Pamela said. "And matter of fact, Alonzo, you probably hear better with respect to this project because Lance is too close to it. Let the Lord lead you and listen to *His* voice. We ain't been doing all this praying for nothing. I *know* God is working."

Cinda smiled a little. "He needed that, Momma Pam."

Pamela got up and hugged Lance's neck from behind. "Y'all know I love my son and respect him as my pastor," she said. "With church stuff I stay quiet—"

"You do?" Lance said, looking up at her.

"When we're *at* church," Pamela said. "I tell you what I think later. But Alonzo and Cinda are family. I had to say what was on my mind."

"Momma Pam, I appreciate everything you said." Alonzo focused on her. "But honestly, I was disappointed about the outcome before I even talked to Lance." He hesitated. "So that was the first thing. We also need to talk about Desiree Riley. Her video's gone viral."

"Wow," Pamela said, sitting back down, "I can't remember the last time I heard that name. What video?"

"We found out about it yesterday from the reporter who interviewed Treva," Lance said. "I haven't watched it, but apparently she talks about her regrets about breaking off the engagement."

"And you didn't mention it?" Pamela said.

"It's been a lot, Mom," Lance said. "I didn't feel like talking about it."

"Yeah, she lays it out there," Alonzo said. "Says Lance is the only man who ever truly loved her, and ending the relationship is a decision she'll always regret."

"Ooh, that's a lot of nerve right there," Pamela said. "After the way she did my son? I don't even know if I could watch that."

"So there's talk of putting her in the movie now," Alonzo said. "Well, not *her*, but you get it—a character who plays her."

"Why?" Lance said.

"Well," Alonzo said, "last year, in preparation for all of this, I asked for names of people I could interview who played a significant role in your life."

Lance nodded. "I remember."

"You didn't mention Desiree," Alonzo said.

"Because she wasn't significant," Lance said.

"But she kind of is," Alonzo said. "She played a significant role in that season of your life. And think about what it adds to the story. If you and Desiree had worked out, there wouldn't have been a Kendra and Lance." He took a sip of water. "Also, the failed engagement makes the Kendra story even more powerful. The fact that you would take such a risk on love *again*."

"That's true," Pamela said. "People want to know how you could go all in and love Kendra, knowing you could lose her in a short time. But to know that this was *after* you went all in and loved someone— and *did* lose her? It doesn't make sense from a natural standpoint to set yourself up for another broken heart. It just shows that it wasn't about you—which is what you want to convey."

"We're meeting about it again this afternoon," Alonzo said. "But her character would only be a minor role, portrayed through a flashback. The team thinks it takes everything up a notch, but I wanted to get you all's input."

"If I was having second thoughts before . . ." Lance heaved a sigh. "*Maybe* it adds to the story, but I'd argue it's nowhere near essential. And now every interviewer will expect me to talk about Kendra *and* Rae. It's a complete distraction. And by the way, she doesn't regret anything. She just wants to grab some spotlight."

"At this point, interviewers will ask about her whether she's in the movie or not," Pamela said. "Like the reporter yesterday."

"I just find it really ironic," Lance said. "Given everything we had to cut from the movie, *this* is the thing that could get included?"

"It's that love story theme," Alonzo said. "But Lance, I feel you. Like I said, I was fighting for the original focus."

"I know you were," Lance said. "And Mom was right. I'm probably too close to this to be able to separate myself and hear what God is saying." Lance let Wes squiggle his way to the floor. "I know you've been seeking Him, and I have to rest in that. It's just been a lot to grapple with at once."

"Can we take a moment and pray together?" Pamela said. "There's a lot happening. All these changes with the movie plus the past showing up all of a sudden. The enemy would love to stir some stuff up right about now." She looked at them. "But I'll tell you this—prayer got us this far and we gon' *keep* praying. God has been *faithful*." She shook her head, thinking about it. "He didn't have to send financing for this movie, but He *did*. Shoot, He didn't have to put Alonzo and Lance on the same path and cause them to connect, but He *did*. And I'm thankful we can trust Him, even when things don't look the way we thought they would. We can trust Him when we don't understand and when we don't like what we see, because He's *sovereign*."

"Amen," Lance said.

"He's just so good," Pamela said, tears welling. "I've *seen* His goodness. He didn't have to deliver me from that prison, but He *did*. Brought me out with a strong hand. I *trust* Him. He is *God*." She paused, overcome, letting the tears stream down her face. "This movie will get made, and it will glorify Him, because this is God's—and He's faithful."

Lance took her hand, lifting her from the chair, and embraced her. "I needed that, Mom."

Treva stood and joined the hug. "I needed it too."

Cinda stood with them. "Can we pray about the million things we need to get done?" She spied Wes trying to scamper from the kitchen and went to get him. "Like the space we need for our production office and base camp."

"How much space do you need?" Lance said. "The Living Water building's got three empty floors. You should go take a look and see if it works."

"See if it works?" Alonzo joined the circle. "God's already provided the perfect house to stand in for this one—right near the church. Now you're telling me we can set up our base camp at the church?"

"What's a base camp?" Treva said.

"The go-to place during filming," Alonzo said. "On a bigger production, it's where you'll find the actors' trailers, hair and makeup trailers, costume department, catering, all of that. For a smaller film like this, it'll be everything to have this kind of space in the Living Water building."

"Look at God," Treva said. "Answering prayer before we pray."

They moved into a circle and joined hands, with Cinda holding Wes.

"Maybe we should just go around the circle and each of us pray as we're led," Pamela said.

"I need to do one thing before we start," Treva said. Her hand in Lance's, she leaned close to him and kissed him. "I love you, babe. And I don't want to give the enemy even a toehold between us."

"That's what I'm talking about," Pamela said, raising a fist. "You kicked us off real good, Treva."

CHAPTER 13

"It's eerie how much these pictures of Brooke look like the ones of Kendra." Faith held up two examples from her spread on the floor. "The hair, earrings, even the clothing is similar."

Reggie looked from behind his laptop on the sofa. "Somebody did an amazing job with the look. What are you working on?"

"Set design for Kendra's room." Faith glanced over at Zoe, fully engaged with her doll's house. "She kept lots of framed pictures on her shelves, especially from high school and college. Brooke did a photo shoot to recreate the looks. I had them printed and got frames." She looked up at him. "I'm in the art department today."

"I thought you were in the wardrobe department today," Reggie said, "all that running around you were doing to different clothing stores. You float to a different department every five minutes."

"And I love it," Faith said. "Remember Alonzo was practically apologizing when he approached me about this job? 'I can't tell you exactly what you'll be doing, sort of an assistant to Cinda and me but also a production assistant when we're shooting—it'll be a hodgepodge—but no glamor whatsoever, lots of grunt work. Plus I haven't thought through the pay . . .'" She chuckled at the way she tried to sound like Alonzo.

"The main thing he wanted and needed was someone he could trust," Reggie said. "I love that you were the first one to come to mind for both him and Cinda." He looked back down at his laptop. "And all that apologizing he was doing, he didn't know this would be perfect for you. And *us*. I still can't believe we'll be working on the Living Word campus together."

"Right?" Faith said. "The question is whether we'll have time to see each other. People start arriving tomorrow, including Mariah and Brooke, which means it's about to be crazy—"

"Here, Mommy," Zoe said, serving her a drumstick and an egg sunny-side-up on a blue plate.

"Oh, this looks delicious," Faith said, taking it. "Did you make this yourself?"

Zoe nodded big as she went to get another, this one with a pepperoni slice and a piece of toast. "Here, Reggie," she said, giving it to him.

"For me?" Reggie said.

Zoe nodded with a smile.

"I can't wait to taste this." He put the laptop to the side, took the red plate, and took a pretend bite of the pizza. "Chef Zoe, I think this is your best yet." He clapped his hands. "Brava."

Zoe started clapping too, and got so tickled she started running around in circles. "Mommy, I bet you can't catch me," she said, laughing.

Faith got up and ran behind her. "You're too fast for me, Zoe."

"Go, Zoe, go!" Reggie said.

The doorbell rang, and Reggie got up to get it. Jesse stood on the other side.

"Aye, what's up, man?" Reggie opened the door wide.

"All good, man," Jesse said, walking in.

"Daddy!" Zoe motored to the door the moment she heard his voice. Jesse scooped her up and brought her into the family room.

"Did I forget you were coming to get her?" Faith said.

"No, I'm meeting Tommy." Jesse paused. "Why are you out of breath?"

Faith chuckled. "Playing with Zoe. Oh, I have to show you." She got her phone from the floor where she'd been sitting and found the video. "Zoe's been playing with the doll's house nonstop. I caught this yesterday after church."

Jesse watched, smiling. "She's really getting into it, huh?"

"Totally," Faith said.

Jesse opened his phone. "Air drop it to me."

"Daddy, can I have juice?" Zoe tugged Jesse toward the kitchen.

"You're asking *me*, Princess?" Jesse said. "What did your mommy say?"

"Please, Daddy?" Zoe pulled his hand. "Want apple juice."

Faith moved into her line of vision. "Yes, what did Mommy say, Zoe?"

Zoe gave a shrug.

"She knows I said no," Faith said. "We cut way back on juice because then she won't drink milk." She eyed Jesse. "But I wonder how much juice she gets at her dad's."

"Uh, I think I'll plead the fifth," Jesse said.

"Sounds serious," Tommy said, coming into the room. "Folk out here pleading the fifth? What's up, man?" he said, greeting Jesse with a hug. "I'm thinking we can go downstairs."

"I didn't even know you had a downstairs," Jesse said. "You've got a lot of space in this house."

"Big family dreams," Reggie said.

"Tax write off," Tommy said.

"Hey, Reg, you should join us," Jesse said. "Tommy's starting a life group."

"That is not what this is." Tommy looked at his brother. "Jesse wanted me to start one, but you know that's not my thing."

"Then we talked about the sermon after service for about twenty minutes," Jesse said. "I told him that's exactly what we could be doing in a setting like this, where we've got more time. So in my mind, this is at least a pilot for a life group."

"I said we could meet and see what God does," Tommy said. "If it's a pilot, then it's a pilot to see if the two of us meet again." He chuckled a little.

Reggie looked at his brother. "So am I invited or nah?"

"You know you can hang," Tommy said. "I just didn't want you to be expecting some deep, theological whatever. This is casual, informal, unprepared—"

"Okay, got it," Reggie said. "Laidback is perfect. I'll be down in a minute."

Reggie saved the article he'd been editing and closed his laptop as Tommy led Jesse downstairs.

Faith looked at Reggie. "I see you and Jesse have gotten chummy lately."

"We would've been cool a long time ago," Reggie said, "if it weren't for you."

Faith raised a brow at him.

"You know what I mean," Reggie said. "Jesse and I met in the context of digging the same woman. Makes things a little complicated. But as time passes, it's not about you anymore. Just brotherhood in Christ." He paused. "And I might've prayed about it."

"Did you really?" Faith said.

Reggie shrugged. "We're part of each other's lives. I would never want Zoe to feel tension between us or to feel funny going from one house to the other because *we've* got issues." He looked over at her as she rearranged bedroom furniture in the doll's house. "So yeah, I was praying."

Faith put her arms around him and kissed him. "Have I told you I love you?"

Reggie brought her closer and kissed her again. "I love you too, baby."

"I wonder if Tommy starting this group—or whatever he's not calling it—is part of the answer to prayer," Faith said.

"I don't know," Reggie said. "Could be an answer to another prayer . . . for Tommy."

❧

"First, let's be clear," Reggie said. "Odds are high that Tommy paid Lance to give that sermon."

"Wasn't it perfect for where I'm at?" Tommy sat forward on an older armchair. "And I hope you felt bad for every time you said I was crazy for being done with relationships, as if that's the 'ultimate situation'."

"Wait, what?" Jesse had the sofa. "You're done with relationships?"

Reggie nodded for his brother. "That's what Tommy's on right now."

"And you can see my brother's been giving me a hard time," Tommy said.

"I understand, though," Reggie said, on the sofa with Jesse. "Because I said the same thing after what happened with my old girl-friend Mia—'I'm done.'"

"You were young and that was your first real relationship," Tommy said. "Nobody took you seriously. Where I'm at is completely different."

"So you're *done* done?" Jesse said. "No marriage, no dating, no nothing?"

"I wouldn't say 'no nothing'," Tommy said. "First Corinthians seven comes to mind, where it says if you're unmarried, you can be more concerned about the things of the Lord. That's why the sermon was perfect, all about clinging to *Him*." He nodded a little. "But yeah, that's what I'm saying. *Done* done."

"You're lightweight blowing my mind right now," Jesse said. "That's like, monk status."

"You know why it's mind-blowing?" Tommy said. "Because people act like marriage is the default status in the kingdom. Like some-thing's wrong if you're not aiming for it. But reading and meditating on First Corinthians seven gave me a whole different paradigm."

"I'm with you on all of that," Reggie said. "As a matter of fact, I spent some time in that chapter after one of our talks. And you're right—the apostle Paul actually says it's good to stay unmarried like he was—"

"And even said he wished all men were that way," Tommy said.

"But right after that he said every man has his own *gift* from God," Reggie said. "So that's the question—has God given you that gift? And if so, is it for a lifetime or only for a season?" He spread his hands in a light shrug. "I know I've been giving you a hard time, but it's all in love. I don't want you to make certain decisions because you're in your feelings, man."

"I know," Tommy said. "I don't want that either. But I just know that right now God is moving me to lean even more into my relationship with Him. That's why the sermon was so on point."

"Yeah, it convicted me," Jesse said. "I've been intentional about dating Jordyn as far as what we do and don't do, and where and when. I'm intentional about texting and calling. I'll buy her little things to let her know I'm thinking about her." He paused. "But how intentional am I with God? When Lance asked that, I didn't have an answer, not one I liked."

"Right," Tommy said. "It moved me to be more intentional about time in the word this week. So"—he opened the Bible beside him and flipped through—"I've been specifically looking at how different people were clinging to God, only a couple so far, but it's rocking me. And based on what I'm seeing, I'm making this list"—he pulled out a folded piece of paper—"with intentional ways to cling to God." He shrugged. "Just want to challenge myself."

Reggie looked at him. "Are you serious right now? We're how many minutes in"—he checked his watch—"and Mr. Nothing Deep or Theological Happening Here tells us, not only about a dope new study —but that he's got a whole Cling Challenge?"

Tommy gave him a look. "If you got all that from these little scribbled notes I just showed you . . . okay."

"Reg, let Tommy be Tommy. We know the deal." Jesse got out his phone. "Who's the first person you looked at?"

"David," Tommy said. "So good."

Reggie got his phone as well and opened his Bible app. "Let's go."

CHAPTER 14

*L*aptop on the kitchen counter, Stephanie hovered near the stove, intermittently checking roasted chicken as she searched travel options. She was convinced more than ever that she and Lindell needed a getaway and they needed it now. But where to?

She clicked between a dozen windows, comparing hotel and Airbnb rates as well as airfare to different destinations. Last minute deals on hotels abounded, even reduced rates on rental homes. But flights were astronomical. At this point she just wanted to find the cheapest island to fly to. If it had sun and water—fabulous.

My fiancée's waiting for me.

Stephanie sighed as her fingers paused on the laptop. Why couldn't she rid herself of Warren's voice? She not only heard it; she felt it in the pit of her stomach.

She opened the oven, peering at the chicken, which wasn't anymore done than when she'd checked two minutes ago.

My fiancé . . .

This time Stephanie heard *her* words, spoken the day she told Warren she'd gotten engaged to Lindell. She could see herself vividly, standing in the doorway to her apartment.

"What's this?" Stephanie had said. "Did we say we were getting takeout?"

"Baby, since when do we have to say we're getting takeout?" Warren moved past her. "I just bring it. And typically you're thankful."

"It's just—you know I've got a lot going on lately." Stephanie followed him into the kitchen. "You have to give some notice. I have plans tonight."

Warren took out cartons of Chinese. "You keep saying you've got a lot going on, but never any specifics."

"That's not true," Stephanie said. "The other night I told you I had an event at church. I even asked if you wanted to go."

"You knew I wasn't going to that," Warren said. "And anyway, I'm talking about *after* the church event, when you were radio silent. And when I asked about it, you said there's just 'a lot going on.'" He looked at her. "So what's up tonight?"

"Just . . . people from church coming over." Stephanie watched him unload more cartons, like he was there for the night. "But I know you'd rather not socialize with them because you think I'm trying to get you to—"

"Nah, I'm cool," Warren said. "We can eat and chill till they get here. No problem."

"Warren, we can't. You can't." Stephanie's heart beat out of her chest. "It's just one person from church coming. And it's . . ." She couldn't believe it had come to this. *Not like this.* She took a breath. "My fiancé."

Warren moved closer to her. "Your what?"

Stephanie's stomach cramped. "I'm sorry, Warren. I wanted to tell you, but there was never a good time."

"Never a good time?" Warren's gaze pierced her. "How about last night—in bed. Maybe *that* was a good time."

"I feel horrible," Stephanie said. "I didn't want to hurt you. For the longest time I wasn't even sure—"

"So you've been out here, not only seeing somebody behind my back, but it's so serious that you got engaged?" He maintained the piercing gaze. "What were *we* doing for the past two years? All the talk about getting married—that was a joke to you?"

"No, Warren, I love you—"

"Stop," Warren said, walking away. "Just stop with the lies."

Stephanie pulled him back, tears in her eyes. "I've lied about a lot of things, but not that. I *do* love you. It's just . . . life is complicated. Warren, I'm *sorry*."

Warren pushed past her, headed for the door. "Enjoy the takeout, you and your fiancé."

The door slammed behind him.

Stephanie stood in the middle of her kitchen now, shaken by the memory. She opened the oven again and looked past the chicken. That was *years* ago. A whole life ago. *What is wrong with you?*

This was why she needed to get away. Seeing Warren had sparked too much. She closed the oven. Lindell had been right. They needed to leave now and work on their marriage, no matter what else was going on. And in the process it would help to bury—

"Steph, hey, you in the kitchen?" Cinda said, walking in. "Mmm smells good in here."

"I thought I'd make dinner," Stephanie said. "That's a long flight from LA. Are they here with you?"

"Just Mariah," Cinda said. "Brooke's on a different flight that arrives in about two hours."

"Okay, let me take this chicken out so I can meet her," Stephanie said, removing the pan from the oven.

Chatter floated from the entryway as Stephanie and Cinda walked out. Faith and Joy stood with the rest.

"Seriously, this is scary." A woman in jeans and a jean jacket with a jet-black pixie cut engaged Joy. "How could you know all of that?"

Joy beamed at her. "I've watched every one of your films, and you even did a reality show here in St. Louis a while back." She shook her head. "I couldn't believe it when Faith told me you were directing this movie." She scanned the circle. "Do you all even understand who she is?"

"We might, just a little," Alonzo said, smiling.

"How about—I was the one who put you on to Mariah," Faith said.

"Oh, yeah, I guess you did," Joy said.

"Mariah, let me introduce you to Stephanie London, the caretaker of the Promises B and B," Alonzo said. "We wanted you to stay here because we know you'll get the utmost in service, but also, Steph is a sister in Christ who keeps it real. And I know you appreciate that even more."

"Okay, now," Mariah said, smiling. "Really good to meet you, Stephanie." She gave her a hug. "And looks like congratulations are in order?"

Stephanie smiled. "Yes, thank you so much," she said. "And it's good to meet you as well. I have to admit I'm not up on your movies—I hardly see any movies—but after hearing Miss Joy's endorsement, I'm about to do a movie marathon."

"Well, clearly you don't have time for movies," Mariah said, glancing around. "You're running this B and B, which looks *amazing*. I can't wait to get a tour. And the Promises name—is that *the* promises? As in, promises of God?"

"You got it," Stephanie said. "It might sound gimmicky but my husband and I named it based on some things God had brought us through. Helps us stay mindful that He keeps His promises." Her own words resonated with her. She needed that reminder even now.

"Listen, if we're about to have church right here in the foyer, just let me know," Mariah said. "I'll make myself comfortable." She shook her head, looking at Alonzo. "You might've miscalculated. Instead of getting to work, I'm thinking this is about to be a spiritual retreat."

"Hey, we're praying for revival in the hearts and lives of everybody who's working on this," Alonzo said. "But sorry, we've also got work to do." He chuckled. "I'll take your bags up."

"Are you ready to go up to your room?" Stephanie said. "Or do you want to take a look around on this level first?"

"Oh, I'd love to see what's on this level," Mariah said.

"Okay, let's go this way to the main sitting room," Stephanie said, leading the way.

"So, Joy," Mariah said, following, "I'm really curious. Why have you followed my career?"

"I love photography," Joy said, "and for the past few months I've been really focusing on learning more about filming video, different camera angles, and things like that."

"That's so awesome, Joy." Mariah paused, looking at her. "How old are you?"

"Almost seventeen," Joy said.

"I wish I'd had this much direction and focus at your age," Mariah said. "I'm truly impressed."

"Thank you," Joy said, smiling.

"Joy, I didn't know you had an interest in that," Cinda said. "I'm even more excited that you'll be joining us as an intern."

Joy stared at her. "I'm going to be an intern?"

"Faith didn't tell you and Sophia?" Cinda said.

"Joy's about to kill me," Faith said, "but it really did slip my mind, given everything we've been doing." She looked at her sister. "And Cinda just told me today, but yes, you and Sophie can be interns. But—"

Joy squealed, whipping out her phone. "I'm calling Sophie right now."

"Joy, just make sure you understand," Faith said. "It doesn't mean you'll be working with Mariah or that Sophie will be working with Cinda. You'll be working with me, doing whatever needs to be done. And the minute you start complaining—"

"Complaining? This is the best—Sophie!" Joy darted off, phone to her ear. "Wait till I tell you . . ."

"I'm sorry," Faith said, looking at Mariah. "I was coming to see what help Stephanie might need for your and Brooke's arrival. When Joy heard me say 'Mariah Pendleton,' she literally jumped in the car. So sorry for holding up your evening."

"No, I mentor young women in the industry, so I love all of this." Mariah's demeanor was easygoing. "I didn't even know we'd have interns. That's awesome."

The front door opened as they continued to the sitting room.

Stephanie looked at Cinda. "Can you take over the tour for a minute? I want to see who that is."

"You know I know this place like the back of my hand," Cinda said.

Stephanie walked to the foyer, surprised to see Lindell. "Hey"—she gave him a kiss—"you're home a little early."

"I'm actually a little late," Lindell said. "You ready?"

Stephanie looked at him. "Ready for what?"

"We've got ten minutes to get to our dinner reservation." Lindell looked at his watch. "Well, less than ten now."

"Tonight?" Stephanie said. "I'm about to serve dinner, and I still need to finish making dessert."

"When did you start making dinner at the bed and breakfast?" Lindell said. "And why tonight, when we already had plans?"

"I thought our plans were for tomorrow night," Stephanie said. "And you know I don't normally make dinner. But Mariah and Brooke are on long flights from LA. I thought it would be nice to serve them in that way."

"This is what I've been saying, Steph," Lindell said. "You don't prioritize our stuff. You didn't even think to add it to your calendar."

"It was a simple mistake," Stephanie said. "Why can't we go tomorrow night?"

"It's the new hot spot," Lindell said. "It's booked the rest of the week."

"I'm sorry, babe," Stephanie said. "Let's go somewhere else tomorrow night and get a reservation for this place next week."

"It won't even matter next week," Lindell said. "We'll be making dinner reservations on an island."

"Well, I don't know," Stephanie said. "I've been checking and flights are too expensive for next week. We need to book at least two weeks out."

"Babe, I've still got miles we can use from my trips to Haiti," Lindell said. "And looks like we've got the perfect destination too. I was planning to tell you over dinner tonight."

"Where?" Stephanie said. "Tell me now."

"I was telling Neil at the office that we never went on a honeymoon," Lindell said. "Of course he gave me a hard time. Then he said his in-laws have a rental house in Saint Lucia. He checked with his folks and look where we're staying." He took out his phone and showed her.

Stephanie did a double take. "This is gorgeous and right on the ocean. But babe, this rental rate. We can't afford this."

"They had people who cancelled at the last minute and forfeited their payment," Lindell said. "Since we're friends, his in-laws said they'd be happy to just let us stay."

"Wow," Stephanie said, taking it in. "So when do we leave?"

"We check in on Sunday and stay till Friday," Lindell said. "God worked it out, babe. We get four full days and five nights. Just the two of us."

"Wow," Stephanie said again.

Four full days and five nights. Just the two of us.

CHAPTER 15

ophomore Year

Tommy rushed into the Student Union and down the stairs. Late, he knew he'd hear about it, but it was just one of those days. Perfect weather. Everybody on the yard. Which meant lots of people to talk to on the way. He pulled open the wooden door—

"Hey, Stranger."

Tommy paused, recognizing the singsong tone, and looked to his left. "Stranger?" He let the door go. "What's going on, Shonte?"

Shonte came closer, hand to a jutted hip. "You were supposed to call me 'right back'. Four days ago."

Tommy heaved a sigh. "It's just been one of those weeks. Midterm. Papers due. You know how it is."

"Yeah, I do," Shonte said. "But I still make time for you. It's like you don't even care. You just forget about me."

"You know I couldn't forget about you," Tommy said, eyeing her. She was definitely fine. "I just need to learn better time management. I'll make it up to you, though."

"What about right now?" Shonte moved closer, inches from his face. "Let's get lunch."

Tommy sighed his regrets. "I wish I had known you were free," he said. "But I'm already late meeting somebody. I was just about to go in here."

"Let me guess," Shonte said. "Your girl is waiting."

"My girl?" Tommy said.

"You know who I'm talking about. Jillian."

"I don't know why you keep—"

"I know," Shonte said. "You're just friends."

"And she's about to help me with this major paper that's due." Tommy opened the door. "Imma call you, though."

Shonte threw up a hand as she walked away. "Whatever, Tommy."

A swell of voices hit him as he walked through the door, and the aroma of fried chicken reminded him that he was starving. But he was late enough. He'd get his food after he let Jillian know he was here.

Tommy spotted her in their usual booth on the far side of the eatery where they could focus. He paused at two tables on the way, saying a quick hello, then slid into the booth opposite Jillian.

"Jilli-Jill, sorry, I was—" His eyes fell on the fried chicken breast and wing on the table, plus fries and a coke. "Aw, you're the best. Have I told you you're the best? Did you know how hungry I was?"

Jillian wore a bare expression. "Who said it was for you?"

"Girl, you haven't had fried chicken since that one time you ate a whole half a wing." Tommy pulled the tray closer. "Anyway, I see you had your burger." He picked up the wing and pointed it at her. "You have no idea how much I'm about to enjoy this. A thousand thank you's."

"You're welcome," Jillian said.

Tommy started on the wing. "What's wrong?"

"Nothing's wrong." Jillian took a red pen from her backpack; her ponytail angled over one shoulder. "You got your revisions for me to look at?"

Tommy paused. "I'm late, and you didn't chastise me for it. Just quiet and grumpy like yesterday." He focused more on her. "And you never wear makeup, but today it looks like it—like all the natural color is gone. What's up, Jill?"

"Nothing's up, except you're late—thanks for acknowledging it—

and I need to get to class soon." Jillian moved her trash out of the way. "So if you want me to check your paper, you need to give it to me."

Tommy wiped his hands, pulled a folder from his backpack, and gave it to her. "I took most of your suggestions, like beefing up the supporting arguments. But I'm not trying to find more citations. I think I've got enough." He took a bite of the breast then looked up. "No rebuttal?"

Jillian looked up from a vague stare at the table. "To what?"

"What I just said." Tommy looked at her. "That I didn't take any of your suggestions so there's no point looking it over."

"Then why are we here?" Jillian sighed, pushing his paper back to him. "I'm heading back to my dorm."

"I thought you had class next," Tommy said.

"You're tracking my schedule?" Jillian said. "Maybe I'm not going to class. Do I need your permission to skip?"

Tommy put the paper in his backpack and pushed his food aside. "Whatever's going on, if you want to talk about it—"

"Why would I talk to you about it?" Jillian said.

"I'm just thinking you might not have anybody to talk to," Tommy said. "Whatever this is, it's got you." He shrugged. "And I thought we were friends."

"On a basic level," Jillian said. "But I don't tell just anybody my business. And for your information, I have someone to talk to. My sister is my best friend—thank you very much."

"Your sister who didn't know which dorm you lived in?" Tommy nodded. "But I do feel better knowing you talked to her."

Jillian looked aside. "I didn't . . ." She took a breath. "I didn't say I . . ." Another breath. "She's busy in law school . . . and just . . . hasn't called back yet." She backhanded a tear. "But it's *fine* . . ."

Tommy passed her some napkins. "Jilli-Jill." He stared at her until she met his gaze. "I'm right here. Talk to me."

Jillian blew her nose and stared at the threadbare carpet. After several minutes she mumbled something that got swallowed by the chatter and the soft rock coming through the speakers.

Tommy leaned forward. "I couldn't hear you."

Jillian let another minute pass before she looked at him. "I said I'm pregnant." She looked away again.

"How long have you known?" Tommy said.

"I took the test night before last." Jillian focused on the table. "I haven't told anyone."

"Not even the father?"

Jillian shook her head. "I'm scared," she said, her voice barely audible. "I don't know what to do." Tears slid from her eyes. "I've never felt so alone."

"You said your sister hasn't called back yet," Tommy said. "She will —it hasn't been a full two days. But what about your mom? She's right here in town. You should go home and talk to her."

"My mom and I . . ." Jillian sighed. "It's hard to talk to her. It's just . . . complicated."

"Well, *this* is complicated," Tommy said. "You need to talk to her. And who's the dude? All I ever see is guys sweating you, and you telling them to get lost."

"That's not true," Jillian mumbled.

"You say it nicely," Tommy said, "but it's true."

Jillian balled the napkin in her hand. "I went to this frat party at Howard a few weeks ago with some people in my dorm."

"A frat guy got you to give up your number?" Tommy said. "I can't see it."

"He wasn't a typical frat guy," Jillian said. "He was really low-key. Wasn't even dancing that much." She sighed. "He just had this vibe about him."

"So he stepped to you," Tommy said, "the two of you connected, you gave him your number, then what?"

"We talked on the phone for weeks," Jillian said. "You know I don't have a car, and neither does he. But a friend of his gave him a ride to my dorm."

"So it became a regular thing? The two of you seeing each other?"

"Just that one time," Jillian said. "We didn't talk much after . . ."

Tommy let out a sigh. "And you're telling me this dude didn't use protection? And you didn't tell him to?"

"It wasn't supposed to go that far," Jillian said. "I told him on the phone that I wasn't ready for sex, that I was a virgin and—"

"Wow." Tommy shook his head.

"Wow, what?"

"You were a virgin, and he knew it?" Tommy said. "How did you even get to where you were talking about sex?"

"We were making plans to see one another, and he asked if he could spend the night." Jillian picked apart the napkin. "I said no, I'm not into all that. So he asked if I was a virgin." She paused as new tears came. "He said he respected that . . . and that this wasn't about sex. He just . . . wanted to see me."

"If he just wanted to see you," Tommy said, "he should've met you somewhere besides your dorm. He came to your room like he wanted to do all along."

"We were just talking for a long while," Jillian said. "And he started kissing me, but I think he was as surprised as I was that it went that far."

"You can believe that if you want to." Tommy's jaw tightened as he shook his head. "I'm telling you, if he walked in here right now, I would knock him out."

"What?" Jillian said. "Why are you getting so upset about it?"

"Because dude is a liar," Tommy said. "He had no intentions of respecting the fact that you didn't want to have sex."

"I'm the one who let him come to my room," Jillian said.

"And you thought you could do so and stay a virgin," Tommy said. "I'm thinking his thoughts were a little different—and he didn't even respect you enough to wear protection." He shook his head again.

"I still don't understand why you're upset."

"Because you were just someone else for him to conquer—and I hate that." Tommy said. "You can call me a basic level friend, that's fine. But to me, you're on a pedestal. I don't know *anybody* like you." He continued. "No hidden agenda. No playing games. You're crazy smart and stupid fine, but I don't know if you even know, humble as you are. And you give up your time just to help me." He shook his finger at her. "You're naive, though. That's for *sure*. You know what—

once we get past this, imma need you to run every guy past me that you're even thinking about dating."

"Once 'we' get past this?" Jillian said.

"Whatever you need, whenever you need it . . . I'm *in* this," Tommy said. "I know you're scared, but you can do this, Jill. Talk to your mom. Your parents are your support system. I bet you'll be surprised how much she's there for you." He added, "And call dude and tell him he's got a baby on the way. Let *him* be scared."

Jillian stared into the distance. "What if I have to drop out of school? How am I going to take care of a baby?"

"Why would you have to drop out?" Tommy said. "You can have the baby and commute from home. But don't stress yourself with all the thoughts. One day at a time. And today, you learned something—you're not alone."

Jillian looked at him. "About that 'basic level friend' comment . . . My upbringing made me so guarded that it's hard to trust people as friends, to even consider someone a friend." She took a breath. "But I literally had no one to talk to. And with something as hard as this, you were easy to talk to. And you cared. I don't think a basic friend could get that irrationally upset." She attempted a wry smile. "Thank you. For being a real friend."

Shonte took a slice of pepperoni from the box and held it in front of Tommy. He took a bite as the buzzer to his suite sounded.

"This pizza was exactly what I needed," Tommy said, leaning next to her on the sofa.

Shonte smiled. "Want me to feed you some more?" She kissed him instead then sighed when the buzzer sounded again. "Are you gonna get that?"

"Probably for my roommate," Tommy said. "And he's gone, so . . ." He shrugged.

"He's gone?" Shonte said. "For the weekend?"

Tommy nodded. "For the weekend." He groaned when it sounded again. "Okay, I'm getting it."

"Now I don't want you to," Shonte said, kissing him again.

"I'll tell whoever that my roomie's gone, so we can get some peace."

Tommy got up and opened the door—and Jillian stood before him.

"Jilli-Jill," Tommy said. "You never come by here."

Jillian's eyes barely met his as she held herself, her jacket zipped up. "Can I . . . come in?"

Tommy stared at her as he backed up and opened the door wider.

Jillian saw Shonte when she walked in. "Oh. I didn't know . . . I'm sorry. I'll go."

Tommy looked into Jillian's eyes. "What's going on?" he whispered. "I've never seen you like this."

Tears welled in Jillian's eyes. "I'm . . . I'm okay. I'm gonna go."

Shonte gave a wave. "Good seeing you, Jillian."

Jillian turned toward the door, and Tommy pulled her back.

"No," Tommy said. "One second." He walked over to Shonte. "I need to see what's going on with Jill."

Shonte shrugged. "Okay."

"I'm saying I'll call you later," Tommy said. "Maybe we can link up tomorrow."

"You can't be serious." Shonte looked over at Jillian then back to Tommy. "I hope you know this is it, Tommy. You can't play me like I'm stupid. If you're choosing your so-called 'friend' over me, I'm done."

"I'm not playing you," Tommy said. "Jillian never comes over here, and I know something's wrong so I'm going to see what's up. We might even be able to kick it again in a couple hours. But if you want to be like that, then I guess we're done."

Shonte got up and put on her jacket. "I'm taking my pizza." She picked up the box and eyed Jillian as she walked out the door.

Jillian took a seat on the sofa, pulling her legs under her. "Sorry about Shonte."

Tommy sat beside her. "How many is that? Two?"

"Two what?"

"Two situations that bit the dust because of you."

"You didn't have to tell her to go."

"She's the one who made it a choice," Tommy said. "She's not my only situation, but you're my only real friend." He looked at her. "You're shivering, and it's warm in here. What's going on?"

Jillian took a moment to respond. "I told my mom, a week ago . . ."

"Okay." Tommy had been waiting for an update but didn't want to press her.

"The first thing she wanted to know was 'Who's the guy?'" Jillian shook her head. "She actually looked a little hopeful when I said he went to Howard."

"Why?" Tommy said.

"My mother went to Howard," Jillian said. "And it was her dream for me to go. She considers it an act of rebellion that I'm here at Maryland. Anyway, when she didn't recognize his family name, she asked me to describe him."

"Describe him?" Tommy said. "What's that about? She thought she might know him?"

"No. To see . . . what the baby . . ." Jillian wiped tears with her jacket sleeve. ". . . would look like. As soon as I said 'dark complexion' . . ." She swiped more tears. "She said . . . She said it would be best to be 'free of the problem.'"

Tommy passed Jillian a pile of napkins.

"So I . . ." Jillian put a napkin to her face, pausing to try to collect herself. "I knew I wouldn't have . . . her support . . . and I . . . got really scared again . . ." She started sobbing. "I went today. I . . . did it . . ."

"Did your mom go with you?" Tommy said.

Jillian nodded, working to get her jacket off. Tommy helped her with it.

"Mom . . . just dropped me . . . at my dorm." Jillian blew her nose. "And I walked . . . over here . . . I couldn't . . . be by my"—she heaved —"where's your bathroom?"

She got up quickly, hands cupped to her mouth. Tommy opened the restroom door and closed it as she vomited. After several minutes she emerged again.

"Come in here." Tommy led her to his room. "My roommate's gone. I know it's a mess." He took some clothes from his bed and threw them over the desk chair. "Lie down right there."

Jillian curled into a ball on his bed, shivering still, tears falling like droplets. Tommy covered her with a blanket.

"Get some rest," he said. "You can stay here tonight. I'll sleep out there. What do you feel like eating? I'll go get it."

"I'm not . . . hungry."

"Let me get you some water."

Jillian shook her head, her loose ponytail flopping to the side.

"You need water and food at some point," Tommy said, "but rest for now." He closed the blinds to dim the last bit of daylight and flicked off the light. "I'll check on you in a little while."

"Can you . . . talk with me . . . until I fall asleep?"

Tommy sat on the floor, his back against the bed frame. "So, I have to ask . . . How did your mom have a problem with you having a baby with a dark complexion, when her own daughter has a dark complexion?"

"She never embraced Treva because of her skin," Jillian said, her voice bare.

Tommy looked back at her. "That can't be true."

"It's true."

"That's sick."

"I know."

They passed the next few moments in silence.

"I just feel so . . ." Jillian's voice broke. "*Sad.*"

Tommy closed his eyes, feeling powerless to help as Jillian sobbed into the pillow. When the tears subsided and her breathing changed, he looked to see if she was asleep. Tommy got up, covered her again, and closed the door, wiping his own tears in his sleeve.

CHAPTER 16

*T*ommy pulled to the front entrance of the Living Water building in Jillian's car, shot her a one-word text—**Here**—and continued his call with Alonzo.

"Man, this is pretty huge." Tommy rested an arm on the center console. "Why would you give the *Post-Dispatch* an exclusive like that?"

"We're not giving the *Post-Dispatch* an exclusive," Alonzo said. "We're giving *you* the exclusive. Two reasons. First, Lance is the one getting most of the interview requests, and he doesn't have the time or desire to talk to all these reporters. This way, there's only one reporter he needs to talk to during filming—you."

"You're assuming that makes it easy for him," Tommy said. "I know enough to ask the really tough questions."

"Nobody said you had to go easy on him." Alonzo had a smile in his voice. "Just speaking from a logistical standpoint. But the other reason is because you're perfectly suited for this."

"How so?" Tommy said.

"You're a well-respected entertainment reporter," Alonzo said. "Plus you're a believer, so you get what we're trying to convey. *And* you know the people involved. Lance discipled you in the faith. You were there when he married Kendra. You can tell the story from so many angles."

Tommy looked up as the doors opened and Jillian walked out—with Silas. "So it sounds like you'd want me on set pretty regularly?"

"Definitely," Alonzo said. "Let's talk more this weekend. Also—Super Bowl. We're having people over, including cast and crew that are in town. Reggie already said you're not doing anything special."

Tommy glanced at Jillian and Silas, lingering just outside the entrance, chatting. "Yeah, we were just gonna watch at the house. I invited Jesse over, though."

"Already got him on the list," Alonzo said.

"Cool. It's a plan." Tommy gave Silas a wave as he passed in front of the car. "I'll catch you later, man." He hung up and his music came back on as Jillian got in on the passenger side. "I was about to get out and let you drive."

"We need to drop you at your house first." Jillian reclined against the headrest. "I can take over from there."

"You must be tired," Tommy said.

"Exhausted."

"Crazy work day?" Tommy pulled away from the curb.

"Well, that too," Jillian said. "Trevor had a slight fever last night, vomited twice. Probably the flu. So that kept me up, plus a middle of the night run to Walgreens for medicine."

"And you didn't mention any of that when you picked me up this morning?" Tommy said.

"Mention it for what?"

"Same way you mentioned Sophie having strep throat last month," Tommy said, "and David needing stitches not long ago."

"You said we needed to 'cut back on everything else.'" Jillian used air quotes. "And you promptly cut back on text messages. Just doing my part to comply." She looked over at him. "*But*, honestly, I can't thank you enough for today. Taking my car in *and* paying for repairs, which were extensive. I couldn't believe it when I called the shop and they told me it was taken care of. Like it or not, I'm finding a way to pay you back."

"I told you I'm not accepting it," Tommy said. "Learn to let people bless you. And as for doing your part to comply"—he cut her a glance —"you conveniently forgot I said we'd catch up when we saw each other. You could've told me."

"Well, I'll tell you this—David is still talking about Sunday," Jillian said. "The concert, taking pics with members of the band afterward. Thank you again for that too." She glanced at him. "He started rattling off other concerts and movies he wants to attend with you, but I told him it was too much."

"Too much for whom?" Tommy said.

"David can't be your little sidekick," Jillian said. "This is your job."

"And I had a blast seeing it through his eyes," Tommy said. "He asked lots of questions, excellent ones. He can roll with me anytime. And you know I wouldn't say it if I didn't mean it."

"I have to say, he wrote a really good review of the concert," Jillian said.

"Yeah, about that," Tommy said.

"Oh, hush. I saw that look you gave me."

"I thought it was way extra at first," Tommy said. "But actually, dope assignment. Sparked a good discussion about what goes into writing a concert review." He looked over at her. "So how did Sunday go? With Silas."

Jillian shrugged. "It was good."

"It was good?" Tommy looked at her. "That's it?"

"Yes, it was good. Nice. I don't know what else—"

"Oh, now we're getting somewhere," Tommy said. "It was *nice.* Your word for, 'I had a *really* good time.'"

"Now you're the one editing conversation?" Jillian said.

"You don't have to downplay it for me, Jill," Tommy said. "Silas is a great guy. I expected you to have a nice time." He glanced at her. "I saw you were trying to look cute too."

"Anyway . . . "

"So when's the next date?"

"There is no next date," Jillian said. "He mentioned dinner as a possibility, but I told him I wasn't ready for that. Dinner just says something more."

"We've had dinner countless times."

"You know what I mean," Jillian said. "Dinner *in that context*." She paused, staring out of the window. "So since we can still catch up . . ."

"Absolutely," Tommy said. "What's on your mind?"

"We would've normally talked about that cling sermon last Sunday," Jillian said. "You've probably got it memorized by now."

"Ha," Tommy said. "*The* most tailor-made sermon I've heard in a while."

"I felt the same way, though," Jillian said. "I've listened twice. Just one of those messages to keep deep in your soul." She looked at him. "It made me want to apologize to you."

"For what?"

"For challenging you about your decision to remain single," Jillian said. "Even if it came from a place of pain, that could be how God is working it for your good." Her eyes rested on him. "I acted like you were settling for something inferior. But as long as you cling to Jesus, you have the ultimate situation."

"Wow, I wasn't expecting that." Tommy focused on the road. "Thank you for that. I know God is still healing me, and you were right that I shouldn't say 'never'. I need to allow room for Him to work." He glanced at her. "But Jill, I'm so hype about this path I'm on. That sermon made me want to go deeper in my relationship with the Lord, so I'm challenging myself to cling. This week the challenge is to talk to Jesus every day like a friend." He paused. "You inspired that."

"How did I inspire that?" Jillian said.

"Because that's what you do," Tommy said. "I do most of my talking to the Lord when I'm going through something. You talk to Jesus about everything, even what to fix for dinner."

"I didn't even realize I mentioned stuff like that to you."

"Because it's normal for you," Tommy said. "You mention talking to the Lord as if you were talking to Treva or whoever. Except, you talk to Jesus way more."

"I guess now that I think about it," Jillian said, "I got that from Darlene, Treva's mother-in-law—well, Hezekiah's mom."

"I knew who you meant," Tommy said, "the one who led you to the Lord."

"Darlene would talk to Jesus *out loud*, in front of us." Jillian smiled. "I always admired her vibrant relationship with the Lord."

"And that's what I admire in you," Tommy said.

"That's awesome that you're challenging yourself like this, Tommy," Jillian said. "So you're doing one a week? For how many weeks?"

"I have no idea," Tommy said. "However the Lord leads. I just know He's working, and it's energizing me."

Jillian pulled up something on her phone and held it up for Tommy.

"What is it?" Tommy glanced over. "I can't read it right now."

"A prayer for you to walk closely with the Lord."

"No way," Tommy said.

"One of dozens of prayers for you in my Notes app," Jillian said. "I know He's working too. God is faithful."

"Have you sent me all those prayers?"

"Nope."

"Why not?"

"Because I'd have to hear you whine about not needing prayers for this or that," Jillian said.

"That's fair," Tommy said. He let a few moments pass as he stared at the road. "Sometimes I think about what it would have been like if we had been believers in college. All those study sessions—imagine if we had had a regular Bible study going."

"And all the prayers we could've been praying," Jillian said. "I've thought about it too. But I also think about this—God knew He would save us. He knew when He brought us together as friends freshman year. And He knew that years later He would bring us together as friends again, and we'd be praying for one another and encouraging one another to cling to Him."

Tommy nodded, taking all of that in. "After Saturday night in the park, I thought today would be difficult."

"Oh, it was about to get bumpy," Jillian said. "I got an attitude when you said I 'conveniently forgot' that we could catch up when we saw each other." She gave him a look. "I didn't forget. I just don't like how you abruptly redefined things—for no reason."

"Sounds like that attitude is working its way back."

"*But*, I remembered the sermon and that I needed to apologize." Jillian sighed. "So the Holy Spirit made me swallow the 'tude."

"You were talking to Jesus right here in the car, weren't you?"

"Venting to Jesus is more like it."

"You said it a few minutes ago—'as long as you cling to Jesus, you have the ultimate situation.'" Tommy gave her a glance. "You decided to cling instead of keeping an attitude, which brought about the ultimate situation—walking by the Spirit. Which brought about a really nice convo."

"So basically, no matter what nonsensical thing you come up with, as long as I cling—"

"That's not exactly—hey, remember this?" Tommy nudged her with his elbow and turned the music up.

Jillian leaned against the headrest. "How could I forget? I liked the song until you played it to death."

"I still remember the cassette," Tommy said. "I might've pushed rewind once or twice."

"Or a hundred."

"You know this was a legit top slow jam—late eighties and nineties." Tommy snapped his fingers. "Listen to the emotion in that simple line—*All I do is think of you* . . ." He sang along with the chorus. "Wait, I have to hear that again." He pushed a button.

Jillian looked over at him, only to shake her head.

"I might even put this on my all-time, old school slow jam list, but a ways down," Tommy said. "Question is whether it makes it into the top twenty."

"Oh, we are absolutely not doing this." Jillian closed her eyes. "I'm way too tired for that debate."

"Who said you had to debate?" Tommy said. "I'd rather you keep quiet than challenge me on *my* list. Anyway, we agreed on most of our top twenty. The issue was always the top-top."

Jillian looked over at him. "You got 'A House Is Not a Home' on this playlist?"

"Nope." Tommy waited a beat before he looked at her. "It's on another one."

She kept eyeing him.

He pushed a few buttons on the dashboard, bringing the song to life, then drove the final stretch toward his house. He pulled into the driveway and put the car in Park.

"You went above and beyond with my car today, Tommy." Jillian picked up her purse. "Thank you."

"One thing you can always be sure of, Jill." Tommy looked at her. "I got you."

Jillian got out and walked around to the driver's side. Tommy got out as well and paused as their eyes met.

Jillian moved first, getting into her car. "And now . . . back to no communication."

"You don't have to think of it that way," Tommy said.

"It *is* that way."

"Jill . . ."

She shifted the car to Reverse. "Thanks again, Tommy."

He backed out of the way and watched her drive off.

CHAPTER 17

$\mathcal{T}$reva slipped into a pair of dark denim jeans as Lance paced the bedroom on a phone interview.

"Would we have gotten married if Kendra wasn't sick?" Lance looked over at Treva to see if she was hearing this.

She met his gaze and shook her head with empathy. The questions people asked.

"No," Lance said. "Our paths wouldn't have crossed because she would've stayed in DC."

Treva put on a mustard-colored sweater and sat on the bed to pull on her boots. Her phone dinged with a notification beside her. She picked it up and saw a text from Jillian.

Running late. Be there in 15. But I know you're running late too.

Treva typed a reply. **I'm at the door waiting... j/k Running late too lol. See you in 15.**

"What if our paths *did* cross and she wasn't sick?" Lance said. "What kind of question is that? I don't see the point in speculating."

Her boots on, Treva moved into the bathroom to freshen her makeup. Thank God Tommy was on board as the exclusive reporter.

Lance only had a couple more of these, which had already been sched-uled. *Lord, please give him patience to make it through.*

"Yes, I do have something to add," Lance said. "Thank you for asking. I'd love for you to note that I'm now happily married to my wife Treva, and we have three daughters and a one-year-old son. . . . Right. No problem. . . . You have a good evening as well."

Lance walked into the bathroom. "So you caught that?"

Treva dabbed powder on her face, looking at her husband in the mirror. "What's up with all of the what if's?"

"Someone asked the same thing yesterday," Lance said. "They want to know whether the DC lawyer would have married the high school dropout."

Treva turned. "You think that's what they're getting at?"

"I know it is," Lance said. "It's a clear mismatch in their eyes."

"I'm glad you shut it down as speculation." Treva touched up her eyeliner. "Because who knows. Maybe the two of you would've still married."

"No, I actually know the answer," Lance said. "Without the illness, Kendra wouldn't have dated me, let alone marry me."

"Lance, you don't know that," Treva said.

"Babe, Kendra and I *talked* about that." Lance came further into the bathroom. "Her circle was filled with JDs PhDs, MBAs . . . She said our relationship was one of the 'hidden blessings' that came from her illness because she wouldn't have dated me otherwise. It was basically the same issue Rae and I had." He eyed her. "If I had been in my right mind, I probably wouldn't have pursued *you*, since you're another one with all the degrees."

Treva eyed him in the mirror. "Oh, you weren't in your right mind when you pursued me?"

"Not at all." Lance tucked a finger through her belt loop, pulling her closer, and turned her around. "My world was lopsided. I still can't believe you did that to me in a weekend." He kissed her. "But that night you shot me down? I thought, oh yeah, what am I thinking? Another attorney."

"I had a lot of reservations about us, and it had nothing to do with schooling," Treva said. "But after that first kiss"—she leaned in for one—"I couldn't remember any of the reservations."

Lance held her. "You're the only woman who has truly loved me for me."

"Kendra loved you deeply, Lance."

"Listen to me, babe." Lance's voice was near whisper. "There was nothing I could do for you. If anything, I complicated your life."

"True," Treva said. "Being so far away, several years younger, in a totally different season—"

"But you fell in love with me," Lance said. "And it didn't take an extreme circumstance. And you didn't try to change me. You just loved me. Unconditionally." He kissed her again, more deeply this time.

"You have this habit," Treva said, "of stirring things up right when one of us needs to be somewhere."

"And think about it—all kids are preoccupied." Lance tightened his arms around her. "Tell Jill you have to reschedule."

"I can't," Treva said. "I'm the one who told her we needed to go to dinner. This morning she realized Trevor's birthday is coming up—his first without Cecil—and the grief hit."

He kissed her again. "How much time you got before she gets here?"

"Not enough."

"You sure about that?"

A ding sounded in the bedroom.

"She's here," Treva sang. She kissed him again and walked out of the bathroom. "We'll pick this back up later tonight."

"How do you know I won't be sleep when you get back?"

"I know how to wake you up."

Treva descended the stairs, hearing voices in the kitchen.

"You're right. I guess I've been a little uncomfortable. I'm coming into this late. Jordyn already knew everybody. And the people who *did* know me . . . knew I wasn't exactly a nice person."

"I haven't been around for more than a decade," Pamela was

saying. "So if you're late, what am I? And if we started swapping stories about who we used to be, we'd be here all night."

"Amen to that," Treva said, walking in. "Jade, it's good to see you." She hugged her and did a quick glance around. "Is Jordyn here too?"

"Only Jade." Pamela sat beside Wes in his high chair, feeding him. "By design. I wanted to get to know her better, outside of Jordyn's shadow."

"That's funny," Jade said, at the table with her. "Jordyn always said she was in my shadow. I guess the roles are reversed when it comes to church stuff."

"I'd like to get to know you better too, Jade," Treva said. "I just wish I'd known so we could've planned for a night when I'd be here."

"That was by design too." Pamela smiled. "I wanted Miss Jade all to myself."

"Jade, you need to know that when you're on Pam's radar, you're locked in," Treva said. "She'll have you covered every way she knows how, especially in prayer."

"I'm seeing that already," Jade said. "I was telling her about my relationship with my mom, and she stopped and prayed."

"And guess what?" Pamela said. "Jade's got me covered too, with my hair. She's going to show me how to care for it. I've got so much to learn about everything."

"Miss Pam, you're doing really good with your hair," Jade said. "I'm just excited to show you how to make a couple of things yourself that'll help keep it moisturized."

"Jade, I wish you had been around to help me care for my girls' hair when they were young, because *whew*." Treva shook her head with a chuckle. "Okay, gotta run. Jill's waiting for me." She kissed Wes, whose face was covered with red sauce. "Look at you, eating all your spaghetti like a big boy. And Mommy loves that you have no idea there's spinach cut up in there."

Pamela chuckled. "Gotta get it in however you can."

Treva heard the front door open and close. "Guess I didn't make it out fast enough, huh?" she called.

"I figured you were in here talking," Jillian said. "Hey Jade, it's really good to see you." She hugged her, then Pamela. "Pam, I owe you a prayer text."

"I thought I owed you one," Pamela said.

"Did Jill get you started with that prayer texting?" Treva said. "I don't have time to type all that out."

"I love it," Pamela said. "Seeing how somebody's praying for me just does something to my soul."

Wes kicked in his high chair, reaching for Jillian.

"Aww, Auntie Jill was ignoring my little man." Jillian walked over and kissed his cheeks as he whined to get down. "I would take you out, sweetie, but I'm really not trying to get red all over my jacket." She chuckled and looked at Jade. "Jade, we should get together sometime. I talk to Jordyn, but I'd love to get to know you as well."

Jade smiled. "I would really like that."

"See, Jade," Pamela said. "We're pulling you out of that shadow."

"Okay, we'd better get going," Treva said. "You all have fun."

Jillian headed out to the car as Treva stopped to get a jacket from the coat closet. She put it on and heard her phone ding. Looking, she saw it was Lance.

You're still down there? Do you know how we could've used that 20 min?

"I had a rush of everything this morning." Jillian sat across from Treva in a booth at The Cheesecake Factory, tossing dressing in her Santa Fe salad. "Trevor's about to turn thirteen, and I remembered this running joke that he and Cecil had." She stared into her salad. "Trevor said he had 'rights and privileges' he'd come into as a teen. Cecil said more like 'rules and responsibilities.' And they both made lists that were long and hilarious to prove their points." She paused. "This morning, I took Cecil's list from the nightstand."

"Oh, wow, you still have it." Treva twirled her angel hair pasta.

"I couldn't stop crying," Jillian said. "I could hear Cecil's laughter as he wrote and the banter between him and Trevor."

Treva nodded lightly. "The whole scene came alive again. I know that was painful, Jill."

"Then I started thinking about how we're coming up on the anniversary of Cecil's passing," Jillian said, "and remembering how sudden it was. I mean we were *all* supposed to be moving out here. Cecil should be serving in ministry at Living Word. We should be settled in a house somewhere—can you believe I haven't even *settled* anywhere yet? The duplex was supposed to be a short-term rental."

"You're not going to stress about the duplex," Treva said. "It's fine, and it's worked well to live so close to each other."

"It's just that feeling of being in limbo," Jillian said. "So it went from Trevor's birthday to the year anniversary to the duplex, then to Sophie's upcoming graduation." She spread her hands. "No money for college whatsoever. Sophie's getting her applications in, and Cecil's the one who would know what to do as far as looking for scholarships or whatever." She sighed. "I feel helpless and stupid."

Their server stopped at the table. "How's the food tasting?"

"We haven't actually tasted it yet," Treva said, "but I'm sure it's fine." She forked up some of the shrimp pasta and ate it as the server walked away. "It's really good."

"This salad is too," Jillian said, tasting it. "First time trying this one."

Treva looked at her sister. "Jill, you know I had a lot of these same thoughts. I understand what you're feeling. And I know you know this —you can't let it all overwhelm you at once."

"I know," Jillian said. "I'm just giving you the real-time thoughts that bombarded me. I even found myself thinking that I should've listened to you and Mama and spent time in the workforce. You've got a hefty savings of your own as a cushion."

"And anytime you find yourself agreeing with something Mother or I said back in the day, you're probably on the wrong track." Treva twirled more pasta and ate it. "You were following *the Lord*, Jill. He moved you to stay home and homeschool, before I knew of anyone else who was doing that."

"I've reminded myself of that at least a hundred times," Jillian said.

"The strong leading of the Spirit, the fact that it made sense to almost no one. But Cecil and I were in full agreement." She took a sip of water. "We couldn't even understand how God was taking care of us through some of those years, but He did."

"He's still taking care of you," Treva said, "and He'll continue to take care of you. But I know it's hard. I definitely want to acknowledge that." She speared a shrimp. "And I'm appointing myself over the scholarship committee. I love researching stuff like that."

"I really appreciate that," Jillian said. "Pam's last prayer text had Scripture about God's provision, so I already know I'll read that a dozen times."

"So you've got all of that happening, which is a lot," Treva said. "And then—what's the deal with Tommy and Silas?"

Jillian looked at her. "That's a really broad question."

"Okay, let's take the easier one first," Treva said, looking at her. "How was coffee with Silas?"

"I enjoyed it more than I expected to," Jillian said. "He's such a nice guy, easy to be around." She ate more of her salad.

Treva kept looking at her. "I was waiting for more."

Jillian stabbed a piece of chicken. "There's really nothing more to say."

"So, any butterflies?" Treva said. "Do you like him?"

Jillian paused her fork. "If this were a random moment in time, and I met Silas and we started dating, I'd probably like him and feel all the butterflies. But it's hard to evaluate, given the season I'm in." She popped a tortilla strip in her mouth. "I know that doesn't make sense, but it's where I'm at. I guess the answer is I don't know."

"And now the harder one," Treva said. "Tommy."

"What about Tommy?"

"What was going on at Zoe's birthday party?" Treva said. "Looked like you two weren't speaking half the time, which was odd, then you left together, then he returned without you."

"Yeah, it's complicated," Jillian said. "Basically, everything changed when I told him I was having coffee with Silas."

"Ohh," Treva said. "He felt a way about that coffee date."

"Which prompted a whole discussion," Jillian said. "That's why we left the party. In a nutshell, we established that we love each other deeply, yet nothing can come of it because—" She extended a hand for Treva to finish.

"Tommy's staying single."

Jillian gave a nod. "So now he's 'falling back' from the friendship and giving me space for potential suitors."

"In other words, he's in his feelings."

"But in fairness," Jillian said, "he's focused on clinging to Jesus. Lance's sermon really spoke to him." She took in another forkful. "I've been praying for complete healing and strength and so much more for Tommy, and I see the Lord working."

Treva nodded. "I've been praying too."

"You have?" Jillian said.

"I was praying for Tommy way back when Allison left," Treva said, "when you weren't even in the picture. And I never stopped praying for him, except now, there's this added dimension." She focused on her sister. "You didn't have to tell me about the love deepening between you two. I've seen it. So that on top of everything he's been through and everything he's grappling with—definitely complicated. I've been praying for the Lord to sort it out for him."

"I would've never thought that one day you and Tommy would be in each other's lives," Jillian said, "and you'd be praying for him."

"Who would've thought I'd be praying, period?" Treva said. "But true. It's not like the three of us were friends in college. It was just you and Tommy. And he was way closer to you than I was, which is kind of hard for me to think about even now."

"You never told me that," Jillian said. "Why?"

"Because you were my best friend growing up," Treva said. "I literally had *no* friends, except you. You did so much for me, made so many sacrifices. Parties you didn't go to. People you didn't hang with. Even arguments you got into with Mother. All because you wanted to be there for me. And I wasn't there for you at all during college and law school." She sighed thinking about it. "I remember that day you broke down in Bible study, sharing about getting pregnant in college.

This was *years* later, and I never knew." She shook her head. "Even now, thinking about what you had to have been going through and how you tried to call me, and I never called you back . . ."

"Treva, we are way past that—"

"I'm just saying, when I think about your friendship with Tommy during that time," Treva said, "I can't help but think of how I failed you as a friend. But now, I can also take myself out of it and simply see what a special friendship you two had." She nodded, almost to herself. "And here you are two decades later, the friendship stronger than ever —in Christ." She ate a shrimp. "Tommy can call himself 'falling back' all he wants. When it's God, it's not as easy as that."

Jillian looked at her. "You really think it's God?"

"The friendship?" Treva said. "No doubt in my mind. Whether it'll ever be more . . . only God knows."

"So I'm changing the subject," Jillian said. "What's the latest with the Desiree situation?"

"They're definitely including her in the movie," Treva said. "Small part, maybe a flashback montage of the two of them falling in love, Lance proposing, then he reads the letter where she breaks things off."

"She broke it off in a letter?" Jillian said.

"Girl, I didn't tell you that part?" Treva said. "He got a Dear John."

"I wonder why it hit her like this all these years later," Jillian said. "She was in tears in that video."

"It's no telling what's happening in her life," Treva said. "I actually started praying for her."

"Oh, that's good," Jillian said. "I'll add her to my prayer list as well." She looked at her sister. "How are you feeling about it now? You were pretty ticked off when you first told me."

"That group prayer refocused me," Treva said. "I'm so glad Pam told us to stop and seek the Lord. Talk about Tommy—I was in my feelings too. And it didn't help that I watched the video and saw how beautiful she is."

"We both know that's an area where the enemy loves to push your buttons," Jillian said.

"Right," Treva said. "Soon as I saw her fair skin . . ."

"I can almost see why Lance dismisses that situation the way he does," Jillian said. "It was actually a two *week* engagement, for all intents and purposes."

"Yeah, well, he still should've told me," Treva said. "But the irony . . . he's all but erased the relationship, and it's probably never mattered to her more than right now."

CHAPTER 18

"*L*ittle man, didn't you eat already?" Lance cut up a meatball and some spaghetti on a small plate and put Wes in his high chair. "You should be in bed, you know that? Your mommy would not be happy about this."

He looked as the doorbell rang. "Be right back, Wes."

Lance went and opened the door—and simply stared.

His brother-in-law Trey stared back at him. "You gonna invite me in?"

"Man, I can't believe my eyes right now." Lance enfolded him in a hug. "What in the world are you doing here? Didn't I just send you an email—to South Africa?" He opened the door wider. "Come in, come in. Completely made my night, man. My brother is home."

Trey set his bags aside and took off his coat, taking in his surroundings. "Man. It feels so good to be here. For real-for real." He heard Wes in his high chair and went to the kitchen, draping his coat over a chair. "Aye, there's my nephew." He removed the tray, unbuckled him, and got him out. "I know you don't know me"—he smiled at him—"but I'm your Uncle Trey. I can't believe I'm just now meeting you."

"He's seen you on FaceTime, though," Lance said.

Wes kept his back stiff as he looked at Trey, studying his face.

"I'm impressed," Trey said. "He basically let a stranger pick him up, and he's not—uh-oh, I spoke too soon." He chuckled as Wes started fussing a little, reaching for Lance.

"It won't take him long to get used to you," Lance said, taking him. "Look at him. He's still checking you out, from a safe distance."

Trey smiled. "I see you. We 'bout to be *good* friends." He looked at Lance. "Where is everybody?"

"Treva's out to dinner with her sister," Lance said. "Joy and Hope are with their cousins. And Mom's downstairs." He put Wes back in his high chair. "But okay, what's up? I thought you were staying in South Africa until you shifted to the long-term missions assignment."

"It was looking like it could take months before that got finalized," Trey said. "I had already been praying about whether to stay and wait or come home for a while. When I heard the movie was about to be filmed, I took that as my answer. I thought I should be here." He sighed. "Honestly, it's been a struggle ever since—"

"Oh, my goodness." Pamela paused, hand to her chest. "I know that's not Trey. What are you *doing* here?" She gave him a big hug. "And you look just like Kendra."

"So yeah, Trey, that's my mom," Lance said.

"Obviously," Trey said, smiling. "Lance sent me the link to your video. I was in tears, thanking God you were out."

"It's so good to meet you finally." Pamela turned to her son. "Lance, you knew Trey was coming and didn't mention it? He's been flying all day. We could've had something special prepared. We should've—"

"Mom," Lance said. "That boy gave no notice. He just showed up."

"Yeah, I kinda just hopped a plane," Trey said. "Alonzo sent me a note that the focus of the movie changed and they were beefing up my part. I took it as an answer to prayer to come home."

"Wow," Pamela said, looking at Lance. "Trey, I can go get you a space ready upstairs."

"Oh, thanks," Trey said, "but I'm staying down the street at my Dad's duplex since he's still in Ghana."

"Okay," Pamela said. "And oh"—she turned—"Jade was about to

leave, but let me introduce you." She waved her forward. "This is Jade, a young woman from our church. Jade, this is Kendra's brother, Trey. Well, not that you knew Kendra, but—"

"I watched that wedding video a dozen times, though." Jade shook Trey's hand. "Weren't you Lance's best man?"

"Okay, that's embarrassing," Trey said. "Nice to meet you, though."

"Why is that embarrassing?" Lance said.

"Not the fact that I was your best man," Trey said. "The video going viral. You don't expect people to recognize you."

"Well, you'd better get used to it," Pamela said. "There's about to be a whole movie."

"But I'm not *in* the movie," Trey said. "The guy who's playing me can get all the attention."

"Oh, and he will," Jade said. "It was trending on Twitter today when they announced that Noah Stiles was cast in the role."

"I didn't even know who he was," Lance said. "Joy had to clue me in."

"And I've been halfway across the world on the mission field for two years," Trey said. "So clue me in."

"He's sort of neo soul, R&B-ish," Jade said. "Plays guitar and piano, writes his own stuff. He was an indie artist first, but once he got signed, the label put him with a hot producer and he hit the top of the charts." She focused on Trey. "What's funny is the two of you kind of resemble one another. He was a great pick, although apparently he's never acted."

"Then I hope he can capture all the nuances of Marlon Woods III," Lance said. "Because if you ask me, Trey might need to play 'Trey.' And it would work because he's not new to drama."

"You're gonna call me out like that, in polite company?" Trey nodded. "Okay."

"It's just facts, man," Lance said. "Drama from the first day I stepped foot in this house."

"Oh, wait, I hadn't put it together," Jade said. "This is the *house*."

"This is the house," Trey said. "Kendra and I grew up here." He walked a few steps, taking a glance around. "It's actually kind of surreal being here now, given all the life changes."

"Wait till you see what we did downstairs," Lance said. "Knocked out a whole wall."

"You want to take a look?" Pamela said. "I stay in the bedroom down there. I'd love for you to see the new space."

"Let's do it," Trey said.

"Come on and hang a little longer, Jade," Pamela said, "unless you've got somewhere to be."

"Not in particular," Jade said. "I just didn't want to take up all of your time."

"Then girl, put your coat and purse back down," Pamela said. "It's Friday night. We're going with the flow."

Lance chuckled at his mom. "Okay, party animal." He got Wes from the high chair and led the way down.

"Oh, wow," Trey said, taking it in. He walked the length of the living area. "Gives the room a whole new look. It's bigger. Brighter too."

"After years in a dingy cell, that's exactly what we wanted for Mom," Lance said. "Bigger and brighter."

"So many memories down here," Trey said, looking from one end to the other.

Lance nodded. "Yeah, the first time I came down here, you and your friends were smoking weed. And I almost got in a fight with the dealers."

"Come on, no way." Jade looked at Trey. "I can't picture that, with you being a missionary and all."

"I need to set the record straight, though"—Trey gave Lance the eye—"You didn't actually *see* me smoking weed. You only smelled it."

Lance looked at him. "Were you smoking weed, Trey?"

"Yup." Trey chuckled a little. "Might've been drunk too." He shook his head. "Those were some crazy days, man." He looked at Jade. "At that point, I would've laughed if you told me I'd be a missionary. I wasn't sure I wanted to be a Christian."

"That's wild," Jade said. "I thought you were a super Christian."

Trey looked confused. "How would you have gotten that impression?"

"Now I'm the one who's about to be embarrassed," Jade said. "So, that wedding video . . . I first saw a clip on the local news. The reporter focused on Lance and that he'd married this terminally ill woman. And I said, 'Who's beside him, though?'" She shook her head. "I might've been a little boy crazy. But I was shocked when my dad said he knew you. Then he said people always talk about Lance's commitment to Kendra, but they miss how devoted her brother was." She shrugged. "I wasn't a fan of church people, so I said, 'oh, he's one of those super Christians.'"

"Ha," Trey said. "Yeah, no. Who's your dad, though?"

"I don't know if you'd remember him," Jade said. "Randall Rogers."

"I definitely remember him," Trey said. "He'd drop by when Kendra was going through chemo and ask what we needed. He supported me on the mission field too." He shook his head. "I was sick when Lance told me what happened to him. Your dad was one of a kind."

"Thank you," Jade said. "Just know that he thought highly of you."

"Trey, I read the updated script," Pamela said. "I know it didn't seem funny at the time, but some of the scenes with your character are hilarious, like the party scene."

"The party scene is in there?" Trey said.

"How could they not put it in there?" Lance said. "Kendra leaves DC after her diagnosis and comes home to St. Louis, thinking she'll get some peace and quiet . . ."

"And I'm having an epic party, drunk, and making fun of the fact that her fiancé left her."

Jade's eyes widened. "You didn't."

"I didn't know about the diagnosis yet, but . . . yeah," Trey said. "Family dysfunction was a thing."

"Oh, your family too?" Jade said.

Lance put Wes down. "They also included the scene when I first come to the door to look at the house."

"Oh, that might be the funniest," Pamela said. "Trey, you were not feeling that."

"At all," Trey said. "I was living my best life. Dad overseas. House to myself. Then Dad calls and says, 'Son, I asked Pastor Lance to move into the lower level and look after the house while I'm gone. He'll be by to check out the place. Show him around, make him feel at home.'"

"Lance was a pastor back then?" Jade said.

"Youth pastor," Trey said. "And he had been *my* youth pastor. But I was older now and in a different place. I did *not* want the man of God moving in and wrecking my game. So I answer the door—"

"Wait, set the scene," Lance said. "Describe yourself."

Trey nodded with a slight grin. "So it had been a while since I'd seen a barber."

"You hadn't met a razor either," Lance added.

"Man, yeah, I forgot," Trey said. "That beard had a wilderness vibe."

"Pants sagging way down," Lance said.

Jade laughed. "I can't picture any of this."

Trey looked at Lance. "Am I telling the story or are you?"

"I just don't want you to miss the details," Lance said. "Matter of fact, we need to go upstairs and see if there's a bag of Doritos or potato chips or something."

"Why?" Trey said.

"So you can act it out," Lance said. "You crunching Doritos as you 'welcomed' me at the door is what makes the scene."

"How do you remember that?" Trey said. "And how am I supposed to act it out by myself?"

"Oh, I'd love to join you. Let's head up—Mom, can you hold Wes?" Lance picked him back up, gave him to Pamela, and started up the stairs. "Except—you be me, and I'll be you."

"Let's go," Trey said, walking up behind him.

Pamela and Jade followed, watching as Lance looked in the kitchen pantry for a prop for Trey to crunch on.

"Lance, are you forgetting Trey's been traveling all day?" Pamela said. "He's got to be dead tired, and you've got him doing all this."

Trey looked back at Pamela. "I'm so good right now. You have no idea. This is exactly what I needed."

CHAPTER 19

*T*ommy walked through the second floor of Living Word Church early Sunday morning, turning on lights and checking classrooms to make sure the various meeting groups had what they needed.

So I'm just saying, Lord, I need You to show me how to re-arrange my days. You know I usually write in the mornings. But with rehearsals starting tomorrow and filming the next week, I won't have that morning time. So how do I find time to write my reviews and other entertainment pieces? Because You know I don't have energy at night . . . although, I know You can give me grace.

Tommy paused inside a room that was used during first service by a parenting ministry. From a quick scan he could tell they didn't have the extra chairs they'd requested. Tommy had asked one of the deacons to handle it last Sunday and had assumed he'd taken care of it that day. He headed for a room near the end of a long corridor that housed extra chairs and tables.

Here's the other thing, Lord. Reggie and Jesse want to meet every week, but that just seems like a lot. Should I put it off until after the filming? Or at least make it every two weeks? But the fellowship was amazing, Lord.

141

Knowing where Reg and Jesse started, hardly able to be in the same room, and where they are now . . . only You could do that.

Tommy stacked several chairs and carried them to the classroom, then got several more on a second trip. Next he stopped inside the room that Cedric used for his Fundamentals of the Faith class, which was also used by a life group that met on Friday nights. The Friday night group liked to put the chairs in circles of eight; Cedric preferred them facing front. Though Tommy had asked the Friday group to put the chairs in their original position when they were done, most Sundays he rearranged them himself.

His phone vibrated on his hip twice as he moved the last of the chairs. *There it is.* When his phone started buzzing with people needing this and that, he knew he no longer had the building to himself.

He paused, gazing vaguely at the floor. *Lord, I'm here every Sunday morning with this place to myself and never thought to spend the time talking to You.* He shook his head. *Show me all the ways I can redeem the time in my days.*

Tommy checked his phone now, seeing a text related to the hospitality ministry—Deneen was always early—and one from the media team. He took the stairs to the first floor and started first toward the media room.

"Tommy Porter, I'm still waiting for your R.S.V.P.," a voice behind him said. "You joining us tonight?"

Tommy turned and saw Debra, head of the singles ministry, coming toward him. "Hey, what's up, sis. Joining who where?"

"Come on, big bro." Debra paused, looking at him. About five feet tall with four-inch heels, her presence was always felt. "The *Singles' Super Bowl Party.* I emailed you a save the date a month ago and a follow-up last week."

"Which email?" Tommy said. "You're probably using the old one that I rarely check." He'd known Debra for years, since she and her parents were long time members. "But sorry, sis, I've already got plans. I appreciate the invite, though."

Debra sighed. "You know I keep trying to get you to join us at *something*," she said. "We need more representation from our older singles—and by the way, your name came up at our monthly meet-and-greet."

"Do I want to know why?" Tommy said.

"Well, I might have *brought* it up." Debra smiled a little. "Because *again* someone asked whether we had 'older' singles in the church, meaning older than twenties or thirties. So I rattled off names, including yours—and *two* women pulled me aside afterward, asking if I know you personally."

"Why would they ask you that?"

Debra gave him a look. "You're an enigma around here. Super friendly. Everybody knows you—but they don't *really* know you. And hello? You're fine." She held her ring finger high. "You know I just got engaged, so I'm not trying to get at you. But I need you to understand how people view you."

Tommy shook his head. "That was a lot. But I appreciate you, sis. I think." He started off. "I need to get going—"

"Can I say one more thing, though?" Debra continued without pause. "I will never understand how Allison got close to you. I always felt a way about her—and I was too through when I saw those Facebook pics she posted." She tossed her eyes. "Anyway, all that to say . . . You need to know there are plenty of *good* women out here, and I can introduce you to two of them myself."

"Debra, I promise I'm good." He checked new notifications. "I've got to run. Later, sis."

Tommy continued to the media room, wondering why Solomon had texted him twice this morning. He hardly ever had an issue.

Tommy opened the door to an area with a window that looked out into the sanctuary. Solomon sat hunched over his computer—Silas beside him.

"Hey, good morning, bros," Tommy said, greeting them both. "I didn't know you were here, Silas."

"I got here early to prep for the sermon, and good thing." Silas sounded frustrated as he gestured to the computer. "We can't get the slides to open."

Solomon looked at Tommy. "The software isn't compatible with our system." He showed Tommy the issue on the computer. "It won't open the file."

"Oh, that's right, today's a big day," Tommy said. "Kicking off launch week for the *Promises* study. Also your first time preaching at Living Word."

"And I can't believe I didn't check to make sure everything was in order before this morning," Silas said. "Solomon said you might be able to help."

"Tommy was the one who pushed for an overhaul of our computer systems and software," Solomon said. "Works beautifully, until it encounters something it deems foreign."

"What did you use to make the slides?" Tommy said.

"Power Point," Silas said. "It's what I used at my former church when I preached."

"Lance started with Power Point at Living Hope," Tommy said, "but we switched to something else, then switched again when we got here. We'll get you up to speed on the current software, but right now we just need to get these slides up on the screen." He thought a moment. "Do you have your laptop with you? We need to try a different way to export the file."

"It's in my office upstairs," Silas said. "But Tommy, I know you're busy. I can tweak my message and try to manage without the slides."

"Nah, let's go," Tommy said, heading for the door. "The sermon is the main thing we do on Sunday morning. I've got all the time to make sure you can communicate what the Lord gave you."

"I really appreciate your help, Tommy." Silas glanced at him as they headed for the elevator. "I was so focused on preparing the message, and now there's this glitch."

"We'll figure it out," Tommy said. "I was just praying for God to make all the rough places smooth this morning. Something comes up every Sunday."

Silas nodded as he stepped into the elevator. "I hardly ever get nervous before I preach, but I can feel it today. I think it's because this is *Living Word*. I always had such admiration and respect for Dr.

Mason Lyles and the church he built. It's surreal to be preaching in his pulpit today." He quickly added, "Which is now Lance's, of course—"

"No, I get it," Tommy said. "Lance felt the same way. Honestly, I'm still not used to Pastor Lyles being gone. He was such a force. Between him and Lance, my life was forever changed."

"I've never heard your faith story," Silas said. "So you were saved through the ministry here at Living Word?"

"Absolutely," Tommy said, walking off the elevator. "I came to St. Louis straight out of college, excited about gaining experience in the field of entertainment news. Got married, started getting more opportunities, career started taking off—but my marriage tanked." He walked with Silas to his office. "I hit bottom, felt like a failure. My sister came to St. Louis and wanted to visit Living Word, because she did the Bible studies. That's how I got here."

"That's incredible," Silas said.

"Sat under Pastor Lyles' teaching week after week," Tommy said. "Lance was the one who actually led me to the Lord and discipled me."

"Wow," Silas said. "Your personal testimony includes two awesome men of God. What a gift." He moved into his office. "And I recently learned a fun fact about your college experience—that Jillian was like a sister to you."

"True," Tommy said.

"So I'll just ask you," Silas said. "Is she as special as she seems?"

Tommy nodded. "Even more so."

"This is why I've always been struck by this particular word in the Bible, especially as it pertains to the promises of God." Silas looked out at the congregation from the podium. "Because we get excited about the promises, as we should. We *ought* to believe God. We *ought* to know and stand on the truth of His word." He paused. "But sometimes you have to what?"

"Wait!" rang out from the congregation as the word flashed on the screen.

Tommy let his eyes linger on the word, unable to get past the irony. All the time he'd spent with Silas to get those slides up on the screen, he'd had no idea this was the theme. More than once, he'd wanted to text Jillian, who was probably in the same service. This was something they'd go back and forth about, with plenty of silly emojis to drive home the amusement. He was confident one of her texts would read, 'I told you so'."

"I'm hearing more enthusiasm," Silas said, nodding. "The first couple of times, you acted as if it was killing you to say it." He gave them a wry smile. "We don't like that word. We wish it wasn't so. But waiting is part of it. And because God is so gracious, waiting itself holds a promise. I told Sister Treva this might be the promise I need to meditate on the most in this study—If I Wait—because my flesh hates to wait. But that's where those powerful testimonies come from —if we would just wait on the Lord." He looked out at them. "Anybody know what I'm talking about? Anybody got a powerful testimony from waiting?"

Hands went up around the sanctuary along with "Yes!" and "Amen!"

"But this is how the enemy gets us," Silas said. "He's the father of lies, but he's always trying to make God out to be the liar. Psalm 25:3 says, 'None of those who wait for You will be ashamed'—so guess what? The enemy wants you to think you've waited and waited, and God didn't come through." He came from behind the podium. "I really want to emphasize this tactic of the enemy. Treva mentioned that they even saw this in real time in the pilot study, with someone who said she'd waited on God, and God hadn't done His part."

Tommy sat forward, his words landing with force. That had to have been Allison. She'd been in that pilot study. And memories now flooded of the two of them arguing about that particular lesson —If I Wait—when Allison got home. She'd started venting about how unhappy she was, how Tommy was smothering her with expectations, how she'd waited so long to get married and it wasn't what she'd hoped. She'd even had an attitude because Jillian had been in town for that lesson. "Your little friend chimed in about how you're such a great communicator—she doesn't *really* know you."

He stared at the back of the pew as he remembered more of the argument.

"So you're upset because you were waiting for God to give you a perfect marriage," Tommy had said, "and you found out life doesn't work that way?"

"I know there's no perfect marriage," Allison said, "but if I'm praying and 'waiting on God,' there's supposed to be a blessing on the other side, isn't there?"

"Oh, you don't count our marriage a blessing?" Tommy said.

"You know what, Tommy, all I'm counting lately are these—the arguments." Allison threw up her hands. "But I guess this is where I'm supposed to wait some more. Wait to feel better about the marriage. Wait for God to turn it all around." She twirled her finger. "And hope that when I get down the road, the waiting will pan out." She shook her head. "How long before you realize it's never going to be what you had hoped?"

"I get it," Tommy said. "You want to see miles down the road and know exactly how things will be. Waiting is a faith move, Allison. You have to actually trust God, which, by the way, happens to also be the Christian life."

Tommy could feel his pulse racing. Had he really said that? Now he'd gone from 'waiting is a faith move' to groaning whenever Jillian spoke the word 'wait.' His stomach churned. *Lord, I became jaded myself.*

"So even though we prayed for my wife to be healed, the Lord chose to take her home," Silas was saying. "Does that mean our waiting was in vain? That God didn't come through?" He moved closer to them. "Listen—God is *always* faithful. Waiting is not about focusing on the outcome *we* desire. It's about seeking the Lord. Keeping a divine focus. That's when that peace you can't explain fills your heart. That's when you get a praise in your spirit despite the tears in your eyes."

Heads nodded around Tommy.

"Waiting isn't passive," Silas said. "If you're waiting, you should be moving—closer to God. Because listen, you never have to wait for *that*. You never have to wait to get closer to God. The Lord's got a promise for you there too—'Draw near to Him, and He will draw near to you.'"

"Amen," Tommy murmured.

"Let me tell you—that promise came alive as I waited and prayed for my wife," Silas said. "The Lord *met* me and ministered to me. He gave me *His* perspective. When my wife went to be with Him, I could rejoice knowing that death has no sting. My wife was with the Lord! How could I say God didn't come through? To live is Christ and to die is gain—she got the gain! She had it better than I did down here on this troubled earth. My God *keeps* His promises."

"Yes!" a woman said in front of Tommy. "Amen!"

Silas went back to the podium. "Let's read this last verse together —Lamentations 3:25." He waited for it to come up on the screen. "'The LORD is good to those who wait for Him, to the person who seeks Him.'" He turned and looked at them. "The LORD is good to those who what?"

"Wait!"

Silas nodded with a smile. "That's your best one yet." He paused. "Not waiting on a thing or a person or a situation to change. To those who wait *for Him*. He's our focus. Always. When you're waiting for Him and seeking Him, you will see His goodness. That's a promise. Let's pray . . ."

⁓

"Hey everyone, before you go . . ."

Tommy watched as his brother spoke from the platform.

"Good morning, my name is Reggie Porter. I serve as part of the online ministry here at Living Word." A contrast to Silas, who wore khakis and a button down, Reggie wore jeans and a polo style shirt. "I have something quick to add to the announcements."

People who had been chatting and gathering their things took a pause.

"Last Sunday, Pastor Lance preached about clinging to God," Reggie said. "In one week, that sermon has been downloaded more than any from the past few weeks. So in case any of you may be interested, starting today on the Living Word site, we're featuring a Cling Challenge."

Chatter started up again, this time about the announcement.

"The goal is a closer walk with the Lord," Reggie said. "Here's how it will work . . . Every Sunday for about the next month we'll upload a new challenge. This week's challenge is this—Jesus calls us friend, so build up that friendship by talking to Him throughout the day, as you would a friend." He added, "Just want to say thank you to my brother Tommy for inspiring this challenge and leading us each week in this. Check the site for more details."

Tommy headed toward the front of the sanctuary, where Reggie was talking with Lance. He paused near Silas, who had a line waiting as he talked with someone. "Needed that sermon, man," he said. "That was a good word."

"Appreciate that, bro," Silas said.

Reggie looked as Tommy approached. "I told you he'd come for me."

"I'm the one who told him to make the announcement," Lance said.

"You told him to put the 'Cling Challenge' online too?" Tommy said.

"He told me about it before service," Lance said. "I took a look and said he should announce it. What's the problem?"

"It's not supposed to be all that," Tommy said. "I only mentioned that I was challenging *myself* each week. It wasn't meant to be hyped up, posted online, and broadcast to the church." He looked at Reggie. "What is that about?"

"It's part of my job to track the analytics," Reggie said. "When I saw how many downloads that cling message got—and obviously it impacted you as well—I thought others would benefit from the challenge. I didn't mention it because I knew you'd object. So I had to go to the top." He nodded toward Lance with a smile.

"I don't see how you could have a problem with it," Lance said. "It's not hype. It's making the message practical in a way I hadn't thought about. Giving people tangible ways to cling. Changing people's habits, man. This is powerful."

"But now I'm responsible for coming up with a new challenge each week," Tommy said. "When it's between me and God, it's whatever. I can move as I'm led. Now I'll be thinking about whether it's suitable for others."

"Oh, that's easy," Lance said. "Don't think about it. If I had to think about whether my sermon was suitable to everybody, I'd never preach. Be led by the Spirit and let that be enough."

Tommy looked at his brother. "Still, Reg, I'm just saying—"

"I see you out here making ministry moves, bro." Alonzo squeezed his shoulder from behind then clasped hands with him.

"That's not at all what you see," Tommy said. "But what's up, bro? Good to see you. And good to see you too, Cinda," he said, hugging her.

Alonzo gestured behind him. "I brought them up here to meet Lance, but I want you to meet them too."

"I know that's not Tommy Porter."

Tommy turned. "Mariah Pendleton. I was so excited when I heard you were directing this movie." He hugged her. "Look at you, back in St. Louis, at my church."

"Oh, it's *your* church, huh?" Mariah smiled. "Cinda and Alonzo said it was *their* church."

"They haven't been here long enough to call it theirs," Tommy said. "They've only got a partial claim."

"So y'all know each other?" Alonzo said.

"We worked together way back in the day, at a local network," Tommy said. "She's phenomenal."

"You know I know," Alonzo said.

Mariah cocked her head at Tommy. "Don't be saying 'way back in the day,' making me look old."

"But you're old *and* phenomenal," Tommy said. "There's a praise in there."

"If I'm old, then you're old," Mariah said. "But I'll give it to you—going smooth on top with the light beard action?" She nodded. "Looking good, my friend."

"Appreciate that, Mariah," Tommy said. "Likewise."

"And Tommy," Alonzo said, "this is Brooke Shelley."

"The one who's playing Kendra." Tommy shook her hand. "Heard lots of great things. Good to meet you."

"Really nice to meet you as well," Brooke said.

"All this time I've been working on pre-production," Mariah said, "I had no idea you and Lance knew each other."

"Lance discipled me," Tommy said. "We've been close for years. That's why I can't figure out why nobody wrote me into the script."

"While you're over there whining," Alonzo said, "I was about to mention that we'll be seeing Tommy on set. He's the exclusive reporter during filming."

"Oh, for real?" Mariah said. "That's big news. Congrats."

"Not as big as yours," Tommy said. "I'm so proud of you. Congrats to you as well."

"That means a lot, Tommy. Thank you."

Tommy moved on as they talked with Lance, thinking about the rest of the morning. He needed to run to the ministry building for a quick meeting then back to the church building for a meeting about the Tuesday night launch event. Before he left for the day, he needed to go by the youth building—

"Tommy, do you have a minute?" David came up to him outside the sanctuary.

"Hey, how's it going, David?" Tommy said. "Nothing's wrong, is there? I hardly ever see teens in this building till after third service."

"No," David said. "I just realized I didn't have your number, and I wanted to catch you while no one's around."

Tommy glanced at all the people coming and going. "No one's around?"

"Well," David said, "while my mom's not around."

Tommy gave him the eye. "You must want to go to a concert and your mom said no. David, you're not putting me in the middle. If Jill said no, then the answer's—"

"No, it's not that," David said. "Not exactly. So Trevor plays bass and I found out there's this concert coming up with this bassist I've heard him talk about—"

"Who's that?" Tommy said.

"Her name is Tonina, I think?"

"Oh, yeah," Tommy said. "She's from here."

"So I asked mom if we could surprise Trevor with tickets," David said, "but it's a smaller venue and it's sold out. Then I said I could ask you if you could get tickets, and she said not to bother you."

"That means you're putting me in the middle, David." Tommy shrugged. "I can't help you."

"But I don't think she really meant it," David said. "She started crying when we saw that it was sold out because she's been emotional about Trevor's birthday and wanting to make it special without Dad." He breathed a sigh. "So if you *could* get tickets, she would ultimately be glad I talked to you. Right?"

CHAPTER 20

"'m seeing a difference already." Jesse leaned against the back of the pew after service. "When did we meet, Thursday?"

"Yeah, this is the third day," Reggie said. "I didn't think it would be much different than the time I spend praying. But, man . . . talking to Jesus like a friend has meant talking to Him *more*."

"Real talk—it was kind of awkward at first," Jesse said. "Like, 'Hey, Jesus . . . umm . . . how are You, today?'" He chuckled. "But I'm getting into a flow. You realize how many things cross your mind and nobody's there to talk them over with—but Someone *is* there. Jesus."

Faith nodded. "When Reggie first told me what you all were doing, I told him I wanted to do it too. I'm pumped that the challenge is online."

Jade held up her phone. "I pulled up the site before Reggie could finish the announcement. I need this. The cling sermon was depressing."

Jesse looked at her. "Why do you say that?"

"I just don't know how you get to where you feel a closeness with God," Jade said. "So I'm willing to at least try the challenge." She turned to her sister. "Are you doing it?"

The only one still sitting, Jordyn focused on her phone.

"Jordyn," Jade said.

"Huh?" Jordyn looked up. "What?"

Jade shook her head. "Girl, never mind."

"Hey, Reg," Jesse said, "are you hearing anything about who might replace Lance at Living Hope? After that sermon today, seems like Silas should get a look."

"I haven't heard anything since they appointed an interim pastor over there," Reggie said. "But that doesn't mean they're not talking about it." He nodded. "That crossed my mind too, even before the sermon. Silas has a shepherd's heart."

"Hey, there's Trey. We were with him at dinner last night." Faith waved him over, waiting for him to move through people in the aisle. "Trey, let me introduce you"—she turned to the rest—"this is Trey Woods, Lance's brother-in-law. Trey, this is Jesse, Jordyn, and Jade," she said, pointing them out.

Jesse moved toward him. "Heard so much about you from Lance. Good to finally meet you." He shook his hand.

"You too, Jesse," Trey said. He greeted Jordyn then moved to Jade. "The homie." He high-fived her. "You are hilarious."

"You already know each other?" Faith said.

Jade nodded. "I was visiting Miss Pam when Trey got there Friday night. Ended up staying an extra two hours because Trey and Lance got on a roll." She shook her head with a slight chuckle. "I found out they don't have any sense."

"Nah, that's you," Trey said. "Trying to act all subdued at first. But she had me weak when we got into, 'You know you're from STL if . . .'"

Jordyn looked at her. "You didn't tell me all that."

"I said we had a dope time," Jade said.

"Wait, I'm just catching this—twins?" Trey said, looking one to the other. "Very cool."

A few people moved into their row and sat down.

"That's probably our cue to get out of here," Reggie said.

"I thought you all were here for second service," Trey said.

"We went to first," Jesse said. "Just hanging and talking. But yeah, we better move out."

Faith and Reggie headed out, and Jordyn got up, typing something on her phone.

"Jade," Jordyn said, "I've got some errands to run. I don't know if you want to go with me or take an Uber?"

"An Uber?" Jade said. "Just take me home before you go. You already knew I wasn't up for errands. I specifically asked if you were coming straight home from church. I would've driven myself otherwise."

"Why is an Uber a big deal?" Jordyn said.

"The big deal is that you're switching things up," Jade said. "Just let one of your errands be to take me home."

"I can take you," Trey said, "but you'd have to wait until after service. Although, that might get you home at the same time as if you ran the errands."

"Not hardly," Jade said. "She's about to hit several stores." She thought a moment. "I wouldn't mind hearing the sermon again, if it's no trouble taking me."

"I can't guarantee that," Trey said. "I jumped in my dad's car, and it was on 'E'. I didn't have time to put gas in it."

Jade gave him a look. "If we run out of gas I'm not walking."

"If you'd rather sit in the car, in the cold with no heat, while I walk to find gas," Trey said, "that's fine."

"I need you to explain how you didn't have time, though," Jade said. "Service hasn't even started yet. I think you just like living on the edge still."

Jesse and Jordyn looked at one another and slipped away as the two of them continued.

"Well, that's something." Jordyn took a glance back at them. "My sister made a friend?"

"Jade's got a lot of layers," Jesse said. "But once I got past, 'I'll cut you if you look at me wrong,' I was surprised how real she could be, even a little funny." He headed toward the exit. "I think you should forget those errands and go with me to get something to eat. I miss you."

Jordyn smiled, putting on her fleece jacket over a bulky sweater and jeans. "We went to the movies last night and service this morning. How can you miss me?"

"I don't understand it either," Jesse said. "I just always want to be near you. I need to fix that."

"You'd better not fix that," Jordyn said, walking outside as he held the door.

"I'll call you before I pick you up for the Super Bowl party," Jesse said.

"I'll probably just meet you there," Jordyn said. "Jade was right—I'm about to hit all the stores."

"You sure I can't convince you to come with me?" Jesse walked her to her car.

"Hey," Reggie said, walking up with Faith and Zoe. "We just picked up your Princess from the nursery. You two want to get something to eat?"

"Ugh," Jordyn said. "Y'all are making it hard. I've already got plans."

"Daddy, Daddy!" Zoe said, reaching for him.

Reggie put her down, and she toddled over to Jesse, who scooped her up.

"Brother Edmonds?" Reggie said. "You got plans too?"

"Nah, I can roll," Jesse said. "I'm definitely hungry. And I can tell you what I was looking at in Second Samuel. Blew my mind, man."

Faith looked from one to the other. "Seriously, what is happening?"

CHAPTER 21

"*W*e'd better go." Sophia backed up from an alcove on the second floor of the main church building. "The youth service is starting."

Lucas took her hand and tugged her back to the shadows. "Wait, I want to know. Was that really your first kiss?"

The sound of that made her heart rate accelerate even more. Did she really just kiss Lucas? "You're surprised?"

"Well, yeah," Lucas said. "You're eighteen. And the prettiest girl I know. You're telling me you haven't had at least *one* boyfriend?"

"I was seeing someone back home in Maryland," Sophia said. "Even went to his prom. But I was afraid to take that step, to kiss him."

"Afraid of what?" Lucas said.

"Of where it would lead," Sophia said. "After my cousin Faith got pregnant, she had a lot of talks with us about taking things slowly with guys."

"I can understand that," Lucas said. "You're okay, though, with kissing me just now?"

Sophia nodded. "But I'm gonna go. I know Joy's wondering where I am."

"Okay," Lucas said. "I'll wait before I head out."

Sophia took the stairs and made her way out of the building. A cold breeze lifted her thick, sandy hair and she remembered she hadn't stopped to get her coat. She'd had a question for her mom about the move to the B and B, but Jillian's phone had been turned off. Sophia had intended to dash to the main building, catch her between services, and dash back. She shuddered a little as she quickened her steps. How had it come to all of that?

She opened the outer door and walked inside, praise and worship music pulsating in the building. She made her way to the youth gathering, and Joy waved to let her know where she was.

"What took you so long?" Joy leaned close, talking above the music.

"First I had to find Mom," Sophia said. "Then you know how you run into one person after another?" She shrugged. "Took longer than I thought."

"So you guys are moving to the B and B right after church?" Joy said. "I'm so jealous that you get to stay there with Mariah Pendleton."

"We're only there for a few days," Sophia said.

"But think about all the opportunities you'll have to talk to her," Joy said. "We won't be able to do that as interns—girl, there he is." Her gaze shifted to Lucas as he walked in. "I was wondering where he was, then I figured he went to hear his dad preach."

Sophia's stomach dropped. Joy was always looking for Lucas. Not for any particular reason. Just to fawn from afar.

Joy nudged her. "He's headed this way."

Sophia focused on the praise and worship team. *Keep going, keep going . . .* She took a peek when he didn't pass by. He'd stopped near a group of guys.

"Do you think he's shy?" Joy said. "He doesn't say a whole lot."

Sophia shrugged. "I think guys are just hard to figure out."

She took a breath, her heart beating out of her chest. How could she bring herself to tell Joy what happened? But even now, the sequence of events was replaying a thousand times in her head.

Sophia had found her mom in the sanctuary, and while they were talking, Silas and Lucas had walked by.

"Hey, you two know each other, right?" Silas said.

Sophia nodded, though she and Lucas had never exchanged more than a few words. Jillian started talking to Silas about his message, and Sophia moved on, Lucas walking with her.

"We actually don't know each other," Lucas said. "But funny that our parents do."

"Yeah, but they both work here, so . . ." She shrugged.

"What about that date, though?" Lucas said.

"What date?"

"Last Sunday after church," Lucas said. "Dad tried to be nonchalant about it, but when he asked which shirt he should wear, I knew he had to have a thing for your mom."

Sophia's insides churned. "Her mom was dating—Pastor Keys? What did *that* mean? Why hadn't she mentioned it?

"Anyway," Lucas said, "maybe we can double date one day."

"Double date?" Sophia said. "Who?"

"My dad, your mom, you, and me," Lucas said.

"Yeah, not gonna happen," Sophia said, butterflies swirling. She'd thought Lucas was cute from the moment she'd first seen him. And being around him in youth group the past few months, it was hard not to develop a crush. But she didn't know Joy had been feeling the same until a couple weeks ago. Still, it was no big deal. Sophia had let it go.

But she'd never considered that Lucas might like her.

"So you're saying you'd never date me?" Lucas said.

"I meant the double—anyway, it's odd that you'd mention a date when you've never said a whole lot to me."

"You're always with your cousin," Lucas said. "And you're a little intimidating."

"How am I intimidating?" Sophia said.

"Even now, that pointed look with those green eyes . . ." Lucas said. "And you don't say a whole lot yourself, so I figured you didn't like me."

"Interesting."

"That's it?" Lucas said.

"I'm just saying, it's interesting to hear your perspective," Sophia said. "This is the most we've ever talked."

"I like it, though," Lucas said. "Talking one on one like this. We're always surrounded by a million people in the youth ministry building."

"Well." Sophia glanced around. "There might be a million people here too."

"You know what I mean." Lucas thought a moment. "I've got an idea," he said. "We've got a little time before youth worship starts. We should find a quiet spot where we can talk and get to know each other better. Just a few minutes."

"Like where?" Sophia said.

"I'm in this building a lot with my dad," Lucas said. "I know where we can go."

Sophia hesitated. "I don't know."

"What's wrong with talking?" Lucas said.

"Nothing, I guess." Sophia thought a moment. "Only a few minutes."

Sophia followed Lucas up the stairs, down a main corridor, and into a side hallway.

"Where are we going?" Sophia said.

"I love mazes," Lucas said, "so I'm always looking for passageways that lead this way and that. I might be a little nerdy."

"I never would've thought that about you," Sophia said. "My brother says I'm nerdy for always having a puzzle I'm working on."

"How is that nerdy?" Lucas settled near an alcove midway down the hall. "It's been a while but the last one I did was this zebra puzzle—"

"Oh man, I did that one," Sophia said. "Wait, I've seen two of those. How many pieces was the one you did?"

"Ten thousand," Lucas said. "One-thousand would've been a waste of time."

"Right?" Sophia said. "Except, this past year I've been doing one-thousand pieces because that's all we've got room for."

Lucas looked at her. "You're talking about . . . since you lost your dad?"

Sophia nodded. "We had to move and make adjustments." She paused. "Sometimes it's the little things that remind me he's gone. Like no more humongous puzzles. He used to help me with them."

"For me it's books," Lucas said. "Mom made it her mission to make sure I had a stack to read. I used to complain, but now that there's no stack . . ."

"How long has it been?" Sophia said.

"Two years." Lucas stared vaguely a moment. "But everything changed before that even, when she got sick."

Sophia sank into her own thoughts. "The hardest part is realizing that life could literally be over tomorrow. That's what hit me when I lost my dad. And I haven't been able to stop thinking about it." She looked at him. "We're supposed to be making all these future plans—college, career, family. Who knows if we'll even be alive?"

"I think about that all the time too," Lucas said. "I even had that thought about you."

"What do you mean?" Sophia said.

"I kept telling myself to go up and talk to you," Lucas said. "I'd imagine the entire conversation, then I couldn't get up the nerve. So I'd say, 'Okay, next Sunday.' But then I'd also think, 'There might not be a next Sunday.'"

"That sounds super pessimistic," Sophia said. "But I totally get it."

"That's why I asked if we could go somewhere and talk," Lucas said, "instead of putting it off till whenever . . . and whenever might not get here."

"I'm actually glad you did," Sophia said.

"Okay, that's huge," Lucas said. "This whole time I didn't know if you were just tolerating me, looking for a way to tell me to get lost."

"I would've told you downstairs," Sophia said. "In a nicer way, but still . . ."

"So does that mean maybe you sorta kinda, at least a little bit, if the sun is shining and you get out of bed on the right side—"

"Okay, stop."

"I'm really wondering, though," Lucas said, "if there's a chance that you could . . . potentially . . . like me."

Sophia glanced downward a moment. "Probably more than potentially."

"That's everything," Lucas said.

"It doesn't necessarily *mean* anything."

"I get that," Lucas said. "But at least, maybe we can meet again next Sunday."

"Maybe," Sophia said. "Well. We'd better go."

"You go first," Lucas said. "Then I'll follow a little after."

Sophia walked away, her insides flipping this way and that. When she got to the end of the hall, she turned back. Lucas was in the alcove still.

"What happened?" he said.

"Nothing," Sophia said. "I was just thinking . . . what if there's no next Sunday?"

Lucas looked confused. "Then it's good we got to talk today."

"True," Sophia said. "It's just . . . I've been curious about something . . . and I've never done this, but with everything we just said about who knows if we'll be here tomorrow, now just seems like—"

"What, Sophia?"

Sophia swallowed, goose bumps dotting her arms. "I just . . . want to know what it's like . . . to kiss."

"So I'm a random guinea pig?"

"And what if you are?" Sophia said. "Does it matter?"

"Yeah," Lucas said, "I don't want to be your first kiss if it doesn't mean anything to you."

Sophia took a breath. "Fine. I've had a crush on you. For a while."

"And you had me sweating all this time with those mean green eyes bearing down on me?" Lucas shook his head. "I don't know, Sophia. Are you sure this is how you want to—"

Sophia leaned in and kissed him.

Lucas cleared his throat and looked at her, and they kissed again.

"So is it what you imagined?" Lucas said.

"Better."

Joy nudged her. "Sophia?"

Sophia's heart beat out of her chest even now. She couldn't remember sitting, but praise and worship had ended and all eyes were on the speaker. "Yeah?" she said.

Joy leaned closer. "I was just thinking . . . If Lucas is shy, maybe I should be the one to strike up a conversation. What do you think?"

Her mouth dry, Sophia searched for words. "I mean, it's just conversation. Why not?"

CHAPTER 22

Stephanie boarded the plane ahead of Lindell, texting Jillian as she walked down the aisle. **Forgot to tell you... I put two loaves of gluten free bread in the laundry room freezer. Brooke is gluten free—preference not medical—and she loves toast with breakfast.** She sent the text and paused as the woman in front of her put her luggage in the overhead bin.

"Babe, top of the list is Pigeon Island." Lindell read from his phone. "It's got these military ruins that sound awesome—you know I love stuff like that. And they've got tour guides who give a history lesson about the battles that took place for control of the island—we're in this row, babe."

Lindell put their carry-on bags and coats overhead and moved into the row first, taking the window. Stephanie lowered herself into the middle seat.

"It says to get there early in the morning for the best experience," Lindell said. "And look, there's this other historical site—"

"Babe, I could see all the touristy stuff if we were heading some-place like London or Rome, but an island?" Stephanie extended the seatbelt over her belly and clicked it in place. "Anyway, I can't do all of that in my condition."

"All of what? Walking?" Lindell said. "You know I'm the first one to look out for your health and the baby's. But walking is actually great for your cardiovascular health. Plus exercise helps you sleep better, minimizes risk of gestational diabetes, kicks up the endorphins—"

"Okay, I get it," Stephanie said.

"How can we go *anywhere* and not learn some of its history?" Lindell said. "You just want to hang at the beach all day, every day?"

"That would be perfect," Stephanie said. "Oh, wait—I didn't tell Jillian about the cookies." She started texting. "She can still serve them if she starts making them now. I need to tell her which recipe folder it's in."

"Steph, we barely made it to the airport on time because you had endless instructions for Jillian." Lindell looked at her. "Now you're texting her every five minutes. When are you going to let it go?"

"Babe, I've never left the B and B in anyone's hands," Stephanie said. "And we happen to have a full house. I have to make sure our guests are taken care of."

"Meaning—you're not going to let it go?" Lindell said.

"What does that even mean?" Stephanie said. "Never check to see how things are going?"

"Steph, have you forgotten?" Lindell shifted, focusing on her. "One of our main problems is the B and B. We're going on vacation to get away from all of that."

"And we *will* be away from it," Stephanie said. "But it's still my responsibility. I can't completely abandon it for several days."

"Or several minutes," Lindell said. "You act like people can't survive without a late afternoon cookie."

"Fine." Stephanie tossed her phone into her purse. "I won't send it."

"Now you're being ridiculous," Lindell said. "You typed it up. Send it."

"Nope," Stephanie said. "I'll hear about it the entire trip." She folded her arms. "I just want to know what I'm supposed to do if Jillian has a question. Or maybe I should turn my phone off, so I won't even know she has a question."

"This is great." Lindell shook his head. "We're headed to the vacation of our dreams, and the B and B is still front and center."

Stephanie gritted her teeth. *If you had just let me send the stupid text in peace we'd be on to something else by now.*

"But to your point," Lindell said, "maybe we *should* keep our phones off, to get the most out of this vacation." He got his phone and powered it down. "Done."

"Of course you can do that." Stephanie ran her hand across her stomach as the baby kicked. "You've got an office full of people who can cover for you."

"And you've got the perfect person covering for you," Lindell said. "I love how Jillian broke it down as she scooted you out the door."

"I bet you did," Stephanie said, glancing at him. "And I know she was right. If she could handle several school subjects for four different kids, plus extracurricular activities, meal prep three times a day, and generally take care of the house *for years*—she can handle the B and B."

"Exactly," Lindell said.

"Still, I can't just totally check out," Stephanie said. "Anything can happen, and Jillian needs to be able to reach me."

"Okay, Steph."

"You have an attitude because I won't turn my phone off for several days?" Stephanie said. "How is that fair?"

"I'd love to see you this protective of us and our time," Lindell said. "If you gave our marriage half the energy you give the B and B—"

"Am I not going on the trip?" Stephanie said. "And right in the midst of all the excitement with the movie. Hollywood is in St. Louis —*at my B and B*—and I'm leaving town. But it's not enough for you."

"If your heart were in it, maybe it *would* be enough."

"My heart *is* in it," Stephanie said. "It just might not look the way you want it to look. You have to stop micromanaging everything."

"*I'm* micromanaging?" Lindell said. "Who's worried about cookies?"

"That's part of my *job*." Stephanie sighed. "I'm so tired of all the—" She sighed again. "Never mind."

"No, go on. Tired of what?"

Stephanie took a moment to respond. "For the longest time I felt I didn't have any purpose. You had medicine, and I pretty much felt useless." She looked at him. "The B and B gives me purpose. I'm using gifts I didn't know I had, like hospitality and service. But I feel bad about using those gifts because you're always comparing what I do as a caretaker to what I do as a wife."

"How can I not compare when I'm getting the short end of the stick all the time?" Lindell said.

"How is it the short end when I'm *on the trip?*"

Her phone chimed, loud and proud in her purse. Stephanie stared ahead, conflicted about whether to check it and mad that she had to feel conflicted.

". . . and at this time all portable electronic devices, including cell phones, tablets, e-readers, electronic games, and MP3 players must be switched to airplane mode . . ."

Stephanie got her phone and saw Jillian's reply on the home screen.

Gluten free bread . . . got it. Now stop worrying about the B and B and ENJOY. Praying, girl.

Stephanie opened her phone and sent the text about the cookies, then switched to airplane mode. She tossed it back into her purse.

"So you and your husband are heading on a vacation?"

Stephanie turned to the woman on her right, who looked to be about her mother's age.

"Yes, ma'am," Stephanie said. "We've got a connecting flight to Saint Lucia."

"Oh, how wonderful." The woman moved her head closer. "Some of my fondest memories are of stealing away from the demands of life with my Jacob and spending time together alone." She smiled a little. "So many things I thought were important never cross my mind anymore. Just those precious moments with my husband, rest his soul."

So the woman wasn't even going to pretend she hadn't heard the entire conversation? And had no problem easing her way into her business?

"Thank you for sharing," Stephanie said. "Sounds like life has taught you a lot of lessons."

"Mostly it's God that taught me," the woman said. "Can I share something else?"

"Sure," Stephanie said.

"I pray for a lot of the younger couples in my life," she said. "You've got constant intrusions that we never had to deal with. Who knew it would be possible to take a phone with you? *Everywhere.* People shouldn't be able to get in touch with you at all times. And we act like we have to respond at all times. You don't have to live under that kind of tyranny." She patted Stephanie's arm. "I just felt led to share that. I hope you don't mind this, but can I get your names and add you to my prayer list?"

"No, I don't mind," Stephanie said. *Except you're obviously telling me we've got issues and need prayer.* "I'm Stephanie, my husband is Lindell. And thank you again."

"It's my pleasure, Stephanie."

"What was that about?" Lindell whispered.

"Tell you later," Stephanie mouthed back.

She took a magazine from her tote and flipped through it, then took out a novel she planned to read on the beach—and closed it soon after she started.

Okay, Lord . . . You're just gonna make that woman's voice loop through my mind?

Stephanie sighed. *Fine.* She got her phone and held it a moment. *For how long, Lord? Please not for the entire trip. I feel like that's a form of claustrophobia. All my thoughts and energy—all my focus—on Lindell?*

She sighed again and powered down her phone.

CHAPTER 23

*J*illian put an assortment of cookies on a silver serving tray and carried it to the main sitting room, placing it on a side table. Checking the coffee carafes, she brought the decaf to the kitchen and started a fresh brew.

"Mom, why haven't we been doing this at home?" David held up a chocolate chip cookie as he walked in. "Afternoon cookies need to be a thing."

Jillian scrubbed a baking pan. "Why did I know that was coming?"

"Did you hear the breakfast menu?" Sophia ate a green apple as she sat at the kitchen table with Joy. "Pancakes *and* muffins, eggs, grits, bacon, sausage, and more . . . every day."

"So basically," David said, "we need to turn our home into a B and B, with Trevor, Sophie, and I as guests."

"That's funny," Jillian said, "because you're not guests *here*. Did you see your list of chores?" She nodded to a sheet of paper on the island.

"How is this fair, Mom?" David said, perusing it. "We're not the ones who volunteered to do this."

"Okay then." Jillian rinsed the pan and put it in a dish rack. "I'll see if you can stay at your Aunt Treva's this week."

"Yeah, come on over, David." Joy peeled back a banana. "So we can both be missing out."

"No way am I leaving," David said. "But are we supposed to be cleaning this entire B and B?"

"A cleaning service does most of the heavy lifting." Jillian filled the carafe with fresh coffee. "I just need you all to help with the breakfast service, keeping the kitchen tidy, washing sheets and towels, that kind of thing."

Voices sounded in the entryway.

"Oh, let me go out there," Jillian said. "That must be Alonzo and Noah."

"Mom, what?" Sophia looked at her. "Is Noah Stiles staying *here*?"

"He's taking the third room," Jillian said.

Sophia and Joy turned wide eyes upon each other, then Sophia looked back at Jillian. "And you didn't say anything?"

"Why would I have said something?" Jillian said.

"This is *so* not fair," Joy said. "I'm packing my bags and coming back over here. I don't care if I have to sleep on the floor."

Jillian took the carafe to the sitting room, where Alonzo and Noah stood talking to Brooke. She set it down on the side table.

"Well, just know that I'm a fan," Brooke was saying. "It's really good to meet you, Noah, and I look forward to working with you."

"Hey Noah, this is Jillian Mason," Alonzo said, turning to her. "She's taking care of the B and B this week."

Jillian shook his hand. "Noah, very nice to meet you. I'm here for whatever you need. We want you to feel at home."

"I appreciate that, ma'am." Noah glanced at the side table with a boyish smile. "I was wondering about those chocolate cookies."

"Ahh the chocolate volcanoes," Jillian said, smiling. "Please help yourself."

"And that's Sophia and Joy," Alonzo said. "They'll be interns on set."

Jillian turned and saw that the girls had followed her.

"Nice to meet you," Noah said, shaking their hands.

"Nice to meet you too," they both said in unison.

"Hey, there he is." Mariah came into the sitting room and gave Noah a hug. "Glad you made it safely. How was your flight?"

"We got delayed a couple of times, so definitely glad to be here," Noah said. "I thought I might miss the Super Bowl."

"Speaking of which," Alonzo said, "after we take your things to your room, we'll head to my house. Cinda's getting everything ready."

"And you got the email I sent before you took off, right?" Mariah said. "I wanted to answer your questions about the start of rehearsals tomorrow."

Jillian gestured to Sophia and Joy and they slipped out, returning to the kitchen.

"That did *not* just happen," Sophia said.

"I wanted to ask for a picture, but it didn't seem like a good time," Joy said. "How is he *cuter* in person?"

"And taller," Sophia said. "And did you see those dimples?"

"And those *eyes*."

"I hope you guys know he can hear you," David said, his head in the fridge.

"No, he can't," Sophia said, her voice a near whisper now. She moved near the sink. "Mom, do you think he heard us?"

"David's just messing with you." Jillian washed the mixing bowl now. "But how do you two even know about him? And how old is he?"

"He's twenty," Joy said. "And how could we *not* know about him. He's got millions of followers, and his music is everywhere right now."

"I've been following him and his music for a long time," Sophia said, "way before he got popular."

"Well, just remember, all of you—no crazy fan stuff toward any of the guests." Jillian rinsed the bowl. "We're here to serve. And where's Trevor?"

David shrugged, drinking lemonade. "Probably playing video games upstairs."

Sophia motioned to her cousin. "We need to go get changed."

"Don't leave without your brothers," Jillian said.

"Mom, why?" Sophia said. "Then we can't talk about stuff. Why can't they ride with you?"

"I'm not leaving until everyone else leaves," Jillian said, "to make sure the B and B is in order. And I want to prep a couple of things for breakfast."

"And I want to get there early," David said, "to network."

Sophia groaned. "Little brothers are so irritating." She left out with Joy.

"So, Mom"—David moved closer—"I've got an update about Trevor's birthday."

"You came up with another idea?" Jillian put the mixing bowl back in a cabinet.

"The same one," David said. "The Tonina concert. Tommy can get tickets."

She looked at him. "You asked him after I told you not to?"

"Actually, you said not to bother him," David said. "And if I thought I'd be bothering him, I wouldn't have asked."

Jillian gave him a look.

"Mom, it's the best birthday gift we could give him." David grabbed a banana and started off. "Trev's gonna go crazy."

Cinda crossed paths with David, stopping just inside the kitchen. "Hey, Jillian, Noah dropped his things in his room, and we're about to take off. Brooke's coming with us too."

"Okay, see you there," Jillian said.

"Oh," Cinda said, "and you got a request to bring those cookies to the party. Noah said it was the best cookie he's ever had."

"I'll be sure to bring some," Jillian said.

She took out a notebook Stephanie left for her and skimmed to figure out what she could prep for breakfast tomorrow. She heard footsteps and voices, Alonzo among them, and then the door opening and closing. She'd try to leave within the hour, but since the night could go long, she wanted to get a handle on—

The doorbell rang, and Jillian wondered if someone had left something. But wasn't the door unlocked?

She went to see who it was and opened it—and saw Tommy.

"Oh," Jillian said. "Hey."

"Hey, yourself," Tommy said.

"Certainly wasn't expecting to see you," Jillian said. "Come in."

Tommy walked in wearing jeans, one of his nice pairs, and an army green cable knit sweater. He looked at her. "Jill, David told me you were upset about Trevor's birthday, and I was worried about you. That's something we would've talked about." He held her gaze. "I felt bad about that."

"I appreciate that," Jillian said, "but it's okay. I'm okay." She glanced away a moment. Measuring words with him felt odd. "You know you're David's hero, coming through with tickets again. Thank you. Trevor will be excited."

"Happy to do it," Tommy said. "But you slid past the other part. Are you really okay, Jill?"

"Being here at the B and B is nice," Jillian said. "I'll have too much to do to focus on things like that for too long. But it means a lot that you would drop by to check on me, Tommy. How'd you know I was here? David?"

Tommy hesitated. "Actually, I . . . didn't—"

"Sorry for making you wait, Tommy." Mariah hustled down the stairs. "Oh, good, Jillian's keeping you company."

Jillian looked at Mariah, who had changed from jeans to leggings and boots, back to Tommy.

"Mariah and I were talking after church," Tommy said. "I told her I'd give her a ride to the Super Bowl party."

"Oh, I thought you left with Alonzo," Jillian said.

"I didn't know Alonzo would be here," Mariah said. "But this works. I get to hang with my old buddy." She looked at Tommy. "Ready?"

Tommy looked at Jillian. "You good, Jill? You need a ride?"

"I'm good," Jillian said.

"Okay, we'll see you there," Mariah said, heading out the door.

Jillian started for the kitchen.

"Jill," Tommy said.

She continued on and seconds later heard the door close.

∼

"Come on! What kind of call was that?" Reggie stood and moved closer to the flat screen on the wall. "He caught the ball in bounds! Put six points on the board!"

Jillian watched from the kitchen, which had a view to the lavish great room. She glanced over at Faith. "Watching Reggie is almost as entertaining as watching the game. You can tell he used to play."

Faith nodded. "He gets into every down, analyzing every move, to the point of getting stressed. Super Bowl magnifies it times ten." She popped a nacho with cheese into her mouth.

"They'd better overturn it," Alonzo said, eyes on the screen. "That's the second questionable call, and this one is huge."

"Maaan, look at that replay," Tommy said. "You see how he jumped, caught the rock, and landed with his toes inside the line? Straight acrobatics."

"Right!" Reggie was pacing now. "He did all that, and they gonna call it *out*? Nah!"

"I'm trying to figure out how the ref even made that call," Cedric said. "Is he blind?"

"And if he couldn't see the play well," Noah said, "he shouldn't have made the call."

"I'm sayin'!" Cedric said. He glanced at the space next to him on the love seat. "Aye, anybody seen my wife? She disappeared."

"All the women disappeared." Lance held a sleeping Wes as he angled his head toward the kitchen. "They've got their own party in there."

Jillian surveyed the great room. Not all the women. Mariah hadn't left her spot beside Tommy.

Cinda stirred a pot of chili. "It's been a while since we've all been together," she called over her shoulder. "Lots to catch up on."

"Like the *Promises* release celebration Tuesday evening." Cyd smiled from her spot at the kitchen table. "Our whole team is excited. Y'all are planning to be there, right?"

"I've been waiting for this," Cinda said. "That study will always have a place in my heart."

"Cinda will be sharing Tuesday night," Cyd said. "Pam too." She turned to her. "Pam, the other day as we were working on the event, I got tears in my eyes thinking about how we used to meet every week for this study—and you were still behind bars. And look what God did." She shook her head. "The study is coming out, and here you are —*free*. And you'll be testifying at the celebration. You put His promises on display. I'm so in awe of God."

"If you're in awe, then I need a bigger word," Pamela said. "Treva had told me about the study, and I was praying for your weekly meetings. I never would've thought . . ." She lifted a hand in praise. "Treva was the one who believed that was possible. I'll be talking about that Tuesday night."

"That could be a movie all by itself." Brooke leaned against the counter. "I can see it—group of women over here in the *Promises* study; Miss Pam in her cell praying for the study; God working over here to get you out"—she shifted her hands—"which then gives you a testimony about His promises."

"Ooh, I love that," Cinda said.

"Then you can write in the part where I'm heckling Jordyn for going to the study." Jade poured herself some Ginger Ale. "Could not understand why she'd want to be in a group like that or why she'd want to study the Bible." She shook her head. "When I think about some of the things I said . . ."

"Jade, you should've seen me at my first Bible study." Treva sat at the table as well. "Jill had to twist my arm to get me there. And I heckled *everybody*—in my head and out loud sometimes too."

Jade stared at her. "I can't picture it. You're way too poised and— were you like—a teen?"

Treva chuckled a little. "Girl, I was fully grown with all three of my kids."

"Yeah, sorry, I can't see that either." Cinda moved closer to the table. "Are you sure you're not exaggerating a little?"

Treva looked at her sister. "Jill?"

"Nope, she's not exaggerating," Jillian said. "We had six women in our group, and I remember reading Psalm 139 one time. One of them said the psalm let her know, 'you're all that because God is the one who put you together.'" She cleared her throat. "And Treva said, 'I'm pretty sure you thought you were "all that" anyway.'"

Jade gasped. "I am so shook right now. That sounds like something *I* would say. It's still so hard to imagine, Treva."

"I could help you out with some stories myself," Faith said, smiling. "I saw my mom change as she went through that study."

Treva nodded. "Jade, I need you to know that God is able to do a *work*. He takes us from glory to glory." She got up and hugged her. "We have a lot in common. And I can see God working in you even now."

"I'm missing all the good chit chat." Mariah breezed in with her bowl. "But I love football, and this game is so good." She moved toward the stove. "Cinda, I need the recipe for this chili. It's delicious. I hope it's okay to get more."

"Of course," Cinda said. "And thank you. I'll definitely get you the recipe."

"Actually, let me get two." Mariah got a second bowl from the cabinet and started scooping chili from the pot.

"I really appreciate you sharing all of that," Jade said, looking at Treva. "I was already planning to come Tuesday evening, but now even more so. It also makes me more motivated to do this cling challenge. Maybe I can find out what it's like to go from glory to glory."

Mariah turned from the stove. "Oh, Tommy was telling me more about that challenge. It sounds *amazing*. I told him I might crash their study group." She laughed as she carried both bowls back to the great room.

Jillian looked as she handed Tommy the second bowl and sat down beside him. The two of them fell back into their own chatter and laughter as they watched the game.

"Can we talk about what a small world it is?" Cinda said. "I can't believe Tommy and Mariah already knew each other."

"And Mariah said they even dated a while," Brooke said. "How crazy is that?"

Treva got up and eased beside Jillian. "You okay?" Her voice was a whisper.

Jillian nodded. "I think I'm gonna go, though."

"Jill, don't go," Treva said. "It's not even halftime."

"It's a chance to get some alone time," Jillian said, "plus I have to be up really early."

Treva looked at her a moment and gave a nod.

Jillian slipped out as the conversation continued and headed downstairs to the game room, letting her kids know she was leaving. Back at the B and B, she transferred a load of laundry from the washer to the dryer then retired to her bedroom on the third floor. After a shower, she put on her PJs and lay across the bed, staring at the ceiling.

Lord, I just wanted to leave the party and be with You. I don't feel like talking to anybody but You. Nobody understands but You anyway . . . Jillian could feel the tears gathering. *Sometimes I don't feel like I belong anywhere, Lord. My life was intertwined with Cecil's for more than two decades—and You took that. You took it, Lord.* She swiped tears. *We were happy. You were healing us and restoring us, and without any warning, he was gone.*

Jillian's chest heaved as tears cascaded down her cheeks and onto the bed. *I know Cecil is with You. I know he's got the 'gain,' as Silas said this morning. But what about us? I'm raising four kids, trying to be strong for them, and I can't even get through the planning of a birthday without breaking down.*

Jillian closed her eyes, reflecting on all of that. *But Lord, thank You that You never leave. Thank You that I can just be with You, here in Your presence. You're my refuge, my strong tower. You're my rock. Thank You that I can be honest about how I'm feeling and know that You care. Thank You that I can even come to you about nights like tonight, when I'm not even sure how I feel.*

She sighed, staring vaguely now at a piece of wall art. *You know it hurt, Lord. Tommy said nothing at the Super Bowl party. All that talk about "we'll catch up in person"—whatever. I'm giving the friendship to You, Lord. If it's over, it's over. I have enough in my life to worry about—that I'm trying not to worry about. Please help me to cling to You, Lord. I know it's true—as long as I cling, I've got the ultimate situation . . .*

CHAPTER 24

"Reg, you see that?" Jesse sat forward in his seat, eyes on the screen. "That's what I've been saying about the pass protection."

"Exactly, man," Reggie said. "The offensive line is struggling. I'm looking at the left tackle like—dude, you in the game or what?"

"Right!" Jesse said. "Opening up all kinds of holes." He got a notification and checked his phone, but it wasn't the one he'd been looking for. Why was Jordyn so late? He dialed her again and got her voicemail.

"So Jesse, who's your team?" Mariah said.

"I'm from the DMV," Jesse said. "Skins all the way."

"I see we've got a whole contingent from that area," Mariah said. "Jesse, Tommy and Reggie, Treva and Faith—"

"And me," Brooke said, raising a hand.

"Wow, that's right," Mariah said. "Brooke too."

"Brooke is a homie?" Reggie said. "Where'd you grow up?"

"Mostly in the Fort Washington area," Brooke said. "Went to Catholic schools."

"What high school?" Jesse said.

"Elizabeth Seton," Brooke said.

178

"Come on," Jesse said. "I went to DeMatha."

"You did not," Brooke said, sitting up in her seat. "Did you know Matthew Murphy and Roland Griffin?"

"*Of course*," Jesse said. "Roland was my boy. So you must know Robin Hudson."

"This is so ridiculous," Brooke said. "I literally talked to her the other day."

The doorbell rang and Jesse watched Cinda move to get it. *Finally.* He was starting to worry about Jordyn, especially since she wasn't answering her phone.

He turned back to Brooke. "I went to grade school with Robin, and our mothers are friends. Tell her I said hello next time you talk to her."

"Will do," Brooke said.

Trey walked in, taking off his jacket.

"Trey, you made it," Alonzo said, rising from his chair.

Lance got up as well, and they both talked to him.

"Hey Noah, where are you from?" Brooke said.

"Grew up in Kansas City," Noah said. "So not too far from here. About four hours."

"Your family's still there?" Mariah said.

"Still there," Noah said. "Mom, Dad, and my little sister."

Jesse felt his phone vibrate and looked at it. He sighed relief when he saw Jordyn's name.

Lost track of time. Almost there.

Jesse typed a reply—**You ok? Been trying to reach u for 2 hours.**

Jordyn replied a few seconds later. **Yes, I'm fine. Didn't mean to worry you.**

Jesse typed another reply—**Where u been? Why weren't u answering ur phone?**

He waited a couple of minutes for Jordyn's response.

Long story. I'm here, tho. Parking.

Jesse got up and walked outside, glancing around for Jordyn's car. Spotting it down the street, he went and opened the passenger door and got in.

"You had me worried, J." Jesse leaned over and hugged her. "You always respond quickly to texts and calls. Mine anyway."

"I'm really sorry, Jess," Jordyn said. "Like I said, I just lost track of time."

"With what, all the errands?" Jesse said.

Jordyn stared at the steering wheel as several seconds elapsed. "Kelvin wanted to meet."

It took a moment for it to register. "The guy you used to kick it with? The married dude?"

"That's why he reached out," Jordyn said. "To tell me he's no longer married." She looked at him. "And I debated whether to meet him and only planned on staying a few minutes . . ."

"So you're telling me that all afternoon and into the evening—you were with him?"

"Again, I didn't realize how much time had passed," Jordyn said. "He just, started opening up about what he was thinking and feeling back when we were, you know, together—"

"Wait," Jesse said. "So you didn't have any errands. You were texting dude at church."

Jordyn looked aside with a slight sigh.

"Okay, got it," Jesse said. "You were lying the whole time. Continue."

"Jesse, it's just that I always thought it was purely physical on his part." Jordyn stared at nothing in particular. "So I was shocked when he said he'd fallen in love with me and—"

"Where'd you meet him?" Jesse said.

Jordyn paused. "When he moved out, he got an apartment—"

"So you were with Kelvin, in his apartment." Jesse nodded. "And what happened, Jordyn?"

"Jesse, I didn't sleep with him."

"Did you kiss him?"

Jordyn stared downward.

Jesse got out and walked toward the house.

Jordyn cut the engine, got out, and followed. "Jesse, wait. I told him that I was seeing you."

Jesse turned. "Was that before or after you kissed him?" He walked back toward her. "We've been dating for seven months, Jordyn. I haven't kissed you *in seven months*, because I wanted to build something deep and meaningful. You tore it down in an afternoon." He shook his head. "I guess it wasn't as special as I thought it was."

"That's not true," Jordyn said. "It's just—the situation with Kelvin was complicated. I wanted to hear him out."

Jesse continued toward the house.

"Jesse, wait," Jordyn said. "It didn't mean anything. Talk to me."

"I heard everything I needed to hear," Jesse said.

He moved inside and waited for Jordyn, closing the door after she entered. They walked into the gathering, and Cinda and the rest of the women greeted Jordyn. Jesse returned to his spot beside Tommy and Mariah.

Moments later Jordyn walked in with a bowl of chili, doing a double take at the sight of Noah. A true fan, she couldn't get enough of one of his songs. Jesse had been looking forward to introducing her, but now . . .

Jordyn sat next to Jesse, leaning close to his ear. "Jess, can we go to another room and talk? Cinda won't mind."

"Interception!" Reggie jumped up. "That was too smooth! Take it on home!"

"Ain't nobody catching him." Jesse got up as well, looking at Tommy. "Didn't I tell you he was gonna make a big play?"

"Yeah, you did," Tommy said, nodding.

"Touchdown!" Reggie said, his arms lifted with the referee.

"Only the third quarter," Alonzo said, "and this game is a wrap."

"It was competitive for a minute," Cedric said, "unlike most Super Bowls. But I ain't mad. We can start the card game early."

"Who's your partner tonight, Tommy?" Lance said. "Reggie or Jesse?"

"Those two can partner up," Tommy said. "I need to get going."

Reggie turned and looked at him. "You're leaving before the game's even over?"

"And he's never *not* played a card game," Lance said. "Somebody check his forehead."

Tommy rose with a shrug. "It's been a long week. I think it's catching up to me."

"I'll walk you out," Alonzo said. "We can talk logistics for rehearsals tomorrow."

Alonzo and Tommy walked out as Cedric and Lance set up the card table.

Jordyn leaned in. "This would be a good time to go talk."

"I was serious, Jordyn," Jesse said. "I heard all I needed to hear."

"You're not being fair," Jordyn said.

"Really?" Jesse said. "You're going with a fairness argument?"

"I'm just asking you not to shut me out," Jordyn said.

"Daddy, Daddy, look what I got!" Zoe skipped over, holding a brownie.

"Mommy said you could have it?" Jesse said.

Zoe pointed a finger behind her. "Miss Shinda."

"Didn't you already have two?" Jesse said.

"Not really," Zoe said.

"Two is enough, Princess." Jesse rose and picked her up. "Let's wrap it up, and you can eat it tomorrow." He glanced at Jordyn as she rose and followed him to the kitchen.

"Hey, Faith," Jesse said, moving toward her. He noticed Jordyn moving to talk to Cinda. "I told Zoe we're going to wrap up this brownie and save it for tomorrow."

"Little girl, where'd you get another brownie?" Faith said.

"Miss Shinda," Zoe said.

Faith and Jesse gave one another a look, hiding their smiles.

"Let's get some Saran Wrap for it," Faith said. "You wanna tear it off?"

Zoe wiggled down and went with Faith.

"Jess," Jordyn said, joining him again, "Cinda said we can go down the hall to the home office to talk."

"Why are you pressing me to have a conversation?" Jesse said. "I'm not feeling it, Jordyn. And we're about to play this game."

"We only got two minutes outside," Jordyn said. "I don't want to leave it like that."

Jesse took a deep breath and exhaled. "Let me tell Reggie I'll be right back."

He walked back into the great room with Jordyn and talked to Reggie, then headed back out.

"Hey, Jesse, I've got a message for you," Brooke said.

Jesse turned back, looking at her.

"From Robin," Brooke said. "I told her we were at a Super Bowl party together, and here's what she said."

Jesse looked at it—**What?!? That's my guyyy. Tell Jesse he can't be letting yearrsss go by without hitting ppl up. Love that two of my fave people know each other now.**

"That's tight," Jesse said. "Tell her we'll connect this week. Can you send me her contact info?"

"First I need *your* contact info," Brooke said.

They exchanged information and Jesse continued on with Jordyn. They stepped into a spacious office with two workstations, a seating area, and multiple built-in shelves.

Jordyn turned to him. "I just need to know if we're okay."

"Jordyn, I said you tore down what we were building," Jesse said. "Does that sound like we're okay?"

"I know I shouldn't have gone over there, and I'm sorry, Jess," Jordyn said. "But you're taking this to an extreme. How can you say I tore it all down?"

"Maybe the question is—what were we building?" Jesse looked at her. "I thought we were trying to grow in trusting God and one another. I knew my track record, so I wanted you to be able to trust that I was in this, that there was no one else in my life, that I would honor and respect you as a woman of God. I thought all of that was mutual."

"Jesse, it is—"

"Jordyn, if I had spent time at a woman's apartment and kissed her, you'd have every reason not to trust me."

183

"But it's not what it seems," Jordyn said. "It was just . . . stupid. I was caught up in the moment."

"Well, there you go," Jesse said. "You got your moment."

"That wasn't *the* moment," Jordyn said. "Jesse, I won't ever see him again."

"That's the problem, Jordyn," Jesse said. "You want me to trust that. I can't. You know why? Because I didn't think Kelvin could hit you up, get you to come over, and kiss you—and I was wrong."

Jordyn looked at him, tears in her eyes. "So what are you saying? That we're over? Because of one mistake?"

Jesse took a moment as he looked into her eyes. "The other day, I told you how special you were to me. I should've been the one asking you." He gave a nod. "Now I've got my answer."

He turned and Jordyn grabbed his hand. "I love you, Jess."

Jesse walked out and re-joined the others.

CHAPTER 25

*J*ade stood in Alonzo and Cinda's office, processing what she'd just heard as she stared at her sister. "This might be the dumbest thing you've done, besides seeing Kelvin in the first place."

Jordyn looked up at her just to roll her eyes as tears streamed her face. "You didn't say that at the time."

"I *clearly* remember telling you that you were dumb," Jade said. "Because you got caught up, thinking he was leaving his wife."

"Well, newsflash—he's divorced," Jordyn said.

"A year and a half later," Jade said. "And if she had any sense, she's the one who left. But that's not the point." She looked at her. "Kelvin calls, and you go running over there? First dumb thing. *And* you're supposed to be here *with Jesse* at a Super Bowl party? Multiply the dumb thing times ten."

"Obviously I didn't plan to be late," Jordyn said. "But you know I was shocked that Kelvin called and curious what he had to say."

"He could've told you on the phone." Jade shook her head. "I thought *I* had issues."

"You do."

"And wait a minute—is that why you were all distracted at

185

church?" Jade said. "And why you couldn't take me home? Because —Kelvin?"

"Jesse basically asked the same thing."

"Wow," Jade said. "You actually set up a cuddle call in the church house, sitting beside your man. Multiply the dumb thing times a thousand."

"Will you stop," Jordyn said. "That's not what it was. And I get it. It was dumb."

"You had a man who actually cared about you," Jade said, "and was committed to you."

"Why are you talking about Jesse and me in the past tense?" Jordyn said.

"Are you with him at the party right now?" Jade said.

"No."

"Did he indicate that the two of you were over?"

"Well. Yeah."

"Past tense," Jade said.

Jordyn stared downward. "I should've lied about where I was. Or at least about kissing Kelvin."

"That's your takeaway?" Jade said. "I'm thinking you need to back up several steps as to what you should've done."

"So now you're Miss Christian?" Jordyn said. "Got all the answers?"

"I have very few answers," Jade said. "But I don't need many to know that that was dumb. And why were you kissing Kelvin anyway, after all your talk of 'boundaries'?"

Jordyn sighed. "When Kelvin said he loved me and wanted us to be together, I don't know . . . It just hit me some kind of way. That's what I always wanted to hear him say. It's not like Jesse has ever said he loves me."

"Jesse has *shown* you way more than Kelvin ever did."

"I *know*," Jordyn said. "I'm just trying to figure out what was in my head at the time. And it's not like I was *kissing* Kelvin. We only kissed once."

"Please tell me you have no intention of talking to him again," Jade said.

"I don't," Jordyn said. "But I don't know what to do. You're right. Jesse is the first guy who truly cared about me. If it's really over . . ." She backhanded tears. "I just don't know what to do."

"Well, you can't hide out in here all night," Jade said. "Get up off this floor, head home, and get some sleep."

"What if somebody sees me on the way out?" Jordyn said. "Look at my eyes."

"I'll go check," Jade said. "If all's clear, I'll text you a thumbs up."

"Are you about to leave too?"

"No," Jade said. "Miss Pam and I are in the rotation for the card game."

"I'm sure Trey has something to do with it too," Jordyn said. "At church looked like the two of you are becoming friends."

"I don't know about all that," Jade said. "He's nice, but I really don't need to complicate my life."

∾

"Seeing you two side by side takes it to another level." Jade took a picture of Trey and Noah along with others beside her. "Even the height and build are similar."

"When the casting director sent me Noah's picture, I saw the resemblance right away." Alonzo stood nearby. "I said, 'He's perfect if he can play the part.' And he nailed it. I felt the sincerity."

"I'm just blown away by the opportunity," Noah said. "I've always wanted to act, and I figured I'd start with projects nobody would ever see. But when they said I'd get to be in a movie with *you*? That was everything, man."

"We were really glad you could do it," Alonzo said. "Things are blowing up for you, and I know there are a lot of demands on your time. And we didn't give you much notice."

"I wasn't missing this," Noah said. "I told my team we had to make it work." He looked at Trey. "I don't know what your time's looking like tomorrow, but I'm hoping I can talk to you about . . . you." He smiled a little.

"I'm here for all of it," Trey said. "Whatever works for you."

"Hey, can somebody send me a pic of Noah and Trey?" Alonzo said. "I want to put it in my story."

"I got one, Zee," Cinda said, showing him.

Hope stepped forward. "Umm . . . can we get a picture with you, Noah?"

"Hope," Treva said, "we told you all—no fangirl stuff."

"Mom, we waited till the game ended," Hope said. "He's just standing here."

"It's no problem," Noah said. "Because I'm about to be a fan and ask Alonzo to take a pic." He moved to take pictures with Hope, Sophia, and Joy.

Trey looked at Jade. "You about to get in line and take a pic with Noah?"

"What's funny is that would've totally been me." Jade lowered her voice. "Except—and I'm embarrassed to say it—my fangirl obsession was Alonzo."

"So how did you and Cinda work *that* out?" Trey said.

"That's a long story right there," Jade said. "It got ugly."

"For real?" Trey said. "I was kidding."

"Yeah, if you google you'll see some stuff. Unfortunately."

"But you're here, though, at their house," Trey said. "So sounds like there's a story there too, a good one."

"But being here does feel slightly like—which one of these doesn't really belong?" She raised a hand partway.

"Life is like that, man," Trey said. "I feel that way all the time."

"Like you don't belong?" Jade said. "That surprises me."

"I felt that way on the mission field," Trey said. "And again this afternoon."

"Oh yeah, you went to see your friends after you dropped me off," Jade said. "So it didn't go as you expected?"

"So here's the context," Trey said. "Molly was my best friend. We did everything together, knew everything about each other. Matter of fact, she even stayed at the house for a while and helped Kendra when she was sick."

"Okay," Jade said, listening.

"Molly married a mutual friend of ours, Timmy," Trey said. "So between that and me leaving for the mission field—"

"Things changed," Jade said.

"Exactly," Trey said. "I drove a couple hours to see them, and it was nice. But on the way back, I'm like, where do I fit anymore? Everything's shifted."

"You just described my life since being saved," Jade said. "I never really had any friends, and even the pretend ones are gone now."

"Hey, Jade." Pamela called across the room. "You ready to whup these two?" She eyed Lance and Cedric. "Reg and Jesse couldn't do it, so as usual, they've gotten cocky."

"Mom, it's not cocky when it's the truth," Lance said. "We happen to be the best." He gave a slight shrug. "For years now."

"I'm ready, Miss Pam," Jade said. "It'll be awkward, putting a beating on my own pastor, but we do what we've got to do."

"Yeah, I used to feel bad about showing no mercy at the card table," Lance said. "But you have to honor your gifting."

"And make no mistake," Cedric said, shuffling the cards, "it's a gift."

Trey walked with Jade across the room. "So you can play?" he said.

Jade nodded. "My dad taught me."

"So, Jade, Momma Pam," Trey said, "this has gone on for far too long. You *have* to silence these two."

"Oh, that's the goal," Pamela said, taking her seat opposite Jade.

"You playing tonight, Trey?" Lance said.

Trey pulled up an extra chair to the table. "Nah, not tonight. I'm just here to cheer on my new friend."

CHAPTER 26

"This can't be real." Stephanie traversed the length of the master bedroom of their island villa. "Do you see this? The bedroom takes up the entire second floor." She gasped. "And look—there's a patio on both sides."

"I remember reading that the house has panoramic views of the Caribbean Sea and the Atlantic Ocean," Lindell said. "I can't wait to see it all in the morning."

"Let's see what it's like on the patio, babe." Stephanie opened the door and stepped out. "Oh, wow . . . The way the water is glistening in the moonlight, the view is incredible even at night."

Lindell joined her at the railing, listening to the waves lap the shore. "Can you imagine living like this all the time?" he said. "This is stunning, and tranquil. I could sleep out here."

"I was thinking of some other things we could do out here," Stephanie said, eyeing a double chaise lounge. "Be right back."

She went to the master bath area, got a couple of towels, and came back out.

"What are you doing?" Lindell said.

"You know I'm funny about lying on other people's stuff." Stephanie spread the towels.

"I mean, why are you doing all of that right now?"

"Because it's such a romantic vibe." Stephanie entwined her fingers with Lindell's, pulling him toward it. "Come here, babe."

She lowered herself onto the cushioned chaise, Lindell beside her. Wrapping her arms around him, she nestled close and kissed him.

"It's definitely romantic," Lindell said.

Stephanie reclined further, pulling him closer, deepening the kiss.

"Babe"—Lindell sat up a little—"I was about to say it's definitely romantic, but it's been a long travel day. I can barely keep my eyes open."

"Who said you had to keep your eyes open?" Stephanie reached under his shirt and massaged his back.

"I'm just saying I have zero energy," Lindell said. "I was actually about to bring the luggage up and get some sleep." He looked at her. "You're not dead tired?"

"I probably would be, if I weren't out here with an abundance of stars overhead, a tropical breeze, and the sound of waves against the shore." Stephanie continued massaging his back. "That doesn't put you in the mood?"

"Maybe so, if I weren't dead tired."

Stephanie sat up. "Okay, babe. I know it's been a long day."

"So you don't mind if I go get the luggage?" Lindell said.

"Go ahead," Stephanie said. "I'm staying out here a while longer."

"Those weren't all the towels, were they?"

"No, there's more."

Lindell went back inside, and Stephanie got up and walked back to the railing, the light breeze blowing her hair. Watching the waves, lulled by the sound, she could feel the onset of tears. It *had* been a long day, mostly emotionally, starting with the strife about the B and B on the first plane ride. She'd turned her phone off and kept it off even during their three-hour layover. And as she and Lindell grabbed dinner then sat at the gate, she could feel it. The distance.

When they weren't talking about the baby or his job, silence engulfed them. And she didn't dare mention the B and B. Without their phones to retreat to, Lindell had buried himself in a newspaper and Stephanie a magazine. She'd kept thinking about what lay ahead —four days and five nights in a dreamy house on a dreamy island— and dread had filled her. Was this how it would be? Were their issues only about to be magnified?

And here it was—her answer. Stephanie swiped tears. She'd tried not to think about what their love life had been lately. This trip was the chance to change all that. And when she saw the patio and felt the vibe, she saw them giving themselves to passion and spontaneity in a way they seldom if ever did. She'd wanted to make love as if it were the first night of the honeymoon they'd never had.

Instead, she was reminded how mismatched they were and how frustrating their love life had been.

Stephanie sighed, staring into the inky sky, her heart quickening as Warren floated through her mind. The man everyone thought she'd marry. Stephanie did love him, but she loved status and financial security more, which pointed her toward Lindell. Still, despite her motives, God had done a miracle in her life and marriage, saving both her and Lindell and giving them a heart to live for Him.

But sometimes . . .

Stephanie closed her eyes as her emotions rode the waves. Sometimes she wondered what her life would've been like with Warren. Like tonight. Fatigue wouldn't have entered his mind. He would've given himself to romance. That's what he always did, despite the situation.

Like the night the power went out during a winter storm. Stephanie had searched her apartment for flashlights, and when she got back to the kitchen, it had already been lit—with several candles. Warren proceeded to ignite the gas stove and cook by candlelight, after which they ate then transported the candles to her bedroom.

Stephanie heaved a sigh, looking out. She knew she shouldn't pull up those memories. She was a different person then, living outside of God's will. But as she moved from dwelling on the past, her mind could only switch to . . . *what if?*

What if she hadn't been so focused on status and money and married the person she loved? And what if she and Warren were now living their lives together, for God? True, their marriage would have issues—everybody's did—but what if the issue *wasn't* their love life? What would *that* be like?

"Babe, you're still out here?" Lindell stuck his head out. "Just took a shower and about to head to sleep. You coming?"

Stephanie glanced back at him. "I think I'll stay out here a little longer."

"Okay, get some rest, though," Lindell said. "I want to head out at eight to take the historical tour."

Lindell closed the patio door, and Stephanie stared at the water, mind full of *what if's*.

CHAPTER 27

*T*ommy trudged into the kitchen, the aroma of eggs and bacon in the air, and went to a cabinet, opening it.

"This visual is giving me so much life," Faith said, writing on a white board. "'My soul clings to You.' That's enough to meditate on right there. But *then* David says"—she started writing again—"'Your right hand upholds me.'" She looked at the words. "It's like—dual clinging."

"The fact that David says it's God's *right hand* upholding him is everything," Reggie said. "Tommy shared a lot of Scripture on the significance of God's right hand."

Tommy looked back at the two of them. "So this is what y'all do? Go deep at the crack of dawn?" He closed the cabinet and opened another.

"Reggie's been talking about what you all studied the other night," Faith said. "So I said we should do it in our devotion time. Psalm 63:8 is now one of my fave verses."

Tommy opened another cabinet. "That verse got me too, especially since David uses the word 'cling'—hey, don't we have some Tylenol, Advil, *something* around here?"

Faith walked over to a different cabinet. "Here it is." She handed him the bottle. "You're not feeling well?"

"Thank you," Tommy said. "I can't shake this headache. Kept me up all night."

"And right when we've got a big day with the start of rehearsals," Faith said.

"I don't think I congratulated you on being the exclusive reporter for the movie," Reggie said.

"Only during rehearsals and filming." Tommy opened the refrigerator and got a bottled water.

"Still, man, that's awesome," Reggie said.

Faith nodded. "Do you know how many media requests are rolling in right now? But you're the guy."

"Which is exciting," Tommy said, "when my head's not pounding."

"Mommyyyy!"

"Aaaand the day just kicked into another gear." Faith headed out of the kitchen. "Tommy, help yourself to breakfast," she called over her shoulder. "I cooked lots."

Reggie looked at Tommy. "So the headache, lack of sleep. Should we pretend it has nothing to do with you and Jillian?"

"It's too early for all that." Tommy shook out a pill and downed it with water.

"Come on, man." Reggie kept his voice low. "You left the party early—something you never do—and it happened to be right after Jillian left. Then you have a sleepless night. You know why?" He stood and moved closer to Tommy. "Because you refuse to be honest with yourself. Now it's affecting you physically."

Tommy drank more water. "I've never been more honest with myself in my entire life."

"Really?" Reggie said. "Saying you want to be single for life is being honest with yourself? You know that's not what you want."

"So, mind reading? That's your spiritual gift?"

"It's just painful to watch." Reggie leaned against the counter. "It's like before, when you and Jillian weren't speaking, and Faith and I had to intervene on our wedding night to get you in the same room."

"*Had* to intervene?" Tommy said. "You could've just minded your business."

"But here's the thing," Reggie said. "It *worked*. You became friends again. *Closer* friends, seemed like. But for whatever reason, you're back to the weirdness." He started for the fridge then backtracked, looking at Tommy. "And *please* tell me what was up with you reconnecting with your old flame in front of Jillian?"

"What are you talking about?" Tommy said.

"You and Mariah hanging strong all night," Reggie said. "Then we discover that you two used to date."

"Who said we used to date?"

"Faith told me last night," Reggie said, "after Brooke told all the women in the kitchen."

"Are you serious?" Tommy blew out a sigh.

"I'm just saying," Reggie said. "Seems like you've been trying to push Jillian away. And last night you probably succeeded."

"That's not what I'm trying to do," Tommy said. "It's just—" He looked as Zoe breezed into the kitchen. "Morning, Zo Zo."

"Morning, Unca Tommy." Zoe barely looked at him as she made a beeline for the markers on the white board. She ripped the cap off and started drawing.

"Zoe girl, that's what's up?" Reggie said. "No morning hug?"

Zoe ran over, wrapped her arms around Reggie for half a second, and went back to the board.

"I had no idea she'd be so fascinated with that thing." Faith walked in behind her. "She'd rather scribble on the board than play with her toys." She looked at Reggie. "We might be able to get a little more devotion time in while she eats."

"Y'all work it out," Tommy said, grabbing his keys. "I'm headed to rehearsal."

"Already?" Faith said. "You're not eating?"

"I'm not hungry," Tommy said. "Doing an interview before the day gets started."

"Who are you interviewing?" Reggie said.

"Alonzo and Mariah," Tommy said.

"Praying you feel better," Faith said.

"I'll be praying too," Reggie said.

Tommy turned to give him a look.

"What?" Reggie said. "You don't want prayer?"

"Depends on what you're praying."

What do I do, Lord?

Tommy had been debating whether to call Jillian most of the way to Lance's house, the site of morning rehearsals. Reggie had confirmed his fears—last night was bad. And Reggie didn't know the half of it. He hadn't seen the look on Jillian's face when she realized that Tommy hadn't come to the B and B to check on her. That moment she realized he was there for Mariah—that's the look Tommy had seen as he lay awake all night.

I'm asking what I should do, Lord, but I'm not sensing any direction. If I call, will it only make things worse? What does clinging to You look like in this situation?

Tommy's hands gripped the wheel. Reggie said he might've succeeded in pushing Jillian away. That's not what he wanted. He couldn't let her think he didn't care.

With the press of a finger, her number was ringing. And ringing. He sighed and hung up when it went to voicemail. Seconds later he took a breath and tried again.

Jillian picked up. "Is this some sort of emergency?"

"Jill, I wanted to talk," Tommy said, "see how you're doing."

"Why?" Jillian said.

"Because . . ." Tommy exhaled. "I hate what happened last night. I didn't know you were at the B and B, and—"

"I get it, Tommy," Jillian said. "It's fine. Is that it?"

"So that's what we're doing?" Tommy said. "You won't even talk to me?"

"What do you want me to say?" Jillian said. "I said I get it. I'm simply asking if that's it."

"Jill, don't do this," Tommy said. "I couldn't sleep last night because I was worried about you. Worried about us. Our friendship. Talk to me."

"What friendship, Tommy?" Jillian said. "We don't communicate, other than a quick convo if we run into one another, *maybe*. You didn't say two words to me at the Super Bowl party."

"Thank you for that," Tommy said. "I feel like we're getting somewhere." He pulled up to Lance's house and let the engine run. "I couldn't say what I wanted to say with everybody there. And at the same time, I didn't want to just chit-chat as if I didn't care what happened at the B and B. Because I did care."

"Cinda and Alonzo have a dozen rooms we could've gone to if you had actually cared to talk," Jillian said. "And as far as 'what happened at the B and B,' you probably think the issue was my realizing you came for Mariah and not me. And yes, I felt a little stupid thinking you had actually come to check on me. But the main issue, Tommy, was your acting as if you were worried about me and asking if I was okay. You *only* asked because you were thrown that I answered the door. So stop with the fake concern."

"Jill, why are you even going there?" Tommy said. "You know I care about you. I'll never stop caring about you. That's why I called just now—to check on you."

"And about that," Jillian said. "You don't get to call me when it randomly suits you. You're the one who said we couldn't talk or text. And I get that now too. Follow your own rules."

The phone went dead.

CHAPTER 28

"Originally I asked Shane to direct because he's a beast and we work so well together." Alonzo took a croissant from a tray on the table. "When production got delayed and he had a scheduling conflict, I was disappointed. But we prayed, and God brought us Mariah. Now I couldn't imagine doing this without her."

"It's a definite God-story," Mariah said. "On my end, I had been developing a script for over a year, excited about an opportunity to do my first action film. The project fell through, and I was licking my wounds. Then Shane called me."

"So wait," Tommy, said, "was Shane instrumental in your coming on board?"

"I would not be here if Shane hadn't called me," Mariah said. "I've never wanted to direct a Christian film. The scripts that have come my way have been cheesy and unrealistic. We don't get but so many opportunities in this industry, and that's not what I wanted to be known for." She sipped her coffee. "But Shane said, 'Mariah, you need to look at this script. It's not a typical Christian film—obviously, or I wouldn't have signed on.'" She spread cream cheese on a bagel. "I read it, googled the real-life story, and couldn't believe it was based here in

St. Louis, where I'm from. Through all of that, I was praying and found myself wanting to be part of the project."

"So you signed on toward the end of last year, when the movie still needed additional financing," Tommy said. "What was that like—having to get up to speed, but not even knowing for sure that there'd be a movie?"

"I said, 'Okay, Lord, this seems just about right.'" Mariah chuckled. "He's been teaching me a lot lately about depending more on Him." She ate a piece of her bagel.

"She put in the work, though," Alonzo said. "I was waking up every morning to messages she'd sent in the middle of the night." He paused, looking at Mariah. "You're still doing that. I had one this morning."

"Mariah was known for her work ethic," Tommy said. "When she was locked in and focused, everybody knew she meant business."

"So what's the story?" Alonzo said. "You worked in the same newsroom?"

"This was when Tommy first started doing an entertainment news segment," Mariah said, "and I was a producer for the 'live at five' news program."

"Weren't you a producer on the six o'clock news program?" Tommy said.

Mariah thought a moment. "I think you're right. I was on the six o'clock by then. So the plan had been to go to LA after film school, but my mom got sick, and I came home." She looked up as Lance walked into the kitchen. "Good morning, Lance," she said. "Anyway, story of my life. Never the path I want to take. Mine are filled with delays, twists, and unexpected turns."

"That better be the story of everybody's life, or I'll feel cheated." Lance got a mug from the cabinet. "Good morning, and who let you all into my house so early?"

"Your momma," Tommy said. "Made us coffee, set out some pastries. You would do well to mimic her hospitality."

"Were we talking too loud, Lance?" Mariah said. "I'm sorry if we woke you."

"No, I was just kidding, it's cool." Lance poured himself some coffee. "I knew you'd be here."

"Lance, thank you again," Alonzo said, "for allowing us to kick off rehearsals here this morning. I know it won't be easy to walk us through the house, re-living old memories, many of them painful."

"I've been up for a while, praying," Lance said. "It actually moved me to thank God, because I've made so many new memories in this house. But yeah, today won't be easy."

"I have to say ditto," Mariah said. "We really appreciate you for doing this. It's one thing to rehearse in the house that's staged to look like this one. But I felt we needed to be *here*. I want us to feel this."

"That's an interesting angle," Tommy said, scribbling notes. "I'd like to get more of your thoughts on your rehearsal process."

"I'd love to talk about that," Mariah said. "It's not so much about perfecting scenes. It's about bonding as a cast. You get this emotional honesty on film."

The doorbell rang, and the door to the lower level swung open. "That's Jade," Pamela said, moving toward it.

Jade walked in with a camera bag and tripod. "Morning, everybody."

"Morning, Jade," sounded in the kitchen.

"What you got going on, Mom?" Lance said.

"Last night I was telling Jade—"

"Before or after that whupping y'all got?" Lance said.

"Don't start," Pamela said. "As far as I'm concerned, we can do a rematch right now." She waved a hand at him. "Anyway, I was telling her about the movie site and how I update it every Monday morning with requests and answers to prayer. She took a look and said I should do video updates to make it more personal."

"People already feel connected to her because of the video she did about being released from prison," Jade said. "And Miss Pam is so passionate when she talks about prayer. I just think it'll take it to another level for people to see that."

"And since I don't know anything about making videos and too old to learn," Pamela said, "Jade said she'd do it for me."

"I'll record you then edit it right here on my laptop," Jade said. "That way we can upload it to the site this morning like usual."

"You can do it that quickly?" Pamela said.

Jade nodded. "It's nothing compared to other stuff we edit."

"You all got my wheels turning." Alonzo got up from the table. "Now I'm wondering what to do about the devotionals."

"What devotionals?" Pamela said.

"I want people to be able to come to the movie site and get dope ministry content," Alonzo said. "So I wanted to post devotions and topical articles, the way they do on the Living Word site, but related to the themes in the movie." He looked at Jade. "Based on what you told Momma Pam, maybe the devos should be recorded on video?"

"If you're asking my thought on it," Jade said, "it's super unimaginative."

"Ouch." Alonzo turned more toward her. "I've been praying on this, so if you've got ideas . . ."

Jade thought a moment. "Okay, so—"

The front door opened and Trey walked in. "Aye, I thought I was early. I'm hungry and forgot to buy groceries."

"Yesterday you were driving on empty," Jade said. "Now you didn't think to buy food." She aimed a thumb at him. "Is he always like this?"

"Always," Lance said.

Trey came into the kitchen and poked his head in the fridge.

"Okay, Jade," Alonzo said. "I feel like you were about to drop something. I'm listening."

"So you've got an opportunity to reach people like me," Jade said. "At least, where I used to be. People who don't know they need ministry content. Maybe don't *want* ministry content. People who would never post up on a blog and read a devo but they're into this movie because they love a good love story or they love Alonzo Coles."

"Or Noah Stiles." Joy had come downstairs and eased into the group. "Two of my Maryland friends suddenly want to come visit after I posted a pic with him. They can't believe this is my life right now."

"Exactly," Jade said. She turned back to Alonzo. "That's what you want to give people—that inside look. Take them behind the scenes. Make them feel like they're part of this, and then minister in the midst of that."

"Okay, I'm feeling that," Alonzo said, nodding. "But I'm not seeing what it would look like."

Trey took the tripod and camera bag from her and set them down.

"Thank you, Trey," Jade said, glancing at him. "So typically, if we get behind the scenes footage, it's after a movie wraps, and it's just a few quick clips," she said. "It would be tight if you did a daily vlog from the set and posted it to YouTube. Real moments with people they love and people they'll come to love. In addition to fun, behind the scenes stuff, each vlog could feature someone—Alonzo, you could do the interview, a short one—but it would be someone connected to the movie who shares something that ministers." She paused. "You could call it a 'ministry moment.'"

"Wow," Alonzo said. "I forgot who I was talking to, the woman who can put together a killer social media campaign. Ask me how I know."

"Okay, how do you know?" Trey said, eating a bowl of cereal.

"I really didn't mean to say that," Alonzo said. "I'm not going there."

"It's fine," Jade said. "I did a couple of not-so-nice videos about Alonzo that went viral. And wouldn't you know—that's what God used to save me."

"Wait, I didn't know that," Alonzo said. "What do you mean?"

Jade sighed. "In the video I mocked you for being 'too Christian' because you started talking about Jesus in interviews, refusing to do sex scenes, and all that. And I was quoting things you said. I actually put the quotes on screen to show that you were now this—"

"'Weird Jesus freak,'" Alonzo said.

"Right." Jade sighed again. "So fast forward. My world was caving, and it came to a head the night before my mom's wedding. We blew up at each other, I drove back to St. Louis in the middle of the night, and as much as I wanted to be mad at her, all I could think was how selfish I was. And mean. And hateful." She spoke at a fast clip. "This went on for days. Every time I wanted to focus on how messed up my life was, it turned into how messed up *I* was. Then one night I was about to edit a video, and when I opened the software program, I saw the video I did about you." She paused. "And I clicked it on."

"I'm getting chills again," Pamela said. "Like when you first told me this."

"So I'm watching," Jade said, "and I hear myself quoting you, saying, 'If Jesus can save somebody like me—as messed up as my life was—He can save you too, no matter where you are right now.'"

"I said that in an interview?" Alonzo said.

Jade nodded. "In the video I was like, 'Now he's Mr. Evangelist.' But as I watched that night, you were talking to me, saying the same thing I said—'messed up life'—but you gave the solution." She took a breath. "I kept rewinding, listening to every quote I mocked you for, tears running down my face. And I didn't know what to do so I looked up the testimony video you did with Jordyn, where you shared the gospel and prayed. And I prayed with you to receive Jesus as my Savior."

"I'm stunned," Alonzo said. "How am I just hearing this?"

Jade gave him a look. "Like I'm trying to bring up what I did to you?"

"So this is what you meant last night when you said, 'if you google . . .?'" Trey looked at her. "But Google won't give you the 'but God.'"

"You're taking the words out of my mouth," Alonzo said. He looked at Jade. "You should be the first ministry moment. Like you said, that video went viral, so a lot of people know what went down between us. But what if they could see us together and hear your story? That is, if you're willing to tell it."

"I don't know," Jade said. "I've never shared about my faith publicly, not even on my own channel. I don't know if I have the right words."

"What was that we just heard?" Pamela said. "Sounded pretty powerful to me."

"Let me tell you," Lance said, "that was moving, especially knowing how much Randall prayed for you and Jordyn for so many years. The way the Holy Spirit weaved your testimony together . . . Trust me. He's already given you the words."

"But we need to back up a minute," Alonzo said. "I love the vlog concept, Jade, but I heard you say *daily*. That's a ton of work. I don't mind doing the ministry moment part, but we need somebody to capture the footage, edit the vlogs, actually to handle the whole social media campaign."

"That sounds like a full-time job," Pamela said.

"And then some," Alonzo said. "But it wasn't my idea." He let his gaze rest on Jade.

Jade looked back at him. "I know you're not offering me the dopest opportunity ever right now."

"I need to look at the budget, though," Alonzo said. "So later maybe we can—"

"There's no time for 'later'," Jade said. "It's day one of rehearsals, which means the vlog needs to launch *today*." She started pacing. "I've got my camera, so that's good. I can set up all the socials this morning —Alonzo, you need to do an Instagram live, get people excited about rehearsals kicking off. Then tell them to go subscribe on YouTube to get daily vlogs throughout the filming. When Noah gets here, he needs to do the same." She thought to herself. "Day one video gets uploaded tonight, then tomorrow we'll—"

"Uh, Jade?" Alonzo said. "You're about to immediately go hard? Not even knowing what you'll get paid?"

Jade shrugged. "It's only for a few weeks, and I can still do what I do for my own channel, just late nights or whatever. Honestly, I'd do this for free."

"I wouldn't let you," Alonzo said. "Did you hear your own job description? It's brutal."

Jade gave a nod. "But I'm feeling this deep down. Like I've finally got a purpose." She looked at him. "I have to thank you, Alonzo. It was one thing to forgive me. But to make me part of the team like this . . ."

"Only because I know you'll kill it," Alonzo said.

"I'm adding you to the prayer list," Pamela said. "This is a big job you're taking on. And actually, I'd love for us to pray for you now." She looked at everyone. "Can we gather around Jade?"

Jade took Pamela's hand, staring downward. A moment later, she swiped a tear. "I'm sorry. I hate showing emotion. I just . . . wasn't expecting all of this."

Alonzo took her other hand as the circle filled. "It's a God thing," he said. "I might be wrong, but I could tell you still felt uncomfortable around me."

"Well," Jade said, "how could I not?"

"Listen," Alonzo said, looking at her, "you and Cinda are sisters, which means you're my sister. Sister in Christ too, so you're double fam. I've got nothing but love."

Jade nodded, her head bowed.

"Amen," Pamela said. "What the devil meant for evil . . . Alonzo, why don't you start us off?"

Alonzo bowed his head. "Heavenly Father, we praise You because You're the God who heals . . ."

CHAPTER 29

*P*amela stood in the bedroom that once belonged to Kendra, praying silently for her son as he shared with cast members pivotal moments that took place there.

"I'm seriously trying to hold back tears," Brooke said. "You were right, Mariah. We needed to be here. We needed to feel this."

Tommy nodded soberly. "I was at the house many times during Kendra's illness, but never upstairs. Being here where she spent hours a day wrestling with every sort of pain and hearing these stories . . . man, this is hard."

"All of it's been hard as we've moved from room to room," Mariah said. "But Kendra's room . . . Definitely the hardest so far."

"Lance," Brooke said, "I know it's in the screenplay, but can you tell us in your own words about Kendra's first day of chemotherapy?"

Lance stood near a bed that now belonged to Hope. "That was when everything was still new. Me living here, Kendra moving back from DC, and of course, the diagnosis."

"And her fiancé leaving her was still new," Brooke said. "I've been thinking about how that would cloud everything."

"Absolutely," Lance said. "Kendra was determined not to need anybody for anything, like when she told me she had a ride to chemo."

"That part moved me to tears," Brooke said, "calling a taxi to go to chemo. The whole ordeal is scary enough, and she had to be feeling incredibly alone on top of it."

"And I was being a jerk at this point," Trey said. "So Kendra hadn't told me yet that she was sick. I didn't know about the chemo."

"So when she got home," Lance said, "I knew I needed to see how I could help. I knocked on her door, but she didn't say anything. Then I heard vomiting."

"This is where I've been trying to get in your head," Alonzo said, "to understand how your immediate response was to clean it up—and you barely knew her. I'm not wired like that, man."

"Well, how else was it gonna get cleaned up?" Lance said. "Chemo had wiped her out. But yeah, the fact that it wasn't a thing for me to clean it up was all God. He had prepared me through all the years of taking care of Mom."

"The way it's written in the script brought me to tears," Pamela said. "One minute we see Lance cleaning up after Kendra, then a flashback of Lance as a boy cleaning up after me."

"Oh, that got me right there," Mariah said. "Lance's heart for his momma is an even bigger love story to me. That's what got him expelled from high school." She turned to Lance. "You were fierce when it came to your mother."

"Those were painful years, though," Pamela said. "Lance shouldn't have had to grow up with an addicted mother. He shouldn't have had to be the parent. He shouldn't have had to fight to defend me at school because I'd had sex with one of his friends in exchange for drugs. I hated myself for years for the things I put him through."

"But Mariah, I appreciate what you said." Lance looked at her. "I hadn't thought of the mother/son story as a love story, but that's what it is. Years of pain, despair, even hopelessness, but the love was always there." He nodded, clearly feeling the emotion. "Then for God to love *us* so much that He'd allow me to lead her to Jesus . . ."

"Glory to God," Pamela said. "He's a Redeemer. And lover of our souls."

"And a deliverer," Lance said. "He delivered us from bondage to sin *and* delivered you from that prison." He shook his head. "I thank God every day for that. You're *here* now. I get to see you, talk to you face-to-face, take care of you, still . . . but in a different way—'cause I'm always gonna take care of my mom." He hugged her, his frame overwhelming her petite one. "How did I even get here?" He looked at Mariah. "You did this, making this morning all emotional."

"Come on, Jesus, and show up in here." Mariah raised a hand. "We give You the praise."

"Oh, yes, we do." Pamela raised hers now. "King of kings and Lord of lords, we praise Your holy name."

"I love this." Jade moved discreetly, capturing footage. "Another type of ministry moment."

"So that's what we're doing?" Lance said. "Praise and worship break? I'm with it."

"I wish we had time for a whole praise and worship break," Mariah said. "But we've got a schedule to keep. After this we transition to the other house, eat lunch, and continue rehearsals."

"Do I have time to ask another question?" Brooke said. "I wanted to hear about Kendra confronting Lance over cleaning up the vomit."

"Yes, definitely," Mariah said.

Pamela eased out of the room, closing the door, but it opened again as Tommy slipped out as well. They took the stairs together.

"You headed out?" Pamela said.

"Just seeing if there's more coffee," Tommy said. "I'm still trying to wake up."

"I was wondering," Pamela said. "You don't seem like yourself."

"I don't?" Tommy said.

"You've been on the quiet side this morning." Pamela led the way to the kitchen. "And last night, leaving the party early—definitely not like you." She started a new pot of coffee. "Actually, every time I've seen you this past week you seemed off."

"I'm all right, Momma Pam, if that's what you're asking." Tommy took a seat in the kitchen. "And that fresh brew is everything, thank you."

"I'm not asking," Pamela said, "because you would only say what you said." She looked at him. "I just want you to know I love you like a son. And I pray for you about as much as I pray for my son."

"Now that's saying a lot," Tommy said. "But should I be worried that you feel the need to pray for me that much?"

"It's not that I feel the need," Pamela said. "The Lord just puts you on my heart and mind. And it's no small thing when He puts you on somebody *else's* mind. I try to pay attention to things like that." She poured him a cup and placed it before him. "Black, right?"

"Yes, ma'am." Tommy took a sip. "Perfect. Thank you. And by the way, I already claimed you as my second mom so we're even."

"That's good to know," Pamela said. "That means I can be free to say some things."

"Oh, is that what that means?" Tommy chuckled. "Since when have you *not* felt free to say what's on your mind?"

"You might be surprised," Pamela said. "I keep most things in prayer." She paused. "But I'll say this—I feel what you're feeling, Tommy. At least in part. God does that too. He'll burden you with what's burdening someone else, to move you to pray."

Tommy drank more of his coffee. "That's interesting because I don't even know what I'm feeling half the time."

They both looked as footsteps and voices approached from the stairs.

"Mom, I've got about ten errands to run." Faith walked in with Treva and Wes. "It doesn't make sense for Grandma Pam to ride with me." She looked at Pamela. "Unless you want a taste of production assistant life."

Treva put Wes in his high chair. "Pam, I'll see if you can ride with Lance, because I'm not going till later."

"Lance is headed to church after this," Pamela said. "But it's no problem. I can catch a ride with whomever."

"Uh, hello?" Tommy said. "Momma Pam, you can ride with me."

"Are you sure it's not a problem?" Pamela said.

"Why would it be a problem?" Tommy said. "We're headed to the same place."

"Because you might have business on the way," Pamela said. "That's something I've noticed—people take business calls and such while driving. I don't want to be an imposition."

"She's got this thing about 'imposing' on people for help with this and that, especially rides," Treva said. "We've been trying to tell her it's not a big deal."

"And it's only temporary," Tommy said. "You'll have your driver's license again in no time."

"I never had a driver's license," Pamela said. "I took the bus everywhere."

Voices floated downward as more people descended the steps.

"So you're saying you don't know how to drive?" Tommy said. "Do you want to learn? Do you *want* to get a license?"

Pamela sighed. "Lance has been telling me I need to learn, but I've gotten through this much of my life without it, so why now? Anyway, getting behind the wheel is a scary thought."

"Oh, you shouldn't have said that last part," Tommy said. "You can't be out here *afraid* to drive. You pray about everything. Have you prayed about *that?*"

"It's just not that big a deal." Pamela wiped the counter. "And I'm past sixty. What's the point in doing that now?"

"Momma Pam, you've got more faith than just about anybody I know," Tommy said. "So I'm sorry, I can't get past the part where you said it's scary. We're gonna start some lessons. Today."

"Don't be ridiculous," Pamela said. "For one thing, there's no time. You heard Mariah say there's a schedule to keep. You've got a job to do."

"Hey, babe," Treva called," your mom's about to get driving lessons."

Lance joined them in the kitchen. "What? You finally decided to go for it, Mom?"

"I didn't decide any such thing," Pamela said. "Tommy's talking crazy."

"I told her we're starting lessons today." Tommy looked at her. "And we are. Real simple. You'll just sit behind the wheel and learn the basics. How to put your foot on the pedal, the brake, handling the steering wheel, starting the car . . ."

"Mom, that's perfect," Lance said. "Start there and see what you think."

Pamela felt a stirring in her gut, that feeling she always got when God was moving her toward something . . . a feeling she knew she couldn't ignore. She took a breath. "So, baby steps? I won't actually be driving?"

"Momma Pam, I'm not *that* crazy," Tommy said. "I can't have you crashing my car." He chuckled a little. "Right. No driving just yet."

"And maybe this could even confirm that driving isn't for me."

"Whatever you need to tell yourself." Tommy took his keys from his pocket. "Let's go."

Pamela looked over at Treva and Lance. "I need all the prayers."

Lance smiled. "You know we got you, Mom."

"And *God's* got you," Treva said.

Pamela put on her coat, got her purse, and headed outside. She spied Tommy's SUV by the curb, with Tommy in the passenger seat.

So this is what we're doing, Lord? If I had known, I would've put myself on the prayer list this morning.

CHAPTER 30

Stephanie walked into the villa and straight up the stairs. "I told you, Lindell. You could've stayed."

"Why would I stay on the tour without you?" Lindell followed her. "I just hate that we wasted our money."

"I didn't even know you had bought tickets for the half day tour." Stephanie looked back at him. "I would've said no way. Who wants to spend half the day touring an island?"

"I thought we both had input on the agenda," Lindell said. "Plus they had a great price for that package, and I was actually enjoying it."

"But we didn't have to do it first thing in the morning, on our first day here." Stephanie kicked off her sneakers. "Still, I tried to be accommodating, but it was too much." She turned, looking at him. "I'm *pregnant*, babe. Yes, walking may be good for me, but not endless amounts of it. I'm tired. I need rest."

"I'm sorry, babe," Lindell said. "That's why I was trying to get you to go to bed early last night."

"If I had gone to bed the moment we got here," Stephanie said, "I would've still been tired after *three hours* of walking."

"Actually, I didn't realize the walking would be that extensive," Lindell said. "I'm sorry about that too. It was just fascinating to me, hearing everything, and I should've been checking to see if you were okay. Big oversight on my part."

Stephanie fished her swim tankini, shorts, and coverup from her luggage. "It's okay, babe, I get it. Sometimes you just nerd out."

Lindell looked at her. "What do you mean, 'nerd out'? I've never heard you say that. You think I'm a nerd?"

"I didn't put any thought behind the word," she said, changing. "It just came out."

"But I want to know—do you think I'm a nerd?"

"Lindell, it's not a negative thing. It means 'intellectual' or 'studious.'"

"Or 'awkward' or 'socially inept.'"

"That's not how I meant it," Stephanie said.

"I'm not asking how you meant it," Lindell said. "I'm asking do you think I'm nerdy? Like—awkward?"

Stephanie pulled the tankini over her head and adjusted it over her belly. "No. I don't."

"Why'd you hesitate?"

"Oh, goodness," Stephanie said. "Can we let this go and get to the beach?"

"I think it's important," Lindell said. "You used the word 'nerdy,' and out of the heart the mouth speaks. I really want to know how you see me. Isn't that what this trip is about? To understand each other better and connect better."

"And how does your question get us there?" Stephanie said. "If I say, 'yes, you're nerdy'—we'll connect better? Somehow, I doubt it."

"Sounds like that's your answer," Lindell said. "Just say it. I'm nerdy."

"*I already answered.* I said I don't think you're nerdy or awkward." Stephanie searched her luggage for flip-flops. "I only hesitated because last night *felt* awkward, but that's an entirely different thing."

Lindell sat on the edge of the bed. "Why did it feel awkward?"

"Babe, I'm super tired and still a little perturbed about this morning." She found the flip-flops and put them on. "It's not a good time to go into all of this. Just let me lay out on the beach and get my mind right."

"But you can't just tell me last night was awkward and leave it at that," Lindell said. "Awkward how? Because I was sleepy and went to bed?"

"You're really making me do this right now?" Stephanie looked at him. "Lindell, I was vulnerable and told you our love life basically wasn't satisfying. That's part of what sparked this trip." Emotions from last night began to swirl. "So we get here, the bedroom is amazing, patio couldn't be more romantic, and I wanted to make love. And yeah, we were both tired, but I thought *that's* what this trip was about —putting some life back into our marriage. So yes, when you half kissed me and got up, it felt awkward, to say the least."

"Steph, I could barely keep my eyes open," Lindell said. "You're penalizing me for that?"

"But wait," Stephanie said. "Then you open the patio door to tell me we're taking an early morning tour. So instead of being able to wake up leisurely and, I don't know, just a wild thought—maybe make love in the morning—"

"You should've said you didn't want to go."

"Lindell, I was dumbfounded that *you* would want to go," Stephanie said. "Did it not enter your mind—hey, my wife's frustrated with our love life; I'm tired but I'll make it up to her in the morning?"

"I figured we could get the tour out of the way before it got too hot," Lindell said. "We've still got the whole rest of the day. Why is this a problem?"

"You're not hearing me." Stephanie threw up her hands. "You're not even acknowledging how I was feeling last night. I mean, Lindell, do you understand how real First Corinthians seven is?"

Lindell's brow creased. "You're throwing Scripture at me now?"

"It's what I had to turn to in the middle of the night," Stephanie said, "to understand what I was dealing with."

"What does it say?"

"Basically," Stephanie said, "stop depriving one another so Satan won't tempt you because of your lack of self-control."

"So what are you saying? You felt tempted somehow?"

Stephanie walked into the bathroom, a suite in itself. "All I'm saying is that it's real. The word is true. When we make love, it's more than making love—it's spiritual warfare. And when we don't, it can open the door."

Lindell followed her. "What were you dealing with?"

"Just . . . thoughts." Stephanie put her hair into a loose bun. "I'm just asking you to understand—"

"What thoughts?" Lindell said. "You're talking about temptation. Was it about somebody in particular?"

"Lindell, we just need to focus on *us* and what we need to do," Stephanie said, "not get distracted by—"

"Warren," Lindell said. "I'll bet anything it was Warren."

"Once again, you're not hearing me. You simply will not attempt to understand how I'm feeling." She got the sunblock and started re-applying it. "Please let's chill on this for a while and go to the beach."

"Just tell me," Lindell said. "Was it Warren you were thinking about?"

Stephanie looked aside.

"How absolutely ironic," Lindell said. "Before we were supposed to leave on our first honeymoon, you were telling Warren you missed him. Now, all these years later, here's Warren again."

"You can't compare the two," Stephanie said. "I can't help what thoughts come into my head. I try to battle them. You have no clue how much I've prayed. But I'm telling you it would help—like, for real —if we simply had sex."

"So you're saying this is a regular thing?" Lindell said. "These thoughts about Warren? I guess I shouldn't be surprised. You already admitted why you married me. He's the one who was everything to you."

She hated that she'd ever told Lindell her initial reason for marrying him, in another vulnerable moment. "So that's what you wanna do? Feel sorry for yourself instead of addressing the core issue?" She grabbed her beach bag and transferred a few things from her tote. "I'll be back in a couple of hours."

"So now you're going to the beach by yourself?" Lindell said. "What, you want time alone to fantasize about Warren?"

Stephanie paused, looking at him. "So I try to be transparent about what I'm dealing with, and you throw it back in my face." She moved closer. "Babe, let me be clear—I don't want to think about Warren. Did you hear me say it would help if we simply had sex?" She dropped her bag on the floor. "I don't want anybody but you." She stripped off her cover-up. "I need you, baby. Make love to me."

Lindell stared at her. "How am I supposed to get in the mood when you just told me you've been thinking about another man?"

Stephanie pulled him onto the bed. "I'll help you get in the mood."

"I'm just saying . . ." Lindell sat up. "You dropped a lot just now."

Stephanie stared at him as tears clouded her eyes. "You know what?" She moved off of the bed. "The longer I'm here in this romantic place having zero sex with a husband who refuses to get a clue—the more I *will* be tempted to fantasize. As beautiful as this place is, it's a stumbling block to me." She took her phone from her tote and powered it on. "I'm checking on flights for home."

"For when?" Lindell said.

"Today, tomorrow, whenever I can get one."

Lindell looked at her. "You can't be serious."

Stephanie turned, tears streaming. "I can't do three more days of this." She shook her head. "I can't do it."

CHAPTER 31

*J*ordyn jumped up from her bed when the apartment door opened and closed and went to meet Jade. "Jesse is literally ignoring me." She held up her phone. "Can you believe he still won't respond to my calls or texts?"

"Jordyn, he broke up with you." Jade moved toward her room with her camera bag and tripod. "What's there to talk about?"

Jordyn followed. "But how could he move on so easily? He claimed to care so much about me, but now it's whatever?" She plopped on Jade's bed.

"You claimed to care so much about him, but you kissed Kelvin." Jade set her things down. "I guess it *is* whatever." She looked at her. "Have you talked to Kelvin?"

Jordyn hesitated. "Not really."

"So, yes." Jade shook her head. "Wow."

"He called, and I told him I shouldn't have kissed him," Jordyn said, "and that I won't be talking to him." She sighed. "You were right—it was the dumbest thing I could've done. I think part of me was looking to justify the fact that I slept with a married man. If it wasn't just sex— if he actually loved me—then maybe it wasn't so bad." She groaned at herself. "But it *was* all bad. And I had asked God to forgive me and tried to put it behind me, then I run over there when he calls? What is *wrong* with me?"

"Honestly I thought you were in the perfect place." Jade looked at her from her desk chair. "I've watched you and Jesse over the past few months, and it seemed like you had everything. He respected you, prioritized you, tended to you, treated you better than any guy has ever treated either of us."

"Just hearing you say it like that . . . I *know*." Jordyn stared downward. "How could I mess that up?"

"But clearly it *wasn't* everything," Jade said, "or Kelvin wouldn't have been an issue." She paused. "I keep thinking about Lance's cling sermon. He said some of us have holes we're looking to fill, wanting people to affirm us, let us know we have value. And these are holes only God can fill." She looked at her sister. "When he said it, I thought about the two of us and the pain from our biological dad rejecting us. We have to have holes. Maybe that's why, despite everything Jesse's done for you—he wasn't enough. And you went to see Kelvin."

Jordyn gave a slow nod. "That's actually pretty insightful, which is unusual for you." She unlocked her phone and started typing. "I'm telling Jesse what you just said. Maybe if he would just try to understand the issues I'm dealing with, it'll give him a whole new perspective."

"How did you miss the whole point?" Jade said. "I didn't say that so you could make a case for Jesse to take you back. I'm saying maybe *this* is what you need, to get closer to God so He can fill up what's missing."

Jordyn stared downward, thinking.

"Well, I've got to get to work," Jade said, powering up her laptop.

"On what? Did you do an outfit of the day or something?"

"Oh, man," Jade said, turning toward her. "So I went to shoot a quick video for Miss Pam. Ended up getting hired by Alonzo to do a daily vlog for the film and handle all the social media."

"What?" Jordyn said. "And you're just now telling me?"

"It happened on the spot, and I've been working all day." Jade took the media card from her camera. "And still working. About to edit today's vlog."

"So you'll be on set every day?" Jordyn said. "Did you think to ask if we could do it together?"

"Why would I ask that?" Jade said. "We don't do anything together, not even the videos on our channel." She started uploading the footage. "What you should've done is positioned yourself to be able to do makeup on set. You were supposed to be developing your own line and taking your skills to the next level."

"You know that got delayed when Dad died," Jordyn said. "And you were never supportive of me doing that without you anyway."

"And you kept saying you were doing it regardless," Jade said, "so don't put that on me."

"You're the one who brought it up," Jordyn said. "But, great. Now I can sit home alone with no boyfriend while you're having the time of your life on set."

"You don't have to sit home alone," Jade said. "Do something productive. You haven't gotten together with Jillian in a while."

"Because I was always busy with Jesse," Jordyn said. "She left me a voicemail saying she missed me at the Super Bowl party and wants to get together for lunch."

"Well, there you go," Jade said, clicking around on her computer.

"I just don't feel like talking to anybody right now," Jordyn said. "Unless . . . Maybe I can get her to pray for me and Jesse."

Jade turned around just to give her a blank stare.

CHAPTER 32

*J*illian stood outside of her cubicle, looking on as Cyd spoke to the Living Water ministry team.

"I just want to take a moment to encourage you all," Cyd was saying. "The *Promises* study released today, and—"

"Woohoo!" rang out in the open space.

Cyd smiled. "Yes, we *should* celebrate, and we'll celebrate tonight as well because it's been a lot of work. But I wanted to encourage you because you really do work as unto the Lord, giving your best because of who *He* is. And I know it gets tedious sometimes." She took a glance around. "Like Carrie answering customer emails or Jillian double-checking every punctuation mark on a page or Tisha designing graphics for social media—"

"And trying to get you to post more often," Tisha said.

"Yes, Tisha, you do," Cyd said. "I'm sure that's tedious for you too." She smiled. "I just want each of you to know how valuable you are to this ministry. God handpicked each of you—I know He did. The Spirit of the Lord is in this place. And you get it *done*, with excellence. I couldn't ask for a better team." She looked at Tisha. "You're filming this?"

Tisha nodded. "For Living Water's insta-story," she said. "You don't believe it, but people want to see more of you. And this is perfect, getting a glimpse of how you lead and encourage us."

"That's all I've got," Cyd said. "But to be continued tonight!"

A couple of people cheered as everyone went back to work.

Cyd stopped near Jillian. "Hey, let's go into my office," she said. "I want to run something by you."

"Okay," Jillian said, grabbing a notebook from her desk. She followed Cyd to her office, taking a seat in one of the chairs.

"So two things converged," Cyd said, taking her seat. "I've been meeting with our publishing team because we want to develop more topical studies. Then this morning I talked to Alonzo about putting together one or two companion studies to be released with the movie." She paused at a knock on the door. "That might be Treva. She's supposed to be joining us. Come in," she called.

Jillian glanced behind her, surprised as the door opened. *Silas?*

"I wasn't sure if you were ready for me," Silas said. "Is this a good time?"

"Yes, perfect," Cyd said. "Thanks for making the time. Please, have a seat."

"Good to see you, Jillian," Silas said, taking the chair next to her.

"You as well, Silas."

"I was giving Jillian some background," Cyd said, "but I'll just cut to it. We want to produce a new topical study. Based on our market research, there are very few books on the topic and even fewer Bible studies. So we believe there's a void that we can fill, which would serve the body of Christ. The topic is grief."

"I remember searching for resources on grief," Jillian said, "and wondering why I couldn't find a whole lot out there."

A knock sounded on the door and Treva stuck her head in. "Opal said I should go in."

"Absolutely," Cyd said. "We've already gotten started. I just told them we want to produce a study on grief, which we were planning independently. But I learned this morning that Alonzo would love for it to be a companion study to the film."

"Remember that grief workshop Lance and I did at the women's conference?" Treva said. "The room was packed."

"It's been on my mind ever since," Cyd said. "The interesting thing was that people said the teaching applied on so many levels, to things we don't even realize we're grieving. We didn't have Living Water then, but I love that now we can actively plan and produce our own Bible study on grief."

"I love that too," Jillian said. "So Treva, are you going to take what you did at the workshop and develop it into a study?"

"I would if I had the time," Treva said. "I'm already stretched with the women's ministry. But Cyd and I talked about it, and I told her you would be perfect."

"You said *I* would be perfect for this?" Jillian said.

"And I agree," Cyd said. "I would love for you to head up the study."

"What does 'head up the study' mean?" Jillian said.

"You would work on developing an outline," Cyd said, "pulling in key passages of Scripture, identifying sub-topics, but you wouldn't be doing it alone. People grieve differently, and I think it's important to pull from varied perspectives. So although Treva can't take on the project herself, she said she could help you develop it."

Treva nodded, looking at Jillian. "All the conversations we've had about our own grief and how we're getting through or the times it gets hard—that will all be helpful in thinking about ministering to others. Lance could give input as well."

"And we've got Silas," Cyd said, turning to him. "In your sermon Sunday, you touched on grief. And Lance told me you preached a whole series on grief at your former church."

"It was initially supposed to be one Sunday,'" Silas said. "But based on the response, I was asked to do another week, then another. I was grateful, given the work it was doing in my own heart as I engaged the topic."

"It's perfect because you had to develop an outline, determine which passages of Scripture you would incorporate, and so on," Cyd said. "The very things Jillian will need to do."

"Well, if I agree to do this," Jillian said. "I'm still trying to understand the parameters. You said I would develop the outline, but who would actually write the study?"

"Oh, I'm sorry it wasn't clear," Cyd said. "You would also write it."

Jillian looked at her. "That's so far outside my lane. I'm a staff editor. I don't write the actual studies."

"Who encouraged me when I said I wasn't a writer?" Treva said. "I think you said something like, 'It's not about what *we* can do. It's all God's grace.'"

"And Jillian, I already know you can write," Cyd said. "I see it in your edits. But even more importantly, I know you've had a heart for going deep in God's word for a number of years. And I know that this past year, you've had to stand on what you know from the word through the storms of grief." Her eyes were warm. "This is actually very much in your lane."

"But there's also the emotional aspect," Jillian said. "I don't know that I'm ready to engage this topic in depth. And besides, I think someone should write it who's got a perspective of *years*."

"I'm not so concerned about the latter part," Cyd said, "because we'll have the input of others. But I am very sensitive to the question of emotional readiness. I remember how difficult it was for Treva to agree to teach on grief at that women's conference."

"That's why you got Lance to teach it with me," Treva said.

"I would absolutely want you to seek the Lord about this, Jillian," Cyd said, "and know that this is something He is calling you to do."

"Jillian, just so you know," Silas said, "my sermon notes and whatever else you may need are at your disposal. And I'll add—I didn't think I was ready to engage the topic either when I preached on it. But by delving into what the word had to say about grief, I was comforted and strengthened." He rose from his chair. "I've got to run to another meeting. Was there anything else?"

"That's all I had," Cyd said. "Thanks, Silas."

"I appreciate your willingness to help," Jillian said. "If I decide to move forward, I'm sure your sermon notes will be invaluable. And how can I hear the sermons themselves? Are they online?"

"They are," Silas said. "I'll send the link after my meeting." He started for the door then turned. "Also, I've got a couple of books on my office shelf that I think would be helpful to you."

"Thanks so much, Silas," Jillian said.

He walked out and closed the door.

Treva looked at Cyd. "So did you know before you invited Silas to the meeting?"

"Know what?" Cyd said.

Jillian looked at her sister. "It better not be what I think you're about to say."

"About the date," Treva said. "Jill and Silas."

"What?" Cyd said. "No, I didn't know. This was recent?"

"Please tell me how this is relevant," Jillian said.

"It just struck me as familiar," Treva said. "Cyd was the one who put Lance and me together to work on the grief workshop. I wondered if she was matchmaking again."

"I didn't know I was matchmaking then," Cyd said. "But no, that wouldn't have entered my mind. I thought if Jillian pursued anything with anyone, it would be Tommy."

"Aren't you two supposed to be here in your official capacities?" Jillian said. "As in, mature, responsible heads of two women's ministries? How did this devolve to the two of you tracking my so-called dating life?"

"Girl, you know nothing's official when it's just us," Treva said. "We're all sisters first."

"Amen to that," Cyd said. "And since Treva and I are the elder sisters, it's sort of easy to . . . you know . . ."

"Be in our business," Jillian said. "Stephanie and I need to form a support group." She shook her head. "But I can't talk. I inserted myself into the Treva and Lance dating situation, because Treva was about to mess it up." She gave her a glance. "Did you ever thank me?"

"Oh, speaking of Lance and dating"—Cyd looked at Treva—"what is the deal with this video Desiree Riley put out? I couldn't believe that. Someone forwarded it to me this morning."

"So you knew her?" Treva said.

"Not well," Cyd said. "She started coming to Living Word with Lance, and even came to a Bible study I was doing at the time. I remember she had questions after class and kept working in the fact that she was about to get her Master's. Another woman chimed in and told her I had a Ph.D. and a tenured faculty position at WashU. Her whole attitude toward me changed." She paused. "I never said anything to Lance about her, but I thought she did him a favor when she broke off—"

They turned as the office door opened.

"So all three of you—here together—and nobody's phone is turned on?"

Jillian, Cyd, and Treva stared as Stephanie entered the room.

"I've been texting and calling all over the place from the time my plane landed," Stephanie said. "I took an Uber because I figured y'all were here at work, but is this a security compound? All contact with the outside world blocked?"

"Steph, what are you even doing here?" Cyd said. "Did something happen? Is the baby okay?"

Stephanie took the empty chair and sank down in it, heaving a sigh. "I'm glad you're together so I can tell you at the same time. But I hope nobody's got to get right back to work. It's gonna take a minute."

"So it's my honeymoon all over again," Stephanie said. "But worse. This time I made it to the island and found out it wasn't paradise."

"I remember that honeymoon story," Treva said. "Well. The honeymoon that wasn't."

Who could forget that story?" Stephanie said.

"I'm just stunned that this is how the trip turned out," Treva said. "I was praying you'd have the time of your life, even got on Instagram to see if you had posted any pictures at the beach."

"I should probably feel accomplished," Stephanie said. "Not many people can travel to an island and never make it to the beach."

"I can't believe you left." Cyd stared at her sister. "You actually got on a plane and left your husband in Saint Lucia."

"That was his choice," Stephanie said. "He could've returned with me."

"Steph, why didn't you call me to talk it out?" Cyd said. "You could've released all of your frustrations, we would've prayed together—"

"I wanted to call you that first night," Stephanie said. "But like I said, we put away our phones, so I was trying to abide by that. Then the next day things escalated pretty quickly. When I turned on my phone, it was to find a flight home."

"I assumed things were going well when I didn't hear from you again," Jillian said. "I was glad you'd gotten your mind off the B and B." She sighed. "I'm so sorry, Steph. I feel like the enemy won. I wish we could pray right now and send you back with fresh hope."

"I had fresh hope two days ago," Stephanie said. "When we walked into that island villa, when I felt that romantic vibe on the patio . . . And just like that"—she snapped her fingers—"it was gone." She looked at Jillian. "How many years have we been talking about my marriage and praying for my marriage? I get moments when it looks like victory is in sight, but it's never long before I get the reminder that this is not the marriage of my dreams."

"The marriage of your dreams?" Cyd said. "Steph, we've talked about that a dozen times. Nobody's living a 'dream.' Marriage is work —you know that. It's sacrificial. It's a picture of Christ and His church. You can't just run away when things aren't going your way."

"I knew you'd make me out to be the bad guy," Stephanie said, "because you have no idea what this feels like. You can't name one time when you wanted to make love and Cedric turned you down—I know you can't. But I need you to try to imagine it—then imagine it happening repeatedly. I need you to acknowledge that it's not a frivolous thing."

"I'm not trying to minimize what you're going through," Cyd said. "With Cedric and me, it happens in the reverse. I'm the one who says I'm too tired or whatever. I *know* it's not a frivolous thing. How can it be when the word of God speaks to it? I love that you raised the First Corinthians verses with Lindell."

"Me too," Treva said. "Every time I've heard someone talk about those verses, it's toward the wife, telling her not to deprive her husband. It's always assumed that the husband wants sex all the time. But Scripture speaks specifically to the husband as well, so God already knew it would be an issue." She looked at Stephanie. "I wish you had stayed too and tried to work through it with the Lord's help. But at the same time, I hope Lindell seeks the Lord about his part in this."

"What did Lindell say as you were walking out?" Cyd said. "He probably didn't think you'd actually leave."

"He kept saying it was ridiculous," Stephanie said, "and if I cared about our marriage, I would stay." She shifted in the chair, resting her hands on her belly. "I told him I couldn't stay *because* I care about our marriage. Who wants to see your issues magnified by a thousand?"

"How are you feeling physically, Steph?" Jillian said.

"Pretty good," Stephanie said. "Just exhausted."

"You should go to my house," Cyd said. "I can run you over there. You can take some time to yourself, get a nap."

"Yeah, I hope you're not planning to jump back into B and B life," Jillian said. "As far as I'm concerned, you're still gone till Friday."

"Oh, and the *Promises* celebration is tonight," Cyd said. "That's actually really timely."

"Timely for whom?" Stephanie said. "I'm not in the mood to hang out. And I don't have any maternity clothes to wear to something like that."

"I've got some things at the house that could work," Cyd said.

"Wow, really?" Treva said. "You've still got maternity clothes?"

"I saved them thinking I could pass them to Steph one day," Cyd said. "And I'm so glad that it worked out. She's been able to wear a lot of the pieces."

"For running errands and life at the B and B," Stephanie said. "For events, we don't exactly have the same style."

"It's maternity, Steph," Cyd said. "And it's church. I'm thinking you'll be fine."

"Well, I'm still not in the mood."

"See how you feel after a nap," Cyd said. "But I'm telling you, you should go. You'll be glad you did. It's times like this when you need a fresh reminder that with God, all things are possible."

CHAPTER 33

Trey sat in a folding chair together with Pamela and Tommy, watching as Mariah rehearsed a scene between Brooke, Noah, and the woman cast as Trey's best friend Molly.

In relaxed jeans and a hoodie, Mariah exuded a command of the set, while also showing deference to Brooke and Noah, who were new to this. "So Trey and Molly come through this garage door and into the kitchen," she said, demonstrating. "Lance has just gotten back from visiting his mom at the Florida prison. He was surprised to see Kendra at the house—and of course she was surprised to see him living in her childhood home. They're now eating and Kendra has just told Lance, 'I'm dying of cancer.'"

Noah nodded. "This is after the big party the night before, right? I'm trying to keep things straight, since we're not rehearsing that scene."

"That's right," Mariah said. "The big party was last night. Loud music, everybody drunk, including Trey. Kendra left DC and returned home—to *that*. This is the next day, so she's rather disoriented, about *everything*."

"Oh, that's a great way to think about it." Brooke was already in place at the kitchen table. "Right before this scene I almost fainted on the stairs because I haven't eaten, so I'm weak and dizzy—physically disoriented. And I'm disoriented because I'm back home and because of the *reason* I'm back home. But I'm also disoriented because Lance is here and my brother's tripping. Thanks, Mariah. That's good."

Alonzo stood watching. "I know we're not doing the Kendra and Lance part right now, but do you want me at the table?"

"Yes, go ahead and get in place," Mariah said. "I want Noah and Brooke to get a sense of the added tension of exchanging words in front of this new house guest who's also a youth pastor." She paused to talk to one of the crew members.

Jade walked over to Trey, her camera poised on a mini tripod. "How weird is this for you? This is the first scene where you get to see Noah playing *you*."

"The whole thing is weird," Trey said. "Watching Brooke play my sister, hearing Kendra's words out of her mouth, even seeing Alonzo say and do things that I saw Lance say and do . . . it's all surreal."

"Okay, let's run through it," Mariah said.

Trey watched as Noah and the actor playing Molly came through the garage door and into the kitchen.

"Aye, I was hoping dinner would be ready." Noah walked in, checking out what they were eating. "Oh, it's the leftover soup? I didn't like it. That's the only reason it's still in there."

"Hello to you, too, Trey." Brooke sat back, eyeing him. "How are you? How was your day? Nice to see you."

Noah frowned a little. "What's that about?"

"It's called trying to have a conversation," Brooke said, script in hand, "since I haven't seen my brother in months, and the one I saw last night I didn't recognize."

Noah stepped closer to her. "So you decide to come home when it suits you—because heaven forbid you should come home and help your mother when she's sick—and you expect everything to be like you remember."

"You're going to stand there and accuse me of not helping Mom?" Brooke pushed her soup bowl aside. "For your information, I offered to come home and stay for a while, but she said not to, that she had plenty of help."

"Which was mostly me, since Dad was always busy at work."

"And you're throwing it up in my face?" Brooke said.

"I'm just saying you hardly came home at all. Always so busy. Kendra, the high-powered DC attorney." Noah opened the fridge and got a bottled water. "You're only here now to lay low because you're embarrassed about the wedding. I heard you got dumped."

"Who told you that?" Brooke said.

"Your maid of honor called to see how you were because you wouldn't answer your phone," Noah said. "She thought I knew." He paused, looking at her. "And do you know *why* she thought I knew, Kendra? Because in normal families, they share things. In normal families people don't keep secrets for years. But we all know this family is far from normal, don't we?"

"Wait, Noah, you must not have the updated script," Mariah said. "We took that out."

"Which part?" Noah said.

"The part about family secrets. The secrets are all gone now," she said, chuckling a little.

"Nobody told us it was that easy to put the secrets behind us," Trey said. "Just push a delete button." He added, "I hadn't seen the script yet, but I figured you wouldn't have time to get into *all* the family drama."

"Yeah, we're having a hard enough time trying to fit in the family drama with Lance and Momma Pam," Alonzo said. "We did a version where we attempted to fit in more family stuff on Kendra's side, but it was too much. I don't even know how you got that one, Noah."

"Probably me doing too much in the middle of the night," Mariah said. "Sent out the wrong script."

"I'll get you an updated one," Faith said.

Tommy raised a hand. "I need a script myself if it's no trouble."

"No trouble at all," Faith said.

"I don't know if it's okay to ask," Noah said. "But can we know what family secret Trey was referring to, since it was almost in the movie anyway? I think it would help me understand more of the dynamics between them."

"I don't mind sharing it," Trey said, "if there's time."

"Please, Trey, go ahead," Mariah said.

"Basically," Trey said, "our Dad had an affair with a fellow professor on campus, and we got a little sister as a result."

"Oh, wow," Noah said.

"We didn't meet her for years," Trey said. "Mom was battling cancer, so that's where our focus went. But we got to know her—Brooklyn's her name—before Kendra died, which was a blessing." He paused. "That's also about the time we found out that mom had had an affair of her own, so . . . yeah."

"I keep hearing real-life drama that would make for a good movie," Brooke said. "This is right at the top."

"Unfortunately true," Trey said.

"Okay," Mariah said, "let's run through it again . . ."

Trey took a roast beef sandwich from the lunch tray, a bag of chips, and a water and joined Jade, who had found a spot in the living room which, for now, was overrun with equipment.

"So this vlog's got you working during breaks too, huh," he said, pulling over a seat.

Jade focused on her laptop. "I want to see the footage I got this morning, make sure there's a variety." She looked at him. "But I wouldn't include what you shared. If anything, just you interacting with Noah and the others, but no sound."

"That day one vlog was sick." Trey opened the chips. "The tight edits and the music . . . you got skills."

"You don't have to sound so surprised," Jade said.

"Hey, I didn't know." Trey ate a chip. "That first night at Lance's, you were like, 'Oh, I just do hair videos.'"

"That *is* what I do," Jade said. "But I try to add some swag when I edit those too."

"Let me see," Trey said, pulling out his phone. "Airdrop the link to your channel."

Jade did so from her laptop, and Trey checked it out.

"This one looks intriguing," he said. "'My Wash and Go Secrets.'"

Jade stayed focused on her footage.

"Okay, okay," Trey said, nodding as he watched. "Music knockin', swag shots with the different looks, all attitude, of course."

"What do you mean, 'of course'?"

Trey kept watching. "Yeah, your editing style is dope. Now you look into the camera and tell all the 'secrets'." He looked over at her. "Is that what you're rocking right now? What's it called?" He looked back at his phone. "A wash and go?"

"Uh, no," Jade said. "This is a Bantu knot out."

"First time I've heard of it," Trey said. "But it's fire."

Jade paused and looked at him. "So what's all this about?"

"All what?" Trey said.

"You coming over here to eat," Jade said. "Complimenting my videos and my hair. And I wanted to ask about your comment Sunday night, when you called me your new friend."

Trey finished a bite of his sandwich. "What did you want to ask about it?"

"You said it after I said I didn't have any friends," Jade said. "But you don't have to do the fake, buddy-buddy Christian thing. I know you're a missionary, but I'm not a charity case."

He crunched on a chip. "I didn't hear a question."

"What?" Jade said.

"You said you wanted to ask about the comment from Sunday," Trey said. "All you did was rant."

"That wasn't a rant," Jade said. "Trust me." She turned a little, focusing on him. "But okay. What was up with the comment? With all of this, even offering me a ride home after church?"

"I've hated the fake, buddy-buddy Christian thing longer than you have," Trey said. "It became an issue on the mission field, a big one. I have no interest in being around people who aren't real." He looked at her. "You're real. And funny, when you stop being guarded. And you're not the only one who needs a friend." He took a swig of water. "That's why I came over here to eat with you."

"I said I didn't have any friends," Jade said. "I didn't say I *needed* a friend. And I don't think the two of us could be friends anyway, because I thought you were cute the first time I saw you, and what I *don't* need is a friendship moving to something else because I'm trying to wean myself off of needing to be with a man and—"

"Jade, it's not a problem," Trey said. "I'm not attracted to women."

Jade stared at him for a few seconds then blew out a sigh. "Okay, that's a relief."

"Well, that's a different kind of response," Trey said.

"I've just never met someone that I wanted to kick it with," Jade said. "That I felt I could be myself around—because I know I can rub people the wrong way. And I was like *man*, he'd be the perfect friend without the 'cute and complicated' part—and now that's gone."

Trey smiled. "Dang, I'm not cute anymore?"

"Not complicated cute," Jade said. "You're 'little brother cute' now."

"Except, we're about the same age."

"Whatever," Jade said. "It works." She sat back a little, looking at him. "So we just heard about all the stuff that was swirling in your family. I'm guessing this was part of it."

"I dealt with it on my own for years," Trey said. "Prayed and prayed for God to change me. It felt like something was missing because I didn't think in terms of falling in love with a woman one day and getting married. But you want to talk about relief?" He exhaled. "When I came to understand that God had given me a gift of singleness, and I was able to embrace that. Changed my whole life."

"How long ago was that?" Jade said.

"A few years," Trey said. "Kendra and Lance helped me with that. But I've learned the importance of friendship because I do get lonely sometimes. Still, it's hard to connect on a real level and be able to trust people. I learned some hard lessons on the mission field."

"Hey, Jade," Alonzo said, walking toward them, "how do I turn off YouTube notifications? I'm getting comments every two seconds. That day one vlog is blowing up."

235

Jade's eyes widened as she pulled it up on her phone. "I've been so busy I haven't checked." She gasped. "Are we really over a million views?"

"You're surprised?" Alonzo said. "You're the one who pitched the vlog concept and said it would connect with people."

"Yeah, but I just uploaded it late last night." Jade went to the settings. "Okay, notifications are off. And you're right—I shouldn't be surprised. Just about anything you touch goes viral."

"That only goes so far," Alonzo said. "I'm seeing the comments. People love the up close and personal vibe. They feel like they're in there with the cast and crew. That's all you."

"Check out these comments about the ministry moment," Trey said. "People remember the video you put out, Jade. Somebody said *you're* 'too Christian' now—ha. But look at this one—'I cried watching the part with Alonzo and Jade. That's the power of forgiveness and redemption.'"

"That's it," Alonzo said. "That's the kind of conversation I want to generate around this film." He held up his hand and high-fived Jade. "You killed it, sis. The whole thing. Now you just have to do it again today, tomorrow, the next day, the day after that . . ." He chuckled.

"Your encouragement is everything, Alonzo," Jade said. "And that means I need to keep pushing." She looked at Trey. "You want to be today's ministry moment?"

"What would I be talking about?"

Jade didn't hesitate. "The importance of friendship."

CHAPTER 34

*J*ordyn took a deep breath and rang the doorbell, folding her arms against the cold. She'd never had to do this—stand at the door waiting. Jesse would have the door open before she got out of her car. But that was when he knew she was coming—when he welcomed her coming. Now she had to show up and hope he was home, and if so, hope he'd answer. For all she knew, he'd spied her from a window and decided to ignore her.

"Come on, Jess, I see your car in the driveway," Jordyn muttered, glancing back at it.

She didn't have a lot of time, since she wanted to get to the *Promises* celebration. But if she had to skip it so they could talk through their issues, so be it.

After several seconds, she debated whether to ring the doorbell again. Sometimes he couldn't hear it, depending on where he was in the house. But was she really going to stand here ringing the doorbell—

Her insides stirred as the door came open. Jesse stood in sweat-shirt, jeans, and a ball cap, looking at her.

"Hey." Jordyn looked into his eyes. "I was hoping we could talk."

"I said I don't have anything else to say," Jesse said. "I didn't answer your texts, so you just show up?"

Jordyn felt the sting. "Jesse, we had one conversation, in the heat of everything that happened. You don't think our relationship is worth more than that?"

Jesse hesitated then backed up finally, opening the door wider, and she walked in.

"Hey, Lancelot," Jordyn said, petting the big dog. He turned his head this way and that, soaking it up. At least *he* was glad to see her.

Jordyn followed Jesse toward the kitchen. Her eyes took in her handiwork—the color scheme she'd helped him choose, furniture she'd suggested, artwork. In the kitchen her gaze fell on an area of shelving accented by pictures in frames, mostly of Zoe. But the one of Jordyn and Jesse, taken around Christmas, had become her favorite of the two of them. Jordyn's eyes swept the frames as she walked past, and again when she took a seat at the kitchen table. It was gone.

Jesse glanced at the fridge. "Can I get you anything?"

"I'm fine," Jordyn said, feeling the distance. She'd been helping herself to whatever she wanted for months now.

Jesse sat opposite her and leveled a gaze under his cap. "So what's up?"

"What's up?" Jordyn said. "You sound as if none of this matters to you. It's like you flipped a switch and I don't even know you."

"Interesting," Jesse said. "I could say the same."

"I didn't flip a switch," Jordyn said. "I made a mistake, but my attitude toward you is the same as it's always been."

Jesse looked aside.

"I'm just having a really hard time understanding," Jordyn said. "One minute you say I mean so much to you, and the next you're blasé about the whole thing. It was super easy for you to end it."

"Super easy." Jesse nodded slightly. "Okay."

"See?" Jordyn said. "No feeling whatsoever. I even told you I love you, and you didn't care."

"So you can read my mind now," Jesse said. "You know what's super easy and what I do or don't care about."

"I don't have to read your mind," Jordyn said. "Actions speak louder."

"Actions speak louder." Jesse said it almost to himself, then rose from the chair. He got something from the cabinet by the desk and set it on the table, sliding it toward her. "What does this say, Jordyn?"

Jordyn began to shake as tears pooled in her eyes. "That can't be what it looks like."

Jesse picked up the box and opened it toward her, showing a beautiful diamond. "I was planning to propose in June, on the anniversary of our first date. I knew I was a bit eager, buying the ring so early. But I believed in us, Jordyn. Couldn't go a day without hearing your voice. Kept thinking about the day we'd be married and you'd move in here with me. That is, if you would've said yes."

"You *know* I would say yes." Jordyn swiped tears that fell nonstop now.

"I love you, Jordyn." Jesse looked aside again. "Ending this was one of the hardest things I've had to do."

"But you didn't have to." Jordyn leaned in. "Jesse, we love each other—why would we walk away from that? Why won't you forgive me?"

"It's not about forgiving you," Jesse said. "I can forgive you, but it doesn't mean we should be together. You said it yourself—actions speak louder. You *wanted* to talk to Kelvin, get in your car and go see him, stay for hours, and kiss him." He shook his head. "But I'm supposed to believe you love *me* and you're committed to *us*?"

"Saturday was one stupid moment," Jordyn said. "For seven months it's just been you and me. Why can't we focus on *that*? Why can't we get back to that?"

"Tell me how I'm supposed to ignore what happened." Jesse focused steely eyes on her. "How am I supposed to trust that it won't happen again? Part of your heart is tied to this guy. Are you even seeing that?"

"That's not true." Jordyn's eyes grazed the box he'd left open and fresh tears fell. "Jesse, you're the only one I want."

Jesse got up and took a pitcher of lemonade from the fridge. He poured Jordyn a glass and set it before her, then poured one for himself. He took his glass to the windowsill, taking a sip as he looked out.

"When I think back on everything between us . . ." Jesse took a moment to continue. "We had the thing that happened when you got into my bed—"

"Could you please not bring that up?" Jordyn cringed still at the remembrance.

"It's just part of it," Jesse said. "I knew we had to separate, and we did. Then you did the video about giving your life to Jesus and being changed." He paused, staring out still. "But it didn't mean you were ready to date. I should have left you alone, given you time."

"Where is this coming from?" Jordyn got up and walked toward him. "I'm the one who wanted us to date, long before you did. And you were careful about *how* we dated."

"Still. I don't know . . ." Jesse thought a moment. "Time alone might've helped you work through some things." He turned toward her. "I'm just saying, it's not all on you. I played a part in this."

"You're making everything sound so final." Jordyn searched his eyes. "Jesse, I get why you're upset with me. I do. And I get that you need time to rebuild trust. But I know it's possible. Don't throw us away."

He moved away, leaning against the opposite counter. "I don't want you to think I'm reacting out of hurt. I've been praying, maybe more than I ever have." He looked at her. "And this study I'm doing with Tommy and Reggie is timely, all about focusing on our relationship with Jesus. That's what I want to do. I honestly just want to focus on Jesus right now. And you should do the same. We can't go wrong putting our energy into the relationship that matters most."

"Jade basically said that earlier today," Jordyn said. "But it sounds at least a little hopeful coming from you. So you're thinking this works in our favor because ultimately, as we focus on Jesus, it'll be good for our relationship?"

"Jordyn, that's not what I'm saying at all." Jesse set his glass down. "If you want to know the truth—no. I can't see us getting back together. I'm just telling you what I *do* see—a higher purpose in all of this."

Jordyn let her gaze wander to the kitchen table, and the little box with the diamond shining forth. She got a tissue from her purse and dabbed her eyes. "I love you so much, Jesse," she said, the words barely audible. "I don't know how I can get past this . . ."

She moved out of the kitchen toward the front door, needing to leave—everything in her wanting Jesse to call her back.

The silence echoed as she closed the door behind her.

CHAPTER 35

*R*ested from a long nap, Stephanie left Cyd's house, locking the door, and headed for Jillian's car in the driveway. The first thing she noticed was extra bodies in the car.

The passenger window came down. "Hey, I was surprised to hear you were back," Mariah said.

"Well, not completely." Stephanie opened the back door and got in beside Brooke. "I don't even have my car. Thanks for coming to get me, Jill."

"No problem at all," Jillian said, glancing behind her as she backed out of the driveway. "And is that Cyd's dress? It looks good on you."

"Yeah, when I tried it on, I had to admit it was cute," Stephanie said. She clicked her seatbelt, looking at Mariah and Brooke. "It's good to see you two. I thought you'd be working into the night."

"Brooke and I caught Jillian leaving and hopped in," Mariah said. "We had a full day and I'll get back to it later this evening. But instead of grinding twenty-four-seven, I wanted to do something for my spirit."

"So how's it going at the B and B?" Stephanie said. "Jillian treating y'all right?"

"Jillian's been amazing," Mariah said. "She makes these spinach frittatas that are to-die-for."

"My weakness is the banana pancakes," Brooke said. "I had to keep telling myself I'm not on vacation. I'm working. Can't be putting on five pounds."

"Jillian, what you need to do is let everybody get one plate and then close the kitchen," Mariah said. "The freedom to pile-on might be lawful but it ain't expedient." She chuckled.

"Okay, Miss Jillian," Stephanie said, "now I know who to go to if I transition from B and B life. You can take over."

"Only if we're trading jobs," Jillian said. "You get three teenagers. Built-in babysitters."

"Ha," Stephanie said. "I couldn't handle three of anything. One baby is beyond me."

"I admire you, Jillian," Mariah said. "It can't be easy to keep keepin' on given what you've had to deal with. I'm encouraged by your strength."

"I appreciate that, Mariah, thank you."

"Listen, don't sleep on Jillian," Stephanie said. "When I first met her and Treva, I thought Treva was the strong, no-nonsense one, and Jillian was the really nice, homeschool-sweet—"

"Homeschool-sweet?" Jillian looked at her in the rearview mirror. "What is that?"

"If you're a homeschooler, I figured you had to be extra sweet, infinitely patient, all that, which you *sort* of are," Stephanie said. "But when you decided to leave everything you've known and move out here after losing your husband, I saw a whole different side. I said oh, this sister gets it done."

"That was nothing but God," Jillian said. "You know I could barely function at the funeral. But moving out here made all the difference."

"Jillian, I didn't know you lost your husband," Brooke said. "I'm so sorry to hear that. Where did you and your family live before you moved to St. Louis?"

"We were in Maryland," Jillian said. "I was born and raised in the DC area."

"We were just talking about that at the Super Bowl party," Mariah said. "That we had a lot of people from the DMV."

"Like me," Brooke said, smiling. "And then you can break it down to the people who went to the University of Maryland. Jesse and Faith, and didn't Treva say she went there?"

"She did," Jillian said. "I went there as well."

"Really?" Mariah said. "Tommy too. Did you know each other? I know Maryland is pretty big."

"Yeah, it's a big campus," Jillian said. "But we knew each other."

Stephanie looked at her. "Weren't you like, best friends?"

"Yeah, we were," Jillian said.

"Wow," Mariah said. "You and Tommy were that close? I had no idea."

"How do you know Tommy, Mariah?" Stephanie said.

"We worked together years ago at a local station," Mariah said. "Now he's the exclusive reporter on set, which is nice."

Jillian pulled into the parking lot at Living Word and navigated toward an open space. "We're early, and there are still lots of people here already."

"Since we're early," Brooke said, "I'd love to see the production offices and where base camp will be set up."

"I can show you," Mariah said. "I got a tour on Sunday." She looked at Jillian. "We'll meet you guys in there."

Stephanie walked with Jillian toward the main building. "Things that make you go hmmm."

"What are you talking about?" Jillian said.

"Mariah's interest in you and Tommy," Stephanie said. "At least, that's the vibe I got. And you acting like he was some random guy on campus."

"I said I knew him," Jillian said. "That was enough."

"Okay, what's going on?" Stephanie pulled Jillian to a stop.

"It's nothing," Jillian said. "And anyway, you've got enough happening in your own life."

"Don't try it," Stephanie said. "We're sisters. And after years of praying together, we know stuff about each other that nobody else knows. I'm always here for you."

Jillian sighed. "Basically, Tommy and I aren't friends anymore."

"Okay, the only other time you two iced the friendship . . ."

"No, nothing like that." Jillian greeted a group of women that passed. "But it's too much to get into right now."

"See, this is what happens when we're not having regular prayer time," Stephanie said. "We miss all the updates."

"Not to mention the power from the prayers," Jillian said, walking. "I thought about that when you were telling us what happened on the island. We need to get back to it."

They moved inside the building, where chatter hit from the women who were gathered.

Stephanie leaned in as they walked. "At least tell me this. Why didn't you want to say that you and Tommy were best friends in college?"

"I didn't want it to get weird," Jillian said, "since they dated before."

"Who dated?" Stephanie said.

"Tommy and Mariah," Jillian said, "when she lived here."

"I love how you said it all casually," Stephanie said, "like no big deal."

"Because Brooke said it all casually," Jillian said, "in Cinda's kitchen at the Super Bowl party."

Stephanie looked at her. "How was I gone only two days and missed all this?"

They walked into the annex area where the event was being held.

"Hey, you made it," Treva said, hugging Stephanie. "How are you feeling?"

"Much better after that nap." Stephanie took a glance around. "Okay, I didn't know this was a whole *event*. They're setting up a dinner buffet? And who was responsible for decorating these tables? They're gorgeous."

"Which means I'd better get moving," Jillian said. "I'm setting up the book displays." She started off.

"Stephanie?"

Stephanie looked left and her eyes went wide. "Roni? What are you doing here? I thought you were still living in Cali." She hugged her. "It's been way too long."

Veronica beamed. "I know, can you believe—wait, girl, are you having a baby? Congratulations!" She hugged her again. "Girl or boy?"

"We want to be surprised," Stephanie said. "So far anyway. I keep thinking we'll change our mind—oh, let me introduce you to Treva Alexander, our pastor's wife. Treva, this is my high school bff, Veronica."

"I came early, hoping to meet you." Veronica said. "I got an early copy of the study from Living Water in exchange for a review. Treva, that study was everything I needed—and everything I didn't know I needed. I'm looking at my life and God differently. I just had to tell you that. And can we get a picture?"

"Of course," Treva said. "And I'm thanking God that the study impacted you in that way. That's an answer to prayer."

"Here, I'll take it." Stephanie took Veronica's phone and snapped a few.

Treva looked as someone called her. "It was really good meeting you, Veronica," she said, moving to see what was needed.

Stephanie shook her head at her friend. "I'm still tripping that you're here. Are you visiting? What's the deal?—and why do you look so good? I can't with you and the same clothes size. Do you eat?"

"Girl, I'm at least two sizes bigger with *no* pregnancy." Veronica chuckled. "But it's been a whirlwind. I moved back early last fall, been getting re-acclimated to the area." She took a breath. "But you've been on my mind. I wanted to get in touch because—" She lifted her left hand to show a diamond.

Stephanie held her hand, eyeing it. "Roni, you're engaged? That ring is gorgeous." She looked at her. "Okay, who's the guy? Someone you met in California?"

"He's a St. Louis guy." Veronica's gaze fell and seconds elapsed before she looked at her. "Steph, it's Warren."

Stephanie could feel her pulse race. "Warren? My . . . old boyfriend Warren?"

"We ran into one another at the Galleria," Veronica said. "And he remembered me."

"Why wouldn't he?" Stephanie said. "He met you through me, all the times I invited you to hang out with us."

"Right." Veronica cleared her throat. "So we stood talking in front of Macy's for the longest time, and it was obvious that there was this . . . connection. We kept in touch and things moved pretty quickly— only as far as getting to know one another. He was transparent about not wanting to have sex. He said he was on this new journey with God."

Stephanie could feel the heat rise to her face.

"He's really different," Veronica said. "Even in the time we've been dating, I've seen him growing in the Lord. Both of us, really." She hesitated. "And Steph, I know this is uncomfortable—for me, for sure. I haven't started coming to Living Word for church yet because I wanted to talk to you first. I was hoping to see you tonight as well."

"Why couldn't you just call me?" Stephanie said.

"I kept putting it off," Veronica said, "because honestly, part of me felt guilty. I didn't even want to pursue a relationship with Warren at first. But I realized—you and I haven't talked in about four years. And you've been happily married for years. So if this is a whole new season and God has brought Warren and me together, why would I reject that blessing?"

Stephanie felt her head give a nod.

"Actually," Veronica said, "when you reached out to Warren a while back, I wanted him to tell you about us. But he thought I should be the one——"

"Roni? It's so good to see you." Cyd hugged her. "Steph, you didn't tell me Roni was coming."

"I'm just as surprised as you," Stephanie said.

"Girl, what are you doing here?" Cyd said.

"Thanks to Living Water," Veronica said, "I got an early copy of the study and loved it. I wanted to come meet Treva. And I wanted to see Steph as well."

"Roni and Warren are engaged," Stephanie said.

"Roni and—oh, *Warren?*" Cyd said.

Veronica nodded. "He proposed on Christmas day."

"Wow, congratulations," Cyd said. "Do you have a date?"

"We're thinking a June wedding," Veronica said, "and Warren is really hoping Lance can conduct the ceremony. He is so into Lance right now." She smiled. "I love him too. Been watching the sermons online, but I'm about to start coming as well."

"Well, we're a big church, so let me know if I can help with your transition," Cyd said.

"It's been so long since I've been part of a church," Veronica said. "I can't wait. Okay, I'm going to check out the displays over there."

Stephanie looked at Cyd as Veronica walked away. "Can you believe that?"

"Quite interesting," Cyd said.

"She knew more about Warren and me than anyone," Stephanie said. "Knew how much I loved him and struggled with choosing between Lindell and Warren." The more she thought about it, the more it stung. "And Warren knew how close Roni and I were. Why would he pursue a relationship with someone who was a really close friend of mine?"

Cyd looked at her. "Steph, you can't be suggesting that Warren owed you anything. After the way you broke his heart?" She sighed. "Please don't add to what you're dealing with by thinking about those two. But it's a blessing to hear that they're serious about their spiritual growth."

"Yeah, but I wish they'd grow someplace else," Stephanie said. "I don't want to be running into them—"

"Hey, Cyd," a woman said. "We need you to look at the program. We had to change the order of the testimonies."

"Okay," Cyd said. "Steph, let me know if you need anything."

She walked away, and Stephanie's gaze landed on Veronica, in conversation with someone, head thrown back in laughter, about the happiest Stephanie had ever seen her.

Stephanie sighed. How was she miserable in Saint Lucia *and* miserable here?

CHAPTER 36

$\mathcal{L}$ive music and lively chatter filled the annex as Cinda moved with Alonzo past lavender and silver accented tables. Her hand in his, she couldn't help but catch the double takes and whispers. Alonzo stood out as one of only a handful of men in the room. But also, in a large setting like this where most didn't know him, he stood out as the Hollywood actor.

Cinda checked the text she'd gotten. "Faith says they're toward the front, left side."

"I see her waving at us," Alonzo said.

They weaved past another table—

"Excuse me," a young woman said, getting up from her seat. "My mom just said this isn't the time or place, but I had to—I'm your biggest fan and I'll never get this chance again." She lifted her phone, her face pleading. "Could I please get a picture with you?"

Cinda felt his hesitation. Alonzo knew that if he took the picture, others would ask.

"Really quickly?" the young woman said.

Two others eased behind her, forming a line.

"I'm sorry," Alonzo said, looking behind the young woman. "I'm doing a quick pic with her, but that's all I've got time for. Maybe later."

The others walked away, and the young woman beamed as Cinda took her phone. She took a couple and gave it back to her.

The young woman checked the pictures and smiled big. "Thank you *so* much."

Cinda and Alonzo moved to the table where Faith sat with her sisters, Treva, and Stephanie.

"Heyyy, sorry we're late," Cinda said, hugging everyone around the table.

"I'm surprised you could make it at all," Treva said. "I thought you'd be working late this evening."

"The production office is right here," Alonzo said, dispensing hugs as well. "Cinda told me she was sharing her testimony tonight, so I wanted to come through for a while then go back."

"Wait, I'm just realizing"— Cinda settled in her seat—"you're not supposed to be here, Steph."

Stephanie met her gaze across a floral centerpiece and flickering tea candles. "Yeah, everyone keeps reminding me."

Faith looked at Cinda. "I said the same thing when I got here."

"Is everything okay, though?" Cinda said. "With you and the baby?"

"Yes, baby and I are fine," Stephanie said, attempting a smile.

Cinda nodded, knowing Stephanie wouldn't say much at an open table. She'd text her in a minute to tell her they'd talk later.

"Hey, you two." Pamela walked up from behind and placed plates in front of them. "I saw you come in and wanted to make sure you got some food before we clear the buffet."

"You even included some cake." Alonzo looked up at her. "You bring the A-list service, always. Thank you, Momma Pam."

"I know—*always*." Cinda turned to hug her. "Love you, Momma Pam."

"Y'all are my babies," Pamela said. "You know I have to look out for you."

"Hey, Alonzo"—Faith leaned past Cinda—"I just told Reggie you were here, and he said you're making him look bad. He wanted to come support Mom—and I told him he should—but he kept saying it was promoted as a women's event and he didn't want to be the only guy here."

"Tell him, number one—that's lame." Alonzo cut into the baked chicken. "Two—it's not too late to bring his second-guessing self up here."

"We did call it a girls' night out after some discussion," Treva said. "We hadn't had one in a long time, and the women got excited about it. But *of course* my son-in-law and whoever else could come. Tell him to come on."

"Alonzo"—Joy called from across the table—"you lit up my Instagram."

"With what?" Faith said.

"He took a boss pic with Sophie and me," Joy said. "So you know *we* posted it. But I couldn't believe it when Alonzo put it in his story and tagged us."

"Jade's been on me about capturing moments on set and putting them in my story," Alonzo said. "You two are interns, so I definitely wanted you in there."

"The notifications have been crazy," Joy said. "A few guys even proposed in my DMs."

Cinda took her phone out and texted Stephanie. **I don't know what's wrong but how can I pray for you?**

"Why am I the only one who's missing out?" Hope said.

"You're not, sweetheart," Treva said. "David and Trevor aren't on set either."

"But they get to see people at the B and B every day," Hope said. "And anyway, I'm in Lance's family. I should get special privileges."

"You are absolutely right," Alonzo said. "And you are absolutely welcome to come to the set. Faith can let you know when it's a good time."

"But don't expect me to come get you," Faith said. "I work pretty much nonstop."

"If I can only come once or twice," Hope said, "that'll be really cool."

"Oh, that's easy," Alonzo said.

"Good evening again, everyone." Cyd smiled from the platform, striking in a long sleeve, muted pink dress. "We've had some good conversation, some good food, our stomachs are full, but no—now is not the time to get sleepy. We're about to get this celebration started. Amen?"

"Amen" rang out from the tables.

"We want to be clear about something," Cyd said. "We're not just celebrating the release of the *Promises of God* Bible study. We're praising God tonight because He's the God who *keeps* His promises." She nodded as more "amen's" sounded. "How many of you believe we serve a God who keeps His promises?"

Reaction sounded in the room, and a moment later, Cinda's phone vibrated. A reply from Stephanie—**Pray I can believe that God keeps His promises.**

"I'm so excited about tonight," Cyd said. "We've got praise and worship, we've got testimonies—get this: women will share testimonies regarding each promise in the Bible study and how God fulfilled it in their lives. We'll hear from Treva, of course, and we've also got a special surprise—Treva doesn't even know." She looked down at their table with a smile.

Treva glanced around the table. "Okay, what is it?"

Each of them looked at the other.

Faith shrugged. "I have no idea, Mom."

"But right now," Cyd was saying, "we've got a little surprise before the main surprise. Come on out here, Lance!"

Lance walked out from the back and came first to their table. He lifted Treva by the hand and hugged her tight as cheers went up, then brought her up to the platform with him. She looked gorgeous in a long ruched charcoal evening dress.

Lance took a microphone someone passed to him. "Treva just said, 'What are you doing here?'" He smiled, his hand in hers. "I told her I was coming later to hear Mom's testimony." He looked at her. "Did you really think I would miss any of this?" He turned back to the crowd. "I hope you all don't mind, because I'm about to talk about my wife for a minute. . . ."

CHAPTER 37

esiree Riley stepped into the annex feeling a rush of emotion. She'd felt it when she walked through the doors of Living Word, but unlike the times she'd been here before, the entryway and corridors were mostly empty. As she made her way to the annex, she could feel the anticipation building. And when she got to the registration table and heard cheers of excitement—and Lance's name—she could barely breathe. She had her answer—he was here.

She'd had to convince the woman at the table to let her in, since the event was sold out. Desiree told her she'd just flown into town and was part of the movie that was being made—all true. She was still shocked that her video had moved the producers to include her part in Lance's life in the film. Still, *she* wasn't in the film. She didn't have any real purpose in being here. She just felt she had to come. From the airport she'd gone straight to her parents' house, showered, and changed into a midi length black dress. The entire time as she'd gotten ready, she couldn't help but think of the moment she would see him.

"We're here for it, Pastor," someone called out amid cheers. "You better honor our First Lady."

Desiree looked up at the platform and her heart reacted. *Lance.*

She moved alongside the wall toward the back, glancing around for a place at a table, her eyes seldom leaving the platform.

"I don't know if you all understand how much I love my wife." Lance looked into her eyes. "I was thinking this morning about how God knew this was coming—that I'd be pastor of Living Word and over a worldwide ministry, which is still crazy to me. And I thought about how—knowing all that—He sent me you."

"Yes, He did!" a woman near Desiree said. "Glory!"

Desiree had been blown away a few days ago when she checked the Living Word site. Lance had been elevated over all of Living Word? How did that happen? Even now, just looking at him, she could tell he was different. She'd never seen him with such presence and authority.

"I have no problem acknowledging that everything involved with this church and ministry is beyond me," Lance continued. "I know I need the Lord daily." He paused, letting his gaze linger on his wife. "And He knew I needed you."

"Woo!" several in the room called out. "All right now!"

Desiree slipped in a vacant seat, taking in more of Lance's appearance. He somehow looked the same yet different. Probably the facial hair. He'd been clean-shaven back then. Now he wore medium stubble, nicely trimmed. Part swag, part distinguished. Typical Lance. He'd always had that special something. And he still looked really good.

"I hope y'all don't mind if I take my time," Lance said. "Can I take my time?"

"Take your time, Pastor!" many called out.

Desiree watched as Lance got a bottle of water from the podium and took a drink. Her mind drifted to a picnic in the park, Lance packing her favorite things, including Fiji, her favorite water. She'd brought her camera and they'd taken loads of pictures, mostly silly ones, as he taught her different techniques. She could see his smile even now in those pics. Lately that smile haunted her at night.

"I don't tell you enough how much I value everything you do," Lance was saying. "How much I value *you*." He focused on his wife.

"You are evidence in my life that God keeps His promises. You shouldn't even be here. Treva, you *coded* in that hospital room . . ."

Treva closed her eyes a moment, dabbing her eyelids.

"We gathered in that waiting room as a church family," Lance said. "We prayed and sang praises as a church family. And it was your words, written for this Bible study, that got us through as a church family. Your words helped us believe."

Desiree focused on Treva. She was beautiful, even more so in person. And from what Desiree had read about her online—writing the Bible study and also leading the church's women's ministry—she was perfect for Lance. But Desiree had never doubted that Lance had moved on, and happily so. She was the one forced to reckon with her own decision.

"Whether you receive it or not," Lance said, "you are anointed for such a time as this. I praise God for His hand on your life and His calling on your life." He looked out at them. "And can I just praise Him for giving me the *love* of my life?"

Cheers rang out as Lance took Treva into his arms and kissed her.

Desiree blew out a breath. *Why am I here?* This was stupid. The filming gave her a reason to come home and see her parents for the first time in a long time. She'd also planned to see if she could visit the set and do a little filming herself, for her vlog. But what did that have to do with being *here*? On the Living Word site, she'd seen the announcement about the celebration tonight. She'd wanted to slip in and just . . . see him. Or maybe, see her life as it once was, when she went to church. See what was missing that she needed to get back.

But she hadn't considered the impact of seeing him with his wife.

Treva took the microphone then took a breath. "I know Cyd's got a program," she said, "and it's not my time to talk."

"Let the Spirit flow, girl." Cyd spoke into her mic.

Desiree remembered Cyd from her time at Living Word. She'd even gone to one of her Bible studies.

"I'm just having a moment right now. Most of you have no idea . . ." Treva wiped tears. "First of all"—she looked at Lance—"I know it seems crazy to you to be pastor of this church and over this global ministry, but none of this surprised me. I knew God's hand was on you, Lance. The night before our wedding, I prayed that whatever He called you to do, I would have a heart to walk alongside. And it's my privilege to do so. I love you, babe."

Lance hugged her and held on for several seconds.

"Oh my gosh, I just love those two," a woman at Desiree's table said. "They are goals."

Treva lifted the mic again. "What Lance said about being anointed for this . . . For years I literally felt useless. I was *told* I was useless." She took another moment. "My own mother told me not to dream, not to hope, because hopes and dreams were only for *some* people—and I wasn't one of those people. 'You'll never be anything that's worth anything, Treva,' she said." She pointed a finger upward, tears streaming her face. "*But. God.*"

Women began to stand around the room.

Desiree found herself listening. Her parents had encouraged her dream of traveling the world. And over the past decade, she'd been told countless times that she was living the life most people only dreamed of. But now she was realizing what it cost her.

"I thought I was a mistake," Treva said. "I thought I had no purpose. I thought I'd never feel *wanted*. But Jesus saved me. *Me*. I did nothing to deserve it, but He *died* for me."

"Glory! Hallelujah!" rang out in the room.

"I found out that in Christ, I *do* have a purpose." Treva looked out at them. "And no matter what you've been told, you need to know that in Christ, *you* have a purpose. God prepared works for you to do before He spoke this world into existence. Guess what? That's a promise!"

More people came to their feet.

"In Christ, every one of us is anointed to be and do all that He has called us to be and do." Treva walked the platform. "And you'd better stand on *all* His promises. He calls you an overcomer in Christ. That's another promise—you *will* overcome. Who's standing on that?"

Lance raised his hand along with others in the room.

"Stand on the promise that He is *with* you, whatever you're going through," Treva said. "Stand on the promise that He'll supply your every need. Stand on the promise that nothing can separate you from His love. And listen—if you've ever felt unwanted like I did, you need to know that the Lord *chose* you." She paused. "I don't think you heard me. *Almighty God* chose you. And He will *keep* you. His love never fails. That's another what?" She cupped her ear.

"Promise!" rang out.

"We praise You, Lord." Treva's eyes closed as she lifted her hands, face turned upward. "We praise You, Jesus. You are worthy."

A piano began playing and the praise team came out.

"Before we hear our first testimony"—Cyd spoke in a low tone —"let's spend some time in worship."

As people around her stood and sang, Desiree bowed, head in her hands, ash brown hair falling overtop. Something about Treva's words. She wished she could replay them, understand what it was. It wasn't the testimony itself. Desiree had always felt loved and wanted by her parents. Maybe it was the part about promises and purpose. Wasn't that what had been bothering her of late, questions about her purpose?

She pondered it a few seconds more then stood with the rest. She'd seen enough, and now was a good time to slip out. She moved toward the door, taking one last glance toward the front. But too many people were standing. She couldn't see Lance and Treva's table.

It was just as well. Seeing Lance from a distance was already more than she could handle.

CHAPTER 38

*L*ance took Wes from Pamela outside the annex hall. "When do you give your testimony, Mom?"

"I'm last," Pamela said. "But I told you, you don't have to stay. Wes needs to go to bed."

"He'll be fine," Lance said. "I'm not missing that. I just need to go to my office for a little while so text me when it's almost time."

"If you need to do some work," Pamela said, "you know you can take Wes to the nursery."

"What you wanna do, little man?" Lance leaned closer to him, as if listening. "Wes said he wants to hang with Daddy in the office."

Pamela smiled. "As long as you're sure." She fished through the baby bag. "Everything's in here—diapers, wipes, two bottles—"

"Tell your grandma we got it," Lance said. He took the bag and put it in the stroller bin, then waved Wes's hand at her. "Bye Grammy Pam. Have fun. Don't come check on us."

Wes laughed as his hand went up and down.

"See you soon, sweet boy." Pamela kissed his cheek and went back inside.

Lance put Wes in his stroller and navigated two long corridors, making his way to the elevator. As he approached the area outside the fellowship hall, he smiled. "Who let the riff-raff in this time of night?"

Tommy turned. "The riff-raff got the keys, bruh."

"And I appreciate you," Lance said. "You make sure everything's in order whenever anything is happening here." He caught up to him. "Where you headed?"

"Why? You need something?" Tommy bent down. "Look at you, riding in style. Give me a high-five."

Wes slapped his hand, smiling.

"I'm wondering if you've got a minute," Lance said.

Tommy stood. "For?"

Lance gave him a look.

"I'm just saying . . . if you're asking as Pastor Lance, I've got a minute. Otherwise, I was about to check the delivery room because I've been waiting for these cables we need for the media—"

"I'm asking as Pastor Lance," he said. "Fifteen minutes give or take, in my office?"

Tommy hesitated. "Why do I feel like I'm being called to the principal's office?"

Heels sounded behind them in the corridor and Lance looked—and saw her.

Desiree continued toward him. "Lance. Hi." She looked beyond him. "Hey, Tommy."

"Hey, Desiree," Tommy said.

"What are you doing here?" Lance said.

"I . . ." She glanced at Tommy then back to Lance. "Can we talk for a minute?"

"No," Lance said. "I have nothing to say. You shouldn't even be here."

"I know you hate me," Desiree said. "If we could talk privately, just for a minute—"

"He said no, Desiree." Tommy looked at her. "And just so you know . . . If I'm around and there's breath in my body, you will not get near him."

Desiree looked at Tommy then at Lance. She walked around them and continued down the corridor toward the exit.

Lance headed to the elevator. "That's one thing you don't have to worry about, Tommy. I meant it. I have nothing to say to her."

"I'm not worried," Tommy said. "Just keeping watch. I can't believe she showed up here."

"That was actually unbelievable." Lance pushed the stroller into the elevator and pressed the button for the third floor.

"And if she was bold enough to do that, I don't put anything past her," Tommy said. "I always thought she was suspect anyway."

"Yeah, you did."

"Acting like she was doing you a favor because she was with you." Tommy headed to Lance's office with him. "Think she'd be here if there wasn't a movie being made about you? Or if you weren't the senior pastor? She better not try it. She ain't stepping up in here and wrecking *nothing*."

"And now she's fully aware that you've changed careers," Lance said, "from entertainment reporter to security."

"You best believe it," Tommy said.

They moved into Lance's office, and the moment the stroller stopped moving, Wes started whining, fighting to free himself.

"You're probably hungry, huh?" Lance said. "Let's see if a bottle will do it."

Wes saw the bottle and kicked his legs, reaching for it. Lance handed it to him, and he nestled back into the stroller, gulping it down.

"Now that Wes is settled," Lance said, taking a seat at the round table, "I can focus on my other son."

"Uh-oh," Tommy said, joining him. "You whipped out the Pastor Lyles hat."

"I did, didn't I?" Lance chuckled a little. "Whenever he called me 'Son,' I knew he was about to say something that would stretch me. It's different with us because you're older. But still, you're my spiritual son."

"Which you only bring up when you want to stretch me," Tommy said. "Now I'm really wondering what's up."

"I'm trying to think where to start because I already hear your objections," Lance said. "How about this? Let me lay out what I want to say, and you save your objections till the end."

"Man," Tommy said with a sigh. "If that's your intro . . ."

"Agreed?" Lance said.

"Fine."

Lance got his laptop from his desk and brought it over, clicking a few keys before he turned it around. "Check the subject lines on those emails."

Tommy leaned forward to see. "People are emailing about the cling challenge?"

"Last week I was getting emails about the cling sermon," Lance said. "People wanted me to make it into a series. Now I'm getting emails from people who are excited about the challenge and want to meet with others who are doing it."

Tommy sat back. "Okay."

"Next thing," Lance said. "At the Super Bowl party after you left, Reggie and Jesse started talking about the Cling study you're doing—"

"There's no 'Cling study,'" Tommy said. "Just Reg, Jesse, and me getting together informally."

"Aren't you looking at how people in the Bible are clinging to God?"

Tommy gave a nod.

"Call it what you want," Lance said. "They got hype talking about it, and a lot of people in the room got hype."

"Okay."

"Next thing," Lance said.

"Come on, bro, really?"

"Is that an objection?" Lance said.

"Go on."

"I was with Alonzo in the production office earlier this evening," Lance said. "You know he's been praying about ways to minister through this movie."

"Yeah, I was there when Jade elevated the blog idea to a vlog."

"Right," Lance said. "So the vlog is reaching people who are following the movie. And Living Water is producing companion studies that'll come out at the same time as the movie."

"That's dope," Tommy said, nodding. "Different ministry for different audiences."

"But Alonzo also wants something that'll minister to the cast and crew during filming." Lance checked on Wes and moved the stroller closer. "He mentioned that Cling study."

"I can talk now?" Tommy said.

"I haven't gotten to my pitch," Lance said. "Remember I told you on Sunday that the challenge filled an important need? Now I'm seeing that a lot of people could also benefit from the study you started with Reggie and Jesse." He paused. "I want you to pray about opening it up and meeting here at the church on Sunday morning. Also—"

"*Also?*"

"Also," Lance said, "you're a writer. I'm seeing a post on the Living Word site each week, where you write up that week's study. People from around the world could follow along online. And last thing—all of this would only take place during filming. Four weeks. So time would fly by." He sat back. "Done. Go."

"I don't like it."

"Of course, you don't."

"I like the small group dynamic," Tommy said. "We can talk about things that people don't want to talk about in a larger setting."

"You can always keep meeting with Reggie and Jesse," Lance said. "But also, a lot of the larger groups break into smaller groups. Or I've seen where they get into deep discussions even in the larger group. The Spirit can move in any setting."

"Second objection," Tommy said. "I don't write devotion type stuff. That's Reggie's lane."

"How long has Reggie been writing?"

"On the job?" Tommy shrugged. "Two years maybe."

"How long have you been writing?"

Tommy simply looked at him.

"Humor me," Lance said.

"Over twenty."

"Next objection."

"Okay," Tommy said. "You're talking about leading a group *and* writing something up. Who has time for that on top of everything else?"

"Now *that* objection I was waiting for," Lance said. "Remember when you were telling me about your call to singleness and you pulled out the verse about having so much more time to devote to the Lord?"

"Oh, you're real funny."

Wes started fussing again and threw his bottle down.

"Trust me, Wes, I feel you," Tommy said, taking him out. He sat him on his lap.

"You're done with your objections?" Lance said.

"Here's another," Tommy said. "You're not talking about a prepared study situation where I'm only facilitating. I'd have to come up with study material week to week and basically teach it." He shifted Wes over his shoulder. "You can't just stick somebody in a position like that. You have to look at gifting. That's not my gift."

"Who said it's not?" Lance said.

"What do you mean?" Tommy said. "It's just not."

"I remember when we launched Living Hope," Lance said, "a lot of people wanted to continue the weekly Bible study I had been doing. Cedric took it over but you filled in a lot of weeks."

Tommy thought a moment as he patted Wes's back. "How did I forget about that?"

"Probably because it only lasted a few months," Lance said. "But you prepared study material and taught it. Cedric and I both felt you were gifted to teach."

"Neither of you said anything," Tommy said.

"He wouldn't have asked you to continue if he didn't think it was in your lane," Lance said. "But you became a deacon around that time and *that* was so much your thing that the teaching went by the wayside." He paused, thinking. "That was unfortunate. I wish I had nurtured that more in you."

"We were doing a thousand things starting a new church," Tommy said. "You can't be going back wishing you had done a thousand and one."

"Yeah, but you didn't even remember," Lance said. "And with everything that's happened, you mostly just shy away from opportunities to minister, like you're doing now." He looked at him. "You don't want to minister because you think you've been disqualified."

Tommy focused on Wes, bouncing him on a knee.

"Another divorce," Lance said. "So your spiritual gifts need to stay in hibernation until you can earn your way back into God's good graces."

"How am I in hibernation when I'm the head deacon, in charge of the buildings in the Living Word complex, and twenty other things?"

"I'm not minimizing that," Lance said. "Your servant spirit is a tremendous blessing to this body. But you can do that in your sleep. Anything that requires faith and trusting God or believing that God wants to use you—you push back." He sat forward. "That's why I'm excited about this cling challenge. I see God working. I just want you to lean all the way into it. Receive the grace He's made available. Let Him use you."

"Hey, hey! The brothers." Cedric appeared in the doorway. "Y'all need to come down to the annex."

"I was waiting for Mom to tell me when she's giving her testimony," Lance said. "But meanwhile I'm talking to Tommy. Why, what's up?"

"There's this surprise that came together at the last minute," Cedric said. "That's all I can say. But I want you two to see it."

"Is it happening right now?" Lance said. "How much time do we have?"

"I think they have about three more testimonies," Cedric said. "Probably thirty minutes or so."

Lance nodded. "Cool. Come in. Before we do that, let's do this."

"What?" Cedric said, walking in.

"Let me read something." Lance got his Bible from his desk and flipped to the verse he wanted. "Paul said to Timothy, 'For this reason I remind you to kindle afresh the gift of God which is in you through the laying on of my hands. For God has not given you a spirit of timidity, but of power and love and discipline.'" He set the Bible down. "I've been talking to Tommy about walking in faith and the gifts God has given him. I'd love for us to lay hands on him right now and pray over him."

"I can't think of anything better to do with my time." Cedric moved closer to Tommy. "Matter of fact, I'll return to do the same every night this week, if we have to."

Tommy gave him a look. "And what exactly are you trying to say?"

"I'm not *trying* to say anything," Cedric said. "I'm *saying* hallelujah, glory to God, ditto, and amen to whatever Lance told you."

Tommy nodded soberly. "So it's like that, huh?"

"It's like that." Cedric stood over Tommy and placed his hands on his shoulder, next to Lance. "All in love, my brother."

CHAPTER 39

*J*ordyn walked across the annex toward her table, hoping not to distract as a woman gave her testimony on the platform. Moving back into her seat, she collected herself, unsure about the decision she'd just made.

"Where'd you go?" Jade whispered.

Jordyn leaned toward her. "I was talking to Mom."

"Why would you be talking to Mom?"

"Because she's our *mom*."

"You know what I mean," Jade said. "When you're upset about something, Mom is not your go-to."

Jordyn took a glance around to make sure they weren't talking loudly. Brooke sat to her left, but she was preoccupied with her phone.

"I had to call her," Jordyn said. "I need to get away."

Jade looked at her. "You're going to visit Mom and the husband?"

"No need to call him that anymore." Jordyn leaned even closer. "Mom said their marriage has been annulled."

Jade gave her a blank stare. "So basically the wedding I refused to attend never happened." She shook her head. "Why was it annulled?"

"She called him a cheat and a fraud or something," Jordyn said, "but I really didn't care. I was just glad he wasn't there because it made me sure about my decision. I asked if I could come for an extended visit."

"How extended?" Jade said.

Applause rang out as the testimony ended.

"I don't know," Jordyn said, clapping with the rest. "I just need some time."

"We've got one more giveaway," Cyd said, taking to the platform, "before our last testimony . . ."

Brooke touched Jordyn's arm. "You're good friends with Jesse, right?" She smiled, phone in hand. "Is he always hilarious? We're on a group text with our mutual friend in Maryland—you should see how long the text chain is—and I cannot stop laughing."

Jordyn didn't know what to say, but turned out she didn't need to say anything. Brooke's thumb was moving a mile a minute as she replied to the next text that popped in, laughing out loud. Jordyn turned and looked at Jade.

"What?" Jade said.

She leaned to Jade's ear. "I'm ready to go."

"Oh, but this time *I'm* the one who drove," Jade said. "And I want to see Miss Pam's testimony." She shrugged. "Feel free to Uber home."

Jordyn rolled her eyes.

"Hey, Jade." Mariah called from across the table. "This is the first time I've had a moment to check out the vlog. You're planning to do this every day?"

"Only during the week," Jade said, "when you're rehearsing or shooting."

"This is excellent." Mariah looked back down at it. "I'm impressed with your editing."

"Wow, that's everything," Jade said. "Thank you for even taking a look."

"Yeah, me and a million others," Mariah said. "Couldn't ask for better marketing."

"Every testimony we've heard tonight has been incredible," Cyd said. "And this last testimony you're about to hear . . ."

"Oh my gosh—he did not say that!" Brooke whispered to herself, but she may as well have had a megaphone.

Jordyn grabbed her purse from the table and leaned toward Jade. "I'm getting an Uber."

"Jordyn, no," Jade said. "I was just kidding."

"I knew I wasn't in the mood to begin with," Jordyn said. "I should've stayed home."

"But it's almost over," Jade said.

"I'll see you at home."

Jordyn left the annex with Brooke's giggles in her head. Jesse's mood certainly wasn't affected by the breakup like Jordyn's. He was having a good ol' time.

She opened the app as she walked, scheduled a ride, and heard the giggles again. How did they wind up at the same table anyway? *Oh.* She knew why. Jade was now fast friends with Brooke and Mariah. She'd seen them looking for a table and waved them over. Jade, the rising star in Alonzo's production company. Next thing you know, he'd appoint her over marketing for all of his independent films. Or maybe Mariah would tap her to join her editing team. Something big and amazing while Jordyn camped out with a broken heart and a mother she could barely stand.

She waited in the foyer and spied a flyer for tonight's event. *Promises of God.* Yeah. Whatever.

CHAPTER 40

*J*illian stood in the shadows listening as Pamela shared her testimony. The two of them had spent the evening serving along with others and missed parts of the program. So she was thankful she got to hear this powerful wrap-up.

Her phone vibrated and she looked at it. A text from Stephanie— **Wondered where you were and just spotted you. You've been moving all night. Come sit with us. Joy and Hope left so I've got a seat right beside me.**

Jillian had seen it. But she'd also seen Lance and Tommy come in and sit at that same table.

She texted a reply. **Thanks girl, but I'm fine.**

Jillian's phone vibrated a moment later.

This entire evening sucks and I need somebody who gets my misery. SO WHAT if Tommy's at the table. :/

Jillian texted—***heavy sigh***—and made her way over there, scooting into the chair.

Stephanie leaned to her ear. "You love me."

Jillian whispered back. "You owe me."

"That's the thing about believing." Pamela walked the platform in black pants and a chic white blouse, her salt and pepper hair in a twist-out. "You get disappointed, knocked down—and you have to believe *again*. When my petition for release got denied, there was nothing in me that wanted to believe again. Disappointment *hurts*. You start thinking you were crazy to believe the first time. So when Treva said she was appealing the decision, my faith said—*I'll sit this one out*. Anybody been there?"

Jillian and Stephanie looked at one another as chatter bubbled throughout the room.

"But the Lord wouldn't let me rest," Pamela continued. "Anybody been *there*? Where He keeps nudging you because you can't let your faith ride the bench. Without faith it's impossible to please God!"

"Bring it, Mom," Lance uttered. "So good."

"He kept telling me to believe," Pamela said. "He kept reminding me that with Him, all things are possible. So I said, 'I need help, Lord. Help my unbelief.'" She paused near their table. "God answered that prayer through Treva. She didn't give up when that first petition was denied. She said, 'Pam, the door is still open. How is this too hard for God? I'm appealing and I'm believing.' Her faith helped increase *my* faith."

Lance put his arm around Treva and whispered something to her as she held Wes, who was asleep.

"God will do that," Pamela said. "He'll put people in your life who will believe *for* you and help you get up off that bench. It's a problem if everybody around you is riding the no-faith bench. Get some people around you with big faith!"

A few people stood, affirming what she said.

"Here I was, all pessimistic about the appeal," Pamela said, "and God had put someone on the appeal board who knew and loved this church and Pastor Mason Lyles. *And* He moved Treva to mention that my son preached the eulogy at Pastor Lyles's funeral. I suddenly had *favor* on that board. Twenty-year prison sentence with nine more years to go, but I was *free*."

Almost all stood to their feet now, praising God.

"All things are possible," Pamela said. "We have to believe, then believe again, and no matter what it looks like, believe *again*." She paused. "I wasn't planning to say this part but the Spirit is prompting me to tell on myself. I had to believe again just this week." She started walking. "I never learned to drive and didn't think it was possible at my age. I was *afraid* to learn—let me put it like that. But Tommy Porter—I call him one of my sons—believed *for* me."

Stephanie elbowed Jillian. Jillian nudged her back.

"He's got me taking baby steps, but today I started studying to get my permit." She waited for the cheers to die down. "But pray for me, y'all. Tommy said I'm getting behind the wheel and driving as soon as I get it."

Chuckles sounded in the room. "You can do it, Miss Pam!" someone yelled.

"I know I'm past my time," Pamela said. "I just want you to know that it doesn't end. You'll keep being challenged to believe. And we have to keep believing. All things are possible—with God."

Applause and chatter filled the room as Cyd returned to the platform. She hugged Pamela on the way.

"Praising God for you, Pam," Cyd said, "and for all of the women who shared tonight. I don't know about you all"—she looked into the crowd—"but these testimonies have challenged me to believe on a higher level. God has moved mightily—not just in the lives of people in the Bible—in the lives of people here in this room. That should encourage us."

Jillian turned to Cinda. "Yours brought me to tears, the way you talked about finding your father after all those years, then losing him tragically, then how your heavenly Father drew you with *If I Come*." She shook her head. "My heart was all over the place."

"You see I couldn't hold it together myself," Cinda said.

"And if you didn't receive one of the giveaways," Cyd was saying, "I'm excited to tell you that if you'd like a copy of the *Promises* study, it's yours. We'll have them on your way out." She paused as people clapped. "But we're not done yet." Cyd stepped aside as two stools

271

were brought onto the platform. "I told you we had a surprise, and I can finally share. I won't even get into how it came together—I'll just say it was nothing but God. But it means so much to me personally because this is my sister-in-law."

"What?" Stephanie sat up in her seat. "Is Kelli here?"

"But some of you may know Kelli and her husband Brian, also known as Alien, from their Grammy and Dove-award winning albums." Cyd waited again for the clapping to die down. "Kelli has written a song specially for this celebration, called *Promises*, and they're here to perform it tonight. Come on out, Kelli and Brian!"

Kelli and Brian walked out to excited applause, many of the people standing. Stephanie had been the first at their table to stand. Hands to her face, she was already overcome.

Kelli and Brian sat on the stools, mics in hand, gesturing for people to sit.

"It's so good to be home!" Kelli smiled as people cheered at that. She glowed in denim, a glittery top, and heels. "St. Louis is home, but also—Living Word is home. Brian and I were part of this church for many years before we moved to Nashville. We love this place, don't we, babe?"

"Living Word will always be home to us." Brian had on black jeans and a black leather jacket. "Shout out and much love to Pastor Lance and Treva. This is our first trip back since Lance became pastor, but we're always in touch. We travel a lot, so Lance hits me up, like—'Are y'all good?' And if you know Lance, what he's *really* saying is—'Whatever with the so-called fame—are you keeping your head and heart in check?'" He looked over at them. "I love you for that, Lance."

Lance tapped his heart and pointed at him.

"And I met Treva almost three years ago when she came here for the women's conference," Kelli said. "*And* I was in the room when she met Pastor Lance so I feel like I saw the initial spark." She smiled at them. "Treva, I told Cyd I needed a Bible study that would remind me of God's faithfulness, and she sent the *Promises* study. I can't begin to tell you how it ministered to me, so much so that I heard a song in my head. And I couldn't let it go. I told Brian we needed to record it, and it didn't make sense because we had just finished recording our next album. But I just knew we needed to."

"So we did," Brian said. "And we loved how it turned out, so Kel sent it to Cyd. And Cyd got excited about playing it tonight during the release celebration."

"Then at the last minute one of our dates fell through," Kelli said. "And Brian and I looked at each other, thinking the same thing—what if we actually went?"

"So we thank God for the opportunity to be here with you tonight," Brian said. "And we hope you enjoy this song."

Kelli got up and went to the grand piano as Brian moved the stools out of the way.

She started playing the keys softly. "One more thing I want to say before we get into the song . . . I love how God works. Miss Pam just gave her testimony on the promise that if we believe, all things are possible with God. And she said sometimes you need people in your life who will believe *for* you." Her fingers glided across the keys with a beautiful melody. "I'll never forget a season in my life when the person who helped me believe was my sister-in-law, Stephanie London."

Stephanie looked more intently at Kelli, as if hearing the story for the first time.

"I didn't believe God could use me in music," Kelli said. "I wasn't pursuing it and didn't think it was possible. And Steph *kept* reminding me of that promise—'All things are possible, Kelli. *All things.*' She got me to go to a songwriter's conference, which led to a string of events that got me back with Brian, my high school sweetheart, in a collab on his second album." She looked out at the crowd. "Steph, we wouldn't be here if you hadn't let God use you in such a big way. Your faith inspired *me* to believe and made God's promises come alive in my life. This song is dedicated to you."

Jillian swished in her purse and handed Stephanie a pack of tissues for the tears streaming down her face. She put a hand to her shoulder. "Cyd knew you needed to be here."

Kelli changed up the chords and moved into the song.

273

All things are possible with You

She sang slowly, deliberately.

But is it possible for me to believe?

Oh, is it possible for me to believe . . . Her voice hung in the air then she paused before finishing—*believe all Your promises to us.*

The music track kicked in, and Kelli got up from the piano, taking the mic with her. Brian came back on stage, moving with the up-tempo beat.

"Come on and praise with us," Kelli said. "Here's the hook!"

Even though I stumble
You've got me by the hand
That's Your promise to us
You strengthen us to stand
If I believe
All things are possible with you because
That's Your promise to us

The whole room was on its feet, clapping and moving to the beat, including Cedric and Cyd who were near the front.

"This is my testimony," Kelli said. "Can anybody relate to this?" She continued singing—

No, I never been the one with giant faith
I never even believed I could go big when I prayed
Don't need a lot of suspense
Doubt just seemed to make sense
No use trying to raise my expectations
But the more I spent time in Your word
It's like a fire that got everything all stirred
Your promises for us
Abundant in Your love
I'm trusting every word

Brian came center stage, rapping his part. Kelli stayed alongside, moving with him.

Lord, I'm trusting every word
But it's so hard to believe
I'm just being honest, Lord

See, my heart is on my sleeve
And I don't know the future
But I do know how to cling
So I'll cling to the promises You made to me
Every one You gave to me
"Say it with us!" Kelli said. "Sing it like you believe it!"
Even though I stumble
You've got me by the hand
That's Your promise to us . . .

~

Jillian hugged Treva at the table as the evening concluded. "What a night. So amazing."

"What a night, indeed," Treva said. "Desiree was here."

"What?" Jillian said. "She was halfway around the world when she filmed that video."

"Lance ran into her earlier this evening," Treva said. "She said she wanted to talk to him."

"No way," Jillian said. "And what happened?"

"He told her he had nothing to say," Treva said. "And Tommy told her she wasn't getting near Lance."

"Tommy and that protective nature." Jillian glanced over at him. "I wonder why she came. And what could she possibly have to say to Lance?"

"Girl, I don't know," Treva said. "It'd be one thing to come to a church service. Why would she come tonight—"

"Mamamamamama!"

"Are you calling me, sweet boy?" Treva took him from Lance as he continued to babble with excitement. "This little boy is so off his schedule. It's late and he's about to be up for hours."

Jillian chuckled as Wes replied with greater excitement. "Yup. You had your party, now he's about to have his."

Treva nodded as Lance motioned to her. "All right, we're heading out," she said, hugging her again. "Thanks for everything tonight, Jill."

"My pleasure," Jillian said. "Your little sis is thrilled about all that God is doing in your life."

Jillian shouldered her bag, ready to go herself. She needed to be up extra early to fix breakfast, but Mariah and Brooke were riding with her. And Mariah was talking to Tommy.

She glanced around. Stephanie had left with Cyd and Cedric. Cinda was gone. Jillian had wanted to talk to Jordyn to see what was going on, since she seemed sad, but looked like she was gone too.

Jillian walked over to Brooke. "You guys about ready to go?"

Brooke looked up from her phone. "I don't know about Mariah, but I'm ready."

Jillian sighed inside. Would it sound dumb to ask Brooke to go get Mariah? Or maybe Brooke could tell Mariah to get a ride back with Tommy. Or maybe if they started making their way toward the exit—

"Hey, sorry, was I holding things up?" Mariah said, joining them. "This was such a great night."

"It really was," Jillian said, walking out with them.

"I'll tell you," Mariah said, "between the testimonies, worship music, and Kelli and Brian's music ministry, my faith got *such* a boost. I feel like God is saying, 'Stop with the wavering belief.'"

"Amen," Brooke said. "I don't know how many levels of conviction I'm gonna get about my life right now, but in a strange way, it feels good. Like God is bringing me out of one season and taking me into another."

"Wow, Brooke," Jillian said, "that's a testimony in itself."

"And it's about to make me shout," Mariah said. "That's what I've been praying for—a new season. I'm thankful for what God is doing with my career, even for the freedom I've had to pursue certain things. But on the personal side, I've been saying—how long, Lord?"

Brooke looked at her. "As far as getting married?"

Mariah nodded. "For a long time, I didn't think about it much. Then you look up and *years* have gone by." She moved closer as a group of women passed. "I was starting to think it was too late for me. But the way God moved to get me on this project, and everything that's stemming from it, including tonight . . . I know He's saying —*believe*."

"Okay?" Brooke said. "I think we *all* got that word tonight."

Jillian pushed the door and held it for them, then continued outside, suddenly unsure whether she even had a takeaway from this evening.

CHAPTER 41

"And I thought you were bawling because you missed us so much." Kelli sat with Brian on the loveseat in Cyd's family room.

"That *is* what started the waterworks." Stephanie had the reclining chair. "But you're Lindell's sister, so I thought about how much he'd hate that he wasn't here to see you. Then I thought—*I'm* supposed to be on an island upset that I wasn't here."

"I'm confused, though." Brian leaned forward. "I get that you and Lindell had an argument on vacation—it happens. But how did you actually get on a plane and leave the island?"

"What do you mean—how?" Stephanie said.

"Like—who does that?" Brian said.

Cedric chuckled from the sofa. "All these years of knowing Steph, and you're surprised by that?"

"Meaning what?" Stephanie said. "I'm trying to see if I should be offended."

"Hey, I don't know what the argument was about"—Cedric spread his hands—"but I know when you've had it—you've had it. You packed up and left Hope Springs *and Lindell* the weekend of that women's conference. And you know what? My brother needed the wake-up call. Maybe he needed this one too."

Cyd leaned against the sofa, on the floor with their dog Reese. "It sounds like the tears were partly because you felt you should still be on the island. Do you regret leaving, maybe a little?"

Stephanie thought a moment. "Maybe a little. But I mostly regret that I'm not the person Kelli talked about in that dedication. That's what really moved me to tears. I can't believe I was the 'all things are possible' cheerleader. Maybe I wouldn't have left the island if that had been *anywhere* in my mind." She sighed. "It's hard to even remember that mindset."

"My memory is vivid," Kelli said. "You were like a drill sergeant the weekend of that songwriter's conference, telling us we were believing —*period*. Remember Cyd?"

"Oh, goodness, yes," Cyd said. "We said if nothing happens for Kelli, at least we'll have a weekend together as sisters. Steph chastised us for having low expectations."

"And that's how you flowed through that whole weekend," Kelli said. "We found out it was too late for me to submit a song for critique, and what did you do? You prayed for God to move the mountain!"

Stephanie shook her head at the remembrance. "What was I *on*?"

"Then you came up to me and introduced yourself to see if I could get Kelli's music heard," Brian said. "Kelli wasn't even speaking to me at the time. But because you believed, you gave me an opportunity to help her. And ultimately, you helped me get back into her life."

Stephanie stared vaguely. "I don't know how to get back to that place. I don't know how to believe like that again." She heaved a sigh. "But what I *do* know is that it's hard to ignore you two showing up to remind me of all of this."

Kelli nodded. "And dedicating a song to you about God's promises when I didn't even know what you were going through."

"If I ever wondered whether God speaks to me . . ." Stephanie sighed again. "But why is it always the stuff I don't want to hear?" She thought a moment. "I feel like I need to go back to the island, but how dumb is that? I literally just got here."

"Got here in time to get some encouragement," Kelli said, "so you can go back and finish the week strong."

"But it doesn't make sense to go back," Stephanie said. "Lindell used all of his miles on our tickets. And if I buy a last-minute, astronomically priced ticket, me and cost-conscious Lindell will have something else to argue about. *And* how about—I'm in my third trimester. I can't be doing all this flying."

"What did your OB say?" Cyd said. "I know you talked to her before the trip."

Stephanie sighed. "She said she had no worries. That baby and I are doing well and I'm free to travel until I hit thirty-six weeks. But still—insert my other reasons. I don't need to go. He'll be back soon enough."

"And you'll be back in the whirlwind of B and B life," Cyd said. "The very thing you needed time away from. That beautiful island setting is still the best place for you two to be right now."

"Well, too bad I can't blink or click my heels together to get there."

"Can you wake up at five in the morning?" Cedric raised his phone. "Found you a flight. I'll book it."

"Why would you do that?" Stephanie said. "I wouldn't even let you."

"Listen," Cedric said, "you all reminded me of everything God did with Kelli back then. There's nothing I wouldn't do for my little sister, but Steph, God used *you* to spark healing, direction, purpose, and even love in her life. And all of that has multiplied in the form of ministry to others." He spoke with sincere earnestness. "Honestly, that would be enough right there. I would bless you just for being a huge blessing to Kelli." He paused. "But that's not what this is."

Stephanie focused on Cedric, wondering where he was going.

"You're my sister too, Steph," Cedric said. "Through Cyd *and* Lindell—I couldn't get rid of you if I tried." He smiled. "I want you to know there's nothing I wouldn't do for you as well. I know this is a hard time, and I want to be there for you and Lindell. Let me buy the ticket."

Stephanie bowed her head a little. "I wish y'all would stop tugging on my emotions tonight." She let a moment pass before she looked at Cedric. "Thank you, bro. You know the love is mutual. But as far as the ticket, I haven't talked to Lindell. What if he's planning to fly back tomorrow?"

"He's coming back Friday," Cedric said.

"How do you know?" Stephanie said.

"I texted him ten minutes ago," Cedric said. "I wasn't buying a ticket and convincing you to go without making sure he'd be there."

"So now I have no excuse," Stephanie said, "except—did I say how dumb this is? How am I supposed to get on a plane and go back to that island?"

Brian quirked his brow at her. "Did you really just ask the same question that I asked?"

"Nope," Stephanie said. "It's totally different in reverse."

~

I know, Lord. Sometimes You hear from me. Sometimes You don't.

Stephanie boarded the early morning flight with the same bags she'd packed a few days before. She settled into a window seat.

I talked to You about my frustrations on the way to the island. But I don't think I said a word once we got there. I know I wasn't talking to You while I was thinking about Warren on that balcony—which is when I needed *to talk to You, to ask for help.* She shook her head at herself. *And I certainly didn't consult You in my decision to leave. Forgive me, Lord.*

Stephanie stared out of the window. *It's hard to talk to You in those times, Lord. When my flesh kicks in, I want what I want and I figure I'll deal with the consequences later. Which makes no sense because I never like the consequences.* She sighed. *I know I'm strong-willed. I know my will needs to be submitted to Yours. But when I'm in the moment—*

"Ma'am, your bag needs to go all the way under the seat."

Stephanie nodded at the flight attendant and pushed her bag with her foot then closed her eyes as people filed by.

Lord should I let him know I'm coming? I didn't plan to. I was just gonna show up, mostly because I still don't know what to say to him. Plus I have an attitude because he only reached out once, to ask if I made it back safely.

She opened her eyes as a couple joined her in her row, acknowledging them with a smile. Thankfully, they were engaged in conversation with each other. She closed her eyes again—then opened them. And got out her phone. The nudge was unmistakable.

Lord, why do You always answer clearly when it's something I don't want to do?

Stephanie stared at the empty text screen. *What do I say, Lord? I can keep it simple, right? What about just—I'm on a plane headed back.*

She contemplated a few moments more, then typed it out. **I'm on a plane headed back.** She paused another few seconds. *Why should I apologize, Lord? How about he be the one to apologize?*

The announcement sounded to switch phones to airplane mode. Stephanie had no problem waiting until her layover to finish the text, but she couldn't ignore the prompting she felt. She continued.

I'm sorry for leaving. I prioritized myself and my feelings over our marriage, and I'm feeling a little convicted—she backspaced—**I'm feeling convicted.** She paused again, wondering how to end it. **I come with no expectations**—she sighed and backspaced—**I'm praying.**

Stephanie stared out of the window as the taxi pulled up to the house. Arriving just as the sun set, she was reminded how breathtaking the villa was. She could even see the sun glistening off of the ocean behind it. If nothing else, she'd be sure to get in some beach time. As for Lindell, who knew? He only "liked" her text to let her know he saw it.

Stephanie paid the fare and got out, waiting as the driver took her bags from the trunk. She'd taken off her jacket on the plane, leaving a white V-neck and coral colored kimono. But the breeze from the ocean was making her long for that jacket.

The front door opened, and Lindell came out in long beach shorts and a tee, looking like he'd been fully enjoying himself on the island. He extended his credit card to the driver.

"I already paid him," Stephanie said.

Lindell put it in his pocket, grabbed her bags, and walked back into the house.

Stephanie moved aside as the taxi backed out and left, then stood in place, staring after him. Did he really just come out here and not greet his wife?

This is that stuff that makes me want to go off, Lord. After I traveled all this way, he has nothing to say? Help me not to go in with guns blazing. But can I take 'em out of the holster?

Stephanie moved up the walkway and into the house, taking it in once again. From the entryway, she could inhale the ocean air, savor the sound of seagulls. She moved into the living space on the first floor. Open and airy with tall ceilings and windows all around, she could see him on the patio, looking out at the water. If the setting itself weren't so inviting, she might leave him to himself. But it helped her do what she knew she needed to do—go talk to him.

She opened the patio door and walked out, the cross breeze lifting the fringes of her kimono. She should've gotten her jacket. That was her first thought. But she continued to a chair next to Lindell, and they sat quietly, both watching the waves and a smattering of people walking the shoreline.

Lindell looked at her. "Are you and the baby doing okay?"

"As far as I can tell," Stephanie said.

Several seconds elapsed.

"I was angry that you would leave like that." He stared out at the water. "It took me a while to pray, and when I did, I prayed that God would convict you. But I'm the one who got convicted."

"About what?"

Lindell let a few more seconds pass. "I need to be honest about something." He looked over at her. "I already knew you'd been thinking about Warren."

Stephanie's heart lurched. "What do you mean?"

"One evening a few months ago I came home," Lindell said, "and you were having a prayer meeting with Jillian in the dining room. And I heard you say . . ." He paused. "I heard you say you were unfulfilled in our love life and that you'd been having thoughts about Warren."

Stephanie felt her arms begin to shake, and it wasn't from the breeze.

"And then you said—"

"I know what I said." She couldn't bear to hear him go on. "So, I was confessing some things to Jillian and asking for prayer, and you stood there and listened? And didn't tell me?"

"I could say the same to you," Lindell said. "You could've told me what you were dealing with." He looked away again. "But once I heard that, no, I couldn't talk to you about it. It was demoralizing. Whatever issues I already had in the bedroom—they only got bigger."

"But the fact that I was asking for prayer—didn't you see that as a positive?"

"I didn't walk away with anything positive." Lindell looked at her. "My wife had another man on her mind."

Stephanie was the one to look away this time.

"But I did realize later that you were obviously concerned about it," Lindell said. "And I knew that you—*we*—needed prayer. The vacation seemed like the perfect answer." He let more time elapse. "I really was tired that first night. And you were talking about how romantic everything was, and I just felt like you expected the night of a lifetime. I didn't want to disappoint you."

"Lindell, I didn't have any huge expectations," Stephanie said. "I just wanted to be with you. It felt like you were avoiding all romance."

"I know it's hard for you to understand," Lindell said. "When everything seems perfect for romance, I feel like I can't measure up. If I'm honest, I have more confidence when *you're* tired. Then I feel I won't let you down." He sighed. "And to be fair, I've always felt that way. It just shot through the roof after I heard that conversation."

"Babe, I'm so sorry." Stephanie turned more toward him. "I hate that you heard that. It sheds so much light on the issues we've had. But it gives me hope that we *can* get past this."

"How does it give you hope?" Lindell said. "I was even more discouraged when you said you were thinking about Warren *again*, right here on vacation."

"But that's my point," Stephanie said. "He didn't come to mind until I felt rejected and alone. If we communicate what we're thinking and feeling, I believe we'll get to a better place." She paused. "But I'm sorry again for leaving. I should've—"

"No, I'm sorry," Lindell said. "You wanted to make love, and I was in my feelings about Warren."

"And I understand that even more now."

"But I gave him too much of a place in my mind," Lindell said. "The reality is that your relationship with him ended years ago. And whatever memories you're battling, it's only that—memories. He's not even in the picture at this point."

Stephanie nodded, her heart racing. Now was not the time to tell him.

"I read the 'warfare' verses you talked about in First Corinthians seven," Lindell said. "That's a big part of what convicted me. No matter how I'm feeling, we do need time together."

Stephanie nodded again, making no assumptions, certainly no overtures.

Lindell got up and extended his hand, helping her up.

"You ready to go to dinner?" Stephanie said.

"We definitely can," Lindell said. "I'm sure you and the baby are hungry." He paused. "But I was thinking we'd head upstairs."

"I got a turkey wrap in the terminal when the plane landed," Stephanie said.

"You think that'll hold you?"

Stephanie followed, her hand in his. "There's no doubt in my mind."

CHAPTER 42

"*A*re you two gonna play or kiss for real?" Jade looked at Alonzo and Cinda through the back of her camera.

"Is this supposed to be like an on-screen kiss?" Alonzo said.

"Do you kiss your real-life wife like you kiss on screen?" Jade said.

"It's no different," Alonzo said.

Cinda pinched his side.

"*Ow.*" Alonzo wrapped his arms around her. "You know I'm messing with you, baby. Kiss me."

Their lips came together, Cinda's arms encircling his waist, Alonzo pulling her closer still.

"Woo-hoo!" A few crew members stopped packing up and came near, clapping.

"Yessss!" Jade said, smiling. "That's the energy we need!"

Cinda covered her face. "So embarrassing."

"Oh, stop it." Jade watched it back on her camera. "Wait till you see how I'm about to edit this."

"But it's a ministry moment," Cinda said. "Zee interviews me about my faith story and how God put me on the path to be a stylist. And then we just *kiss* after that?"

"No, silly, that's not how it'll look on the vlog," Jade said. "The ministry moment will be its own segment. But since you're the ministry moment, we *have* to play up the fact that you're Alonzo's wife." She did a quick YouTube search on her phone. "Look at this —'Every Alonzo Coles Kiss On Screen.'"

"Somebody put a video together like that?" Alonzo said.

"Several somebodies," Jade said. "It's a thing. You're known for romance. So I'll edit up a similar montage, the music will build, and it'll be like—*boom*—none of that compares with his *real* leading lady." Her shoulders did a jig. "The vlog for the fourth day of rehearsals is about to be fire."

"I'm with it," Alonzo said. "You need another take?"

"The only other take I'm doing is at home tonight," Cinda said.

"Aye, I'm with that too," Alonzo said. He stole a kiss from her before moving to talk to Mariah.

"Cinda, thank you for doing the ministry moment," Jade said. "When I heard your testimony at the *Promises* celebration, I knew we had to include it in the vlog." She packed up her camera bag. "It was hard to hear, though."

"I was trying not to delve too much into what happened between me, you, Jordyn, and your mom," Cinda said. "I didn't want it to be awkward."

"But that's your testimony," Jade said. "We treated you horribly. Basically drove you out of the house. God led you to the B and B, and you literally got saved there." She shook her head. "I don't have a problem with you keeping it one hundred. You heard my own testimony on day one of the vlog. I *know* how awful I was."

Cinda extended her arms and Jade walked into them. "I think we need these regularly, just because."

"I am so not a hugger," Jade said. "But yours are low-key special."

Cinda sighed. "I wish Randall were here with us now. Sometimes I think about what it would be like, with all of us together as a family. And how's Jordyn doing, by the way? I haven't talked to her since she left for Chicago."

"I haven't talked to her either," Jade said. "She texted to let me know she got there, though."

"I'm praying for her," Cinda said. "This breakup with Jesse hit her really hard."

"For her to go stay with Mom?" Jade nodded. "Yeah, she's going through."

Brooke walked up. "Cinda, I'm headed with you to wardrobe, right?"

"Yes, ma'am," Cinda said. "We're working on the wedding dress."

"Ahh," Brooke said, beaming. "Why am I so excited about that?"

"Because you already know," Jade said. "When I first saw Kendra walking down the aisle in that video, I said, 'Ohhh, is *that* what we're doing??'"

"Exactly," Brooke said. "And you know I'm about to soak it up as if I'm really getting married."

"Girl, you'd better," Jade said, smiling.

"Okay, we need to get moving." Cinda had three bags in tow. "The original designer of the dress is meeting us over there."

Brooke looked at Jade, wide-eyed.

"Cinda really did just drop that like it was nothing," Jade said. "Soak it up for both of us." She shouldered her camera bag and a tote bag and followed them toward the door.

"Hey, are we leaving?" Trey called from the kitchen.

Jade looked back. "I don't know about 'we,' but *I'm* leaving."

"I love that you're mean by default," Trey said, walking toward her. "I thought we were doing the dinner thing."

Jade looked at him. "You can't be serious. I had a vlog to edit last night, but you got me to go grocery shopping *and* cook for you. And you think we're doing it again tonight?"

"Not the grocery shopping, obviously," Trey said. "But don't you have to cook anyway?"

"Not necessarily," Jade said. "I'll order delivery in a heartbeat."

"But you *can* cook," Trey said. "And I've got all this food now. So I figured you could whip something up and we could talk—or not. You can focus on your editing. But you have to admit we had a good time talking, and you still got your work done."

"Later than I wanted to," Jade said. "But you're right, about the fun. I haven't laughed that much since . . . never." She added quickly, "If I'm cooking, it'll be something easy like spaghetti. And I'll make meatballs with the turkey, Caesar on the side, and some garlic toast. That's it, so if you don't like it, too bad."

Trey took a moment to respond. "I probably shouldn't tell you my alternative was a can of soup."

～

Jade hunched over her laptop at the island in Trey's kitchen. "So can we talk about how you ended up on a mission field?" She looked up. "I can't imagine giving up life as I know it and spending two years in Africa. What made you do that?"

Trey put their plates in the dishwasher. "Didn't you just say we needed to stop talking so you could work on the vlog?"

"That was a few minutes ago," Jade said. "Right now I'm uploading clips, so I can multitask."

"All right, I'll give you the brief version." Trey sat next to her at the island. "I heard this missionary at Living Word one Sunday morning —hadn't been to church in forever. This was during Kendra's illness."

"What made you go that particular day?" Jade said.

"Lance was at the house and in my ear," Trey said. "So God was working on me day and night. One Sunday I woke up and just felt this urge to go. When I got there, I knew why. I needed to hear that man's message."

"I'm guessing he was sharing about his experiences?" Jade said.

Trey nodded. "Told stories, gave us a picture of what life was like. But then he started talking about *our* lives—how we want everything comfortable and predictable. He said, 'But some of you are called to live outside the box' . . . I moved to the edge of my seat. Everything in me was like—*pay attention.*"

"Okay, this is interesting," Jade said.

289

Trey continued. "He said, 'You might not realize it yet, but your life is not meant to be ordinary. You're not meant to have the comfortable spouse, kids, cat, and dog. Maybe you won't marry at all.'"

"Whoa."

"But wait, it gets better," Trey said.

Jade gave him a look. "Depending on your perspective."

"True," Trey said. "But that's why it hit me the way it did. I had never heard this perspective. I had never heard somebody say *out loud* the things that were in my head."

"Okay, tell me how it got 'better.'"

"He went beyond 'maybe you won't marry' to—it could even be *wonderful* if you don't get married." Trey shifted more toward her. "Then he said—'Singleness is not a second-class gift. It's a true gift. And if that's your gift, embrace it.'"

"Ooh, that's what you were telling me before," Jade said, "that you learned to embrace it. This was the time period?"

"Exactly," Trey said. "I had never thought of it as a gift. I just knew I didn't want to get married. I'd even tell my mom that, and she thought I'd grow out of it. But listening to this guy, I thought—*I'm not crazy. I can have these thoughts. And*—the gift is from God."

"I'm thinking this isn't the brief version, but I'm here for it." Jade pushed her laptop aside. "I'm loving the progression."

"Don't turn around and complain when you're up editing late," Trey said.

"You know I will," Jade said. "But go ahead."

"So the guy basically exhorts us to go wild for Jesus." Trey got his bottle of water and drank some. "To do all the things that 'comfortable' people can't or won't do because of family and career obligations. I had never thought of myself as having an advantage, so to speak; it always felt like a deficit. But now I'm like, wow, I can *devote* myself to Jesus, in ways that are unique to this gift of singleness."

"And you did, right?" Jade said. "You ended up in South Africa doing the thing."

"Not right away," Trey said. "During Kendra's illness and then after she died, I just wanted to be with family. And Lance moved forward with starting Living Hope Church, and I wanted to be part of that."

"And you were there with my dad," Jade said.

Trey nodded. "But I finally did a couple of short-term missions trips and loved it. Then I had this mid-term missions assignment, which technically ended a few weeks ago. The plan was to stay there and shift to a long-term assignment. But I started struggling with what I wanted to do and was praying about it. When I heard filming was about to start and the focus had changed, I was led to just come home."

"So it sounded like you were all in," Jade said. "Then you started struggling? You know I'm wondering what happened, but if you don't want to go into it . . ."

"I've kept you from your work long enough," Trey said. "I need you to get it done so I won't hear it the next time I want you to cook."

"It'll get done," Jade said. "You took me this far into the story. I want to hear the rest."

Trey got another piece of garlic toast from the baking pan. "Want one?" he said.

"I'm full," Jade said.

He broke off a piece and ate it. "So we were at the church one night after Bible study, only a handful of us left, all guys." He sat back down with the toast. "And one of them asked for prayer for something he was dealing with, then someone else opened up about a personal struggle, then the next. And I'm hearing these powerful prayers going up." He ate the rest and drank some water. "So I'm sitting there like, *Lord, should I share?* I knew I needed prayer. And Lance was the one I usually talked to. But I said these are my brothers in Christ. I can trust them."

"Uh-oh. The way you said that."

Trey nodded with a sigh. "I told them the Lord had given me the gift of singleness, and that I wish that meant I didn't have to battle loneliness. 'But lately,' I said, 'the battle has been intensifying.' I asked for prayer that God would strengthen me with respect to the loneliness." He shook his head, thinking about it. "They said the singleness part was the problem, that it's a rare gift, and 'You're a handsome young man; why would you take that path?'"

"I know I'm new to this," Jade said. "But what does being young and handsome have to do with it? Does God only give the gift to old, ugly people?"

"If you could have been there to deliver that one line . . ." Trey smiled a little. "One of the guys said, 'Let's pray for the Lord to send Trey a wife,' and they all started saying what a blessing it would be to find a wife on the mission field.'"

"Like—hello?" Jade spread her hands. "Did you not ask for prayer on the issue of battling loneliness? How they gon' switch up your prayer request like that?"

"They're all older," Trey said, "and felt they could understand my life and what I needed better than I could. And I get that. But they didn't know my whole story." He sighed again. "So I said, 'Listen, I appreciate everything you all are saying, and I know you're trying to help. But it's more complicated than that. I'm . . . just not . . . attracted to women.'"

"Let me guess," Jade said. "Now they *really* had some new prayers for you."

"They told me I needed prayer for deliverance, then they said I needed to repent. I said, 'Repent for what? An inclination?'" Trey looked at her. "They acted like I had done something wrong. Literally bombarded me with condemnation, all the things I used to think and feel about myself. Things that Lance ministered to me about in the past." He shook his head. "I walked out."

Jade could feel tears welling. "I mean, here you are trying to live super devoted to Jesus, doing stuff I've never even heard of—who *embraces* singleness, gift or not?" Her chest stuttered with a sigh. "I *do* wish I had been there to tell them a thing or two. What happened after that?"

"I had some follow-up conversations with the local leadership," Trey said, "and I could just tell that they saw me differently. The timing of this movie was everything."

Jade looked at him. "I just went through every emotion in the past thirty minutes. I was with you in the joy of finding your purpose and loving the mission field, and then sadness over what happened." She took a breath, thinking on it. "So how have you been feeling since you got back?"

"That first night," Trey said, "Lance and I stayed up talking about everything. It was really good. I thank God for giving me Lance as a brother. But that loneliness I was battling . . . I told you I drove to see my friends on Sunday, and it was just different. Now we're in rehearsals and about to start filming, and I'm constantly reminded of my sister and how much I miss her. So it's still a battle." He stared downward a moment. "I'll just do my own psycho-analysis. You being here is about more than getting a meal. I could go to Lance's for that. It's just . . . I've been praying and I feel like God sent someone who could be a real friend."

"The thought that I could be an answer to someone's prayer . . ." Jade heaved a sigh. "I don't know how to be a real friend, Trey. I'm not even building a friendship with Jesus like I wanted to with this cling challenge."

"I heard that announcement on Sunday," Trey said, "but I haven't gone online to check it out. What is it?"

"Oh, I don't think you were here for Lance's cling sermon," Jade said. "You should listen to that first, then check out the challenge. The goal is to have an intimate relationship with the Lord. This week we're supposed to talk to Jesus like a friend."

"Wow," Trey said. "So I'm battling loneliness and praying. And soon as I get back, there's a challenge happening to get closer to Jesus *and* there's suddenly this mean person in my life who's not at all about friendship, but might be *the* friend for me."

Jade sat silent for a moment. "I'm just thinking," she said, "maybe we could do the cling challenge together. You probably wouldn't need help staying on track with it, but I do." She hesitated. "And maybe as I learn to build a friendship with Jesus, I could learn to be a friend . . . to you." She put her head in her hands. "That was way too vulnerable."

"Can we incorporate meals as part of the challenge?"

Jade looked up. "Did you really just say that in my vulnerable moment?"

"Well. Yeah."

Jade shook her head. "You're a piece of work, you know that?"

"That's what Kendra used to tell me," Trey said. "I feel like we just bonded even more."

CHAPTER 43

"You can't be getting my blood pressure up." Pamela's hands gripped the steering wheel. "How am I supposed to remember all this? I told you I'm not ready to be behind the wheel."

"You'd never be ready if it were up to you." Tommy looked at her from the passenger seat. "That's why I wanted you to take that test for your permit, so you could get to this step before you talked yourself out of it. And see? You passed it."

"But that wasn't driving," Pamela said. "I just had to know rules of the road and recognize some signs."

"It was an important step," Tommy said. "And by the way, I sent you a link to take practice tests online, and you did it—which shows you're into this more than you might think." He glanced at her. "I thought you'd be celebrating the fact that you passed a little more than you did, though."

"What would I be celebrating?" Pamela said. "That I get to do something I'm not ready for?"

"You get to see that you can do this—sit in the driver's seat with the engine running, press down on the gas, and go," Tommy said. "You'll be amazed how quickly it becomes second nature."

Pamela heaved a sigh. "But it's so much. Checking *this* mirror and *that* mirror but making sure I'm focused on the main window, plus navigating the wheel, and what if I have to turn—oh, Lord, where's the turn signal?" Her eyes roamed the dashboard.

"Momma Pam, we're in a parking lot for a reason," Tommy said. "No need to constantly check the mirrors—although I do want you to get practice with that. And don't worry about the turn signal until we get to it. Now this is what I want you to do." He pointed straight ahead. "Drive toward the end of the parking lot then do a U-turn. So you're going to turn the steering wheel to the left"—he demonstrated with his hands—"until you're headed back this way."

"But I see two cars down there. What if I hit them?"

"Those cars are parked," Tommy said. "The only way you'll hit them is if you turn a sharp right when you get to them. You'll be fine if you keep the wheel steady like we talked about."

"Okay," Pamela muttered. "Wow. Am I about to actually drive?" She could feel her heart palpitating. *Jesus, please help me.* She took a breath. "Okay. So hands like so, right foot on the gas . . ."

"Lightly," Tommy said. "We'll get to acceleration later."

Pamela shot him a look. "You're not expecting me to drive on the highway, are you?"

"Absolutely," Tommy said. "Eventually. Why wouldn't I?"

"Because it's the *highway*," Pamela said. "Cars whizzing by at ungodly speeds. Do you know how many people get killed out there?"

"How many die in their sleep?" Tommy said. "You avoiding that too?"

"We don't have to be gung-ho about this, is all I'm saying." Pamela examined the dashboard again and looked in the rearview mirror. "It's enough if I can run an errand or two on local roads."

"One day at a time, how about that?" Tommy said. "But is there a reason we're just sitting here?"

"Oh." Pamela sat up straight and checked the position of her hands on the wheel. "Because I can't hold a conversation and drive at the same time."

Tommy chuckled a little. "And we do want you to concentrate."

Pamela pressed the gas pedal, and the car lurched forward.

"Lightly," Tommy reiterated.

"Okay," Pamela said.

She tapped her foot on the gas and the car started rolling.

"See?" Tommy said, beaming. "Just like that—you're driving."

"Ooh," Pamela said. "I can call this driving?"

Tommy took out his phone. "I'm sending Lance a video."

"I'd look at the camera and smile," Pamela said, "but I don't want to crash into those two cars."

"Much appreciated," Tommy said.

Pamela steadied her hands and tightened her grip on the wheel as she passed the cars. Nearing the end of the lot, she began turning the wheel with both hands and heading left. "Like this?" she said.

"You go, Momma Pam," Tommy said. "Get your swerve on."

Pamela focused, completing the U-turn. "Hey, I did it!" she said, the car headed the opposite direction.

Tommy smiled. "Of course, you did. You're doing great. Okay, keep going until you get to that fire hydrant up there."

Pamela navigated the car to the designated point, but it kept rolling. "Oh, shoot, do I brake with the left foot or the right?" She tried each one as she said it, the car jerking twice.

"Think about it like this," Tommy said. "All your driving controls are toward the center." He motioned, showing her. "So it's your right foot—the one closest to the controls—that's part of the action. It works the gas pedal and the brake."

"That's good," Pamela said. "That helps."

"So the car is stopped," Tommy said. "If you take your foot off the brake, will the car stay in place?"

Pamela studied the controls for a moment. "Oh, I didn't put it in *Park*."

She shifted the gear, and she and Tommy got out and traded places.

Tommy glanced at her, smiling as he pulled off. "So, congratulations. You drove a car for the first time in your life."

Pamela couldn't help but smile as well, with a sigh on its heels.

"But the thought of driving on an actual road with cars all around me —*moving cars*—is even scarier now that I see all the things I need to pay attention to."

"Wow, you had a victory today," Tommy said, "and that's what you're coming away with? It's even scarier?"

"It's not unusual, you know," Pamela said. "I had friends in prison who got out and were anxious about re-learning their driving skills. So if *they* were anxious . . ."

"I just need you to acknowledge that you took a gigantic step today," Tommy said, "more than you ever imagined."

Pamela gave a nod. "That's very true. I never imagined myself—" She paused, her phone ringing. "See, this is what I don't want to get used to, folk being able to reach you at all times." She fumbled around in her purse to find it.

Tommy chuckled. "Momma Pam, there's an 'off' switch."

"Then I'll wonder what I missed."

Tommy shook his head at her.

"Oh, it's Lance, on that Face thing." Pamela clicked it on, and Lance and Treva came into view.

"We're calling to congratulate you," Treva said, beaming.

"I almost fell out of my chair when I saw that video," Lance said. "You were *driving*, Mom. You conquered your fears."

"I didn't conquer any such thing," Pamela said. "I hope you could tell that was only a parking lot."

"Mom, you were behind the wheel, foot on the gas, making the car go," Lance said. "Huge step."

"Please tell her," Tommy said, glancing into the phone. "Maybe if ten of us say it, it'll get through her head."

"Pam, you probably don't realize it, but you looked so excited behind that wheel," Treva said. "I could see it in your eyes—you *want* to learn. And you *will* conquer your fears."

"We just wanted to celebrate with you the minute we saw it," Lance said, "but we'll see you when you get here."

Tommy glanced at her when she hung up. "Since we both plan to be on set, I'll just pick you up every day during filming."

"That would be a blessing," Pamela said, "if I didn't know what it meant."

"It's still a blessing," Tommy said. "A double one. You don't have to worry about how you'll get there, and yes, it means you'll get in some drive time every day. You'll progress quickly."

Pamela looked at him. "It's no coincidence that you started this cling challenge the same week I started these driving lessons. You and God teaming up against me." Her gaze shifted to the road. "He really dealt with me about this week's challenge—talk to Jesus like a friend. I love that—but I thought I was already doing it."

"I feel like *I've* heard you talking to Jesus like a friend," Tommy said.

"The Lord let me know I wasn't talking to Him about my fears," Pamela said. "I didn't even think of them as fears." She thought for a moment. "It's jarring how much has changed since I went to prison, especially all the technology and what not. And given my age, I keep telling myself there's no point learning this or that, but really—and this is what I'm realizing—I have this fear that time has passed me by. Like, what's the use? I missed out on the prime season of my life and now it's basically over."

Tommy looked at her. "I was waiting for the part where you said the next thing you realized was how foolish that was."

Pamela sighed. "Some of it's just a fact, like my age. And some things *did* pass me by. It's a consequence of my own bad choices. I have to reckon with that."

"So God moved in a mighty way to get you out of prison *early*," Tommy said, "but it's actually too late and 'real life' is behind you." He glanced at her. "Who got people around the world praying for everything concerning this movie and the people involved with it? You prayed in the financing." He turned to her again. "I'd love to see you *act* like your life is basically over and sit somewhere for five minutes. You couldn't do it. So the devil's gonna have to take those lies somewhere else."

"So this is what it's about to be like every day, huh." Pamela cut her eyes over at him. "I feel like the Lord's giving me a *daily* challenge."

"Happy to serve," Tommy said.

"But that means I'll see you more, which will lead me to pray for you more."

Tommy looked over at her. "I never got to ask what you were praying."

Pamela stared at the road. "Oh, lots of things."

"You're gonna do me like that, Momma Pam?"

"I might tell you one day." Pamela gave him a wry smile. "When you're ready."

CHAPTER 44

*J*unior Year
The energy in the Atrium went through the roof as the deejay teased with snippets of Doug E. Fresh. Hands in the air, people moved to the crowded floor, bodies swaying to the groove.

Jillian moved to the beat, chatting with girlfriends—and felt the tug of a hand as she got pulled away.

Tommy walked in front of her, tightly given the crowd, bopping his head as he led her to the floor.

"Boy, you better go dance with Regina." Jillian yelled over the music.

Tommy leaned back. "You're the one who said I was dumb for trusting her." He claimed a spot and started dancing.

"Actually, I said you were a fool"—Jillian danced with him—"but you're still with her and everybody's out here, so you know she wants to dance."

"All I know is she's acting funny tonight and this is my jam, so . . ." Tommy kept grooving.

"The other thing is—I was keeping an eye out for Deon."

"Nah, Jill," Tommy said. "That's my boy, but don't be standing

301

around waiting for him. You'll see him when you see him. Let him find you."

The space grew tighter and bodies bumped one another as more and more people flocked to the floor, spurred by the flow of the deejay.

"You hear the way he dropped that Eric B. & Rakim?" Tommy said. "He is going *off* right now."

Jillian caught sight of Regina weaving through bodies to get to them. "She's headed this way."

"Who?" Tommy said.

"Who else? Regina. And don't act funny."

"I just said *she's* the one acting funny."

"But if she's trying to make up, don't act funny to pay her back for acting funny."

"You should be *telling* me to act funny since I shouldn't trust her."

Regina pressed in beside them and started talking to Tommy, the movement of her head signaling her displeasure.

"Aaaayyyyeeee" thundered in the room as they heard the whistle from "Set it Off."

Jillian could tell by Tommy's eyes that he'd shot back something dismissive. He tried to keep dancing, but Regina wouldn't let him. She had her finger going now, with a glance or two back at Jillian.

Jillian felt another tug of her hand and turned around. Deon hugged her and they fell into the groove, dancing as they exchanged helloes.

"I see Tommy and Regina doing the usual," Deon said, looking over at them. He returned his gaze to Jillian, leaning in so she could hear him. "And you're looking fine as usual."

Jillian felt herself blush as they continued to dance. She'd taken extra time to get ready, selecting a nice top to go with her jeans and putting on light makeup, knowing she'd see him. He looked good himself, in a beige sweater she hadn't seen. They'd been getting to know one another since earlier in the semester.

"Looks like everybody came out tonight," Deon said.

"Yeah, last party till the break." Jillian leaned in a little. "You get some studying done?"

Deon nodded. "A few hours at the library." He smiled at her. "You gonna come study with me tomorrow?"

Jillian returned the smile.

"Oh, you're good," Deon said. "Get my hopes up with the smile, but you ain't said *nothing*." He shook his head. "Why does *Tommy* get all the study time?"

Jillian shrugged. "It just works. We've been studying together since freshman year."

"I'm not tripping," Deon said, "'cause I've got *this* with you."

Deon moved closer, and Jillian tingled as his arms circled her waist. All around them people bounced to an accelerated groove, but Deon had shifted them to half-time. Her head near his neck, they swayed as she took in the faintness of his cologne.

"You gonna miss me over the break?" Deon spoke into her ear.

Jillian had thought about the fact that he'd be in Jersey, and she wouldn't see him for about a month. "We don't leave for another three weeks or so."

"You didn't answer my question."

Jillian smiled to herself. "Maybe."

"Mine is more than a maybe," Deon said. "I'm definitely gonna—"

"Aaaaayyyyyyeeeee!" sounded again, this time because the deejay switched to go-go music. A new set of people flocked to the floor as some moved off.

Tommy came up beside them, taunting Deon with the words to the song—"Do you know what time it is? Tell me, do you know?" A little taller than Deon, he smiled as he bopped to the syncopated beat.

"Whatever," Deon said. He'd told Tommy he couldn't get with go-go music. "Glad all the DC folk are happy." He gave the peace sign as he backed away. "Y'all can have this one."

Tommy moved into his place, and he and Jillian started moving to the local band Rare Essence.

"Where's Regina?" Jillian said.

"Somewhere with an attitude."

303

"Which is only getting worse with you dancing like you don't care."

"I don't."

"You do," Jillian said. "If you didn't, you would've let her go a long time ago."

"Can you stop talking and messing up my groove?"

"We should do an unplugged. I feel like there's a lot to talk about."

"The problem is—you're trying to start it now," Tommy said.

"I'm just saying we need one," Jillian said. "We can do it tomorrow."

"Fine."

"After our study session."

"*Okay.*"

"Or before. Either one works."

"See that?" Tommy pointed in the air. "The song is over. You are so annoying."

The deejay switched to house music, prompting cheers from the Baltimore people who quickly took to the floor. Jillian and Tommy gathered with Deon and others who were talking about where they were headed next. Regina walked over as well, drawing Tommy into a private conversation.

Deon moved closer to Jillian. "You going to the after party?"

Jillian shook her head. "I'm tired. Heading back to my room. What about you?"

"I was waiting to see what you were going to do," Deon said. "I can walk you back."

Tommy came over. "Hey, Regina wants to go somewhere and talk, but I told her I'm walking you to your dorm first."

"You don't have to do that," Deon said. "I just told Jillian I'd walk her back."

"I hear you," Tommy said. "It's just something we do." For the past year, he'd walked Jillian back to her dorm after parties and other late-night events. She'd asked him to, to avoid compromising situations.

Deon looked at Jillian. "I don't get it—is Tommy your bodyguard? We hardly ever get one-on-one time. I just wanted to talk."

"Man, why I gotta be all that?" Tommy said. "You know Jillian's like a sister to me. If I want to make sure she's safe, imma make sure she's safe."

"From *me*?" Deon said. "I thought I was your boy."

"Tommy, it's fine," Jillian said. "Deon can walk me back, and you and Regina can go talk."

Tommy let his gaze rest on her a second to be sure, then said his goodbyes. Jillian and Deon left the Student Union and headed toward her dorm. The daytime temperature, fairly mild for November, had dropped several degrees. Jillian held herself against the cold.

"Here," Deon said, taking off his jacket.

"Thanks," Jillian said, wrapping herself in the warmth and that scent she loved.

They walked a ways in silence along the winding sidewalk that led to her dorm. This time of night, it remained mostly isolated with sparse lighting. Since most of her girlfriends had moved to the south side of campus, she'd grown accustomed to taking a shuttle at night or finding someone to walk with. Tonight she felt butterflies as she walked.

Deon slipped his hand in hers as they wound their way around the football stadium. "So how did you and Tommy get so close?"

"We had classes together as freshmen, and I started tutoring him in writing," Jillian said. "Then I went through some things last year, and he was there for me."

Deon looked at her. "And the two of you never . . .?"

"Never," Jillian said. "But I'm sure you already asked him that."

"It's just hard to believe," Deon said. "I also asked him if he was blind."

"It's just not like that," Jillian said. "He's the one who connected the two of us, remember?"

"Yeah, after he gave me the third degree."

"The third degree?" Jillian said.

"He wanted to know if I was really trying to get to know you or if you were just a . . . you know . . ." He shrugged.

"A situation?"

"How do you know about that?"

Jillian returned the shrug.

Deon shook his head. "Y'all really are close."

"So what'd you tell him?"

"I said I wanted to get to know you," Deon said. "And that's what we've been doing." He held her hand tighter. "It's been nice."

Jillian nodded. "You're different than I thought you were."

"How did you think I was?"

"Seeing you around Tommy and the other guys," Jillian said, "y'all are always joking, so I thought you were charged all the time. But when it's just us, you're quiet and thoughtful."

"So, boring."

"Not at all," Jillian said. "Because you choose your words carefully, it makes me more interested in what you have to say."

"Okay," Deon said, sounding surprised. "But now I'm afraid I'll say something stupid."

Jillian shrugged. "It's just me, so who cares?"

"That's something I didn't expect," Deon said. "Being around you, I don't know, I thought I had to be on point all the time. You know? Because you just seem so together." He looked at her. "But you make it easy to be around you. I like being around you."

Jillian walked a few feet in silence. "I like being around you too."

"Now that's something you haven't done," Deon said. "Tell me straight out what you're feeling about me."

"I didn't say anything surprising," Jillian said. "If I didn't like being around you, I wouldn't be around you."

"But hearing you say it is different. Vulnerable."

Jillian gave a nod. "Looks like we're learning a lot about each other this evening."

Their pace slowed as they crossed into the courtyard area in front of the dorm.

"Thank you for walking me," Jillian said.

"Any time." His hand in hers still, he brought her closer and kissed her.

Jillian felt the flutters, even more as his arms circled her waist.

"It's really not that late," Deon said, his voice a whisper in her ear. "We should keep learning about each other."

"Meaning?" Jillian said.

He kissed her cheek. "We should go inside and keep talking."

"Well, it's late enough," Jillian said. "And I don't want you to get the wrong idea, because I'm not having sex."

"Okay, that was to the point," Deon said. "But Jillian, I would never pressure you to go where you don't want to go. Trust me—my respect level for you is high. I just want to enjoy your company a little longer."

Deon looked into her eyes and brought her closer still, kissing her again, more deeply this time. Jillian's heart thumped in her chest, knowing he should go but unable to muster the words. And anyway, what would be wrong with talking and enjoying each other's company . . . just a little longer?

"Hold up." Tommy's brow quirked as he looked at her. "You told D you weren't down for sex, and *that* was his next move? He knew *exactly* what he was doing with the 'no pressure' pressure kiss."

"Or he was just in the moment like I was." Jillian sat at a table with him in a study room in her dorm. "You think everybody's got ulterior motives."

"And you think everybody's motives are pure," Tommy said. "I know guys, and I know D."

"Then why'd you set me up with him, if his motives are so bad?"

"First—I didn't set you up with him," Tommy said. "I made the connect after he *kept* asking about you—and only after I had separate convos with both of you." He leaned back in his chair. "I'm not saying he's a bad person. But it's like I told you—*most* guys are out here trying to have sex. And they don't really care that you don't want to. They make it their mission to persuade you otherwise." He came forward. "And by the way, he said he had a high level of respect for you because I said that's what he better have. But I meant *show* it, not just say it."

"So how should he have shown it?" Jillian said.

"You said, 'it's late' and 'no sex,'" Tommy said. "That was the time to say goodnight, not to try to turn up the heat." He looked at her. "So what happened? You left me hanging."

"You're the one who said, 'Hold up,'" Jillian said. "I gave him his jacket and said goodnight."

"That could've been two hours later."

"He didn't go inside."

Tommy sat back again with a sigh. "I thought I was gonna have to pull him up."

"If anything had happened, it would've been on me," Jillian said. "You don't have to be so protective of me."

"And yet, I am." Tommy smiled. "Did you catch that?"

Jillian tossed her eyes. She'd been talking about effective uses of 'yet' versus 'but' in his papers.

"But for real," Tommy said, "you went *through* last year. I was there when you would break down and couldn't stop crying. It messed *me* up. So I don't care if you don't like it—*I'm protective of you.*" He shook his head. "It's a trip, though. It didn't just mess me up—it messed up my situations too."

"I remember when you said you weren't even using that word anymore."

"It started bothering me," Tommy said. "Like—why do I need to be talking to all these women? I kept thinking, what if *I'm* the reason somebody's breaking down in class, in Roy's, in the middle of a football game—"

"I didn't break down at a football game."

"You didn't cry for one whole quarter?"

"Silent tears. That's not breaking down."

"Anyway," Tommy said, giving her a look, "now that I think about it, that's how things got more serious with Regina, because I wasn't doing the usual. But then *I* end up being the one who gets played."

"Oh, tell me about the talk last night," Jillian said. "We've been focused on Deon and me this whole time."

"Can't really call it a talk," Tommy said. "Things blew up when ol' dude showed up."

Jillian's eyes widened. "Mitch showed up after I left? And you're just now mentioning it? What happened?"

"So he walks in with a couple of his boys," Tommy said. "Regina and I are about to leave, but we stop to talk to some people. Next thing I know, the two of them are off to the side carrying on a conversation."

"No way," Jillian said.

"Literally had me waiting," Tommy said. "Then gonna ask if I'm ready once they're done, like it's nothing." He blew out a breath. "We got outside and I said, 'You already know he's an issue—people telling me they're seeing you two together, you saying it's nothing—and now you're gonna connect with dude in front of me?'"

"You already knew she'd say they're just friends," Jillian said.

"And her favorite line—'You and Jillian aren't the only ones who can be close friends.'"

"Right," Jillian said. "Except nobody could ever say they've seen us all hugged up, because it's never happened. Not the case with Regina and Mitch." She looked as someone passed by the glass wall. "So you two have been here before. Where'd you leave it this time?"

"Bottom line," Tommy said, "we broke up."

"You've been there before too."

"I know," Tommy said. "She already left two messages this morning. I think she thinks it's temporary."

"What about you?" Jillian said.

"I don't know," Tommy said. "I'm not even sure what I'm feeling. Seeing the two of them last night . . . I don't know if I got upset because I felt she dissed me or because I still care about her."

"Could be both," Jillian said.

"Thanks for the help."

"I'm supposed to know what you're feeling?"

"You usually act like you know," Tommy said.

"I've got an idea," Jillian said, "but you won't do it."

"And just because you put it that way, I want to know."

"When you've got a paper to write," Jillian said, "you always say it's hard to come up with your thesis and main points. Even when we talk it out together, you're fuzzy. But when you start writing . . . that's when your thoughts start rolling."

"I'm definitely fuzzy right now because I have no idea where you're going."

"Write Regina a letter," Jillian said, "but not with the intent to give it to her. Just start writing. No filter. Let your thoughts flow. Your own words might tell you what you're feeling."

Tommy frowned. "I don't even know if I care enough to put in that much work."

"It doesn't have to be long," Jillian said. "But that'll be another indication—how much comes to you." She shrugged. "Depending on what you write, you could wind up with a love letter that you can give to her."

Tommy looked at her. "You're actually serious."

"I'm just going by what I've seen," Jillian said. "Some people think best when they're writing." She shrugged again. "Writing is your thing, Tommy. You're good at it."

"You've never told me that," Tommy said.

"I'm always telling you how well you write," Jillian said. "But the red marks speak louder to you."

"Man, that red makes it seem *all* bad."

"I wouldn't be so nit-picky if I didn't see so much in what you write," Jillian said. "And it just keeps getting better."

"I *know* you've never said that," Tommy said. "I feel like the teacher just gave me a gold star." He smiled a little. "I think imma try your crazy idea and see if it works." He took some paper from his backpack.

"Right now?"

"Might as well, while you're here," Tommy said. "You can check it, like everything else I write."

Tommy hunkered down and Jillian took out a binder for one of her classes, popping a can of Mountain Dew as she studied her notes. She glanced over at Tommy every now and then as he'd get up and pace a little then sit back down to continue. Between them they consumed two bags of Funyuns and half a pack of Starbursts, Jillian taking the strawberry and orange, Tommy the lemon and cherry.

"Done." Tommy pushed the papers toward Jillian.

Jillian gathered them up. "Wow. Three pages?"

"Way more than I thought," Tommy said. "But you were right—it helped me process what I was thinking and feeling. Go ahead and read it."

Jillian got two paragraphs in and paused. "Okay, wow. You went back to how you were feeling during your very first conversation?"

"Wild, right?" Tommy said. "That's what came to me. I wanted to be real about how I felt something even then. How she captured me and I wanted to get to know her."

Jillian continued, turning to the back. "This is deep. I didn't know you saw yourself in a long-term relationship with her early on."

"I just realized it myself," Tommy said. "I wasn't used to giving somebody that kind of attention. Spending time together, making time to talk—and not just about superficial stuff—*and* I don't have any situations on the side? I was thinking if I'm giving all this and she's giving the same—why wouldn't we be together for a long while?"

"Whoa," Jillian said, eyes on the page.

"What?"

She looked at him. "You said you've learned something about yourself, that you'd rather love one woman than have several that you could get with at any time."

"Yeah, that just came to me too."

"That's a pretty big deal, Tommy."

"Is it?" Tommy said. "I actually don't miss all that other stuff. What really could compare with having one woman on your mind and knowing you're on her mind? Just thinking about where you could go that's special or what you can do to make her smile . . . You know?"

Jillian stared at him. "Who are you and what have you done with my best friend?"

"You can't say you haven't seen me changing," Tommy said. "We just talked about it." He paused. "But something else came to me as I was writing that. I wasn't just impacted by what you went through. I've been impacted by our friendship. The way I see you and the way I feel a guy *better* treat you—why wouldn't I shoot for the same as far as a relationship?"

"I'm blown away," Jillian said. "But I'll say this—it's exactly what I said could happen. This is turning into a love letter."

She kept reading, turning another page, then looked at him. "'And yet'?"

Tommy gave a wry smile. "How's the placement?"

"Perfect," Jillian said. "I just wasn't expecting it."

"That's the whole point, isn't it?"

Jillian kept reading. "Wow, Tommy. You wrote paragraph upon paragraph about how you had turned into this guy who wanted love and romance and one woman to heap it on. Even said you thought she was the one—until it became clear she wasn't." She looked at him. "Are you planning to give this to her?"

Tommy shook his head. "It's over, and it'll stay over. She doesn't need to know all that. But I'm glad *I* know."

"It's beautifully written," Jillian said. "Only saw a couple edits." She smiled at him.

Tommy heaved a sigh. "Craziest idea ever, but I needed that."

"You're welcome," Jillian said. "We should probably focus on studying now."

"Let's do it." Tommy dumped the contents of his backpack on the table. "Hey Jilli-Jill."

She looked through her notes. "What."

"Think we'll be best friends forever?"

"What does that even mean?" Jillian said. "Nothing is forever."

"If there were such a thing as forever," Tommy said, "think we'd stay best friends?"

"No."

"Why not?"

"Life doesn't work that way." Jillian got a pen from her backpack.

"Think your pessimism will last forever?"

Jillian gave him a look.

"I want it to," Tommy said. "To last forever. Not your pessimism—this friendship. That's something else I realized as I wrote that."

Jillian looked at him. "You asked if I thought it would last forever, not whether I wanted it to."

He held her gaze.

Jillian gave a slight nod. "I want it to."

CHAPTER 45

It reminds me of a vacation my husband and I once took to the quaint island of Nantucket. We went in October—in-between season—when bustling crowds have diminished to a manageable horde. Of course, the weather can be tricky that time of year as one could encounter a snarl of wintry elements. But thankfully we had daytime temps so inviting that our jackets draped our shoulders as we strolled the beaches, watching waves crash wildly into the sand. . . .

Jillian paused her reading of the manuscript and skimmed further down the page, then turned to the next, seeing that the story went on. She added to the note she'd been writing to the author—"Great, descriptive storytelling, but I find myself forgetting what biblical point you're making. Let's cut back on some of the stories and spend more time illuminating the actual verses. At Living Water, our readers really do appreciate a lot of word in their Bible studies. But you're such a gifted storyteller that short, vivid examples will go a long way."

She went back to the document on her laptop screen and continued reading.

And can I just tell you about the delicious breakfasts we enjoyed on this vacation? One particularly delectable culinary experience consisted of a combination of poached eggs with crab . . .

Jillian's thoughts drifted to Boston, the last vacation she shared with Cecil, where they savored their favorite foods—shrimp, crab, lobster, and fresh fish. The New England clam chowder was a favorite memory in itself. Cecil would order a bowl wherever they went, for breakfast if he could. He said it would never taste as good anywhere else.

After dinner they'd take extended walks downtown, hand in hand, which wasn't a casual reflex. They'd just endured one of the biggest trials of their marriage. Her hand in his had been evidence of God's grace in healing and restoration.

Jillian's eyes folded to a close. *We saw Your faithfulness and Your goodness, Lord. You kept us. You blessed our family. Why would You do all of that and then take him from us?*

Jillian sighed softly. She'd asked the Lord these same questions countless times. She knew she'd never understand why, not in this life. But it helped to share her heart with Him, to grieve *with* Him so He could comfort her. Lately so many things triggered a memory, which then triggered grief. With the one-year anniversary of Cecil's passing approaching, she knew it would happen more and more. And she would run to the Lord more and more.

Your God has commanded your strength.

Jillian's heart quickened. One of her favorite go-to verses. She'd been spending a lot of time in the Psalms, and that verse—Psalm 68:28—always lifted her. *Thank You, Lord, for reminding me again and again that You're with me.*

Jillian put her eyes back on the screen, knowing she needed to get back to work. Almost everyone was gone already, but she'd been arriving at work later than normal this week in order to cook and serve breakfast at the B and B. She needed to make up the time, and she loved working this time of day. The quiet helped her focus . . . as long as her own thoughts didn't get in the way.

"Hey, I wasn't expecting you to still be here."

Jillian looked up to see Silas with two books. "Oh, hey."

"I was planning to leave these on your desk," Silas said. "The books on grief that I mentioned the other day."

"Okay, thanks." Jillian stood, taking them. "I still don't know whether I'll take on the project. Whenever I think about it, it's so immense on many levels." She put the books down. "But I watched the first sermon in your grief series. Took me by surprise."

"How so?" Silas said.

"I think given the subject matter, I thought it would be on the somber side," Jillian said. "You had a Holy Ghost fire."

"Well. Remember I said God did something with that message?" Silas came further into her cubicle. "I went into sermon prep thinking it *would* be somber. But I could feel the opposite happening as I studied."

"What do you mean?" Jillian said.

"I couldn't read about death without it being checked by life," Silas said. "Christ died. The One who was in the beginning, through whom all things were made—*died*. But the grave couldn't hold Him. He rose again!" He pumped a fist.

"Oh, and I loved the part about Lazarus," Jillian said. "Mary and Martha grieving, and Jesus was like, 'I thought you knew—I'm the resurrection and the life'—"

"'He who believes in Me will live even *if* he dies.'" The passion shone in his eyes. "What is death? *What is death?* Jesus abolished it. Yes, I grieve the loss of my Audrey, but all of that sermon prep made me focus more on the truth that she's *alive*, with Christ."

"It encouraged me so much," Jillian said, "focusing on that truth with respect to Cecil. And you know what really surprised me about your message? The way you brought in the book of Revelation. You just don't hear preaching about Revelation, and for you to weave it into a message on grief . . ." She leaned against her desk space, gesturing for him to take her chair. "When you said Audrey is going to be riding on a white horse, clothed in white with the armies of heaven, coming with Christ . . . that was so powerful."

"That's what really ignited me," Silas said, sitting back in the chair. "I wasn't planning to bring in Revelation at all. But the Holy Spirit kept bringing to mind verses from that book—it's one of my favorites

—so I turned to it and read it in light of the topic of grief. It cast a different light on everything."

"So, admission," Jillian said. "That's the one book of the Bible I haven't studied inductively. I read it years ago. But I always thought if I study it deeply, I'll get into the twenty million interpretations and grow discouraged because who knows what it all means. So . . ." She shrugged.

Silas nodded with a slight smile. "Let me rephrase that for you. The one book of the Bible that shows a resurrected and glorified Christ *in heaven*, with angels and other living creatures worshiping Him, who alone is worthy to take the book of life and break its seals, who then takes the book of life and begins to execute judgment because He is King of kings and Lord of lords, who, as part of that judgment, will see to it that the devil is thrown into the lake of fire, and who will Himself descend from the heavens in power and glory . . . You're avoiding *that* book."

Jillian gave him a blank stare. "You weren't supposed to challenge me to do a deep dive into Revelation. I'm used to people saying, 'Girl, I feel you.'" She chuckled a little. "But I got this stirring inside as you broke that down, just like when I heard you preaching about it. I know it's the Lord telling me to do it."

"Amen," Silas said, "I can't tell you whether you should do the grief study or not. I *can* tell you that you need to study Revelation. It'll impact you in ways you don't expect." He rose from the chair. "And by the way, at my former church I taught a 'Jet Tour Through Revelation' class to give people an overview and get them excited about studying the book. For you, I would do it for free and throw in dinner to make it semi-painless."

Jillian narrowed her eyes at him. "It was free at your church as well."

"Minor detail," Silas said.

"You would actually use Revelation to get a dinner date?"

"I'm all about object lessons," Silas said. "Dinner highlights the promise in Revelation that 'they shall hunger no longer.'"

Jillian shook her head, trying to stifle a smile. "Are you talking about tonight?"

"One thing we'd cover is time references throughout Revelation," Silas said. "Words like 'quickly' and 'no delay.' So, yes. Again, object lessons."

"You know you're a trip, right?"

"Just trying to help a fellow saint get a vision of the glories to come."

"Uh-huh." Jillian packed up her laptop, then put her Bible, notebook, a couple of pens, and a highlighter in her bag and shouldered it. "All right. I'm ready. For Bible study." She shook her head at herself. "At least I can say it's not a traditional date."

"I thought you would say it's not a date, so I'll take that." Silas led the way out. "And lest you think I'm just a coffee and wings guy, Lucas and I found this great place." He looked at her. "Do you like Mexican?"

Jillian's stomach tightened as she and Silas strode toward the restaurant. Of all the Mexican spots in St. Louis, she was certain he couldn't be heading to this one. But by the time it became clear that he was, it was too awkward to object.

It's not a big deal. Jillian exhaled, her breath a cloud in the cold air. No need to feel funny about going places that she and Tommy frequented. They attended the same church, which was also her workplace, and that wasn't an issue. As long as she and Silas didn't sit in the booth. *That* would feel odd.

"I was hoping to introduce you to a new place, like that coffee shop." Silas pulled the door open for her. "But maybe it's even better that I chose a place you love."

"What are the odds, right?" Jillian said.

They moved toward the hostess stand, which had someone Jillian hadn't seen before.

"Good evening," Silas said. "I called ahead. Keys. Reservation for two."

The hostess checked. "Yes, Mr. Keys." She grabbed two menus. "Right this way, please." She looked back at them as she walked. "We're a little crowded tonight. I hope you don't mind a table."

"No problem at all," Silas said as they followed. "Hey," he said a moment later, "there's Tommy."

Before Jillian could register what he'd said, Silas had veered away. She followed with her gaze and saw him talking to Tommy. With Mariah. In the booth.

The hostess stopped at a table right near the booth, and Jillian glanced around, ready to ask for a different one. But there wasn't an empty table in sight.

The hostess placed the menus on their table. "Enjoy," she said.

Jillian stood by her seat, knowing she needed to go say hello. *Just go and get it over with.*

She took a deep breath, turned, and moved to the booth, her eyes falling on the fajitas they had both ordered.

"It's so incredible to meet you," Silas was saying. "You have no idea —that was my wife's favorite movie."

"I have to say it was one of my favorites as well," Mariah said. "The location, the cast and crew, everything about it was special. Although"—she glanced at Tommy—"the experience on this film is quickly eclipsing that one—hey, Jillian."

"Hey, Jill," Tommy added.

"I don't want to interrupt," Jillian said. "Just saying a quick hello."

"I'm the one who interrupted them," Silas said. "I'll let you all get back to it. Mariah, really good meeting you."

"You as well," Mariah said.

Jillian and Silas went back to their table. Silas helped her with her coat and placed it in a free chair, then pulled out her chair for her. She sat with her back to the booth.

"Running into the director of the indie film you've seen at least three times," Silas said. "Who would've thought?"

"Mariah is staying at the B and B I told you about," Jillian said. "Really down to earth. She's a believer too."

"That's great to hear," Silas said. "You mentioned that people from the movie were staying there. I had no idea she was one of them."

Jillian opened the menu she knew by heart and stared at the words.

"Jillian, I hope you don't mind if I ask a question," Silas said.

"Not at all," she said, looking at him.

"You mentioned that you and Tommy were best friends in college," Silas said. "But that's the second time I've been around you two when it seemed sort of tense. But there was also the time he drove your car to pick you up from work."

"Good evening, guys." A server dropped off two glasses of water, chips, and salsa, looking rushed. "I'll be right back to take your order."

Silas looked at Jillian as the server walked away. "I just want to make sure I'm not treading on anything."

Jillian took a moment to respond. "You really do speak your mind, and I appreciate that because it makes it easy for me to do the same." She took a sip of the water. "You're not treading on anything, Silas, because you and I aren't doing anything. If Cyd hadn't met with us about the grief study, we wouldn't have had that conversation at work this evening, and we wouldn't be here right now." She sighed. "But I apologize. I said dinner was a step I wasn't ready to take, and I should've stuck to that no matter the circumstance." She closed her menu. "I think we should just go."

"Jillian, I'm the one who should apologize," Silas said. "I told you before—I enjoy your company. As we were talking earlier at the office, I didn't want it to end. I really did want to inspire you to study Revelation. But I also thought a jet tour through the book would be a great, no-pressure way to continue to get to know one another." He glanced at the booth. "Then I went and made it awkward with the comment about you and Tommy." He looked at her. "If you want to go, I understand. But I'd love to still take you through Revelation. And I'll try my best not to enjoy it."

Jillian thought for a moment, then got her Bible, notebook, and pen from her bag and laid them on the table. "Yeah, from what I recall . . . wrath of God, plagues, earthquakes, unchained demons . . . this won't be enjoyable at all."

CHAPTER 46

aughter emanated from Jillian and Silas's table, drawing Tommy's attention. Again. He wondered what could be so funny, since Jillian had her Bible open and pen in hand, jotting notes. It was Silas doing most of the talking, and she was clearly enamored.

"I'm sitting here flabbergasted." Mariah looked at Tommy. "Your wife decided that marriage was too confining? She wanted her freedom—and actually left?"

"Moved in with her old boyfriend," Tommy said. "Got pregnant by the guy—"

"Waiiiit." Mariah leaned in, fajita in hand. "She wanted freedom and ended up with a baby?" She ate the last of it.

Tommy gave a nod.

"Oh, Tommy . . ." Mariah drank some of her iced tea. "This was recent?"

"She left about a year ago," Tommy said. "Divorce was final last summer. She just had the baby."

"That had to be so hard for you," Mariah said. "I'm blown away by all of it. First of all, the fact that you even got married."

"How is that the 'first of all'"? Tommy said.

321

"Because I remember you saying—'I doubt I'll marry again.'"

Tommy finished a bite of his fajita. "I forgot we connected soon after my first divorce."

"I don't know if 'connected' is the word," Mariah said. "You were giving 'emotionally unavailable' vibes the whole time we were dating. But to be fair, you told me where you were. That was a hard divorce too."

"First marriage and I failed," Tommy said. "I had a lot to sort through. Dating wasn't on my radar. I don't even know how that happened."

"Talking about this and that at work," Mariah said. "Then we'd continue after work over a meal, sort of like this." She took a glance at her empty plate. "It went from there."

Tommy nodded, glancing over at Jillian and Silas. Why should he be surprised to see them out together? They worked at the same place, and Silas made it clear that he wanted to pursue her. Still, Jillian had said dinner was a step she couldn't take yet.

"Excuse me," Tommy said, catching the server. "We'll take the check."

"Are you sure?" Mariah said. "You didn't eat a whole lot."

"I'm not real hungry," Tommy said. "I'll take it home."

Jillian's voice rose in laughter once again, and Tommy gave another glance. She looked awfully comfortable for somebody who claimed she wasn't ready.

"I always wonder what would've happened if I hadn't moved away," Mariah said. "Even with the emotional space you were in, we had a good time together."

"I thought you just said we didn't connect."

"I'll put it this way," Mariah said. "We didn't connect as deeply as I would've liked."

The server laid the check on the table. "Whenever you're ready. No rush." She reached for his plate. "Should I box this up for you?"

"Yes, please, thanks," Tommy said, taking a credit card from his wallet. "Thanks for doing this interview, Mariah. I'm excited to write this profile about your rise in Hollywood as a premier director. It's your time to shine."

"Thank you, Tommy. I love that we got a chance to catch up as well." Mariah took out her own credit card. "And I've got that. I'm the one who wanted to go eat. And this was really good."

"I'm glad to hear that," Tommy said, although he was kicking himself for bringing her here. Mariah said she had a taste for Mexican and asked if there were any new places in town. This was the first that came to mind. "But I can't let you do that." He waved the card. "Business expense."

"Fair enough," Mariah said. "But dinner's on me when you come to LA for the premiere of the movie."

"Sounds good," Tommy said. He looked as Jillian got up and walked to the restroom.

"I meant to tell you I heard something interesting the other day," Mariah said. "That you and Jillian were best friends in college."

"Yeah, we were," Tommy said.

"So what did that look like?" Mariah said. "Did you date at some point before you settled on being friends?"

"Not at all," Tommy said. "She was just my closest friend, and it was all platonic."

"And you stayed in touch all these years?" Mariah said.

"We got back in touch a few years ago," Tommy said, "when she came to Living Word for a women's conference."

"It's such a God thing when a friend comes back into your life," Mariah said, "like with the two of us. It makes you pay attention to what He might be doing and even seek His purpose in it." She looked at him. "Marriages don't last forever, but friendships in Christ do. I don't think we think about that enough—how much God values friendship among believers." She stirred her tea with her straw. "I would love for us to build up our friendship, Tommy."

Tommy stared downward, feeling like he'd been hit with a divine two-by-four. Thoughts swirled in his head as he processed it, his pulse racing.

"Tommy?" Mariah said.

"I'm sorry, I just . . . I need a minute."

Jillian's phone vibrated on the table as she ate a taco with grilled chicken. "Sorry, Silas. I think the kids are taking turns as to how often they can bombard me with questions tonight."

Silas had a beef enchilada in hand. "You know I understand."

Jillian looked to see which kid had texted—and looked twice at the name on her screen, even more so at the message. **We have to talk.**

She wanted to turn around and ask if he was crazy. Why was Tommy texting her right now? She replied—**I have nothing to say.**

The second she laid her phone down, it vibrated again. **I have something to say.**

Jillian's jaw tightened even as she tried to look casual. The audacity. Was the world supposed to stop because *he* had something to say? Who did he think he was to interrupt—

Vibrate. **And I need to tell you tonight.**

Jillian looked at Silas. "I'm really sorry. I need one more sec."

"Take your time," Silas said. "No problem."

Jillian's thumb flew across the mini keyboard. **You have so much nerve. Why should I care what you have to say? And if I DID make time to hear it—big IF—it certainly wouldn't be tonight. Why are you texting me anyway? Didn't you outlaw that??**

She could see him typing and kept her phone open for the response. It was short—**Are you clinging?**

Jillian fired a response. **Meaning what?** She took a sip of water, ready to tell Tommy *enough.* She was done with the back and forth.

His text came before she could type hers. **Meaning—did you ask God what HE thinks about talking tonight? Or was that *your* answer? Just trying to get the ultimate situation.**

Jillian couldn't type fast enough. **I seriously can't stand you.**

She dropped her phone into her purse.

Silas looked at her. "Nothing's wrong with the kids, is there?"

Jillian cleared her throat. "No, they're fine."

Silas wiped his mouth with his napkin. "So I was saying I love that there's this interlude before the seventh seal where John sees a great multitude in heaven that no one can count, praising God before His throne. . . ."

Jillian nodded, her stomach cramping.

"So in the midst of horrible judgments happening on earth," Silas continued, "God gives us this glorious scene in heaven. It's just an amazing—"

"Silas, I hate to interrupt," Jillian said. "I need to run to the restroom."

"Oh, of course," Silas said.

Jillian got up and took her purse, knowing her behavior seemed strange. Not to mention—she'd just gone to the bathroom ten minutes before. She walked in, locked herself inside a stall, and leaned against the divider with a sigh.

Lord, what is happening? I thought this evening couldn't get any crazier —then Tommy starts texting in the middle of dinner, from ten feet away? What could be so important that he needs to talk tonight? But he was right, Lord. I gave him my response. I didn't acknowledge You.

She paused as someone walked in and went into a stall.

I don't know what this is about, Lord. But if it's Your will for us to talk tonight, let it be done. Bend my will toward Yours, Lord. 'Cause that's the only way it'll happen. And if it's not Your will—

Jillian felt her phone vibrating with a call. She took it from her purse and shook her head as she answered. "How are you calling me?"

"I took your cue and went to the restroom," Tommy said.

"It wasn't a cue," Jillian whispered.

"Did you talk to Jesus about it?"

"I'm hanging up."

"Jill, wait, can you meet me at the church?" Tommy said.

"At the church?"

"I'm trying to think of a place to talk," Tommy said. "It's too cold to go to Forest Park." He paused. "I need to tell you how God convicted me a few minutes ago."

"Why are you acting as if it can't wait? I'm *sure* it's not urgent."

"You know that feeling when the Spirit is telling you to move and to move *now*?" Tommy said. "I'm not saying it's *urgent*. I'm just trying to obey the prompting of the Spirit."

"Nice. Phrase it in such a way that it's hard to say no."

"It's hard to say no because you prayed about it, and your spirit is bearing witness."

Jillian sighed into the phone.

"See you when you get there, Jill."

Jillian walked up to the main entrance at Living Word, and Tommy pushed the door open for her.

"Hey, Jill," he said.

"Hey," Jillian said.

She entered the building and waited as he locked it back. Taking off her coat, she cast a glance at the corridors beyond them. The foyer was lit but from what she could tell, all else was darkened.

Tommy turned and started walking with her. "So, thanks for coming."

"Where are we going?" Jillian said.

Tommy led her to the elevator. "Fourth floor."

Jillian followed him on. "What's on the fourth floor? I've never been up there."

Tommy pushed the button. "You're about to see."

"Are we the only ones in the building right now?"

"If we aren't then we've got a problem."

"I'm used to being in the Living Water building with only a few people at night," Jillian said, "but not the main church building. But I guess this isn't strange to you."

Tommy shook his head. "It's what I do."

The elevator doors opened and Jillian was struck by the lights that had already been turned on. She followed Tommy as he went left.

"Okay, I thought this would be out of the way storage space or dingy office space," Jillian said. "I was not expecting this." She glanced upward and all around. "The hanging lights from the slanted wooden rafters. The skylights—I can't imagine how this must look during the day. And who tends to these gorgeous plants? They give it an atrium feel." She paused a moment, taking it in.

Tommy kept walking, taking them past a couple of rooms and down another hallway that led to arched wooden doors with stained glass windows on either side. He opened it for her.

Jillian stopped just inside. "I told the Lord I thought this evening couldn't get any crazier." She looked at Tommy. "It just got crazier."

"So you *were* talking to Jesus," Tommy said. "Let me get that," he said, taking her coat.

Jillian moved further inside, surveying the pews and even bigger stained glass windows up front and on either side. "Living Word has a chapel on site? How did I not know that?"

"A lot of people don't know," Tommy said. "We had small ceremonies here years ago, but we basically grew out of it."

"It's so beautiful." Jillian moved up front, examining the detailed architecture and the stained glass. She turned and saw Tommy unscrewing a bulb that had gone out on a wall sconce—and wondered why he was looking so fine lately. She rolled her eyes at him.

"So why are we here?" Jillian said.

Tommy put the bulb where he'd laid their coats. "We needed a place to talk."

"We could've gone to the fellowship area or a hundred other spaces you have access to," Jillian said. "Why the chapel?"

He looked at her. "I wanted someplace special."

Jillian's breath caught. "I have no idea why, but okay." She took a seat in the front pew, her heart rate accelerated. "What did you have to tell me?"

Tommy joined her, the silence engulfing them for a few. "I'm not sure where to start." He took another moment. "When you told me you were having coffee with Silas, it hit me. Hard." He looked at her. "I was jealous, Jill. I knew he was pursuing you, and *I* wanted to be free to pursue you. I wanted to be in a different place with a different mindset and a different past and different hopes for the future. But I wasn't there, and that hurt."

Jillian turned more toward him, listening.

"But it was more than that," Tommy said. "We talk about being best friends in college, but you're my best friend *now*. You know me better than anyone. Our conversations *stay* at the soul level. It irritates me but you even know what I'm thinking half the time."

Jillian wanted to say *that* was what she missed—not being able to talk at the soul level. But she kept listening.

"We can kick it doing whatever, laugh about stupid stuff, talk about the Lord and His faithfulness—any and everything. And you pray for me more than anybody ever has." Tommy took a moment before he continued. "I saw you getting swept off your feet and our friendship getting tossed to the wind. And the thought of that *really* hurt."

"So you decided to fall back," Jillian said.

"I told you I didn't want to complicate things for you," Tommy said. "I told myself that too. But I was just trying to protect myself from what seemed inevitable."

"Which didn't make any sense," Jillian said. "You can't even know what's inevitable. You reacted and jumped fifty feet ahead based on a *coffee* date."

"At least you're now calling it what it was," Tommy said.

"You said you didn't want to complicate things for me," Jillian said, "but I kept saying I didn't want anything to change as far as our friendship. So you actually *did* complicate things, by redefining it."

Tommy looked at her. "I was in my feelings, Jill. And I've been miserable every day that I couldn't talk to the one person I want to talk to."

Jillian gave him a look. "You weren't miserable at that Super Bowl party. Nor at dinner tonight." She paused. "And since you admitted to feeling jealous, I'll admit the same. It felt like you tossed our friendship aside and replaced it a minute later with Mariah."

"As if that were even possible," Tommy said. "Jill, you hung up when I called to talk about that Super Bowl party. I *was* miserable. I left soon after you did. Didn't play cards afterward. Didn't even stay for the end of the game."

"That's never happened," Jillian said.

"I felt I had let my friend down," Tommy said. "You were hurting over Trevor's birthday and thought I had come to check on you. Then I left with Mariah and even though, in my mind, I'm sitting and watching the game, she's beside me, talking. I knew it felt like—*whatever, Jill*. And next thing I knew, you were gone. I didn't feel like staying either."

"I couldn't sleep that night," Jillian said. "I thought our friendship was a gift, and I couldn't understand why it was basically over. But I kept saying, 'Lord, Your will.'"

"Then tonight happened," Tommy said. "I was kicking myself for going there—until I saw God show up." He got up and paced a little. "Mariah was talking about how much God values friendship among believers. She even made the point that unlike marriage, friendships in Christ last forever. And I felt this strong conviction."

"Why?" Jillian said.

"Our friendship *is* a gift from Him," Tommy said. "And I backed away from it—not led by the Spirit, but by the flesh." He paced some more. "It hit me so hard tonight—I wasn't clinging to the Lord when I did that. I was just feeling sorry for myself." He looked at her. "I'm sorry, Jill. And I hope you can forgive me because if I've lost my best friend . . ."

Jillian stared downward. "It was a lot. Losing my husband and grieving him. Then feeling like I'd lost our friendship and grieving that. Besides my father, there are only two men that I *know* God put in my life. Cecil . . . and you. And you *both* were gone." Several seconds elapsed. "I was praying that His will be done, and if that was His will, I knew He'd be with me, and I'd be okay. But hearing you say all of this . . . I'm thankful to God." She looked up, tears welling. "You know I forgive you."

Tommy blew out a sigh. "Thank you, Jill." He sighed again. So you heard me say I wanted someplace special." He went and stood near the front. "Can you come up here, please?"

Jillian's insides were a jumble as she got up and joined him. "What are you doing, Tommy?"

"You said we had this unwritten rule where we don't talk about feelings," Tommy said, "and that I have a hard time saying what's on my mind." He paused. "I'm going to tell you exactly what's on my mind."

Jillian blew out a breath. "Okay."

Tommy looked into her eyes. "I love you more than I ever knew was possible." He took a moment, holding her gaze. "But this place I'm in . . . I don't even understand it fully. I know there's pain, and fear, lots of doubt about a lot of things." He paused. "And I know God is working on me. Maybe that's why I feel called to singleness, because of the work He's doing. Maybe I won't know it's time to do something else until He lets me know it's time. But I'm not saying 'never' about the future anymore. I'm clinging and praying. If it's God's will for me to be in a relationship, I pray He'll do enough of a work in me that I'm willing. And I pray it won't be too late for that person to be you."

Jillian's heart reacted as his eyes filled with tears.

"But I truly feel that our friendship is the treasure." Tommy paused, taking a breath. "In Christ the friendship is what will last eternally. And I'm grateful that I don't have to be in a particular place in order for us to be friends. I can still be in the Refiner's fire. I can still be broken—"

"Tommy . . ." She wiped his tears as her own began to flow.

"This is really a praise I'm feeling," Tommy said. "God gave us friendships in Christ to help one another, and you've been there for me. So I want to express my commitment to the friendship, especially after I almost messed it up." He took out his phone. "I was moved to look up all the 'one another' verses I could find, about how believers are to treat each other. I put them in my notes."

"When did you have time to do that?" Jillian said.

Tommy navigated on his phone. "While you were taking your time to finish that extra-long dinner with Silas."

"I bet that felt really good to say."

"You have no idea." Tommy took a breath. "Okay . . ." He held his phone before him. "Jilli-Jill, as your friend in Christ and as called by God, I promise to encourage you and to build you up, to bear with you and to bear your burdens, to serve you, to seek after that which is good for you, to pursue the things which make for peace, to be kind, tender-hearted, and forgiving, to clothe myself in humility toward you, to regard you as more important than myself, to pray for you, and to love you." He'd been looking up intermittently but now he focused on her. "Not a dreamy or romantic love. I promise to love you with Christ's love, the kind of love that lasts forever."

Jillian couldn't see for her tears.

"I promise to be your friend." Tommy's voice broke as he said it. "And unless and until you get swept off your feet and tell me this season of friendship is over, I ain't going nowhere."

Jillian got tissues from her purse and gave him one, using the other herself. "Give me that," she said, taking his phone. "Tommy-Tom, as your friend in Christ and as called by God . . ." She repeated everything he said, but with a different ending. "I promise to be your friend and to love you with Christ's love." She looked into his eyes. "I promise to love you through the brokenness."

Tommy took her into his arms and held onto her. She could feel emotion emanating from his chest, even as her tears wet his sweater.

"Oh my gosh." Jillian took a step back, looking at him. "Oh. My. Gosh."

"What is it?" Tommy said.

She wiped her face with the tissue. "I said there was no such thing as forever."

"Huh?"

"We were studying for finals," Jillian said. "And you asked if I thought our friendship would last forever."

Tommy thought for a moment. "Wow," he said. "I forgot all about that."

"So did I," Jillian said. "It just popped into my mind."

"How crazy is that?" Tommy said. "Way back then, I wanted our friendship to last forever. Why would I even say that?"

"I've got goose bumps," Jillian said, holding herself. "We had no concept of forever. Didn't know Jesus. Didn't know anything about eternal life."

"But God knew that one day we *would* know Him," Tommy said. "And that this thing that seemed impossible—a forever friendship— would be real. In Christ." He paused, processing it. "How mind-blowing is that? He knew that decades later we'd connect that moment to this."

"Moments like this I'm so in awe of God's sovereignty," Jillian said. "How He moves across time and seasons and people's lives. It's mind-boggling."

"I already know I'll be thinking more about tonight and how everything unfolded," Tommy said. "It's confirming for me that God really is working."

He turned out the lights, and they got their coats, Tommy tucking the light bulb into his pocket before they walked out.

He fell into a silence, turning out additional lights as they went. "Thinking back to that time in college," he said, "I remember how protective I was of you." He looked at Jillian. "I hate that I didn't protect you when I fell into that emotional tailspin. I hate that that happened between us, Jill. I wish our record before God was spotless. You don't know how many times I've gone to the Lord—"

"Tommy." Jillian stopped and looked at him. "I have a good idea how many times, by the number of times you've expressed it to me. And you know I have the same regrets. I was in my own emotional tailspin. We didn't cling to God, and we experienced the pain that comes from that." She looked at him. "But we just had a whole cele-bration the other night, praising God for His promises. You already know this promise, but hear it is again, First John 1:9—'If we confess our sins, He is faithful and righteous to forgive us our sins and to cleanse us from all unrighteousness.' And Psalm 103:12—'As far as the east is from the west, So far has He removed our transgressions from us.'" She paused. "Now ask me how I know those by heart."

"I know it weighs on you too," Tommy said.

"We have to believe those promises just like all the others," Jillian said. "Our record *is* spotless before God, because the blood of Jesus covers our sin."

"That's mind-blowing too," Tommy said, walking. "You know? The fact that Jesus would shed His blood for us. We're the ones who sinned, but He *died* for us." He hit the down button.

"We'll praise and thank Him forever," Jillian said.

Tommy walked onto the elevator. "Thank you, Jill."

"For what?" She joined him, pushing the button for the first floor.

"Forgiving me like Christ does," Tommy said.

"Well, it's one of the 'one another's,'" Jillian said. "Part of our friendship vows."

Tommy looked at her. "Friendship vows. I like the sound of that."

Jillian met his gaze. "I do too."

CHAPTER 47

$\mathcal{S}$ophia descended the stairs at the B and B close to midnight, texting Lucas as she listened to music. In touch every day now, he'd even come to church during the *Promises* celebration so they could see each other. Sophia had slipped away during one of the testimonies and met him in their secret hallway. She would've stayed longer if Joy hadn't texted that she and Hope were moving to her table.

She walked into the kitchen and flicked on a light as she read his latest text. **Ppl at school keep talking abt Hollywood in STL... and you're PART of it. You LIVE w them.**

Sophia opened the fridge and got a Coke, thinking about that. A lot of her friends from back home had reached out with that same sentiment, almost making her feel like a celebrity herself. She popped open the soda can, took a sip, then typed a reply. **Not for long. B&B life is over soon. Excited to be an intern tho.**

She went into the pantry and sifted through the snacks, deciding on a bag of salt and vinegar chips as her phone dinged again.

You should send me that pic you posted.

She typed back. **The one with me, Joy & Alonzo? Why?**

"I see I'm not the only one raiding the kitchen."

Sophia looked up, her pulse accelerating at the sight of Noah in joggers, a hoodie, and slides. She'd seen him at breakfast every morning this week, and they'd exchanged a few words. But he still had an aura about him.

"Yeah, just grabbing some chips." She'd come down in leggings and an oversized shirt. "Did you want some?"

"Any pretzels?" Noah came closer, looking.

"Yup." Sophia passed him a bag. "And did you want the Hershey's?" She felt silly asking, but by now, they all knew hot chocolate was his thing.

Noah smiled. "That was next on the list. Thanks." He took the box. "And do you know if any of those chocolate cookies are left from earlier today?"

Sophia's phone dinged, and she silenced it. "They're over here." She took her earbuds out as she led him to a cookie jar on the counter.

"That's everything I need," Noah said. "Thanks, Sophia." He started filling the teakettle with water.

"I'm surprised you remember," Sophia said.

Noah looked back at her. "Remember what?"

"My name."

"We're staying at the same house," Noah said. "And y'all are hosting us. It would be rude not to remember your name."

"Actually, we're just filling in," Sophia said. "It's our last night." She watched him take a packet out of the box. "Have you ever made it with the actual cocoa? Where you heat the ingredients on a stove?"

"Nah, I'm always on the go, in a hotel or something," Noah said. "It's hard enough to find a microwave to heat the water for the packet."

"As much as you love that stuff, you should try the real thing," Sophia said. "It only takes about five minutes."

"You mean you could make it right now?" Noah said. "You've got the ingredients?"

"I think so," Sophia said.

She went back to the pantry and got the Hershey's cocoa and some sugar. Then she got vanilla extract from a cabinet and milk from the fridge. She looked at him. "You want a mocha cocoa?"

Noah smiled, nodding. "You already know."

Sophia added coffee to the ingredients on the counter, then got a saucepan and followed the directions on the Hershey's container.

Noah watched as she mixed sugar and cocoa in a saucepan. "You said it's your last night here. But you're an intern, right? You'll be on set?"

"Only sometimes," Sophia said. "But I'm looking forward to it."

Noah opened his pretzels, watching her stir. "So you're in college? High school?"

"I'm a high school senior." Sophia added milk once it came to a boil and kept stirring. "So you do this every night, get a midnight snack?"

"Not really," Noah said. "My producer sent some tracks we're working on for my next album, so I'm up listening."

Sophia looked at him. "Richie Brazil?"

"You're up on my music?" Noah said.

"Ever since you dropped 'So Long' on Soundcloud." Sophia removed the pan from the heat. "I used to love when you'd play your guitar and sing on YouTube too."

"Come on," Noah said. "You go back to Soundcloud days?"

"I remember when you had something like three thousand Instagram followers." Sophia added the vanilla and instant coffee and beat the mixture with a whisk. "I kept wondering when you would blow up, because the music was so good."

"I can't believe you're one of the day-ones." Noah took out his phone. "What's your IG?"

"Why?" Sophia said.

"Imma follow you," Noah said.

She got her phone and showed him her handle. "Why are you following me?"

"I appreciate the support," Noah said, clicking the follow button.

Sophia ignored the butterflies. He followed hundreds of women. "Okay, ready to try it?" She got a mug from the cabinet and poured him some.

"That looks really good," Noah said. "Are you pouring some for yourself?"

"I was about to head back up with my Coke and chips," Sophia said.

"You don't like hot chocolate?"

"I do," Sophia said. "My mom used to make it like this for us. But I already had my Coke, so . . ." She shrugged.

Noah glanced over at the kitchen table. "You should get a cup and listen to the tracks with me."

Sophia's eyes widened. "You would let me hear?"

"You're a for-real fan of the music," Noah said. "And that energizes me. I'd love to hear your thoughts. I can run up and get my laptop."

"I would love that," Sophia said. "But first, taste it," she said, nodding to the mug.

Noah blew the steam and took a sip. "Ohhh, this is a problem," he said, his dimples showing. "I can never go back."

"Told ya," Sophia said.

Noah took another sip and left to get his laptop. Sophia poured herself a cup and took a seat at the table, checking her phone. She saw several texts from Lucas, wondering where she'd gone.

Sorry. Noah walked in and we started talking. Sending the pic.

Sophia sent Lucas the picture and thought about texting Joy to tell her she was hanging with Noah. But she was probably sleep. She'd tell her in the morning.

Noah returned, placing the laptop between them on the table.

"You should use the earbuds," Noah said, "so you can hear the nuances."

Sophia took a sip of cocoa. "That's the only way I listen to music."

Noah hesitated. "I'm always nervous when it's a new project and I'm just starting to share it. So I want your feedback, but just know my stomach is in knots."

"That's hard to believe," Sophia said, even as she noted the cute furrow in his brow.

"It's real," Noah said. "It's hard to put yourself out there. But I want you to be honest. You're one of the first to hear this."

"Okay, then." Sophia put in her earbuds and plugged them into his laptop. "Play the first track."

~

"Soph, are you sleep? During a test?"

Sophia roused herself, lifting her head. "Huh?"

Joy pointed at the computer screen. "You fell asleep during your Latin test."

"No, I finished it." Sophia yawned, rubbing her eyes, then looked at the screen. "Oh, no, I didn't send it!" She clicked it and checked the clock. "Ten more minutes and it would've been a fail, literally. Thanks, girl."

"Good thing I had to come back for my camera." Joy got the bag from among her things. "Jade's letting me get footage of wardrobe and the production office for the vlog, while she gets footage from the last day of rehearsal on set."

"This is the perfect setup," Sophia said. "You think Aunt Treva'll let us do our school work in her office more often? We're close to everything."

"I don't know," Joy said, checking her camera bag. "Depends on what she's got going. And she's still not totally used to homeschooling, so she feels like she needs to oversee everything." She looked at her. "So what's up with you today? That's the second time you fell asleep."

"Oh, we've been busy with school so I hadn't had a chance to tell you." Sophia turned more toward her. "I was up late listening to some of Noah's music."

"You always listen to music as you fall asleep," Joy said.

"No, I was listening *with* Noah," Sophia said. "To some new music he's working on."

Joy focused on her. "How did you not have a chance to tell me *that*? That should've been the first thing you said when you picked me up this morning."

"You know how cranky I am when I don't get enough sleep,"

Sophia said. "I didn't feel like talking. And I was still processing it. It was unbelievable."

Joy came and stood near her. "How did it happen?"

"Really random," Sophia said. "We were both getting a snack and started talking in the kitchen. Then I ended up making hot cocoa for him—"

"What?"

"He loves hot cocoa," Sophia said. "Then he found out I was a long-time fan, so he let me listen to some tracks for his upcoming album. We were there till past one o'clock."

"I've got shivers," Joy said. "So what was it like? Being near him like that? And what was *he* like?"

"He mostly just sat back and let me listen and give feedback," Sophia said. "And he'd share the story behind the songs. I loved that part."

"I'm waiting to hear what it was like being near him," Joy said.

"Kind of unreal," Sophia said. "I thought he'd be constantly on his phone or something, but he actually focused on what we were doing." She thought a moment. "I felt like I got to know him a little, which I didn't expect." She sighed. "But it didn't mean anything. We move back home today, so . . ."

"Mind. Blown." Joy sighed, shaking her head as she took the camera bag. "Off to get footage. Cinda said she could use you in wardrobe when you're done with school."

"Why didn't you say that when you first came in here?" Sophia said.

"I was still processing it," Joy said.

"Ha. Ha."

Sophia packed up her books, though she had a little more work to do. If Cinda could use her now, she'd rather spend time in wardrobe and finish her work tonight. She headed for the elevator as her phone dinged.

U still here? Just pulled up.

Sophia replied. **What are u doing here? Omw down.**

As she approached the entryway, Lucas came into the building in jeans and a jacket. He put his hands in his coat pocket. "I don't live far, so since you said you were hanging out here today"—he shrugged —"thought I'd stop by after school."

"I wish I had more time," Sophia said. "I'm headed to the wardrobe department in the other building."

"Okay, before you go . . ." Lucas looked a little shy. "I wondered if you might want to go out this evening. Maybe a movie. Or we could get something to eat."

"Oh, I don't think that'll work," Sophia said. "We're moving out of the B and B this evening."

"What about tomorrow?"

"Tomorrow's my brother's birthday," Sophia said, "so we're all going to this concert."

"Sunday?" Lucas said. "That is, if you even want to go out with me."

"I do," Sophia said with a smile. "Can I let you know tomorrow?" She also still needed to find a way to tell Joy.

"Tomorrow sounds good," Lucas said. He hesitated a moment. "So what was that with you and Noah?"

"Me and Noah?" Sophia said.

"Last night," Lucas said. "We were texting then you checked out."

"He and I were talking, like I told you," Sophia said. "And I didn't check out. I sent you that picture you wanted."

"But I texted a few more times after that and . . ." Lucas waved a hand. "Never mind. I started getting these crazy thoughts about you dating Noah, and I knew I couldn't compete with that."

"Definitely a crazy thought," Sophia said. "You and I aren't even dating yet."

"I'm your first kiss, though."

Sophia felt the heat in her cheeks. "About that . . . I don't want you to think that's going to be . . . regular."

"Yeah, if you tried it again," Lucas said, "I was going to tell you we can't make it a thing."

"Ha," Sophia said, putting on her jacket. "By the way, why'd you want that picture?"

Lucas opened his phone and passed it to her. The picture, cropped to show only Sophia, was on the screen.

"You made me your wallpaper?" Sophia passed it back. "Okay, that's creepy."

"No one'll see it but me," Lucas said. "And you look way better than anything else I've had on my screen."

"I'm cringing," Sophia said, opening the door. "Just know that I'm not sending you any more pictures."

"I'll take my own, on our date," Lucas said. "And hey, how about your mom and my dad going to dinner last night? I guess they're a thing now. Anyway, I'll talk to you later."

Sophia took out her phone as she started toward the building.

Just got some news. We need a meeting.

CHAPTER 48

*B*rooke checked a new text message and sighed, increasingly irritated by her boyfriend's tone. She just wanted to enjoy the impromptu celebration they were having for the end of rehearsals.

"Congrats again, everybody," Mariah was saying. "We accomplished so much in rehearsals this week." She had a spot on a sofa in the B and B sitting room. "The goal wasn't to become more familiar with your lines, but to get more acquainted with each other and with the soul of this story. I saw that happening more and more each day."

"I love that our core cast is small." Alonzo sat with Cinda on another sofa. "We've been able to get to know one another relatively quickly. Like Noah and his insane love of Hershey's."

"I'm not the only one who loves chocolate," Noah said. "If you're coming, I know I need to hide some of the chocolate volcano cookies."

"So that's why there weren't as many today, huh?" Alonzo said.

"Food's here," Faith called, coming through the front door. "I'll set it up in the dining room."

"Right on time," Mariah said, rising. "I love this Friday night party we've got going."

Cinda got up as well. "I've been texting and spreading the word. People are on their way."

Brooke hung back as everyone moved to the dining room, checking the series of texts she'd been ignoring. Cornell had had an attitude before she even left. He'd wanted to come with her, and she'd told him this wasn't the time. Besides the rehearsal and shooting schedule, she'd wanted to use this time to reconnect with God. Still, he'd found a way to keep her preoccupied with complaints that she was ignoring him.

Avoiding was more like it. Time away had given her the clarity she needed to end their living arrangement. But she knew it would be hard. They'd moved in together because neither could afford a decent place on their own. Brooke had already been talking to Cinda and Alonzo about possible roommates in LA. Cornell would have to scout out the same. She just didn't know how to tell him.

As Brooke pondered how to answer his latest texts, more group texts came. She, Robin, and Jesse now had a daily thread of current events, randomness, and silliness. She skimmed to Robin's last text—

So it's Friday—what's happening in STL tonight? You two hanging?

Brooke felt a flutter. Was Robin suggesting that Brooke and Jesse get together? She was about to text her privately and tell her not to go there—and Jesse's response came.

No big plans. Got a text about a get together at the B and B, so I'm on my way. Always down for food lol. Brooke, maybe I'll see u there?

Flutter. Brooke shook it off and replied—**Yup, we're all here.**

Brooke heard additional voices coming in and went to join everyone. She'd reply to Cornell later.

"Good to see you, Brooke," Treva said, hugging her.

"It's good to see you too," Brooke said. She hugged Lance next. "Thank you again for everything this week. I understand so much more about Kendra just from the things you shared with us."

"I wish I could've been around more," Lance said. "But if you ever have a question, don't hesitate to ask." He smiled as Pamela and Tommy walked up beside them. "How was the lesson today?"

"First, let me tell you—I got to go with Tommy to the news station, where he does his Friday entertainment thing," Pamela said. "I got such a kick being behind the scenes."

"Momma Pam, you're behind the scenes of a movie production every day," Tommy said. "That news segment isn't a big deal. Tell them your big news with the driving."

"I drove on the street for the first time," Pamela said, "with cars, stop lights, and everything."

"You go, Pam," Treva said, hugging her.

Brooke clapped as Lance hugged her next. "That's awesome, Miss Pam," she said. "After you told us about your driving lessons at the *Promises* celebration, I definitely wanted to hear updates."

"Thank you for that, Brooke," Pamela said, smiling. She elbowed Tommy. "Tell them what you got me."

"What did I get you?" Tommy said.

"The sign!" Pamela said.

"Oh, goodness," Tommy said, chuckling. "Momma Pam was so elated to see the 'student driver' sign I put in the back window."

"It took some of the pressure off," Pamela said. "Nobody honked at me."

"They didn't honk because you were handling your business," Tommy said. "I told her she did such a good job."

"To be fair, we only went three blocks," Pamela said.

"Mom, you do it every time," Lance said. "You get excited about your progress, then you minimize it. You went three blocks with actual moving cars, and you were *driving*. That's a praise!"

"What's all the excitement over here?" Mariah said, walking up.

"Just reporting my driving progress today," Pamela said. "Tommy had me out on the street. I drove three blocks."

"Way to go!" Mariah said, hugging her. "I've been praying for you."

"I'm so thankful," Pamela said.

Mariah looked at Tommy. "You must've gotten my text about the party. I'm glad you came."

"I did get it, thanks," Tommy said. "That's why I brought Momma Pam, knowing she could ride home with Lance and Treva. I was coming anyway, to help Jill with all the stuff she brought over here."

"I forgot that Stephanie and Lindell were returning this evening," Treva said.

"There's Jill now," Tommy said, looking across the room. "Let me see what she needs."

Brooke looked across the room herself—at Jesse. He'd just arrived and was talking to someone. She moved to the buffet that had been set up and started making a plate.

"All right, let's get this party started for real." One of the guys on the crew set up a smart speaker on a side table. "Alexa, play Noah Stiles."

The room erupted as one of Noah's jams started playing. Then phones went in the air, recording as Noah grabbed Sophia and started dancing.

"Okay, Sophia!" Brooke called. "You better hang with Hershey!"

Noah laughed. "You *know* you're gonna get it for that, Brooke."

Brooke added two kinds of pasta and salad to her plate and got some plastic silverware.

"You're just now eating?" Jesse said, coming beside her.

"Yeah, I've been talking," Brooke said. "And hey to you too."

"Haven't we been texting all day?" Jesse got a plate himself. "I feel like we said hello hours ago."

"That group text is too funny," Brooke said. "I don't know who's crazier between you and Robin."

Jesse smiled as he added chicken Parmesan to his plate. "Always been that way. We bring out the crazy in each other."

Brooke felt awkward waiting as Jesse got his food. Why would she assume they'd be eating together? "I'm heading to the sitting room," she said.

"Good idea," Jesse said. "I want to sit and eat, and all the chairs are taken in here."

Brooke led the way, surprised the room was empty. She sat on the sofa and Jesse joined her.

"Hey, did Cinda come through here?" Faith said, popping in.

"I have no idea," Jesse said. "Literally just got here."

"Okay, thanks."

"Hey, Faith," Jesse said, "I'm assuming *somebody* is taking care of Zoe? I got nervous when Reggie walked in a minute ago."

"I know, right?" Faith said. "*Everybody*'s here—except Hope. She's got your princess."

Jesse put a hand to his heart. "Ahh, all is well."

Brooke looked at him as Faith walked out. "I saw you with your daughter at the Super Bowl party. She's so adorable." She paused. "So you and Faith, huh?"

Jesse forked up some ravioli. "For a moment in time. And thank you. Zoe's my heart."

"Faith is from Maryland too, right?" Brooke said. "How'd you both end up in St. Louis?"

"Faith moved out here when her mom married Lance," Jesse said. "She was pregnant with Zoe at the time." He ate more of his food. "After she had the baby, I transferred to WashU here in St. Louis to finish my graduate degree, to be near Zoe."

"Just Zoe?" Brooke took a bite of French bread.

"There's a story there," Jesse said. "But in the end, yes. Just Zoe." He cut into the chicken Parmesan. "What's the story behind your moving to LA? You always dreamed of being an actor?"

"For as long as I can remember," Brooke said. "Always auditioning for school plays, then community theater. Majored in drama at UVA. Then I had to ask myself if I was going to go for it or not. I'm not a big risk taker, but it felt like I was putting everything on the line if I moved to LA."

"But you did it," Jesse said. "And you're about to be a big star. Is that trippy?"

"I'm not about to be a big star." Brooke ate some of her salad. "It's an amazing breakout role, though. And yes, every day is trippy playing opposite Alonzo—oh, and Alonzo announced that the Cling study is starting Sunday at the church. So thanks for telling us about it. From what I hear, that's what sparked it."

"Yeah, the church sent an email today," Jesse said. "So you're going?"

Brooke nodded, eating her pasta. "They said they'll find rides for people who want to go."

"If you want to go, I'll come get you," Jesse said.

"That's a lot, Jesse," Brooke said. "The class is early, during first service. So you'd have to leave that much earlier in order to swing by here."

"You said that like it's a problem," Jesse said. "I can take whoever's here that wants to go."

"Well, wow," Brooke said. "That's really—"

"Oh, hey, somebody else had the same idea." Jade walked in with Trey.

"Hey, guys," Brooke said.

"Trey, I've been wanting to get with you man," Jesse said. "I think I mentioned before . . . I used to meet regularly with Lance, and he told me a lot about you."

"Uh-oh," Trey said, taking the love seat.

"Let me put it this way," Jesse said. "He said I reminded him of you in a lot of ways."

"So we can keep it real then," Trey said.

"Exactly," Jesse said. "I know you just got back and you're busy with the film. Just wanted you to know I'd love to connect when you get time."

"Let's do it," Trey said.

"Speaking of connecting," Jade said, "Brooke, I would love for you to do a ministry moment for the vlog. I heard you say that God was getting your attention when you got this role. If that's something you'd be willing to talk about, I think it would be perfect."

"I would love to," Brooke said. "I'm not sure how I would talk about it, though, since things aren't resolved yet." She thought a moment. "Or I could just be vague-ish about the particulars. That could work."

"No pressure and no rush," Jade said. "We'll be doing this throughout the shoot. So think about it, pray about it, and whatever you decide is cool."

"Okay people, I'm coming for y'all." Mariah motioned for them to get up. "We moved the table back and made a bigger dance floor. Let's get it!" She moved toward the library and started rounding people up in there.

"I'm so glad I brought my camera," Jade said. "We haven't had any footage like this on the vlog."

"How are you getting footage *and* dancing?" Trey said.

"Obviously, I'm not dancing," Jade said.

"But you are." Trey got up and pulled her up by the hand. "It'll make my night just to see if you know how to let go and have fun on the dance floor."

"You trying to say I can't?"

"I'm saying if you can, it'll be a wonder."

"One song just to prove the point," Jade said, following him out. "Then I'm taking out my camera."

Jesse looked at Brooke. "Are we following orders or rebelling?"

Brooke got up. "I'm gonna go in. It'll be fun."

"I was about to rebel," Jesse said, rising. "But since you shamed me."

Brooke and Jesse walked into the dining room, which had been transformed. Lights dimmed, music knocking, it had a club vibe as several people had taken to the floor.

Jesse looked at her. "If we're in here, might as well dance."

"Is that your way of asking?" Brooke said.

"Nope," Jesse said. "Because I'm still lightweight rebelling."

They moved a few feet onto the dance area as an up-tempo song played through the speaker. Jade and Trey danced next to them, Jade feeling the groove.

"Hey, Trey, I guess it's a wonder, huh?" Jesse said.

"I'm shocked she knows how to have fun," Trey said.

Brooke smiled. "This is definitely fun. And I love this song." She lifted her arms, enjoying the groove herself. "You don't look like you're rebelling *too* much, Jesse."

"I actually can't remember the last time I danced anywhere," Jesse said. "So I guess it's *kinda* fun."

"I see you meant it when you said one song." Jesse laughed as Jade took footage of them and others dancing.

"You knew I wasn't playing," Jade said. "This is way more important." She moved to the other side of the floor.

"Where's Jade's sister?" Brooke said.

Jesse shrugged. "No idea."

Brooke looked confused. "I thought you two were together."

"'Were' being the operative word."

"Oh," Brooke said. "That's pretty recent. I'm sorry."

"No need to be," Jesse said.

"Heyyy, welcome back!" rang out from several voices.

Brooke turned and saw Stephanie and Lindell come into the room. The music stopped and Mariah walked toward them.

She hugged Stephanie. "First, welcome back," she said. "Second, I take full responsibility for the fact that the furniture is rearranged and we've got a full-on party happening. I know it's been a long trip, so we'll shut it down so you can rest."

Stephanie exchanged words with Lindell and looked at everybody. "Y'all, we had two long flights and we are *tired*. But that was *the* best vacation ever, so we're ready to party *with* you. Turn the music back up!"

Cheers went up, the music came back on, and Stephanie and Lindell went around the room greeting people.

Brooke looked at Jesse. "I won't shame you if you're ready to sit back down."

"Nah," Jesse said. "This is the good time I didn't know I needed." He smiled at her. "You wanna dance?"

CHAPTER 49

*J*illian stood on a ladder in her kitchen Saturday morning, trying to stretch a vinyl birthday banner from one side to the other. Twice she'd affixed it to one wall, but because of its weight, it fell before she could affix it to the opposite side. On this third try it was looking good, staying in place. *Please let it work this time, Lord.* The end of the banner in hand, she climbed the ladder rungs slowly and affixed it to the opposite wall with a heavy piece of industrial tape.

Jillian removed her hand, seeing if it would stay in place, then walked back down and took a look. She sighed relief. *Finally.* This was a family tradition, hanging the birthday banner so the birthday kid would see it first thing in the morning. David and Sophia had both opted against tradition on their birthdays. It was too hard doing what they'd always done, without their dad. So instead of a family breakfast at home, they'd gone out to eat. And instead of dinner at a favorite restaurant, they'd eaten at home. But Trevor said he wanted the family traditions, and as hard as it might be, she wanted to give that to him.

Earlier this morning she'd gotten two bouquets of mylar and latex balloons. She attached them now to weights and arranged them on the island. Next she sprinkled "13" confetti on the kitchen table and counter, then checked the frittata mini muffins in the oven. Trevor not only wanted breakfast—he wanted a smorgasbord such as they'd had at the B and B all week.

Thank You, Lord, that Trev's birthday fell on a Saturday, so we could have this time as a family.

She took the mini muffin tins out and turned to get something from the fridge—and the banner fell, clipping her shoulders before the vinyl hit the floor.

Jillian stared at it. She couldn't do it again. Couldn't move the ladder to the other side to fix the one end to the wall then stretch it to the other, hoping the first end didn't fall, then climb the ladder again to the top—she *hated* climbing ladders—to fix the other end when the stupid thing would keep falling anyway. This was *Cecil's* thing. If he ever had any issues, she never knew about it. He just did it.

Her mind went to Trevor's last birthday when Cecil hung the banner early and took the boys to play basketball at his school. They never complained about being awakened before dawn when it meant they could get in a game with their dad. For Cecil it was about the quality time, but it also gave Jillian time to decorate the kitchen and cook. She hadn't asked him to do it. He just knew. They were a team. Now she daily got reminders in one form or another that he was no longer with her.

Jillian kicked the banner aside and opened the fridge but couldn't remember what she'd wanted. She groaned aloud and closed it back.

Lord, it's the little things like that stupid banner. I lose it over the little things. Please help me. I woke up feeling the grief, couldn't stop crying in the shower, but You gave me strength to get moving. I got the balloons, started cooking, actually felt pretty good. Then a banner sends me over the edge.

She opened the fridge again, remembering it was eggs. Eggs for the chocolate cake mix waffles. *That's why I don't think I'm the one to do this grief study, Lord. Shouldn't it be someone who has a better handle on her emotions? Someone who can celebrate a kid's birthday without crying a river? Your will, Lord, always. But I don't mind telling Cyd—*

She looked as Sophia walked in wearing sweat shorts and a wrinkled top, her hair in a messy ponytail.

"Good morning, Soph," Jillian said, turning on the waffle maker.

Sophia stepped over the banner and came near, hugging her. "Morning, Mom."

"What are you up to this morning?" Jillian poured the chocolate cake mix into a bowl.

"So we've been busy with B and B stuff, and I hadn't had a chance to ask you," Sophia said. "Are you dating Pastor Keys?"

"Where did that come from?" Jillian said.

"Lucas," Sophia said.

"I didn't even know you talked to Lucas." Jillian cracked the eggs.

"Yeah, I was going to get to that after this," Sophia said. "First he told me you and his dad had coffee. Then yesterday he told me you went to dinner. He said you two are a thing now."

"No, we are not a thing." Jillian paused, looking at her. "Dinner was spur of the moment and related to a Bible study project we might be working on. I didn't mention that or the coffee because I know it's a lot to swallow, just the fact that I'm out with someone. I didn't want to say anything until I felt it was truly—"

"So you two are just casually talking?" David walked in looking confused. "As if I couldn't be Trevor right now? And if I *were* Trevor, my eyes would've hit midair—because that's where the banner is supposed to be. But where is it?" He shook his head as he picked it up and stretched it out. "The moment would be ruined."

Jillian watched as David went to a cabinet, got a hammer and nails, and moved the ladder to the other side of the kitchen. Climbing the ladder with the banner in hand, he nailed one side of it to the wall, then did the same on the other side. It hung perfectly.

He went back to the entrance to the kitchen and gave a sigh. "Now the young man can have his moment."

"Come here, David." Jillian hugged him. "You don't know how much that blessed me."

Sophia looked at her brother. "So, David, they're not a thing."

David looked at her. "You're not supposed to give the intel *in front of* Mom."

"What's going on with you two?" Jillian said.

Sophia and David looked at one another.

"When Lucas told me about the coffee date," Sophia said, "I told David."

"Which I already knew about," David said, "since I saw you and Pastor Keys when you were leaving church."

"Then I told David about the dinner," Sophia said. "So we've had a couple of meetings—"

"A couple of meetings?" Jillian said.

"In the tradition of the family meeting that you and Dad started," David said. "You can call these . . . committee meetings." He glanced at Sophia. "Which is why it should've stayed in committee."

The doorbell rang, followed by several knocks.

"Who could that be?" Jillian said.

Before she could go see, they heard the door open and close.

"Okay, what's happening right now?" Sophia said.

They moved out of the kitchen and gasped at the sight. "Courtenay?!"

Courtenay beamed as she set down her bags and came toward them. "Surprised?"

Jillian embraced her. "You drove up here? Through the night?"

"Where'd you get that jacket?" Sophia hugged her. "I'm borrowing."

"You're too old for hugs now, David?" Courtenay waved him over. "Get over here."

"I don't have a problem with hugs." David embraced her. "I get lots of hugs in youth group."

Jillian looked at him. "Oh, really?"

"Look at him, Mom." Courtenay took off her jacket and laid it on the sofa. "He's fifteen, getting tall, filling out. And he's a cutie."

"I'm so not ready," Jillian said. "So what in the world are you doing here, Courtenay?"

"I wanted to surprise Trevor," Courtenay said. "It's a big birthday for him, and I could tell he really wanted it to feel special. I drove up yesterday and stayed at Faith's last night so I could *really* surprise him, on the day."

"You surprised all of us," Jillian said. "It couldn't be more special—ahh, and there he is, the birthday boy."

Trevor came down the stairs looking half asleep. "I heard all these voices, and I thought I must be dreaming when I heard Courtenay."

"Not a dream." Courtenay went and gave him a big hug. "Happy Birthday, Trev!"

Jillian hugged him next. "It's official, Trev. You're a teenager."

"Still a youngin', though." David mussed Trevor's curly hair. "You'll always be the baby."

"Happy Birthday, baby brother," Sophia said, hugging him. She turned to the others. "Anybody notice we hug a lot as a family? Are we weird?"

"Group hug!" David said, pouncing on Sophia and Trevor.

Sophia squirmed. "Boy, you're pulling my hair."

Courtenay brought Jillian into the fray, all of them laughing, arms around one another.

"To answer your question," David said. "Yes. We are weird."

"This right here is called a blessing," Jillian said, arms around them still. "The love, the laughter . . . God is so good."

"Oh, let me see," Trevor said, breaking from the pack.

Jillian followed as he walked toward the kitchen, looking up before he got to the entryway. A smile appeared when he saw the banner, and got bigger when he spied the balloons and confetti.

"I didn't know what this birthday would be like, honestly." Trevor turned toward them. "I knew it would be sad, but I didn't know if it would be *mostly* sad or if I would feel guilty if I didn't feel sad enough—"

"Oh, honey, no," Jillian said. "You don't *have* to feel sad. Joy is a gift from above. I've been praying for you to be filled with joy today."

"Okay, because seeing you all and knowing the kind of breakfast we're about to have . . . I'm hype." Trevor paused. "Anybody happen to plan anything for this evening?"

Jillian and the other kids looked at one another.

"I think you're on your own," Jillian said. "I figured you'd do the usual. Video games and such."

"I'm immensely here for part of the day," Courtenay said. "Then I'm getting together with Faith again."

"Which means I can get a ride," David said, "because I'm hanging with Reggie tonight. But you're thirteen now, Trev. You can do your own thing, right?"

Trevor stared at them. "I mean . . . I guess . . ."

"I can't do it," Jillian said. "His poor face looks so sad." She put an arm around him. "Trev, you know we've got plans. We're not telling you what they are just yet, but your evening is booked."

His face lit up. "I really wondered."

"I know you guys are hungry," Jillian said, "so I need to get back to making breakfast."

Trevor looked at his brother. "Sounds like we've got time for video games—with the birthday pass for unlimited screen time."

"Let's go," David said.

"You never heard me say 'unlimited'," Jillian called after them. She moved back to her waffle station.

"Mom, what can I help you with?" Courtenay said.

"I think it's under control," Jillian said. "I prepped some things last night that only need to be warmed up." She got a measuring cup. "So Soph, you were about to tell me about Lucas?"

"Hmm, who's Lucas?" Courtenay slid into a seat at the kitchen table.

"Remember we got a new pastor a few months ago?" Jillian added water and oil. "It's his son."

"He's a senior like me," Sophia said, sitting with Courtenay. "And we've been talking and texting all week. He wants to take me out tomorrow night."

Jillian started the mixer. "Out where?"

"Either a movie or something to eat."

"So, wait," Courtenay said, "How did the two of you connect?"

"I came to the main church building to talk to mom a couple weeks ago," Sophia said, "and it was right after his dad preached, so he was there too."

"I remember that," Jillian said, turning the mixer off. "You hadn't connected before then?"

"Not really," Sophia said. "We ended up going to the second floor to talk and get to know each other." She paused. "And I'll just say it—I finally had my first kiss, in the hallway with Lucas."

"Okay, wow," Courtenay said.

"I wanted to see what it was like, so I just . . . kissed him," Sophia said. "But I told him it won't be a regular thing. I really have been listening to the things you and Faith have said."

Jillian looked over at her. "I love that you were willing to share that, Soph. You're eighteen, and it's so important for us to be able to talk about things like this. I didn't have that with my mom when I was your age."

"Grandma Patsy didn't know when you had your first kiss?" Sophia said.

"She didn't know anything I was doing," Jillian said, "until I had to tell her I was pregnant."

Sophia stared at her with wide eyes then looked at Courtenay. "Did you know?"

"Mom told me last summer when I was going through everything," Courtenay said.

"How old were you?" Sophia said.

Jillian came closer. "Nineteen. I was a sophomore, and I had an abortion." Whenever she said it, she felt an ache in the pit of her stomach. "So everything you've heard from Faith and Courtenay about regrets—I can't begin to describe what it's been like for me." She paused a moment. "After I was saved, I had the hardest time believing that Jesus would forgive me for that. His grace is astounding. But it's still hard . . ."

"You've got tears in your eyes even now, Mom," Sophia said.

"It's especially hard on a day like today, when it's one of your birthdays," Jillian said. "I wonder how old my son or daughter would be now."

"Did Dad know?" Sophia said.

Jillian nodded. "I told him all about it." She brushed the tear. "But let's get back to you. Tell me what you like about Mr. Lucas."

Sophia thought a moment. "He's cute, but he's also quirky. And he doesn't try to act like he's all cool. And I like that we can text about lots of different subjects."

"Mom," David said, walking in. "I couldn't say anything when Trevor was down here, but shouldn't I ask Tommy if we can get another ticket for tonight, for Courtenay?"

"We already talked about it," Courtenay said. "I was at Faith's, remember? Tommy said he can get me a ticket—oh, and Mom, I'm staying for Tommy's Cling class tomorrow. Reggie and Faith got me excited about it."

Jillian smiled. "I'm so glad to hear that, Courtenay. He sent me week one of the study to edit, but I haven't had a chance to look at it yet."

Sophia put a hand over her mouth and coughed. "Intel," she muttered, looking at David.

"You could never go undercover," David said.

"What's going on?" Courtenay said.

"That's what I've been trying to figure out," Jillian said.

"So, Mom, we know you've got things under control here," Sophia said, rising. "And we can finish the Lucas convo later." She pulled Courtenay up and hooked an arm in hers. "Don't you need to go upstairs and put your things away? I'm thinking you might be interested in our committee . . ."

CHAPTER 50

*J*ordyn opened a bag of Cheetos on the sofa and hit the play button on Jade's latest vlog. She'd uploaded it later than normal—midday—and Jordyn hated that she'd actually been waiting. Was this what her life had devolved to? Living vicariously through her sister's experiences on a movie set?

But she'd watch these vlogs even if Jade weren't involved. They were that good, though Jordyn hadn't told her. She hadn't even told Jade she'd been watching, mostly because she simply didn't feel like talking.

Her phone rang with a call from Jillian, interrupting the video. Jordyn debated whether to answer, given her non-talkative mood. But on the fourth ring, she clicked. "Hey, Jillian."

"Jordyn, hey," Jillian said. "I've been trying to reach you. Is everything okay?"

"I know, I'm sorry I haven't called back," Jordyn said.

"And I was looking for you last night at the B and B party," Jillian said.

"What B and B party?"

"The cast and crew got together to celebrate the end of rehearsals,"

Jillian said, "and Alonzo and Cinda invited a lot of other people as well. I was hoping to see you so we could catch up."

"Was Jesse there?" Jordyn said.

"Yes, he was there," Jillian said. "That's why I was surprised that you weren't."

"Well," Jordyn said, "we broke up, and it's been really hard."

"Oh, sweetie, I'm so sorry."

"And it was my fault," Jordyn said. "Remember the married guy I was seeing? He's divorced now and wanted to see me, and I went. And kissed him. And it was stupid, and Jesse won't ever trust me again. And I'm just basically feeling sorry for myself. That's why I haven't returned your calls."

"Jordyn, let's get together and talk and pray," Jillian said. "I want to see you and spend some time. We're celebrating my son's birthday today, but what about tomorrow afternoon or evening?"

"Oh, I'm in Chicago, at my mom's house." Jordyn wasn't sure she'd get together even if she could. Jillian would focus on Jordyn's relationship with God, like Jade and Jesse, probably more so. And she didn't like the answers she'd have to give. "I'm not sure how long I'll be here. I needed some time away."

The garage door opened and Jordyn glanced toward the kitchen. Her mom was back home.

"Okay," Jillian said. "Well what if we talk for an extended time tomorrow? And I'd love to pray right now, if you've got time."

Janice came into the living room, looking at her.

"Um, my mom just walked in," Jordyn said. "Can I text you a time to talk tomorrow?"

"You sure can," Jillian said. "I'm looking forward to it. I'll be praying for you."

Jordyn hung up and looked at her mother. "Hey, mom."

"Well, good morning—or afternoon, I should say. Glad to see you're finally up."

"I've been up, Mom," Jordyn said. "I was in the room."

"In the bed, under the covers," Janice said. "That's not 'up.' And why is your hair all over your head?"

Jordyn patted it, sighing to herself. A mass of tangles. She never let her hair go like that.

Janice came closer. "What'd you eat, besides those Cheetos? I told you about filling up on that stuff."

Jordyn took one from the bag and crunched into it. "I don't have an appetite for anything else."

"I had a mind to throw all of it away this morning," Janice said. "Just sitting around sulking and eating junk, and for what? A breakup?" She threw up her hands. "Guess what, Jordyn? He's not the only man out here."

Jordyn ate more Cheetos. "And I bet you didn't go through *anything* when your marriage ended."

"That man thought he could marry me and get his hands on the money Randall left me," Janice said. "*And* told his little side chick his plan before we got married." She got a gleam in her eye. "I kicked his behind out with great joy because I had grounds for an annulment."

"So how'd you find out?" Jordyn said.

"Emails," Janice said. "He thought he deleted them but was too dumb to empty the 'trash' folder."

Jordyn shook her head. "So you cheated on Dad with a loser who turned around and cheated on you—oh, and also only married you for your money. Stellar."

"I knew you and Jade would gloat," Janice said. "But what did your man do? I'm sure he's not much better."

"I'm the one who messed things up," Jordyn said. "I got caught up with Kelvin and kissed him."

"He broke up with you over a *kiss*?" Janice said.

"This is why I can't talk to you about it, Mom," Jordyn said. "We're in different worlds."

"Wait, Kelvin?" Janice said. "The guy who was lying about leaving his wife? The one I put out of your party?"

"He actually did leave his wife," Jordyn said. "That's why he wanted to see me. He said he loves me."

"So he was serious about you after all?" Janice said. "Well, what's the problem? If I recall, he's got a good job, making good money. Instead of crying over what's-his-name, you could be with Kelvin."

Jordyn sighed. "Who cares about Kelvin's bank account, Mom? I love Jesse, and one of the things I love about him is that he loves Jesus." She navigated back to the video. "Jade was right. This is one of the dumbest things I've ever done."

"Is Jade giving relationship advice now?" Janice said. "Has she *ever* had a relationship that meant anything?"

"It wasn't advice," Jordyn said. "It was an assessment, an obvious one." She curled her legs under her. "You're still upset because Jade didn't want any part of your wedding or your new married life, and turns out she called that right too."

"Jordyn, why are you here since you're obviously still hostile toward me?" Janice stared down at her. "You can eat Cheetos and cry on your own couch."

"Because if I stayed I'd see Jesse at church," Jordyn said. "And I'd be hearing about Jade's great life every day and comparing it to my sucky one. I needed time away."

"What's happening with Jade?" Janice said. "What great life?"

"She's filming behind the scenes videos and doing social media for Alonzo's new movie, the one about Pastor Lance," Jordyn said. "And she uploads these vlogs every day." She showed the video on her phone. "I just started watching the latest one."

"Let me see it," Janice said, sitting next to her. "They've been talking about the movie on *Entertainment Now*."

Jordyn started it from the beginning. "This is from the last day of rehearsals."

"So she's actually on set?" Janice looked closer. "That's the director, Mariah Pendleton. How did Jade get this kind of access?"

"It's her job, Mom," Jordyn said. "That's why I said it's a great life."

"I like how she's capturing the camaraderie they're building," Janice said.

"Yeah, this part with Alonzo and Noah walking and talking outside has all the feels," Jordyn said.

"Now what's this part?" Janice said.

361

"There's a ministry moment in every episode."

"I'm sure Alonzo's behind that," Janice said. "He can't do anything these days without 'Jesus' all over it."

"That's sort of the point of the movie, Mom," Jordyn said. "To minister to people." She listened for a moment. "This is interesting, hearing her talk about how God opened the door to being a key grip for the movie."

"I didn't even know what a key grip was," Janice said. "I'll say this—nice touch with Alonzo conducting the interview. Anytime he's on screen, it's a win. Also, it shows camaraderie with cast *and* crew."

They continued watching as the interview concluded and the music shifted to a funky beat.

"It usually wraps up after the ministry moment." Jordyn looked closer. "Wow, they're showing the party at the B and B?" She looked closer for a glimpse of Jesse.

"Looks like they're having a good time, too," Janice said. "Look at Alonzo and Cinda. Reminds me of the time we didn't know she was the woman on the dance floor with him. I still can't believe she snuck into that premiere like that."

"She didn't sneak in," Jordyn said, "and why would you still be talking about that?"

"Who's that dancing with Noah?" Janice said.

"Aww look at Sophia," Jordyn said. "That's Jillian's daughter."

"And Jillian is . . .?"

"Remember I told you?" Jordyn said. "Jillian's the one led me to Jesus. She's my spiritual mom. That's who I was talking to just now."

Janice sighed and kept watching. A moment later she leaned in. "Isn't that Jesse?"

Jordyn spotted him at the same time, in the background at first. Now the camera got closer.

"So he's with a Hollywood actress now?" Janice said. "I'm starting to see Brooke everywhere." She nodded a little. "Okay, Jesse."

"What do you mean—'okay, Jesse'?" Jordyn said. "He's not *with* her. It's just a dance. I was with him when he met Brooke at a Super Bowl party."

"And you're no longer with him," Janice said. "So how do you know he's not with *her*?"

Jordyn thought a moment. What if Jillian knew and didn't want to tell her? What if everybody knew? She got up, Cheetos spilling to the floor. "I need to make a call."

"First, you're going to pick up those Cheetos before they stain my carpet," Janice said. "And tell Jade I said hello."

Jordyn picked up the Cheetos, threw them in the trash, and went up to the room she was staying in. She clicked to dial Jade. It rang and went to voicemail, and Jordyn called again.

Jade picked up. "I have to call you back."

"Is something going on with Jesse and Brooke?" Jordyn said.

"What did you not understand about my needing to call you back?"

"You're not doing anything for real," Jordyn said. "You're not on set today, are you?"

"I just pulled up to Lance's house," Jade said. "I'm filming Miss Pam's prayer video."

"If you're still in the car, you've got a minute," Jordyn said. "Was that a random dance between Jesse and Brooke or did it look like more?"

"So you watch the vlogs, huh?" Jade said.

"Yes, Jade, and they're really good," Jordyn said. "But since your time is limited, can we get to Jesse?"

"I have no idea what's up with Jesse and Brooke."

"Were they *only* together on the dance floor?" Jordyn said. "Or did you see them talking or flirting or whatever?"

"I didn't see any flirting," Jade said. "But yeah, they were talking and eating in the sitting room when Trey and I walked in."

"Then what?"

"Then all four of us were talking," Jade said.

"And you said you had no idea," Jordyn said. "That was like a double date."

"Do you know how ridiculous you sound?"

Jordyn paced the floor. "Why would you sit and talk with the guy who broke up with me?"

"Why wouldn't I?" Jade said. "I don't have a problem with Jesse. He did nothing but treat you well."

"And why would you include footage of them in the vlog?" Jordyn said. "You know when people see it, they'll be asking about the guy who's with Brooke. You just made Brooke and Jesse a couple."

"Nobody's checking for Brooke like that yet," Jade said. "But you need to stop worrying about what Jesse is doing. I thought the whole point was to get away from all of that."

"It was," Jordyn said. "Then you put him in your vlog." She paused, staring vaguely. "What if he and Brooke do like each other? What if he starts seeing her?"

"While you drive yourself crazy with speculation," Jade said. "I've got to go."

Jordyn sighed and clicked off, then went back to the vlog, to the part with Jesse and Brooke. She hadn't noticed it before, the way they smiled and acted playful, as if they knew each other. She thought back to the *Promises* celebration, all that laughing Brooke was doing as she texted . . . with Jesse. She stared at them a moment more then tossed the phone on her bed, her stomach tightening.

If she were honest, she'd wanted Jesse to wonder where she was. To miss her. Call and see about her.

Jesse wasn't thinking about her at all.

CHAPTER 51

 esiree stared at her laptop screen in her old bedroom in her parents' house, needing to finish this video and get it uploaded by evening. She loved editing video almost as much as shooting it. And the footage she'd captured in Malaysia was more incredible than she remembered. But she'd been unable to focus all week, since the event Tuesday night.

She took a sip of coffee and played a clip from inside a bat cave on the island of Langkawi. The sound creeped her out anew, that and the sight of hundreds of bats on every surface of the cave. But it motivated her as well. She'd determined early in her career to live outside her comfort zone, to take risks and be fearless as a travel vlogger. And she'd done just that, from scaling mountains to sky diving to getting close-ups like this of creatures that made her skin crawl. She'd gained a sizable following in doing so. But more than that, she'd confirmed for herself time and again that she was doing exactly what she'd been made to do.

So why was she suddenly unsure about the direction of her life?

Desiree sighed, her eyes falling on the *Promises* study. She'd gotten a copy on her way out the other night, and it had become a complete distraction. She'd pick up the book and read another page. Or the same page. Sometimes just the same few lines because she couldn't get past them. Treva had a way of delving into issues that cut to the core, things Desiree had never thought about, things that made her uncomfortable. More than once she'd told herself the study wasn't for her. Yet she'd find herself back in it.

She picked it up now, opening to her bookmarked page in the *If I Dwell* chapter.

Where do you live? The answer seems obvious. Your current city comes to mind. Maybe you've never left the area in which you grew up. Maybe you're acclimating to a new town. But it's not a difficult question. You know where you live, in a physical sense, at least.

But where do you live spiritually? And by live, I mean live. *When you get up and go about your day, is God on your mind? Do you talk to Him? Do you care what He thinks? How much does He factor into your decision making, if at all?*

Desiree paused, staring vaguely. Second time she'd read it, and she still didn't know what to do with it. Since she had no fixed address, even the easy question was hard. She didn't live anywhere. She'd been traveling from place to place for years. And spiritually? She wasn't sure she wanted to know where she lived.

She sighed, her eyes floating to the next paragraph.

As you ponder these questions, turn to John 15 in your Bible. We're going to spend time focusing on one word—abide.

She skipped to the next paragraph, which had a definition of "abide"—"It means to stay, to remain." The words seemed targeted—at her. As if she could never claim them given the life she'd chosen. She couldn't take an entire chapter of feeling that her whole life was off. *No, thank you.*

Desiree closed the book and moved her gaze to her laptop screen. She had to focus. This was a sponsored video for a brand she'd recently landed, so the pressure was on to not only get it done but make it impressive. Adding clips from the bat cave, she then debated what to follow it with. Footage of herself riding a scooter through the town? Didn't seem quite right. What story was she telling? Typically it fell into place with little effort but right now she only had a collection of sights and experiences with no narrative to pull it together.

Desiree heaved a sigh. She should've edited the Bangladesh video first. She'd taken a paddle steamer overnight from the capital city to Barisal, and the timeline itself made it easy to build a story around. She pulled up some of the footage of the floating market to reacquaint herself with what she'd shot that morning—then let out a groan. How did it make sense to start editing a whole new video when *this* one was time sensitive?

She needed more coffee.

Desiree took her mug to the kitchen, her thoughts a jumble. Maybe she was dealing with burnout. A fellow travel vlogger had done a video about it recently. How the hustle had taken its toll. There was no finish line to their work. Just the next destination and the next and the next, filming, editing, uploading. The pace energized her, but she couldn't deny that it was a grind. Maybe she'd hit a wall and simply needed a break.

She stared at the coffee pot, pondering her upcoming trips—six countries in the next five weeks. She could easily make a case for burnout—and the thought of calling it burnout made her feel better. That she could deal with. Schedule time off on a beach somewhere, rejuvenate, then get back at it.

Facing the truth was infinitely harder.

Sighing, Desiree leaned against the counter. *Okay, God . . . Okay . . .* She sighed again. How long had it been since she'd prayed? She wasn't even sure what to say.

Just talk to Him.

Her heart raced. She could see Lance's face, hear his voice. He'd taught her much about God, including how to pray. Lately her thoughts filled with so many of their conversations.

"What do you mean, just talk to Him?" Desiree had said. "Talk to Him how? What do I say? You know I didn't grow up with all this."

"I didn't either," Lance said. "I'm saying it's not a formula. No magic words. Just talk. Tell Him what's on your mind."

"But when we pray together, it sounds like you're quoting Scripture sometimes," Desiree said. "I can't do that."

"It comes out because it's in me," Lance said. "But I talk to God all the time, and most of the time it's whatever's on my mind." He took her hands into his and bowed his head. "Lord, I pray you give Rae a real comfort level in talking to You. Let talking to You be like breathing. Natural. Regular. And as she draws near to You, I pray You draw near to her, in Jesus' name."

"Amen." Desiree half smiled at him. "Let me guess. That 'draw near' part. Bible verse?"

Lance's eyes twinkled. "Maybe. Now your turn."

"My turn for what?" Desiree said.

"To pray." Lance bowed his head.

"You mean out loud? And what am I praying about?"

"Whatever's on your mind," Lance said.

Desiree let a few seconds lapse. "Lord . . . thank You . . . for Lance. For giving me a man who helps me do things like this." Head bowed, she squeezed Lance's hands. "It's scary, Lord, learning to live for You. I'm not even sure what that really means or what it looks like. But I know you've put Lance in my life to show me." She paused, tears welling. "And I love him more than I've loved anyone. But even *that* is scary. I guess I'm just asking, Lord . . . Help me to . . ." She looked at Lance. "What's the word you always use?" she whispered.

"Surrender," Lance said.

Desiree took a breath. "Help me to surrender."

Lance took her into his arms. "That was beautiful."

Desiree swiped tears. "I don't know where all that came from."

"Yeah, what was up with that one part?" Lance said. "I didn't know loving me was scary."

"How could it not be?" Desiree said. "You've shaken up my entire life. And I happen to like being in control."

Lance nodded. "That's dope self-awareness."

"But scary or not"—Desiree stared deep into his eyes—"I love loving you."

Lance kissed her. "Not as much as I love loving you."

. . .

Desiree brushed the tears from her face and closed her eyes. *Lord, I feel like part of me wants to run to You and another part wants to run away. I don't know if I'm afraid to face You . . . or if it's that I'm afraid to face myself. . . . I feel lost. Which is crazy because I remember feeling lost when I met Lance, and then I felt I'd finally* found *something. Someone. You. How am I in that same place of feeling lost again?*

Desiree pondered that a moment, but she had no answers.

And I don't know what to do with all these thoughts, Lord. I keep thinking . . . What would've happened if I had stayed? What if I had kept learning and growing? What if . . . What if I had married Lance?

She took a deep breath. She'd been avoiding that question. It was pointless. But whenever she grappled with matters of faith, it was hard not to think about the man who'd led her to faith. But faith—where she was with God—*that* was the burden of her heart. Not Lance.

Still . . .

She added fresh coffee to her cup, her hand shaking. What was she thinking, doing that video, pouring out her heart about Lance? Maybe it was part of the burnout, coming to the end of herself. When his wedding video went viral and he was doing the national interviews, it didn't have a big affect on her. But a lot had happened in a few years. For one, she'd gotten engaged again. Finally. But a few months ago, she ended that one too when she realized he didn't compare to Lance. No one did. That was the hard truth. No one loved her or cared for her or poured into her like Lance did. And the realization had made her sick. Her life had started mocking her. *What a fool.* She'd thrown away true love, and she'd never find it again. Just cheap imitations.

When she heard about the movie and saw the Living Word site, the mocking got louder. And the regrets. And the pain as she remembered how she treated Lance. She recorded the video as a form of therapy. Unscripted, she shared for the first time on her channel that she'd been engaged to Lance—"yes, *that* Lance," she'd said. She'd broken down into tears as she told how she ended it and how much she regretted it. She even said she'd always love him.

Desiree sighed, sipping her coffee. In her mind she was talking to the people who subscribed to her channel. She didn't use any tags related to Lance or the movie because she didn't want to trigger an algorithm. Still, it went viral. Now the world knew what she was grappling with. And it had yielded a call from the producers of the movie. But it was far from therapeutic. If anything, she only felt worse.

Desiree took her coffee back to her bedroom and started editing the Malaysia video again.

Where do you live?

She paused, the words practically ringing in her ears.

She sighed, answering aloud. "I don't know. I've lost my way."

CHAPTER 52

*T*ommy straightened the chairs in the Living Word classroom Sunday morning. *Lord, I never thought I'd be getting a room ready for something I'd be teaching. You know there are quite a few others who are more qualified and could do a better job. But I couldn't shake the sense that this was Your will.* He paused. *Which doesn't make it easy. But more and more, Lord, I just want to do Your will, whatever the cost.*

He moved to the front, trying to decide whether he wanted to use the podium on top of the table or—

"Morning, Tommy-Tom." Jillian breezed in with coffee cups and an Einstein Bagel bag. She set them down on the front table and took off her coat.

Tommy looked at her. "What are you doing here?"

"Coming to your class." Jillian passed him a coffee and took a sip of hers. "Nice look with the V-neck sweater vest and the button down with open collar."

"What are you doing here *this early?*"

"I was planning to edit what you sent me in my quiet time this morning," Jillian said. "But when I got ready to pull it up, I was moved to just come and do it with you."

"Like we used to do," Tommy said.

Jillian nodded. "Except we've never worked on content like this together."

"Which is what I told Lance," Tommy said. "This isn't my lane. But you're equipped to help with the technical aspects of writing *and* with this type of content. This is what you do every day. God is good." He took a sip of coffee. "Thanks for this."

"And thank you again for the tickets to last night's concert," Jillian said. "We knew Trevor would enjoy it, but I think we all have a deeper appreciation for the bass now. It was really good."

"I thought you'd enjoy it," Tommy said, opening the bagel bag. He smiled. "You got me a French toast bagel."

"Comfort food." Jillian reached in and got a wheat.

"Are you sure that's not the real reason you came early?" Tommy said. "Because you think I'm anxious about the class."

"You *are* anxious about the class." Jillian took a seat and started arranging her things on the desktop. "But we've already been praying. I wouldn't have come early because of that."

"Well, I appreciate it anyway," Tommy said, pinching off a piece of bagel. "It's comforting just to see you and to know you care." He watched her open her laptop. "Have you given it a first read?"

"Not yet," Jillian said. "But I know it needs to be uploaded this morning, so I'm ready to jump into it."

Tommy sat next to her, checking a couple of text messages. The building was waking up. Thankfully, he could handle these concerns with a simple reply.

"Ooh, can we talk about this title?" Jillian said.

"I thought it might be too simple, but—"

"No, I just wasn't expecting this angle—'Clinging Through Fear.'" Jillian looked at him. "I thought you were looking at ways in which different people in the Bible were clinging to God."

"That's how *I* was doing it," Tommy said. "But when I started praying about how to prepare for the class and the online version, it didn't sound right to put something like, 'David, King Hezekiah, and Paul' as a title." He broke off another piece of bagel. "So I looked at what different people were facing and made that the title. Basically the same thing but around a theme."

"Look at you," Jillian said, "clinging during the writing process."

"I wonder who told me to do that," Tommy said. "I could feel the difference. The Spirit was definitely guiding me."

"I love that you put the people you're covering at the top, with Scripture references," Jillian said. "Visually, I think a bullet list would work better, though."

Tommy nodded, responding to the texts as Jillian made the changes.

"Are you thinking you'll get through all of this in class?" Jillian said.

"I wasn't sure how much we'd have time to cover," Tommy said. "But I figured with the online version, people could space it out during the week if they want."

"Oh, wow," Jillian said, her eyes on the screen. "I thought the main issue would be trying to get you to share something personal, which is outside of your comfort zone. But with devotional content, that's the connection point." She looked at him. "You're actually talking about your fears."

"I was waiting for you to get to that," Tommy said. "I found out something about writing in this lane. God uses it to dredge up stuff you don't want to talk about. It's more about the work He's doing in you than to whomever you might be writing." He drank some of his coffee. "It would be much easier to write about something I conquered five years ago than something I'm still dealing with."

"Yup," Jillian said. "That's why I'd rather not do the grief study—the dredging up part."

"What grief study?" Tommy said.

"I thought I told you about that." Jillian thought a moment. "I guess it came up during the time we weren't really talking. Cyd asked if I would work on a Bible study on grief that would be released with the movie."

"That's big," Tommy said. "And definitely needed. You're praying about it, I hope."

"I am," Jillian said. "I just don't know about the timing, given that I'm still in-process. And I said what you said—it's not my lane, since I edit rather than write." She paused. "If I *do* do it, I would definitely incorporate different voices in terms of how one grieves. Also, Cyd asked Silas to work on it with me."

"You and Silas would write it together?" Tommy said.

"I'm not sure how it would work exactly," Jillian said. "But that's what led to that dinner, because I had listened to a sermon he did on grief."

"That's how Lance and Treva got together," Tommy said, "bonding through grief."

"Right," Jillian said. "But I really didn't mean to take us on a tangent." She turned back to the screen. "Tommy, wow. You put it out here—'I've been divorced twice, and my fear—well, one of them—is that life won't ever be what I thought it would be . . . what I prayed it would be.'" She looked at him. "I don't think I've heard you put it like that."

"I hadn't thought of it like that myself," Tommy said, "until I started writing."

Jillian continued aloud. "'As believers, we're supposed to walk by faith, not fear. It's hard to even talk about your fears with fellow believers because everybody's quick to tell you *faith over fear*. But God welcomes our thoughts. He knows them anyway, before we do. Talking to God about our deepest fears is a way to cling to Him. He not only listens; He gives the perspective we need. Let's look at how these people in the Bible reacted in the midst of fear, and how God responded . . .'"

"Aren't you supposed to be editing? You're just reading"—Tommy looked up from the text he was composing—"you've got tears in your eyes?"

"I've been praying for you"—Jillian dug in her purse for a tissue —"to be real with the Lord about your fears, and I'm—"

"You've been specifically praying that?"

Jillian dabbed her eyes then opened her phone and showed him the prayer in her notes.

"Wow," Tommy said. "It's right there."

"I'm just in awe of God right now." Jillian stared at the screen. "This is beautiful, Tommy. It's hard to edit when it's ministering. But trust me, I'm working. I only see a couple of minor changes so far." She looked at him. "I wonder what it'll be like, with you talking about personal things like this in class."

"I have no idea," Tommy said. "I don't even know who will come. I'm hoping for a small group so we can have some real discussion."

"I don't know what your idea of 'small' is," Jillian said. "But when that email went out about the class, it began with—'By request . . . .'"

"Hey, what have we here?"

Tommy looked as Reggie and Faith walked into the classroom. "What are you talking about, Reg?"

"My big bro. My Aunt Jillian." Reggie stood before them, nodding. "I do believe this made my morning."

"Jill was simply editing my post for the Cling study," Tommy said.

Reggie smiled. "And I'm simply saying we love to see it."

"That's how I felt Friday night at the B and B," Faith said, "when Tommy carried Aunt Jillian's luggage downstairs. Like *awww.*"

"Something's wrong with you two," Tommy said.

Jillian chuckled. "I'm saying *awww* about you two being the first ones here this morning, showing love for Mr. Tommy-Tom."

"Ah, but we're *not* the first ones." Reggie gave her a look as he took a seat up front. "And I'm not just here to show love. I was into that first discussion we had and our group morphed into this. So as a charter member, I'm excited about this next lesson."

"And it's so good," Jillian said. "We just finished going through it."

Reggie nodded at them. "Just keeps getting better. You two have your own private study time before the group study."

"Like we do, Reg," Faith said.

"And when you bond around studying the word," Reggie said. "*Whew.* That's that deep, strong stuff."

Tommy shook his head. "I can't with the two of you."

"Morning, good people," Cedric said, walking in with Cyd.

Tommy eyed Cedric. "You're supposed to be getting ready for *your* class right now. And Cyd, you're always in first service. What's the deal?"

"You're tripping if you think I would miss this," Cedric said. "My class is fine. I had two people training under me to lead a group, so we're covered." He gripped hands with Tommy and hugged him. "I'm all the way here for you, bro. You know I've been praying. I had to see the Lord at work in you."

Cyd hugged him too. "You know you're family, Tommy. When I got the email that you were leading this class—as well as the subject matter—I had to pause and praise God." She looked into his eyes. "I couldn't miss this. I've been praying for you too, and God is clearly working."

Tommy didn't have time to respond as more people walked in, including Lance, who got held up just inside the doorway with people greeting him.

Tommy went toward him. "Excuse us," he said, pulling Lance aside. "What do you need? Something with the audio-visuals?"

"I'm straight," Lance said. "I came to see how you're doing."

"Like you have time for that," Tommy said.

"And speaking of audio-visuals," Lance said, "Solomon is coming to set up to capture sound."

"That doesn't work well for interactive classes like this," Tommy said. "You can't hear what other people are saying."

"It'll still be good to get your end," Lance said, "for people who can't be here."

"My two favorite guys, right here together." Pamela hugged them both.

"Are you by yourself, Momma Pam?" Tommy said. "Did you drive?"

"You're funny," Pamela said. "I'm ready for tomorrow, though. Let's do double—six blocks."

Tommy smiled. "Okay now, Momma Pam. Let's go!"

"I think I better take over the driving lessons if I want to keep my primary spot in the family," Lance said. "All right, I'm headed down."

Momma Pam took a seat next to Jillian, and Tommy talked to various people who came in, watching as the room filled up. He'd scheduled the class during first service, thinking fewer people would come. But the idea of a small group dynamic was dwindling by the minute.

"Good morning, friend." Mariah hugged him. "How are you feeling?"

"I'm good," Tommy said. "How about yourself?"

"I'm good too," Mariah said. "You just seemed a little distant at the party Friday night. I was hoping everything was okay."

"Everything is good," Tommy said. "Actually, better than it's been in a while."

"Oh," Mariah said. "Okay, good to hear. Hope we can talk later." She moved to find a seat with Brooke.

"Man, I thought we were good on time." Jesse glanced around. "It's filling up already. How are all these people showing up for *our* group?" He smiled.

"The seats up front are the last to go," Tommy said. "There's a spot by your fellow charter member over there."

"Aye, bet," Jesse said, heading over there.

Tommy picked up the microphone. "Good morning, everybody. We'll get started in about five minutes, so go ahead and find a seat. And why are y'all avoiding the front? We've got some nice people down here who promise not to bite."

Camera flashes started going off, prompting Tommy to look toward the door. Alonzo and Cinda had walked in.

Tommy picked up the mic again. "I know some of you aren't used to seeing brother Alonzo, but we don't do the celebrity stuff up in here. No pics or video. And seriously, the dude can't even play Spades, so my admiration fell off a long time ago."

He greeted more people as Alonzo came and hugged him. "You already know, man," Alonzo said. "I'm so pumped about this class. We've got eleven people from the cast and crew in here this morning."

"Are you serious?" Tommy said.

"God is moving, man," Alonzo said. "Just wanted you to know. Keep letting Him use you."

Tommy moved to the front, ready to begin. Another influx of people came, and he waited as they got settled. Among them were Courtenay, Sophia, and Joy, and Stephanie and Lindell. And Silas.

Tommy watched as Silas moved to a section of seating up front, past several bodies, landing in an open seat . . . beside Jillian.

CHAPTER 53

*B*rooke sat with her Bible open, feeling an eager anticipation already about the class.

"I shared a little about my life and struggles so you would know that I'm not coming at this as someone who's got it all together," Tommy was saying. "I started the challenge and the study for myself, because *I* need to learn how to cling to the Lord more deeply. And this lesson on fear really spoke to me." He walked across the front, looking at them. "Anybody else dealing with some fears you want to get past?"

A majority of the hands went up in the room, including Brooke's.

Tommy nodded. "I see you. I've been praying that the Lord will set us free through this study." He got his iPad from the podium, which had the Bible app open. "So we're looking at how people did or didn't cling to God in the midst of fear, because we can learn a lot from both sides. I'll tell you what really got me—Adam and Eve. Can someone read Genesis 3:8-10?" He waited for them to find it then pointed to a guy with his hand raised. "Go ahead."

The guy stood. "'They heard the sound of the LORD God walking in the garden in the cool of the day, and the man and his wife hid themselves from the presence of the LORD God among the trees of the garden. Then—'"

"Wait a second," Tommy said. "We have to pause right there. We know this is after the serpent has tempted Adam and Eve, after they've sinned. Prior to that, what was their relationship with God like?"

"Adam was naming the animals with God," one guy said.

Tommy nodded with a smile. "Isn't that something? God was actually bringing the animals to Adam to see what *he* would call them."

"They were walking and talking with God," one woman said. "Enjoying His presence."

"Yes," Tommy said. "Enjoying His presence. Now what are they doing?"

"Hiding from His presence," the woman said.

Tommy heaved a sigh. "That really hit me when I was preparing this. They were *created* to cling to God, to have an intimate relationship with Him. And they *were* clinging to Him, every day walking and talking to Him. And sin broke all of that." He paused, closing his eyes. "Lord, thank You that in Christ we don't have to hide from You. Help us to enjoy Your presence always." He looked at the guy who was reading. "Okay, please continue."

"'Then the LORD God called to the man, and said to him, "Where are you?" He said, "I heard the sound of You in the garden, and I was afraid because I was naked; so I hid myself."'"

"Thank you," Tommy said. "Check that out." He walked with his iPad. "Sin enters the world and right with it—fear. Adam and Eve never experienced fear when they were in God's presence. Now they're not only experiencing shame for the first time, but fear as well. It had to be *strange* to them. Like—*what is this I'm feeling? I want to run.*" He sighed. "Instead of running from the serpent, who did they run from?"

"God," rang out in the room.

"How crazy is that?" Tommy said. "But don't we do that? What are some reasons we run from God?"

Several hands went up. Tommy pointed to the first person.

"We run because we're afraid of what He might call us to do," a woman said. "We don't want to surrender."

"Good one," Tommy said. "Been there, done that."

"Because we're angry at God," a guy said.

"Yes," Tommy said, then pointed at the next.

"Out of shame, like Adam and Eve," a woman said. "That was me."

"What I want us to get," Tommy said, "is that fear wants to come between us and the Lord. I'm seeing that even more as I'm standing here, and it's rocking me. Family, when fear comes, we can't run from the One who can help us. We *have* to run to God."

"Amen," Brooke murmured, along with several others.

"Turn to First Samuel 17," Tommy said. "Most of us know this story—David and Goliath. What's wild is that fear is what jumpstarted it." He moved closer to them. "You've got the Philistine army on the mountain on one side, the army of Israel on the mountain on the other side, with a valley between them. What happens next? The Philistines send out one man from the ranks—Goliath. Why?"

"To invoke fear," one guy said.

"Did it work?" Tommy said.

"Absolutely," the guy said.

"Goliath issues a challenge," Tommy said. "Choose a man to fight me. If he kills me, we become your servants. If I kill him, you become our servants. What was the reaction from Israel—verse 11?"

"'When Saul and all Israel heard these words of the Philistine, they were dismayed and greatly afraid,'" a woman read.

"Man," Tommy said. "Dismayed and *greatly* afraid. And listen, these are not ordinary citizens. This is the *army*. This is the king!" He started walking again. "Okay, so they're 'greatly afraid.' Does King Saul call for corporate prayer? Does he take a moment himself to send up a prayer to God?" He shook his head as "No" sounded in the room. "No, Saul had already demonstrated that he was a king who had no interest in clinging to God, so God told him two chapters ago that He was taking the kingdom from him." He gave them a look. "When you've got a king who ain't clinging, you're in trouble." He paused. "*But God.* He had been training up a cling-er."

"Oh, I love that," one woman said. "I want to train up my children to be cling-ers."

"Amen," Tommy said. "Somebody tell us how this shepherd boy named David had been trained to cling?" He pointed to Faith.

"When he was taking care of his father's sheep," Faith said, "and a lion or bear took one of them, he would actually go after the lion or bear and rescue the sheep. Then when the lion or bear went after David, he'd kill it. But the main thing is that David said it was *God* who delivered him from the lion and the bear. So he had learned to cling to God and trust Him in that way."

"So he couldn't just read a book and learn to cling?" Tommy said. "He had to go through some stuff?" He sighed. "We hate the trials"—he raised a hand—"and trust me, I'm talking to myself. But God *uses* them. They perfect us. Because David learned to cling in the pastures, he didn't flinch when it came to clinging on the battlefield." He looked out at them. "Anybody have experience with that? Where you learned to cling in one area, despite your fears, and that built up your strength to cling in another?" He looked in front of him. "Jesse."

"This is hard for me," Jesse said. "The story's actually on YouTube, but telling it in a class like this . . ." He took a breath. "I was seeing someone in college, she got pregnant, and I got scared and tried to run. I wanted her to have an abortion. She didn't, thank God." He took another breath. "But I was still afraid of what kind of father I would be—I never really knew my own father. Long story short, I was saved during that time and—I didn't think of it like this at the time—but I learned to cling to Him as I started walking out fatherhood. I was surprised by how much I *loved* being my daughter's father."

Brooke focused on Jesse, moved by his vulnerability.

"That experience taught me to cling in relationships," Jesse continued. "At first I was afraid of how I would look, the guy who's not about sex and wants to take everything slow. That wasn't me—but now it *was* me. I know it might sound silly, but I struggled with what women might think of me." He paused a moment. "As I'm listening to this, I know that learning to cling in fatherhood has helped me to cling to God when it comes to women."

"That's so good," Tommy said. "Thank you for sharing that, Jesse."

Brooke's hand went up, and Tommy pointed at her.

"This is hard for me too," Brooke said.

"Let me say this," Tommy said. "As the Spirit moves in here and people share, we need to keep it confidential. We need to be able to trust each other. Amen?"

A chorus of "Amen's" sounded in the room.

"So my situation is the opposite of Jesse's," Brooke said. "I *haven't* been clinging to God in my current relationship. I moved to LA and moved in with my boyfriend, with all the justifications—it's expensive; I'm a starving, wannabe actor." She shook her head as she thought about it. "And it's hitting me that it was *fear*. Fear that I couldn't make it otherwise. And it's really hitting me that I've been running from God." She blew out a breath. "He's been trying to get my attention these past two weeks, and I'm *still* running. Still making excuses. . . . So yeah, I'm the example of what it looks like *not* to cling."

"Tommy," Cyd said, "can we pray for Brooke after class, whoever wants to stay?"

"I was thinking the same thing," Tommy said. "Is that cool with you, Brooke?"

Brooke nodded soberly. "Thank you."

Mariah put an arm around her and hugged her when she sat back down.

Tommy walked with his iPad again. "Okay, so shepherd boy David brings lunch to his brothers in the army." He paused. "How crazy is that? This boy was the UberEats delivery guy. Bringing food to his big, brave brothers in the army." He continued walking across the room. "Goliath comes out *again* and challenges Israel. Look at verse 24—'When all the men of Israel saw the man, they fled from him and were greatly afraid.' But this time David is there. He hears the giant. He sees the fear in his brothers, his king, all the men. And he says, 'Who is this uncircumcised Philistine, that he should taunt the armies of the living God?'" He paused again. "*Come on!* That's what it means to cling! You *immediately* bring God into it. That giant wasn't taunting Israel's army. He was taunting *God's* army. The *living* God. This boy had no fear because he was clinging to his God!"

"Glory to God!" Several people lifted their arms in praise.

"I promise y'all, I'm not trying to preach up in here," Tommy said. "But this thing is giving me *life*."

"Preach on, Tommy!" one woman said. "It's giving me life too!"

"So look at this," Tommy said. "David asked what would be done for the man who kills the giant because he is *all in*. His oldest brother —one of the ones who was greatly afraid—is rolling his eyes because baby brother is out here flexing. So he tells David, verse 28—'Why have *you* come down? And with whom have you left those *few* sheep in the wilderness? I know your insolence and the wickedness of your heart; for you have come down in order to see the battle.'"

"There's always a hater," one woman said.

Tommy shook his head. "There *will* be people in your life who can't stand that you're clinging to God. You're supposed to be a slave to people's opinions and people's approval, like they are. You're supposed to be afraid to move by faith, like they are. But look how David responded." He chuckled before he even read it. "He said, 'What have I done now? Was it not just a question?'—and that boy turned away! He's like, *whatever. I ain't got time. I'm clinging!*"

"Amen's" sounded in the room and two people stood up, raising a hand to speak. Tommy called on the first one.

Brooke's phone vibrated and she looked at it. Jesse? He'd only sent one text outside of the group, and that was to tell her this morning that he was on his way. She opened the text to see it in full.

That last part you said isn't true. By sharing, you're now an example of what it looks like *to* cling.

She typed a reply. **I need to take some steps before I can claim that.**

Brooke listened to the person who was sharing, then looked at her phone when Jesse replied.

Claim it and let it strengthen you for the next step. You didn't have to share that. The Spirit moved and you chose to cling.

Brooke took a breath. **Thank you for not judging me.**

Jesse replied in seconds. **Huh? Did you hear my story? Thank YOU.** He sent another before she could respond. **Hope it was ok to text you. We can take it back to the group.**

Brooke sent him a reply. **I didn't mind at all.**

She kept an eye on her phone, but Jesse didn't send another text.

Brooke cast a glance down at him in the front row. He'd been nice enough to give them a ride, but he'd chosen not to sit with them. Now he'd texted some encouragement, but she wouldn't read anything into that either. They had an easy camaraderie because of their mutual friend Robin. That's all it was.

And it just so happened that she enjoyed every interaction she had with him.

CHAPTER 54

*S*tephanie's insides had been in knots from the moment she and Lindell took their seats near the back. She'd spotted them—Warren and Veronica—sitting several rows up. And all she could think was *how?* How could she not have anticipated that this could happen? And how could she not have told Lindell that Warren was attending Living Word? She'd told herself it didn't make sense to ruin part two of their vacation. But after all the discussion this morning, she knew what it really was—fear. The very thing she was feeling this moment.

"I'm loving this discussion," Tommy was saying, "but I have to hold off on the last two hands. Our time is running out already. I thought we'd be able to get to Joshua and Caleb, King Jehoshaphat, Daniel, Shadrach, Meshach, and Abednego, Peter . . ." He threw up his hands. "I know—what was I thinking? But it's online for whoever wants to continue the study this week." He took up his iPad. "But we *cannot* leave without finishing this scene with David and Goliath."

Stephanie looked as Veronica whispered something to Warren. They'd had their heads together the whole time, commenting on the class, no doubt. Veronica had even raised her hand and spoken.

Stephanie's heart nearly pounded out of her chest as she wondered if Lindell would recognize her.

"David has given Saul back his armor—we talked about that," Tommy said. "So Goliath is fully decked in scale armor made of bronze, a bronze helmet, all that, and David's got *no* armor. All he's got is a stick in one hand, five stones that he put in his shepherd's bag, and his sling. And Goliath is *mad*. How they gon' send this boy with sticks to fight me?" He chuckled a little. "Goliath is like—this is light work. Come on and let me kill you real quick."

"You can't come for the cling-er!" somebody yelled out.

"Right!" Tommy said. "And don't you love how David goes *off*? He lets *everybody* know he's clinging. Look how many times he mentions God—'I come to you in the name of the LORD of hosts, the God of the armies of Israel, whom you have taunted'; 'This day the LORD will deliver you up into my hands'; 'that all this assembly may know that the LORD does not deliver by sword or by spear.'" He looked up. "And this—'for the battle is the LORD's and He will give you into our hands.'" He looked at them. "How many of you need a reminder every now and then that the battle is the Lord's?"

Stephanie raised her hand with the entire class.

Tommy had his hand up and his eyes closed. "Lord, thank You that You love us. Thank You that You *see* us and You care, even when it may not look that way to us. Help us to remember that the battle is Yours—and if it's Yours, that means You're fighting for us. Thank You for *fighting* for us, Lord. We need You. We can't make it without You. In Jesus' name."

"Amen" sounded in the class.

"So look," Tommy said. "It says Goliath got up and came to meet David. But David *ran quickly* toward the battle line." He was walking again. "Everybody else paralyzed in fear. The cling-er *runs* to the giant. He knew the battle plan and he didn't have to hesitate. How did he know the battle plan?"

"He's clinging!" a few people said.

Tommy nodded. "He's clinging to the Commander of the army, the One who has the plan. So David runs quickly to the line, takes one

stone from his bag, slings it, and it strikes Goliath square on the forehead. He drops dead." He looked at them. "Listen. One man who was
willing to cling changed the fate of a nation. What kind of difference
can you make in your family, on your job, in ministry, in your
community, in this local church . . . if you get serious about clinging to
God?"

"That's the truth," Lindell said.

"Is fear an issue for you?" Tommy said. "Ask yourself. I need to ask
myself. And if so, here's the cling challenge for this week . . ."

Stephanie watched as Veronica turned a page in her notebook, pen
poised.

"The challenge is to seek God specifically about your fears,"
Tommy said. "Deal with it, even if it's hard, even if it hurts. Ask the
Lord to shine a light on it, help you understand it, and to help you be
free of it. Cling to Him in this. This includes meditating on Scripture
related to fear. I've included verses in the online lesson." He checked
his watch. "Sorry for running over, guys. Great class! Brooke, come
down front so we can pray for you."

"I need to tell Tommy how good this was," Lindell said. "Plus, we
should go down to pray for Brooke since she's staying with us."

"Okay," Stephanie said, putting her notepad in her purse, lingering.
Warren and Veronica hadn't budged from their seats. How long did it
take to get up and go?

Lindell looked at her. "What are you doing? Brooke's down there
already."

"Okay," Stephanie said again.

She took another glance. Warren and Veronica were at least
moving toward the door. She took her time walking, looking at her
phone.

"Hey Steph, isn't that your friend, Veronica?"

Stephanie's stomach cramped as she looked and saw Warren and
Veronica joining the prayer circle. *Are they serious? Why?* "Yeah, I saw
her at the *Promises* celebration and was surprised to hear that she's
coming here."

"Aren't you going to say hello?" Lindell said.

"They're getting ready to pray."

"Steph, hey!" Veronica's tone was low as she approached. "I didn't know you were in here." She hugged her, then Lindell. "It's so good to see you, Lindell—been way too long."

"You too, Veronica," Lindell said. "Things are good?"

"Real good," Veronica said, beaming. She flashed her ring. "I got engaged."

"Congratulations," Lindell said. "Someone from Cali?"

Veronica smiled. "That's the same thing Steph said. Nope. It's Warren." She looked over. "Hey, baby, come here."

Stephanie looked downward. *Lord, please let the floor open up and swallow me whole, I beg of You.*

Warren came over, first looking at Veronica like—*why?* Then to Stephanie and Lindell—"Good to see you two."

"You as well," Lindell said. "Kind of surprised to see you here."

Warren glanced at Stephanie. "I've been here about a month or two now."

"Veronica got you to come?" Lindell said.

"No, he started coming before I did," Veronica said.

"We should get to the prayer circle," Stephanie said.

Warren and Veronica headed over there. Stephanie took a step—

"Did you know Warren was here at Living Word?"

Stephanie looked at him. "We can talk about it later, babe."

"Did you?"

She looked at the prayer circle a few feet away and back to Lindell. "It's not the time," she whispered.

"Then let's make time," Lindell said. "Forget the prayer circle."

Lindell headed out and Stephanie followed, her legs growing limp by the second. He continued down a hallway until they were alone.

"I'm asking again," Lindell said. "Did you know Warren was coming here?"

"Yes," Stephanie said. "I ran into him before service a couple weeks ago."

"And you didn't mention it?"

"Mention it for what?" Stephanie said. "I already knew Warren was a touchy subject. Why would I bring him up?"

"Because it's a big deal that your old boyfriend is attending our church," Lindell said. "And not just any old boyfriend. Somebody you almost married. Better to mention it than for us to run into him like we just did."

"Hindsight is twenty-twenty," Stephanie said. "At the time, I didn't want to argue about it."

"Why would we argue about it?" Lindell said. "You can't control who comes to Living Word."

"Well, true—"

"But I'm wondering why he'd choose to come after all these years?" Lindell said. "He didn't even come when you were dating."

"You never know when God is going to move in somebody's heart," Stephanie said. "And Lance's ministry draws a lot of people who've never been churchgoers."

"Did you ask him why now?" Lindell said. "Seems like a natural question to me."

"Well, yeah, and that's what he said, that God had been moving in his heart to go to church." Stephanie wanted to leave it at that, but she couldn't ignore the conviction. "And he was moved to come to Living Word in particular after . . . we had a brief conversation."

Lindell looked as if he was processing what she'd said. "You've been talking to Warren? Behind my back?"

"It was one phone call, months ago," Stephanie said. "And afterward—"

"Were you the one who made the call?"

"It was a low moment," Stephanie said, "and yes, I reached out—but I told him I shouldn't have called, and that was it."

"Until he shows up here at Living Word."

"Which is obviously nothing," Stephanie said. "You see he's engaged."

"And you're married," Lindell said. "But it doesn't stop you from thinking about him."

"That's not fair," Stephanie said. "We just got past all of that."

390

"We didn't get past anything," Lindell said, "because you were still hiding this. We were on vacation, talking things out, putting everything on the table. And you were still lying."

"I wasn't lying," Stephanie said. "I was just afraid to tell you. We had gotten to such a good place. I know it was wrong to call him, and I'm sorry. But there was nothing to it, and I didn't want it to affect the progress we were making."

"And yet, it was going to come up at some point, because he's *here*," Lindell said. "In our faces, because *you* reached out to him. But hey, it's all good. You get to run into your former love every Sunday and fantasize about him."

"Lindell, I cannot believe you would—"

"How did you feel seeing him just now?" Lindell said. "I bet you hate that he's with your old BFF."

"I knew you would blow this way out of proportion," Stephanie said. "It was *nothing*. The fact that he's with Roni should tell you it's nothing."

"Maybe it *is* nothing on his part," Lindell said. "You're the one who needed prayer concerning him. You're the one who called him. And now you're the one who gets to see him regularly. From your standpoint, it's not nothing."

Stephanie looked as a couple passed by. "Can we please continue this at home?"

"No," Lindell said. "I'm the one who needs some time now. I'm going to get a few things and stay with Cedric and Cyd."

"Lindell, please don't do that," Stephanie said. "We need to work this out just like we worked things out last week."

"How many years have we been married, Steph?" Lindell said. "And you are *still* reaching out to him. *Still*. And you know what's funny?" Equal parts anger and hurt filled his face. "If you had married him, you would *never* be thinking about me. You've *never* loved me like you loved him." He shrugged. "Maybe he still loves you too. I think you should work on getting him back before he walks down the aisle with your BFF."

He turned and Stephanie pulled him back, tears in her eyes.

"Lindell, you're talking crazy," Stephanie said. "I *love* you. I only want you. And we've got a *baby* coming—do you not care about that?"

"I'm the one who said it was the happiest time of my life," Lindell said. "You're the one who couldn't agree. And you know I care about our baby. I'm here for our baby, and I'm here for you too, Steph. The slightest hiccup, I'm there—whatever you need. As far as the marriage, I don't know." He paused. "I just don't know."

Lindell walked away and Stephanie stared after him, thinking of the times their marriage had hit a rough spot. She'd always been the one who needed time, even the one who'd left altogether. But she was the impetuous one. Lindell, even with diagnosed PTSD, had never packed a bag and said he needed time away from her.

She felt herself shaking as she stood alone and very pregnant. *Lord, how do we come back from this?*

CHAPTER 55

"*I* don't know if I want to go to youth church today." Sophia walked with Joy to the building. "It was nice going to Bible study as part of the film crew. Maybe we should go to the main service with the rest of them."

"I'm definitely going to youth church." Joy typed on her phone as she walked. "I've been texting with Lucas since yesterday, so I'm looking forward to seeing him."

Sophia slowed her steps. "You've been texting with Lucas? How did that happen?"

"I picked up my phone and saw a text from him, asking what I'm up to," Joy said. "I couldn't believe it. Look."

Joy showed the initial text, and Sophia could see an entire chain that ensued thereafter.

"How did you not tell me about that?" Sophia said. "That's something you would have forwarded the moment you got it."

"I don't know," Joy said. "I thought about what you said about processing what happened with Noah. I guess I wanted to process this too."

"I get that," Sophia said, glad she hadn't told Joy about her and

Lucas. "But the fact that he texted you out of the blue . . . that's really wild."

"Not as wild as Noah putting you in his story yesterday," Joy said. "You know people are wondering who was dancing with him." She tossed Sophia's hair. "And girl, your curls are popping today. I don't know why you don't wear it like this all the time."

"Same reason you don't," Sophia said. "Takes too long to style it this way." She'd taken the time this morning, thinking she and Lucas would be going out tonight, though she hadn't gotten confirmation from him. Looked like now she knew why.

They walked into the building, through several pockets of conversation, Joy leading the way. Sophia knew she was headed wherever Lucas was. Fine. Sophia wanted to see him herself.

They moved into an area with assorted beverages and doughnuts. Sophia spotted him, but not before Joy. She went straight to him, engaging him in conversation as Sophia looked on from a slight distance. Lucas looked over at her and Sophia stared him down. He looked away.

"Soph, why are you back there?" Joy waved her over.

Sophia moved closer. "Hey, Lucas."

"Hey, Sophia," Lucas said.

"I'm gonna get a doughnut," Joy said. "You guys want anything?"

"I'm fine," Sophia said.

Lucas nodded. "Me too."

Joy walked away and Sophia looked at him. "I'm guessing you changed your wallpaper," she said.

"Yeah," Lucas said, "after I saw the real reason you couldn't go out Friday night. You had plans with Noah."

"I did not have plans with Noah." Sophia kept her voice low. "The cast and crew had a last minute party at the B and B, and we danced. It was no big deal."

Lucas hesitated. "I thought, when I saw Noah's story . . ."

"And instead of getting actual facts," Sophia said, "you ignored my text to confirm our date for tonight and hit up my cousin?"

"I figured you just didn't want to tell me," Lucas said. "I thought you were playing games."

"Now who's the one playing games?" Sophia said. "My cousin thinks you're really into her. I can't believe you—"

"They had the chocolate glaze today," Joy said, licking her fingers as she spoke. She looked at them. "Ready to go to class?"

"I'm going to the main service," Sophia said. "I'll see you later."

Sophia left the building and checked her phone, her insides stirring when she saw a text from Noah.

Breakfast isn't the same. Miss u.

She read it three times then measured her reply. **I miss those breakfasts too.**

Noah replied. **U don't miss me?**

Butterflies swirled. Sophia typed—**Maybe :) was hoping you'd be at church.**

Woke up late. Maybe nxt Sun

Sophia typed a quick reply—**OK**—and kept moving toward the main building.

Or u could come get me.

Sophia paused again, wondering what he meant. **For church?**

Yup.

Sophia's mind raced. Was he serious? But why would he say it if he wasn't? She could pick him up and be back in time for third service. How would that look, though, if she walked in with Noah Stiles? But then, she was part of the movie crew, loosely anyway. And cast and crew were there today. She was doing her part, picking up the cast member who woke up late.

Be there in 20.

"I'm wondering how many people will recognize you." Sophia glanced at Noah as she drove. "We were talking about the movie last night, and I was surprised my sister didn't know who you were."

"I'm not surprised," Noah said, in jeans and a long sleeve shirt.

"People listen to whatever they're into. Somebody can be huge in country music and unknown to the person who listens to hip hop." He looked at her. "What kind of music is your sister into?"

"Gospel and praise and worship," Sophia said.

"There you go," Noah said. "Probably the case for most of the people at your church, which is cool. I like being in spaces that give me a different perspective, outside of the world I live in."

"I can't imagine living like you do," Sophia said, "with all the traveling and shows and fans wanting a piece of you." She gave him a glance. "But you actually seem normal. Somewhat."

"Somewhat?" Noah said.

"It can only be so normal to have millions of followers," Sophia said. "But you don't act super entitled and you're not a jerk."

"All of this could be gone in a minute." Noah snapped his fingers. "My manager was in an R&B group in the nineties, and he talks about how they had a hit single on radio and thought that was everything. They started touring, got a taste of fame." He talked with his hands. "The next single didn't do as well. Third single did even worse. The label dropped them. It was over that fast." He looked out at the road. "Knowing this won't last forever helps me stay grounded. That and Vikki Deandra Stiles."

"Who?" Sophia said.

Noah smiled. "My mom. She's *big* into her church and always telling me that fame doesn't mean anything if you're not living for God."

Sophia smiled a little. "You believe that?"

"She says it so much it's hard not to." Noah thought a moment. "I know she's praying for me. I'm not into it like she is." He looked over at her. "She would love you, though. A for-real church girl."

"How would you know I'm for real?" Sophia said.

"I can tell," Noah said. "I think that's why I like you."

Sophia pulled into the crowded parking lot, once again trying to ignore the butterflies. She waited for a family to back out of a space and took it. They got out and made their way into the building.

"Have you been over there yet?" Sophia said, pointing. "To the production offices and wardrobe and all that?"

"I came once in the evening," Noah said. "But I couldn't take it all in. It's like a mini campus out here. And I was *not* expecting all these people."

"I know," Sophia said. "I thought our Maryland church was big."

They walked inside the main doors, the air filled with chatter and laughter given the second service ending and the third set to begin.

"There's an area with coffee and pastries and stuff," Sophia said. "Or we could go straight to the sanctuary."

"I ate *well* this morning, so I'm good," Noah said. "We can just go in."

She led the way, moving through the crowd—

"Sophia, hold up."

She turned and saw that Noah had been stopped by three young women.

"I knew you were in town filming the movie about Pastor Lance, and I was *hoping* you would be here today." The woman smiled ear to ear.

"I was looking for you when I saw Alonzo and some of the others from the movie this morning," another said. "I was like aww, he didn't come. But we are *here* for the grand entrance."

"Not a grand entrance at all." Noah shrugged. "Just couldn't get up this morning."

"I know you hear this a lot," the third woman said. "But I'm your biggest fan—you have no idea. I drove to Chicago to see you in concert because your tour didn't come to St. Louis—*please* come to St. Louis next time."

"For sure," Noah said. "I'm thinking by the end of this shoot, St. Louis will be my second home."

"Can we get a picture?" the first woman said. "But I don't want a group pic. I want my own pic."

The other two echoed the same sentiment, so they took turns taking a picture with Noah. They got a goodbye hug and looked at

Sophia as Noah rejoined her. The two of them continued to the sanctuary, where people from the second service still milled about.

Alonzo spotted them and waved them forward as he talked with a group, many from the movie. Sophia saw her mom among them.

"Excited to see you, man," Alonzo said, greeting Noah. "How'd you get here?"

"Sophia brought me," Noah said.

Jillian moved closer to Sophia. "You left to get Noah?" she said, near whisper.

"Yeah, he texted me," Sophia said. "He woke up late but wanted to come."

"I didn't even know you two talked like that," Jillian said. "How does he have your number?"

"We had breakfast every morning at the B and B, Mom," Sophia said. "Plus there was a late night snack and music thing—I'll tell you about it."

Courtenay walked up to her. "So that's Mr. R&B superstar? You gonna introduce me?"

"He's not a superstar," Sophia said. "And be nice." She tapped Noah on the shoulder. "Hey, this is my sister Courtenay. Courtenay—Noah."

Noah shook her hand. "Nice to meet you. I think I know the whole family now."

"Heard a lot about you," Courtenay said. "I'm looking forward to checking out your music."

"I appreciate that," Noah said.

The praise and worship team came onto the platform, signaling the start of service. Second service people started cutting their conversations and filing out.

"Hey, Noah," Alonzo said, "we're headed to the production office so just meet us there after service. We'll get you back to the B and B afterward."

"Okay, sounds good," Noah said.

Sophia looked at him as they headed for a pew near the back. "You excited about the first day of filming tomorrow?"

"Remember I was nervous about you listening to the music?" Noah said.

"Yeah," Sophia said.

"That was nothing compared to how I'm feeling about tomorrow."

Noah moved into the row, and Sophia felt a hand to her shoulder.

"Girl, I had to come over here and find you," Joy said. "Everybody's over there talking about Noah being here today. Somebody saw him walking in with you." She glanced at him. "How did that happen? I was *just* with you."

"He needed a ride to church so I went to get him," Sophia said.

"He *texted* you?"

"We exchanged numbers the night I listened to his music."

"I had to come see for myself, but let me get back." Joy smiled. "Lucas and I are sitting together."

"Joy," Sophia said, "I need to talk to you about that later."

"About what?" Joy said.

"Lucas."

"What about him?"

"I can't tell you now," Sophia said. "Service is starting."

"Well, you can't mention it and then make me wait," Joy said. "What is it?"

Sophia sighed. "Let's go out there."

Sophia and Joy left the sanctuary and moved to a quiet spot.

"It's really hard to tell you this, but I have to," Sophia said. "You're my cousin and my best friend and—"

"Soph, what is it?"

"Lucas isn't being real with you," Sophia said. "He texted you because he was upset with me. He and I were actually supposed to go on a date tonight."

Joy stared at her a second. "How were you supposed to go on a date with Lucas tonight? You never mentioned anything about you and Lucas."

"I was waiting for the right time because I knew you liked him," Sophia said. "But Joy, I wasn't planning anything—it just happened—and I wanted to tell you—"

"What 'just happened'?" Joy said. "You said the date was supposed to be tonight."

Sophia exhaled. "I kissed him."

"You *kissed* him?" Joy said. "You kissed *Lucas*? When?"

"A couple of weeks ago in a hallway upstairs," Sophia said. "We were talking and he said he had a crush on me, and I had a crush on him but I wasn't going to act on it because I knew *you* had a crush on him." She took a breath. "We've been talking and texting every day. But when he saw the Insta-story with Noah and me, he got an attitude. Texting you was a way to get back at me."

"First of all, we're cousins but we are *not* best friends," Joy said. "You didn't tell me about Lucas, and it took you forever to tell me about you and Noah."

"Joy, I told you the next day—"

"And I don't even know if you're being straight about Lucas," Joy said. "Maybe you tried to get at him, and he turned you down. Sounds like you're the one who's upset because he doesn't want to take you out tonight."

"Joy, I can show you the text messages between me and Lucas," Sophia said. "You'll see that what I'm saying is true."

"There's a text that says he reached out to me to get back at you?"

"No, he told me this morning," Sophia said, "while you were getting your doughnut."

"Even if that was his initial reason, it doesn't mean it's *still* the reason," Joy said. "We texted for several hours yesterday and we've been hanging today in church. Or maybe you think it's not possible for him to like me once he gets to know me."

Joy walked away, and Sophia walked back into the sanctuary, feeling heavy. She scooted past the people in her row and stood next to Noah as praise and worship continued.

He lowered his head next to hers. "What's wrong?"

Sophia wished she could change everything with Lucas, starting with saying no to that initial hallway conversation. "I think I just lost my best friend."

Sophia felt Noah take her hand, and she couldn't ignore the butterflies.

CHAPTER 56

$\mathcal{T}$rey cut a hefty piece of sweet potato pie in the kitchen of his dad's duplex and put it on a dessert plate. "So what's your biggest fear?"

Jade poured a cup of coffee. "That I won't be able to eat a meal in peace ever again."

"After that roast you whipped up today?" Trey said. "And a pie too? I'm here to tell you that's real. But besides that." He poured a cup as well.

"I'm not even sure what my biggest fear is," Jade said. "And if I did know, I doubt I would want to tell you." She carried her coffee to the living room. "What's yours?"

"You're not getting any of this pie?" Trey said.

"I'm too full," Jade said.

Trey sat on the floor with his pie and coffee, his back against a leather sofa. "My biggest fear is that I'm destined to be lonely." He savored some of the coffee. "But it's like Tommy said in class this morning. You can't really talk to people about your fears. They don't give you room to be human."

Jade sat cross-legged on the love seat across from him. "I thought you could talk to Lance, though."

"True," Trey said. "Lance listens and understands for the most part. And he knows me better than anybody at this point. But it's hard to keep bringing up the same stuff. You know? Like—'Come on, Trey, you're not past that yet?'"

"Lance wouldn't say that," Jade said.

"I know. He wouldn't even think it. It's just me wishing I *was* past it." Trey paused, tasting the pie. "Okay, I'm supposed to believe this is your first time making this?"

"It *is*," Jade said. "I've been learning to cook different things but didn't want to start baking because I'd be tempted to eat it all. You're my taste tester."

"You better go get some so you can see how good this is," Trey said.

"Really?" Jade went to the kitchen as Trey ate another forkful.

"So anyway," Trey said, "as far as the loneliness, sometimes I wonder—is this my thorn? The thing that God is using to show me that His grace is sufficient? Or maybe it's a perpetual trial to perfect me and teach me to endure." He forked up another bite. "But either way, that's my fear—that it'll always be an issue."

Jade returned with a sliver of pie. "And you're thinking this because of life on the mission field, especially given what just happened?"

"Yeah, you don't know whether there will be somebody on your team that you vibe with like a friend," Trey said. "And so far I *haven't* had somebody like that. But if I'm called to missions, it's something I'll have to deal with."

Jade tasted the pie, pointing her fork at it. "Not bad," she said, smiling. "I can't believe I made sweet potato pie. Anyway, don't you think David had to be lonely at times?"

"Where did that come from?"

"We're talking about loneliness," Jade said. "And we were talking about David this morning—oh, wait, did I tell you how wild it was to actually read the David and Goliath story? I only knew the pop culture reference—little guy versus the giant. No idea that it's *really* about how he was trusting God. That blew me away."

"Soooo, wow. I forget you didn't grow up with this." Trey finished his pie.

"Nope," Jade said. "You've probably heard the story a hundred times. I was like, *Ahhh, did David really take off the armor? How is this about to play out?*"

Trey chuckled. "That was everything I needed, in that one statement." He shook his head. "Jade, Jade, Jade . . . experiencing Christian life through you is priceless. But tell me about the lonely part."

"We talked about David being a shepherd, out there fighting lions and bears." Jade ate another forkful of her pie. "How much time must he have spent with no one but the sheep? Plus he was the youngest. His brothers weren't even home—they're off to the battle. He *had* to get lonely. But seems like he turned alone time into God time."

Trey stared at Jade. "So one minute you gon' be the one who doesn't know *the* Sunday School story, and the next you're dropping a whole gem?" He let out a sigh. "That's the power of the Holy Spirit, for real. I've never thought of the mission field as anything like David's sheep field, till this moment. I'm about to put 'alone time is God time' on a mug, shirt, *something* to remind me."

"I need that myself," Jade said, picking up her phone. "It's going in my notes." She typed it in there then stared downward a moment. "I think my biggest fear might be rejection."

"Thought you didn't want to tell me," Trey said.

"Oh, hush," Jade said. "But it's dumb because I've already experienced my greatest rejection. Can you fear something that's already happened?"

"What was the rejection?" Trey said.

"My biological father," Jade said. "As much as we loved Randall, we wanted to meet him." She paused. "Well, what we really wanted was a relationship with him. But he didn't . . ." She shrugged. "He didn't want anything to do with us."

"So now you're afraid that any and everybody might reject you," Trey said. "If you ask me, your biggest fear is showing people the real you. You don't have to worry about it when you've got twenty walls up. You reject them before they can reject you."

"Did I ask you for an analysis?" Jade said.

"But man," Trey said, sighing. "I hate hearing that about your biological dad. I can't imagine the pain you felt. You probably wondered what was wrong with you, that he would reject you. But something was wrong with *him*, Jade. That wasn't the right response. Period. That was *not* the right response."

Jade looked aside for several seconds. "Why are we talking about this? I need people who only talk about trivial stuff." She sighed. "You might be right about my biggest fear. I used to give away my body quicker than I'd let someone get to know me. How crazy is that?"

"I'm trying to picture you interacting with a guy," Trey said, "pretending to be nice."

"That was never happening," Jade said. "I was just good at flirting."

Trey cocked his head, looking at her. "Nah, I can't see it."

"The funny thing is *I* can barely see it now," Jade said. "I thank God I'm not that person anymore." She ate the last bit of pie and set the plate on the coffee table. "But now that you've got us *way* off the lesson . . ."

"This *is* the lesson," Trey said. "We were talking about Shadrach, Meshach, and Abed-nego and how they didn't fear the fiery furnace."

"Then you had to stop and get pie, and went on a tangent about *our* biggest fears—"

"Which isn't a tangent because that's the challenge this week."

"It *is* a tangent because we weren't finished with the story," Jade said. "I want to see what happens. I mean, I know they survived, but I want the details. And yes, I know—another story everybody learns in Sunday school."

"Well, real talk," Trey said. "I heard these stories growing up but they were just that—stories. I didn't see the faith behind them or how to actually apply them to my life. Even now, I'm seeing this new perspective of how they're clinging to God." He got his Bible from the coffee table. "What verse are we on?"

"Twenty-one," Jade said. "After the king got mad and turned the furnace up seven times hotter because they said their God was not only *able* to deliver them, but that He *would* deliver them. I love that!"

"The level of faith is ridiculous," Trey said. "To know and *trust* God like that . . ."

"And it seems like a whole different type of clinging than David fighting Goliath," Jade said.

"Why do you say that?" Trey said.

"These three are clinging in obedience," Jade said. "Right? They're refusing to worship the golden statue because God said not to worship other gods. So it's rocking me that they fear God more than they fear the king or that fire. *Man . . .*"

"Didn't fear people's approval either," Trey said. "Imagine all these dignitaries and rulers there for the dedication of this image. A command goes out that when you hear the music, you have to *fall down* and worship—you can't even play it off. But these three dudes—with government appointed positions—are *obviously* the only ones standing." He looked at her. "I think it's your turn to read."

Jade looked down at her Bible. "'Then these men were tied up in their trousers, their coats, their caps, and their other clothes, and were cast into the midst of the furnace of blazing fire.'" She looked up. "If I'm believing God to deliver me from the fiery furnace, I'm wanting a deliverance *before* I get to the furnace. Strike the king dead. Make the fire go out. No, God lets them get tied up and thrown into the actual fire."

"That'll preach," Trey said. "Who wants to go *through* the fire? But all the glory in this story—and the reason it's even in pop culture—is because they went *through* the fire."

Jade read the next couple of verses then paused. "You want to continue?"

"Nope," Trey said. "This is the best part. You take it."

Jade smiled. "'Then Nebuchadnezzar the king was astounded and stood up in haste; he said to his high officials, "Was it not three men we cast bound into the midst of the fire?" They replied to the king, "Certainly, O king." He said, "Look!" I see four men loosed and walking about in the midst of the fire without harm, and the appearance of the fourth is like a son of the gods!"'" She looked at him. "Wow. The only thing I knew about the story was that three men got thrown into the fire and didn't get burned. I had no idea that a *fourth* person was in there with them. Was that an angel?"

"Some say an angel," Trey said. "Some say it's an appearance of Christ. But either way, it was supernatural, and it was from God."

"I just got chills," Jade said, holding her arms. "They were clinging to God in the fiercest way, and their obedience and trust *mattered* to Him. He showed up! He was with them."

"And we don't have to wonder if it's Jesus who's with us, which is huge." Trey thought about his own words. "But do I act like it's huge day to day? Am I making the most of His presence?" He sighed. "I've got a lot to pray about with the challenge this week."

"Can we pray together to kick off the week?" Jade said. "What you said about not wanting to show people the real me . . . I feel like part of my challenge is learning to take down these walls. This is about to be a tough one."

"We said we're in it together," Trey said. "Prayer is part of it. And I'm definitely here for the construction project."

Jade gave him a look. "Who said you'll be involved?"

"You can go ahead and start now," Trey said. "That's a wall."

Jade heaved a sigh. "Fine." She took another moment. "I wouldn't be thinking about taking down my walls if you weren't willing to help me, and if you weren't there to listen. So . . . yeah."

"Just to show you how much I appreciated that, I'll cook tomorrow."

"You don't know how to cook."

"I can cook easy things," Trey said. "Like grilled cheese."

"I'll cook," Jade said.

"Just remember that I offered."

"Trey, just pray."

CHAPTER 57

*B*rooke descended the stairs of the B and B at six-fifteen Monday morning, greeted by the now-familiar, delicious breakfast aroma. She could hardly sleep for all the jitters about the first day of filming. Well, that plus the blowup with Cornell. So she'd gotten up before dawn and spent time doing Bible study and going over her lines. Now she had roughly twenty minutes before the car would arrive to take her to base camp for hair, makeup, and wardrobe.

Brooke walked first into the dining room, which was empty save for an assortment of breads and pastries on the sideboard, as well as coffee, assorted teas, and pitchers of juice and water. She put her phone on the table and went into the spacious kitchen. Stephanie stood over the stove in a house robe and slippers, scrambling eggs.

"Good morning, Stephanie," Brooke said.

Stephanie turned, taking out her earbuds. "Good morning, Brooke," she said. "I've got your oatmeal right here"—she pointed —"and I'm about to plate your eggs. Bread is in the toaster." She tended to the eggs. "How are you feeling this morning?"

"Nervous," Brooke said, shaking out her hands. "And tired for lack of sleep. But definitely excited." She added oatmeal to her bowl then sprinkled a little brown sugar. "Stephanie, are you okay? I hope it's all right to ask. You just . . . don't seem yourself."

Stephanie got a plate and transferred the eggs onto it. "Thank you for asking, Brooke. I didn't sleep well either, but all is well. I really wanted to make sure you all had a great start today." She handed her the plate. "Oh, and Mariah already left. She was in focused, director mode."

Brooke got her toast. "That just made me more nervous."

"You'll be fine," Stephanie said. "I'm cheering for you. Praying too."

"Thank you so much, Stephanie."

Brooke took her food to the dining room, got coffee and a glass of water, and settled at the table. Checking her phone she saw a flurry of group texts from the past five minutes, starting with Robin acknowledging Brooke's big day and Jesse chiming in.

She smiled as she typed her reply. **What are you guys doing up? And thank you! Pray for me, y'all. Feeling nervous.**

Brooke tasted the oatmeal as another flurry of texts came in response. She intermittently replied and ate her breakfast, then saw a single text from Jesse. She went to it.

Hey, didn't put this in the group to respect your privacy. Just seeing how you're doing after the prayer y'day.

Brooke replied. **A lot happened after. Can update you but I'm rushing. It'd be faster to talk if you're able.**

Her stomach dipped slightly as Jesse's name flashed on her screen with a call.

"Good morning," Brooke said. "Are you always up this early?"

"Pretty much," Jesse said. "I walk my dog in the morning. But also, I've got my daughter this week so I'm trying to get some time in the word before she wakes up."

"Hey, me too this morning." Brooke scarfed down some of her eggs. "I was doing the Cling study. King Jehoshaphat got me hype."

"That's crazy," Jesse said. "I just read that. I know you don't have time to get into it, but it got me hype too. So what's the update?"

"First, thank you for being part of the prayer circle," Brooke said.

"After those prayers, I thought God would move. But I didn't think He'd move that fast." She drank some juice. "Cornell called last night, upset because he watched the vlog with the two of us dancing Friday night."

"Oh, for real?" Jesse said. "I haven't seen it. He thought something was up?"

Brooke sighed. "He already had an attitude because we haven't been talking like normal. So he tried to say that was why, because I'm supposedly out here having a good time with you." She bit into her toast. "Forgive me for eating, by the way. So anyway, things spiraled and next thing I knew, he was breaking up with me."

"Oh, wow," Jesse said. "That's the last thing you needed, something to upset you the night before the shoot."

"That's what got me," Brooke said. "I wasn't upset. I saw it as an answer to prayer. I had been trying to find a way to tell him that we needed to get separate places. And I felt bad because he's not working right now—well, just small jobs—and I knew he'd feel the strain. But breaking up solved the problem. *He* said he was moving out, like it would hurt me."

"Look at God," Jesse said. "It just makes you think—why am I not praying about *everything*?"

"I thought the same thing." Brooke looked up as Noah walked in. "But thanks for checking on me. I really appreciate that."

"Absolutely," Jesse said. "Go kill it today."

Brooke smiled. "Thanks, Jesse." She hung up, looking at Noah. "How can you eat all that so early in the morning?"

"All what?" Noah blew his hot chocolate and took a sip. "This is less than I normally get."

"Pancakes *and* biscuits?" Brooke eyed his plate. "Plus hash browns, eggs, bacon and sausage?"

"Somebody has to show appreciation for Stephanie's efforts," Noah said.

"You are certainly doing your part," Brooke said. "You all set for today?"

"I've only got one scene, and I think I've got my lines," Noah said. "What about you? You're in every scene."

Brooke spooned up more oatmeal. "That's why I was nowhere to be found on Saturday."

Noah's phone lit up on the table with a FaceTime call. After several rings, he decided to get it. "Hey, I have to call you later."

"I know you're busy. Just saying good luck with everything today. Why am I on speaker?"

"Because I need to eat and get out of here," Noah said. "I'll call you later, though. And thanks."

"Kk. Miss you."

"Miss you, too," Noah said, clicking off.

"Your mom calling to wish you well?" Brooke said.

Noah stabbed some of his pancakes. "I won't even tell Alyssa you thought she looked old enough to be my mom."

"I wasn't looking at the phone," Brooke said.

"That was my girlfriend," Noah said.

"Oh," Brooke said. "You've never said anything about a girlfriend."

Noah added more syrup. "And I didn't know you had a boyfriend till I just heard you say you broke up."

Brooke nodded. "Touché." She looked as Faith walked in. "Good morning, lady."

"Hey, good morning, guys," Faith said. "Updated call sheets." She handed them out. "Just so you know, I'm taking you two to base camp. I need to talk to Steph, but I'll be ready in ten."

"Umm . . ." Brooke focused on the call sheet after Faith left. "They added a scene that's toward the second half of the movie."

"Mariah told us they don't film everything in sequence," Noah said.

"I know, but I'm trying to remember what's going on with Kendra's hair at this point." Brooke finished her eggs. "I'm sure they've got it figured out. But great—now I've got more lines to memorize."

"Part of being a star," Noah said. "Suck it up."

Brooke narrowed her eyes at him. "Why does it feel like you really are my little brother? An annoying one."

"Just trying to help you get the right mindset," Noah said. "Bottom line, big sis—you 'bout to blow up." He forked up hash browns and eggs. "And when your ex tries to get back, tell him it's too late."

"Yeah, that won't be happening," Brooke said. The next man in her life needed to be someone who was serious about God—serious about clinging to God.

She put her dishes in the kitchen and started up the stairs, checking to see if more group texts had come. Checking for Jesse.

"Oh, I was prepared to style your hair in a ponytail today," Abby said. "That's what the scenes called for."

Brooke looked in the mirror at her. "Right. But here's the updated call sheet." She showed her again. "In this scene they added, Kendra's hair is in a head wrap. I just wanted to make sure you saw that." She looked over at Alonzo. "Hey, the scene where Lance is about to move out . . . are we shooting it this afternoon?"

Alonzo occupied a chair a few feet away, talking to his barber as he trimmed his hair. "I'd say it'll be afternoon when we get to it, yes. Why? Did I miss something?"

"It's not a problem," Abby said. "Brooke, you know how to do head wraps, right?"

"Not at all." Brooke looked at Alonzo again. "In that scene, Kendra's wearing a head wrap. But Abby doesn't know how to style the head wrap."

"Well, I had a plan," Abby said. "I was going to learn by going through tutorials on YouTube, and I assumed I'd have enough notice." She reached for her cell phone. "I'll call Maggie."

"The production designer?" Brooke said.

"That's who I report to," Abby said. "I want to see what she advises."

"I'll call Maggie," Alonzo said, getting up. "We had a lot of back and forth on this."

"Head wraps?" Brooke said.

"All of your hair needs during production," Alonzo said. "And here we are on the first day and—" He sighed, clearly peeved. "Brooke, sit tight. We'll get it handled."

"Well, meanwhile let's finish getting you ready for the first scene this morning," Abby said.

Brooke chuckled as the group text lit up. She'd told Robin and Jesse about her head wrap issue and they both sent memes with women wearing beautiful turbans and head wraps. Then Robin sent a video tutorial, telling her she'd better skip lunch and get her skills down.

"Brooke, sorry," Abby said. "I need to run to the restroom. Too much coffee."

Jade walked in with Alonzo soon after Abby left.

"This is why I keep thanking God for not only answering prayers with this movie, but *anticipating* prayer needs," Alonzo said. "So after I talked to Maggie, I went to get Cinda's input and Jade was with her in wardrobe."

Brooke's face lit up. "Oh, that's right, Jade, you do hair videos. I should've known you could do head wraps."

"Uhh, not for real," Jade said. "I've done them, but I always pull up a tutorial. And the one I pull up is my sister's. She's a beast with head wraps."

"Cinda's calling her right now," Alonzo said. "Unfortunately, she's out of town, but close enough that she could get here by afternoon, if she's willing. Jade can get you through today, if need be, though. And hopefully—prayerfully—Jordyn will agree to come on board."

"Wow, I really appreciate that you would bring Jordyn on board just to handle head wraps." Brooke said.

Alonzo moved closer. "Well," he said, his voice lower, "we knew head wraps would be featured in the movie and I wanted Jordyn from the beginning. But we were already battling about where to film and —" He sighed. "I won't get into the politics, but you'll learn that people are very territorial about their departments. Anyway, Jordyn will do a lot more than head wraps, if she agrees. She'd be your personal hair-stylist for the shoot."

Brooke's phone vibrated with another text in the group thread, this one from Jesse.

We got you on prayers for a head wrap expert. Let us know who God sends.

Brooke started typing . . .

CHAPTER 58

Stephanie dried the frying pans, griddle, and baking pans and put them back in their respective cabinets. Next she disposed of the trash and wiped the counter of crumbs and pancake mix residue. Felt good to make a big breakfast and see smiles of appreciation. Now they were gone—and they'd be gone for hours. She knew what she needed to do with the time.

Lord, I just want to curl up in a ball in bed all day. I want to cry and feel sorry for myself and be mad at Lindell for leaving. It would be awesome to get hit with an overwhelming bout of third trimester fatigue as an excuse to lie back down. But no. Can't even get a Braxton Hicks contraction when you want one.

Stephanie sighed and popped a couple of grapes in her mouth from the fruit tray she'd prepared. She'd eaten when she first came down and was starting to feel hunger pains again. She ran her hand over her stomach. "I know. Mommy needs to feed you...."

"Hey, Steph, I'm here," Jillian called. "You downstairs?"

"In the kitchen," Stephanie said, moving to meet her.

She walked straight into Jillian's arms and let her head rest on her shoulder. All morning she'd had to hold her emotion in front of the guests. Now a rush of tears came.

"It means so much that you would come." Stephanie held onto her. "I know you have to go to work."

"I just wish I could've come yesterday," Jillian said. "But between seeing Courtenay off and the kids having different things going on—"

"There was too much happening here anyway," Stephanie said. "Now is perfect."

"Let's go into the sitting room," Jillian said. "I know you've been on your feet cooking and cleaning all morning."

"I need to get a plate I put in the microwave," Stephanie said.

"I'll get it," Jillian said. "Go get comfortable."

"Make yourself one too," Stephanie said. "There's some leftovers."

Jillian brought Stephanie's plate and a bottle of water, plus a small fruit plate for herself.

"Thanks, Jill," Stephanie said, removing the cap and taking a sip. She put the bottle on the coffee table and sat back on the sofa with a sigh.

Jillian sat facing her. "I know we've been going back and forth through texts, but tell me how you're feeling. What's on your mind right now?"

Stephanie heaved a sigh. "My fears."

"Your fears?" Jillian said.

"Tommy and that stupid cling challenge," Stephanie said. "I didn't even hear most of the class yesterday, just like I didn't hear most of the cling sermon when Lance preached it. Both times I was preoccupied with seeing Warren." She ate some eggs. "But this morning the Lord had me listen to Lance's sermon online."

"Oh, and the class was recorded," Jillian said.

"Girl, already listened to that too," Stephanie said. "I was like, Lord, why do you have me texting Tommy all early to see if he recorded the class?" She ate some more. "Of course he was up and got it to me within minutes, because—God."

"So, wow, you listened to all of that this morning?" Jillian said.

"During breakfast prep and cleanup," Stephanie said. "Then I prayed and asked God to show me my fears." She ate some hash browns as she thought about it. "Prior to yesterday I would've said

415

'ditto' to Tommy. My main fear was that life would never be what I thought it would be—particularly, my marriage. And I know we have to put aside the 'fairytale' thoughts and all that, but even with basic compatibility things." She sighed. "Anyway, you already know all that. *Now* my main fear is that my marriage is over and our baby won't have two parents who are together."

"Steph, you know Lindell isn't leaving you and the baby." Jillian speared a cantaloupe. "He just said he needs time."

"But Warren was already a problem, when we were only dealing with the *thought* of him," Stephanie said. "Now we could run into him at any time. I don't know if our marriage can handle that constant source of friction." She drank more water. "I almost texted Roni to tell her they need to find another church."

"I actually thought about that," Jillian said. "I don't know how you would word it, though."

"Exactly," Stephanie said. "'Roni, I'd appreciate it if you and Warren could find another church. This is *my* church—you know, the one I grew up in? And I know it's been several years, but Warren is still an issue with me and Lindell.'" She scooped up more hash browns. "Umm. No. Don't want her to know that. Anyway, I didn't pray about it. I really want us to pray about what to do."

"Amen," Jillian said. "Which reminds me about that other prayer that Lindell heard. When you told me that the other day . . ."

"That's what I'm saying—*that part* was already complicated and challenging and painful," Stephanie said. "I made it *worse*." She broke off a piece of biscuit. "Lindell said I've never loved him like I loved Warren and I should get back with him. He *actually* said that. And I know he was hurt but I think he really thinks he doesn't measure up to Warren in my mind. That's what could cause him to walk away for good. Well, that's my fear, anyway."

"But thankfully," Jillian said, "the point of the challenge is not to identify our fears and wallow in them. It's to bring them to the light and let God deal with them." She shifted more toward her. "So we're not only going to pray; we're going to believe that God will work *all* of this for good and for His glory. He's able, Steph. We're giving God all the lies you're believing. Let's put everything on the altar."

"I can't believe you just said that." Stephanie sat up a little. "That's what's been on my heart after listening to those messages—put *every-thing* on the altar for the sake of my marriage." She thought a moment. "The B and B. Worry about what to do with respect to the marriage. All my marriage expectations . . . if there's little passion, so be it—"

"But Steph, you can have expectations in prayer," Jillian said. "It's called faith. Again, *God is able*."

"Have we not prayed for years about passion in the bedroom?" Stephanie said. "Even when things are going well, there's not much passion. And I keep letting it be a source of discontentment. I have a husband who loves me and would do anything for me—at least, I did, before all of this. I want to focus on *that*."

"I'll tell you one thing," Jillian said. "I've never seen you this passionate about wanting your marriage to work. Seems like God is already working things for good. Fear of losing your marriage is showing you how much you want it."

"That's true," Stephanie said. "After you leave I'm planning to spend time doing the Cling study, reading every passage of Scripture Tommy put in there. Typically I'd be doing laundry, administrative stuff, cleaning . . . But that's my priority today." She heaved a sigh. "I do want my marriage, Jill. So you know what else I'm putting on the altar—again? Warren. Every stinking thought about him and the past. I need the Lord to take those thoughts and kill them."

Jillian raised her hands. "Yes! Praise the Lord!"

"But," Stephanie said, "that's a fear too, surrendering *everything* to God. I want us to pray that I'll be able to cling to Him and trust *His* will for me, whatever it may be." She paused. "But our prayer time is never one-sided. What are you putting on the altar?"

"Uh, who said I'm putting something on the altar?" Jillian said. "I could have a dozen other things to pray about."

"But wouldn't it be powerful if that's what our prayer time is about?" Stephanie said. "Both of us giving everything to God and letting Him do what He will? Then we can both be nervous about the outcome." She finished her eggs. "I know one thing you could put on the altar."

Jillian looked at her. "What."

"Don't be so enthusiastic. The grief study."

"Really?"

"You're stressed about whether to do it, then you say you know it could help people, then you wonder if you're really ready," Stephanie said. "Stop the back and forth and just put it on the altar. Let God decide. In fact, girl, put 'readiness' on the altar."

"What do you mean?" Jillian said.

"How many times have you said you don't know if you're ready to do this or that because of whatever grief timeline is in your head?" Stephanie threw up her hands. "What does 'ready' even mean from God's standpoint? What are we *ever* ready to do, apart from Him? All you need to know is whether His grace is there, and *that* means you're ready."

Jillian gave her a look. "I thought I was coming over here because *you* needed help."

"You want me to keep going?" Stephanie said.

"With what?"

"With what you need to put on the altar," Stephanie said.

"Not really," Jillian said. "But go on."

"Tommy, Silas, dating, and marriage."

Jillian gave her a blank stare.

"I love that you and Tommy are friends again," Stephanie said. "But who said friendship is all that God has for you two? Because *Tommy's* not 'ready' for more? Give that thing to God and see what *He* says." She put her plate on the side table. "On the other hand, you've determined that you won't allow Silas to pursue anything with you—again, the 'readiness' thing. I need you to seek the Lord about that. Because have you not noticed that Silas is a serious—and handsome—man of God who *is* ready for more? Put *that* on the altar and see what God says. And on the *other* hand—"

"Seriously?"

"I think you think you're supposed to get past some marker for it to be 'okay' to consider dating or marriage again," Stephanie said. "Is it in God's hands or *your* hands? Could you put that on the altar, ma'am? Because I'm eager to see the plans He has for you."

"Now that you spent all that time telling me what my prayer request is," Jillian said, "I need to go because I'm about to be late for work."

"Ha," Stephanie said. "This altar prayer got me fired up. We're about to pray right now, for as long as we're moved to pray. I'll call Cyd myself and tell her you've got an excused late note from the Holy Spirit."

Jillian moved closer and took both of Stephanie's hands. "I'll admit I'm fired up myself. Let's shake some stuff up in the spirit, Steph. We need God to move mightily."

"Amen," Stephanie said, bowing her head. "And let me start with repenting openly for reaching out to Warren, which opened a door for all of this . . ."

CHAPTER 59

id-afternoon Jordyn turned onto the street where filming was taking place. She'd left Chicago soon after Cinda's call, but highway construction had made traffic heavy. She'd kept Faith updated about her progress, and Faith had kept her updated about the shoot—until the past two hours. Jordyn knew they were busy, but she wondered if Brooke had already shot the scene with the head wrap.

She couldn't believe it when she got the call, which she'd missed at first. Still asleep, her mom had to wake her to tell her that Cinda was trying to reach her. As Cinda explained the issue, Jordyn thought she might be dreaming still. She'd basically spent the past couple of days with Brooke. Googling photos. Perusing her social media. Reading her industry bio. Jordyn would've hopped up and made the drive no matter whose hair she was styling, simply for the experience. That it was Brooke made the experience more intriguing.

Flatbed trucks, vans, and a portable storage container let Jordyn know which house she needed. She found a parking spot several houses away and texted Faith to let her know she'd arrived. By the time she walked up to the house, Faith was coming outside.

"Hey, so glad you made it," Faith said, hugging her. She raised a finger as she listened to something on her walkie-talkie and sent a reply.

"I'm sorry I couldn't get here sooner," Jordyn said. "Traffic was awful."

"It worked out," Faith said. "They're almost finished rehearsing the scene right now, then Brooke needs to go back to base camp for hair and makeup."

"Base camp?" Jordyn said.

"The area we're utilizing at Living Word," Faith said. "You're about to get well-acquainted with it. Let's head inside for a minute."

Three crew members came out as Jordyn followed Faith inside the home.

"Watch your feet," Faith said. "And your head."

Jordyn ducked beneath a piece of equipment and tried not to trip over wires and cables that extended every which way. They came into a living room area where Brooke and Alonzo were working out a scene with Mariah and a couple of other people. Several crew members tended lights and cameras.

Faith waited at the entryway to the room. "I just want Brooke to know you're here," she whispered.

"Who are those other people with Mariah?" Jordyn whispered.

"The DP—Director of Photography—and assistant director," Faith said.

Brooke and Alonzo moved into position and said a few lines, all of them nodding afterward as if satisfied. Brooke glanced their way and smiled, making praying hands to thank Jordyn.

"Okay, she can breathe easier knowing you're here." Faith started walking, answering someone else on her walkie-talkie. "So next we need to go to base camp so you can meet all the necessary people and fill out some paperwork. But as soon as Brooke gets there, she's the priority."

"Got it," Jordyn said.

"Hey, I'm done," Brooke said, walking up behind them. "Am I riding with you, Faith?"

"You are now," Faith said, telling someone on the walkie-talkie. "Brooke, you've met Jordyn Rogers, right?"

"At the Super Bowl party." Brooke extended her hand. "So good to see you again, and I can't thank you enough for coming."

"No worries," Jordyn said. "I'm glad to be able to do it."

Faith paused as something else came through on the radio device. "Okay, I need to wait till Alonzo's done and take him back. Brooke, do you mind riding with Jordyn?"

"I don't mind at all," Brooke said. "Jordyn and I are about to be spending a lot of time together."

"These head wraps are gorgeous." Jordyn ran her hand across them on the clothing rack from which they hung. "The colors and textures . . . They'll be a prominent part of your character."

"I'm just seeing them myself," Brooke said. "Cinda really did get some beautiful fabrics."

"And I've got a list right here of which head wrap goes with which scene," Jordyn said. "Today's is the bright blue one. But first let me prep your hair."

Brooke settled in the chair as Jordyn took her hair down.

"So you wore a ponytail in the earlier scenes?" Jordyn said.

Brooke nodded. "Those were scenes after Kendra got the diagnosis, when her hair was the last thing she was thinking about. So loose pony with flyaway hairs."

"But we don't want *your* hair to be the last thing we're thinking about," Jordyn said. "This kind of hair tie causes breakage. And was anything put on your hair to retain moisture?"

"Not that I know of," Brooke said, texting.

"Okay," Jordyn said. "We'll make sure we get you tight on pony days as well." She parted a section of hair and applied a dime size amount of styler. "I know you've got a short window. Right now, I'm cornrowing your hair real quick."

"Real quick?" Brooke said. "Do you know how long it would take me to cornrow my hair? That is, *if* I knew how."

Jordyn smiled, already on the next section. "After this, I'm going to wrap your hair in a black satin scarf. It's never been used, just so you know."

"I'm not worried," Brooke said.

"The satin scarf will help your hair retain moisture," Jordyn said, fingers moving, "but also prevent any oils from seeping into the head wrap and potentially discoloring it."

Brooke chuckled then looked at her. "Sorry, that wasn't related to what you said. My friends wanted an update on the head wrap situation. I was so worried this morning. I told them help has arrived." She looked at Jordyn. "I thought Jade was going to do it, which would've been a step up, for sure. But when she said *you* were a beast at head wraps, I was so glad you could come."

"My sister said that?"

Brooke nodded. "But I feel bad that you had to drive all that way. Did someone say you were in Chicago?"

"Yes, at my mom's," Jordyn said.

"Aww, that's nice," Brooke said. "Now I really feel bad, cutting short your visit with your mom."

"No, trust me, it's fine," Jordyn said, cornrowing the last section. "I had been there a few days already."

"Oh yeah, I asked about you . . ." Brooke paused. "It was nothing. Just the other night at this get-together for the end of rehearsals. Your sister was there."

Jordyn put the satin scarf on then got the head wrap and folded it in half. "I saw that actually, in the vlog." She placed the fabric at the nape of the neck and brought it forward, covering her ears, then tied it in a double knot.

"I didn't realize so many people watch the vlog," Brooke said. "But it keeps coming up."

"Looked like a good time," Jordyn said.

Jade walked in, filming.

"You can't just show up with a camera and no heads-up," Jordyn said. "Look at me. I've been traveling for hours."

"I actually *can* show up with a camera," Jade said. "It's my job. And Jordyn, really? That sleek bun is killing."

"Thanks," Jordyn said. It had taken time to detangle her hair and style it. But no way was she showing up to do Brooke's hair without her own looking on point.

Jordyn tucked the ends of the fabric into the wrap, making sure Brooke's hair was completely covered. "So the note says that for this scene, Kendra hasn't had a whole lot of experience doing head wraps. So I did a basic style. And it's a little askew on purpose, but it's fixed in place. I'll be there to adjust as necessary."

"Askew?" Brooke said, rising. "This is amazing." She checked herself out in the mirror. "Okay, I've got to run to makeup. Thank you so much, Jordyn."

"You're welcome," Jordyn said. She looked at Jade once Brooke had left. "Thanks for talking me up."

"I only told the truth," Jade said. "It would've been ridiculous *not* to use you." She sat in the chair. "So how did it feel, doing her hair after you stalked her?"

"Who said I stalked her?"

Jade gave her a look.

"Only a light stalk," Jordyn said. "She was texting her friends while I did the head wrap, and I think I saw Jesse's name."

Jade shrugged. "And?"

"What do you mean—and?"

"Jordyn, what *if* she likes Jesse?" Jade said. "What if Jesse likes her? What if they're just friends?" She threw her hands up. "Who cares? You can't obsess about it. *Or*, if you want to keep obsessing about it, don't do her hair. It's creepy to do both."

Jordyn sighed. "You're right. I know you're right. But it's hard not to obsess about it."

"Then tell them you can't do it."

"I'm not telling them that," Jordyn said. "I want this on my resume."

"Well then do something about the obsession," Jade said. "Put your energy into something else. You should do the Cling study."

"That's what Jillian told me," Jordyn said.

"Oh, you talked to Jillian?" Jade said. "That's good."

"I didn't *talk* talk to her," Jordyn said. "She wanted to, but I knew she'd ask if I've been praying or in the word. And I'd have to tell her not really."

"Did you at least pray *with* her?" Jade said. "That's what you normally do, and you always say it makes a difference."

"Not yet," Jordyn said. "But she sent me the link to the Cling study yesterday. She said she thought it was exactly what I needed and that we could talk about the lessons together."

"Do it, Jordyn," Jade said. "Seriously. I'm doing the study with Trey, and I'm in the Bible more and praying more. I'm seeing a difference already. If you don't do it with Jillian, you could do it with us." She got up from the chair. "At least go online and check it out."

Jordyn gave a slow nod. "Okay, I will." She stared vaguely for a moment. "Why do I hate that Brooke is actually nice, though? I bet Jesse thinks she's really nice."

Jade threw up a hand. "It's hopeless," she said, heading for the door. "Please just tell them you quit."

CHAPTER 60

Treva sat at the round table in her office at Living Word, jotting down ideas for the theme of the next women's conference. She and Cyd had been talking informally about it, and Treva was excited to move to this next phase of nailing down a date and a theme. The last women's conference would forever be etched in memory, and not solely because she met her husband there. The messages in the main session, the workshops, the praise and worship, the fellowship, and the late night gatherings—all of it made for an unforgettable time.

Treva looked as her door opened and her assistant Ellie walked in.

"Treva, I've got a call that came in from the main church line," Ellie said. "A woman says she'd like to talk to you, but she didn't give her name."

"You're saying you asked for her name, and she wouldn't give it?" Treva said.

"That's right," Ellie said.

"Okay, send it in," Treva said. "Thanks, Ellie."

She picked up on the first ring. "Treva Alexander."

"Treva . . . thank you for taking my call," the woman said. "This is . . . my name is Desiree Riley."

Treva sat back, crossed her legs. "I know who you are. What can I do for you?"

"So, I wasn't sure you'd actually get on the phone." Desiree paused. "I'm calling because . . . I guess the best way to put it is . . . I was at the *Promises* event, got the study, and started going through it." She paused again. "I'm sorry if I sound funny. My heart is beating so fast."

Treva got up and walked a little. "You're fine, Desiree. I'm listening. What's on your mind?"

"I just . . . have so many questions," Desiree said. "It's been a long time since, well since I've been to church or read the Bible. And there's something about your voice in this study. It's speaking to me. Even when I heard you at the event. And I just . . . wondered if we could meet."

Treva's brow went up a little. "You want to meet?"

"I know it sounds crazy," Desiree said. "But so many things are gnawing at me as I read. For example, in one chapter you ask, 'Where do you live?' and my answer is 'I don't know. I've lost . . . I've lost my way.'" Her voice broke. "And I don't know what to *do* with that. You talk about knowing Jesus, and I don't know if I do or don't at this point. I feel . . . yeah, *lost*." She took a stuttering breath. "And this idea came to just call you. But I know Lance told you about me, and right —as if you'd want to meet with me. But I just don't know what else—"

"I'll meet with you, Desiree," Treva said.

She took a moment to respond. "You'll . . . meet with me? I wasn't expecting that."

"Can you meet this afternoon at three?" Treva said. "I had a conference call that got rescheduled."

"Yes, I can," Desiree said. "Where do you want to meet?"

Treva thought a moment. "I don't know where you're located, but if we could meet near here at a coffee shop or something, that works best for me. I need to be back for another meeting."

"Whatever works for you," Desiree said. "How about the Starbucks about a mile from there?"

"Perfect," Treva said. "See you there."

She walked out of her office and into Lance's. "You'll never guess who I'm meeting today."

~

The moment Treva walked in she spotted Desiree at a table for two. Head bent over her phone, her hair fell in wispy layers, the ends dusting the table. She looked up as Treva approached.

"Treva, thank you for coming." Desiree stood and shook her hand, her light eyes penetrating. "It's so nice to meet you."

"You as well, Desiree." Treva hung her coat on the back of the chair. "I think I'll get a latte. Did you want anything?"

"Oh, I was waiting for you," Desiree said. "Tell me what you want, and I'll go get it."

"A grande nonfat vanilla latte would be great," Treva said. "Thank you."

Desiree got their drinks and gave Treva hers, then went to the condiment bar.

Treva took a sip as she waited, fighting thoughts of the past that were trying to creep up. Years of being compared to women like Desiree. Years of being reminded that her dark skin didn't measure up. Thankfully, those battles were few and far between now. But something about coming face-to-face with a woman who once had her husband's heart . . . It was hard not to focus on her outward appearance.

Treva's phone vibrated and she took it from her purse. A text from Jillian.

Praying. God's got you. This is spiritual. Focus on her soul.

Treva let out a silent sigh, typing a quick reply as Desiree returned. **You know me so well. Thank you. Love you.**

Desiree looked at her. "I thought I'd start the conversation here, though it's really awkward. I assume you saw the video?"

"I did, yes," Treva said.

"I record a lot of personal things on my channel," Desiree said. "Life updates, how I'm feeling about this or that. When I'm alone in a rented cottage in Thailand or wherever, it's easy to turn on the camera and start talking." She took a sip of her drink. "But the day I recorded that . . . It was a low point. I had recently ended an engagement, then here's Lance back in the news . . . It made me assess my life, and I didn't like what I saw. Then I started your study. And it's making my mind spin, but it's also connecting some dots for me."

"What do you mean?" Treva said.

"I was focused on Lance and my regrets as far as the two of us— I'm sorry, please tell me if this is too much."

"Straightforward is my language," Treva said. "We're good."

"Okay," Desiree said. "And I won't lie—I do have regrets as far as that. But now I'm thinking that what I mostly regret is drifting from God."

"I could see that," Treva said. "The two are simultaneous. Lance is the one who led you to the Lord, so he's in that mix of emotions."

"Yes, that's exactly it." Desiree seemed to ponder it even now." She paused. "So he told you about that, about our relationship."

Treva sipped her latte. "Yes, he told me."

"Thinking back on it," Desiree said, "it was such a heady time, getting to know Lance as I was getting to know the Lord. Two relationships that quickly became the foremost relationships in my life." She thought a moment. "When I broke things off with Lance, I didn't intend to also make a break in my relationship with God. But in hindsight, I guess that's what happened."

"Well, Lance had plugged you into a faith community at Living Word," Treva said. "Now you were overseas, and unless I'm mistaken, traveling from place to place—"

"That's right," Desiree said. "I talk about the nomad life on my channel."

"So how did you go about growing in the faith and staying plugged into a community of believers?" Treva said.

Desiree looked downward a moment. "I didn't. At first I was torn about the decision to end the engagement, so I threw myself into the travel and building up my channel. Moving from country to country, barely remembering what city I was in—there was hardly time to breathe. Now it's years later . . ." She sipped her drink. "I've been every place I dreamed of visiting and amazing places I didn't know existed. The channel has grown beyond what I dreamed too. But . . . I'm sitting here feeling lost."

"So tell me why you wanted to meet?" Treva said. "What is it that I can do?"

Desiree took the *Promises* study and a notebook from her bag. "I wrote down questions that came to me as I read the study, questions keeping me up at night. I wondered if you could explain some things I didn't understand." She paused. "Basically, I wondered if you could help me assess where I am and how I can get back . . . back to where I was . . ." Her voice trailed off.

"When you were with Lance?"

"Well," Desiree said. "In so many words, yes."

"I'm willing to answer your questions as best I can," Treva said, "and prayerfully it'll help. But first, I have a couple of questions I'd like to ask myself."

"Sure," Desiree said.

Treva looked at her. "You recorded a video about Lance and days later hopped a plane. Did the decision to come back to the States have anything to do with him?"

"Only as far as the movie," Desiree said. "It was a chance to come home for the first time in a long time. And I'm hoping it's also a chance to get some footage for my channel from the set."

"Why did you come to the *Promises* event?" Treva said.

"Now I admit that did have to do with Lance," Desiree said. "Once I made the decision to fly back, I started thinking about Living Word, since it was my church home for a time. I pulled up the site to get updated and couldn't believe Lance was the senior pastor. Then I saw that an event was happening the night I got into town. Curiosity got hold of me. I wanted to see him in this role that was so far from the Lance I knew."

"And why did you want to have a private conversation with him that night?"

"You're right," Desiree said. "Straightforward is your language." She cleared her throat. "I didn't expect to run into him on my way out. So seeing him like that, for the first time in so many years . . . I think I just wanted to apologize for the way I handled things. Sending a letter instead of calling because I couldn't bear to hear his voice . . . It's one of the things that still haunts me."

"You should know that Lance didn't want me to meet with you," Treva said. "He doesn't trust you. And given that you declared publicly that you'll always love him, then showed up at Living Word—"

"Oh, Treva, please know I would never think of trying to come between the two of you," Desiree said. "And nor could I. Being there Tuesday night, it was abundantly clear how much he loves and adores you. I greatly respect that."

"Okay," Treva said. "I'm asking you to also respect the fact that Lance said he has nothing to say to you. I'm asking you to respect that boundary."

"Of course," Desiree said.

Treva drank more of her latte. "I came because I was already praying for you. I believe the Lord is drawing you back to Him. Before we get to your questions, let's pray . . ."

CHAPTER 61

*C*edric leaned against the bathroom counter as Cyd washed her face, preparing for bed. "I thought for sure Lindell would've gone home by now," he said. "This is the fourth night."

"And looks like he'll be here a while longer," Cyd said, rinsing. "Did you see all the groceries he bought today?"

"Are you serious?" Cedric said. "I've been trying to talk to him to understand why it blew up again. They had the issue on the island, Stephanie went back down there, and they were *good*. Now just because her ex showed up at Living Word, he leaves? She's *pregnant*. Make it make sense."

"There's more to it than that, babe." Cyd dabbed her face with a hand towel. "And I don't think you even understand the history."

"I know Steph was in love with the guy," Cedric said. "And Lindell canceled the honeymoon because he found some email she sent him. But how many years ago was that?" He watched as Cyd applied face cream. "He keeps saying he doesn't want to run into dude every week. The only reason he ran into him was because they were in the same class. Living Word has thousands of people. It won't be an every week thing."

"Okay, let me see if I can help you." Cyd took his hand and led him into the bedroom where they sat on the bed. "That weekend we met at Steph and Lindell's wedding . . . What if I was deeply in love with another man and started seeing you both at the same time?"

"I'm supposed to be able to imagine that?" Cedric said.

"And you find out that I've got this other guy, and it's a serious relationship," Cyd said. "So from the beginning you're comparing and thinking you won't measure up."

"Nah, I would've been like—whatever with dude." Cedric leaned forward and kissed her. "She 'bout to be mine and totally forget what they had."

"That right there," Cyd said, pointing at him, "is the difference between you and Lindell. You've always been confident—arrogant even—when it came to women. Lindell has always been self-conscious and awkward with women."

Cedric thought a moment. "He used to say he could never compete with me when it came to women, and I'd tell him it's not a competition. We're just different." He shrugged. "I could never be a doctor. But he was always brilliant when it came to science."

"So think about this from Lindell's perspective." Cyd adjusted the satin scarf on her head. "He meets Stephanie and falls for her. And Stephanie happens to be in love with Warren—a guy that's a lot like you, good-looking and confident. In his mind he can't compete with that."

"But Lindell gets the girl," Cedric said. "That's why it doesn't make sense to me. She chose *him*. They're married. Why is this still a problem, years later?"

"Well, we know the real reason," Cyd said. "The enemy. He knows where Stephanie is weak and where Lindell is weak. He basically took the dynamic they started with and caused it to snowball into the present." She paused. "But as far as the details, you should talk to Lindell about it."

"I've tried talking to him," Cedric said. "He won't open up."

"Babe, I've heard you say things like—'Man, you're tripping. Your wife needs you,'" Cyd said. "Try talking from a posture of wanting to understand from his perspective. Is he still up?"

433

"In the family room like usual," Cedric said. "I've never seen him watch this much television."

"I think it's a good time to talk to him," Cyd said, "while Chase is asleep."

Cedric eyed his wife, looking irresistible in a nightshirt. "I had something else I wanted to do while Chase is asleep." He kissed her then sighed. "But okay, I hear you. This is important." He sighed again as he got up.

"I'm praying," Cyd said.

"That's good," Cedric said. "Stay praying. So you don't fall asleep."

"I can't promise, babe."

Cedric paused. "Can you promise that if you fall asleep, you'll stay in bed a little longer in the morning?"

"I can promise that regardless," Cyd said.

"See, that's why I love you." He walked back over to her and kissed her.

Cyd let it linger. "Is that the only reason?"

"Do I need more than one?"

Cyd chuckled. "Boy, go talk to your brother."

"You told your wife to try to get back with this dude?" Cedric looked bewildered. "Lindell, I'm honestly trying to understand. Do you really believe Steph still loves this guy?"

Lindell sat in the reclining chair, staring at the television, his jaw set.

"And before you answer," Cedric said. "I don't want anything from your feelings. I want to know if you *really* think Steph is still in love with him."

Lindell let some seconds pass. "I don't know if she's still in love with him, but—"

"No, we're not moving till this is settled." Cedric got the remote and clicked off the television. "Has she told you that she still loves this man? Yes or no."

"No," Lindell said. "She claims she doesn't."

"Okay, so she actually said she *does not* love him." Cedric spoke from the sofa. "What makes you think something is still there?"

"She called him a few months ago," Lindell said, "claiming it was one conversation to catch up. But it's not that simple. He'd been on her mind."

"And how do you know that?" Cedric said.

"Because I overheard Steph talking to Jillian during their prayer time." Lindell took a moment to continue. "She said she needed prayer for our sex life and for help to stop thinking about Warren." He looked downward. "She said . . . she was tempted to compare the two of us."

"How long ago was that?" Cedric said.

"Some months ago," Lindell said.

"Okay." Cedric took a breath. "Let me pause and say I know that was crushing. No man wants to hear that. Period. Steph was asking for prayer, trying to kill all of that. But because you heard it, it probably only made things worse."

"That's exactly what happened," Lindell said. "I wanted to have sex even less and when we did, I was more self-conscious. And of course she could feel that."

"So the blowup during vacation," Cedric said, "was that related to all this?"

"When we got to the house the first night," Lindell said, "it had a romantic vibe and Steph was in the mood. I was tired from traveling —don't say it. I already know."

"I didn't say a word," Cedric said.

"Anyway, the next day, we had this argument because I scheduled a morning tour—"

"Your first morning there?" Cedric said. "The morning after you were too tired for sex?"

Lindell sighed. "I know. I'm just telling you what happened. So Steph proceeds to tell me how important it is for us to have sex, that it's basically spiritual warfare according to First Corinthian seven— wait, you're clapping?"

"*Yeah*, I'm clapping," Cedric said. "Come on, sister Steph! She's out here fighting *not* to think about Warren. I know how that is."

"You do?" Lindell shifted more toward him.

"Cyd and I struggled with our sex life in the past," Cedric said, "especially when Chase was smaller and she had the demands of her job and ministry. It felt like our love life got put on a shelf." He blew out a breath. "So I started having thoughts about women I used to date. Not like I was *trying* to think about them. I'd be in a meeting or walking the dog and suddenly those memories were in my mind. I knew it was spiritual warfare."

"What did you do?" Lindell said.

"The same thing Stephanie did—asked for prayer," Cedric said. "Lance was praying with me. But part of the warfare was what Stephanie said—sex. That's what that verse is talking about."

"We looked at it together," Lindell said. "I knew she was right. And when she came back to the island, I told her why those romantic moments are hard for me. I even told her I heard the convo with Jillian and how it affected me."

"That's good," Cedric said. "Praise God." He looked at him. "You also had sex when she came back, correct?"

"Yes, we had sex," Lindell said.

"Glory to God," Cedric said. "So you get to that place, you come back from vacation, and you see the guy at church. Now you're here in my family room instead of with your very pregnant wife." He spread his hands. "Why?"

"That's when I found out that she called him a few months ago," Lindell said. "He supposedly felt God was moving him to go to church, and because she called, he ends up at Living Word."

"So he probably came to mind one day," Cedric said, "and instead of killing it and winning the battle, she gave in and called. But it was one call?"

Lindell nodded. "That's what she said. And that she told him she regretted it and wouldn't be reaching out again. But now he's at our church—"

"He and his fiancée," Cedric said.

"Still," Lindell said, "*he's* there. That's the main part. And I don't care what the odds are—she and I *will* run into him and it'll be a constant reminder for both of us that I don't measure up."

"Finish the sentence," Cedric said.

"I did finish."

"It'll be a constant reminder that you don't measure up . . . how?" Cedric said. "You're a medical doctor, Lindell. Do you know how many people wish they could measure up to *you*? To your intellect, your know-how, your ability to connect with patients. I could keep going. How is it that you don't measure up?"

Lindell stared downward again. "In the bedroom."

Cedric nodded. "Now it makes sense. You think it's a losing battle. That you'll never have confidence in the bedroom. Basically that you can't satisfy your wife." He paused. "So let's praise God right now because none of that is true."

"What are you talking about?" Lindell said. "How is it not true?"

"You're treating this like something you can't get better at," Cedric said. "This isn't like a shoe size, something you can't change. You can learn to be a better lover."

Lindell looked confused. "What do you mean 'learn'?"

"We can talk about how you can improve," Cedric said. "Like what you could and should be doing to learn more about your wife, that sort of thing."

"Why am I just now hearing this?" Lindell said. "You've never told me that before."

"Because you're just now telling me it's an issue in your marriage," Cedric said. "We could've had this talk a long time ago." He leaned forward. "You know MJ is one of my favorite ball players. He said, 'Get the fundamentals down and the level of everything you do will rise.' That's *so* on point for where you are. We just need to talk about the fundamentals. Your confidence and everything else will rise."

"You really think this could make a difference?" Lindell said. "For me?"

"It'll make *all* the difference," Cedric said.

"Can we start tonight?" Lindell said.

"One second." Cedric got his phone and typed a message to Cyd. **It'll be a while. Looking forward to the am. Love u.**

He got a reply seconds later. **Aww I was still up and waiting.**

Cedric sent a fast reply. **Don't play with me. I'll be like Lindell who?**

Cyd replied again. **lol...your brother needs you...love you, babe**

Cedric put his phone down and looked at Lindell. "Okay, let's pray first because it's important to recognize that the Lord is *for* a husband and wife having great sex."

"That sounds so weird," Lindell said.

"That's why you need this clinic, Dr. London," Cedric said. "So we'll pray and then get into maybe two fundamentals."

"Which are what?" Lindell said.

"That's part of the prayer," Cedric said. "It's not like this is a course I teach. But I'm thinking maybe . . ." He nodded to himself. "Speed and touch."

CHAPTER 62

$\mathcal{T}$ommy walked into the Living Water building Thursday evening, texting Jillian that he was on his way up. Shooting hadn't wrapped for the night, but he'd gotten the coverage he needed for the day. He looked forward to catching up with Jillian over a bite to eat.

He moved toward the elevator and heard voices coming from a common area down the hall. Curious, he went to check it out and saw a small group gathered with food, Bibles, and notepads.

"I'm still getting used to people hanging out in my buildings at night," Tommy said. "I know there's the usual mayhem upstairs with the production crew. But what are y'all doing?"

Trey looked up at him. "Dinner break with some eats from crafts services. But like you said—it's mayhem upstairs. So we're doing the Cling study down here."

"The Cling study?" Tommy said.

Reggie lifted his phone to show him. "You know Faith and I normally do devos in the morning, but she has to be up and out super early now. So we switched to doing it over the dinner break, which works well since I'm already up here."

439

"We thought we discovered a new study spot this evening," Faith said, "and Trey and Jade had beat us to it."

"Tommy, this study is changing my life." Jade had her Bible in her lap. "We've been focusing on different people every night. And I'm seeing that these are real people who needed to cling to God just like we do. Thank you for doing this."

"It's changing my life too, Jade," Tommy said. "I love that you all decided to do it together."

"We are having a *time*," Faith said. "This discussion is so good. I hate that I only have a few minutes."

"Hey, there you guys are," Jordyn said, walking up. "Jade, you didn't get my text?"

"Oh, I haven't looked at my phone," Jade said. "I thought you were working, though."

"I've got a few minutes so I wanted to see what you all were up to," Jordyn said.

"You should join us," Faith said. "We're doing the Cling study."

"I don't think I have enough time to get into that," Jordyn said.

"You don't have time for much else either," Jade said. "So come on and sit with us."

"I'll leave you all to it," Tommy said. "But I have to tell you . . . seeing this was special."

He rode the elevator up, past the production floor, and got off at the main floor for Living Water's offices. Walking toward Jillian's area, he felt a stirring when he saw her, only a profile view as she talked to Treva. But she was captivating. Seemed like obvious things he'd always known about her now captured him.

Treva met him as he approached. "I have to give you a hug," she said, embracing him.

Tommy looked from Treva to Jillian. "Why, what's going on?"

"I'm sure I've got black smudges under my eyes," Treva said. "I was in tears when Jill told me about the friendship vows. And the fact that you did it in the chapel—all of it—that was beautiful, Tommy."

"You were there, Treva," Tommy said, "all those years ago when the Lord started building this friendship, before we even knew Him. It's astounding to think about. I was just moved to honor what He's done."

"Yes, I was there," Treva said, "and I was jealous of your friendship, which was dumb. I was too self-absorbed to be a good friend to Jill. But you were there for her." She took a breath. "I want you to know I'm thankful for the friend you've been to my sister, Tommy, both then and now."

"Great, now *I've* got smudges," Jillian said, dabbing her eyes with a tissue.

"I don't even know what to say to that," Tommy said.

"You don't have to say anything," Treva said. She glanced at Jillian. "I already know how you feel."

Tommy gave a nod. "Then I guess we'll leave it right there."

"Yes. Let's." Jillian gave her a sister a look.

"What?" Treva said. "I have big sister prerogatives."

Jillian shook her head and looked at Tommy. "Ready?"

"Definitely," Tommy said.

They left the building, stopping in the parking lot to talk to a couple of people on the production crew, and got into Tommy's SUV.

He started the engine. "So where are we going? Did you decide?"

"Yup. Cantina Laredo."

"So we're headed back, huh?" Tommy said. "You gon' make sure you get your fajitas fix."

"That's the thing," Jillian said. "I didn't get fajitas last week because I couldn't order the way we do it. Now I really have a taste." She shifted toward him. "So you've had a big week so far, hanging on a movie set. What's the experience been like?"

"Because I was part of Lance and Kendra's life, watching them film these scenes is surreal." Tommy flicked on the turn signal. "But I've never been this close to a movie production, so I'm gaining a lot of insights I can use as an entertainment reporter."

"Sophie can't stop talking about it," Jillian said. "She put in a few hours Tuesday afternoon and was actually excited about having to be there by seven this morning. Normally I'm the one dragging her out of bed, but she was rushing me because she didn't want to be late. If you and I didn't have plans, I would've driven myself so I could have slept longer."

"So she's loving the experience?" Tommy said.

"Over the top," Jillian said. "She texted fifty emojis today because she got to stand in for Brooke while the lighting and camera crews prepped the scene."

"I saw that," Tommy said, "plus other things Sophia and Joy got to do. I'm thinking about writing an article highlighting the internship side of the production. The importance of giving young people a vision and inspiring them to dream." He looked at her. "What do you think about me interviewing them?"

"I think it's awesome," Jillian said. "And I know they would love that." She looked at him. "I read your latest article that came out this week, the profile on Mariah that you didn't ask me to edit."

"Yeah, I thought that might be a little awkward," Tommy said.

"It wouldn't have been a problem," Jillian said. "I got to know Mariah at the B and B last week, and I like her. We also rode together to the *Promises* event—which was interesting, since both coming and going, she made it pretty clear that she wants back whatever you two had." She glanced at him. "The article was well done, by the way. She came across as one to be reckoned with, an up-and-coming power player in Hollywood."

Tommy looked over at her. "Go ahead and ask."

"Ask what?"

"You want to know about my relationship with Mariah."

"If you know that I want to know, I shouldn't have to ask," Jillian said.

"Spoken like classic Jilli-Jill," Tommy said. "So you know we worked together. This wasn't long after my first divorce, and I was sorting everything out. Not looking to date. But you know how it is. There were very few of us there who were young black professionals, so we gravitated to one another, talking about workplace politics and whatever else was going on. Then we started meeting after work at happy hour, getting drinks, something to eat." He shrugged. "We sort of fell into whatever it was. But she knew from the start that I wasn't trying to be in a relationship."

"How long did it last?" Jillian said.

"A few months," Tommy said. "It ended when she moved to LA. And no, I'm not feeling like I want to recapture any of that. You already know where I am as far as relationships."

"Wait, I should get this," Jillian said, looking as her phone rang. "It's Steph." She answered and mostly listened for several seconds. "Oh, wow. Okay . . . okay, praise God. . . amen. . . Oh . . . No, I know . . . Okay, I will. . . . I know . . . You're welcome. . . Okay."

Jillian sighed. "I'm bummed because it looks like I won't be able to make your class this Sunday. But God is answering prayer, so I'm thankful for that." She put her phone back in her purse. "I can't go into it, but Stephanie's moved to attend another church this Sunday, and she wants me to go with her and have prayer time beforehand."

"I'm praying from the other end, so I get it," Tommy said. "I'm bummed too, though. I loved having you in class."

"I still get to preview the lesson when I edit it," Jillian said. "And I'm claiming special one-on-one study time with the teacher sometime next week."

"Done," Tommy said.

"I can't go into Stephanie's side of things," Jillian said, "but I was planning to tell you my side over dinner. Might as well start now." She looked at him. "We had a powerful prayer time, putting everything on the altar. And it was spurred by your cling challenge about fear."

"You know I want to hear more," Tommy said.

"We thought about the things we've been holding onto—things we've been clinging to," Jillian said. "And we wanted to give it all to God and just cling to *Him*." She spoke at an excited clip. "So for me, I realized I've had a fear about moving forward. I haven't even begun looking for a permanent place to live. And Stephanie helped me see that I need to put 'readiness' on the altar. Instead of saying I'm not ready to do this or that, let God decide."

"Wow," Tommy said. "That's powerful."

"And a little scary in itself," Jillian said. "When I say I put everything on the altar, I mean everything. Things like when to start looking for a house, where, and what price range. What to do about college for Sophia. Whether to do the grief study, without focusing on whether I feel equipped or emotionally ready. Just Lord, what's Your will? And even my notions about dating."

Tommy looked at her. "What do you mean?"

"I keep saying I'm not ready to date or think about marriage," Jillian said. "I'm realizing fear is part of it, even the fear that I might somehow dishonor Cecil's memory. So I put all of that on the altar too. God's will. God's timing. That's what I want. As long as I cling to Him, I've got the ultimate situation, right?"

"Right," Tommy said, parking the car. "That's a comprehensive prayer. No telling how God might respond or what He could lead you to do."

They got out and walked toward the restaurant.

"That's why I said it's a little scary," Jillian said. "But we also prayed that the Lord would increase our faith and trust in Him. It was so freeing to pray like that, to just surrender."

"Amen," Tommy said, nodding.

He opened the door for her and they walked up to the hostess stand.

"Good evening, do you have reservations?" a guy said.

"We don't," Tommy said. "Do you have a table for two?"

He looked down, checking the seating chart.

"Hey, you two, good to see you!"

Jillian smiled at the hostess they'd come to know. "Good to see you as well."

The hostess grabbed two menus. "I've got it," she told the guy, and led them to their favorite booth. "There you go." She left them with the menus. "Your server will be right with you. Enjoy."

"Thanks so much," Jillian said, settling into the booth.

Tommy took off his jacket. "I'm thinking about everything you said, Jill. That's really deep."

"God is using you with this study, Tommy," Jillian said. "I don't know if I would've had the courage to pray that prayer without the challenge and 'cling to God' hanging like a neon sign in my mind."

"Do you know where you're going to church this Sunday?" Tommy pushed the menu aside since he didn't need it. "I guess you have time to figure it out."

"That was easy," Jillian said. "Living Hope. That way it still feels like home. I actually miss that smaller church feel sometimes."

"Silas is preaching there this Sunday." He opened the menu, stared mindlessly at it.

"Is he? Why?"

"They're looking at him as possibly serving as the senior pastor at Living Hope," Tommy said. "This is a first step." He turned a page. "I'm sure he'll feel good seeing familiar faces."

"Hey, guys," Emily said. "How are ya tonight? I've got your water— one with lemon, one without—and your chips and salsa. I'll be back shortly to take your order." She scurried to a table that had flagged her.

Jillian glanced at Tommy, her phone in hand. "Put your earbuds in and check your messages."

Tommy quirked a brow as he got them from his coat pocket. He looked at his phone, a smile creeping onto his face. "You sent 'Zoom'? You know it's on my playlist already."

"I sent it because I know that's what you feel like doing right now, flying away." Jillian focused on him. "And because I won't let you—I think that's friendship vow 6.0 or something. And because it's in your all-time top five. So instead of flying away, you can listen and get that throwback feel-good vibe." She put in her earbuds.

"We're listening together?"

"Yup."

Tommy put his earbuds in, and they put their phones on the table, clicking play at the same time. He felt it right away, his head bobbing. "That hi-hat at the beginning, man. And the way the horns come in . . . Then they had the nerve to add strings."

Jillian's head was moving too. "Then Lionel comes in all smooth."

"At his finest," Tommy said. "You can feel the passion."

"You guys ready to order?" Emily said. "You going with the usual?"

"Can we get a few more minutes?" Tommy said.

"Of course," Emily said, moving to the next table.

"Wow," Tommy said. "Searching for horizons he's never seen. That just hit me a whole different way."

"The song is so plaintive," Jillian said. "You can feel it—the longing."

Tommy looked at her. "We've never done this. I'm loving it."

"I thought you might."

"Can we do 'Voyage' next?"

"I knew you'd say that too."

CHAPTER 63

*J*esse wheeled Zoe into the Living Water building early Friday evening, navigating her stroller through the entry-way. "You ready to see Mommy?"

Zoe kicked her legs out. "Mommy!" She turned to look up at him. "Where is she, Daddy?"

"You'll see her in one minute, Princess," Jesse said, rolling her toward the common area.

As they drew closer, Jesse could see the group spread out at a round table, a group that included Jordyn.

Faith saw them coming and jumped up, beaming. "Zoe girl! What are you doing here?" She took her from the stroller and picked her up, hugging her tight. "You miss Mommy?"

Zoe nodded big, her hands in Faith's face. "But Daddy gives me juice!"

Faith chuckled. "I love that you love spending time with your daddy." She looked at Jesse. "I can't believe you did this. How did you know when the dinner break was?"

Jesse pointed at Reggie. "This was all his idea."

"Baby, wow," Faith said, walking toward him, Zoe in tow.

Reggie stood, and the three had a group hug.

"Your schedule's been crazy now that production has started," Reggie said. "I know how much you miss your Zoe girl."

Jesse moved toward the table. "What's up, Trey? How's it going?"

"I'm good," Trey said. "How about yourself?"

"Hanging in there," Jesse said. "Good to see you, Miss Jade," he said, looking at her.

Jade got up and hugged him. "I love seeing you with Zoe, Jesse."

Jesse moved around the table as chatter filled the air. "How are you, Jordyn?"

Jordyn looked up at him. "I'm okay. What about you?"

"Things are good," Jesse said.

"Heyyy, you're in the building!"

Jesse turned as Brooke came near. "I thought you'd be tied up," he said. "I was just letting you know I was in the neighborhood."

"It's the perfect time." Brooke smiled, her hair in a ponytail. "We're on a break before the final scene."

"The play-by-plays in the group text are everything," Jesse said. "I feel like I'm up on how a movie is made."

"You want a tour of our base camp?" Brooke said. She heard Zoe talking and turned. "Aww is that your little girl? Can I meet her?"

"I'd love for you to meet her," Jesse said. He walked Brooke over and introduced her as Zoe sat with Faith.

"I've heard so much about you, Zoe." Brooke leaned down, smiling. "It's so good to finally meet you."

Zoe smiled back . . . then her gaze went past Brooke. "Jordy! It's Jordy, Mommy!"

Jesse sighed to himself. Zoe had been asking where Jordyn was.

Zoe squiggled down and ran over to Jordyn. Jordyn picked her up, hugging her.

Jesse looked at Faith. "Hey, do I have time to take a quick tour?"

"I've got Zoe if Faith has to leave," Reggie said.

"Cool, thanks." Jesse looked at Brooke. "Let's do it."

Brooke walked with him to the elevator. "So in this building there's hair and makeup, wardrobe, craft services, and the production offices. We've also got 'trailers'—I told y'all about that, right?"

Jesse joined her on the elevator. "Complete with selfies of you in your actor 'trailer' with chairs and a desk." He chuckled a little.

"I love it, though," Brooke said. "It's a place to get away and have our own personal space. Even has a little sofa so I can take a power nap." She led him off of the elevator. "Okay, we've got separate rooms for hair and makeup. I'll show you where I get my hair did."

"How's it going, having Jordyn as your stylist?" Jesse said. "When you told us they brought her on board, I couldn't react like I wanted to in the group chat."

"How did you want to react?" Brooke said.

"With some emojis like"—Jesse made a shocked face.

Brooke laughed. "I didn't know if I would feel awkward, given that you two just broke up, and you and I were becoming friends." She paused. "And it actually *was* awkward when she mentioned the vlog."

Jesse looked at her. "What did she say about the vlog?"

"Just that she'd seen it," Brooke said. "But that meant she saw us dancing, and it probably hit her like it hit my ex." She stopped at the entryway. "But to answer your question—I'm loving having Jordyn as my stylist. I've got zero worries knowing my hair—and head wraps—are in her hands." She led him inside. "Here's the room that's been made into a salon."

"Okay, I didn't think they'd bring in actual salon chairs," Jesse said, glancing around. "And mirrors and hooded dryers and what not? This is cool."

"Jordyn and I will be in here shortly," Brooke said, "getting me ready for tonight's scene."

"What's the scene about?" Jesse said.

"It's an early scene between Kendra and Lance," Brooke said. "Where she finds out he dropped out of high school, sold drugs, and went to prison."

"Man, when you say it like that . . ." Jesse shook his head. "It's hard to believe that's *our* Lance. But that's why this movie is so powerful. That verse about becoming a new creature is real."

"That reminds me," Brooke said. "I haven't had a chance to tell you because I didn't want to put it in the group text. But what you shared in class about your daughter and relationships was moving. And that part about being afraid of how you might look as the guy who's not about sex and wants to take things slow . . . There are women out here *praying* for that guy to come along."

"I appreciate that perspective," Jesse said. "And can we just give each other permission to text outside of the group? Unless that's a problem for you."

"Not a problem at all," Brooke said. "I would've suggested the same but I didn't want to go outside of whatever bounds were in place."

Jesse gave a light shrug. "I just agree with what you said, that we're becoming friends."

Brooke showed him the makeup room and craft services, then headed down another hall. "My classroom/trailer is down that way," she said. "I'll give you a peek if you want."

"The tour is absolutely incomplete without a peek at the classroom/trailer," Jesse said.

"I might have clothes on chairs and empty snack bags on the table," Brooke said as she walked. "So no judgment."

"I won't even tell you what my house looks like with my daughter there," Jesse said. "So you're safe."

Brooke opened the door but Jesse stayed just outside.

"Why are you smiling?" Brooke said.

"Because all week you've been texting like *you're* on a tour or a field trip as you experience everything for the first time." Jesse pointed. "Check out that sign on the door."

"It's just my name," Brooke said.

"'It's just my name,'" Jesse echoed, up a pitch. "No matter what the 'trailer' looks like"—he walked further in—"you need to grasp that it's *yours*. Only Hollywood actors get them, and you're a Hollywood actor. I love that you're humble, but I don't want you to miss what God is doing. This is huge, girl."

"I do recognize that," Brooke said. "I know it's a blessing to get this opportunity. But I find myself getting anxious already about whether I'll get another one. This shoot will be over quickly."

"How long is it scheduled for?" Jesse said.

"Four weeks for the St. Louis shoot," Brooke said. "Then a few days in Florida."

"So you only have three more weeks in St. Louis?" Jesse said.

"That's what I'm saying," Brooke said. "This week is gone. It'll be over in no time."

"Wow." Jesse followed Brooke back out. "But you can't be worrying about what's next. You're stealing all the joy from *this*. You know God'll come through. Just like He did when your ex thought *he* was ending the relationship."

Brooke sighed. "It feels like such a weight has been lifted with that."

"You two were together a long time, though," Jesse said, walking with her. "I know you said you weren't upset, but do you think it'll hit you at some point?"

"God had been preparing me for it," Brooke said. "I'm sure it'll hit at some level, but I'm mostly just thankful." She stared ahead. "That feeling when you're finally where God's been trying to get you to." She turned to him as they waited for the elevator. "But your breakup is just as fresh. How's it been for you?"

Jesse thought a moment. "I was upset, but not at the level I thought I would be. I asked if you thought it would hit you at some point because that's what I'm wondering myself."

Brooke looked at him as they got on the elevator. "Sooo I don't want to pry, but . . ."

"We broke up because Jordyn got with this guy she used to see and kissed him," Jesse said. "The other part you need to know is that she and I hadn't kissed in several months, specifically because of our past and wanting to make things special."

"Okay, you weren't playing about taking it slow," Brooke said, leading him back to the hair department. "And I can definitely see how you'd be hurt behind that."

"Add to the mix that I had already bought Jordyn an engagement ring and was planning to propose in June."

"Oh, Jesse," Brooke said. "Yeah, I would think you'd be crushed."

"And really I've just been praying and weighing things." Jesse

451

thought about it even now. "I love Jordyn. She's the first woman that I can say I truly poured myself into. And I think I thought, okay, I'm trying to do things God's way for the first time, so this has to be the one. But that's not necessarily the case." He walked slowly. "Jordyn says I overreacted by breaking up, and I'm being cold. I'm not trying to be that way. I forgive her. But does that mean I have to give it another try because of what I *thought* we had?"

"This is deep, Jesse." Brooke took a moment herself. "Part of me wants to tell you—but you *love* her. You bought a *ring*. You *are* crushed; you just won't let yourself feel it." She looked at him. "But you're so calm and rational." She paused. "No. Spiritual. That's the word. You're on a spiritual level with all of this instead of an emotional level."

"I really have been clinging to God in this," Jesse said. "Asking Him to show me what to do. Praying to have His mind so I can think what I should think. Even asking Him to feel what I'm supposed to feel." He gave a slight shrug. "Right now I'm not moved to try again."

"Which could change," Brooke said. "Maybe God is working in Jordyn's heart in such a way that she *will* be the one for you when you come back together. I was just saying that I'm finally where God's been trying to get me to. Maybe that's the journey that Jordyn is on."

"I hope she is," Jesse said. "I told her that. But that doesn't mean it has anything to do with me."

He looked as Jordyn came toward them. She avoided eye contact and went into the room.

"I guess it's time," Brooke said. "I'd better get in here."

"Hey, thanks for the tour," Jesse said. "And for listening."

"Likewise," Brooke said. "I'm really glad we're becoming friends."

"While the clock is ticking," Jesse said. "Before the shoot is over, we should do something. Hang out a little, if you have time. I know how busy your schedule is."

"I would love that," Brooke said. "I'll make time."

CHAPTER 64

"Why are you ringing the doorbell?" Lance looked at Trey in the doorway. "That should let you know it's been too long since you've stopped by. What have you been up to?"

Trey walked in, taking off his jacket. "Uh, there's a movie being filmed. Maybe you're familiar?" He hung up his jacket.

"I feel bad I haven't been on set," Lance said. "Too many obligations. Mom's keeping me updated, though."

"Hey, Trey, how are you?" Treva called from the kitchen.

"Real good now that I'm catching that aroma." He walked with Lance to the kitchen. "Where's Wes?"

"Still taking a nap," Treva said. She turned from the stove and hugged him. "We've missed you. You're supposed to be dropping by at least every other night for dinner."

"It's been early mornings and long nights all week with the filming," Trey said.

"Yeah, but we didn't see you last week either," Lance said.

"Oh, true," Trey said. "I've been hanging with Jade. We're even doing the Cling study together." He got a banana from the fruit basket. "And by the way, I told her she could meet me over here for dinner.

Hope that's okay. It sounded like you were just having a casual group of folks."

"Jade is more than welcome." Treva cut the fire on the stove. "It's definitely casual. Silas wants to talk about our experience at Living Hope. That's why Lance wanted to see if you could make it, since you were part of the launch."

"That and we figured you'd want a meal," Lance said.

"What'd you fix, Treva?" Trey said. "It smells delicious."

"All I made is the rice," Treva said. "Lance put some chicken and vegetables in the slow cooker with this za'atar seasoning he can't get enough of."

"It's my first time making this recipe, though," Lance said.

Trey lifted the lid to the slow cooker. "I've never heard of za'atar seasoning, but I can tell this is about to be an experience."

"Hey babe," Treva said. "Everything is ready. I'm going to check on Wes."

"Okay," Lance said, taking a seat at the kitchen table. He looked at Trey. "So hanging with Jade, huh? Why am I having visions of you and Molly?"

"It's so different, though," Trey said, joining him. "Molly and I were close, but for a while, we were drinking and smoking weed together. When all that changed and we started living for God, it was Molly, *Timmy*, and I who were hanging—which is how they ended up married." He ate some of the banana. "With Jade, it's been this purposeful friendship from the start, where we're intentionally seeking God and going deep in His word. I've never had anything like that."

"I love that," Lance said. "I've been praying for the Lord to send you a friend."

"I know," Trey said. "And before you know it, I'll be leaving again, so you might as well keep praying."

"Speaking of that," Lance said. "I finally got a chance to talk to Pastor Fuller this week about your experience with the last missions assignment."

"You didn't have to do that, Lance," Trey said. "I already talked to him."

"As pastor I'm head of our global team," Lance said. "I absolutely needed to talk to the missions pastor about what happened. We need to decide if we're going to continue to partner with that organization, and if so, what kind of training needs to be put in place. We've scheduled a phone conference with them." He checked a notification on his phone. "Also, he mentioned that you haven't gotten back to him about the mid-term and long-term options he emailed you about."

"I'm praying about it," Trey said. "After the shoot I'll have more time to focus on it." He peeled back more of the banana. "But if I'm honest, I'm in no rush. It feels really good to be home."

"Rest is good," Lance said, nodding. "You know I'm praying as well. So you've been at the shoot every day?"

"Every day," Trey said. "Can you believe it's a wrap on week one already?" He got up and got a bottle of water from the fridge. "It's probably good you're not there, though. It's one emotional wave after another."

"I have no desire to relive all of that," Lance said. "Mom said she saw some people on the crew in tears during a scene."

"More than one scene," Trey said. "Maybe if Alonzo and Brooke didn't act so well." He downed some water and checked his phone. "Jade said she's walking to the door. I'll get it."

Lance checked his own phone and replied to a text from Cedric.

"Pastor Keys and his son were pulling up too," Trey said, returning with the three of them.

"Please call me Silas," he said. "And it's good to finally meet you, Trey."

Treva rejoined them with Wes as they all greeted one another. A moment later, Joy and Hope came downstairs.

"Mom said she might be late," Lance said, "so we can go ahead and pray."

They gathered and bowed their heads as Lance prayed. At the sound of "Amen" the door opened and closed.

"Must be Mom," Lance said. "Right on time."

Pamela walked in smiling, Tommy with her.

"Can't wait to hear today's report," Lance said. "And don't minimize it right after."

"So you know we've been driving earlier in the day at break time," Pamela said, "because the shoot doesn't end till late." She focused on Lance. "Well. Today we went *after* the shoot so I could learn to drive at night." She shuddered even now. "Goodness. Turning on the headlights and getting used to everybody else's bright lights in the mirrors and what not . . ." She elbowed Tommy. "Tell him how I did."

Lance and Tommy looked at each other in amusement. Pamela liked to set up the situation then let Tommy finish.

"First, let's give God a praise that Momma Pam is no longer protesting for thirty minutes before she tries a new level of difficulty," Tommy said.

Applause sounded in the kitchen, and Pamela turned. "I didn't know y'all were listening," she said. "But Tommy, stop exaggerating. I never protested thirty minutes."

"How long then?" Tommy said.

"Fifteen at the most."

"Let's also give God a praise," Tommy said, "that Momma Pam now gets into the driver's seat, makes her own adjustments with the seat and mirrors, starts the car, and is ready to roll—like a pro."

"Go, Grandma Pam!" Treva said, clapping Wes's hands together as more applause sounded. Wes squealed louder than the applause.

"And on her first time driving at night"—Tommy looked at her —"you should tell it."

"No, you tell," Pamela said.

"Okay, so Momma Pam was driving behind this car," Tommy said, "on a main thoroughfare—that's the first thing, not a side street. And the guy in front of her suddenly brakes, reacting to something in front of him. But Momma Pam reacted quickly as well. She put on the brakes, and because she had left plenty of room between her and the driver, it was no problem." He looked at her. "But the biggest news is that she wasn't rattled and kept on driving. Can we give God a praise for *that?*"

Pamela got a standing ovation as Lance took her into his arms again and rocked with her. "Praise God, Mom. That fear is conquered."

"Well, there's still the highway," Pamela said. "But one step at a time. And listen, I've got a praise of my own. I couldn't do this if it weren't for Tommy's patience and encouragement. I feel like God has given me a second son. And I already told him I pray for him like he's my son."

"Ooh, that's big," Treva said. "Tommy, you're about to see some mountains moving. And side note—Lance and I are doing the Cling study in the evenings. It's so good."

"I told him," Lance said. "I love the way it's challenging us—literally." He shook his head. "I don't know about this 'second son' stuff, though. You better be glad you're family already."

Pamela smiled. "You're staying to eat, aren't you, Tommy?"

"Just dropping you off," Tommy said. "I'm not trying to interrupt the evening plans."

"Nah, man, stay and eat," Lance said. "We're talking to Silas about Living Hope, and you were there too from the time it launched."

"Grab a plate and help yourself, everybody," Treva said, showing them the food. "We're eating in the dining room—thank you, Hope, for setting the table." She added, "Oh, but we need a couple of extra chairs and place settings."

"Old habits die hard," Trey said, grabbing a kitchen chair. "That was my job when we had Bible studies here at the house—more chairs."

"I've got the place settings," Hope said.

Lance moved Wes's high chair to the dining room and got the plate Treva made for him. Then he got his own and sat next to Wes so he could feed him.

"So how's the filming going?" Silas took a seat with his plate. "People were talking about it at the barber shop this week. It's a pretty big deal in town."

"I love what I've seen so far," Pamela said, sitting as well. "But I had no idea how tedious it would be. Several takes from one angle, then several more from a second angle, then a third set from close-up. Hours to do *one* scene."

"With breaks for lighting changes between each of those," Trey said, adding another chair.

"Wait a second," Silas said, glancing at his plate. "What is this we're eating? It's really good."

"I was about to say the same thing," Pamela said. "I saw Lance fiddling around in the kitchen earlier, but I didn't know what he was making. This is delicious, son."

"Yeah, I was wondering if I could get the recipe," Jade said.

"Oh, we gon' make sure you get this recipe," Trey said, savoring a bite.

"I'm glad you all like it," Lance said. "Jade, remind me before the night is over. I'll get that recipe to you."

"So Joy, did I hear you're an intern on set?" Silas said. "What kinds of things are you doing?"

"Mostly random stuff," Joy said. "Running errands and helping out wherever needed. And I now know how to make coffee." She smiled. "But it's the coolest job ever."

Lucas sat beside her. "I'm hoping there will be scenes where they need extras."

"They'll be filming at church," Trey said. "Not sure when, but they'll definitely need extras for those."

"Alonzo and I talked about that," Lance said. "We'll send out an email to let members know in advance, for anyone who wants to take part."

"Tommy, I really enjoyed the piece you did on Mariah," Silas said. "I'm a fan of her work, and you highlighted her signature trademarks as a director, like her use of music, which I love. I could tell you're a fan of hers as well."

"Even more so after watching her this week," Tommy said. "Her work ethic and her instincts are phenomenal."

"So to let everybody know," Lance said, "Silas is preaching at Living Hope this Sunday, and I've asked him to consider serving as interim pastor there. Our current interim pastor is moving to

Kentucky for an opportunity. This is an informal gathering to give our perspectives about Living Hope." He turned to him. "Silas, whatever you want to ask."

"Thank you, Treva and Lance, for hosting this evening," Silas said. "I'm humbled by the opportunity to preach at Living Hope this Sunday and, as I've told you, Lance, taken aback that I'd be considered for the interim pastor position." He glanced around the table. "I just really want to hear from you all what the experience was like there."

"I'll just say," Trey said, "the dynamic is obviously very different because it's a much smaller congregation. When I left, Lance was still at Living Hope. Coming back and going to Living Word . . . I'd forgotten how big it is. I loved that everybody knew everybody at Living Hope. It felt more like a family."

"Definitely," Tommy said. "People said they felt seen. We knew what was happening in their lives and could jump in and help. We try to foster that at Living Word, and we address a lot of people's needs. But the dynamic isn't the same."

"Also a huge difference—one service." Treva affixed the top to Wes's sippy cup and gave it to him. "And not just from the perspective of preaching. It makes a big difference for members as well, seeing everyone in the same service. And you don't have to hurry up and leave the sanctuary as the next service starts. A lot of connecting and bonding happened as we lingered after service."

"I see that at Living Word too," Lance said, "especially with the fellowship areas. But again, a different dynamic. At Living Hope, it was like family hanging after church, then a big group would end up going to brunch or lunch."

"That's a great point," Jade said. "For someone like me who's not uber social, I hardly ever go to the fellowship area at Living Word. But I've been in those conversations that happen organically in the pews after church. And yup, then it's like—time to get out." She chuckled.

"The church we came from is a little bigger than Living Hope," Silas said. "And as an assistant pastor, I did appreciate getting to know people on a personal level, especially the young adults. It's such a pivotal age."

"You should know then," Lance said. "Living Hope had a disproportionate number of young adults, but the dynamic shifted. Many of them followed us to Living Word last year."

"You were the reason a lot of them joined Living Hope to begin with," Trey said. He looked at Silas. "We had students from different campuses coming to the Bible studies, and they spread the word about the church when we launched." He glanced at Lance. "A lot of single women came too, since the 'amazing love story' had gone viral, but I digress."

"I bet Treva had all of 'em hot and bothered when she walked up in there," Pamela said.

"So this is interesting." Silas set down his fork. "Trey, you called it a digression, but you reminded me that Lance was single when he launched Living Hope. All of my friends who are senior pastors are married, and I found myself thinking it would be odd to step into that position as a single man, even on an interim basis."

"Being single allowed me to devote an extraordinary amount of time to launching the church," Lance said, "and then serving as pastor. Didn't seem odd at all."

"That's really good to hear," Silas said. "Although, while I appreciate the benefits, I'm hoping I won't remain single too long."

"Hmm is that a twinkle in your eye, Pastor Keys?" Pamela smiled. "Let us know if we can be praying for a move of God in that area."

Lance caught a glance from Treva. He focused on feeding Wes. Somehow his mom had missed the dynamics in the room.

"From what I know, Pamela," Silas said. "You're a prayer warrior. The last thing I'd refuse is prayer for a move of God."

"Hey, Hey!" sounded as the front door opened.

Treva smiled. "Faith and Reggie were able to make it after all." She rose as they walked into the dining room. "Aww, there's my pumpkin. Come here, sweetie," she said, taking Zoe from Faith.

As everyone exchanged greetings, Lance went to get the second high chair that they used for Zoe, and Trey got up to get more chairs. Faith and Reggie hung their coats, washed hands, and got their plates, bringing them to the dining room.

"Hope, you didn't get additional place settings?" Treva said.

"It's just Faith," Hope said. "She can get them herself." She saw her mother's gaze rest on her. "Fine," she said, rising.

"Just to catch you up," Treva said as Faith, Reggie and Zoe settled in, "we've been talking about our experiences at Living Hope because Silas is considering an interim pastor position."

"Which is dope," Reggie said. "After you preached, I was hoping you'd get an opportunity like that."

"That means a lot, Reggie, thank you," Silas said.

"And actually," Pamela said, "we had gotten on the subject of being single and praying for a move of God."

"Oh, Tommy's favorite subject," Reggie said.

"What is?" Pamela said.

"Being single," Reggie said, starting in on the meal.

Tommy looked at his brother. "I know you didn't just walk up in here and—"

"Not too often I hear that being single is someone's favorite topic," Trey said. "How did that happen, Tommy?"

Tommy sighed and shook his head, looking at his brother again. "I appreciate you, Reg."

Reggie scooped up more food. "Always much love."

Tommy looked at Trey. "So without getting deep into it," he said. "I know you're doing the study, so you heard me say I've been divorced twice and that life isn't what I thought it would be." He paused. "I basically came to a decision to remain single."

"Seriously?" Trey said.

"Wow, I didn't realize that," Silas said.

"You mean *alone* single?" Trey said. "Not even dating?"

"I don't think of it as alone," Tommy said. "It's like Lance said in his cling sermon—'Jesus is your ultimate situation.' I'm leaning into that. Also, friendships are important so I'm not alone in that sense either." He focused on him. "But you're not new to this, Trey. You've been on the single journey for a while."

"Right," Trey said. "I'm just surprised to hear that you're on it."

"We all are," Reggie said. "What was that you were saying, Momma Pam, about praying for a move of God?"

~

"I had no idea." Pamela talked to Treva in the kitchen after everyone had left. "The person Silas has his sights set on is Jillian?"

"It would appear." Treva loaded dishes in the dishwasher. "Jill said they had a second quasi-date—"

"They've been on a date?" Pamela said. "I had no idea," she said again. "I've been praying that Tommy would get past the hurt and everything else. And I've been praying for God's will to be done concerning him and Jillian. And now I've told Silas I'll be praying for a move of God with respect to finding a wife."

"The good thing is you're praying for God's will," Treva said. "It's complicated on a few levels, but He can work it out."

"You know another situation I'm praying about is the one with Desiree," Pamela said. "Have you heard from her since your meeting?"

"Just once," Treva said. "She updated me as to where she is in the study and asked a couple questions."

"So she thinks you're just on deck for her at this point?" Pamela said. "How do you feel about that?"

"I was surprised to get the text," Treva said. "But I was just as surprised by how the meeting went."

"Yeah, I didn't expect you to be there for almost two hours," Pamela said.

"And you already know how I feel about it," Lance said, coming into the kitchen. "I still can't believe she hit up my wife—or that you actually went."

"I wrote the study that she had questions about, babe," Treva said. "And the meeting was fruitful."

"You could've put her onto Cyd, Mom, Jillian, or a dozen others in the women's ministry alone," Lance said. "Meeting would've been just as fruitful."

"But I don't think it was a coincidence that she reached out to me, especially since I was praying for her," Treva said. "And we were able to speak forthrightly. Her intentions seemed sincere."

"Treva, I don't care if her intentions are good, bad—whatever," Lance said. "I don't want her anywhere near my life—actually, Mom would've been too close. Definitely not *my wife*."

"Well, I doubt she'll reach out again anyway," Treva said. "She's back at it next week with her travels."

"I'll keep praying for her," Pamela said. "But I'm with Lance on this one. She had her chance with my son, and she blew him off. That ship has sailed, little momma, no matter how many tears you want to shed." She shook her head, focused on nothing in particular. "And don't be trying to work your way back to anywhere *near* my son's life, in any form or fashion."

"Tell us how you really feel, Mom," Lance said, smiling.

"Got me riled up, thinking about this." Pamela headed downstairs. "I'm going down here right now to pray a hedge of protection."

Lance put his jacket on. "I'm headed to Cedric's, babe," he said, giving her a kiss.

"What are you guys doing?" Treva said. "It's the second night in a row."

"You know Lindell is still over there," Lance said. "We're talking to him. Guy stuff."

"You and Cedric talking to Lindell about guy stuff, huh?" Treva eyed him. "And if I were a fly on the wall . . ."

"No need to be a fly on the wall." Lance kissed her again, more deeply this time. "You already know everything I'm saying."

"I told you about doing that when you're on your way somewhere." Treva put her arms around him and kissed him again. "Didn't you tell him enough last night?"

"Nope," Lance said. "I saved some of the best for last."

Lance grabbed his keys then came back, kissing her one last time, letting it linger. "Okay, I'm out."

Treva stared after him. "I'm gonna get you back for that."

CHAPTER 65

"I had a best friend in college. Some of you know her—Jillian Mason. She's not here this morning, so I can talk about her."

Trey looked at Jade. "Did you know they were best friends in college?"

"You haven't been here," Jade whispered. "They're like, best friends even now."

"People couldn't fathom that it was possible for us to be 'just friends,'" Tommy said. "Whatever girl I was dating *really* couldn't fathom it."

People chuckled in the room.

"One time, a young woman I was dating challenged me and said, 'What about the guys you hang with? Why can't one of *them* be your best friend?'" Tommy walked across the front. "I said good question. I wanted to know myself why I considered Jillian my best friend. And you know what? I didn't have to think long."

Jade leaned over to Trey. "I can't believe Jillian's not here for this."

"Jillian listened to me way more than my other friends did," Tommy said. "And she didn't just listen to what I said. She heard what I *wasn't* saying. And she took the time to ask follow-up questions to

464

learn even more. You know how some people find a way to make every conversation about *them*? If I was sharing something, Jillian kept the focus on me, uncomfortably so sometimes, until we got to the soul of the matter. *Nobody* else did that."

"*Trey*." Jade said his name like a gasp. "That's what you've been doing with my walls project—listening and asking questions, to the point of discomfort."

"Meaning you finally appreciate it?" Trey said.

"I didn't say all that," Jade said.

"But it wasn't just the listening," Tommy said. "Jillian cared. When she said, 'How are you?' she actually wanted to know. And if there was anything in my answer that indicated something was wrong, she paused whatever she was doing to address it. Caring takes time and energy. And she spent her time and energy on me, over and over again."

Trey elbowed Jade. "You can't ever deny that you're my friend. Cooking is caring."

"As I started thinking about all of this, I said, 'The real question is —why am I hanging with those guys at all?'" Tommy chuckled a little. "It was absolutely clear to me why Jillian was my best friend. She knew and understood me far better than anyone else." He paused and looked out at them. "But what if she did all that listening, and I didn't listen to her? What if she knew me deeply, but I only knew her on the surface? What kind of friendship would that have been? Do you know of any relationship that thrives when it's one-sided?" He started walking again. "So why do we think we can have a thriving relationship with God even if it's one-sided?"

Trey glanced at Jade, who was talking to Jordyn on her other side.

"I know," Tommy said. "We don't think it's one-sided. But God knew us before we were born, even before He laid the foundation of the world." He spoke slowly, deliberately. "Psalm 139 says He's intimately acquainted with *all* of our ways and knows our thoughts before we can think them. He even loved us when we weren't thinking about Him. So clearly, when we're saved through Christ and come into a relationship with Him, it starts off one-sided. Amen?"

"Amen" sounded in the room as Jade took notes.

"God knows us intimately, and as we come into this relationship, we begin to know *Him*—hopefully, intimately." Tommy paused. "How do we do that?"

"Through His word," several people said.

Tommy nodded. "How many of you know that takes time and energy? I had to ask myself how much time and energy I was putting into it. How much time was I spending in the word? Not just to check it off on my to-do list, but really spending time with the Lord? Was I really seeking to *know* Him through His word? Because I can't cling to Him in a real way if I don't know Him well."

"That's where I am right now"—Jade leaned in, whispering—"realizing I didn't know Him well—and loving that I'm getting to know Him."

"I said we'd be looking at how people did or didn't cling to God in the Bible," Tommy said. "This week, the character study we're doing is of God Himself. We're looking at passages that give us insight into God's character, His heart, His thoughts—whatever we can learn about Him—so we can know Him better and cling to Him more tightly." He added, "And don't get me wrong—the whole Bible does that. I chose passages that spoke to me personally. I know some of you are studying in groups during the week. Share some of your favorite passages with one another as well."

"That's your assignment," Jade said.

"What's my assignment?"

"Think about your favorite passages that speak to God's character —I know you've got some," Jade said. "And we'll look at them this week."

"Today, the first passage I want to hit is short, but it *rocked* me," Tommy said. "Can somebody read Genesis 5:21-24?"

A woman stood. "'Enoch lived sixty-five years, and became the father of Methuselah. Then Enoch walked with God three hundred years after he became the father of Methuselah, and he had other sons and daughters. So all the days of Enoch were three hundred and sixty-five years. Enoch walked with God; and he was not, for God took him.'"

"Thank you," Tommy said. He looked at his iPad. "Enoch's entire life—summed up in four verses. What's the main thing that the Holy Spirit wants us to know about his life?"

"He walked with God," sounded in the room.

"We've got another cling-er," Tommy said. "Imagine *that* being the thing you're known for in heaven—you walk with God. What does that mean? Hebrews 11:5 says Enoch obtained the witness that he was pleasing to God. So walking with God has to do with living a life that is pleasing to God." He took a moment. "I didn't plan to go here, but I need to pause." He moved closer to them. "We need to understand that clinging to God is related to obedience to God. Those moments we stray outside of his will—when we get caught up in sin—we are not clinging. I've been there, and it's painful." He nodded soberly. "But I'm here to tell you that God is gracious and merciful. When we repent, He forgives. If sin has put some distance between you and the Lord, don't stay in that place. Ask the Lord's forgiveness and get back to clinging to Him. We *need* Him."

Several people murmured "Amen."

"How long does it say Enoch walked with God?" Tommy said.

"Three hundred years," a couple of people said.

"So Enoch is walking with God *continuously*," Tommy said. "That'll preach, right? Season to season, through ups and downs, no matter what, he's all about living a life that's pleasing to God. But that's from Enoch's side of things. Let's look at God's side. What does this tell us about *Him*? Anybody?" He pointed at someone.

"That God *wanted* Enoch to walk with Him," a guy said. "He welcomed the companionship."

"I love that you used that word 'companionship,'" Tommy said. "And *right*—God *wanted* the companionship. Can we please understand this about the heart of God? He is not some far-off God who's only interested in 'big' things like running the universe. He's interested in companionship. *With us.*"

Tommy pointed at someone whose hand went up. "Go ahead."

A woman stood. "I just want to say that what you shared about your friendship with Jillian is helping me understand companionship with God." She took a moment. "It was a little hard for me to grasp that I could have an intimate relationship with Him. I knew I needed to read the Bible, but I wasn't sure how that translated into a close relationship with Him. But I feel like I'm starting to get it." She nodded a little. "It really is about getting to know Him, like you get to know a friend. And that energizes me to be in the word more, so I can know Him more, so I can have a closer relationship."

"Amen," Tommy said. "It's been energizing me as well." He pointed. "Trey."

Trey stood. "These four verses are rocking me too. I don't know how many times I've heard, 'Enoch walked with God' but didn't really think about all that that meant." He pondered it even now. "It's such a basic thought but it's everything—they were *together*, Enoch and God. They *enjoyed* each other, so much so that God was like—come on up here and let's kick it in heaven." He paused. "I battle loneliness and I'm going to meditate on these verses. I love that it says *twice* that Enoch walked with God. Like—don't miss this. They were *friends*. I'm just thinking of how that had to affect his life every single day. All that he must have heard and learned. Confiding in the Lord as his friend. He was clinging for three hundred years! I act like I can't get through a year or two on my own overseas—*with God*. Lord, help me." He sat back down.

"That's so good, Trey," Tommy said. "And you highlighted something else that we learn about God in these verses. He not only wants companionship with us, He *enjoys* it. Like you said, God wanted more. He *took* Him to be with Him! That blows my mind." He looked at his iPad. "David said in Psalm 18:19—'He rescued me, because He delighted in me.' And Psalm 37:23 says, 'The steps of a man are established by the LORD, and He delights in his way.'" He looked at them. "Do you ever think about God *delighting* in you? And if you're clinging to Him, you *know* He delights in your way. I love what Trey said about the day-to-day friendship. That's real. In Christ, that can be each of us, every day."

Several people stood now, wanting to speak.

Tommy smiled. "I should've known this would happen. I thought we'd get through the short Enoch passage quickly and move on to the others. But hey, we'll camp here as long as we need to. This is good." He pointed at the next person.

A guy stood. "This might seem like a small thing, but what I love about that three hundred years is that God doesn't get tired of us . . ."

～

"I'm sorry, y'all," Tommy said. "We're over our time again. But the discussion was incredible. Only two more weeks to go."

"We need more," one woman said amid the groans.

Tommy smiled. "Oh, and let me tell you the challenge. The challenge this week is to read through a book of the Bible and note all the things you learn about God. Pray as you read and let the Holy Spirit lead you. Have a good one."

"Only two more weeks?" Jade looked at Trey. "Seems like everything is flying by. The shoot will be over before we know it too. And then you'll be off to Timbuktu somewhere."

"I don't know if you know that that's an actual place and an actual possibility," Trey said. "But I get it. And I'm here for the acknowledgment that you'll miss me."

"That's not what I said."

"Is that you or the wall talking?" Trey started heading out.

"I don't know what I was thinking when I asked you to hold me accountable," Jade said. She looked at Jordyn. "You okay?"

Jordyn nodded vaguely, looking at Jesse and Brooke. They had sat together and were walking out ahead of them.

"Hey, Trey," Tommy called, "appreciated your input today."

Trey looked at Jade. "I'll catch up with you guys." He walked over to Tommy. "This class is helping me in a lot of ways, bro. Wanted to let you know I'm thankful you're doing this."

"I felt that, about your battle with loneliness," Tommy said. "I'll be praying for you."

"Thanks," Trey said. "I'll be praying for you too."

Tommy looked at him. "I always appreciate prayer, but any particular reason you said that?"

"Just thinking about what you said at dinner about life not being what you thought and deciding to stay single," Trey said. "Then today I heard you talking about what you have with Jillian."

"Well, I was talking about college," Tommy said.

"It's not the case now?"

Tommy gave a nod. "Even deeper now, because of Christ."

"I'm not trying to analyze your situation, man," Trey said. "I have a hard time analyzing my own. But after listening to you today, I was just moved to pray." He shrugged. "I know what it's like to have the gift of singleness for the long term. God may have gifted you with something else."

Tommy seemed to think on that. "What happened to the young guy who used to just sit and soak things in? You're not supposed to grow up and actually have a word for somebody."

"Aye, it's that Enoch high I'm on," Trey said. "Trying to walk with God and hear some things."

"Seriously," Tommy said, "coming from you at this particular time . . . I think I needed to hear that. And hey, you think God might be already working as far as your loneliness battle? Looks like you and Jade are developing the kind of friendship I was talking about."

"Maybe," Trey said. "If there wasn't a clock counting down the time I've got left in the States." He spread his hands as he started off. "Always a reason to cling, right?"

CHAPTER 66

"Why did I head straight to the same area I used to sit in?" Jillian moved into the familiar row at Living Hope and took off her coat.

"And why am I having all the flashbacks?" Stephanie followed Jillian, glancing around the sanctuary. "So many memories in this place."

Jillian settled into her seat. "The first time I visited was the weekend of that women's conference."

"Oh, that's right," Stephanie said. "Girl, remember we came in that shuttle from the hotel?"

"And I almost missed it going back," Jillian said, "because I waited after the service to talk to Lance about Treva. She was *actually* about to head back to Maryland without saying a word to him."

"I'll never forget when he pulled her off of that shuttle." Stephanie shifted, trying to get a comfortable position. "He took a risk, not knowing what she would say or whether she would reject him. That stuck with me." She sighed. "The things you do for love."

"That's why we're here today," Jillian said. "Because of your love for Lindell and—"

"Good morning, sisters, good to see you back here," Johnelle said.

471

Jillian stood and hugged her. "Good morning, Johnelle. Good to see you too."

Stephanie shifted to look at her. "Sister Johnelle, how have you been?"

"Girl, blessed," Johnelle said.

"I would stand to hug you," Stephanie said, "but it took a lot to get situated."

Johnelle's gaze went to Stephanie's belly. "Wait, are you—?"

"Yes, ma'am," Stephanie said. "Eight months."

"Wow," Johnelle said. "Congrats to you and Lindell. Where is he this morning?"

"We're worshiping in different places today," Stephanie said.

"So you showed up to support Pastor Keys?" Johnelle leaned closer. "I'm already hearing whispers from people excited about us getting another single pastor. But I was wondering if he was *single* single or dating somebody. And seeing you two here . . ." Her eyes rested on Jillian.

"We didn't know he was preaching when we decided to come," Stephanie said.

"Oh, well, good," Johnelle said. "So *is* he seeing somebody over at Living Word?"

"You should ask him," Stephanie said. "He just walked in."

Johnelle turned. "He looks even better than his picture on the website. And is that his son? I know just the young lady I'd love for him to meet. Let me go introduce myself." She made a beeline for them.

"Like I said"—Stephanie looked at Jillian—"so many memories." She rubbed her stomach. "This baby is just kicking away. And lately, whenever the baby kicks, I'm thinking he or she knows something's wrong. Daddy's voice is nowhere around." She sighed. "It's been a week since he's been home."

"I can't believe a week has passed already," Jillian said. "Is he still checking on you and the baby every day?"

Stephanie nodded. "And he wanted the update from my OB appointment a couple days ago. But that's all I get from him."

"Cyd's report was intriguing," Jillian said, "that he's been meeting with Cedric and Lance."

"Yeah, they're probably trying to talk him off the ledge," Stephanie said. "Fifty reasons why you shouldn't leave your wife and baby for good."

"Or they're praying," Jillian said. "Like we've been doing. This morning was another powerful prayer time."

"Jillian, Stephanie . . . what a wonderful surprise." Silas stood at the end of the row.

"Feels good to be back," Stephanie said.

"And congrats," Jillian said, "on your opportunity here."

"Do you have a minute?" Silas said.

"Mm-hm I knew that was coming." Stephanie spoke under her breath.

Jillian elbowed her as she stood. "Sure."

Jillian walked with Silas to an area off to the side, feeling slightly different around him. Probably the prayers she and Stephanie had been praying. Gave her a touch of *what if?*

"I had to tell you that it feels really good to see you here," Silas said. "I wasn't expecting this at all."

"I couldn't believe the timing actually," Jillian said. "Stephanie and I decided to come before we knew you'd be preaching. Again, such a wonderful opportunity for you."

"I wanted to tell you about it," Silas said. "But for whatever reason, we didn't run into each other this week, and we're not at the point where we text, so it didn't feel right to let you know that way." He looked into her eyes. "Even though you didn't know I'd be preaching, I'll take this as a blessing."

"Well," Jillian said, "if our being here is a blessing to you, then praise God."

"I'm starting to think that this opportunity may be God signaling a new season," Silas said. "And I don't think it's a coincidence that you're part of that." He looked beyond her. "Oh, your daughter's here?"

"She planned to meet us here, yes," Jillian said, turning to look. "It was good talking to you, Silas."

"You too, Jillian."

Jillian met Sophia as she came up the aisle. "What's wrong?" she said, seeing her face.

"Why is Lucas here?" Sophia eyed him across the sanctuary. "I came to this service with you so I wouldn't have to see him and Joy at Living Word."

"What's going on with you and Joy?"

"There's no time to get into it, Mom," Sophia said. "Just"—she groaned—"*why* is he here?"

"Because his dad is preaching," Jillian said.

"Why didn't you *tell* me his dad was preaching?" Sophia said.

"Sophie, how was I supposed to know you had whatever going on with Lucas and Joy?" Jillian said. "I don't know why you're worried about it, though. You don't have to pay him any attention."

"Yeah, you're right," Sophia said, following Jillian to the pew. She stopped before she moved into it. "I'll be back," she said with a sigh.

"What's wrong now?" Jillian said.

Sophia showed her phone. "Lucas just texted, asking to talk. I'm curious what he'll say. And since service is about to start, if I do it now instead of after, it'll have to be quick."

Sophia went to meet him as Jillian sat back down.

Stephanie turned to her. "Got a church update from Cyd. Warren and Veronica were in class but not Lindell."

"Wow," Jillian said. "We prayed specifically that Lindell wouldn't run into him. Thank You, Jesus."

"I need to ask if Lindell went to church at all, though," Stephanie said, texting. "What if he's on his way to a backslidden condition? He might never come home."

～

Lindell shut his car door, clicked the alarm, and walked toward the main building. He couldn't remember the last time he'd gone to third service, but he wasn't ready to see Stephanie and definitely didn't want to see Warren. He timed it so he'd even miss all the in-between fellowship. Praise and worship should be well underway by now.

He walked into the building and headed to the sanctuary, then paused just outside. Better to go to the balcony. No one would be up there. He turned and started toward the stairs—and everything stopped as Warren came out of the men's room. Lindell took a quick glance around for Veronica. Nope. It was just the two of them.

He continued toward the stairs.

"Lindell, you got a minute?"

He wanted to say no. Why would he have a minute for Warren? He sighed and turned toward him, waiting.

"I was hoping to see you in class this morning," Warren said. "Actually, I prayed I would see you. So running into you now . . ." He searched for words. "I'm new to praying about things, but this seems like a direct answer. I didn't want to let the opportunity pass."

"What's this about, Warren?" Lindell said.

"Last week after class," Warren said. "You and Stephanie were headed to the prayer circle one minute, then you talked to me and Roni—the tension was obvious—and you left. It made me realize that being here was a problem."

"That surprises you?" Lindell said.

"It wasn't even in my mind," Warren said. "From my perspective, you and Stephanie were happily married, and I didn't matter *at all.*" He moved a little closer. "Lindell, I'm just gonna keep it real. Steph and I had been together for years. We were talking marriage. Then here you come, the doctor, and she fell in love with you. She married *you.*" He threw up his hands. "You won. Then—"

"It wasn't that simple, though," Lindell said. "We didn't even go on our honeymoon because she was emailing *you* saying she'd see you when we got back and she missed you."

"Steph felt bad because I wouldn't talk to her," Warren said. "Why do you think she was emailing? We never emailed. I wouldn't pick up the phone. She knew she'd done me wrong—she didn't even tell me about you until she was engaged. So she kept asking if we could still be friends, and I kept telling her no." He lowered his voice a little as someone walked by. "The email was her trying to meet so she could 'explain everything.' I said no to that too. And I didn't give a second thought to the 'miss you' line. Steph said a whole lot that she didn't mean—obviously." He paused. "But I've been getting a different perspective about all of that. . . ." His words trailed off as if he were thinking about it even now.

"What's that?" Lindell said.

"I mean, man, we weren't even saved back then," Warren said. "I was mad at Steph for playing me, but everything was out of order anyway. I'm just getting that from what I'm learning as a new believer." He focused on Lindell. "But you and Stephanie have been living this Christian life for years now. Are you still holding that email against her?"

"It's not that I'm holding it against her," Lindell said. "I know where we were at the time, certainly not living for the Lord. It just felt like she still had feelings for you."

"Maybe she did at the time," Warren said. "Again—we were seeing each other up till the time you got engaged. I didn't know anything about you." He paused. "Did you know about me?"

Lindell hesitated. "I did. I knew she was in a long-term relationship, and that she was still seeing you."

"And you thought she'd forget about me the minute you put a ring on it?" Warren said. "Come on, man. You went into that with your eyes wide open."

Lindell wanted to rebut him, but he couldn't. It was true.

"But listen," Warren said, "after that email, I didn't hear from Stephanie for *years*. Not until a few months ago." He gestured with his hands. "She called out of the blue, said she wanted to catch up. I found out you two lived in North Carolina for a while, that you did some missionary work in Haiti, and now you've got the B and B. And she was really excited about the pregnancy. Said she couldn't wait until you two had the baby." He continued. "It was like I figured—you two were happy and doing well. Then she texted that she shouldn't have called and wouldn't reach out again. I was like okay, whatever." He shrugged. "I still didn't think we could ever be friends anyway."

Lindell knew he should get to the service, but he wanted to see where this was headed.

"But here's the thing," Warren said. "I had been feeling like God was trying to get me to go to church, and I was fighting it. I kept thinking, I don't even know what church to go to. After Stephanie's call, a lightbulb came on. *Living Word*. She tried to get me to go back in the day, and I never would. I looked it up and saw you had a new pastor and three services. I said, okay God, You got me. I'll visit. And I already knew how big the church was"—he glanced around at the building—so I didn't think I'd even see Stephanie. It wasn't about her. For the first time in my life, I was doing something that God wanted me to do. And for the first time in my life, as I sat under Lance, I heard the gospel and knew I needed to be saved." He paused. "And I thank God for saving me."

Lindell found himself giving a nod.

"But then we ran into you in that class," Warren said, "and it hit me —this is a problem. So I started praying about what to do, and I felt I needed to talk to you. Then I prayed that I would run into you." His eyes held a sincerity. "I just want to say I'm sorry, man, for causing tension and whatever else. I feel like I'm in a sweet spot coming here and being engaged to Roni. But I'm praying for God to show us another church that we can go to and grow in." He spread his hands, backing up. "That's all I wanted to say. No need to respond."

He turned and went on his way.

Lindell stood there a moment, trying to process what had just happened. The one thing that hit him most—Warren seemed to have been praying a lot more this past week than he had.

CHAPTER 67

"*H*ow long are you going to be mad at me?" Sophia backed out of the driveway Monday morning. "I get up extra early to come get you, and you can't even say hello?"

"I didn't ask you to come get me." Joy reached for her seatbelt. "Faith did."

"Oh," Sophia said, switching the gear. "If it's nothing to you, just stay home."

"Fine," Joy said, finger combing her hair. "Thank you for coming to get me." She whisked it into a loose bun with a scrunchie. "Now can we just go so we can be on time?"

Sophia switched gears again. "So why didn't you tell me what happened with Lucas at dinner Saturday night?"

Joy looked at her. "How do you know about that?"

"He mentioned it at Living Hope yesterday."

"You two were at Living Hope together?"

"Not *together*," Sophia said. "I went with Mom, and I didn't know his dad was preaching."

"What did he say?"

"He said, 'I know you know what happened last night,'" Sophia

478

said. "And I didn't. But I didn't want to tell him I didn't." She glanced at her. "So what happened?"

Joy stared at the road for a moment. "I asked him why he stopped texting, and he said things got busy." She gave Sophia a glance. "But he wasn't really talking to me at dinner either, even though we sat side by side. So I said, 'Just admit that you were only talking to me to get back at my cousin. I already saw the messages you sent her.'"

"You didn't, though," Sophia said. "I wanted to show you and you walked away."

"He didn't know that," Joy said. "He admitted it, said it was dumb, and apologized. I have nothing to say to him ever."

"Well, neither do I," Sophia said. "He tried to apologize to me too, for reaching out to you, and asked if we could start over. I told him he was out of his mind."

"I hope you said it just like that," Joy said.

"Actually, I told him he was crazy."

"Even better." Joy looked at Sophia. "I'm sorry. I didn't want to believe you. And I was jealous that you had Lucas *and* Noah interested in you."

"How many girls do you think Noah is 'interested' in?" Sophia said. "That means nothing."

"So what's going on with him?" Joy said. "Anything?"

"Well, at church last week, he held my hand during praise and worship," Sophia said.

Joy turned more toward her. "Then what?"

"Then nothing," Sophia said. "Sat through service then he went to the production office." She thought a moment. "Not much interaction last week, given the shooting schedule. And he didn't text me to come to church yesterday." She shrugged. "That's all the excitement I can report."

"At least you're reporting again."

Sophia glanced at her as she drove. "I'm sorry again for not telling you things right away, especially about Lucas. I was really sad when I thought I'd lost you as my best friend. That's why Noah took my hand, actually."

"I still don't know if I'd call you my best friend," Joy said.

"Who's closer to you than I am?"

"No one."

"Then I'm the best friend you have, whether you like it or not—wait, where's my phone?" Sophia said, hearing it ring.

"It fell on the floor," Joy said, picking it up. "Um, it's Noah."

"Noah?" Sophia said. "He's never just called." She took the phone and answered. "Hey, what's up?"

"Sounds like you're already up and about it," Noah said. "So my call time isn't till a little later this morning, and I don't want to leave super early with Brooke. I was wondering if I could ride with you."

"I'm pulling up to base camp right now," Sophia said, driving across the Living Word parking lot. "Faith gives us assignments once we get there."

"But don't they basically look for stuff for you all to do, so you can get the experience?" Noah said. "If a cast member has an actual need, you don't think they'd be cool with you helping out?"

"Let me call Faith," Sophia said. "I'll let you know." She hung up and looked at Joy.

"I could hear the whole thing," Joy said.

"What do you think?"

"That you should call Faith, like you said. She's always lecturing us about learning to be professional."

Sophia called Faith twice but it went to voicemail. She sighed as she pulled into a parking spot. "He's right. They do look for stuff for us to do, and he needs a ride up here."

"He had a ride," Joy said. "He didn't take it."

"Well, still," Sophia said. "I'll go get him, and I'll leave Faith a voice note telling her what happened."

"All right," Joy said, hopping out. "See you when you get back."

Sophia left the voice note as she headed to the B and B. A few minutes later, Faith's name flashed on her phone.

"Soph, this is not the protocol," Faith said. "Noah shouldn't be calling you about a ride. I'm the one who arranges transportation."

"Well, I think because I was at the B and B and we know each other—"

"I'm not comfortable with that," Faith said. "Come back to base camp and I'll arrange transportation for Noah."

"I'm literally parking at the B and B," Sophia said. "Does it make sense to leave Noah here and head back?"

Faith thought a moment then sighed. "Okay, head straight back with Noah. I'll be waiting. And I'll remind him of the protocol."

Sophia walked up to the B and B and opened the door, the aroma from breakfast still in the air. She looked in the dining room and didn't see anyone, so she texted Noah to let him know she was there. Seeing no one in the kitchen either, she moved to the sitting room. Noah's footsteps sounded shortly after.

"Hey," he said, walking in with a hoodie, black joggers, and slides with socks.

"Hey," Sophia said, rising. She wondered when her insides would stop reacting when she saw him. "Ready?"

"I thought we could chill for a while since I've still got some time," Noah said.

"Yeah, but Faith said to head back," Sophia said. "So if you're ready . . ." She moved toward the door.

Noah tugged her back, his hand in hers. "I didn't tell you I missed you yet."

"I think you just did," Sophia said.

"Not like I wanted to." His fingers tugged her closer and his lips went to hers. He let it linger softly. "Now I'm ready."

Sophia's heart hammered as they walked out the door and to the car. Barely conscious of starting the car or taking off, she kept replaying the kiss in her head.

Noah looked over at her. "Your hair looks cute like that."

"Oh," Sophia said, remembering she didn't have time to do anything with it this morning, just a messy bun like Joy. "Thanks."

"So what'd you do this weekend?"

"Nothing special really," Sophia said. "How about you?"

"Spent time running lines with Brooke," Noah said. "Also worked on music." He gave her a glance. "I started writing a new song."

"For real?" Sophia said. "Do I get to hear it?"

"I doubt I'll record it," Noah said. "Sometimes I just write because stuff wants to get out."

"I knew you couldn't have recorded it that fast anyway," Sophia said. "I wanted you to sing it for me."

"Here in the car?" Noah said.

"Uh, yeah, why not?"

"Because," Noah said. "It's still early, my voice isn't warmed up, and it'll just . . . feel weird. Plus it's not even done yet."

"I'm not looking for a *performance*," Sophia said. "I just want to get an idea. Did you write to a track? Is it on your phone?"

Noah blew out a breath. "I never do stuff like this." He looked over at her. "I don't know why I'm even thinking about it."

"Because you know I love your music and I'm genuinely interested in your process," Sophia said. "I want to hear how you put a song together, from the beginning."

Noah was quiet for a moment. "Besides my producer, I don't think anybody's ever said that to me. Most people don't know or care that I write a lot of my songs. They don't know it reflects my soul." He paused. "My girlfriend doesn't even know."

Sophia glanced at him. "That's the first time you've mentioned a girlfriend."

"We met last year at a music festival," Noah said. "And it's been cool. We have fun together, and I know she cares about me. But she never asks about the process. If I tell her I'm writing, she barely acknowledges it." He shrugged. "I don't know. It just affected me when you said that. Like that night I found out you actually *listen* to my music."

"So after all of that," Sophia said, "I just know you're about to let me hear this song."

Noah gave a sigh as he looked at her then connected his phone to the bluetooth in the car. "You need to understand that the track isn't mixed or mastered. I don't even have my guitar in St. Louis, which is what I *really* like to write with. And this is just the first pass on the lyrics and again—it's not done. I literally just started it yesterday, which means I might've even forgotten how the melody goes—"

"Noah, seriously?" Sophia said. "I'm not listening critically. I just want to hear what you wrote. I want to hear what was in your soul."

"That's the other thing," Noah said. "Lyrics are intensely personal. Once it's recorded and out there, I don't think about it. Even the other songs you listened to—they were further along and I could be more detached. But for you to listen to something I just wrote because I was inspired"—he paused at Sophia's groan—"*okay*. I just needed to say that."

Sophia stared at the road ahead as the track started. "Ohh I thought the tempo would be slower. Love that mid-tempo vibe." Her head moved to the beat.

Noah cleared his throat, looking at the lyrics on his phone.

Used to dream about love
Never will admit
All the longings of my heart
No, they never quit
I get it
Can't be the one who's totally committed
But my heart keeps calling me a hypocrite . . .

He looked at Sophia. "That's all I've got. But on the hook right here I'm thinking something like—'Cause I want a real love . . . da-da-da-da-da-da-da . . . just want a real love . . ."

"That's catchy." Sophia chimed in the next go round. "Just want a real love."

"Heyyy," Noah said. "You sing?"

"Choir only," Sophia said.

"Sounded like more than that to me."

"So a love song, huh?" Sophia said. "And I caught how you effortlessly hit that higher octave near the end of the verse, talking about 'my voice isn't warm.'" She rolled her eyes as she mimicked him. "I'd get five million views if I uploaded a video of you singing that."

"Except you wouldn't see the views because I'd kill you."

"Seriously, though, Noah?" Sophia glanced at him. "That gave me chills. You should do more music in that register. Something about your voice right there. And you should definitely record that song."

Noah smiled a little. "You really like it?"

"*Love* it," Sophia said. "The way your voice sounded and the lyrics themselves. I was intrigued even."

"By what?" Noah said.

"The word 'can't,'" Sophia said. "'Can't be the one who's totally committed.'"

"That's how it feels," Noah said. "Everybody expects me to be a certain way or assumes I'm a certain way. And I'm young so *I* feel like I need to be a certain way. Being committed to one person is so far from that."

"Which is why you have a girlfriend, but you're out here kissing other women?"

"I knew that was coming," Noah said. "But it's not like that."

"Mm-hm," Sophia said. "And by the way, just so you know, we're not kissing again."

Noah gave a nod. "I probably should've asked if it was okay to kiss you anyway."

"Yeah," Sophia said. "You should have."

"What would you have said?"

"Probably no." Sophia thought a moment. "I had my first kiss a couple of weeks ago, just to see what it was like—"

"Only a couple of weeks ago?" Noah said. "You really are a church girl." He turned to her. "Who did you kiss?"

"How is that any of your business?"

"Just wondered if you picked some random guy out of a crowd," Noah said, "since the goal was to see what it was like."

"Ha. Ha." Sophia kept her eyes on the road. "No. But my point is— after that, I decided I wanted a kiss to be something special. So I would've told you no because it wouldn't be special."

"What do you mean, it wouldn't be special?"

"How could it be?" Sophia said.

"I know I'm assuming," Noah said, "but I thought you liked me as much as I like you."

"What does that have to do with anything?" Sophia said.

"If two people like each other, that doesn't make it special?" Noah said.

"Not if they like several other people as well."

"I know you're suggesting I'm the one who likes all these people," Noah said, "and it's not true. But okay. If it wasn't special to you, I can't do anything about that." He gave her a glance. "It was special to me."

Sophia shook her head. "You know what just went through my mind?"

"What?" Noah said.

"Every story my sister and cousin have told me in order to warn me about guys," Sophia said. "Why is that always the line? 'You're *special*.'" She said the word with a swoon face then shook her head again.

"It's not *always* a line," Noah said. "You want to know why the kiss was special to me?"

Sophia rolled her eyes over to him. "Why?"

"Because you don't just see the person I am out in the world," Noah said. "When we're together, you're not trying to take a bunch of selfies with me to post. It's not about who I know or what you can get from me." He looked at her. "You see *me*. You just want to talk and get to know me. And you remind me of the only other woman I know who's not into all that other stuff—my mom." He paused, nodding to himself. "That's why it was special to me."

Sophia pulled into the parking lot and navigated to a space, pondering what he'd said.

"Sophia, I sang for you just now, raw, unplanned, something I've never done." Noah looked into her eyes. "And those were lyrics I didn't plan to share with anybody. You don't think that was special?"

"I mean, that part maybe, but—"

"One more thing," Noah said. "I was supposed to call Faith if I wanted to change up the transportation plan. But I was thinking about how hectic last week was. At base camp and on set, there wasn't any time or space for us to talk." He sighed. "I wanted time to talk to you this morning. Because you're special."

Noah got out and walked toward the building. Sophia watched him, telling herself to reject everything he'd said. Wasn't this part of the game? All the "special" talk so he could manipulate her. And she'd end up with a story to tell like Faith and Courtenay.

She got out and headed inside, resolving to herself that it didn't matter anyway. In a couple of weeks, he'd be gone. And between now and then, she'd do everything she could to avoid him.

CHAPTER 68

"How did rehearsal go?" Jordyn undid the head wrap Brooke wore in an earlier scene.

"Ended up with extra lines to memorize," Brooke said, sitting in the salon chair. "But it was really good. Trey gave us more context surrounding the scene and the added dialogue takes it deeper."

"So two more scenes, and then later today . . ." Jordyn eyed her in the mirror as she began to take out her cornrows. "You're really going to chop all your hair?"

Brooke nodded. "Mariah and I both think it's important for the scene."

"But you could wear a wig and cut *that* hair off," Jordyn said.

"We talked about that too," Brooke said. "But we want the authenticity. And I really think that walking in Kendra's shoes like that, as small a sacrifice as it may be, will make the performance more powerful." She looked up at Jordyn. "Did you big-chop when you went natural?"

"I did," Jordyn said. "We were building a hair channel, so we wanted the whole journey, from transition to big-chop, to phases of growth, all that."

"And your hair looks so healthy, full, and gorgeous," Brooke said.

"Thank you, Brooke," Jordyn said, unraveling another cornrow.

Several seconds elapsed before Brooke continued. "This might be awkward, but can we address the elephant in the room?"

"What elephant is that?" Jordyn said.

"Jesse and I sat together in class yesterday," Brooke said. "And I know you saw us talking here on Friday as well. I want you to know we're just friends." She turned her head as Jordyn worked. "I'm actually hoping the two of you get back together."

"Definitely wasn't expecting to hear that," Jordyn said. "Why are you hoping we get back together?"

"Because he loves you, Jordyn. He told me that." Brooke leaned her head to the side. "I know he may seem detached, but it's not because he doesn't care about you. He really is seeking God about it." She paused. "I just think it would be beautiful to see the Lord leading you back to each other as you both seek Him."

Jordyn clipped part of Brooke's hair out of the way. "So, you have no interest in dating him yourself?"

"I didn't say that." Brooke took a moment. "I've gotten to know Jesse through a group text with a mutual friend, and now we're getting to know each other better as friends. He's the type of guy I'm praying for. And I don't have to tell you why, because you know." She leaned her head forward as Jordyn worked in the back. "I would absolutely be interested in dating him . . . if we didn't live in different worlds, in different parts of the country. I know it wouldn't work, and I'm not big on wasting energy." She continued. "But the way he's focused on the Lord . . . it's helping me do the same. That's why I wanted to say what I said to you."

Jordyn took out the last cornrow. "And I appreciate everything you said, even the rebuke."

"Rebuke?" Brooke said. "I wasn't trying to—"

"No, I know," Jordyn said. "That part about seeking the Lord . . . Jesse even told me that *that* relationship should be our main focus right now. But I haven't been giving it the attention I should. I went to class only because I thought Jesse would be there, and I wanted to talk to him. *He's* been my focus."

"Jordyn, I get that it's hard because you're dealing with emotions from a breakup," Brooke said. "But you've got the perfect setup right now. This Cling study is all about *the* relationship you need. And it's short, only four weeks. You can do this, Jordyn." She looked up at her. "Is there anybody you can study with during the week, to help keep you accountable?"

Jordyn brushed her hair, preparing it for a ponytail. "I've had two people offer to do the study with me, and I haven't taken them up on it. I feel like I'm behind now." She shrugged. "We'll see."

"Ooh, no, that doesn't sound promising," Brooke said with a slight chuckle. "How about this? You and I have to see each other every day, all day. Instead of random conversation, let's be ready to talk about some aspect of the study. Doesn't have to be structured. But it provides an accountability factor—we'll need to do some studying beforehand."

Jordyn looked at her. "You would do that?"

"I'm doing the study anyway, mostly early mornings," Brooke said. "This gives me a way to reinforce what I'm learning."

"You just motivated me to do some studying on my break times today," Jordyn said.

"Now *that* sounds promising." Brooke smiled. "We might even be able to jump into some stuff this afternoon."

"That'll be good," Jordyn said, putting her hair in an elastic hair tie. "You can focus on something besides the fact that all of this"—she held up the pony—"is about to be gone."

Brooke stared in a bathroom mirror, cameras rolling, her hair hanging past her shoulders.

Alonzo stood behind, eyeing her in the mirror. "How much are we cutting?"

Her arms twitched as she hesitated. "Cut it to less than an inch."

Alonzo grabbed the scissors and Brooke turned slightly away from the mirror, closing her eyes. She prayed while in character.

Lord, please let this go well. We've only got one take to get it right. And please let me feel this the way Kendra felt it. Give me grace for this performance.

Brooke could feel the scissors clamp down on a section of hair in back. Her eyes closed tighter and a moment later, a big clump of it was gone. Alonzo moved to another area in the back, then another, working his way around as her hair fell to the floor. When he got to the front and lifted a section of hair, tears fell from Brooke's eyes.

"You okay?" Alonzo said, delivering his line.

Brooke nodded gently, tears sliding from her closed eyes. "Keep going," she said.

Alonzo cut the hair in front then Brooke heard the buzz of the clippers. His barber had walked them through this scene, telling Alonzo how to shape it. He took his time, and when the buzzing stopped, she turned slowly toward the mirror. Her heart beat an unfamiliar rhythm as she stared long seconds at herself, unsure what to think.

Alonzo turned her around by her shoulders. "You look beautiful."

Brooke only stared at him, her face streaked with tears.

"You said I looked intimidating in high school." Alonzo spoke the words softly. "You were intimidating to me too. You were the girl who had everything—beautiful, smart, popular, family had money, and actually lived in Clayton. I was the poor boy who got bused in."

Brooke's gaze was fixed with his.

"All these years later, part of me still saw you as that," Alonzo said. "Untouchable. Unreachable. With your hair gone . . . I don't know. It's like, I see you. And you're beautiful. Not the beauty I saw before. Deeply . . . beautiful."

Slowly they moved closer together, and Alonzo embraced her. Brooke's head went to his shoulder as he held her.

Then suddenly he began to back up. "I'm sorry. I don't want to . . . I shouldn't have." He grabbed the broom leaning against the bathroom wall. "I should just . . . sweep up the hair."

Brooke left the bathroom and the camera closed in as she dissolved into tears.

490

"And . . . cut," Mariah said. "Wow. Just wow."

Mariah hugged Brooke, followed by Alonzo.

"Best actress nominee," Alonzo said. "I keep telling you. You're *killin'* it, girl."

Brooke blew out a breath, wiping her eyes. "Just please tell me we got the take."

Mariah cocked her head. "Girl. We got an *amazing* take."

Brooke took one last look at her hair as someone swept it up. She moved off the set, others hugging her as she went—and saw Jesse watching from the background.

She went to him. "What are you doing here?"

"You sounded big and brave in the group text," Jesse said, "but this was huge. I asked Alonzo if I could be here for support."

Jesse hugged her and Brooke broke down in tears again.

"I'm sorry," Brooke said. "I don't know what's wrong with me." She wiped her eyes.

"It was a lot," Jesse said. "And you put your whole self into it. That was moving."

"But I didn't think I'd feel emotional *afterward*." She sighed. "I prayed to feel at least some of what Kendra felt, and I think God answered."

"So what's next?" Jesse said. "Do you have another scene?"

"Not tonight," Brooke said.

"You heading to the B and B to rest or getting something to eat first?"

"Depends. Am I eating by myself?"

"If you prefer," Jesse said. "But I was gonna roll with you, if you want."

Brooke smiled. "That sounds perfect."

"By the way, I love the look," Jesse said.

Brooke's hand went to her head. "I kinda forgot that I'm standing here looking completely different. Thank you, Jesse—oh! We're supposed to wash it real quick and put conditioner and—"

Her heart thumped as she remembered who was supposed to wash it and apply all the product. She turned—and her gaze fell on Jordyn.

~

"I feel bad because I had *just* told Jordyn that I'm basically rooting for the two of you to get back together." Brooke faced Jesse on the sofa in the B and B sitting room, a slice of pizza in her hand. "And hours later you're on set to see me, and I'm hugging you and leaving with you. Do you know how that had to look?" She took a bite.

Jesse took another slice from the box on the coffee table. "So that's what you're doing? Rooting for me and Jordyn to get back together?"

"Well, pretty much," Brooke said. "I said it would be beautiful to see the two of you seeking the Lord, and the Lord leading you back to each other."

"And you felt the need to tell Jordyn this because . . .?"

"Because we're together all day," Brooke said, "and I knew it had to bother her to see us at the Bible study and at base camp on Friday. I didn't want things to be strained between us." She took another bite and waited to swallow. "I wanted her to know I'm not competing here. I actually want you back together."

"And what did Jordyn say to that?" Jesse ate some of his slice.

"She wanted to know if I had any interest in dating you myself."

"And here's where it gets interesting," Jesse said.

"I'm guessing you want to hear what I said."

"Oh, you can't hold back now."

"I told her I'd absolutely have an interest in dating you," Brooke said, "given that I'm praying for a guy like you to come along." She finished her slice. "And of course, this assumes a mutual interest, which is actually irrelevant because I also said it wouldn't work, given how our lives are set up." She shrugged. "That's why I can root for the two of you."

"Except now Jordyn can see that we actually *are* dating," Jesse said, "and she'll wonder why you took her through that whole convo just to ambush her with the truth later."

"See, don't say that," Brooke said. "You know how bad I feel."

"You told her we're friends," Jesse said. "It's not unusual that I'd be there for support." He drank some of his soda. "I bet she was cool when she washed your hair and all that."

"Jordyn is professional, which I love," Brooke said. "Of course she wouldn't act funny. She went right to work, getting this TWA together."

"TWA?"

"Teeny weeny afro," Brooke said. "You should be up on all the natural hair jargon after dating Jordyn."

"Because we'd be talking about TWA's?"

"I don't know, you might've—"

"Girl, I hear your voice," Stephanie said, approaching. "Let me see!"

Brooke stood up to meet her and took a breath as Stephanie came in. "Really different, right?"

"Aww, look at you," Stephanie said, taking her in from different angles. "Everything is popping even more. Your eyes are gorgeous. Never noticed that mole on your cheek. Even your smile . . . so warm and beautiful. It's perfect on you—hey, Jesse. I didn't mean to ignore you."

"It's all Brooke right now." Jesse was enjoying another slice. "I'm good."

"I'm still not used to it," Brooke said. "Every time I look in the mirror, I'm like—did I really do that?" She exhaled. "But I feel like it's more than the movie. Like I'm making a new start."

"Then you just fired out the gate," Stephanie said. "I see you with those big hoop earrings too, trying to look all cute. All right, I'm headed back up. Just had to get a look. I love it."

"Thanks, Stephanie," Brooke said. She got another slice as she sat back down. "So, I hope you don't feel a way about my convo with Jordyn."

"Other than the wealth of assumptions and presuppositions, not at all," Jesse said.

Brooke gave him a look as she finished her bite. "I already said that the part about us dating assumes a mutual interest."

"It's also an assumption," Jesse said, "that if Jordyn and I are both seeking the Lord, we'd find our way back to each other."

"I didn't assume that would be the case," Brooke said. "I said it would be beautiful if it happened."

"And the assumption that if you and I were to date—it wouldn't work."

"Oh, yeah, I definitely made that assumption," Brooke said. "And it's a confident one."

Jesse continued. "And the assumption that if there were a mutual interest, we would decide to date *even if* it could work."

"Hmm that assumption slipped by me." Brooke finished her slice. "If there were a mutual interest and we felt it could work, why would we decide not to date?"

"Timing," Jesse said. "We're both coming out of relationships. Classic rebound situation."

"Ahh but now *you're* assuming—that that's a problem." Brooke sipped her water. "Two people seeking the Lord and clinging to Him can't get into a relationship soon after one has ended? That could be God's *perfect* timing."

"Okay," Jesse said, nodding. "I love when I'm checked on an old way of thinking." He looked at her. "So only one assumption left on the table."

Brooke looked curiously at him. "Two by my count."

"Nah, there would be a mutual interest," Jesse said. "We're only left with your confident assumption that it wouldn't work."

"Well, it wouldn't," Brooke said.

Jesse nodded. "Given how our lives are set up. Okay."

"Do you have a rebuttal?"

"I just think it's interesting that you and your ex-boyfriend's lives were set up perfectly," Jesse said. "Same industry. Same city. Shoot, same apartment. And it didn't work."

"That's because God said no," Brooke said.

"What did He say about this situation?"

Brooke hesitated. "I didn't talk to Him about it."

Jesse shrugged. "If you hear from Him, at least you're no longer assuming."

"Why do I feel like this conversation has suddenly become a riddle?" Brooke said. "What are you saying, Jesse?"

Jesse leaned in a little. "You said everything I've been thinking. I liked you but didn't know if it was mutual. I was convinced it wouldn't work. Even had the additional issue with timing. So I would've never said anything to you. But hearing *you* say it made me reexamine." He paused. "How did we have the same thoughts, in the midst of a Cling study, and neither of us talked to God about it?"

"Because it seems ridiculous," Brooke said. "*And* you have an engagement ring that you intended to give someone whom you still love. I said timing shouldn't be an automatic issue, but your feelings *are* an issue. You and Jordyn really could get back together. That's another obvious reason why it wouldn't work."

"I'm still waiting for you to touch on the God part."

Brooke heaved a sigh. "This is *so* ridiculous."

"I agree."

"And how is this happening right after I told Jordyn I'm rooting for the two of you?"

"I had nothing to do with you and those pom-poms."

She sighed again. "What if we prayed together, right now? Total 'Your will, Lord' prayer. Inviting God to close the door hard to whatever mutual whatever this might be. And I want us to pray for His will with you and Jordyn too. And let's pray for Him to show us all the ways this wouldn't work that we haven't even thought of. And—"

"Brooke, are you going to keep talking about what we should pray —or pray?"

"Okay, okay," Brooke said. "Should I start?"

"After that prayer essay you just laid out? Yeah, you can start."

CHAPTER 69

"God let Elijah completely show out with those Baal prophets." Jillian sat relaxed in the chapel pew, her Bible and notes spread before her. "He was like, put My glory on display. The fact that it was even set up as a competition—'you call on the name of your god, and I'll call on the name of the LORD, and the God who answers by fire, He is God'—shows that God is a *Boss*. He's like, there is *no one like Me*. And you 'bout to see. I *love* that about God."

"I should've known this was one of your faves." Tommy sat facing her in the pew. "You get fired up about every passage in the Old Testament where God is flexing, especially if He's speaking in first person."

"Ahhhh, you know it," Jillian said. "I was torn between going to Isaiah—*so* many flex verses—or looking at these Elijah verses. Or even the last couple of chapters in Job, where He says, 'Have you ever *in your life* commanded the morning, and caused the dawn to know its place?'" She pumped a fist. "Let 'em know, Lord! You are the Most High!" Her fingers started turning. "Now I want to look at Job for a minute."

"We're staying right here where you've got us, in First Kings," Tommy said. "I'm tripping because I always thought of it as *Elijah* flexing as he mocks the Baal prophets—'Call out with a loud voice;

maybe your god is asleep.'" He chuckled. "But you're right—this tells us a lot about God too, just in the way it was set up, which had to come from Him. They were calling on their god all day—and nothing. Then Elijah prepares the sacrifice, calls on God, and He gets to *show out* by sending fire from heaven onto the altar."

"And look at the result," Jillian said, eyes on her Bible, "people fall on their faces and say, 'The LORD, He is God.'" She looked at Tommy. "He's gonna get the glory. *Period.* Reading passages like this helps me to cling because I'm in *awe* of Him. Who or what else would I cling to? But here's the next part I wanted to show you," she said, turning the page.

Tommy looked at her before he turned. "I love your love for the word. It's infectious."

"You're the one who got us into this study," Jillian said. "So, likewise." She skimmed a few verses. "Okay, so I was headed to chapter nineteen, but can we pause at this last verse in eighteen? This speaks to the character of God too. Look at this—'Then the hand of the LORD was on Elijah, and he girded up his loins and outran Ahab to Jezreel.'" She looked up. "Ahab is in a *chariot*, and Elijah outruns him? We need a whole separate study time on how powerful the hand of the LORD is. I mean, come on! This is who we cling to—He's all-powerful!"

"Jill, I *promise* you I was on that when I first started this study," Tommy said. "I was seeing so many verses that talked about His hand and His right hand, all signifying His power. It made me stop and pray, asking the Lord why I was seeing that and praying for His hand to be upon me."

Jillian looked at him. "His hand *is* on you, Tommy."

"Why do you say that?"

"I see it," Jillian said. "Not that it wasn't on you before. But I see more of His strength at work in you. And it's no wonder. You've been in the word more than I've ever seen you in the word."

Tommy sighed. "It's been so good, Jill. It's been *life* to me. And I do feel His strength, and so much more." He grew quiet a moment. "I just want to stay in this place."

"And you can," Jillian said. "That's the blessing. Just stay in His presence."

Tommy looked into her eyes. "As long as I cling, huh?"

Jillian met his gaze. "As long as you cling."

He looked back at his Bible. "Now what are you excited about in chapter nineteen?"

"Okay, so Elijah has killed all the Baal prophets," Jillian said, "and now Jezebel lets him know that *he'll* be dead by tomorrow. So Elijah's afraid and runs for his life. Goes into the wildness and asks God to take his life."

"Man, this hits last week's lesson on fear," Tommy said. "Dude *just* faced the Baal prophets—*four-hundred-fifty* of them—and he killed them! Then this one woman threatens his life and fear takes hold." He shook his head. "Talk about needing to cling twenty-four-seven."

"And I love that he does cling when he gets to the wilderness," Jillian said. "He says, 'O LORD, take my life'—can't you feel the depths of despair?—but he's talking *to God*. It's a cry for help to the only One who *can* help him." She put a finger on the page. "And look how God responds—this is what I wanted to get to. The same powerful God who rained fire from heaven sends an angel who gives him food and water—"

"Nah, you can't just say 'food and water,'" Tommy said. "This angel served up a bread cake baked on hot stones! Do you *know* how good that had to taste to Elijah in the wilderness?"

"Exactly," Jillian said, smiling. "The angel could've fed him some berries or figs. He got a hot meal! Then the angel tells him to rest and feeds him *again*." She looked at Tommy. "This is the God we cling to as well, a loving and caring God who understands our emotions and our needs . . . a God who is good to us."

"Man, Jill . . ." Tommy stood with a sigh and walked a little. "This captures what my walk with God has been lately. Feeling like He understands my emotions. I give them to Him, and He can handle *all* of them. And in return, He ministers to me. He truly is a loving and caring God." He looked over at her. "We need to do this every day."

"I'm wondering why you didn't think to suggest it before today," Jillian said. "Studying together in this chapel . . . issa *vibe*."

Tommy chuckled. "You clearly got that from one of your kids." He came and sat by her again. "It's definitely a vibe, though. Beautiful and peaceful. And I don't think I can ever come here now without thinking about our friendship vows."

"And speaking of the friendship," Jillian said, "all week my coworkers have been mentioning what you said about me in your post. I didn't even know they were doing the study." She looked at him. "I still can't believe you put that in the lesson this week."

"I can't believe you let me keep it in there."

Jillian shrugged. "Why wouldn't I? I was surprised when I saw it. But it was relevant, showing how we can build intimacy with God."

"I was praying for an illustration," Tommy said, "and when the Lord showed me, it was so obvious." He thought about it even now. "If it weren't for our friendship, I don't know if I'd know how to relate to the Lord *as a friend*. Sometimes I'll be talking to Him about something, and I'll go off on this tangent and that tangent, and I'm like—am I *rambling*? Then I'll think—but Jill gets me when I do that so God definitely does." He paused, checking a notification on his phone.

"Almost time?" Jillian said.

"They're gathering people in the youth building," Tommy said, reading the text, "about to give instructions. Faith said a lot of people showed up to be extras."

"That's why I'm able to be here right now," Jillian said. "Cyd gave us the afternoon off because just about everyone in my office wanted to take part."

"I've got a few minutes before I need to get back," Tommy said. "Was that everything you wanted to share from the Elijah verses?"

"I had one more thing." Jillian looked back at her Bible. "This is also the chapter where God tells Elijah to stand on the mountain. And there's a strong wind, but God wasn't in the wind. An earthquake, but He wasn't in that. A fire, but He wasn't in that."

Tommy nodded. "And after the fire, a still, small voice."

"I was really meditating on that in light of this lesson about knowing God." Jillian took a moment. "He *is* mighty and can bring the strong wind, earthquake, and fire. But when He speaks to us by His Spirit, it's that gentle voice." She looked at him. "It's what you were saying a moment ago. There's nothing like the sweetness of His presence."

"I love that you ended on that note." Tommy rose and picked up his jacket. "That's definitely where I want to stay—where I'm *praying* to stay. I feel like I'm hearing His still, small voice more and more." He paused. "Jill, it's amazing."

"Adding that to my prayer list for you," Jillian said, typing on her phone. She gathered her Bible, notes, and jacket and followed Tommy out.

"Are you going to be an extra in the scene?" Tommy said.

"I was willing if they needed more people," Jillian said. "But it sounds like they're covered."

"Yeah, they waited till late afternoon because they mostly wanted high schoolers, since they're filming a youth service." Tommy walked onto the elevator and pushed the button for the first floor. "But adults are always in the service, so you could definitely be in it."

"So Alonzo gets to preach today," Jillian said. "I might go just to see him play the youth pastor. That'll be fun."

The elevator stopped at the third floor. When the doors opened, Silas stood before them.

"Well, hello," Silas said, stepping inside. "Is this going down? I've never been on the fourth floor. What's up there?"

"A handful of offices," Tommy said, "plus some storage space and a chapel."

"A chapel?" Silas said. "I never knew that. So you've got a second office up there, Tommy?"

"I've got a hard enough time keeping the one office straight," Tommy said.

"Are you heading down for the shoot?" Jillian said.

"Not so much to be in the scene," Silas said. "It's a great opportunity to see Mariah Pendleton at work."

They got off the elevator and walked toward the exit.

"Hey, Jillian, do you have a moment?" Silas said.

Jillian paused, giving a glance at Tommy as he continued on. "What's on your mind?" she said.

"I didn't get a chance to talk to you after church on Sunday," Silas said, "but I wanted to invite you to go to dinner. I know you consider that a big step. But given that we've already had a dinner outing—which, I realize, we kind of backed into—I thought you might be willing." He added, "And I'm not looking for a quick answer. Just that you'd think and pray about it."

"Thank you for the invitation, Silas," Jillian said. "And I appreciate the space to think and pray on it. I definitely will."

"Are you excited about the filming?" He moved ahead and opened the door.

"I'm sort of like you"—Jillian walked out—"interested to see how it all happens. Sophia's been talking a lot about it."

"Lucas too," Silas said. "By the way, I think he's got quite the crush on Sophia."

Jillian nodded slightly. Sophia had told her about the ordeal between her, Lucas, and Joy. "I don't know about you, but I find it hard to keep up with who the latest crushes are. They can be pretty flighty at this age."

"Oh, I agree," Silas said. "But he said something about making a dumb mistake and could I arrange for the four of us to go out—and no, I wasn't inviting you on a double date. But it let me know that this appeared to at least be an upper level flighty crush." He took in the scene as they walked into the youth building. "Wow. This looks like a Sunday crowd."

Jillian moved between groups of high schoolers. "Can you see what's happening up ahead? Because back here it's light chaos."

"Looks like we're part of the overflow," Silas said, craning to see. "The doors to the auditorium are closed up ahead."

"Oh, well," Jillian said. "Guess I'll head back to the office. I love working when it's quiet anyway."

The outer door opened behind them and Faith walked in with two others, all of them with badges and walkie-talkies.

"Aunt Jillian, what are you doing out here?" Faith said. "Everybody's inside."

"Everybody who?" Jillian said. "I just got here."

"Come with me," Faith said.

"Can Silas come also?" Jillian said.

Faith nodded, waving them along.

Jillian and Silas followed them through the crowd of mostly young people and into the auditorium, where there was an even bigger, more organized crowd.

"Did you want to be in the scene?" Faith said.

"Just here to watch," Jillian said.

"Then you can hang over this way." Faith motioned to the area. "They're giving instructions to people who want to be in it."

"Okay, thanks, Faith," Jillian said, moving to the designated area with Silas.

"I see Treva, Lance and others closer to the front," Silas said. "How fun if they're planning to be extras."

Jillian smiled. "That would be awesome."

They watched as crew members positioned the high schoolers in certain seats. Jillian spotted Sophia and Joy helping with the effort, looking official in their badges. A moment later she saw David coming toward them.

"Mom," he said, an earnest look in his eyes.

"Did you speak to Pastor Keys?" Jillian said.

"Hi, Pastor Keys," David said.

"Hi, David, good to see you," Silas said.

"Mom, can I talk to you?" David's eyes shifted to indicate *not here.*

Jillian walked with him a few feet. "What's going on?"

"Mom, this is now a handful of times you've been aggressively with Pastor Keys," David said.

"Aggressively?" Jillian said.

"It's just a saying, Mom." David said. "Has it moved to dating now?"

"David, please tell me why you sound so distressed." Jillian spoke in a near whisper.

"Because first I saw you going to coffee with him," David said. "But

I didn't think it was a thing until Lucas told Sophie it was a thing. Then you went to dinner—but you said *that* wasn't a thing." He spread his hands. "Now you're at the shoot with him."

"We both work here, David," Jillian said. "I saw him coming down the elevator and we walked over."

David sighed. "So that was it?"

"Well, on the way, he did invite me to dinner, as an official date," Jillian said. "I haven't given my answer yet."

"But you're thinking about it?" David said.

"I told him I'd think and pray about it," Jillian said. "Sweetheart, I'm assuming this has something to do with the 'committee' you and Sophie were talking about. I think it's time to extend it to a family meeting so I can hear what's on your minds. I knew that if and when this day came, it would be hard on you all to see me with anyone other than your dad."

"I mean, yeah, but that's not why I'm asking." David leaned in closer. "What about Tommy?"

A blank stare came over Jillian. "Okay, this is not what I thought it was. Let's definitely plan to talk tonight."

"I don't know if tonight will work, Mom," David said. "Tommy said I could shadow him till the shoot ends this evening. I get to be an extra *and* do behind the scenes stuff."

"When did you arrange that?"

"When he got here a little while ago," David said. "I wanted to come talk to you when I saw you. But I have to get back."

Jillian joined Silas again, hoping he hadn't overheard a word of that. Then, as if David had set it up, Tommy walked toward the back and out of the auditorium.

"That was a nice tribute that Tommy wrote," Silas said, "to your friendship."

"Oh, in the study?" Jillian said. "It wasn't meant as a tribute, just an illustration."

"But a tribute nonetheless," Silas said. "A lot of people long for a friendship like that, especially one that's time-tested." He paused a moment. "I have to admit, I was a little relieved when Tommy said he was committed to being single."

Jillian looked at him. "When did he say that?"

"Over dinner at Lance and Treva's the other night," Silas said.

"And you were relieved?"

"Well, I've made no secret of the fact that I'd like to know you better," Silas said. "Tommy already knows you well, and there's clearly a strong connection. So yes, I admit I'd be worried if he weren't decidedly single."

"I'm just curious," Jillian said. "How did that come up at dinner?"

"We were talking about Living Hope," Silas said. "I hadn't realized that Lance was single when he launched it. I felt it would be odd for me to serve as a single senior pastor, but Lance said it was beneficial. I said that's great, and added—but I don't want to be single for long." He glanced at someone who walked by. "That's how it started. Reggie chimed in and said singleness was Tommy's favorite subject."

"Ah," Jillian said. "Now it makes sense."

"I'll go ahead and share this too," Silas said, leaning closer. "Pamela heard my comment about not wanting to be single for long and said she'd pray with me for a move of God. The only person anywhere near my orbit is you, so I took that as encouragement from the Lord to pursue that official date." He nodded a little. "That's also why I didn't think it was a coincidence that you came to Living Hope on Sunday."

Jillian stared vaguely, unsure what to say.

"I'll tell you this," Silas said. "When you pray in faith, God is a master at making you wait. But when the appointed time comes, it *comes*. And you rejoice that you endured instead of giving up."

CHAPTER 70

Stephanie sat in a reclining chair in her bedroom Thursday evening, legs propped and Bible in her lap, wondering what she'd gotten herself into. Determined to stick with the Cling study, she'd listened to the audio from Sunday's class and taken up the challenge for the week. Reading through a book of the Bible and noting what she learned about God didn't seem like *too* much, if she picked a short book. She'd flipped through, debating which to choose, and landed on Lamentations.

It fit her current mood. Almost two weeks and Lindell still wasn't home. With all the praying she and Jillian had done, she'd been trying to trust and cling. But as the days mounted, it was getting harder to do so. Why not wallow in despair with verse after verse in Lamentations?

But now as she moved into chapter three, she was ready to bail and jump to another book. She'd never actually read Lamentations and hadn't quite grasped how heavy these laments were. God's people had been taken into captivity because of their sin, and the land God had given them was now a desolation. Words like "distress," "affliction," "groaning," and "there is no one to comfort" dominated chapters one and two. And now in chapter three, the prophet Jeremiah was lamenting that as he cried out for help, God had shut out his prayers.

She read the next line, verse eighteen—"My strength has perished, and so has my hope from the LORD."

Stephanie closed her Bible. *Okay, Lord, yes, I chose a short book because I was too tired to spend a lot of time in Your word. And yes, I thought I wanted to wallow in despair. But I thought there'd eventually be* some *hope. The point of the challenge was to learn more about You so I can cling tighter. But now I feel like You're telling me that my strength and hope have perished. Fantastic.*

Her mind went to the scenarios she'd been imagining of her and the baby on their own. It could happen. People prayed all the time for miracles, for God to intervene and turn an upside-down situation right side up. But sometimes He chose to let it stay upside-down. Sometimes He chose to let you groan and feel the distress. Seemed like no one liked to acknowledge that, but it was true. And it had been true for her marriage for years. Truth be told, she'd seen this coming for years, she or Lindell walking out for good. Although, she'd always thought it would be her. The miracle was that she was here, praying for God to move in her marriage—and her husband was nowhere in sight.

Stephanie stared at her Bible, ready to put it on the nightstand and get ready for bed. But she found herself reopening it and flipping to other books of the Bible. She read the first couple of verses of Joshua before checking herself. Twenty-four chapters? Psalms could work. She could read only a few of them. But somehow she felt the urge to go back to Lamentations.

Okay, fine, Lord, I don't know if this is You or some form of depression taking hold. But I'll wallow some more and finish the book.

She went back to where she'd left off in chapter three and continued reading—and immediately sat up straighter. *This* is what I was about to get to? She hadn't even realized it was in this book. Her eyes took in line upon line.

This I recall to my mind,
Therefore I have hope.
The LORD's lovingkindnesses indeed never cease,
For His compassions never fail.

They are new every morning;
Great is Your faithfulness.
"The LORD is my portion," says my soul,
"Therefore I have hope in Him."
The LORD is good to those who wait for Him,
To the person who seeks Him. . . .

Stephanie paused, tears in her eyes, and read the verses again slowly. She took notes as to what they told her about God, then closed her eyes, overcome. *Your lovingkindnesses never cease, O God. Your compassions never fail. Great is Your faithfulness, Lord.* She wiped her eyes. *I do have hope. You are my portion! You are good to those who wait for You. I will cling and wait, Lord. Give me strength to cling and wait.*

Stephanie put up the groceries from a late night trip to the market. Running low on a few items, including Noah's beloved Hershey's, she'd decided to go now rather than hope they could make it through breakfast. Felt good to have a freshly stocked fridge and pantry.

She put on a kettle for a cup of tea and turned at the sound of footsteps. "Hey, Mariah, I hardly ever see you in the evening."

"I know," Mariah said. "When I'm in production mode, I'm consumed from first thing in the morning until late at night, and sometimes through the night."

"I hope you're getting the rest you need," Stephanie said.

"I'm always sleep-deprived during filming," Mariah said. "It's only a few short weeks, and I have to make sure we get it done and get it done well. But I do need replenishment." She smiled as she ducked into the pantry. "And hey, I want to share this with you," she said, emerging with snacks. "We've been checking the weather closely to see when to hold this outdoor wedding scene. Lance and Kendra got married in October, so we knew we were at a disadvantage, filming in February."

"Yeah, Brooke was saying they'd probably be freezing out there, acting like it's a balmy fall day."

"I think Miss Pam was praying about the weather harder than anything else," Mariah said. "We thought we'd shoot the wedding scene the final week, but today the forecast shifted. Looks like temps will climb to the upper fifties next Wednesday, which will at least *feel* balmy since it's been in the thirties and forties. I thought it would be special to have 'wedding guests' in the scene who were actually at the wedding. So I'm hoping you and Lindell can come."

Stephanie hesitated at the mention of his name. Given Mariah's schedule, she probably had no idea that he hadn't been around. "I think that would be special too," she said. "I don't know if Lindell can make it, but I'll plan to be there."

"I'll let you know the time as we get closer," Mariah said.

"Where are you shooting it?" Stephanie removed the kettle as it began to whistle.

"Lance's house," Mariah said. "People know that setting from the video, so I'm excited to capture the wedding in the same location."

"Oh, *that's* what'll make it special," Stephanie said. "Maybe even emotional."

"It won't be the first time with this shoot," Mariah said. "Headed back up to look at dailies." She started off then came back. "Stephanie, just want to say that staying here has made such a difference for me with this shoot. It's such a homey atmosphere, and my room feels cozy. And the Scripture here and there reminds me where my help comes from, that all of this is not on me. Had to tell you that."

"Thank you, Mariah," Stephanie said. "I really appreciate that."

Stephanie made her tea, thinking about Mariah's words. Ever since she'd prayed and put the B and B on the altar, she'd wondered what God would do. Comments like that reminded her that the B and B was a God thing from the start. When Mrs. Cartwright had first brought the idea to her of being a caretaker, Stephanie couldn't see herself stepping into that role. She didn't even like being around strangers. But God moved in her heart to do it and surprised her with a love for serving people in this way. Still, if the season were ending, she'd have to move on and see what was next.

She carried her tea upstairs, hand to her stomach as her lively little one started kicking. That was the other thing. If the season *wasn't* ending, what would life be like, running a B and B with a newborn? With or without Lindell, it would be challenging. But she'd been reading blogs of others who'd done it, some rearing several kids in a B and B. It was simply a lifestyle, and guests knew from the website what to expect. One blogger even said that guests would feed the baby, if need be, while she cooked breakfast.

Stephanie closed her door and rested the tea on a tabletop beside the recliner. After changing into her robe, she sat down with her Bible. She'd read through all of Lamentations last evening, taking additional notes, and wanted to choose another book for tonight. She'd noticed a difference when she went to bed. Her thoughts were filled with what she'd read—with the word of God and the promises of God. She wanted that same peace tonight. If she could—

Stephanie sat forward a little, listening. She was used to the floor-boards creaking on the stairs, but the footsteps seemed to be coming up instead of going down. Maybe Mariah had a question. She lowered the footrest and got up—and the door opened before she could get to it.

She looked at him, almost confused. "Lindell?"

"Hey, Steph." He put his bag down and closed the door. "Can we talk?"

Stephanie could feel the beat of her heart. Why did his tone sound heavy? What was he about to say? She moved to the bed and sat with her back against the headboard, a pillow her cushion. Lindell hung his jacket then sat on the edge beside her.

"I didn't know I'd be gone this long." He stared down at his khakis. "I was hurt, but it was more than that. I was dealing with insecurities that I've basically had for the life of this marriage. But Warren said something that stuck with me."

Stephanie's eyes went wide. "You talked to Warren?"

"Ran into him at church," Lindell said. "He said he prayed for an opportunity to talk to me. Anyway, he asked if I was still holding that email against you—"

"You talked about the email?"

"Steph, I know how this must be hitting you," Lindell said, "but can I say this without the interruptions?"

Stephanie nodded. "Go ahead.

"I deflected the question," Lindell said, "but I knew the answer. Yes, I was still holding that email against you, all these years later. And here was Warren, a new believer, letting me know that I hadn't grasped a core concept of the faith—forgiveness." He sighed. "It was also clear after talking to Warren that I hadn't given prayer its proper place. I stayed with Cedric and Cyd an extra few days to focus on praying and seeking the Lord. I didn't want to come back until I had truly forgiven you, for the email and for reaching out to him."

Stephanie could feel her heart beating as she hung on every word.

"But Steph, you *did* give prayer its proper place," Lindell said. "You got Jillian to pray with you—to *fight* with you—as you battled those thoughts. I couldn't appreciate that. *I* should've started praying for you after I heard that. But instead, I filtered it through my insecurities, which, as you know, made things worse as far as intimacy between us." He turned toward her. "I'm sorry for that, Steph. For making it about me and not recognizing that the enemy was playing both of us." Emotion slowed his words. "I'm sorry for not forgiving you and for not standing with you in prayer."

Stephanie felt the emotion welling up inside. "And I'm sorry for calling Warren, Lindell—"

"Steph, you already apologized," Lindell said. "I know you're sorry. I just want you to know that I forgive you. And I won't keep throwing it up in your face like I've done with the email."

"But he's at Living Word because of what I did," Stephanie said. "And I hate that I've put you in the position of possibly running into him week to week. But babe, if you're willing, we can both go to Living Hope. I went this Sunday and—"

"Wait," Lindell said. "You weren't at Living Word this past Sunday?"

"I didn't want to see Warren," Stephanie said. "And I wanted you to know that I was serious about doing everything I could to get him out of my head."

Lindell leaned over and kissed her. "Thank you for that, babe. We'll see about Living Hope. Warren said he's praying for God to show him another church he and Veronica can go to."

"Sounds like this conversation went on and on."

"I do believe it was God, as crazy as it seems." Lindell ran the back of a finger down Stephanie's cheek. "I missed you."

Her breath stuttered as tears gathered. "I thought you might not come back."

Lindell moved further onto the bed and held her in his arms. "I love you, Steph. I needed that time, and by God's grace, I believe it made me a better husband. I prayed for you and for us more this past week than I can remember."

Stephanie held onto him. "I love you, too. And I realized something, which is even truer now that you're back. This really is the best time of my life."

Lindell kissed her and then kissed her again, slowly taking it deeper. He moved down her neck with a trail of kisses, then untied her robe and let it fall aside. Stephanie watched as he got up, took off his shoes, then stationed himself at her feet, slowly massaging them. He moved so methodically and sensually that by mid-calf, she couldn't take it anymore.

"Um, sir, you are driving me crazy. If you don't get your clothes off right now . . ."

CHAPTER 71

"So I've shown you all some of the base camp, and this is the actual production office for the movie." Desiree held her camera in front of herself, filming. "Like I said, I wanted to be on set today while my part was being filmed and show you guys that, but they keep it tight over there, understandably." She walked as she talked. "But this has been an incredible experience. And you know what I just realized? I've talked to you guys from dozens of cities all over the world, but never from my own city of St. Louis. So I'm loving this," she said, smiling.

Someone in the production office walked past, giving her a glance.

"I've gotta run, guys." Desiree lowered her voice. "I hope you enjoyed this little glimpse of a real, Hollywood production. Until next time . . ."

Desiree shut off her camera and tucked it into her bag then walked around to one of the cubicles. "Thank you for allowing me to film in here," she said to the woman.

"You're welcome," the woman said. "Have a great evening."

"You, too."

Desiree put on her jacket, wrestling still with her plans—a flight to New York tonight, connecting to London. She'd told herself it was the only thing that made sense, continuing with the pace. This was her life, after all. But the deeper she'd gotten into the study, the more she'd questioned that life. Did she need to take a break? Maybe put her career on pause? She didn't know. And with no definite answers, she'd resolved to keep moving.

Desiree took the elevator down, head in her phone as she checked the status of her flight. The elevator stopped one floor down, and two guys got on.

"So who's going tonight?" one of the guys said.

"Me, Tommy and Jesse, maybe Alonzo, plus you, if you're going," the other guy said. "We're heading out now, though."

"Yeah, definitely," the first guy said. "Did y'all check with Lance?"

Desiree glanced up at the guys, whose backs were turned to her.

"Duty calls," the guy said. "He's in the office late tonight."

The elevator opened and they walked off, continuing their conversation. Desiree walked off as well, her heart pounding. Was that a sign?

She stood in the entryway, contemplating. It was Friday night and the shoot had wrapped for the day. When she'd arrived earlier, people were everywhere. Now from what she could tell, the building was near empty. And Lance was only yards away in another building, another empty building. And she really wanted to talk to him.

For days as she'd pondered what to do with her life, Lance kept coming to mind. He knew her. Had a way of speaking straight to her soul. And he always broke down advice about God in a way she could understand. She wanted to ask—how do you know if God is moving you to do something? To change your life?

She'd texted Treva to see what she thought, but Treva had put her in touch with Cyd. And Desiree didn't have time to explain her whole life situation to Cyd.

Now, on the night she was flying out, she heard *that* in the elevator? Maybe she could talk to Lance after all. If he'd only take a moment to listen, he'd have the perfect advice. She just knew it. In the end, she might not have a flight to catch.

Desiree put on her jacket and headed outside.

I'm asking you to respect that boundary.

She paused with a sigh. She'd told Treva she would, but that was before she cut off contact. And Desiree's life was at a crossroads. What was she supposed to do? Odds were—Lance wouldn't talk to her anyway. And if he did, he wouldn't talk long. But she had to try. If she missed this opportunity, she doubted there'd ever be another one.

Desiree walked to the main church building and pulled the outer door, relieved it was open. Her mind went back to the last time she'd walked through these doors with Lance.

"Are you really about to leave me?" Lance had taken her hand as they walked into the building. "What am I supposed to do for two weeks?"

"That's cute," Desiree said. "Between your job and everything you're involved in here at church, you're always busy."

Lance leaned over and kissed her. "Never too busy for you, though."

"And I love that," Desiree said. "But should you be kissing me in church? I feel like there's a rule against that."

"I'm taking all the kisses I can get," Lance said. "I miss you already."

"I'll be back before you know it," Desiree said. "But look what I'm taking with me." She paused, pulling a bridal magazine from her purse. "I'll be dreaming about wedding gowns on the plane."

Lance smiled. "A fall wedding. It'll be here before you know it." He kissed her again. "I still can't believe you said yes."

Desiree looked into his eyes. "I love you, Lance. You're the best thing that ever happened to me."

Lance paused, looking at her. "You sure about that? You don't always act like it."

"What do you mean?"

"Sometimes I think you're hoping you can change me," Lance said, "or at least my job."

"I just think you could do so much more," Desiree said. "You've got more potential than you realize."

"But if I'm fine where I'm at," Lance said, "would you be fine with it too?"

"Why would you be fine with that, though?" Desiree said. "I want the best for you. For *us*. One more"—she kissed him then started walking. "And you *are* the best thing that ever happened to me. You led me to Jesus. You help me understand the Bible. I mean, wow . . . I just got a Master's degree, but I knew next to nothing about the word of God. You changed that. Gave me a whole new life. . . . It's scary, though."

"Why do you always throw that in?" Lance said, walking into the sanctuary.

"Because it is," Desiree said. "The whole concept of surrendering and God being in control. I've got lifelong dreams. I don't know what He'll do with those."

"Do you want *your* dreams or the dreams He has for you?"

"That's the part that's scary," Desiree said. "Who *knows* what God's dreams are for me?"

"But His dreams and plans are better than anything we can come up with on our own," Lance said, moving into a pew.

"How do you know that, though?" Desiree said.

Lance looked at her. "I trust Him."

Those last words lingered as Desiree walked toward the elevator. Lance trusted God, and look where he ended up. She wasn't ready to hear all of that at the time, but now . . . Now she just wanted to sit and listen.

Her heart pounded as she walked into the elevator. What if there were others working upstairs? She shrugged it off. She'd simply leave if she ran into anyone. She looked at the buttons, remembering that classes were on the second floor and offices on the third. She pushed '3,' her heart pounding again.

The elevator doors opened, and she looked both ways as she walked off, deciding to go left. Looked like that's where the offices were. She passed one with the lights off—"Silas Keys"— and kept going. Further down, she saw an administrative area outside of a main office—no, two offices. She slowed her pace. No one sat at the outer desk, and one of the offices was dark. As she got closer, she saw the name on that one—"Treva Alexander."

Desiree continued, everything racing within. Lights shone in the other office, and the door was open. She paused and took a breath, then walked in.

Her heart reacted when she saw him at his desk, typing on a laptop.

Lance looked up and looked right back down, shaking his head. "I don't know what you think you're doing, but you need to leave." He continued typing.

Desiree came closer. "Lance, I need to talk to you."

"So you're hard of hearing." He picked up his phone, engaging it. "Do I need to call security?"

"Lance, stop," Desiree said. "I'm not a criminal. Why won't you talk to me?"

Lance continued with his phone. "Didn't you say something to my wife about respecting boundaries?"

"I'm in a crisis right now," Desiree said. "I literally don't know whether to get on a plane this evening or put the traveling on pause. I'm trying to figure out what God wants me to do. I need to talk to someone who knows Him, whose counsel I can trust—someone who knows *me*."

Lance looked up. "You want my counsel as to what you should do about traveling? Please consider the irony."

"I know the irony, Lance." Desiree took another step toward him. "That's the other thing. I wanted to say I'm sorry. I hate the way I handled things. I can't sleep at night, thinking about how I treated you—"

"Rae, that's your issue, not mine," Lance said. "I sleep really well. Take it up with God, a psychologist, whoever—not me. I don't need your apology. Until a reporter told me about your video, I hadn't thought about you in *years*."

"I know you've moved on, Lance." Desiree looked at him, though he wasn't looking at her. "Your life is clearly blessed. Congratulations, by the way, on everything you've accomplished—"

"I didn't accomplish anything," Lance said, looking up. "None of this came by my own strength, nor was I seeking it. I was fine in that camera shop. It just became clear that God had other plans."

"See, that's what I'm talking about," Desiree said. "How did you know that? How did you know what His plans were? I need your help to understand that for my own life."

Lance stood. "Rae, I want to be really clear right now. I am not here for you, in any type of way. I am not here to give you counsel. I am not here to talk you through any aspect of your life. I am not here to pastor you or to expound on any aspect of God, His ways, or His word." He walked toward the door. "I hate that I have to be this cold, but you made me go there. You are not welcome here. When it comes to my family, this ministry, the calling God has on my life—"

"Hey, babe." Treva walked in with her phone in hand.

Lance brought her close and kissed her. "Hey, babe. Thanks for coming."

"Oh, I wouldn't have missed it," Treva said. "And the convo was entertaining."

Desiree looked at them, confused.

"I was with my sister in the Living Water offices," Treva said. "Lance called and left the line open so I could hear. He also texted and told me to come."

"Well, it's not like anything was going on," Desiree said. "I meant it when I said I'd never try to come between you two. I just needed counsel."

Treva moved further inside, clearing the doorway. "I heard your dilemma, Desiree. I'm praying you hear the Lord clearly and follow His will."

Desiree nodded, walking out, replaying Lance's words. If she were honest, part of her wanted to hold a place still in his heart, just enough to move him to respond if she really needed him. To at least *talk*.

She took the elevator down and walked off. Now she knew. All ties were completely severed.

But not with Me.

Desiree's heart pounded, in a different way. She stopped short of the exit. Was this *God* speaking to her? She heard it deep in her heart, an assurance. *Hope.*

She continued outside and to her car.

If this is You, God, I don't know what to do. Please help me. Do I catch this flight? Or do I stay in St. Louis?

CHAPTER 72

*J*ade sat focused at her laptop Friday night, headphones on, reviewing clips she'd captured earlier in the day. First, she wanted to make sure she'd gotten good footage of the prank Alonzo played on Noah. They were filming the scene of the big party Trey threw the night Kendra came home, with extras poised to party with him. When Mariah said, "Action," random music was supposed to play. Instead, Noah's music boomed from the speakers. He was so thrown he couldn't remember his part in the scene.

Jade chuckled as she watched it again. She'd even caught Trey's reaction. *Perfect.* She imported the clips into the vlog, already thinking about how she'd edit to tell the story. Next, she previewed a clip she'd recorded with Brooke. She nodded, loving what they'd gotten, and—

She looked as her bedroom door came open.

"You're home before me tonight?" Jordyn said. "What's that about?"

Jade kept the clip playing in her headphones. "I'm working on the vlog, like I do every night."

"Usually while hanging with Trey."

"Oh, they've got a guys' night out thing tonight," Jade said.

"Who?"

"Trey, Jesse, Tommy, Reggie, and whoever else."

"Well, good," Jordyn said, coming in. "We can have a girls' night in. We haven't had a chance to talk since we've been grinding with this shoot." She sat on the bed. "So, tell me. What's the deal *now* with you and Trey? I know you're not still claiming that you're just friends."

"Jordyn, really?" Jade said. "A girls' night in? The headphones aren't an indication that I'm *yet* grinding?" She took them off with a sigh. "To your question, Trey and I are very much 'just friends'."

"Jade, you're together every evening," Jordyn said. "If you're not eating at base camp, you're cooking for him. That's more time than Jesse and I used to spend together."

"You didn't mention the Cling study," Jade said. "That's primarily why we get together. We study, talk about what we study, and pray."

"And *nothing* else?" Jordyn said. "I find that hard to believe."

"Like when you claimed that you and Jesse weren't kissing?"

"It was true," Jordyn said.

"And so is this," Jade said. "Why would I lie?"

"But why, though?" Jordyn said. "He's cute and the two of you are cute together. And you're clearly compatible. I've never seen you so comfortable and free around anybody, the way you are with him." She lay down, leaning on an elbow. "Do you think it'll become more?"

"Nope," Jade said. "Trey isn't attracted to women, which makes this one of the best and safest friendships I've ever had."

Jordyn stared at her. "I had no idea."

Jade shrugged. "It's not a secret. But I only told you so you'd stop with the 'it's inevitable that you'll be a couple' stuff."

"But you never know," Jordyn said. "Could turn out to be a situation like Marisa Herman."

"Who?"

"She goes to our church," Jordyn said. "She'll tell you she was never attracted to men in general, and still isn't. But God sent one man that she found herself drawn to and fell in love with. They're married with two kids now."

"I mean, that's great," Jade said, "but you're acting like it's not as great a story for God to send a friend. Like the friendship can't be enough."

"I'm not saying that at all," Jordyn said. "Because honestly? As someone who knows you better than anyone, I know what a miracle it is that God sent you a trusted friend."

"You didn't have to give it miracle status," Jade said.

"You know how you are," Jordyn said. "I'm saying I agree that it's huge and it's awesome. But I'm *also* thinking about the main promise in Treva's study—with God all things are possible."

"Which you want to apply to romance," Jade said. "For me, that promise is everything with respect to, again, friendship. God bringing Trey and me together as friends, and it doesn't have to be about all that other stuff—the fact that *that's* possible. Man, that's so dope to me."

Jordyn grew quiet a moment. "I wonder if I should think that way about Brooke and Jesse."

"What do you mean?"

"Earlier in the week Brooke made a point of telling me that she and Jesse are 'just friends.'" Jordyn sat up. "Then Jesse shows up to watch the scene where she gets her hair cut, and it looked like they went out together afterward." She paused. "I keep thinking there has to be more—but that's what I was thinking with you and Trey."

"I wonder why Brooke felt the need to tell you that," Jade said. "It's not like you and Jesse are together."

"But we *just* broke up," Jordyn said. "And she probably knows *how* we broke up, and that it's not something I wanted. Since we're working closely together, I guess she wanted to let me know she wasn't a threat—oh, and she and I are sort of doing the Cling study together ourselves."

"What do you mean 'sort of'?" Jade said.

"We talk about it as I do her hair," Jordyn said. "Like today we talked about a couple of the Psalms and what they tell us about God."

Jade nodded. "I'm glad you're doing that, Jordyn. I told you I think this study is exactly what you need right now." She turned more toward her. "So have you talked to Jesse at all?"

"Just two seconds that time he brought Zoe to Living Word,"

Jordyn said. "I stopped calling and texting, since he was only ignoring me. I'm just praying he forgives me."

"What if he's forgiven you," Jade said, "but he still doesn't want to get back together?"

"Do you know how tortured I would be? Knowing he bought me a ring and I messed it up—over Kelvin? I don't even want to think about it." Jordyn looked over at the laptop. "So who's your ministry moment for today?"

"Um . . . Brooke."

"Of course," Jordyn said. "What's it about?"

"She's talking about how she was always looking to God to fulfill her dreams," Jade said, "but missed the importance of walking in obedience. She also talks about a lesson she just learned about prayer."

"What's the lesson?" Jordyn said.

"That she needs to take everything to God," Jade said. "She said she assumed a certain situation couldn't work, but then she realized she hadn't prayed on it. She said you can't assume you have the answers about *anything* without going to God, which is a needed message."

"She's talking about Jesse."

"Huh?" Jade said.

"I asked if she was interested in Jesse," Jade said. "She said yes, but that it wouldn't work because of the distance and everything. So, great." She lay back down on the bed. "Now we're both praying . . . about a relationship with Jesse."

CHAPTER 73

"*H*ey, I was hoping I'd catch you here early." Mariah walked into the classroom Sunday morning.

"Hey," Tommy said. "You're by yourself? How'd you get here?"

"Good ol' Uber," Mariah said. "I won't take much of your time. I figured you might be preparing for class."

"Actually, working on the online piece." Tommy closed his laptop. "What's on your mind?"

Mariah took a seat next to him. "I think we know each other well enough that I can be straight with you."

"You know you can, Mariah."

Mariah took a moment to begin. "Seeing you here at Living Word and knowing you'd be around for the shoot—that was a nice surprise. And it felt like old times when you picked me up for the Super Bowl party and we hung out. We always had a good time together."

"Very true," Tommy said.

"And we got to chat a lot during rehearsal week," Mariah said, "and even went to dinner and again had a great time catching up."

Tommy nodded, though the main thing he remembered from that night was Jillian sitting across from them, and the evening culminating with friendship vows.

"But things seemed to break down after that," Mariah said. "And it could very well be me because once a shoot starts, I'm singularly focused. But you seemed to grow a little distant, like at that B and B party. And I wanted to talk to see if I'm imagining things." She hesitated. "I guess what I'm saying, Tommy, is I thought I felt a renewed spark between us. And if I'm wrong, I want to know. Because the first time around, the miles between us seemed insurmountable, and we didn't even try to continue the relationship. But now I'm old enough to know that if everything else clicks, especially spiritually, distance doesn't have to be the deal breaker."

Tommy nodded soberly. "I really appreciate that we can have a straight conversation, Mariah." He took his time. "Seeing you again, hanging out at the Super Bowl party . . . all the convos really did feel like old times, but even better with the God component." He took another moment. "The first thing I have to tell you is that in all honesty, I can't say I felt a spark between us. There's a connection as far as being old friends, but not a spark in terms of anything future. We didn't get to this at dinner, but after my last divorce, I came to a place where I decided to stay single."

"Indefinitely?" Mariah said.

"I'm putting more prayer on that lately," Tommy said. "But yeah, unless God says differently."

"Wow. I'm glad I asked."

"As far as feeling that I grew distant," Tommy said, "it has everything to do with timing. When you got here, Jillian and I were going through something as friends. Usually at a get-together like the Super Bowl party, she and I would be hanging. Once it got smoothed out, it was back to the norm. So, at the B and B party, I was with Jill, helping her move out." He paused. "I apologize if it felt like my attitude had changed toward you."

"No, it's making sense now," Mariah said. "Things seemed tense between you two when we saw her at dinner. Then last week you wrote about your friendship in the study." She nodded, mostly to herself. "You spoke of the college years, but you were describing the way it is now as well."

"That's true," Tommy said. "Even more so."

"Everything is clear now," Mariah said. "Thank you for being forthright, Tommy. I feel a little silly, though, thinking there was a mutual spark."

"Please let that go," Tommy said. "We will always be cool. We better be, because I get *all* the clout from knowing Mariah Pendleton, the power Hollywood director."

"Yeah, you really gassed me up in that article," Mariah said. "Even my mom was like—are you all *that?*" She chuckled.

"You are absolutely all that," Tommy said. "I was a fan before you *had* fans. So just know—" His gaze went to Jillian as she walked in. "Hey, Jill."

"Hey, good morning," Jillian said. "I can come back—"

"No, I'm headed to the production office," Mariah said, rising. "Thanks, Tommy. And Jillian, good to see you."

"You too, Mariah." Jillian took off her jacket. "Ready to finish this edit so you can upload it?"

Tommy looked at her. "First, how are you, Jill? The reminder came up on my phone this morning."

Jillian sighed as she sat down. "I woke up with a knot in my stomach, like my body's gearing up for the big emotional hit."

"I started praying," Tommy said. "That's why I scheduled the reminder." He paused. "I bet that's why David asked if he and Trevor could shadow me tomorrow. I didn't make the connection till now."

"He asked if he *and* Trevor could shadow you?" Jillian said. "That's way too much. Does he realize it's a movie set, not a concert or a theater? And they've got school work to do—"

"Jill," Tommy said, "if your body's gearing up, you know they're feeling it. They were there with their dad." He shook his head. "It's not too much. I will *find* ways to keep them engaged. I'm glad they knew what they needed and asked." He looked at her. "But what do you need? How can I help?"

"You're already doing it," Jillian said. "Prayer is everything. Thank you, Tommy." She thought a moment. "I want to get up earlier than normal tomorrow and spend extra time with the Lord. I just want to fill up. And I thought the kids and I would have a special dinner tomorrow evening, but I didn't know they were making their own plans."

"I'll make sure they're home in time for dinner," Tommy said. "Even if we're not done on set, I'll get them home."

"By now you know David well enough to know that if the shoot is still happening, he won't want to leave," Jillian said. "When he shadowed the other day, they were filming here at church. He'll love actually being on set. Just let them get the full experience."

"Then you should come eat with us during the dinner break," Tommy said, "so you won't be alone."

"I don't know," Jillian said. "I hardly ever have the place to myself. I might enjoy that alone time."

"I hear that," Tommy said. "See how you feel tomorrow. If you're cherishing that time, soak it up. If it feels like the walls are closing in, you'll know where we are."

"I like that," Jillian said. "Meanwhile"—she looked at him—"can we get to your Week 3 study and challenge? I wasn't ready."

"You think I am?" Tommy said.

"What made you go there?"

"I had a whole different lesson and challenge for Week 3," Tommy said. "I scrapped it after I spent time with the Lord yesterday morning." He opened his laptop. "I had to think about why I started this—to challenge myself. To do what I need to do to cling to God. And Enoch kept coming back to me. We had such a great discussion about him last week."

"Sophia told me. She said y'all were on Enoch for most of the class."

Tommy nodded. "And I kept thinking about Hebrews 11:6—'And without faith it is impossible to please Him . . .'—and the fact that it's a continuation of the Enoch verse right before it. Enoch walked with God and was pleasing to God—because he walked *by faith*."

"And there's that promise we all love in that verse," Jillian said. "'. . . for he who comes to God must believe that He is and that He is a rewarder of those who seek Him.'"

"Exactly," Tommy said. "I want to up my faith walk, Jill. How can I cling if I'm not clinging *in faith*? So, I started looking at everybody mentioned in Hebrews 11, all the faith stories. I've read them before, but this time I prayed as I read them, asking the Lord to teach me more about walking by faith. And He moved me to make that the focus of Week 3."

Jillian looked at him. "All I can say is wow. I already know that going deeper into this week's study will challenge me—before I even get to the actual challenge. This is inviting God to shake some stuff up."

"You already did that," Tommy said, "when you put everything on the altar."

"Putting everything on the altar and saying, 'Have your way, Lord' is one thing," Jillian said. "You took it to another level. You've got us like Peter, saying, 'Lord, command me to come to You on the water.'"

CHAPTER 74

"*W*hy are you so surprised that I'm doing the study?" Sophia sat with Joy, waiting for class to begin.

"Because we only came to hang out with the movie crew," Joy said. "I've never heard you mention the study otherwise."

"Well, we weren't even talking for about a week," Sophia said. "But remember Courtenay was here the first week? She really liked it and wanted to continue. She asked if I'd do it with her, probably just to get me in the Bible. But we've been having some good talks around it."

"You could've told me," Joy said, "or even included me."

"It's a short study," Sophia said. "And it's packed. A lot of stuff we couldn't get to. So maybe when the shoot is over, we can all do it again, and also include Faith and Hope."

Chatter in the room rose as eyes focused on the entrance.

"Guess who's here," Joy said.

Sophia looked and saw Noah walking in with Alonzo, Cinda, and Brooke. They came to the section near them, which had seats open on Joy's side.

"Hey, Joy," Noah said. "Would you mind switching?"

Joy traded with him, and Sophia gave him the eye as he sat.

"Why did you do that?" Sophia said.

"So I could sit next to you," Noah said. "You can talk to your cousin anytime." He leaned closer. "Why did you ignore me all week?"

"I don't know what you mean," Sophia said.

"If I walked into crafts services, you walked out," Noah said. "If you were on set and we had down time, you made sure you weren't anywhere near me."

"You made things weird with the kiss."

"And I said it wouldn't happen again." Noah's inflection rose, though he kept his voice low. "But now you won't even speak to me?"

"Why do you care?" Sophia said. "Judging by the stares, there are plenty of women in here alone that you can talk to."

"I didn't get out of bed early on a Sunday morning to talk to them," Noah said. "I came to talk to you."

"Except, this isn't a social gathering," Sophia said, glancing toward the front as more people came in. "It's a Bible study. Do you even know what this class is about?"

Noah took a glance around. "Not really. But Tommy's leading it, so it can't be too bad."

Sophia focused on him. "It's about intimacy. With God. You've got maybe two minutes to make your escape."

"Is that supposed to scare me?" Noah said. "I grew up in church, Sophia. None of this is new to me."

Sophia gave a light shrug. "Okay."

"Good morning and welcome, everybody." Tommy stood at the front of the class. "We're about to jump into Week 3. Are y'all ready?"

"Ready!" several voices shouted.

"We'll pray to start," Tommy said. "But real talk—I'm excited and anxious at the same time about this week. "We're gonna cling *for-real-for-real*. Amen?"

A chorus of amen's resounded in the room.

Noah leaned to Sophia. "What does 'cling' mean?"

∽

529

"By this point, I know we won't get to half of what I thought we would," Tommy said. "But I thought we'd spend most of our time on Abraham, Noah, or Moses. How are we spending all this time on Gideon? We've only got a few more minutes." He pointed. "Jesse."

"You know what's blowing my mind right now?" Jesse said, standing. "We're talking about walking by faith, and I tend to think that I have to generate all this faith to please God. No. He *helps* us build the faith. First, He tells Gideon"—he looked at his phone to read it —"'Arise, go down against the camp, for I have given it into your hands.'"

Tommy nodded with a smile. "And if that's you, you're thinking, okay, this is God. He's saying it's done. I need to believe and go do it."

"*Right,*" Jesse said. "But *then* He says, 'But if you are afraid to go down, go with Purah your servant down to the camp, and you will hear what they say; and afterward your hands will be strengthened that you may go down against the camp.'" He looked up. "*Really?* So if my faith isn't where it ought to be—if I'm a little scared—God is able to give grace like *that?* He gave *added* assurance that He's got it."

"But you've got to take it home, bruh." Reggie looked at him. "God gave one of Gideon's enemies a *dream. That's* what he heard when he went down to the camp." He smiled. "Imma let you have it."

"That's where it gets *ridiculous,* right?" Jesse said. "Gideon goes down *right when* the enemy is relating a dream about a loaf of bread tumbling into the camp and striking the tent. Then the other guy says, 'This is nothing less than the sword of Gideon . . . God has given Midian and the camp into his hand.'" He had a bewildered look. "God actually gave his enemy a dream *and* gave the interpretation—you better be afraid of Gideon!" He blew out a breath. "I'm about to pray for God to build *my* faith like that. It's crazy that He knows what we need to believe—and that He's willing to give us that."

"I didn't get to Gideon in my personal study last week," Tommy said. "This is speaking to me too. If we're clinging to God, we don't have to be giants in the faith to do what He calls us to do. We can trust that He'll give us the strength to walk by faith, from circumstance to circumstance. This is powerful."

Sophia raised her hand partway, only half sure about chiming in.

Tommy saw her. "Okay, last one. Sophie."

Sophia stood. "That part when God said to Gideon, 'your hands will be strengthened' . . . really moved me." She let a moment pass. "When my dad passed last year, it was sudden, and I felt I had no strength . . . to do anything. I was afraid. I didn't know where we would live or *how* we would live—my mom had basically never worked. And even though I was raised to know God, my relationship wasn't deep or anything. To be honest, my faith was just . . . weak." She took a breath. "But this is helping me to see all the ways God has been building my faith, including being in this study. Tomorrow will be one year since my dad went to be with Jesus, and I can say that I'm not where I was. God has strengthened me."

Sophia stared downward as applause rang out in praise to God.

"Thank you for that, Sophie," Tommy said. "You're not the only one who has felt that you had no strength. I've been there too this past year. But praise God that when we're weak, we're perfected in *His* strength." He moved across the room. "Okay, the challenge. This week is all about the truth in God's word that without faith, it is impossible to please Him. If you're here and you have not placed your faith in Christ for salvation, that's where you start. We talked about that at the beginning of class and we've identified people who can pray with you." He continued walking. "If you've placed your faith in Christ, this week is about remembering that it's a faith *walk*. We *still* need faith to please Him, day by day. So, the challenge is this—ask the Lord to show you one step of faith that you need to take this week—and take it."

Reaction sounded immediately throughout the room.

"I know, I know, I get it," Tommy said. "Just one step. Ask the Lord what *your* step of faith is. No matter what, He's got you. He'll help you take it. Keep clinging and have a good one!"

Sophia typed notes in her phone to share with Courtenay as others around her prepared to leave.

Noah looked at her. "That's the first time I've heard you talk about your dad."

Sophia finished the sentence she was typing only to look at him and shrug. "It never came up."

"Unless the schedule changes, it's mostly Alonzo and Brooke tomorrow," Noah said. "Maybe we can do something."

Sophia continued typing. "Why?"

"I just thought it would be nice, so hopefully the day won't be as hard."

"I was already planning to intern all day tomorrow," Sophia said, "for that reason."

"But you don't have to," Noah said. "You can do something else, with me."

"I appreciate the thought, but I don't think so."

"Can you at least look at me?" Noah said.

Sophia sighed and looked at him.

"Why are you being like that?"

"Because I'm not going to be one of the people you pretend to like when your girlfriend's not around." Sophia's voice was a whisper. "You really should try commitment. That's what you want deep down anyway."

She got up and moved past him, looking at Joy. "Ready?"

"You have to admit," Joy said, walking out with her. "It did seem kind of special for him to come today to talk to you."

"It's part of the game," Sophia said. "I talked to Courtenay about it the other day, and she didn't think he was being real either."

"But what if he *is* being real?" Joy said. "What if he really thinks you're special?"

"What would it matter?" Sophia said. "He'll be gone soon. Special wouldn't be special for long."

Sophia unwrapped two tacos in the dining area of craft services at the dinner break Monday evening.

"I can't believe we got to shadow today." David ate a turkey club sandwich. "The fight. The fake blood. Such an epic scene."

"It was way too intense for me," Sophia said.

"Especially when the other guys jumped in," Joy said.

"Uh, Soph, and Joy, they were acting," David said.

Sophia crunched into her taco. "But I kept thinking, this really happened."

Faith cut some of her chicken sandwich and gave it to Zoe. "I was trying to picture Lance fighting like that. I couldn't see it."

"That's why the movie needs that scene," Tommy said, eating with them. "They can't just talk about how Lance used to be. They need to show it. I was excited to see that."

Trevor looked at them. "Did Uncle Lance actually break that teacher's nose?"

"*Yes*," David said. "That's why it's so epic. Uncle Lance got *hands*. He probably could've been a boxer."

"I concur," Reggie said. "Who wants to tell him he missed his calling?"

"You know what was funny?" Faith said. "How did I forget that Lance and Kendra went to high school together? It threw me when I saw Brooke in the scene, witnessing the fight."

"That's a big part of the story," Tommy said. "The fact that they went to high school together but from totally different circles."

"Like you and Mom," David said, "except it was college."

"Umm, what?" Sophia said. "Mom and Tommy weren't in totally different circles. They were best friends, so obviously in the *same* circle."

"I'm saying they were *from* different circles," David said. "Weren't you, Tommy?"

"Yeah, I'd say that's fair," Tommy said. "By the way, have you guys checked on your mom?"

"I guess we've kind of been busy," David said. "But she checked on us a couple times."

"You should ask how she's doing," Tommy said.

"I'll send her a text right now," Sophia said, typing.

David looked at Tommy. "Have *you* checked on her?"

"David, you just took it from zero to sixty," Reggie said. "And I'm here for it."

Tommy continued eating. "I've checked on her, yes."

"Why do I feel like there's some undercurrent happening?" Faith said.

"Can we talk about it?" David said.

"No," Sophia said, looking at her brother.

"I don't see why not," David said. "We're all family here."

Sophia looked as Noah walked in and came to their table, saying something to Tommy. Tommy got up, and they moved away to talk.

Faith looked at her cousins. "Why are you two talking in code?"

"We had a family meeting last night," Sophia said. "And David is about to say some stuff he shouldn't."

"Okay, that's deep," Reggie said.

"I just think Tommy should know he has our full support," David said. "Desperate times call for desperate measures."

"Mom would kill you," Sophia said. "And I'd tell her the minute you said it. And no more shadowing for you."

David groaned. "I didn't consider the shadowing part."

"Why are these desperate times, David?" Faith said.

David leaned in. "Pastor Keys asked Mom out on an official dinner date."

"Ohh," Joy said. "And he said he doesn't want to be single for long."

"See," David said. "I didn't even know that part."

"Okay, back up," Faith said. "What was the family meeting about specifically?"

"So, when Courtenay was here," Sophia said, "David and I told her about Pastor Keys and Mom semi-dating or whatever. She had the same reaction we had, but she wasn't sure we should say anything." She looked to make sure Tommy was still preoccupied. He and Noah had taken a seat at another table. "Yesterday I called her after church to tell her the cling challenge—ask the Lord what step of faith you should take. She called back that evening and said we needed to have a family meeting."

"Which was perfect," David said, "because Mom had already said she wanted to hear what was on our minds."

"This is wild," Reggie said. "So what happened at the meeting?"

"Courtenay started it off," Sophia said. "She talked about the night she stayed with Faith. That was her first time being around Tommy for an extended time. She said y'all were swapping college stories."

"Yeah, we were up late that night," Reggie said. "Courtenay was asking Tommy about his college days with Aunt Jillian. And you know how Tommy tells stories. It was hilarious."

Sophia continued. "Courtenay told Mom she could see how they became best friends. Then she said, 'Mom, you and Dad were perfect for one another. And in this season, I think you and Tommy are too.'"

"Whoa," Reggie said.

"Right," Sophia said. "Courtenay said that was her step of faith, that she felt she had to tell Mom that."

"At which point," David said, "since Mom is big on essays, I proceeded to read an encomium I had written for the occasion."

"You actually wrote something?" Faith said.

"Desperate times," David said.

"I have to say it was well done," Sophia said. "All the things he appreciated about Tommy, with a thesis and supporting statements."

"Come on, seriously?" Faith looked at Reggie.

"You all have no idea," Reggie said. "Faith and I *been* on this train. But after all of that, I'm sure your mom told you that Tommy is super single."

David sighed. "A conundrum for sure."

"That's where my step of faith comes in," Sophia said.

Everyone looked at her.

"I'm back," Tommy said, rejoining them at the table. "What did I miss?"

CHAPTER 75

March

"I can't get over this purple wedding dress." Brooke stared down at it from atop a riser. "It's so gorgeous."

"Roxie did an amazing job." Cinda tended to the hem. "Just a couple little adjustments."

"I can't believe she remade the actual dress." Brooke snapped a picture in the mirror to put in the group text. "The feel and flow of it. The richness of the purple satin with the chiffon. The way the beading sparkles on the bodice. It looked stunning in the video, but the video couldn't fully capture it."

Faith walked into wardrobe, walkie-talkie in hand. "Just got an unofficial report from Mom. The house is filled with crew members plus the guest extras that are arriving. It's a little too chilly for the extras to wait in the backyard, but thank God the sun is shining. And they're almost done with the set in the back. She said it's beautiful."

"I'm almost done with Brooke," Cinda said, crouching down. "And while she's in hair and makeup, I'll be working on Zee and then Noah. We're looking good as far as time."

"What about the maid of honor and flower girl?" Faith said.

536

"They're getting ready next door," Cinda said. "They'll be done before Brooke."

"Okay, I'll send an update," Faith said. "And Brooke, that color is gorgeous on you."

"Thank you so much, Faith," Brooke said, smiling.

Brooke checked her notifications. Robin replied with a dozen heart emojis. Jesse replied to Brooke personally.

You look amazing.

Brooke could feel herself blush. She replied—**You're kind, especially since I haven't been to hair and makeup.**

Jesse's reply came in seconds. **Even better. Raw beauty.**

Brooke took a steadying breath. Since the evening she and Jesse prayed together, she'd only seen him once, at church on Sunday, and all of their interaction had been within a group of people. There hadn't been much texting either. She wanted to hear clearly from God without the beat of her heart weighing in . . . like now.

She felt her phone vibrate and looked at it again.

I got invited to your wedding. Leaving work early so I can go.

"Looking good." Cinda backed up and checked her on all sides, making more adjustments. "Okay, today you'll go to makeup first then hair."

Normally she did the opposite. But she went to Amber first, the one who did her makeup. And when she got to Jordyn, she got a reaction.

"Oh, wow," Jordyn said as she walked in. "Who is *that?*"

"Right?" Brooke checked herself in the mirror again. "I'm unrecognizable."

"You're always beautiful," Jordyn said. "But I see why it took you so long with Amber. That was sheer artistry happening. Such an exquisite look for the wedding."

"It's an amazing team here," Brooke said, "you included." She took a seat in the chair. "I know we don't have much time. Who are we talking about in Hebrews 11 today?"

"I actually got off on a tangent last night," Jordyn said, putting a satin scarf on Brooke's head. "Since we're talking about people who had all this faith, I automatically thought they must have lived perfect lives. But I saw that that's not the case at all."

"Ooh, this is good," Brooke said. "Who did you look at?"

"We spent the last couple of days looking at Abraham's faith—how he left his family and country when God called him and even offered up his son when he was tested." Jordyn got the royal purple head wrap from the rack. "But I had no idea that he had a whole *other* son, Ishmael, because they got ahead of God."

"Girl, yes," Brooke said. "God had promised a son and they waited a while, then Sarah was like, 'Just get with my maid. That's how we can have this child.'"

"It was so interesting to me that they didn't have the faith at first to believe God could give them a son *through Sarah*, because of her age." Jordyn began to wrap the fabric around Brooke's head. "That encouraged me, to know you can get it wrong and be way outside of God's will, and He'll be gracious to set you on the right path again."

"Wow," Brooke said. "I need to meditate on that. Were you in class when I shared about living with my boyfriend in LA?"

"No, but I saw your ministry moment," Jordyn said, "when you said God was teaching you about walking in obedience."

"Yeah, that's what I was mainly referring to," Brooke said. "What you just said made me think about that. He really can set us on the right path. When I get back, I'll have a whole new living arrangement. That's a praise right there."

"But I was also thinking," Jordyn said, "sometimes you have to deal with the consequences. The notes in my study Bible said that Ishmael's descendants were some of Israel's greatest enemies." She continued working with the head wrap. "When we move outside of His will, God is gracious and forgives. But consequences are real."

"Okay, I was on a high with that first part," Brooke said, "then I took a hard fall."

"Sorry," Jordyn said. "That's kind of where I'm at, swinging between being thankful for God's grace and kicking myself for the stupid stuff."

"But you know what's also encouraging?" Brooke said. "Knowing

Abraham and others lived imperfect lives, you can read Hebrews 11 with a new perspective. They were remembered for their acts of faith, not the other stuff." She paused. "I really need to pray about this week's challenge and the step of faith."

"But you basically did the challenge before it was a challenge," Jordyn said. "You took the step of faith of ending your living arrangement, which I'm sure wasn't easy, especially from a financial perspective."

"Yeah, but my boyfriend broke up with me," Brooke said, "so I didn't have to do anything. I don't think that counts for a step of faith." She chuckled. "Are you praying about what to do for yours?"

"I actually had some prayer time with my spiritual mom, Jillian," Jordyn said. "And I decided . . ." She hesitated. "Can I ask you a question first?"

"Of course," Brooke said.

"You addressed the elephant in the room last week, which I really appreciated," Jordyn said. "I'm wondering if there's a different elephant this week. Like I said, I saw your ministry moment. Did something change between you and Jesse?"

"Somewhat," Brooke said. "We're not dating, but we prayed about whether we should, whether it could work." She glanced up at Jordyn. "It was unexpected. I had even told Jesse that I was rooting for the two of you. I hope you don't think I was being disingenuous last week."

"I actually don't," Jordyn said. "But I'm glad I asked because it confirms the step of faith I need to take." She took a breath. "I've been clinging to Jesse more than I've been clinging to God. It's just been hard to let go, but I know that's what I need to do. That's my step of faith." She gave a nod. "Letting go."

Brooke stared out of the backseat car window as they approached Lance's house. The street had been blocked off, with a traffic attendant at the entrance, and trucks and storage trailers lined the road. As they drew closer, she could see a few people dressed in wedding attire in front of the house, along with several crew members.

From the passenger seat, Faith had been trading messages on the walkie-talkie. She turned to Brooke. "You're gonna go upstairs until they're ready for you. We've got food and drink up there, and your glam team will be there for last minute prepping."

"Got it," Brooke said.

A crew member opened Brooke's door, and she got out, taken aback by the stares until she remembered she was dressed as a bride. The crew member escorted her toward the house then got a signal to wait as a few guys toted lumber and other materials out of the house.

"So that's how they do you, huh? Leave a beautiful bride stranded on the sidewalk. Where's your entourage?"

Brooke smiled as she turned, hugging Jesse, but carefully so she didn't mess anything up.

"I thought you'd already be inside," she said.

"I wanted to leave work earlier," Jesse said, "but some things came up that I needed to handle." He took a step back, eyeing her. "I'm not even a fan of purple, but that's a good look. I'll say it again—you look amazing."

"Thank you, Jesse," Brooke said. "But it's my glam team—they're amazing." She looked at him. "You don't look bad yourself. Nice 'fit with the slacks and sports jacket."

"I try every once in a while," Jesse said. "So shouldn't you be pulling up in a limo and getting out with your wedding party? I know how it's supposed to go. I've seen the video."

"Ah yes, you're up on it," Brooke said. "We shoot that scene tomorrow. The wedding ceremony itself commands all the focus today."

"Hey, Jess," Faith said, walking up.

"Faith, any way I can get into the ceremony?" Jesse said. "They said they've got enough people back there."

"I'll take you back there," Faith said.

"Just like that?" Jesse said.

Brooke chuckled. "Faith fills twenty roles with this production company, including personal assistant to Alonzo and Cinda. She can do what she wants."

"Not at all," Faith said. "But it's not hard to get Jesse into the ceremony." She looked at him. "You ready?"

Jesse raised his phone. "Do you have time to take a pic of me and Brooke?"

"A quick one," Faith said, taking the phone.

Brooke moved beside Jesse, their arms sliding around the other. Faith took a few shots and gave him back his phone.

The crew member with Brooke motioned to her. "We can go now."

The group of them moved toward the house.

Jesse looked at Brooke. "This might be the first time I've ever asked a bride what she's doing after her wedding ceremony."

"Might be?" Brooke said.

"Can I comment?" Faith said.

"Ha," Jesse said. "No."

They moved inside the house and into a swell of people moving in a dozen directions. A different crew member halted them.

Jesse moved closer to Brooke. "One, I'm praying for you. Two, you may not have time, but yeah, it would be nice to hang out later."

"Agreed," Brooke said, looking at him. "And it would be nice if you'd send me a copy of that pic."

"I don't know," Jesse said. "We're still waiting to see how God answers, so you might not want it 'cause . . . we look cute."

The crew member prompted Brooke forward. She looked back at Jesse. "Send it."

CHAPTER 76

$\mathcal{L}$ ance stood in the back, behind the rows of white chairs filled
with extras, many of whom had attended his and Kendra's
wedding. He could see everything from here—Brooke just
walked up the aisle to meet Alonzo under the trellis—including the
cameras, rigs, boom mics, and lights. He needed this wide perspective
to remind himself that this was only a production. Until today, he'd
been able to avoid the shoot and the emotional toil that came with it.
But since this morning, he'd been fighting to stay one step ahead.

It started with the landscapers showing up early to transform the
backyard, just as they'd done on the morning of the wedding. And
that had been the mood all day, crews converging on the house,
making changes that took him back. Seemed they hadn't missed a
detail, which meant the entire setting was a carbon copy of their
wedding day. Which meant he couldn't help but recall all the
thoughts, hopes, and emotions that went with that day.

A gasp sounded as instructed as Brooke slumped over suddenly
and Alonzo caught her, carrying her to the front row. Cyd and Cedric
switched seats to make room, as they'd done on that day. And Lance
closed his eyes, remembering the panic and fear wrapped in the
moment. He'd prayed for God to strengthen Kendra for their wedding

day, and it had looked as if they wouldn't even make it to the vows. It was a knock against the hope he'd had, hope that Kendra would defy the odds and they'd live a long life together. If she couldn't make it through the ceremony, could that mean . . . *No.* The Bible spoke of hope against hope. He would believe for her. He would hope for her. For *them.* And he did that until . . .

Emotion pressed its way and Lance took a breath, ready to leave. He didn't know why he'd been around all day anyway. Treva and his mom had told him they'd handle everything, knowing it would be difficult for him. Still, it was a lot and he hadn't wanted to leave it all on them. But the bulk of the work was done now, except for the actual filming, so it was a good time to—

"There is no me without you . . ."

Lance's breath caught at the sound of his vows.

"You're a gift from God that I will treasure all of our days," Alonzo continued, his voice thick with emotion. "I can't love you with my love because it's not enough. I promise to love you with the love God gives me for you . . . and He tells me it's endless. I promise to seek Him for your every need, to trust Him with every one of our days, and to believe that His goodness and lovingkindness will follow us all the days of our lives."

Alonzo paused where Lance had paused, because the commotion had caused him to forget the rest of the vows he'd prepared. From there, he'd simply said what was on his heart.

"For better, for worse, for richer, for poorer, in sickness, and in health? Girl, I would lay down my life for you. I will cherish you, protect you, pray for you . . ."

Lance looked as Tommy rose from his seat. Near the back, he wasn't in the shot, so he moved down the row, up the aisle, and into the house.

Lance followed, dodging equipment and crew people inside. He caught sight of Tommy walking toward the front door.

"Tommy," Lance called. "You leaving? I was about to go too. Maybe we could—"

The door opened and Tommy left out.

Lance moved to the door and walked out after him. "Tommy!"

"I have to go, man," Tommy said, barely audible as he kept moving.

"Tommy, come on, man," Lance said. "What's going on? Stop and talk to me."

Tommy slowed his pace but continued toward his SUV near the end of the street. Lance caught up to him seconds later.

"We can talk about it later, Lance." Tommy kept walking. "I just need to go somewhere alone."

"I'm going with you," Lance said.

"Because you don't know what 'alone' means?"

"Because I feel like I should go."

They walked the last few yards in silence. Tommy clicked his remote, unlocking the driver side.

Lance stood by the passenger door and heard the second click. They both got in.

Tommy started the car, shifted into gear, then paused with his hand on the gear shift, as if unable to go further.

"Put it back in Park," Lance said. "Tell me what's going on."

Tommy shifted back and stared out of the front window. After several seconds he looked at Lance, fresh tears in his eyes. "How did you do it?"

"Do what?"

"I was there when you married Kendra," Tommy said. "I was there as we prayed for healing and you were *believing* for healing." He back-handed the tears as more came. "I saw how much you loved her and how broken you were when she was gone. How did you come *back* from that? How did you get to where you could give your whole heart to someone again?"

"You know it wasn't easy, Tommy," Lance said. "I really did believe God would heal Kendra. I was broken, like you said. Hurting. *Angry.* I felt God had let me down." He focused on him. "And just now in that ceremony I felt it all again. I was about to leave because this entire day has been hard. The pain didn't magically disappear; it just ebbs and flows."

"But you met Treva, fell in love, and went all in *again*," Tommy said. "Which means you did that twice, given what happened with Desiree. That's a risk, man. When your heart's been broken and you *know* how it feels, it's a risk to put it out there again." He stared downward. "And when you love someone to the core, and you don't know what you would do if it didn't work . . . Because if *this* didn't work, my heart would be torn to pieces." Tears streamed as he looked at Lance. "I love her, man. I love Jill so much. I heard your vows and all I could think is that's exactly how I feel about her."

"You think I don't know that, Tommy?" Lance said. "I've been praying. Mom's been praying. Treva's been praying. And that's just *this* household. We aren't the only ones."

Tommy looked at him. "Are you serious?"

"Why do you think you got pushback when you were talking about a call to singleness?" Lance said.

"But that was real," Tommy said. "I wasn't just saying that."

"And I believe God did call you to singleness for a season," Lance said, "to get your mind focused on Him, and to heal you and strengthen you. He even stirred up your teaching gift and lit a fire in you to cling to Him. Now it's time to let go of the fear." He paused. "Didn't you cover that in week two?"

Tommy gave him a look.

"You asked how I did it," Lance said. "It's not a mystery, man. Same thing you're doing—I had to cling to God. And I had to trust that the story didn't end with Kendra. God was still writing my story, and He had Treva in mind." He looked at him. "You know how you give us a hard time because we can't keep our hands off of one another? He had *that* in mind for me."

Tommy nodded soberly. "That's actually a dope point."

"I could give my whole heart and love again because I'm not loving with my love," Lance said. "I'm loving with *God's* love. And His perfect love casts out fear. Yeah, it *was* a risk. Treva had her own life with her kids all the way on the east coast. She tried to distance herself from me twice. I had to step out in faith—which, by the way, is what you're covering this week, right?"

Tommy sighed. "And I covered fear and faith because I knew I needed it."

"But let me tell you how I got the courage to take that step," Lance said. "The weekend Treva and Jill were here for the women's conference, remember they visited Living Hope?"

"I remember," Tommy said.

"Treva didn't say a word to me," Lance said. "She was determined to leave town and never see me again because she was like you—afraid to risk again. But Jill told me to give it another try, to talk to Treva. Because of her encouragement, I took the step of faith and got Treva off of that shuttle." He shifted toward Tommy. "I owe Jillian one. So I'm telling you, my brother—go get her off the shuttle before someone else does. Take the step or you'll regret it, Tommy." His brow furrowed. "And *please* tell me what risk you're taking. Jill is your best friend. And you already know she loves you as much as you love her."

Tommy nodded slightly, staring at the road again. She was the first to say it all those years ago. He'd been thinking about that day a lot lately, remembering what he felt. What he said and didn't say. What he let get away . . .

CHAPTER 77

Senior Year

Tommy walked into a mostly empty Roy Rogers, feeling tightness in his chest. He spotted Jillian right away, in their usual booth, always on time. He noticed her hair too, sandy colored ringlets flowing past her shoulders. Without her ponytail, the vibe seemed different. Or maybe it was just him. Or what they were about to do— say goodbye.

"Hey, Jilli-Jill," Tommy said, sliding into the booth.

Jillian looked at him with a slight smile. "Hey, Tommy-Tom."

Two seconds of silence felt like two hundred.

"I wasn't sure if you'd be hungry or not," Jillian said.

"Not really, since it's late afternoon," Tommy said. "I ate around lunch time."

"Me too," Jillian said.

"Feels strange not to have any papers that need editing."

"It's celebration time," Jillian said. "Classes *and* finals are over. Graduation's only days away. We made it."

Tommy looked at her. "I wouldn't have made it without you, Jill."

"You would've totally made it without me," Jillian said. "Just maybe with some different scores on your papers."

Tommy smiled. "That's the truth. And I wouldn't have landed this opportunity to work for a newspaper in St. Louis. I had to submit three writing samples, all of which you had a hand in. You helped me build my skills so that I can actually write for a living. That's *crazy*. I can't thank you enough."

"When we first started with the tutoring," Jillian said, "I thought it was for that one class we were in. I don't know how you got me to look at every paper this entire four years, especially the last year or two. You were fine on your own."

"I wanted to do cartwheels when it got to where you'd only put a few torture marks," Tommy said. "But you always have constructive feedback, so I wanted your eyes on everything I wrote." He looked at her. "I'm gonna miss that."

"I'll miss it too," Jillian said, "and this booth, and the aroma of your fried chicken."

"I should've gotten some fried chicken just because." Tommy sat back in the booth. "Know what else I'll miss? Our study sessions."

"We just had a slew of them the past two weeks," Jillian said. "I don't know how we ever got actual study time in with all the talking."

"But man, those talks . . ." Tommy nodded. "I think *that's* what I'll miss most. Therapy sessions, unplugged sessions, just being silly sessions, and for you—Relationships 101 for the Naive sessions."

"Oh, you're funny," Jillian said.

"I can't call it that?"

"I admit it's a little accurate," Jillian said, "especially the first couple of years. But it's a two-way street, buddy. The past two years, those sessions were primarily for you."

"Okay, I'll give you that," Tommy said. "Seemed like as soon as I started to actually care about relationships, *I* became the naive one. I'm out here thinking, heyyy, I'm into you, you're into me, this is about to be a 'make it last forever' type of thing."

"Leave it to you to work in a song title," Jillian said. "But true, last semester it looked like Beverly might last, at least longer than she did."

"Case in point," Tommy said. "She was the only person I was

seeing. She said I was the only person she was seeing. What she failed to add was—*on this campus.*"

"What happened with the one in your class this semester?" Jillian said. "You talked about her early on and it sounded like you were connecting. Then I didn't hear anything more about her."

"Oh, Linda," Tommy said. "When she found out we were best friends, she said the only way we'd have a chance is if I cut you back." He shrugged. "That was that."

"Sounds like Deon," Jillian said. "He did *not* like the fact that I told you everything."

"Because that meant he couldn't play you," Tommy said. "Then he tried to tell me it was none of my business if he played you."

"I don't know why he thought an ultimatum would move me," Jillian said. "He actually said 'me or Tommy.'" She shook her head.

"All the drama these four years," Tommy said, "and both of us ended up spending this last semester with no relationship."

"Just a friendship," Jillian said. "And we got to build it up even more."

Tommy nodded. "A lot more walks on South Hill."

"Oh, I'll miss those," Jillian said. "I know you're moving home this evening, but your dorm's over that way anyway. We should do one of those walks right now. It'll probably be the last time."

"Last time. I hate the sound of that."

"Yeah. I'm sure this is our last time in Roy's." Jillian took a glance around. "I was sad thinking about it on the way here."

Tommy sighed. "Why did we have to graduate on time?" He slid out. "Let's walk."

They left the Student Union, heading across campus on a warm spring day. An unfamiliar silence fell between them once again, Tommy finding that he could hardly look at Jillian. Whenever he did, his thoughts became a jumble.

He stared ahead as they walked. "So you move out of your dorm in the morning?"

"My mother will be there bright and early," Jillian said, "so I need to have everything packed and ready to go tonight."

"And you're still thinking about what you want to do as far as work?" Tommy said.

"Yup," Jillian said. "I'll get an earful from my mother. She's fond of saying I lack ambition."

"So if I said, what do you see yourself doing in five years, what would it be?"

"Married with kids."

"Wow," Tommy said. "You didn't hesitate."

Jillian walked a ways in silence. "It still grieves me, what happened sophomore year, because I've always wanted kids. I just hate that I . . ." She heaved a sigh. "I don't think I'll ever get past that." Several more seconds elapsed. "But yes, that's what I see myself doing. That's what I *want* to do. So meanwhile, my sister and her husband are expecting. I'm thinking about staying with them and helping to take care of the baby." She looked at him. "What do you see yourself doing in five years?"

"Entertainment reporter," Tommy said. "Picture me in a job where I *have* to listen to music and go to concerts." He smiled. "But also, definitely married with kids."

"That sounds about right," Jillian said, "now that you're in 'make it last forever' mode."

"Yeah." Tommy's eyes fell on her and his insides reacted. He moved his gaze back to the campus scenery.

They continued walking, slowly when they reached the bricked pathway on South Hill.

"It feels like we're about to be a world apart," Jillian said. "I know what I'll miss most." She looked over at him. "My best friend."

Tommy looked into her eyes, certain he felt a thousand things. A thousand things he didn't know what to do with. "I said I'll miss the talks the most, but that's what I was really saying. I'll miss my best friend."

Jillian turned toward him. "I don't know if I ever thanked you for the way you took care of me that day . . ." She looked away, letting a few seconds pass. "And for always being there, even protecting me when I said you didn't have to. And for making me laugh. I hardly ever heard laughter growing up." She looked into his eyes again. "I don't know what I would've done without you these four years."

Tommy brought her close and they hugged each other, something they hardly ever did. Jillian's head rested on his chest.

"I love you, Tommy." Her words, soft yet assured, sent waves through him.

He closed his eyes and spoke from the depths of his soul. "I love you too, Jill."

Tommy could feel his heart beating as they lingered there. He wanted to freeze time. That's what they needed—more time. To talk, figure things out. Didn't they need to figure this out? What *was* this? And why now, when they were about to be a world apart?

"We can try to keep in touch," Jillian said, in his arms still.

"For sure." Tommy's words were almost a whisper.

He'd never wanted to think of her as anything but his best friend. Never wanted to ruin what they had. But right now, all he wanted was to hold her forever.

Jillian's arms fell from him. "I know you have to go. I guess this is goodbye."

"Don't say it like that," Tommy said, feeling a miserable lack of everything—words, understanding, *time*. What could he do? "We'll definitely . . . keep in touch."

Jillian nodded, backing up. He watched as she turned and walked away, hands to her face as if wiping tears. He watched her until she faded from his sight.

CHAPTER 78

"So between hearing about the women and the bizarre behavior, twice we're told that Samson judged Israel for twenty years." Jade lifted the lid to the Dutch oven to see if her chicken and white beans had come to a boil. "I want to know what he was doing during *that* time."

Trey chopped romaine lettuce in his dad's kitchen. "I have never in my life wondered what Samson was doing as a judge. You be tilting everything from a different angle."

"Because I'm hearing about him through Hebrews 11," Jade said. "After reading about different people and their acts of faith, with Samson I'm like . . . ummm?" She lowered the heat to a simmer. "But who knows what he did by faith during all that time as a judge."

"Now you've got me wondering," Trey said. "I would love to see a whole book of Samson, breaking down that time. Can you imagine some boring, responsible, non-riddle-telling, no preoccupation with women years?" He put the lettuce in a salad bowl and got the shaved parmesan. "But on the faith part . . . He did believe the word that was spoken by the angel to his mother. He never cut his hair, knowing he was dedicated to God. And he knew every display of strength was from God."

"But that's where he throws me." Jade turned from the stove. "All that, and you gon' tell Delilah the *secret* to your strength? *Obviously* she was setting you up."

"We could have a whole *separate* discussion on properly stewarding your gifts." Trey chuckled a little. "But we're talking faith. The Philistines cut his hair, captured him, gouged out his eyes, then made him the entertainment at their celebration. And what did Samson do?"

"Asked God to strengthen him one more time so he could take 'em out."

"That's faith, right?" Trey added croutons and started tossing with tongs. "He brought down the house on all of them, which was also God's plan. Remember the angel said he would begin to deliver his people from the Philistines."

"This is what stands out to me from his story," Jade said. "God sent the angel to announce Samson's birth. God told the plan for what Samson would accomplish. And the Spirit of God came upon him when he displayed strength." She took the rolls from the oven. "So you know what I'm taking away from this? Given how messy I can be, I need God to be the beginning, the middle, *and* the end."

Trey nodded. "So if we could sum that up in one word . . ."

They both said it. "Cling."

"We're good to go on the food," Jade said, cutting the fire on the stove.

"You wanna pray?"

Jade took one of his hands and bowed her head. "Thank You, Lord, for this food." She paused a second. "Thank You that we can cling to You. But we need help to do that. I wondered how Samson could've been so reckless, as if I didn't live years of recklessness. Help us to cling to you, Lord. Thank You for Jesus and for saving us." She paused again. "And thank You for this friendship with Trey. Please bless the food and this friendship, in Jesus' name, amen."

"Amen," Trey said, looking at her.

"What?" Jade said.

"I didn't expect to hear that in your prayer," Trey said. "That you're thankful for our friendship."

"How could I not be?" Jade got a ladle and scooped the chicken and beans mixture into a bowl. "It's literally changing my life."

"Mine too," Trey said.

She paused, looking at him. "It makes sense that it's changing my life. I've never studied the Bible or prayed like this, plus the way you're helping me with my walls. But how is it changing your life?"

Trey served himself some of the salad. "I've never studied the Bible or prayed like this either, not with a friend. Not where we go deep with it, on all the tangents, being vulnerable about what we don't get or not ready to get, asking questions, taking everything to God in prayer. I feel the difference in my life." He paused. "But also, the friendship is helping with some of my walls too."

"Oh, *now* you're admitting you've got walls?" Jade moved to the salad. "When all the construction focus has been on this end?"

"I don't know if I realized I had them," Trey said, switching to the chicken and beans. "But again, I'm seeing the difference. I'm seeing how much I share with you, when I tend to be guarded. And not just share in terms of telling, but I share *myself* with you. I don't filter things based on what you might think or whatever. I can just be me, and I didn't know how much I needed that. I can breathe around you."

Jade thought about that a moment. "And then we remember that this isn't the real world. The shoot and the study are about to end, and we'll resume our normal lives—and your norm will take you halfway around the world."

Trey took a seat at the island with his food. "I was planning to update you on that. I exchanged a couple of emails with Pastor Fuller, the one who's over missions."

Jade joined him. "What's the update?"

"He told me about two opportunities he thought I'd be interested in," Trey said. "One would be serving mid-term in Ethiopia. The other is a long-term assignment in Uganda."

"When would you leave for those?" Jade said.

"They would both start in April." Trey started on his salad.

"Next month?"

"Everything is already lined up," Trey said. "I wanted us to pray about it this evening, as far as which assignment I should take." He tasted the chicken and beans. "You're batting a thousand. I don't even like beans for real, but these are tasty."

Jade smiled. "You like it? Really? I wasn't sure about this one. But it's tasty to me too. I guess it's a keeper."

"Definitely a keeper." Trey spooned up some more. "So you'll be getting back to your YouTube channel?"

"Yeah, neither of us has uploaded a video lately," Jade said. "We've got enough on the channel to sustain us in periods like this. But I'll be getting back to it."

"After working at this pace with the vlogs, it'll be nothing for you to edit your next hair video." Trey looked at her. "What's that called?"

"An easy high puff." Jade smiled at the way she said it. "And you got that right. Hair videos will be a breeze." She took a moment to eat more of the food. "I've got something to pray about too—the step of faith."

"I thought we already prayed about that," Trey said.

"We prayed about what the step of faith should be," Jade said. "I think something came to me, so now I need prayer on *that*."

"What is it?" Trey said, eating.

Jade sighed. "Sharing the gospel with my mother."

Trey looked at her. "Which is hard when you don't even want to talk to your mother."

"You already know," Jade said. "And the fact that I've seen her hostility toward the gospel, in the way she treated our dad."

"You were hostile too, though," Trey said. "And look what God did." He drank some water. "We should start praying regularly for your mom."

Jade nodded. "I'd love for you to go with me so she can meet you."

"You'd love for me to go with you to make it easier."

"Well, you're the missionary," Jade said. "Sharing the gospel is what you do. I wouldn't even know what to say."

"You're the one who's in relationship with her," Trey said. "It really starts with you opening up communication and showing her grace through forgiveness. But we can also talk about how to talk about the gospel."

"That works," Jade said. "Except now I need prayer to be able to show her grace. When I talk to her and she says one thing that hits me wrong, the old Jade pops up." She ate some of the Caesar salad. "But I was serious about wanting her to meet you."

"I'd love to meet your mom," Trey said. "But why do you want her to meet me?"

"After Dad died, I had guys staying the night with me at the house," Jade said. "Mom didn't care and I loved having the 'freedom' to do that." She paused, eating. "I want her to see the type of guy I'm hanging with now, and that it's not about sex. And I just . . . want her to meet my closest friend."

Trey nodded. "I told my dad about you."

"When?" Jade said. "And what did you say?"

"Earlier this week." Trey got up and went to the Dutch oven, adding more to his bowl. "He wanted to know how the movie shoot was going. After I updated him, I said, 'You should probably know who's been cooking in your kitchen.'"

"Okay, wow." Jade handed him her bowl.

Trey added more to hers and gave it back. "I told him who you were and that we were hanging out here a lot, cooking, studying together, all that." He sat back down. "Clear uptick in enthusiasm in his voice. I know he's been praying for me as far as the loneliness. And he's probably wondering if this is an answer to his prayer for God to send 'the one.'"

"He told you he's praying that?" Jade said.

"He's really supportive of where I am on this singleness journey," Trey said. "But one time when I was feeling low, he said, 'I just think it's important, son, that you don't limit God. Nothing is too hard for Him. I'm not saying marriage is the be-all, end-all, but what if that's what God has for you down the road? Would you hear His voice?'"

"Whoa," Jade said.

"Then he said he just wants God's will for me." Trey paused, savoring the food. "So he said he's praying that if it's God will, that He'd send one woman that I'd fall in love with. And if it's His will that I stay single, that He'll give me grace for that continually."

"How did you feel about that prayer?" Jade said.

"I couldn't argue with it," Trey said. "I want God's will. Anyway, when I told him about you, I'm sure he heard all kinds of stuff I didn't say." He shrugged. "I knew that would be the case, though. I guess we're thinking the same way. I wanted him to know who God *did* send —you. My closest friend—in the *non-real* world, according to you."

"You know I'm right about that," Jade said. "And the real world is coming hard and fast. Honestly, I don't know whether to make the most of your remaining time or to cut and run. It'll only get worse as April approaches."

"What'll get worse?" Trey said. "The friendship?"

"No," Jade said. "How much I'll miss you."

Trey cocked his head, looking at her. "You just be saying stuff now. With no coaxing." He ate a bite of food. "You could come with me."

"What?" Jade said. "Come with you where?"

"To Africa."

"On a missions trip? For *years*? Do you know how insane that is?"

"Okay," Trey said.

"Why'd you even say that?"

Trey shrugged. "It just crossed my mind a couple times."

"But why would it cross your mind?" Jade said. "I'm pretty sure I've said I could never be a missionary."

"More than once. That didn't stop it from crossing my mind."

"What crossed your mind when it crossed your mind?"

"I just thought it would be dope to be on the same team," Trey said, "serving in ministry, making an impact for Christ."

"Why would I leave my entire life—everything I'm doing, how I make a living—to do that?" Jade said. "That's not my calling. *At all.*"

"Okay."

"That's all you're gonna say?"

Trey ate the last of his food. "At least we'd be in the real world."

"So you think this is funny," Jade said. "I shared a vulnerable sentiment that I would miss you. And you respond with a ridiculous, unrealistic, non-solution."

"I'm not trying to be funny," Trey said. "But cool." He went to rinse his bowl. "Let's drop it."

"And for me to do something like that would make no sense at all," Jade said. "For the sake of a friendship? We can email, can't we?"

"Yup." He put the bowl in the dishwasher.

"See, there you go," Jade said. "I'll be the best pen pal ever. I'm feeling better about the distance already." She picked up her fork and put it back down. "And you know what else makes it nonsensical? The time factor. You're leaving *next month*. I can't completely change up my life in one month's time. You had everything lined up and ready. I don't. I'd have to—I don't even know what I'd have to do. A million things. A million hard, life-turned-upside-down things I don't even want to do. Because my *friend* is going? Who *does* that?" She shook her head. "No. No. And nope."

Trey opened the freezer. "Did you want some of this ice cream?"

Jade stared into her bowl. "I just feel like you wanted to mess me up with that. It has to be a *calling*, Trey."

"How did it mess you up?" Trey scooped ice cream into a bowl. "You rejected it the second I said it."

"But now my stomach hurts."

"You want some tea?"

"I want to move to a different topic."

"Okay," Trey said. "Let me show you these pictures my little sister sent me today." He got his phone from the counter. "I told you she and her mom are in Seattle now, and—"

"Trey." Jade looked at him. "How do you know if something's a calling?"

CHAPTER 79

Stephanie walked with Lindell hand in hand into the Cling class Sunday morning, eyes flitting across the landscape. They'd had precious time together going through the prior week's lesson and wanted to attend the last class. But they were also very aware that Warren might be there. She exhaled. Still early, but so far, so good.

Jillian got up the moment she saw her. Stephanie went to talk to her as Lindell went to get seats.

"First, you're glowing and looking too cute in this jersey knit top," Jillian said, hugging her. "Second, you know I'm about to get on you."

"Girl, I owe you so many updates." Stephanie guided her to the side of the room. "All that praying we did and I keep thinking, I need to tell Jill how God is answering. But I did tell you he was home and things were going well."

Jillian gave her a look. "That doesn't cut it on a basic level for us. I was like, if she can't get on the phone or send a detailed text, *at least* send a voice note. Then I didn't run into you at church last Sunday. And at the wedding shoot, there was too much going on. But at the same time, I was *really* excited that you were too busy to update me."

She smiled. "Just seeing you two walk in this morning . . . I know you can't get into it now, but ma'am, you'd better make some time."

Stephanie got a gleam in her eye. "I have to tell you this part right now." She pulled her further aside and leaned close. "Jill." She blank-stared her. "How am I having *the* best sex *of my life*—at eight months pregnant? Girl, every night since he got back. Is this exceeding abundant or *what*?!"

Jillian squealed, eyes wide. "Beyond what you could ask or think!" She grabbed Stephanie and rocked with her. "Oh, Steph. We *prayed* for that for so long. Praise God!"

They remembered where they were and glanced around. Enough people and chatter filled the room that they'd largely gone unnoticed.

"What in the world happened?" Jillian said. "I mean, I know it was all God, but still!"

"I'll fill you in," Stephanie said. "But girl, God got the pastor and an elder involved."

"What?" Jillian said. "Involved how?"

"I *wish* we had time," Stephanie said. "I have to tell you about the baby's room we set up too. Maybe we can snatch a few minutes after class. But I want to hear more about how last Monday went. We had been praying about that."

"And thank you," Jillian said. "You definitely took time to see how I was doing. You know I thought the anniversary would be especially difficult. And granted, it was hard. But I didn't expect it to be so sweet."

"Wow, in what way?" Stephanie said.

"After work I had all evening to myself because the kids were at the shoot," Jillian said. "I had mostly avoided looking at photo albums the past few months. But I took out every one that evening and cried for probably two hours straight. But they weren't distraught tears. I was smiling and even laughing through tears as I strolled through the memories. I had tears of gratitude as I remembered what was happening in a particular season and how God showed His faithfulness, even tears just reflecting on how good Cecil was to me."

"Ahhh, that *is* sweet," Stephanie said, hugging her. "God is so good."

"We'd better get to our seats," Jillian said. "But we're definitely snatching time afterward."

Stephanie spotted Lindell next to Cyd and Cedric. She made her way to them, taking the seat Lindell had saved between him and Cyd.

Cyd gave her a side hug. "Girl, how many unanswered texts have I sent you?"

"Jill just gave me a hard time," Stephanie said. "But once you get the full picture, I promise—you'll understand. Oh, wait." She got herself back up, moved past Cyd, and hugged Cedric. "I always knew you were the best brother-in-law on earth, but you took it to a stratospheric level."

Cedric smiled. "So all is well, I take it?"

"Bruh." Stephanie gave him the eye as she sat back down.

"What are you two talking about?" Cyd said.

"Tell you later," Stephanie said. "Although, you already know. You just been holding out on me."

"Already know what?" Cyd said.

Stephanie leaned over to Cedric. "Does she know?"

Cedric gave a nod. "She knows."

Tommy moved to the front to get people's attention as additional people walked in, Silas among them. Stephanie watched as he went to the front row where the empty seats were and sat beside Jillian. A moment later she groaned inside when Warren and Veronica walked in. What was that bit about finding another church? She took Lindell's hand as they moved to the opposite side of the room.

Lindell leaned to her. "Babe, it's fine." He kissed her lightly. "I don't feel any kind of way."

"Must be all that warfare we've been engaged in," Stephanie said.

"Absolutely," Lindell said, kissing her again.

"This is our last week together," Tommy said, "and I can tell you that I'm not leaving the same way I came in. Anybody else feeling that?"

Hands went up throughout the room, along with several "amen's."

"The first three weeks flew by," Tommy said, "but we covered a lot of territory. In Week 1, we looked at how people did or didn't cling to

God in the midst of fear, focusing on Adam and Eve and David here in class. Our challenge was to seek God about our fears and meditate on Scripture concerning fear so we could be free of it."

Stephanie nodded. "I needed that week," she murmured.

"In Week 2," Tommy said, "we focused on knowing God intimately through His word, because we need to know Him to cling to Him. We spent a lot of time on the Enoch passage—man, I was blessed by that. And the challenge was to read a book of the Bible and take notes on what you learned about God." He paused. "All right, be honest—how many of you actually did that?"

Stephanie raised her hand along with most everyone in the room.

Tommy nodded, smiling. "Y'all are serious up in here. That's amazing. Okay, and Week 3 our focus verse was Hebrews 11:6 which says without faith it is impossible to please God. Clinging involves active faith. The goal was to look at the people mentioned in Hebrews 11 and how they acted in faith. The challenge was to ask the Lord what step of faith you could take and to take the step." He paused again. "Did anybody actually take a step of faith last week?"

Lindell's hand went up along with a good smattering of others.

"Praise God," Tommy said. "He's answering prayer and moving in this study." He walked across the front. "In addition to the class, we've got people participating online from all over, and I think the best part for me has been hearing about all the study groups that have sprung up, taking the study deeper during the week." He pointed. "Debra, go ahead."

"I had to comment on that," Debra said. "And I might be telling on myself because maybe we should've asked permission. Anyhoo, we reposted the study on the Living Word singles site and have gotten a lot of positive feedback. I just wanted to let you know another way it's being used."

"It's a blessing to hear that," Tommy said. "The attorney will call you tomorrow about the copyright violation." He chuckled and pointed to someone else. "We'll jump into the lesson after this one."

"You told us at the beginning that this was a personal study, and you hadn't expected to lead a class or anything," the woman said. "I'm just wondering if there's any way we can offer feedback to get Living Word to publish this as a study. Just from the way we run out of time each week, I know there's so much more you would add to it."

"Can I chime in, Tommy?" Cyd said.

"Go ahead, Cyd," Tommy said.

"I'm so glad you asked that," Cyd said, looking at the woman. "I already know I'd love for Living Water to publish this, and it would be great to get your feedback. If anyone else would like to see Tommy write this as a lengthier, published study—"

Clapping started around the room, prompting a chain reaction of people coming out of their seats. Stephanie stood with Lindell, smiling as Tommy's head fell. He looked up again, motioning for people to sit down.

"Amen," Cyd said when it got quiet. "I'll give you guys an email at the end of class to send your feedback."

Tommy had a confused look as he gazed out at the class. "How y'all gonna give feedback that results in *me* doing more work?" He shook his head. "Okay, I'm excited to get into this lesson." He looked to his right. "You probably noticed this cart up here," he said, walking toward it. "Deneen brought it in this morning—thank you, sis." He wheeled the cart to the middle of the room. "Many of you first met Deneen as a visitor. She's the queen of our hospitality ministry, and in the hospitality suite she always has grapes. I arranged for her to bring extra this morning." He took the cloth from the top of the cart to reveal big bowls of red and green grapes.

Stephanie leaned to Lindell. "Why did your baby just kick, as if he or she was salivating for those grapes?"

"I had so many thoughts about where to go for this last lesson," Tommy said. "But as I prayed, this one came out of nowhere. And I knew it was from the Lord." He let his gaze cross the room. "The heart of this study is intimacy with the Lord and being totally dependent upon Him. I love that God used the word 'cling' in Deuteronomy. It gives us a real picture of the intimate relationship He wants with His people. Jesus gave us a picture of that intimacy as well, in John 15:4-5. Can someone read that?"

A guy stood with his phone. "'Abide in Me, and I in you. As the branch cannot bear fruit of itself unless it abides in the vine, so neither can you unless you abide in Me. I am the vine, you are the branches; he who abides in Me and I in him, he bears much fruit, for apart from Me you can do nothing.'"

Tommy took a cluster of grapes from one of the bowls. "Jesus is the vine, as believers we're the branches"—he ran his hand along a branch—"and He says, 'Abide in Me, and I in you.'" He looked at them. "Abide is a word that means to remain, to dwell. Where you abide is where you *live*. You ain't going *nowhere*. That's what it's supposed to be like with you and Jesus, with me and Jesus. A constant flow." He paused. "What does that sound like?"

"Clinging," a few people said.

Tommy nodded. "The branch clings to the vine. It *has* to cling to be worth anything because the vine is the life source. That's why Jesus says, 'Apart from Me, you can do nothing.'—because He's life to us." He lifted a cluster of grapes. "And as the branch clings to the vine—as we abide in Him—we bear fruit." He took some grapes from the branch. "And fruit in your life is just as obvious as these grapes are."

"What does it look like in our lives, though?" a woman asked.

"I'm glad you asked," Tommy said, smiling. "We've spent the first three weeks talking about the importance of clinging to God and what it looks like and doesn't look like to cling. Today let's look at what happens when we cling. Let's look at the fruit, because Jesus says you will bear *much* fruit."

Stephanie raised her hand, and Tommy pointed at her. "Yes, Steph?"

"My baby wants to know if you can pass those bowls around as we talk about fruit."

CHAPTER 80

"*S*top looking over there."

Jordyn caught herself and shifted her gaze. "It's hard not to," she whispered to her sister.

"I thought you were supposed to be letting him go," Jade said. "Tell your eyes to get with the program."

"It'd be easier if he weren't sitting with Brooke, chatting every five seconds." Jordyn turned her attention to the guy who was talking.

"So bottom line, you're saying if you're clinging, it shouldn't be a secret," the guy was saying. "It should show in how I'm treating others. I hadn't made the connection between clinging to God and the fruit of the Spirit, but clearly one goes with the other." He glanced at the woman next to him. "Probably wouldn't work to tell my wife I'm clinging to God, but I'm not showing love, patience, or kindness around the house."

"No, sir," his wife said. "Would not work."

Chuckles sounded in the room.

A woman in Jordyn's row stood. "I love what you said, Tommy, about the fruit of thanksgiving and that verse—what was it?"

"First Thessalonians 5:18," Tommy said. "'In everything give thanks; for this is God's will for you in Christ Jesus.'"

"I used to wonder how I could give thanks in *everything*," the woman continued. "But the more I cling, the more I see God at work. So even if I'm having a trying day, I'll notice that I'm not reacting like I normally would or I'm able to see how it could've been worse, but for the grace of God. Now I'm going to actively thank God in those times."

"I'm seeing a big difference as I do that," Tommy said. "Add in some praise and you just went to another level." He started walking. "Okay, we're about to keep it moving because I want to make sure we've got enough time to talk about these last two. This next one may seem obvious because we've talked about it in every class, but I want us to recognize it as the main fruit of clinging—intimacy with God."

Jade elbowed Jordyn.

"What?" Jordyn said.

"You're looking again."

"Can't you talk to Trey and stop worrying about what I'm doing?"

Jade popped a grape into her mouth. "I can do both."

"I'll confess," Tommy said. "I've had times in my Christian walk when I've spent more time in the word or prayed more because I really wanted God's blessing on something." He sighed. "I wasn't excited about time with the Lord in itself, only about the goal I had in mind."

"Ouch," one woman said.

"But these past few weeks," Tommy said, "I'm *enjoying* my time with the Lord more. *That's* the goal, being in His presence, and I'm seeing how sweet that is." He kept moving. "Two weeks ago when we talked about knowing God, we saw that He establishes our steps and delights in our way, from Psalm 37:23. That same Psalm tells us—'Delight yourself in the LORD'." He looked out at them. "I used to shoot straight to the promise—'and He will give you the desires of your heart.' But now, that first line is everything to me. Clinging is delighting ourselves in the LORD." He paused. "Has anyone else experienced that during this study in particular?"

Several hands went up.

"Ask him how he got there," Jordyn whispered.

"You ask him," Jade said. "It's your question."

"But I don't want to ask with *them* in the room."

Jade sighed. "Tommy, can you tell us how you got to that place where you're enjoying that time?"

Tommy thought a moment. "I saw a difference when I got intentional about my time with Him. I used to grab a few minutes here or there to pray or get in the word, but always felt rushed and distracted. But when I made that *the* thing I was doing, it became something else. I started opening my Bible expecting to hear from Him, talking to Him about what I was reading, talking about my own life and how it applies." He moved closer as he talked. "Then He's showing me things and speaking into my life, and there's this back and forth. I *protect* that time now. Anybody else want to chime in on that?" He pointed. "Jesse."

"That intentional time made all the difference for me too," Jesse said. "I realized I could get up early to walk my dog because I had to, but couldn't get up to spend time with the Lord. So during the study, I started getting up even earlier to spend time in the word before work. I feel like I'm shutting out the world and just focusing on Him. That's *our* time. I even put my phone away now."

"Ouch," a few people said.

Tommy chuckled. "Y'all sound like a choir."

"Also," Jesse said. "I've been surprised by how much comes to me during that time. Answers to prayer, clarity, direction. It's like Jesus is saying, 'Aye, it's about to be My time with Jesse. I got something for him.'"

Tommy smiled. "That's that sweetness I'm talking about."

"I wonder if he got clarity about him and Brooke," Jordyn said.

Jade looked at her. "What did *you* get clarity about?"

"Jesse didn't know it," Tommy said, "but he just touched on the last fruit of clinging that we're covering this morning—answered prayer. Let's look at John 15:7." He picked up his iPad from the podium. "Jesus said, 'If you abide in Me, and My words abide in you, ask whatever you wish, and it will be done for you.'" He looked up. "That's an amazing promise, right? Almost seems too good to be true."

"I feel like I've got more *unanswered* prayers than answered ones," a woman said.

"I hear that," Tommy said. "Let's break down this promise." He looked at the screen. "Jesus said, 'If you abide in Me . . .' That's what this entire study is about. Clinging. Holding tight to Him, and all that that means. A life of surrender and trust. A walk of obedience." He paused. "Not a perfect walk. We talked about that. We're saved but we have a sin nature. We will sin in something we say, do, or even think. And there are sins of omission. But here's more fruit that comes from clinging—being sensitive to the conviction of the Spirit and being quick to repent. Amen?"

"Amen" sounded around the room.

"So we're abiding in Jesus," Tommy said. "Walking daily with Him. Clinging to our life source. But there's more to this promise. What's the second part?"

"'And My words abide in you,'" a few people said.

Tommy blew out a breath. "It just got real. Jesus isn't giving us a blank check, like the book of James says, so we can consume it on our lusts. It's gonna always be about *His* glory. We need *His* words abiding in us so we can ask the right things—so we can ask according to His will." He walked a little. "We need to be clinging to Him *and* clinging to His word. This is a condition to the promise." He pointed. "Sophie."

"You put that bonus part in the study about memorizing Scripture," Sophia said, "and my sister made that part of our challenge. My mom had us memorizing Scripture for years, and I didn't really internalize it. But now it feels like the words are coming alive. And it rocked me when you read that verse, that these are Jesus' words abiding in me."

"Absolutely," Tommy said. "Thanks for sharing that, Soph. You *know* that will bear much fruit." He acknowledged another hand. "Noah."

Almost every eye in the room looked his way.

Noah took a moment. "This is only my second class. Last week I didn't even come for the class, but something you said made me . . ."

He took a glance around. "I don't know what I'm thinking. I can't be openly saying stuff like this."

"Noah, it's up to you if you want to continue." Tommy looked out at everyone else. "And if he does, I don't want to see one phone or iPad recording it. It's our last class. Let's respect this as a confidential space where the Holy Spirit can move."

"I'm not even sure what I want to say." Noah looked down a moment. "Last week in class I heard things I've never heard. Tommy's working on set, so when I saw him, I asked some follow-up questions. The conversation opened up a lot. And now this class . . ." He took another moment. "So, I pray for God to bless my music career and the acting and other things. But to be honest, I don't even think about God until I want Him to bless me. Hearing words like 'cling' and 'abide' . . . I feel like God is *calling* me. Like, personally. And I'm trying to . . . I don't know . . . ." He sighed. "I'm sorry, I know this is off topic and I interrupted the lesson."

"How is it off topic?" Tommy said. "It's exactly what we're talking about. The first step to clinging and abiding is a true relationship with God through His Son."

"But I feel dumb," Noah said. "I grew up in church. I should already know all this."

Tommy looked out at everyone. "How many of us grew up in church, but weren't saved till we became adults?"

Several hands went up.

Jordyn looked at Jade. "I thought if you grew up in church, you pretty much grew up saved."

"Noah, please don't feel dumb," Stephanie said. "It's not about that. I grew up in *this* church, under excellent preaching. Heard the gospel countless times. And I wasn't saved till after I got married. I was rebellious and had a hard heart, for sure. But also, the Holy Spirit draws us at the appointed time." She smiled. "So I'm just gonna sit over here, pray, and get ready to rejoice with the angels because it looks like it's your appointed time."

"I still have a lot of questions, though," Noah said. "Can I talk to you some more afterward, Tommy?"

"You know you can," Tommy said. "And I'm sure Stephanie won't be the only one praying for you."

A lot of amen's sounded.

"Okay, I'm excited to hit this last part," Tommy said. "And let me say this for those who aren't familiar with the gospel of John . . . at this point in chapter fifteen, it's the night before Jesus goes to the cross. He's had supper with His disciples, Judas has left to betray Him, and He's talking with the eleven who remain. He's well aware of what's coming—His death, resurrection, and return to heaven. And He's got some important things to convey to them and all who would believe after them."

Heads nodded around the room.

"Let me repeat the first part of what Jesus said in 15:7—'If you abide in Me, and My words abide in you'—that's the condition." He moved closer. "This is what I want y'all to get—*that's* the path you're on. You're already on it. You have a heart to cling to God. You've been in His word, even memorizing His word. You study on your own and then you get with other people to go even deeper. My prayer is that we continue on this path, that God will give us grace to *stay* abiding and clinging, to the Lord and to His word. Let's build a whole culture of cling-ers in this church and beyond." He had a fire in his voice. "But then . . . We can't stop there, y'all. If we're doing all of that, this promise is *ours*. We've got to believe. We've got to start praying with power."

"Come on here, Tommy," Pamela said, waving a hand.

Tommy looked at his iPad screen. "Jesus said, 'ask whatever you wish, and it will be done for you.'" He looked up. "If He said it one time, it would be enough. He's God. He's the living *Word*. He ain't got to say it but once. Amen? But He put *emphasis* on it. Look how many times He said it." He walked with his iPad. "John 14:13—'Whatever you ask in My name, that will I do, so that the Father may be glorified in the Son.' John 14:14—'If you ask Me anything in My name, I will do it.'" He looked up. "Mind-blowing, right? There's more."

Pamela stood, prompting a couple of others to come to their feet.

"John 15:16—'You did not choose Me but I chose you, and

570

appointed you that you would go and bear fruit, and that your fruit would remain, so that *whatever you ask of the Father in My name He may give it to you.'"*

More people stood in the room.

"Jesus *still* wants to make sure His disciples get this. John 16:23 —'Truly, truly, I say to you, *if you ask the Father for anything in My name, He will give it to you.'"* Tommy looked at them. "Five times in one night Jesus repeats this promise—'Whatever you ask—it will be done.' So now we need to ask ourselves—who's gonna believe the promise?"

Jordyn looked as Jade stood along with Trey.

"You're abiding in Jesus," Tommy said. "His word is abiding in you. Who's going to put aside the doubt and the fear based on disappointment from the past? Who's willing to ask in faith and believe it will be done?" Emotion filled his voice. "That's your challenge this week. *Ask.* Ask *in faith* and *believe.* And if you're not quite there, I need you to say, 'I believe, Lord! Help my unbelief!'"

Jordyn stood now, uttering, "I believe, Lord. Help my unbelief."

Tommy stretched his arms in praise, looking upward as the majority of the room stood, many praising, some in tears.

"Help us to believe Your promise, Jesus." Eyes closed, Tommy's face was turned upward still. "We want to abide in You. We want to bear fruit for Your glory. Give us faith to believe and *ask,* that Your will may be done. Strip us of the fear. Help our unbelief. Strengthen our faith. Fill us with Your Spirit and give us grace to cling to You continually." He wiped tears from his eyes. "We are *Yours,* Lord. We are Yours."

CHAPTER 81

Sophia stood near the front of the room, lingering after class with many of the cast and crew who'd been there each week.

"It's not only the last class. It's our last Sunday here at Living Word." One of the production assistants ran her finger down her cheek to symbolize a tear.

"You all are making me sad," Faith said. "I was all energized and ready to conquer when class ended."

"Me too," another crew member said. "That's *why* I'm sad. I don't want this to end."

Sophia glanced toward the front of the room. Noah and Tommy sat in the front row, heads close, talking. They'd been that way for a while.

"All of this completely surpassed what we prayed for," Alonzo said. "We didn't know there'd be a Cling class and people studying the word during dinner breaks on set and what not."

"I think y'all totally targeted me in your prayers," Brooke said. "'Lord, shake up her life *completely*.'" She shook her head. "It's almost funny, getting a role in a movie based on a real-life story of a current pastor—and end up attending his church during the shoot, whole life impacted."

"Same," Mariah said. "I had no idea Lance's church would play a role in my actual life. We had that step of faith challenge last week, and I realized I was already taking steps of faith. It's been a faith move to put down the work on Sunday mornings, even into the afternoon, and be here in class and at the service. I never do that in production mode. And I haven't seen any difference as far as output."

Sophia looked again as Tommy and Noah stood, still in deep discussion.

"You even got inspired to include some things in the movie," Alonzo said, "because you were at the service."

"See, look at God," Mariah said. "He said, 'Seek first the kingdom'—"

"'And these others shall be added,'" Alonzo said with her, smiling. He took Cinda's hand. "And speaking of service . . ."

"It's about that time," Faith said, heading out with Reggie.

Joy looked at Sophia. "Are you going to youth church today?"

"I think I'm going to the service here," Sophia said. "What about you?"

"I want to go to youth church," Joy said, "but I'm still actively avoiding Lucas. I was hoping you were going."

"Just stay here," Sophia said. "Uncle Lance is in a series—"

"You waiting for me?"

Sophia's insides dipped as Noah spoke from behind. Only a handful of people remained in the class so she didn't have much of an excuse. "Sort of," she said, turning. "I just wanted to say something."

"I'm heading over," Joy said. "Text me if you decide to come."

"I will," Sophia said.

"So you're talking to me today?" Noah looked up as Tommy passed. "Thank you, again, Tommy."

"Looking forward to talking some more this week," Tommy said.

Noah turned his gaze back to Sophia, waiting.

"I wasn't ever *not* talking to you," Sophia said.

"Really?" Noah said. "Not the vibe I got at all. But what did you want to say?"

"I was listening to what you were saying today," Sophia said, "and I felt bad. You asked me questions during class last week, and I blew you off because I didn't take you seriously." She looked as others left the class. "I just wanted to apologize for that."

"No need," Noah said. "I wouldn't have taken me seriously either. I wasn't even serious about being in the class at first. I just wanted to see you."

"But now," Sophia said, "looks like you got some answers."

"Yeah." Noah let out a sigh. "A lot happening in my head and heart right now."

Sophia nodded. "Well. I just wanted to tell you that," she said, turning to leave.

"Hey," Noah said. "When did you commit your life to Jesus?"

Sophia turned again, thinking. "If you had asked when did I become a Christian, I would've told you I prayed when I was young to 'receive Jesus into my heart,' at church and with my mom and dad. But you asked a harder question." She sighed. "I think that's where I am right now, these past couple of weeks."

"You're saying you're just now making that commitment?" Noah said. "You're the super church girl in my eyes."

"Like I said in class," Sophia said, "outer life doesn't always match inner life."

"So why now?" Noah said.

Sophia thought again. "I think a combination of things is making me think about life and where I'm at. I'm about to graduate. This internship has me contemplating what's next." She took a moment. "And I know you won't get this, but when you kissed me, it really made me think about where I'm at. It wasn't like my first kiss. Kissing you scared me. I could see myself going where Faith and Courtenay went, places they warned me about. Then I felt stupid when you said you had a girlfriend, and I knew it was nothing to you. That's why I said not to kiss me again." She spoke as her thoughts came, looking into his eyes. "But it was based on *you* and where you were. And it

574

bothered me that I didn't have my own convictions. So I talked to my sister, and for the first time I heard what she was saying about needing to walk out a real, living faith." She paused. "And that was *way* oversharing. Sorry."

Noah looked away a moment then went and sat down, staring downward.

Sophia looked at him, waiting.

"I'm glad you pushed back on that kiss and stopped talking to me." He looked at her now. "I wouldn't have come to class otherwise. And also . . . I probably would've tried to get you in bed. And whether you did or didn't, I would hate myself right now."

"At least you're admitting it was a game," Sophia said.

"Not like you think," Noah said. "I mean, I don't know. That's just been my life. That's where I try to take things." He looked at her. "But I was serious when I said you were special, even more so now."

Sophia shook her head. "And you actually tried *that* again."

"The problem is . . . I didn't know what to do with that," Noah said. "I still don't. But I want to know."

"Okay, well, I don't know how we got on all of that," Sophia said. "I thought we were talking about faith, but I'm headed to service." She moved toward the door.

"Sophia." Noah got up and walked toward her. "I prayed with Tommy and committed my life to Jesus." He blew out a breath. "I'm not even sure what it all means. I just knew I had to. For the first time I saw myself as a sinner in need of salvation." He took another breath. "Last week you said, 'You should really try commitment.' You said that's what I wanted deep down anyway. And you were right. I just didn't know it was Jesus I needed to be committed to, until today."

Sophia stared at him. "Wow. That's big."

"I'm sure it's even bigger than I realize," Noah said. "It could affect so many things. I haven't wrapped my mind around it yet."

"Your mom's gonna flip."

"Ohhh, she really is," Noah said. "I need to text her."

"Text her?" Sophia said. "That's a FaceTime."

"True, true," Noah said.

Sophia was still taking it in. "You really did that?"

Noah nodded. "I really did that." He started toward the door. "Well, I'm sure we're late for service."

"We could go to the balcony," Sophia said. "It's on this level."

"We?" Noah said.

"Since we're both late."

Noah smiled a little. "Let's go."

Sophia led them to the balcony entrance, where an usher told them to go on in. Only a few people had come up there, and those few were scattered. Sophia and Noah sat in a pew to themselves as a woman read announcements in the service.

"I should've said thank you," Noah said, looking at her.

"For what?" Sophia said.

"For telling me how you got to where you're committing your life to Jesus," Noah said. "That's big too. I just wish I hadn't played a negative role."

Sophia gave a faint nod, looking at the big screen, unsure what to say.

"My girlfriend and I broke up Friday night."

She glanced at him then back to the screen.

"I asked her why she never engages me about my music, only the stuff surrounding the music," Noah said. "And I told her about the Cling class and the convo I had with Tommy last week about the gospel and Jesus. She said, 'I know you're not about to believe that fairytale.'"

Sophia looked at him. "What did you say?"

"I tried to tell her what Tommy told me, and even what I knew from growing up in church," Noah said. "She said she should've known that this movie and these people would be a bad influence on me. We went back and forth, and by the end, we both knew it was over." He looked at Sophia. "And the whole time, I kept thinking it would be a completely different conversation with you."

Sophia stared at the screen again as the choir began to sing.

"Can we talk after church?" Noah said.

"About what?"

576

"Me and you."

Her insides dipped again. "There's nothing to talk about, for a million reasons."

"Will it hurt you to listen?"

Sophia blew out a breath, letting several seconds pass. "I guess it won't hurt."

~

After service, Sophia and Noah took the stairs to the main level and moved through the crowd of those coming and going. He got stopped twice, taking quick selfies, and they left out, heading to base camp in the Living Water building to find a quiet spot to talk.

Sophia's phone vibrated on the way, and she saw a text from Joy. **Just left class. Headed to worship service. You coming?**

Sophia updated her and got another text seconds later.

You HAVE to stop in here w/Noah. It's his last Sunday. Ppl will go crazy.

Sophia replied—**Which is why we shouldn't.**

Joy countered—**Just for a MINUTE.**

Sophia looked at Noah. "Joy wants us to stop by the youth building, where you shot that scene. You saw how they reacted when they saw you that day. She's thinking since it's your last Sunday and all that."

Noah shrugged. "If you think it's okay."

"We'll only stay a minute," Sophia said. "They're moving into their worship service."

Sophia let Joy know they were coming, and she was waiting by the entrance as they walked in.

"Thanks for coming, Noah," Joy said. "I just thought it would be fun for people to see you one more time."

"I love this church," Noah said. "It's not a problem."

As they moved out of the entryway, word was spreading and people were coming, phones raised, flashes going off. Noah was immediately encircled as people asked for pictures.

"Yeah, this wasn't a good idea," Sophia said, looking at Joy. "People are actually coming out of the service."

"Service hasn't even started yet," Joy said. "He's filming a movie here, about our pastor. Why shouldn't people get the benefit of mixing it up with him for a second?"

"Maybe because it's pandemonium?" Sophia said.

"No, it's not," Joy said.

Noah looked back at Sophia, and she came forward.

"This isn't cool," he whispered. "I don't want to disrupt the program over here. We need to go."

Sophia took his hand and pulled him out from among them.

Noah gave a wave. "Just wanted to say a quick hello and thank you for all the love and hospitality during the shoot. See you next time."

More flashes went off as leaders in the youth building came to see what the commotion was.

"You gonna introduce me to your friend?" Lucas said, walking up to them.

"Lucas, this is Noah," Sophia said. "Noah, this is Lucas, one of our pastor's sons."

The two shook hands and greeted one another as Joy looked on, making a face.

Sophia stifled a laugh.

"You ready?" Noah said.

"Okay, that was crazier than I thought it would be," Sophia said as they left out.

"I thought it would be a fun thing to do," Noah said, "but it didn't feel right."

They walked into the Living Water building and down the main corridor, settling on a quiet seating area, taking armchairs next to one another.

Sophia looked at him. "So that guy Lucas you met? That was my first kiss."

"For real?" Noah said. "That's the random dude?"

"I didn't say it was random."

"So why'd you say our kiss wasn't like that one?" Noah said. "What was your first kiss like?"

Sophia took a moment. "I don't know. It was just . . . not scary."

He looked at her.

"I just . . . didn't think about it much afterward."

"So by 'scary,' you meant memorable."

"Anyway."

"And he wanted to meet me," Noah said, "which means he's got a thing for you."

"Which means nothing," Sophia said. "Like this talk we're about to have."

"I thought you said you'd listen," Noah said. "You're already saying it's nothing?"

"Okay, yes, I'll listen," Sophia said. "Go ahead."

"It's not like I've got some big speech prepared," Noah said. "I told you there's a lot happening in my head and heart. I've got all these thoughts and so much I need to understand about this new path I'm on. But right there in the midst of it all is you. I see *you*."

"I don't know what that means."

"Neither do I," Noah said, shifting more toward her, "except I don't want to leave at the end of this week and never talk to you again. Or never see you again. I want you in my life."

"Noah, I feel like my mom right now," Sophia said. "Just think practically with me for a minute. We're young—I'm eighteen; you're twenty. I'm in high school, about to go to college. You're an artist who travels the world." She looked confused. "Be in your life how? How does that even make sense? You'll leave St. Louis and meet the next person in the next city that you want in your life. And that's *fine*. You're just here with me in the moment, but it'll pass."

"Maybe you're right," Noah said. "It doesn't make sense to me either. But I see you, and I can't let it go."

"That's what it means to be in the moment," Sophia said. "When you leave, it'll be gone." She slipped off her jacket. "And anyway, it's complicated enough trying to handle 'simple' relationships. A whole thing just happened with Joy, Lucas, and me that was upsetting. And you think I'd be in *your* life? You just got mobbed *at church*."

"Sophia, I already know the odds," Noah said. "I know better than you do. We don't have to talk 'relationship.' I'm just saying can we try to keep in touch? If I text you, will you respond or will you ignore me?"

Sophia shrugged. "I'll respond if you text me."

Noah sighed. "That's all I wanted to hear."

Sophia looked at him. "It's hard to believe you really care whether I'd text back, though. I'm still trying to figure out what angle you're playing."

"I know," Noah said. "And it's understandable. I just have to show you."

"And even if you're serious," Sophia said. "I'll remind you again— we're young. And fickle. So I won't feel a way if you stop texting two weeks from now."

"While you're coming hard with the pessimism and cynicism," Noah said, "I'm wondering what it might be like if we're both clinging and abiding."

"It would still be aggressively irrational."

Noah looked at her. "I just want to know if I'm wrong in thinking that we both like each other and want to know each other better."

Sophia took her time responding, first with a heavy sigh. "No, you're not wrong."

"Okay," Noah said.

"Okay, what?"

"I think imma take up a cling challenge."

CHAPTER 82

"Is this what it's like the last week on set?" Brooke looked at Alonzo as the crew set up the lighting for the next shot. "Feeling sad and not wanting it to end?"

"Not always," Alonzo said. "There've been times I couldn't wait for a shoot to wrap. But I love that you're feeling that about this one. I feel that too."

"Uh, excuse me." Mariah looked over at them. "This is not the final week for either of you. So don't get us all depressed with the sad energy. Plus I need you fresh for Florida next week."

"Oh, I'll be good for Florida," Brooke said. "But it *is* the final week for the St. Louis shoot. And God has done so much in a short period of time here." She looked to her left. "Miss Pam and Trey, are you going to the Florida shoot?"

"I don't think so," Pamela said. "But the prison scene is of course meaningful to me, since it's the only time I got to see Kendra."

"That was such a pivotal time," Trey said. "Kendra had finished chemo, was cancer free, and felt good enough to ride down and visit you, Momma Pam. I remember thinking, this could be the miracle we're praying for; she just might stay cancer free." He looked at

Brooke. "I'm not going, but I love that you'll get authentic looks from shooting the prison and beach scenes down there."

"The beach scene gets me every time," Alonzo said. "I mean, think about it. It's weeks after the wedding. They're on the road after visiting Momma Pam, and Lance surprises Kendra with this impromptu beach stop, which is basically the honeymoon they couldn't have. They finally get this window of time when her body's not being ravaged by cancer, chemo, or radiation, and they can enjoy one another." He blew out a breath, shaking his head. "Yeah, Trey, everyone who watches this scene will be hoping they can stay right there in that place."

"I'm thinking there will be no vlog footage today," Jade said. "Just letting y'all know. That sad energy Mariah mentioned." She held the camera in her lap. "I'll tell you what, though. Everyone who watches should *also* be thinking about making the most of whatever time they have. Lance *did* that."

"Jade, that's what I'm taking away from this," Brooke said. "Like the scene we're shooting tomorrow when Lance and Kendra went on the photography outing in Forest Park. She took up a whole new hobby and they enjoyed it together. If I don't apply *something* from this to my own life, I'll be through with myself." She sighed. "But now Alonzo's got me thinking about that beach scene. I'm not ready. It's their happiest time but I'll be bawling."

"Alonzo, please talk to us about the wrap party." Mariah looked up from going over a portion of the script in her director's chair. "I'm determined to keep the mood at least one level above gloom."

"Faith is organizing it," Alonzo said. "It's Saturday night, as you all know. Living Water was already planning to transform some of its space into a venue for big events, so we're helping them get there. Contractors got started last week." He nodded. "Expect some good food and good music. Let's be clear—the emphasis is on party."

"Woohoo," Mariah said. "That's what I'm talking about."

"Could be a special appearance," Alonzo said. "Maybe a surprise or two."

"Ooh, is my little brother performing?" Brooke said. "That would be lit."

"Surprises are meant to be just that," Alonzo said.

"Can I vlog the wrap party?" Jade said. "That would be the ultimate finale."

"You definitely can," Alonzo said. "But I thought the premiere would be the ultimate vlog finale."

"Noooooo," Jade said, head thrown back as she groaned the 'no' for several seconds.

"Umm, what did I miss?" Brooke said.

"Jade, I thought you would be hype about vlogging the premiere," Alonzo said.

Trey looked at Jade. "Can I tell?"

"Go ahead," Jade said, her head still back on the chair.

"Jade's praying about whether to do a mid-term missions trip to Africa," Trey said.

"Oh, my goodness," Brooke said. "How long is mid-term?"

"Two years," Trey said.

Alonzo let out a low whistle. "Wow, Jade. That's . . . wow."

"See that, Trey?" Jade lifted her head. "Thank you, Alonzo, for confirming how insane this is."

"It's not insane," Alonzo said. "Just huge. I would've never guessed that you'd consider something like that."

"Didn't I just say God is doing so much during this shoot?" Brooke said. "That's amazing, Jade. To even be willing to pray about it. I'll pray as well."

"Thanks," Jade said. "I think." She sighed. "The team leaves next month, if you can believe that. I've been reading up on it, and even if I felt the urge to go—*huge if*—there's the funding and a bunch of other stuff that stands in the way." She looked overwhelmed even now. "Anyway, I keep thinking of things I'd miss out on, and I totally forgot about this one. I wouldn't even *be* at the premiere."

"But you'd be serving our Lord with brother Trey," Pamela said. "I think that's so beautiful. I've been praying hard on it since you shared it with me, Jade."

"And if God says yes," Alonzo said, "Cinda and I got you on the funding you need."

"Don't tell me thaaaat," Jade said, throwing her head back again.

"Jade," Pamela said, "I'm also praying that if this is the Lord's will, that He'll give you a heart for it. He's so faithful to do that."

"Thank you, Miss Pam." Jade sighed. "I'm about to have *all* the fun at this wrap party."

Brooke checked her phone as they continued talking. Her heart lurched a little at a text from Jesse.

Hey, if you get time tonight, let's talk.

She stared at his words. Sounded like he'd gotten an answer.

Brooke sat across from Jesse in a dimly lit Italian restaurant, a candle flickering between them. With tables well-spaced, they'd had an intimate evening of great conversation and laughter. But she couldn't ignore that she'd felt a little on edge.

"So, Jesse," Brooke said, "we've talked a lot about your life and mine tonight, deeper than we've ever gone. But something tells me that's not what you had in mind when you said 'let's talk.'"

"That's not entirely true," Jesse said. "We're usually around other people at church or the B and B. So I did want to just take some time and go deeper, learn more about each other." He ate more of his tiramisu. "But also, knowing you've only got a few days left, I wanted to see where we might be with that prayer we prayed. Any updates on your end?"

"On my end?" Brooke said. "I'm thinking you should go first since you called the meeting." She eyed his dessert. "Can I get another taste of that?"

Jesse slid the plate her way. "Have at it."

"I just want a little," she said, taking a forkful and sliding it back.

"All right, I'll go first," Jesse said. "So we both started out thinking it wouldn't work to pursue something between us. And we prayed, and I've even prayed about it since then. And I've been paying attention to my thoughts."

"What do you mean?" Brooke said.

"That's what I've been doing lately when I start praying about something," Jesse said. "It's a trip when I notice my thoughts shifting, like when something occurs to me that I've never considered. I start paying attention because it might be from the Lord." He ate another bite of his dessert. "So these are the thoughts that were already in my head . . . Pursuing a relationship is hard enough by itself. When you add distance, that's another level of hard."

"Facts," Brooke said, taking a sip of cappuccino. "That was in my head as well."

"Then you have to ask yourself—if it starts looking like it could work, would I be willing to move?" Jesse took a sip of espresso. "I'm in St. Louis because of my daughter. She's the most important person in my life, and it's important to me that I be an active part of *her* life. So I already know I wouldn't move anywhere as long as she's here, unless the Lord makes that *abundantly* clear."

"I love your love for your daughter," Brooke said.

"And on the flip side," Jesse said, "you moved to LA in order to pursue your dream career, and it's happening. You heard from your agent just today about a role that looks promising. You're not moving anywhere either, and nor should you. So all of that made us think— well, what's the point?"

"Exactly," Brooke said.

"I would love to tell you I got some big, definitive answer from on high," Jesse said. "But I can tell you how my thinking shifted." He pushed his plate aside. "Before, I was thinking, is this a potential relationship? Where we'll building toward something more? If not, she'll head back to LA and do her thing, and I'll do mine." He sipped more espresso. "Now I'm thinking, is this someone I would pour energy into to build a friendship? And that shift came from this guys' night out we had."

"Okay," Brooke said, surprised. "I'm all the way interested. Tell me more."

"I was with Trey, Tommy, and Reggie," Jesse said. "And it was real talk about a lot of stuff. But two big themes were singleness and friendship because Tommy had talked about his friendship with Jillian in the lesson." He paused as their server picked up his dessert plate. "I thought about how I was *never* sincere about friendship with a woman. If it wasn't leading anywhere—meaning anywhere physical— it was a waste of my time. But now I was seeing friendship differently —as a believer." He spoke with his hands. "Then Trey started talking about his friendship with Jade. And Reggie talked about how he and Faith started with a strong friendship, which I saw for myself and did *not* appreciate at the time." He chuckled a little.

"And you're thinking that's our answer—friendship?" Brooke said.

"I didn't want to put it like that," Jesse said, "because it sounds lame, like a door prize. That's why I said—is this someone I would pour *energy* into to build a friendship? Tommy was telling us the difference in his friendship with Jillian now, compared to college, when they weren't believers." He finished his espresso. "When you're coming at it from a gospel standpoint, it's *work*. Bearing burdens, repentance, forgiveness, unconditional love, praying for each other, and so much more." He paused. "And my answer was yes. I would be willing to pour my energy into building a friendship with you. And who knows what God could do in the future—there would be no pressure—but the friendship itself would be sweet."

Brooke nodded. "Fruit from clinging."

"I hadn't thought about it like that," Jesse said. "Yes. That would be some amazing fruit." He sat back. "I did a lot of talking. I want to hear your thoughts. Maybe you had something totally different."

"I've just been torn," Brooke said. "I couldn't get past the obvious obstacles. But I also wasn't feeling—oh, well, that was a really short and sweet almost something, but *bye*."

"Right," Jesse said. "It doesn't have to be an all or nothing deal."

"I think you brought the answer," Brooke said. "Friendship. But not in the way we're used to thinking about it. A Christ-centered friendship. Which means, like you said, no pressure. No expectations of something more. But the crazy texts can continue. And we can build something that glorifies Christ and bears fruit." She paused. "And we don't have to say goodbye."

Jesse looked up something on his phone. "And we don't have to delete this," he said, turning it toward her.

"Aww I love that pic." Brooke smiled. "We *do* look cute." She happy-sighed. "I feel so good about where we landed." She looked at Jesse. "Hey, we prayed about you and Jordyn too. Where are your thoughts with that?"

Jesse took a moment. "I'm not sure where I am with that."

"Hmm," Brooke said with a hint of a smile. "That sounds like a shift to me."

"You've got it on your calendar, right?" Brooke looked over at Jesse from the passenger seat. "Wrap party at Living Water Saturday night."

"I got two invitations," Jesse said. "Faith emailed one and Alonzo forwarded one. It's on the calendar." He glanced at her. "When do you fly out?"

"Sunday," Brooke said. "We've got three days in Florida, then back to LA."

"Imma miss you, for real," Jesse said, pulling up to the B and B. "I should've known you'd become my homie, since you and Robin were close."

"Just know that I'll be picking up the phone to FaceTime you at will," Brooke said.

"Matter of fact," Jesse said, "FaceTime me from Florida and show me the beach while we wait for spring up here."

"Will do," she said, opening the door. "Thanks for everything, Jesse."

"Talk to you later."

Brooke got out and walked up to the front door—which flung open before her.

"Excuse us, Brooke." Lindell had his arm around Stephanie as he ushered her out, a bag slung over his shoulder. "We're on our way to the hospital."

"Oh, no," Brooke said. "Is Stephanie okay?"

"Looks like she's going into labor early," Lindell said.

Brooke turned as they passed. "What can I do?"

Lindell looked back at her. "Please pray."

CHAPTER 83

"How is the world populated with so many people if this is the process to get them here?!" Stephanie lay on her right side, clutching Lindell's hand, feeling the most intense pain yet. "If you think I'm doing this more than *once* . . ."

"Babe, you're doing so good," Lindell said, rubbing her back. "And look how God is blessing you—you just hit thirty-seven weeks, so the baby's not premature, and your labor's progressing quickly."

"But now we're waiting for the doctor who thought it *wouldn't* progress this quickly." Stephanie propped herself up and leaned into him. "And can I *please* go to the bathroom. You're a doctor, babe. Tell her to let me go." She whispered, eyeing the nurse across the room. "I have to *go.*"

"Babe, you can't." Lindell caressed her face. "It's too risky. The baby's too close. But the doctor will be here any moment. I promise—it won't be long. You're doing so good."

"Babe, *seriously* . . ." Stephanie groaned as she tucked her head down. She breathed in and out as the intensity kicked up another notch. "Why are we waiting for the doctor? *You're* a doctor. Deliver our baby, babe!"

"Steph, she's in the building. She'll be here—"

The door swung open and the room was suddenly abuzz with people.

Dr. Ewing smiled and patted Stephanie's leg. "Baby decided to come a little early, huh?"

Stephanie loved her doctor but now was not the time to spout the obvious. *You think?*

She closed her eyes as the next contraction hit, vaguely aware of what Lindell was saying to the doctor. He'd been a blessing, though, advocating for her from the time they arrived at the hospital, knowing exactly what she needed. And he'd gotten in touch with the doctor before they left the B and B.

"How are you doing there, Momma?" Dr. Ewing's voice was soothing as she checked Stephanie and the baby.

Stephanie groaned her response, the contraction hitting on cue. "Dr. Ewing . . ." She leaned forward. "I'm ready to push this baby out."

"That's good news," the doctor said. "Because the baby's ready, too." She turned to the nurse beside her, giving instructions.

"Okay, babe, it's time," Lindell said. "We're about to see our baby."

Stephanie squeezed Lindell's hand and pressed forward when the doctor told her to push. *Help me, Lord. Thank You for watching over us.* She pushed again, groaning as sweat beaded on her forehead.

"You're doing so good, babe." Lindell craned his neck one way then the other, as he kept an eye on her and the baby. "This is the most exciting moment of my life, watching our baby come into the world."

Stephanie pushed several minutes more and heard a "Yeah!" as the baby came forth.

"It's a girl!" Dr. Ewing said.

Her cries filled the room as the doctor held her, and Stephanie stared with wonder at her baby girl, tears in her eyes.

"Babe," she said, squeezing Lindell's hand again. "This is the best moment of my life."

"I think that's the perfect middle name." Lindell sat on the bed beside Stephanie, gazing at his baby girl.

"It had been on my mind as a possibility if we had a girl." Stephanie held the sleeping baby in her bosom. "But I wasn't sure what you would say, and of course, I thought we'd have plenty of time to talk about it."

"I love that we can honor Samara in this way," Lindell said. "The way you bonded with her was nothing but God. You even led her to the Lord, Steph." He nodded. "Yes. Samara, it is."

Stephanie softly stroked the baby's hair. "What are your thoughts for the first name?"

"Well, it's funny," Lindell said. "I wanted an S name, patterned after her beautiful mother. We've got that now with 'Samara,' but I don't mind two." He looked at her. "What were you thinking?"

"I wanted a name patterned after you," Stephanie said. "We've been through a lot, babe. Over time it's been up and down, up and down. But you keep letting God build you up so you can come back stronger. I want to honor you too." She leaned closer to him. "I was thinking maybe Lindzey—L-i-n-d-z-e-y."

Lindell was quiet a moment. "I wasn't expecting that." He rubbed his daughter's back. "Lindzey Samara London. I love it, babe."

He kissed Stephanie then leaned down and kissed the baby's cheek. They sat in silence a moment, their gaze focused on their newborn.

"Ohhh, babe, we've got a problem." Stephanie looked at him. "Breakfast is supposed to be served in a few hours, and we're not there. Our guests are about to wake up to no food."

"They won't miss a beat," Lindell said. "Jillian is there."

"When did you have time to call Jill?" Stephanie said. "How did you even think to call her?"

"I can't take any credit," Lindell said. "Jillian texted when she found out you might be in labor to see if she should head over there."

"I can't believe her," Stephanie said. "But what about the kids? We've got one less room now because of the baby."

"I told her that," Lindell said. "She said she'd work it out."

A soft knock sounded on the door and Cyd peeked her head in. "Can we come in?"

Stephanie smiled. "We told you guys to just wait till tomorrow."

"We had to come see our niece," Cyd said, walking in with Cedric.

"And granddaughter," Claudia said, right behind them.

"All three of you came," Stephanie said. "Where's my Chase man? And Dad?"

"Chase is asleep at Mom and Dad's," Cyd said. "He and Dad will come see the baby tomorrow."

"Awwww," Cyd said, standing over them. "Look at that sweet, little girl."

"Look at those little fingers all curled up." Claudia beamed at the baby. "She is so precious."

"She's absolutely beautiful," Cedric said. "I'm trying to see who she looks like. I think she takes after our side, Lindell."

Lindell nodded. "You know I already said it. I sent Kelli a pic and she confirmed it too."

Cyd and Claudia looked at one another, shaking their heads.

"This little girl is all Sanders," Claudia said. "Do we have a name yet?"

"We just settled on one," Stephanie said. "Lindzey Samara London."

"Oh, I love that," Claudia said.

"Wow, Samara . . ." Cyd said. "That really hit me. And Lindell and Lindzey—I love it." She stared down at mother and daughter. "Can you believe it, Steph? You're a momma."

"Girl, I know," Stephanie said. "Scary thought, isn't it?"

"What was scary was hearing that you had gone into labor," Cedric said. "We thought something was wrong with you or the baby."

"What happened, Steph?" Cyd said.

Stephanie glanced at Lindell. "I was taking a shower and started having contractions. I thought they were the Braxton Hicks. But then my water broke, and I was like *whoa.* Is this it??" She shifted the baby a little. "You know Lindell. He notified the doctor, the hospital, packed my bag, and got us out of there. Good thing too, given how quickly the baby came."

"It's not even fair," Cyd said. "First time pregnancy and only a four-hour labor. And should I say I told you so? I wanted to have your shower a month ago."

"Clearly I thought I had time," Stephanie said. "I wanted to wait until the B and B guests were gone. I had all the plans for the final two weeks of this pregnancy."

A ringtone sounded in the room, prompting everyone to check his or her phone.

Claudia realized it was coming from her purse. "Must be Bruce. No one else would be calling at this hour." She got her phone and looked at it. "Oh, it's your Aunt Gladys. We left her a message about the baby. I'll step out and answer it."

Cyd looked at Stephanie. "Okay, I saw the way you looked at Lindell when I asked what happened. Now that mom's gone, what's the real story?"

"For the record, I have always hated that you know me so well." Stephanie sighed. "Sooo we've got this new nightly ritual."

"Ritual?" Cyd said. "Why does that sound ominous? Like some ancient pagan practice."

"Only you, Cyd." Stephanie paused. "Sex. We were having sex."

Cedric let out a chuckle. "Man, Lindell, you took it *way* beyond. You're out here inducing labor?"

"I wouldn't make that direct correlation," Lindell said.

"Whatever, Dr. London," Cedric said. "We 'bout to come to *your* clinic."

"So wait," Cyd said, "did your water actually break . . . in the act?"

"No, in the shower, like I said." Stephanie leaned into Lindell. "But we wondered if it had some help."

"Again," Lindell said, "from a medical standpoint, I don't think there's a real causal connection."

"But in our minds," Cedric said, "there will always be one. My niece got some *help* making her entrance into this world."

Claudia came back into the room. "Aunt Gladys sends her love. She wants you to call when you get a chance."

"I'll make sure I send pictures of the baby too," Lindell said.

Claudia leaned down, smiling at the baby as she squirmed in Stephanie's arms. "Aunt Gladys also said to tell you she expects a house full of children."

"After what I just experienced?" Stephanie said. "Let's just say that's amusing."

"If you think about it, Steph," Cedric said, "it fits together nicely. The daily ritual can feed the yearly ritual of producing new offspring."

"Did you say yearly?" Stephanie said.

"And what's this about rituals?" Claudia said. "Sounds like some ancient pagan stuff."

Stephanie looked from her mom to Cyd. "How was I born into this family?"

CHAPTER 84

"Morning, sweetheart." Jillian looked at her daughter as she mixed pancake batter. "I didn't think you'd be up this early, given the late night we had."

"We've only got two days left for the shoot." Sophia side-hugged her. "Joy and I are interning all day today and tomorrow, and we'll make up our school work next week."

"I'm surprised you didn't stay with Joy," Jillian said. "I thought that made more sense. Your brothers aren't even here."

"Well, this way I can help you like before," Sophia said, filling a pitcher with orange juice. She paused before taking it to the dining room. "How long do you think Miss Stephanie will be at the hospital?"

"She'll probably come home Saturday," Jillian said.

"Good morning," Brooke said, a touch of concern in her voice. "So what's the news? Did Stephanie have the baby?"

Jillian turned from the griddle. "She had the baby last night— Lindzey Samara London."

"Aww a little girl?" Brooke said. "That's awesome." She got a bowl for her oatmeal. "I was so shocked when I saw them leaving for the hospital. I was praying everything was okay."

"I was just coming for an update," Mariah said, walking in. "Brooke told me what happened last night."

"They had a baby girl," Brooke said, smiling.

"Oh, wow," Mariah said. "She came early."

"Three weeks early," Jillian said. "But mom and baby are in great health, praise God."

"That's so exciting," Mariah said. "I can't wait to see the baby."

"Oh, me too," Jillian said, pouring pancake batter onto the griddle. "I'm stopping by the hospital on my way to work."

"I was about to be fine with some instant oats this morning," Brooke said, scooping oatmeal from the saucepan. "Thanks for this, Jillian."

"It's my pleasure," Jillian said. "I know you guys are on a tight schedule in the morning, so please, help yourself."

"Brooke, you see this?" Mariah stood by the island. "She's back with the frittatas, but mini size. I love it."

"I did that for my son's birthday, and it was a hit," Jillian said, smiling. "So I thought I'd do it this morning."

"You see how I just put five on my plate?" Mariah said. "I'm about to eat more with the minis." She shook her head at herself.

Jillian turned the pancakes as they got their food and moved into the dining area, chatting about the day's schedule. She glanced at Sophia, now stirring a mixture on the stove, Hershey's cocoa and other ingredients beside her.

"You've got a taste for hot cocoa?" Jillian said.

"I'll probably get some, but—"

"Wow." Noah walked into the kitchen, looking at them. "This is a surprise."

"Good morning, Noah," Jillian said. "Did you hear about the excitement last night?"

"No, what happened?" Noah said.

"Stephanie went into labor," Jillian said. "She had the baby and all is well. But you've got some substitutes this morning."

"It's good to see you back," Noah said, his gaze resting on Sophia.

"I took a chance that you wanted blueberry pancakes," Jillian said, removing them from the griddle.

"Yes, ma'am," Noah said, plating the pancakes. "Thank you."

"Here you go," Sophia said, handing him a mug of hot cocoa.

"I had gone back to the instant packets," Noah said. "But once you've had the real thing . . . Thanks, Sophia."

Mariah came back in. "Do you guys know if there's any more green tea with ginger?"

"I'll look for it," Sophia said, going into the pantry.

Mariah paused, looking at Noah's plate. "Why do those look really good? I might have to treat myself."

"You should," Jillian said. "I'll have more ready in a couple minutes."

Sophia came out with the tea. "I'll put this on the sideboard in the dining room, Miss Mariah," she said, leaving out. Noah followed her.

"Uh-oh." Mariah looked as Faith walked in. "I must be running late, and I'm in here getting more food."

"No, you're good," Faith said, putting her jacket on the back of a kitchen chair. "I'm a little early."

"Okay, great," Mariah said. "I've got time to eat pancakes I don't need—and swipe another frittata." She chuckled as she headed to the dining room.

"I'll bring the pancakes out to you," Jillian called after her. She looked at Faith. "How are you this morning, sweetie?"

"Tired," Faith said, grabbing a plate. "And hungry."

"Did Zoe keep you up last night?"

"Zoe slept like a rock," Faith said. "The guys were up half the night."

"Oh, no," Jillian said. "I'm so sorry. David and Trevor were excited to be going over there. They probably kept Reggie up all night too."

"Reggie was a main culprit," Faith said. "And Tommy. The four of them were playing bid whist. Tommy was teaching them."

Jillian looked at her. "You're kidding."

"Nope." Faith helped herself to eggs, bacon, and hash browns. "I told them so many times to keep it down. And of course, as soon as I got to a hard slumber, Zoe woke up." She poured a cup of coffee. "But on the way over here I thought about the sleep deprivation Stephanie's about to have, and I adjusted my attitude."

"Ha," Jillian said. "Are you going by there today?"

"I can't till this evening," Faith said. "But Steph sent pics of little Lindzey. She's adorable."

"Isn't she?" Jillian said. "Give me a hug, girl." She walked over to her. "Praying your strength today. I remember when you were an adorable little baby, first baby I ever cared for. You'll always be special in that way."

Faith hugged her tight. "Love you, Aunt Jillian."

"I love you too."

Faith headed to the dining room, and Jillian scooped the pancakes from the griddle and onto a plate. She walked them out to Mariah. "Your pancakes, mademoiselle," Jillian said, feigning an accent. "Anybody else need anything?"

"No, thanks," Brooke said. "I need to finish getting ready. This was delicious, Jillian." She picked up her empty plate and bowl.

"I'll get that," Jillian said. She glanced at the other end of the table, where Noah and Sophia were engaged in quiet conversation. "Noah, can I get you anything?"

He looked up. "Oh, no, I'm fine. Thank you."

Jillian took the dishes to the kitchen and made her own plate. She ate at the kitchen table, turning on her laptop to check emails and look over some work since she'd be going into the office a little later than normal.

An email from Cyd caught her eye, with "Grief Study" in the subject line. She skimmed the message. Cyd wanted to know if she'd made a decision. If Jillian said no, Cyd would need to ask someone else as soon as possible.

Jillian had another email from a realtor she'd gotten in touch with, with listings of available properties in her price range. This was the third the realtor had sent, but they seemed to come when Jillian was rushed for time. Still, she needed to make time to click the links and preview what was out there. She made a mental note to go through them later today or tomorrow.

"We're leaving, Aunt Jillian," Faith said. She rinsed her plate and silverware and put them in the dishwasher. "Thanks for breakfast. I feel a lot better."

"You're welcome," Jillian said. "I'll have a talk with my boys so you don't get a repeat of last night."

"No, it's okay," Faith said. "I know what it's like when I get together with Courtenay." She put her jacket back on. "But I could only say that after some caffeine."

Jillian opened an email with an updated author manuscript as Sophia walked in. She fixed a plate, warmed it up, and joined Jillian at the table.

"I thought you already ate," Jillian said.

Sophia broke off a piece of bacon. "I was just out there talking."

Jillian looked at her daughter. "So what's going on with you and Noah?"

"What do you mean?" Sophia said.

"Well, there was that day you picked him up and brought him to church," Jillian said. "One Sunday you sat together in class. And this morning he was definitely happy to see you."

Sophia ate some eggs. "I guess you could say we like each other."

"So what does that mean, in your world?"

"Good question," Sophia said. "I'm trying to figure it out myself." She took a moment as she swirled her fork in hash browns. "Can I be honest and you promise not to flip out?"

"I promise," Jillian said.

"We kissed," Sophia said. "A couple of weeks ago. And I told him I wouldn't kiss him again. I even talked to Courtenay about it and decided I would avoid him until he left town because"—she shrugged—"I didn't want to get caught up in something stupid." She ate some of her food. "Then he showed up at class the first time and again this past Sunday. And after he gave his life to Jesus—"

"Wait, what?" Jillian said. "When did that happen?"

"This past Sunday," Sophia said. "He talked to Tommy a long time after class and prayed with him." She paused, eating more eggs. "So Noah and I went to service together in the balcony. And after service, he said he wanted us to keep in touch. I told him it's dumb because we're young and he's an artist who travels all the time and it would never work—whatever *it* would be."

Jillian closed her laptop as she focused on her. *Help me to hear Your voice, Lord, even as I listen to my daughter. Let me not react according to my own understanding. Give me wisdom.*

"But—and I'm not saying I believe him," Sophia was saying, "he said he could see me in his life, whatever that means. Then he said, 'If I text you, would you respond?' And I said I would." She forked up some hash browns and ate them. "But it still seems dumb and I don't think it *means* anything."

"Is that why you wanted to come to the B and B with me?" Jillian said.

Sophia gave a nod. "I hate that I like him, but I do. And I know everything you're gonna say, Mom. Courtenay already said it. *I've* said it to myself. But one huge thing that's changed in the past week is that he and I are both committed to Jesus."

"I know I've told you this before," Jillian said, "but I was your age when I went to college, and I was so naive. You're not as naive as I was, but there's a lot you haven't experienced and don't understand." She looked into her daughter's eyes. "But it's not just about inexperience, Soph. You can have all the experience in the world and find yourself doing something you regret. I've been there." She took a moment. "I guess I'm saying that even with your eyes wide open, boundaries drawn, even with both of you committed to Christ—you can still be way over your head."

"I know," Sophia said. "And it makes me want to run from him. But he said something I can't stop thinking about—'what if we're both clinging and abiding?'"

"I love that that's on his heart and mind," Jillian said. "I also want you to consider the need to guard your heart. What if you really fall for him? How will you feel when he's traveling the world, meeting women in different cities?"

"I could've really fallen for Lucas, Mom," Sophia said. "And next thing I knew, he was flirting with my closest cousin—my best friend. I can get a broken heart right here at church." She sighed. "So if Noah does actually like me, and I like him, and we're both committed to Jesus, should I never talk to him again?"

Jillian stared at her a moment and sighed. "My mom heart wants to protect you, just like I wanted to protect Courtenay when she went off to college."

"And she got hurt," Sophia said. "But were you the one who picked her up and helped her through that?"

"The Lord did," Jillian said. "He brought me in to help in the midst."

"Maybe this thing with Noah will fizzle by next week," Sophia said. "But if I do fall for him, and I'm clinging to God in the process, and I get hurt—do you trust God to help me?"

"One thing I know—God is faithful." Jillian got up. "Come here, you." She embraced Sophia. "I see so much spiritual growth in you, sweetheart. I'm so thankful to God. And thankful we can have these talks."

"Me too, Mom" Sophia said, embracing her still.

"I just want to emphasize something you said."

"What's that?" Sophia said.

"Keep clinging to God."

~

Jillian walked into Living Water mid-morning, after a short but sweet visit with Stephanie, Lindell, and the baby. These days she never knew what activity might greet her when she walked into the building. Crew members populated different spaces and now contractors were coming and going. It would seem strange when life got back to normal next week.

She took the elevator up and walked into Living Water's office space, and saw Silas and Cyd talking. He must've gotten the email too.

Jillian continued to her cubicle, greeting coworkers along the way, and set down her things. Taking her laptop out of her bag, she got ready to hunker down and get to work. But first, a cup of tea. She left her cubicle and walked toward an area with coffee, tea, and other refreshments—and heard her name.

Jillian paused, looking to her left, and saw Silas coming toward her.

"I saw that you're just getting here," Silas said, "so I won't hold you. I don't know if you got Cyd's email, but she wants to know where we are with the study."

"We might as well step over here," Jillian said, leading him to a quieter area. "I did get the email. Did Cyd add anything when you talked to her?"

"Just that she'd like to know by the end of this week," Silas said.

"That's tomorrow."

"That's why I came to talk to you," Silas said. "My answer is the same as it was from the beginning. I'm in. Willing to roll up my sleeves and help however I can, from gathering resources to helping to outline the study. Or to just be a sounding board. Whatever you need."

"I hadn't decided whether to do the study," Jillian said. "But if the deadline is tomorrow . . ." She thought a moment. "I've been leaning toward no, so maybe this just gives me the courage to say it. I'll let Cyd know."

"I'm surprised to hear that," Silas said. "And I feel bad because I know how much Cyd wants you to do it."

"Why do you feel bad?"

"I'm sure I'm part of the reason you declined," Silas said, "especially given our last conversation."

"I don't think that had much of a bearing on it at all," Jillian said. "I had a lot of factors to consider."

"But I complicated matters with the 'official' dinner invitation," Silas said. "I just . . . I read that wrong. And I apologize."

"For asking me out?" Jillian said. "That's not even apology territory. And as for the study, I put a lot of prayer on it, and I don't think it's for me to do it. It's just that simple."

Silas nodded. "I guess that's that then." He paused. "One more thing. I'm still thinking about that conversation we had. I was disappointed with your answer about dinner, but taken by your candor. And your faith. I wanted you to know that."

"I appreciate that, Silas," Jillian said. "Actually, I think God used you to speak something to me. At that shoot in the youth auditorium, you said, 'God is a master at making you wait. But when the appointed time comes, it *comes*. And you rejoice that you endured instead of giving up.'"

"Wow, I'm not sure I even remember those words," Silas said.

"It stayed with me because you used the words 'wait' and 'endure,'" Jillian said, "which is, well, long story . . . but it's a thing." She paused. "Once you said it, I couldn't let it go. I felt God was answering a prayer."

CHAPTER 85

"*L*indzey, you need to know how special this is." Stephanie sat up in bed, lightly rocking the baby. "You've got the senior pastor *and* the First Lady here to see you."

"Girl, if you don't cut that out." Treva stood by the bed. "Can we please talk about this little lady's eyes?" She smiled at Lindzey. "Look how alert she is. Taking in *everything.*"

"Yesterday she was asleep for every visit," Stephanie said. "She's trying to hang a little today."

"She really is taking you guys in," Lindell said, looking on from a chair beside the bed.

"Think she'll let Uncle Lance hold her?" Lance took off his jacket and placed it on the arm of a second chair.

"Wash your hands, babe," Treva said. "I'll wash mine too."

"Oh my gosh," Stephanie said. "Treva, can you be here for every visit and let the people know?"

They washed and dried their hands, then Lance lifted the baby gently from Stephanie's arms. "Hey there, Lindzey, it's your Uncle Lance," he said, holding her close. "I can't wait for you to meet your little cousins Zoe and Wes."

Treva chuckled as she rubbed the baby's back. "Watch them grow up thinking they're actual cousins."

"They are, as far as I'm concerned," Stephanie said. "That bond was formed back when Zoe was in the womb. Remember?"

"I'll never forget that period of time," Treva said. "You connected with Faith when I couldn't reach her. You helped her get through a critical time."

"You know that was God," Stephanie said. "It was a critical time for me too, and she helped *me* through." She paused. "And how did I just come through *another* critical time? I think I get more than my fair share." She shook her head. "But Lance, I haven't had a chance to say thank you. Lindell told me about the 'clinic.' I am *here* for the marriage ministry training conducted by our leaders."

Lance smiled. "Brother Cedric pulled me in on that. And trust me —I do consider it a vital part of marriage ministry. We started and ended with prayer."

"Prayers were answered," Lindell said. "We serve a mighty God. And for real—I'm thankful for two brothers who are willing to engage in real talk like that from a godly perspective. You told me things I *did not know*. And it set me free from a lot."

"I was wondering about those late-night trips Lance was taking over there," Treva said, looking over his shoulder at the baby. "I agree that it's vital. I've had talks like that with young women who are getting married. We've got all the admonitions for singles but too uptight to help the married people."

"You know how you and Lance did that video for the *Promises* study?" Stephanie said. "I want you to do one called 'Marriage Ministry That Will Rock Your World—Unplugged.'"

Lance nodded, as if thinking, then turned and kissed Treva. "What you think, babe?"

Treva gave him the eye. "You know they ain't ready." She checked the notification on her phone. "Faith says they're setting up the Abby Singer shot."

"The what?" Lance said.

"She's typing," Treva said. "She says that means they're on the next to last shot and we need to get over there." She set her phone down.

"But I need to get my turn with this precious girl." She slipped the baby from Lance's arms.

"So this is about to be it for the whole production?" Lindell said.

"The St. Louis portion," Lance said, "which is the majority of it. We wanted to be there when it wraps."

"How much have you seen of the filming?" Lindell said.

"Part of the wedding scene because it was filmed at the house," Lance said. "That's about it."

"You thought you'd be there for a lot more of it," Treva said.

"It's been nice, being a little detached from it," Lance said. "I haven't even had to do interviews, other than with Tommy."

"Well, I love that you're showing up as it wraps," Stephanie said. "I can understand not wanting to watch a painful part of your life recreated. But I'm sure it'll be nice for them to see you there today."

"And I'm looking forward to celebrating tomorrow night," Treva said.

"I *so* want to be there," Stephanie said. "But we'll be enjoying our first night at the B and B with this little lady."

The door opened and Cyd and Cedric walked in with Chase.

"Chase-man! Come here and hug Aunt Stephy!"

Chase ran over and gave her a big hug.

"Y'all started the party without us?" Cedric said.

"We're on our way out," Lance said. "Trying to catch the last part of the shoot."

"I guess I have to give you up, little Lindzey." Treva kissed her forehead.

"Ooh, I'll take her," Cyd said, holding out her arms.

"Not till you wash your hands," Treva said.

"Your Auntie Treva's got your back, baby girl," Stephanie said, chuckling.

"Hey Steph," Cedric said, "did you tell them your labor story?"

"We didn't get to that," Stephanie said. "But we talked about the video Lance and Treva are about to do, called, 'Marriage Ministry That Will Rock Your World—in Seven Easy Steps.'"

"Oh, the name changed?" Treva handed the baby to Cyd.

"Yup," Stephanie said. "That one's more on point."

"What in the world?" Cyd said.

"Oh, I'm with that," Cedric said. "Let's put it on the production schedule."

Lance chuckled, shaking his head. "Treva, Cedric and Steph are now in the same room. If we don't leave right now, we'll never get out of here."

❧

"Cut!" Mariah said. "And that's a wrap!"

Cheers rang out from cast and crew, and Alonzo, Brooke, and Noah shared a group hug.

"I know it's not *over* over, but I'm gonna miss you guys!" Brooke said. "Can we do this every week for forever?"

They got their phones and took group pictures, many of them silly.

Treva smiled and looked at Lance. "I love how they bonded. Such a great team."

"Lance, come over here—you too, Treva," Alonzo said. "Hey, those of you who are in here." He put an arm around Lance as a couple dozen people gathered. "This man entrusted me to tell his story, and it hasn't been an easy road for him. But he did it because he wanted this movie to make an impact for Christ." He looked at him. "So Lance, because you haven't been around for a lot of the production, we've got a little something for you. You need to know that your willingness to do this has *already* made an impact."

"Oh, babe"—Treva put her hand in his—"I've got goose bumps already."

A middle-aged guy stepped forward. "My name is Robert. I'm a lighting technician in the electrical department. Been doing that for a lot of years, but never been part of a Christian film. My wife and I go to church when we can, but I can't say it's a top priority. So anyway, I didn't pay much attention to the prayer time at base camp every morning. I'm just doing my own thing, getting coffee and breakfast." He glanced around at his fellow crew workers. "But something made me go one morning, and I heard the strangest thing. Somebody asking for prayer because a toilet got flooded back home, which messed up the ceiling below it. I thought—you can pray for stuff like that??"

People chuckled in the room.

"My wife told me the night before that our basement had flooded from the rain," Robert continued, "and we didn't know how we'd pay for the damage. Miss Pamela prayed, and long story short, we found a contractor who's a friend of a friend and he gave us a rate we could afford. I'm praying about *everything* now."

Whistles and cheers went up.

"This'll be hard to get through." A soft-spoken woman stood a few feet from Robert. "I lost my mom to breast cancer. She was a believer and trusted God to the end." She took a moment. "As she grew worse, it actually made me upset that she kept praising God. I was thinking, if God is so good, why won't He heal you?" She let out a sigh. "But as the script supervisor, I got to hear all of the dialogue. And there's a scene where Kendra and Lance talk about eternal life . . . For some reason, it just clicked. I finally got that Mom had a greater hope." She looked at Lance. "Thank you."

Lance nodded, overcome.

A young woman moved partly into the circle that had formed. "I feel like it's testimony time back in the day at church—giving honor to God, who's the head of *my* life . . ." Her head fell as she chuckled. "Okay, imma stop playing."

"Amber, don't start up in here this evening," another woman said, chuckling.

"For real, though," Amber said, "I really do have to testify. I was on this Disney show when I was twelve. I won't even bother to give the name because God said to put it behind me. But y'all, I was literally *on Disney*. Thought I was headed for *all* the stardom. People gassing me up, telling me I'm about to be the next this and that. And over the next two years, I watched every door close. People stopped returning calls. They had moved on to the next thing."

"Oh, my goodness." Treva whispered to Lance. "I thought she looked familiar. Hope used to watch her show."

"I was disappointed for a long time," Amber said, "questioning God because I thought He had a plan for me in entertainment. But it got to a point where I said, 'Your will, Lord.' And you know what happens when you pray that—you better be ready for *anything*." She gave them all a look. "I found myself in cosmetology school and people were feeling sorry for me, like, *this* is what it's come to? But I've always loved dabbling in makeup so I enjoyed it, even if I didn't know where it was headed." She took a breath. "Fast forward—started getting jobs as a makeup assistant and building my portfolio. Then I heard that this movie got the green light. Listen . . . A chance to work on a Christian film? With Alonzo Coles? And I had been following what God was doing with Cinda's career as a stylist. I said, 'Lord, *please* put me on.'" She paused, shaking her head as if still in disbelief.

"He is able!" someone said.

"Y'all." Amber paused again. "You don't even understand the praise party I had when I got the call. They offered me my first gig—not as an assistant—as a makeup artist!"

"And you did a phenomenal job!" Brooke said, leading the rest in cheers and applause.

Amber continued when the applause quieted. "Lance, thank you for saying 'yes' to this project. I'm not leaving the same as when I started. When you have to get up before dawn to go to work and you know it's for the kingdom? It hits different!" She chuckled. "Alonzo, thank you for persevering to get this movie made and for helping to set the tone every day. I've never experienced on a shoot what I experienced here. I heard Brooke say she wants to do this every week for forever. Ditto!" She looked at Pamela. "We have not because we ask not, right?"

"Yes, ma'am!" Pamela said, smiling.

"I could talk about that morning prayer time too," Amber said. "Whew! But let me give somebody else the floor . . ." She stepped back, exchanging dialogue with someone who stood next to her.

Treva watched with Lance as several more came forward, telling how their involvement with the project had impacted them, including a few who mentioned the Cling class and Brooke who spoke tearfully about growing closer to God during the shoot.

"Wow," Alonzo said, "When I heard Lance was coming, I spread the word this afternoon about what I wanted to do. But I didn't expect so many to share. If that's it, we'll start—"

"I'll say something, Alonzo," Sophia said, moving out of the background. "I wasn't going to share because I'm just an intern and Uncle Lance is, well, my uncle." She gave him a glance. "I wanted to be an intern so I could have it on my resume. But mainly, I thought it would be dope to be part of a Hollywood film, meet cool people, and post about it on Instagram." She paused with a wry smile. "Amber said she's not the same, and neither am I. My faith got real during this shoot. I'll be headed to college with Jesus on my mind, and that's not where I was before this." She looked at Lance. "I'm even listening to your sermons now, Uncle Lance."

"Soph, come here, girl," Treva said. She took her into her arms and hugged her tight. "I'm so glad you shared. My heart melted hearing that."

Lance hugged her next. "If I only heard that one testimony, it would've made it all worth it. Praise God, Soph."

"I have to add mine to the others," Jade said. "I'm nowhere *near* the same. Tommy's Cling class had me shook, in a good way. I used to think I could never have the kind of relationship with the Lord that others talked about. Now I actually feel like . . ." She took a moment. "I feel like I'm getting there." She nodded to herself with a sigh. "Also, I'm a twin, so I've always had a built-in friend, and I love Jordyn. But for the first time in my life, I've got a soul mate kind of friend, which I didn't think was possible. And it wouldn't have happened without this shoot." She stepped back to where she was, beside Trey.

"I need to add," Alonzo said, "that the vlogs themselves have made an impact during this shoot. Thank you to everyone who participated by doing ministry moments. And thank you, Jade, for the tremendous work you poured into that."

Applause sounded throughout the room.

"Anybody else before we start packing up?" Alonzo said.

"I'll go," Noah said, stepping forward. "It's a chorus now, but I'll say it too—I'm not the same. I've got a bio that says I grew up singing in church. But I didn't know Jesus." He heaved a sigh. "That Cling class got me. Tommy listened to a lot of my questions and gave me some hard answers." He looked over at him. "I came into this thinking like Sophia, that my resume would change. I didn't know *I* would be changed." He paused. "Tommy prayed with me, and I'm thankful that I now know Jesus as my Lord and Savior."

A chorus of praise went up in the room.

Treva looked at Lance. "Did you know that?"

Lance shook his head. "I had no idea." He went over and hugged him. "Welcome to the family, my brother. Wow. God is so good. I'll be praying for you."

"I really appreciate that," Noah said.

Brooke hugged him as well, along with a few others.

"I knew a lot of these stories," Alonzo said, "but I'm still blown away hearing them all at one time." He paused. "Momma Pam, can you come over here?" He put an arm around her. "Just in case one or two of you don't know, this is the woman who has prayed for every phase of this project, prayed for every one of you by name, and prayed *with* many of you during the filming. And it looks like God has been answering in a mighty way. Can we please thank God for Pamela Alexander?"

Pamela clasped her hands in a praying position, looking upward as cheers rang out.

"Okay, everybody," Alonzo said. "We're gonna end it here because we've got more celebrating to do tomorrow. Who's coming to the wrap party?"

Hands went in the air and some started dancing as they cheered.

"I see y'all are ready," Alonzo said, smiling. "Bring all that energy tomorrow night!"

Lance went over to Trey as people started breaking down equipment and packing up. "Hey, we haven't talked since earlier this week. Any updates?"

"Not really," Trey said. "Still praying."

"I saw Pastor Fuller today."

"So *you're* the one with the update," Trey said.

"He said he assumed you would take the long-term missions opportunity," Lance said, "because that's what you'd been waiting for. He was trying to figure out why the shift to mid-term and a sudden interest in adding this woman to the team."

"I see that smile you're trying to hide," Trey said. "You're getting a kick out of this."

"It's not that I'm getting a kick out of it," Lance said. "I'm just in awe of God. I remember Randall praying for Jade to come to church—just to come to church. He would have never imagined that one day *she'd* be praying about whether to take a missions trip to Africa." He glanced over at Jade who was getting footage. "And on the other side, I've been praying for years for a God-given friend for you and would have never imagined that that friend would be Jade. And then, that she might join the missions team? It's mind-boggling."

"As she keeps reminding me, though," Trey said, "it's a long shot."

"You knew it was a long shot when you suggested it," Lance said. "But now that she's taking time to pray about it, I know you'll be disappointed if she doesn't go."

"I keep telling myself she's not going," Trey said, "to not even think about it. But my mind goes there anyway, picturing us doing ministry and engaging the culture together. Having my friend with me." He looked over at her. "Then I go back to—she's not going."

"Also," Lance said, "I talked to your dad. He asked about Jade."

"Not surprised," Trey said. "I told him about her, but he wanted *your* perspective. Not about Jade herself but whether this could lead anywhere."

"I simply countered with questions," Lance said. "Why does it need to lead somewhere? Haven't we been praying for friendship? If it's God-ordained, is it not enough?"

Trey sighed. "I get frustrated when Dad goes to you, like I'm a child and he needs to check on me. But at the same time, I love it because you say all the things."

"But you know I agree with Marlon," Lance said. "All things are possible with God. He absolutely can awaken love within you for a woman. But I'll always push back on the idea that being single means you're existing at some lower tier. In Christ you've been made complete. And as Joy says—that's point-blank period." He smiled. "I'll keep praying on the missions thing, though. Who knows what God might do."

"Those words used to scare me," Trey said. "Like, yeah, who knows what God might do—and it's probably something you don't want Him to do. But just now when you said it . . . I don't know. Made me feel expectant. Like, what *is* God going to do?"

"Amen," Lance said. "No need to be afraid of God's plan. Just stay praying."

Trey nodded. "And clinging."

CHAPTER 86

"Ooh, this is a whole vibe." Jade paused at the entrance to the wrap party. "I have to capture this," she said, taking her camera from her bag and backing up. "Come *on* with the black, merlot and gold motif. Do you *see* this?" She walked as she filmed. "And check out those gold chandelier clusters."

"I see the black and gold accents," Trey said. "But what and where is the merlot?"

"The deep purplish red table covers on the high tops," Jade said, pointing. "Then they've got dark florals—deep red and purple in that one—in assorted gold containers. Ahhh, I love it so much."

"I wonder if it's meant to be a tribute to Kendra," Trey said. "Reminds me of the colors from the wedding."

"Ohh, could be," Jade said, nodding. "I had the same reaction when I saw the wedding colors." She looked behind her. "What happened to Jordyn?"

"I don't know," Trey said. "Maybe she stopped in the restroom."

"Orrr, she saw that," Jade said, spying Brooke and Jesse. "But she knew they would be here." She put her camera away and walked further inside. "It's popping in here already, and the music is tight."

"Let's see what appetizers they've got," Trey said.

"Of course, food is your first thing," Jade said.

"What else would we do?"

"Uh, mingle?"

"We can mingle with appetizers."

"Jade, you look so pretty," Faith came up and hugged her. "Always stylin'. I show up in a basic black pantsuit, and you step out in a trapeze dress—what color is this exactly?"

"Rust," Trey said. "She corrected me when I said orange."

"This is light years from orange," Jade said.

"And this curly 'fro is giving me life," Faith said. "You are forever changing up your hair. You see I need help with that." She patted her puff.

"Girl, that's your signature look, and I love it," Jade said. "You have to rock what works for you."

Reggie walked up and greeted them both then looked at Faith. "I thought we were headed that way"—he pointed two fingers—"to the appetizers."

"I'm trying to get there myself, Reg," Trey said.

The four of them made their way to a long, beautifully decorated table and perused the selections.

Jade got a plate and added honey sriracha chicken wings, chilled shrimp, barbecued shrimp, and a puff pastry.

"Good to see you, Jade," Jesse said, coming beside her.

"Hey, Jesse, how are you?" Jade said.

"I'm doing well," Jesse said, getting some of the barbecued shrimp. "Did I hear you might be going to Africa?"

"Wow, the grapevine is something else," Jade said. "Nothing certain yet, but I'm praying about it."

"I don't know if I could even consider something like that," Jesse said, "so I think that's dope." He added stuffed mushrooms. "How's Jordyn?"

Jade looked over at him. "She's good. But you could always ask her yourself."

"I know," Jesse said. "Never thought I'd see the day when it would be easier to talk to you than to Jordyn."

Jade got some spinach dip. "She's the same Jordyn you fell in love with, Jesse."

Jesse nodded vaguely, staring downward a moment, then continued making his plate.

Jade found Trey on the dessert end of the table. "So the way it's set up, they want people to stand and eat at the high tops to keep a party flow. But they do have a few tables over there where we could sit." She nodded her head toward the back.

"You said that like I care where we eat."

"I must've had a brain freeze," Jade said. "You'd be fine in a stairwell as long as you had your plate."

"There's Jordyn," Trey said, "on the dance floor."

Jade followed his gaze and saw Alonzo surrounded by Cinda, Jordyn, and Mariah. "Look at Jordyn, actually having fun."

Jade led Trey to a high-top table near the dance floor.

"I'm loving the energy." Jade spoke above the music as she eyed the floor. "It's still kind of early, but people are out there having a good time." She ate one of her shrimp.

Trey dunked a cracker in spinach dip. "Mariah said she wanted to party, and she meant that."

"Right? Not playing at all." Jade smiled as she moved to a different dance partner. "Get 'em, Mariah!" She tasted one of her appetizers. "Oh, wow, did you get one of these?"

Trey found it on his plate and sampled it. He leaned toward her so she could hear. "Some kind of sweet potato something. That's really good."

"I'm trying to figure out what spices are in here," Jade said, taking another bite. "I need to try and make this."

"Yup," Trey said. "Figure it out and give me the ingredients. I'll go grocery shopping tomorrow."

"Um, sir," Jade said, "now that the study *and* the St. Louis shoot are over, you think I'm still cooking for you?"

"Nope," Trey said. "I think you're still cooking because you still need to eat. I'll just happen to be there when it's served."

"You are pitiful."

"Aye, I bet you don't know anybody who appreciates your cooking more," Trey said. "I've never tasted better. Everything is bomb. Flavorful. Never under or over-cooked—"

"I'll cook it tomorrow, Trey."

He pointed the sweet potato bite at her. "And this right here will be poor in comparison."

"I meant it when I said you're pitiful." Jade glanced across the room. "Okay, Treva, you better make your entrance. That black sheath dress is fire." She smiled. "Lance got her on his arm like, this is *my* woman."

"Yours is fire too, though," Trey said. "I meant to tell you that."

Jade looked at him. "At least I can appreciate the distinction," she said. "When you compliment my cooking, it's a means to an end. But a compliment about the dress is real. So, thank you for that."

"Nah, you can't dismiss my compliments about your cooking." Trey leaned his head to hers, his voice elevated. "If it wasn't bomb, trust me, I wouldn't be on you to cook." He picked up another appetizer. "And yeah, your look is always on point. I mean, I'm not blind. I thought you were beautiful the first time I saw you."

Jade's brow furrowed. "You never told me that."

Trey shrugged, eating a wing. "Why would it come up?"

"Uh-oh," she said, eyes on the dance floor. "Brooke and Jesse are out there. Now Jordyn's on her way over here."

Jade looked at her as she approached. "You okay?"

"Can I borrow your lip gloss?" Jordyn said. "I forgot mine."

"That's why you came over here?" Jade took it from her evening bag and gave it to her. "Jesse asked how you're doing."

Jordyn used the camera on her phone to apply the gloss. "He can't ask me himself?"

"That's what I said to him."

Jordyn checked her hair and handed back the tube. "I'm about to go dance with Joel."

"Who?" Jade said.

"The boom operator," Jordyn said, heading back to the dance floor.

"Well, all righty then," Jade said. She bopped her head as the deejay started mixing in Beyonce's version of "Before I Let Go."

"You want to go out there?" Trey looked down at her feet. "If your stilettos can handle it."

Jade answered by taking his hand and dancing her way to the floor, which had gotten more crowded. She moved near Jordyn, and without a word, they fell into simultaneous moves side by side.

"Ayyyeeee!" a few people said, backing up and watching them.

"Twins?" someone else said.

They had fun with it for a minute then did their own thing.

"So you two come up with choreography in your spare time?" Trey said, dancing with her.

"We actually don't," Jade said. "But we've clicked like that since we were little." She saw a few phones in the air and looked across the floor. "I was wondering where Noah was. He and Sophia look really cute dancing together."

Moments later the floor reconfigured as Alonzo and Cinda started a line dance and others joined, including Noah and Sophia.

"Heyyy," Jade said. "Come on, Trey."

Jade and Jordyn got in sync with the group, gliding to one side.

"Hold up," Trey said, watching. "This is new, new to me anyway. You know I've been out-of-pocket for over two years."

Jade got beside him, showing the steps.

"I see you, Trey!" Jordyn said. "You're working it. Now do the bunny hop and drop," she said, demonstrating.

"Yeah, right," Trey said.

"The young people always got something extra," Jade said. "What's that shuffle turn thing Sophia and Noah are doing? I feel old."

"Go up there with Cinda and Alonzo," Jordyn said. "They're trying to get it."

The line dance continued through two more rotations then the deejay mixed in the original "Before I Let Go" by Maze.

"Look at the shift," Jade said as the line dance disbanded and a different crowd took to the floor.

"The grown folk are taking over now," Lance said, coming beside them with Treva.

"Whatever," Trey said. "I always liked this version."

"Me too," Jade said, still dancing. "My parents used to play it."

Jillian and Tommy came to the floor near them, then Cyd and Cedric.

"So it's a sister thing," Trey said. "First you and Jordyn. Now Treva and Jillian."

"Look at them rocking the old school," Jade said, smiling. "I've never seen them dance. And Lance and Tommy hanging right with them. Why do I just want to keep watching?" She shook her head at herself. "And if I want to keep watching, that means I need to be filming."

"I thought about that during the line dance," Trey said.

"Why didn't you say something?"

"Because you were having a rare moment—enjoying yourself," Trey said. "You think there won't be another line dance tonight?"

Jade chuckled. "True."

They left the dance floor and went back to the high top where Jade had left her bag. She got her camera and surveyed the room to see what she wanted to capture first. Her gaze landed on one of the low tables toward the back—on Jordyn and Jesse.

CHAPTER 87

"Well, if that's it," Jordyn said, rising, "I'm gonna get back." Jesse looked at her. "So I ask how you're doing, you ask how I'm doing, and that's all we've got?"

"Apparently," Jordyn said. "And I'm not here for the awkward silence. I appreciate your asking, though."

"Jordyn, can you sit down, please?" Jesse said.

She looked at him for a second and sighed before sitting again. "Why the sudden interest in a conversation, Jesse? Now that you and Brooke are together, this is your way of rising above it all?"

"Where'd you get that from?" Jesse said. "Brooke and I aren't together."

"Well, whatever term you're using," Jordyn said.

"Friends," Jesse said. "That's the term we're using."

"It really doesn't matter," Jordyn said. "Why'd you want me to sit down?"

"When I asked how you were doing, I wasn't looking for a one-word answer," Jesse said. "I wanted to really hear how you're doing, how things are going with you."

"Why?" Jordyn said.

"What do you mean, why?"

"Because whenever I tried to talk to you, you had nothing to say."

"Jordyn, I was *hurt.*" Jesse stared into her eyes. "I bought you a *ring.* I wanted to *marry* you. Then I didn't see how I could trust you again." He looked away a moment. "Yeah, it was hard to have a conversation."

Jordyn stared downward, unable to look at him.

"But that comment about rising above it all . . ." Jesse stared ahead, taking his time. "That's exactly what the Lord helped me to do these past few weeks. To get out of my emotions and focus on Him. Just seek Him and let some time pass. And honestly, it helped to have Brooke as a friend. Even to pray about whether I should pursue something with her. It helped to be that detached from you and me and assess everything from a distance." He turned to her. "So I'm asking again. How are you?"

Jordyn took her time as well. "Better than I've been. I'm in a good place." She added, "I'm sure Brooke told you we were doing the Cling study together, sort of informally. But it made me stay up on it. And that helped." She debated whether to continue. "For my step of faith, I let you go. Which I know sounds stupid since you let me go a long time ago."

"Why was it a step of faith?" Jesse said.

"What do you mean?"

"I'm wondering what made it a faith move."

Jordyn thought a moment. "I couldn't stop thinking about you. About us. I hated what I did and wanted to turn back time, do that whole day over. I just wanted to get back to where we were, and it was consuming me." She sighed. "Bottom line—I was way more focused on you than the Lord. It took a while to even tune into that conviction. So, I knew I had to let you go. And only hold on to Jesus."

Jesse's eyes rested on her. "That's everything, Jordyn."

Jordyn let several seconds elapse. "So did you get an answer, when you prayed about Brooke?"

"It's what I said—friends," Jesse said. "That was the answer."

Jordyn stared vaguely as people flocked to the floor for "Won't He Do It."

"I had been praying about the two of us too, Jordyn," Jesse said.

"And I just wasn't feeling it. I wasn't moved to try again. Then Brooke and I prayed about it together."

"You and Brooke prayed about you and me?"

Jesse nodded. "And the past few days, I noticed my thoughts changing. Just the fact that you were *in* my thoughts. Thinking about the times I went to work tired because we couldn't get off FaceTime. And how I'd miss you if we hadn't texted in three hours. And how we celebrated the anniversary of our first date every month, because we said it was the day our lives changed."

"Why are you saying all this, Jesse?"

"Because I hadn't been thinking about *any* of this stuff," Jesse said. "And I thought it was because Brooke and I prayed. And that's definitely part of it. But now I'm also thinking . . ." He looked at her. "I'm thinking it had to do with your step of faith."

"I'm not sure what you mean," Jordyn said.

"Maybe God didn't want me to feel anything or to even think about you until *He* was on the throne of your heart," Jesse said. "He was waiting for you to put Him first. When you let me go, it's almost like . . . it unlocked something."

"You said we needed to put our energy into the relationship that matters most," Jordyn said. "But when you said it probably wouldn't make a difference as far as us, that's the only part that stuck out to me."

"I thought we were over." Jesse focused on her. "You said it was like I flipped a switch and turned off. Now I'm thinking *God* flipped that switch. He wouldn't let things move forward until they were in proper order."

Jordyn gave a vague nod. "Things definitely weren't in proper order, for me to go see Kelvin." She gave him a glance. "I still hope you can forgive me for that."

"It's already done," Jesse said.

"So you're thinking about us again," Jordyn said, "feeling like something was unlocked. What does that mean, Jess? Or maybe you don't know yet?"

Jesse took a moment to answer. "So much is hitting me right now.

I didn't know what you would say. I just knew we needed to talk." He blew out a breath as he stared downward. "If you could feel the way my heart is racing right now. I think this whole conversation is God's answer. He was waiting to reveal it. Right here. And I'm trying to understand . . ."

Jordyn could feel her heart pulsating as well, even as she tried to contain it. "Jesse, I think I'm gonna go. I just—"

"I'm realizing, Jordyn . . ." He looked at her. ". . . how much I missed you."

"Don't do this to me, Jesse." Jordyn braced herself. "I finally let you go—"

"And I'm glad you did," Jesse said. "I'm thinking about that verse we kept talking about in class, that without faith it is impossible to please Him—and He's a rewarder of those who seek Him."

Jordyn felt tears welling in her eyes and tried to will them away. "I don't know what any of this means. I don't want to get my hopes up."

"Are y'all having a good time tonight?" Alonzo spoke from the platform at the front of the room.

A couple hundred people in the room cheered affirmation.

Jordyn and Jesse looked toward the platform.

"We've definitely been having a good time," Alonzo said. "A few of y'all haven't left the dance floor *at all*. But I have a strong feeling that it could be better, and that it's about to *get* better. Because right now, we're about to bring to the stage a special performance by our very own—Noah Stiles! Give it up for Noah, y'all!"

The lights dimmed even more as people cheered, moving to the front for a better view. Special lights bathed the platform in hues of blue and red, and music boomed from the speakers as Noah walked out, captured by several phones in the air.

"This is a really special night." Noah wore baggy jeans and a white tee under a long plaid shirt he'd left unbuttoned. "It's not a typical performance. I'm here with family."

"Yes!" rang out from the crowd, along with whistles.

Noah smiled. "Normally I kick off a set with an up-tempo song, but my big bro Alonzo had a special request." He walked the platform.

"This is for Alonzo and Cinda—and all the other couples in here who might be feeling this. It's called, 'A Love Like Yours.'"

"This is your jam." Jesse stood and took her hand. "Let's go."

Jordyn held back. "To the dance floor? We can't."

"Why not?" Jesse said.

"Why would we?"

"Jordyn." Jesse looked into her eyes. "Dance with me."

Jordyn's insides stirred as she got up and walked hand in hand with Jesse to the dance floor, which wasn't nearly as populated as before. Most stood near the front, filming with phones. But a few couples swayed as Noah crooned. Cinda looked over at them and smiled.

Jordyn put her arms tentatively around Jesse. "This is the last thing I expected tonight." She felt tears welling once more. "I thought you'd never hold me again."

"Having you in my arms is the best feeling in the world right now." Jesse closed his arms tighter around her and exhaled. "I love you, Jordyn. I've never loved anyone like I love you."

Tears spilled from her eyes. "I love you, too, Jesse. I love you so much."

"I want what we had," Jesse said. "But it would be better than what we had, now that we're all about clinging to Jesus." He looked at her. "Do you still want us, Jordyn?"

"You know I do," Jordyn said. "But what if I fall back to that place where I'm not putting Jesus first?"

"Reggie said he and Faith make time to study the word and pray together," Jesse said. "I love that. I think that's how we keep the right focus."

"I love that too," Jordyn said. "But are you saying . . . are we like, back together? Or maybe you want to pray about it some more?"

"I've been praying for weeks," Jesse said. "And God's been tuning my ear to hear His answer. I heard Him loud and clear tonight." He looked into her eyes. "I'm sure. What about you?"

Jordyn nodded. "You know I am."

Jesse brushed tears from her face. "You took my breath away when you walked in here in this bangin' black dress." He pulled away a little to look at her, shaking his head as he brought her back. "You're beautiful, J."

"Thank you, Jess." Jordyn nestled close. "You're taking my breath away right now wearing my favorite cologne."

Jesse swayed with her. "Know what I miss?"

"What?"

"You getting mad when I do this." He twirled her hair around his finger.

Jordyn ducked her head. "Jesse, stop playing. You'll make it frizz."

He chuckled softly. "I'll stop because this is your part right here."

Jordyn nestled close again. "How do you remember?"

"All the times you'd turn up the radio and tell me to be quiet?"

The bridge on the song ramped up and Noah hit the beautiful falsetto—"a love like yooouuourrs."

"Come on, sir!" Alonzo called out as the crowd responded to Noah.

Jordyn swayed as Noah continued to riff, feeling the passion. "Every time I hear this song now, I'll think of tonight. It's perfect."

Jesse nodded. "This might be our moment."

"Ohhh." Jordyn's voice was a whisper. "It definitely could be. We'd have to both agree."

"I'm giving it 'moment' status," Jesse said.

Jordyn looked into his eyes. "Then that would be two of us."

She closed her eyes, her heart soaring as Jesse put his lips to hers, kissing her, letting it linger a little as her favorite song wound down.

They applauded with the rest when the song ended. Jesse led her off the floor as Noah introduced the next one.

Jade stood waiting, looking at them as they approached. "So y'all just gonna do me like that? I gotta get the news with everybody else?"

Jordyn glanced at Jesse then back to Jade. "See, what had happened was . . ."

"Whatever," Jade said. "This made my night. I need hugs." She hugged Jesse then paused. "But wait, is it real? Official? All that good stuff?"

"It's real," Jesse said. "And Jade, what you said to me earlier made a difference."

"Oh my gosh," Cinda said, walking up. "I was seriously about to stop dancing and come hug you two."

"Girl, me too," Faith said, waiting for her turn to hug.

"Are you guys serious right now?" Jesse said.

"Yes!"

Jade, Cinda, and Faith laughed when they realized they'd said it at the same time.

"And you know what this means?" Faith said. "No more 'Where's Jordy?' Zoe will not let it go. That girl loves you." She hugged Jordyn.

"That means so much, Faith," Jordyn said. "Thank you for sharing that."

Brooke walked up next. "I'm over there listening to Noah but I had to come tell you how happy I was to see this." She looked from one to the other. "My prayer was answered, and it's beautiful just like I knew it would be." She hugged them and went back.

"Let's go up there and watch," Jordyn said, taking Jesse's hand.

They moved through the crowd and settled on a spot with a clear view. Noah sang more of his radio hits, a couple of them filling the dance floor. He'd said it wasn't his typical performance, but he was energized, all over the platform with choreographed moves, giving them a full concert experience.

The music slowed now, a soft piano track playing. Noah got a cloth and wiped his face, then drank some water. He came to the edge of the platform and looked out into the crowd.

"This is my last song tonight. But before I sing . . . Sophia, where are you? Can you come up here?"

CHAPTER 88

Sophia stared at Noah from her spot near the front, heart thumping.

"Girl, go," Joy said, giving her a nudge. "He said to come up there."

"I'm not going up there," Sophia said. "Do you know how embarrassing that would be?"

Noah spotted her and walked to where she was, extending his hand from the platform. Sophia shook her head at him, mouthing, *No*.

"Okay, fam," Noah said, looking out at everybody. "I need y'all to help me get Sophia up here."

The room filled with whistles and cheers that grew louder by the second. Joy took her hand and her purse and led her to the platform stairs, where Noah was waiting. He came down, took her hand, and brought her up to even louder cheers.

Sophia looked at him, certain her face was red. "What in the world are you doing?"

Noah brought a stool from the back of the platform. "Go ahead and get comfortable, Sophia." He spoke into the mic. "It's gonna be a minute."

In jeans, boots, and a camel-colored sweater with fringe around the bottom, Sophia exhaled as she sat, heart thumping all the more.

"You've probably seen concerts where they pick a young woman in the crowd and bring her on stage to sing to." Noah looked out at everyone. "I've never done that. But I had to bring Sophia up here tonight, and here's why."

Sophia kept her eyes on him, his gray plaid shirt swinging as he walked.

"We have this running debate, disagreement, whatever you want to call it," Noah said, "where I tell her she's special, and she thinks I'm playing games. So, Sophia"—Noah turned to her—"I hope this convinces you. You'll be the first person I sing to on stage—and the first person I wrote a song for." He came closer. "I wrote this a few days ago. It's called, 'You're Special' . . . because you *are* special, to me."

Sophia felt her arms shaking. Was this really happening? The whole evening had been a dream, starting with their first date at a restaurant forty miles away. Noah had wanted to take her out on his last evening in town. He googled and found a spot with great reviews and an intimate setting in the middle of nowhere. With extended time to themselves, they'd gotten to know each other better, never once running out of conversation or laughter, yet aware that their time together was quickly running out.

Noah got his own stool as people captured the moment on video, lights from the phones shining toward them. He sat facing her as the track with soft piano increased in volume. It hit her that this was the track to the actual song. He was about to sing her a ballad.

Mic in hand, Noah stared downward a moment, riffing softly over the intro, then looked into her eyes to sing the verse.

Never knew I could
Didn't know I would
Think about you all the time
Things you say stay on my mind

Noah sang slowly, his vocals lush as he focused on her.

You've got ways I never knew
You really do keep me in awe of you
Make me re-evaluate

628

Choices that I used to make

Sophia could barely look at him as she took in the words. Did he really write this about her? Goose bumps rode her arms as he moved to the chorus.

You're special
It's settled
Another level
You're special
You're His vessel
I gotta be careful
Because —You're special
Beautifully unusual
You're special . . .

Sophia closed her eyes, replaying the chorus. The words. The way he took his time with them. And that soaring falsetto on 'beautifully unusual.' She held herself to calm the shivers.

Into the second verse now, Noah's voice grew more passionate, moving Sophia to open her eyes. He locked her in his gaze as he moved to the chorus again, taking the words "you're special" to new heights. His whole body was into it now, punctuating each line as his vocals soared even more.

Sophia could hear the response from the crowd, but she couldn't take her eyes off of him. She'd always loved his voice. Never in a million years would she have imagined him using it to sing to her.

The song came to a close and he pulled her to her feet, hugging her to extended cheers and applause.

Sophia looked into his eyes. "That was beautiful, Noah. I love it. I would love it even if it wasn't for me."

"I love that you love it," Noah said. "I was wishing I had my guitar." He thought a moment. "I'll record it with the guitar and send it to you."

They walked off the platform as the deejay started the music again, many crowding around to get a final moment with Noah and take pictures.

Joy pulled her out from the crowd and stared at her. "Do you even know how crazy that was? *I can't even.*" She gave Sophia back her purse. "You know you're about to be all over social media."

"No, I won't," Sophia said. "This isn't a typical crowd of 'fans' who'll be posting stuff. It's the film crew." She shrugged. "It won't be big like that."

"Yeah, okay," Joy said.

"Soph, I had to bring Jade to talk to you." Cinda walked up with her. "She can help you get your social media ready."

"Told you," Joy said.

Sophia looked at Cinda and Jade. "What do you mean, get it ready?"

"People are about to be checking for you," Jade said. "You know how he just said 'another level' in that song? That's what you're about to experience. Ask Cinda."

"And it was different with me," Cinda said. "I wasn't on social media when Alonzo first posted about me. But it was still crazy, with people trying to find me."

"But Sophia, you're active on social media," Jade said. "I would advise you to make your profiles private and go through your posts. Whatever you don't want the world to see, delete or archive, because they *will* be all in your business. Then—"

"Okay, wait," Sophia said. "Cinda, you dealt with that because Alonzo posted about you, which meant his millions of followers saw it. This was a private concert, and if anyone does post a video, only a few people will see it."

"You're underestimating the reach a video like this could get," Jade said. "With the right hashtags, it'll hit the algorithm and go viral." She gave her a look. "And girl, Noah Stiles wrote you a love song and sang it to you live. It *will* go viral."

"It wasn't a *love* song," Sophia said.

"That's *exactly* what people will call it," Jade said.

Sophia saw her mom coming toward her. "Jade, will you have time to talk later, so I can get more of your suggestions?"

"I'll type up a note and text it to you," Jade said. "Let's exchange numbers."

They airdropped their contact information, and Sophia turned to her mom.

Jillian hugged her. "Wow. You've had quite a night, sweetheart."

Sophia exhaled. "Was that wild or what?"

"You've made an impression, that's for sure," Jillian said. "What I love is that he apparently sees you as special because of who you are in Christ. That part about having to be careful because you're His vessel—that was my favorite."

"Why did I know you'd love that line?" Sophia said. "I did too, though."

"I just want to be clear," Alonzo said from the platform, "the night is *far* from over. We're keeping the party energy going—I see y'all on the floor gettin' it—and we've got another special appearance in a few."

"Mrs. Mason," Noah said, joining them, "I just want to say thank you for everything at the B and B. Even this morning with the bow on the Hershey's tin. You made my last morning special."

"You're very welcome," Jillian said. "And I'll never hear that word again without thinking about the song. Noah, it was really beautiful. You're a gifted young man."

"I appreciate that." Noah glanced at Sophia. "Your daughter is amazing inspiration."

"I'm not good at mincing words, Noah," Jillian said. "I don't know where this is going between you and Sophie, if anywhere. But I want you to know that you're in my prayers. I'm thankful that you see Sophie as special and as God's vessel. I'm praying that your actions toward her will reflect that."

"Yes, ma'am," Noah said. "I appreciate those prayers."

"Have a safe trip," Jillian said, hugging him. "It was a pleasure getting to know you a little at the B and B."

"You too, Mrs. Mason."

Sophia walked with him. "You say all your goodbyes?"

"Not all of them," Noah said, looking at her. "You going downstairs with me to meet the car?"

Sophia nodded.

They stopped in an office where he'd stored his luggage and took the elevator down as Noah focused on his phone.

"So you fly to Toronto first?" Sophia said as they stepped off.

"Yeah, concert's tomorrow night."

"It's crazy you don't even get to go home," Sophia said. "It's just right to the next thing."

"We knew that's how it would be when they offered the part in the movie," Noah said. "But I wanted to do it." He looked at her. "And I'm glad I did. The travel hassle is more than worth it."

They walked across the entryway to the door. "How long before your car arrives?" Sophia said.

"ETA is ten minutes." Noah eyed her. "Check your phone."

"Why?"

"Just check it."

Sophia took it from her purse and looked at the screen. "What's up with all these notifications?"

"I tagged you," Noah said.

Sophia looked at him. "In what?"

"I posted the video just now."

Sophia's eyes widened. "Why would you do that?"

Noah gave her a look. "What's the name of the song?"

Sophia opened the Instagram app and looked at the post. His caption said, "#itsawrap Can't wait for y'all to see this movie! Meanwhile, fun times at the wrap party. Got a chance to sing new music. Special dedication for @sophiemase. Should I release it?"

"I'm actually speechless," Sophia said.

"I wasn't going to post it at first," Noah said. "Honestly, I know it's about to make some people mad, plus I didn't know how you'd feel about the attention. But I prayed about it, which is wild—I'm actually praying about stuff. And I realized it's my first post since giving my life to Jesus. It felt good to do something I wouldn't normally do. It's like, special on top of special."

"Do you realize what you did, though?" Sophia said. "It's gonna be kind of hard for you to give that 'you're special' line in the next city."

"Are you still going there?" Noah said. "So the song and this whole night was just part of the game?"

Sophia sighed. "No, I don't think it's a game. But I still don't see how we'll be able to keep in touch." She gave a hint of a smile. "Airdrop the video, though. I'll play 'You're Special' when you stop texting."

"I'll Airdrop it, but not for that reason." Noah sent it as his phone vibrated with a text. "Driver is two minutes away."

Sophia looked into his eyes, telling herself not to get emotional.

Noah took her into his arms. "Cling and abide. That's what we're doing, right?"

Sophia nodded in his chest. "Right."

"Writing you that song and performing it was my step of faith," Noah said. "Putting my heart out there, learning to do relationships differently. And that's my 'ask' too—asking Jesus to help me do that. Top of the list is staying in touch with you."

Sophia nodded in his chest again.

Noah took a step back and lifted his bags. "Reply when I text you," he said. He walked out to the car as it pulled up.

She stared after him, wondering why he didn't kiss her goodbye. It would've definitely been special.

Sophia took the elevator back up, her phone vibrating as the doors opened. She stepped out, looking at it. Amid endless Instagram notifications was a text—**This is a test.**

Sophia smiled inside as she typed—**I promise to reply to every one you send.**

She went back into the party and sat at a table to herself, replaying the night in her head. It hardly seemed real even now. What would it be like in the coming weeks when all of this was a distant memory? It really did seem ridiculous.

Cling and abide.

Sophia nodded to herself. That was the only thing that made sense —cling to God—the only thing that was sure. That's what she would do. And she and Noah . . . well . . . that would probably always seem ridiculous.

"Okay, everybody," Alonzo said as the deejay paused the music. "We've got our next special appearance . . ."

CHAPTER 89

"I think it's a good time for me to cut out." Jillian stood between Tommy and Treva. "I have to be up early to fix one last breakfast before Mariah and Brooke fly out."

"Okay, party pooper," Treva said. "If I can stay knowing my one-year-old might be up at any time in the night, so can you. We never get to hang out. And we're actually having fun tonight."

"So there's a whole story behind this next guest appearance," Alonzo was saying. "But I can't tell the story as well as she can. So I'm excited to bring to the stage one-half of this Dove and Grammy Award winning duo—please welcome Kelli Howard!"

"Wow, Kelli's here?" Jillian clapped with the rest as she walked out. "Steph is gonna hate that she missed this."

"Thank you, Alonzo," Kelli said, looking classy in black pants, a long, belted black wrap jacket, and glittery heels. "Good evening everybody!" She smiled as people greeted her back. "I'm so excited to be here for the wrap party. I've been excited about this movie from the moment I heard about it, so to be able to come here tonight and worship with you means the world to me."

Jillian leaned to Treva. "Look at Cedric moving to the very front. I love it. He is *the* proudest big brother ever."

"Alonzo said there's a story behind my being here tonight," Kelli said, "and that he can't tell it as well as I can, which may be true. But I can't tell it as well as this next person. So come on up here, Tommy Porter!"

"Tommy?" Jillian looked at him. "What do you have to do with Kelli being here?"

Tommy went up on the platform and greeted Kelli with a hug. She gave him the microphone.

"The story starts way back," Tommy said. "Junior year in college my best friend Jillian told me to do this exercise that I did not want to do." He walked the platform slowly. "The issue was whether I'd continue to invest energy in a relationship with a young woman named Regina. But first I had to figure out how I felt about Regina."

Jillian looked at Treva. "I am so confused as to why he's telling this story right now."

"So Jillian said, 'Tommy, you never know your thoughts on something until you write it down. That's when it clicks for you. So write down what you're feeling about Regina and the relationship—no filter. If you end up with a love letter, get back with her. If you can't come up with a paragraph, maybe not."

A few chuckles sounded in the room.

"I thought this was the dumbest idea," Tommy continued. "But I said, whatever, I'll do it. Ended up with three pages. Discovered things about myself that I didn't realize, and this was the biggest one—that I had a deep desire to love someone and to be loved in return." He paused. "I also discovered that Regina wasn't the one."

Treva looked at Jillian. "Do you remember all of this?"

"Like it was yesterday," Jillian said.

"If you were in the Cling class, you know I've been through some things, including two divorces." Tommy paused with a sigh. "The thing I desired deeply—to love and to be loved—wasn't working out for me." He started walking slowly again. "So in the midst of the hurt and pain, I said, hey, I'm cool just being single. Even felt the Lord had called me to it, indefinitely. That was some months ago. But these past few weeks, I've been really leaning into my relationship with the Lord and experiencing more of *His* love." He paused again. "Let me tell you . . . nobody can love like He can."

Several people around Jillian nodded with "amen's."

"Meanwhile, I'm now doing this Cling class," Tommy said. "And we had a challenge to take a step of faith. Now, I'm the one who came up with challenge, but I hadn't actually taken the step." His words were deliberate as he looked out at them. "I prayed about what my step of faith should be, and Jillian's words from junior year came to mind. *Write*. Write what you're feeling and thinking about this season of your life, about God and your relationship with Him, about the disappointments and failures, about everything—no filter. Just lay it all out there, no matter how much it hurts and let the Lord meet you there."

"Wow," Jillian uttered, mostly to herself, knowing what a step that had to have been for Tommy.

"I started writing, and in no time, I had pages and pages," Tommy said. "And I realized . . ." He paused, staring downward a second. "I realized I was writing to the Lord." He paused again and blew out a breath. "I was venting and questioning and breaking down, tears falling on the paper."

Jillian felt her own tears stirring. *Jesus, this is incredible.*

"The more I wrote," Tommy said, "the more it became this love letter . . . to the Lord. I started seeing things I couldn't see before. God was giving me understanding as I wrote, and I was praising like I hadn't praised before." He stopped walking and looked at them. "Now here's the strange part. I started hearing a melody. Now I've always loved music—hearing melodies isn't the strange part. I've just never heard an *original* melody. I'm sitting there with my paper and pen, and these words start coming to me—words to a song."

"What? Tommy, you wrote a song?" Jillian spoke under her breath.

"I couldn't believe God gave me a *song*, which He *knows* is my love language." Tommy blew out a breath as if still trying to grasp it. "The challenge for the last week of the study was from John 15:7—'If you abide in Me, and My words abide in you, ask whatever you wish, and it will be done for you.'" He walked again. "So I said, 'Lord, if it's Your will, I'm asking that this can somehow be recorded.' And I watched

God do it. Long story short, Noah heard the lyrics and put me in touch with someone who produced the track. And I sent it to Kelli and asked if she would sing it." He exhaled. "That's the whole story behind Kelli's being here tonight. She's here to sing the song, which is called, 'As Long As I Cling.'"

Jillian's heart was already doing back flips—then she heard that title. She went to meet Tommy as he came down from the platform.

"I can't believe you didn't tell me," Jillian said. "You wrote a *song*?! You put "as long as I cling" in a *song*? I can't even think straight right now."

"I wanted to surprise you," Tommy said. "But I'm a little nervous now that everyone's about to hear it."

All eyes focused on Kelli as a mid-tempo track started playing. She closed her eyes as she began to sing the first verse.

It's complicated
When your life isn't what you thought it would be
Is it overrated
When you want to see what you prayed and believed?
"Oh, Tommy, I feel that so much," Jillian murmured.
Kelli looked upward now, extending her hand.
I come to You, feeling broken
So nothing unspoken
Don't wanna give up
Is grace really enough
Help me build my faith up
You give me what I need—it's truth.

Kelli took a step forward as she went into the chorus, looking out at them.
I can overcome
Be perfected from
All the trials that come
You can help me run
As long as I cling.
I can still believe
Have the faith to see

You are all I need
Your presence is everything
As long as I cling to You, Lord.
You are worthy of all glory
No one like You
I'm gonna stay here, in Your presence
The God of heaven
As long as I cling.

Tommy looked at Jillian. "You're crying about the song?"

"There's so much healing in the lyrics, so much strength, so much answered prayer." Jillian couldn't stop the tears. "God is so good. This song is beautiful, Tommy. You even put your heart's desire in there about wanting to stay in His presence."

Kelli moved into the second verse.

It's complicated
When you learn that every kind of love isn't sure
Is it overrated
To be secure, just want a love that endures
I come to You, heart outspoken
Spilling with emotion
How can I get through?
What can I hang onto?
I want a hope that's brand new.
You give me what I need it's truth—

Kelli looked upward again as her voice went into the bridge.

You're the love that never leaves
From everlasting
So here's my life, take all of me
I just want to cling . . .

Arms raised, tears spilled down Jillian's face as she worshiped. This was her heart's cry as well—*here's my life, take all of me; I just want to cling.* But knowing Tommy had penned the words—knowing the whole song was a declaration of overcoming in Christ—made her praise all the more. *Thank You, Jesus. You are so good. So faithful. Thank You, Jesus.*

639

Kelli was praising as well, ad libbing over the track. Jillian wiped her tears and noticed that others were lost in praise, including Tommy.

"You are worthy of all glory!" Kelli said, her voice lifted up as tears streaked her cheeks. "There's no one like You, O God! Just let us stay in Your presence. Help us to cling to You, O God. We give You glory! . . . We give You glory! . . . We praise Your holy name! Thank You that we can overcome in Christ Jesus. Thank You for helping us to run! You are all we need. We praise You, Lord!"

Kelli continued to pray and praise as arms lifted throughout the room.

"And Lord, when we we're too weak to cling, You said Your strength is perfected in our weakness," Kelli said. "Strengthen us continually, O Lord, so we can cling to You continually. There is *strength* in your presence. There is *healing* in Your presence. There is *joy* and *no fear* in Your presence, Lord. Help us to stay right here, in Your presence. We give You glory. . . We give you glory, O Lord. Thank You that we have the victory, as long as we cling. In Jesus' mighty name." She looked out. "And everybody said—"

"Amen!" rang out in the room.

Kelli walked the platform, still praising. Then she exhaled and looked out at them. "So." She smiled as she walked a little. "If you were listening to Tommy's story, you heard him mention his best friend Jillian. I don't know if all of you know, but Jillian is here tonight." She paused, looking out. "Jillian, can you come up here?"

Jillian looked confused and lifted a hand partway.

"I see your hand, Jillian," Kelli said. "But I need everybody to see you, so can you come up here?"

"Okay, this is interesting," Jillian mumbled, moving to the platform.

Jillian watched as Kelli got a stool and placed it in front of her. "She's all yours," Kelli said, moving off the stage.

Jillian turned—and saw Tommy behind her.

"I sound like Noah right now, telling you to take a seat." Tommy had the microphone again.

Jillian stared at him, trembling a little as she lowered herself onto the stool.

"Jill, you were there in the study room when I discovered my deepest desire—to love and to be loved." Tommy stood before her, staring into her eyes. "The following year, right before we graduated, you told me you loved me. And I told you I loved you. But I didn't know what to do with that. You were my best friend, and I didn't want to mess that up. I was so confused." He paused. "But I'm not confused today."

Tommy went down on one knee and the crowd reacted. Jillian exhaled slowly, tears clouding her eyes.

"Jillian, my best friend then, my best friend now, I love you." Tommy held her with his gaze. "And it's a little scary to acknowledge, but my deepest desire is to love you and to be loved by you for the rest of our days." He brushed a tear. "And as long as I cling to Him"—he raised a finger upward—"I know perfect love will cast out fear." He took a box from his jacket and opened it to reveal a ring with three diamonds. "Jill, will you marry me?"

Jillian could barely see for the tears. "Yes. *Yes*."

The room erupted as Tommy put the ring on her finger and lifted her to an embrace. He kissed her then leaned to her ear, amid the cheers. "I love you so much."

Jillian held tight to him. "Tommy, my heart is exploding right now."

They came off of the platform, hugging Kelli first.

"I am so happy for you two," Kelli said, beaming. "Congratulations!"

"Kelli, the way you sang that song . . ." Tommy shook his head. "You ministered so beautifully. I can't thank you enough."

"You know I love your voice, Kelli," Jillian said. "I need that song in my life."

"You didn't say you wrote a *song*." Treva walked up with Lance, shaking her head at Tommy. "That was *so* beyond what I expected. I couldn't stop crying. And the proposal!" She hugged him. "The whole thing was beautiful, Tommy."

"Wait, you told them you were going to propose?" Jillian said.

"I let a handful of people know," Tommy said. "And good thing. Treva had to talk you out of leaving early."

Treva embraced her sister. "You have no idea how much my heart is rejoicing."

"I might have a slight idea," Jillian said, smiling.

"You got her off that shuttle, man." Lance hugged Tommy. "I got a little emotional." He hugged Jillian next.

"He got me off a shuttle?" Jillian said.

"I'll explain later," Tommy said. "Some people want to see you." He nodded to her left.

Jillian squealed. "Courtenay?! You're not supposed to be here till spring break. And David and Trevor? I thought only one of my kids was here." She took all four of them into a group hug. "How did this happen?"

"Tommy called each of us," Courtenay said, "to ask for your hand in marriage."

Jillian looked at him. "You asked my kids for my hand?"

"It was important to me to have their blessing," Tommy said, "and for them to be here."

"He flew me up here," Courtenay said, wagging her eyebrows.

Jillian looked at her kids. "Did you all tell him he already *had* your blessing?"

Tommy looked confused. "What do you mean?"

"We had a family meeting," David said, "basically telling Mom to marry you."

"Then Mom told us it wasn't happening," Sophia said, "because you said you were staying single. So for my step of faith, I fasted and asked for God's will to be done."

"Soph, I didn't know that," Jillian said.

"This whole thing is blowing me away," Tommy said. "Come here, you guys." He took them in and hugged them.

"Tommy, Tommy, Tommy." Reggie paused, looking at him. "I wasn't going to believe it until I saw it. You actually did the thing." He hugged him. "I might be happier than the day *I* proposed, for all the blood, sweat, and tears that went into this."

"I'll give it to you, man," Tommy said. "You wouldn't let up. You knew."

"Then you went full beast mode with the story and the song," Reggie said. "Epic status, man. I didn't know you had it in you." He hugged Jillian next. "I wasn't satisfied with you being my Aunt Jillian. I wanted the connection to come through Tommy, so you'd be my sister."

"Don't make me cry again, Reg," Jillian said.

"I was bawling like a baby," Faith said, hugging them both. "I've got the whole thing on video, every amazing second. And I've already got an idea for the wedding—"

"Okay, wow," Reggie said, "you might be happier than the day I proposed too."

"This is all I've got to say," Stephanie said, walking up. "Lindell came home. We've had our baby. And Jill and Tommy are engaged. I need nothing more."

Jillian smiled, hugging her. "Girl, what are you doing here?"

"You think I was missing this?" Stephanie said. "Cyd told me this morning, and I said I am *there*."

"Oh, so you saw Kelli?" Jillian said.

"Kelli and Brian came to the B and B right before this and visited with the baby," Stephanie said. "And yes, we got here in time for *everything*—come here, Tommy." She hugged him. "We put you on the altar and look what God did. I'm so relieved." She chuckled.

"And I'm so happy for you, Lindell, and little Lindzey," Tommy said. "Where's Lindell?"

"In the back with the baby," Stephanie said. "We only came for the proposal, so we're about to go. Trying to be careful about germs and what not. Oh, and Jill, my mom's doing breakfast at the B and B tomorrow morning. I wanted you to fully enjoy the evening and all that God has done."

"Thank you, Steph," Jillian said, hugging her again.

A familiar piano melody came through the speakers, causing the three of them to look to the platform.

"Y'all didn't think I left my husband at home, did you?" Kelli was back on stage, this time with Brian. "We're excited to share this song that's become an anthem in our household. The *Promises* song! Lord, help us believe!"

"Ahh it's an anthem for me too now," Stephanie said.

"All things are possible with you . . ." Kelli sang.

"Hey," Tommy said, leaning to Jillian's ear. "Let's step out for a minute."

Jillian nodded and took his hand, walking out with him, pausing as people wished them well. In the foyer just outside, they ran into Silas, who was coming back in.

"Congratulations are definitely in order," Silas said, shaking Tommy's hand. "I'm sincerely happy for the two of you."

"I really appreciate that, Silas," Tommy said.

"Thank you, Silas," Jillian said.

Silas looked at Jillian. "You didn't have to wait as long as you thought. You must've prayed some powerful prayers."

He moved inside, and Tommy looked at Jillian as they walked. "What was that about?"

"He asked me on an official dinner date," Jillian said. "I told him I couldn't go, and I told him why." They sat on a cushioned bench in a quiet alcove as she continued, looking into his eyes. "My step of faith was to wait for you, and my 'ask' was that we'd be together, but only if it was the Lord's will."

Tommy seemed at a loss for words. "Why would you wait, Jill? That could've lasted who knows how long."

"Well, for one thing," Jillian said, "I felt it was God moving me to wait. But also, because I love you, Tommy. I didn't need to marry again. Having you and our friendship in my life—that's the treasure, like you said in the chapel. That was enough for me."

Tommy stared long into her eyes and leaned in, kissing her softly. "I love you." He exhaled as he put his arm around her. "This feels so good, just sitting here with you. I wanted a moment with just the two of us."

"I was thinking that when you took my hand." Jillian entwined her fingers with his. "*This* feels so good."

Tommy's head fell next to hers. "Did I tell you I love you?"

"I'll never get tired of hearing it," Jillian said. "I love you, too. And I can't believe we're engaged." She looked at him. "Are we really engaged?"

Tommy lifted her left hand. "We are really engaged. Oh, and I know you might think it was presumptuous to pick a ring for you. This was for the surprise, but I want us to go back and you can see what you like."

"Tommy, this ring is incredible," Jillian said, looking at it. "The only reason I'd say we need to go back is because it's got to be way over budget. An emerald cut diamond in the center plus one on either side?"

"So you like it?" Tommy said.

"I *love* it. But I'm saying if it's too much—"

Tommy silenced her with a kiss. "It's not too much."

"I just want you to know," Jillian said, "that the past two decades I've gotten good at living within a small budget. I don't want you to think you have to buy something like this for me."

"And I just want you to know," Tommy said, "that an upside of being a bachelor most of my adult life—with zero kids—is I've got a nice savings. What matters to me is that you love it."

"I love so many things," Jillian said, leaning into him. "Your story about writing the love letter to God, the way God showed up, *the song*, the way you planned everything tonight . . ." She looked up at him. "And I love that you're my fiancé." She kissed him. "But I don't want a long engagement. Is it too soon to be thinking about that?"

"I was thinking the same," Tommy said. "Long engagement for what? And no big wedding either."

"Ooh, you know what would be amazing?" Jillian said. "You brought up that moment we said goodbye. What if we had an intimate ceremony on Maryland's campus, right on South Hill?"

"Oh, that would be dope," Tommy said.

"And both of our moms can be there," Jillian said. "Plus, of course, your dad and Adrienne, and Darlene too—it's so convenient because they're all in Maryland."

"And a few of us can just fly out there," Tommy said. "I love that. I'll talk to Lance."

"Ask him if his calendar is free for like, next week."

Tommy chuckled softly. "I wish we could plan it that fast." He shifted a little, looking into her eyes. "I was low key staring at you all night, knowing I was about to ask you to be my wife. And I was overwhelmed. I can't believe God did this. He brought me out of a wilderness, Jill. And the fact that it's about to be me and you? How crazy is that?"

"It's not *about* to be me and you." Jillian lifted her hand again. "This means *now* it's me and you. Jilli-Jill and Tommy-Tom. And yes, that's crazy."

He let his gaze linger on her. "You look amazing tonight. I mean, you always look amazing, even when you don't bother with your hair—"

Jillian elbowed him.

"But you are *smokin'* tonight, for real," Tommy said. "Maybe because you wore a dress, which is rare. But that burgundy is hot on you. Makes your hazel eyes pop. And the muted gold strappy shoe is all swag."

"So I get a whole assessment of my look now, huh?"

"But wait, I'm not done." He ran his fingers down a lock of her hair. "Where'd this come from? I've never seen your hair like this."

"Well, now I get it," Jillian said. "Sophie said I should try something different. So she did my hair, made it stick straight instead of curly. She must've thought it would make an impression."

"Oh, it did," Tommy said.

"Now it's your turn," Jillian said. "Want to know what I've thought about you the past few months?"

"What?"

"That if you're bent on staying single," Jillian said, "you need to stop working out and looking better than you did in college."

"What does being single have to do with working out?"

"Because if we couldn't be together, you could at least do me the courtesy of not looking good."

"I'm heavier than I was in college, though," Tommy said.

"It's all muscle, though." Jillian leaned in, hugging him. "In all the right places."

"Are you flirting with me, Jilli-Jill?"

"Absolutely."

Tommy nestled close. "Do we have to go back to the party?"

"Probably," Jillian said.

"But I don't want to move."

"Me either."

Jillian let a few seconds pass then stood and extended her hand. They started back, fingers laced.

"By the way," Tommy said. "Reggie and Faith are already looking for their own place."

"Wow, it just hit me," Jillian said. "I guess I don't need to buy a house."

Tommy squeezed her hand. "No, Jill, you don't."

"Do Faith and Reggie need to move, though?" Jillian said. "Sophia's headed to college, God willing, so it'll only be David and Trevor most of the time."

"Reggie never intended to be there long," Tommy said. "It was just to help them get started. He said it's their wedding gift, giving us space to be newlyweds."

"Did he really say that?"

"You know he did."

"Ooh, you know what else just hit me? The *honeymoon*." Jillian leaned into his arm. "Where should we go?"

"Any place you want," Tommy said.

"You can't say any place I want," Jillian said. "I want to hear your preferences."

"I only have one." Tommy turned to her and held her. "Wherever you are. As long as we're together, baby, I'm good."

Jillian wrapped her arms around him. "Mmm add that to the list of things I love."

"What's that?"

"You calling me baby."

Tommy kissed her. "I feel like this is a dream. Like I need to get a piece of paper and write, 'I'm marrying my best friend' a hundred times before I can believe it."

Jillian kissed him back. "And that's one paper I would not need to edit."

CHAPTER 90

"$\mathcal{I}$ must say again how nice this is." Janice looked across the table at everyone. "It's certainly a first, both of my daughters here with their dates for dinner."

"Mom, for the tenth time, Trey is not my date," Jade said. "Friends. We're *friends.*"

Trey bumped her leg under the table. He'd told her to stop being nit-picky with her mother and to remember the reason they were there. Jade cut an eye at him.

"Jade, I stopped trying to keep up with what you all call various relationships a long time ago," Janice said. "I'm just saying it's nice to actually see the faces of the gentlemen you're with and have a regular conversation instead of them coming and going at night."

"Mom, really? This is what you're doing?" Jordyn eyed her. "This is *why* we don't like to bring people around you. Because *you* don't know how to have a regular conversation."

Jesse cleared his throat. "It's definitely good to see you again, Mrs. Rogers." He glanced down at his plate. "And this roast with the gravy and tender vegetables is delicious."

Jade exchanged a glance and a smirk with Jordyn. Jesse got points for not only calling their mom by the right name—she reinstated her former married name after the annulment—but also for not mentioning the occasion that brought him there the first time, which was her wedding.

"I appreciate that, Jesse, thank you," Janice said.

Jade cut into one of her potatoes. "But I'll just say, Mom, that you're right."

Jordyn gave her a surprised look.

"We did have guys coming and going at night." Jade paused, taking a bite of food. "And this *is* nice, to be able to bring God-fearing men to dinner. I never thought this would be how our lives would look."

"That's true," Jordyn said, making an adjustment herself. "For God to move in my life and Jade's life around the same time is a miracle." She ate some beef with carrots. "And I apologize for going off, Mom. Obviously, we wanted to bring Jesse and Trey, or we would've come by ourselves."

"Which would have been a treat in itself," Janice said, "since Jade's only been here once in the past few months."

"And you know why, Mom," Jade said. "Things have been rocky ever since Dad died and we found out . . . everything we found out. I'm praying we can get past all of that."

Janice cut a piece of her roast. "So, Jordyn, you said you just got back from filming in Florida. How did that go?" She ate a forkful.

"It was a packed three days, but it went well," Jordyn said. "It's a wrap on the whole movie."

"When does it come out?" Janice said.

"I don't know." Jordyn looked at Trey. "Do you know when it'll be in theaters?"

"I don't think there's an official release date yet." Trey broke off a piece of his roll. "But Alonzo said they're thinking by the end of the year."

Janice looked at him. "Now, Trey, what's your connection to the movie?"

Trey finished a bite of food. "Kendra was my sister."

"Oh, my goodness," Janice said. "I'm sorry, I didn't realize. Jade said you did missionary work or something."

"Trey was the best man in that wedding video," Jordyn said. "Remember Jade kept talking about how cute he was?"

"That makes me want to pull the video up," Janice said. "I do see the resemblance now." She looked at Jade. "And I remember you hitting that replay button. Friends, huh?"

"Friends," Jade said. "And I told Trey all about that."

"So now that the production phase is over, what happens from here?" Janice looked at Jordyn. "Will you get an opportunity to style hair on other movie shoots?"

"No, this was a unique situation, with most of the filming taking place in St. Louis." Jordyn said. "Also, the key was that I could style the head wraps."

"I'm just remembering how obsessed you both used to be with Alonzo Coles," Janice said. "He's got this production company now and he's family. I'm surprised you're not doing everything you can to work for him."

"Well, clearly we're not those fangirls anymore," Jordyn said. "And it just wouldn't make sense to try to work for him. Doing what? I'm fine doing what I do for our channel."

"What about you, Jade?" Janice said. "Your vlogs were a marketing hit for them, with millions of views. Will you continue to handle social media for the production company?"

"That was only for this film," Jade said. She paused a moment. "And actually, I hadn't had a chance to tell you, but the next thing I might do is a missions trip . . . to Africa."

Janice gave her a blank stare. "You can't be serious. I'd sooner imagine you on a trip to Mars than a third world country."

"Mom, before tonight you couldn't have imagined me at the dinner table with a guy, especially one I'm not sleeping with." Jade forked up more food. "Things are different. *I'm* different."

"How long would you be there?" Janice said.

"Two years."

"Jade, even your father didn't go that far." Janice's eyes penetrated. "You can't just pick up and leave *life*. You have responsibilities. For one thing, you share an apartment and living expenses with your sister. You would leave her in a lurch?"

"It's not a big deal," Jordyn said. "It's a month-to-month lease, and I'm already looking at one-bedroom apartments, just in case."

"I'm assuming you'd be going on this two-year trip with Trey?" Janice said.

"We would be on the same missions team, yes," Jade said.

"Okay, help me understand," Janice said, "because you haven't even known him that long—no offense, Trey. I'm just looking out for my daughter. Jade, why would you go to the other side of the world with him?"

"Mom, it's not just the two of us," Jade said. "Again, it's a team. And the team is organized and sent by Living Word, which has a whole global missions program." She heaved a sigh. "But you asked why I would go. I won't even lie—it seemed insane to me too, at first. But I've been praying about it and reading about it, and I'm starting to feel this burden to be part of something beyond *me*." She could feel it even now as she said it. "I've been doing hair videos for years, and I'm thankful I can make a living at it. But I realized I had never asked God what *His* plan is for me. For the first time in my life, I'm doing that. I want to know. And if I get the sense that it's His will for me to go, I'm going."

"Well, that was a whole word," Jordyn said. "I started doing those testimony videos last year because I felt burdened, and then I just stopped. Haven't posted anything faith-based in months. And I've never asked God what His plan is for me either." She nodded to herself. "This would be the perfect time. More and more I do want to live for Jesus."

"Oh, your dad would be giddy if he were here," Janice said. "I don't know how it happened, but the two of you are now perfect Randall clones. He would be so proud."

"Mrs. Rogers," Trey said, "from what I could tell, Randall was proud of you also."

Jade slipped him a dubious look, and Trey knocked his leg against hers.

Janice seemed to ponder that as she ate some roast and potatoes. "I didn't connect the fact that you knew Randall," she said. "If he brought me into the conversation, I'm sure you got an earful."

"He only had good things to say," Trey said. "He'd come to the house during Kendra's illness, and we'd all be sitting around talking. I remember he told us how you met—in high school, right?—and how your beauty and intellect captured him. And another time he mentioned what a great decorator you were and how you put so much time and attention into making your house a home for your family."

Janice sipped water from her glass. "I'm surprised to hear that. I assumed he complained about me around his church friends."

"Not at all," Trey said. "And one time I remember he brought some —was it a pasta shells dish?—that you had made. And he talked about what a good cook you were. Kendra couldn't eat it because, well, she couldn't eat most things. But Lance and I tore it up. We were thankful because some days were just really hard, and finding something to eat was an afterthought. It was right on time."

Janice stared down at her plate. "Randall asked if I would make that, and I had an attitude the whole time." She took a moment. "He knew how to cook himself, but I think it was a particularly busy time at his firm. Anyway, I told him it was *his* church and *his* friends, and he couldn't be asking me to cook for everybody who got sick." An audible sigh escaped. "I didn't know till this moment who it was for."

"I get that," Trey said. "You couldn't put a face on it. We weren't personal to you. And the whole church thing was a source of hostility. I've been there."

"You've been there?" Janice said.

"Around the time Kendra got sick, I didn't want anything to do with church because of some things I was going through," Trey said. "Actually, Kendra had stopped going herself."

"But she married Lance, the pastor," Janice said. "And you were his best man. I assumed all of you had, I don't know, a deep faith commitment."

"By the time of the wedding, we were in a different place," Trey

653

said. "But I'm just saying, it's a journey for all of us. I think the four of us here could say we're really surprised by what the Lord has done in our lives." He paused. "You might be saying the same thing one day."

"Oh, Randall tried many times in many ways to tell me why I needed Jesus," Janice said. "It never moved me."

Trey smiled a little. "Jesus hasn't moved either."

"Meaning what?" Janice said.

"He still loves you," Trey said. "He still offers forgiveness of sins and the gift of eternal life. He's still willing to give you the kind of peace and joy you've never experienced. I don't know everything that's happened in this family or in your life personally, but I know it's been really hard. Jesus is still willing to take your weariness and your burdens and give you rest."

Several seconds elapsed as Janice stared down at her food.

"And on another note"—Trey gathered the last of the food on his plate—"you're two for two with these meals, Mrs. Rogers, because this is definitely delicious. Jade *clearly* got her cooking skills from you." He turned to Jade. "Make sure you ask your mom for this recipe."

"You could *not* have told me that we'd end up reminiscing about old times after dinner, in a good way." Jade sat in a recliner in her mom's family room.

"Just the fact that we were laughing with Mom. Like, what?" Jordyn had a spot on the sofa next to Jesse. "Totally didn't expect that."

Jesse looked at her. "Didn't we pray about tonight on the drive over here?"

"And specifically prayed for a good time." Trey had his legs kicked up on the other recliner, engaged with his phone.

"Yeah, but you saw how tense it was for a while there." Jordyn looked at Jesse. "Did *you* think the mood would lighten up?"

"It was definitely tense," Jesse said. "I was praying while we were sitting there. I thought maybe it would be better in the morning before we left. But Trey came in clutch with that story."

"I wouldn't have even thought to bring it up," Trey said. "But when she mentioned Randall being proud, it came to mind. That was all God."

"Well, let's just pray we can get through breakfast with no blowups," Jade said. "Then we can drive back counting the trip a success." She looked at Trey. "That's the first time I've seen somebody talk to her about Jesus, where she wasn't openly hostile."

"We've been praying, Jade," Trey said. "And Randall was praying for *years*. You two forgiving her and loving on her is everything."

"Speaking of the drive back," Jesse said, "since it's on me, I'm about to hit this bed. But uh, we're sitting on it."

"Oh, let's pull it out," Jordyn said, rising. "And I'll get some sheets."

"Trey, I put your stuff in a bedroom upstairs." Jade got up from the recliner. "I'll show you." She looked at him. "*Trey.*"

"Wow, this is crazy." Trey looked up from his phone. "Hey, turn on the news."

Jade got the remote and flipped to cable news.

The anchor spoke into the camera. ". . . so we knew shoes were about to drop, but we didn't know how big. The NBA tonight has made the decision to suspend play altogether."

"What?" Jesse walked closer to the television. "No basketball?"

"Quite frankly everyone is shocked," the anchor continued. "This is a place we've never been. We're now trying to figure out what next steps will be . . ."

"This is incredible," Jordyn said. "All because of that virus?"

Trey nodded. "A lot of shoes are about to drop." He looked at Jade. "The missions pastor just sent out an alert. Based on what they're seeing around the world, it looks like international travel for missions is about to be suspended."

Jade took a moment to process what he'd said. "Wow. I guess that's the answer to all the prayers. I'm not going."

Trey nodded soberly. "Looks like neither of us is going."

CHAPTER 91

"*E*verything is happening so fast." Treva sat on the floor of her living room watching Wes stack blocks with Zoe. "No March Madness, no baseball, no hockey. Even Broadway's going dark."

"Yeah, it was real when I saw that Coachella was postponed." Faith occupied the floor space across from her. "What's *not* affected right now?—Zoe, play nice. Let Wes have that." She paused a moment. "And Mom, did you see the video Desiree Riley uploaded?"

"A new one?" Treva said. "What's it about?"

"You know how we were wondering whether she decided to leave town?"

"I haven't given much thought to where she is as far as a physical location," Treva said. "I've just been praying for the Lord to plant her where she needs to be spiritually."

"Well, Grandma Pam and I were wondering," Faith said. "Turns out, she's in Australia. She said for the first time in her life, she sensed God speaking to her. She didn't know why, but she was moved to change her ticket to Melbourne." She redirected Zoe, who was banging on the piano. "Then the pandemic hits. At first, she was bummed because she would've stayed in St. Louis and quarantined with her parents. But she's renting a room in this house, and she found out the woman who owns the home is a believer."

"Are you serious?" Treva said.

"So they start talking," Faith said, "and the woman is bummed because they've got severe restrictions over there and she can't get together with her Bible study group."

"Come on, Faith," Treva said. "Really?"

"Mom, I couldn't believe it," Faith said. "You have to watch the video. Desiree shows footage of her and the woman studying the Bible together. She said there's so much that God needs to do in her life and heart, and that this quarantine will be all about her biggest journey yet, a spiritual one."

"Is our God an awesome God or what?" Treva said. "That's exceeding abundant!"

"*Mom.*" Hope called well before she came into view. "Can you believe *Disney World* shut down?" She spread her hands, incredulous. "No Mickey?"

"That's the shut-down that made it real for you?" Treva said. "You haven't mentioned Disney World in years."

"But you know it's there if you want to go." Hope plopped down on the floor beside her. "It feels like we're entering an alternate universe."

"Wes, you can't have all the blocks. Share with Zoe." Treva took some from his pile and gave them to Zoe. "Play dates with these two are so comical."

"We hadn't had one in too long," Faith said. "I love watching them together."

"I'm waiting for the day when he tells Zoe to call him 'Uncle Wes,'" Treva said.

"Ha," Faith said. "I think she'll convince Wes to call her 'Aunt Zoe' and we'll have to explain the actual chain of command to him."

Treva chuckled as the front door came open. "Is that who I think it is?" she called. "With what I hope you've got?"

Pamela came and stood before them. "So, the good news is that I went for it. By the grace of God, I got over my fears and actually learned *to drive*, which is practically a miracle, as far as I'm concerned. And I can take the test again."

"Aw, Grandma Pam, you really did go for it," Faith said. "You'll *kill* it next time, for sure."

"And now you know what to expect with the driver test," Treva said. "It'll be a breeze when you go again."

Pamela looked to her left, and Tommy walked in.

"And the bad news," Tommy said, "is that I no longer have a student, because Momma Pam killed it *this* time."

Pamela took the paper from her pocket and did a little dance as she held it in the air, beaming.

"You got it?!" Treva hopped up. "I'm gonna get you for that." She hugged her tight. "I'm so excited for you!"

"Knock, knock—can we come on in? The door's wide open."

"Cinda?" Treva walked to the entryway. "Hey, you two."

"Hey, Treva," Alonzo said. "We told Lance we'd stop by."

"He's been on conference calls the past couple of hours." Treva took her phone from her pocket and started texting. "I'm letting him know you're here. Come on in."

"Ohh, Zoe and Wes playing together?" Cinda walked into the living room. "This is too cute."

"By the way," Treva said. "Pam's got news to share."

"I know it's not what I think it is," Alonzo said. "I know you didn't go out there and conquer on your first try."

"Wait, what?" Lance said, walking in. "Mom, I didn't know you were back." He looked at her. "Well?"

Pamela showed the license, and Lance hugged her so hard she almost lost her balance. Alonzo and Cinda had hands raised, cheering.

"My mom's about to be out here driving in these streets," Lance said, smiling.

"She's *already* out here in these streets," Tommy said. "How you think she passed the test?"

Lance nodded. "You did what I couldn't do, Tommy. Her second son got her out there."

"Wait a minute," Alonzo said, "I thought *I* was the second son."

"I love *all* my sons," Pamela said. "No partiality."

"What?" Lance gave her an incredulous look. "Mom, you *better* show partiality. I'm *your* son. They've got their own mommas."

Tommy chuckled. "He is so serious right now."

Alonzo sat down on the sofa with a sigh. "Y'all, it's been a day. I'm glad you're all here so I can update you."

Lance moved closer to him. "I'm assuming it's about the movie. What's going on?"

"I've been on calls with producers, studio execs, actor friends . . ." Alonzo shook his head. "Projects are already being affected at every level. If they're in pre-production, they're getting shelved. Projects ready for release are now on hold."

Pamela took a seat on the sofa as well, listening.

"It's crazy that we literally *just* wrapped," Alonzo said. "If this had happened two weeks ago, we would've had to shut down production. But we have a completed film."

"Glory to God," Pamela said.

"So we'll proceed to post production and get the film ready for release," Alonzo said. "But we don't know how long this pandemic will last. Theaters could be shut down for the foreseeable future."

"But we're looking at the end of the year or early next year for a release date," Faith said. "It can't last *that* long."

"I pray it won't," Alonzo said. "So much we don't know yet." He looked at Pamela. "I hope you didn't think we were done praying for this movie."

"Not in the least bit," Pamela said. "I wasn't expecting anything like this, but God isn't surprised. He'll guide us just as He has from the beginning."

"We've got even more to pray about." Lance looked at Tommy. "Did you get the emails I forwarded you?"

Tommy nodded. "I read them while Momma Pam was taking her test. I got your text too. I can stay for the next conference call."

"Okay, now I'm super curious," Faith said.

"Right," Treva said. "What's the latest, babe?"

Lance looked at them all. "We're about to shut down Living Word and Living Hope."

CHAPTER 92

"*L*indzey might have enough to get her through to high school." Stephanie sat on the bed, sorting through clothes as the baby slept in a bassinet beside her. "I forgot about this—look at this little track suit." She held it up. "Is this the cutest thing or what?"

Lindell lay across the bed. "That shower was a thing to behold. I just hope she gets to wear all this stuff before she grows out of it."

Cyd went overboard all by herself," Stephanie said. "I don't even know how she got it all together so quickly."

"Yeah, but your mom outdid Cyd," Lindell said. "Lindzey got the full 'first granddaughter' treatment."

"Oh, and all this right here?" Stephanie lifted a pile on her right. "Arrived today from Mrs. Cartwright in a beautiful basket. Wasn't that sweet?"

"One thing I can say about this whole B and B experience," Lindell said. "Mrs. Cartwright has always been really thoughtful. Accommodating too. Didn't blink an eye when you told her we wanted to take some time to adjust to our new normal before booking guests."

"Babe." Stephanie paused what she was doing and looked at him. "Can you believe the timing? We're suddenly in the middle of a pandemic, without having to worry about what to do with guests. But wait till you hear this."

"What?" Lindell said.

"I called Mrs. Cartwright to thank her for the baby gift," Stephanie said, "and she started talking about the situation with this virus. Apparently, a friend of hers in Florida contracted it and is now in the hospital. She told me there was no rush whatsoever in opening to guests. She wants us all to be praying for wisdom about what to do, how to do it, and when to do it. She said, 'For now, you and Lindell just enjoy that baby.'"

"That's a blessing," Lindell said. "I talked to one of my coworkers today who has a background in epidemiology. It could take a long time to develop a treatment or vaccine, so proper safety measures are paramount. He started telling me things we would need to do to ensure the safety of our guests and ourselves. But at least we've got some time before we need to go down that road."

Stephanie folded a baby blanket. "You know what else is interesting?"

"What's that?"

"The B and B was one of the things I put on the altar when I prayed with Jillian," Stephanie said. "It's been a source of tension between us, and I wanted to know what God wanted us to do, especially once we had the baby. Would He tell us it was time to go? I was still waiting."

"Wow," Lindell said. "And now we've got this period of time when we're basically not even running a B and B."

"Which makes our lives almost . . . normal," Stephanie said. "Just you me, and Lindzey, for a while anyway."

"Who would've thought we'd find a little normalcy in the midst of the chaos that's happening everywhere this week?" Lindell got up to check on the baby as she started cooing. "It's still hard to believe that Living Word is shutting down."

"I know," Stephanie said, remembering that her biggest concern not long ago had been whether Lindell would run into Warren in the church building. "Life in every other respect is about to be everything *but* normal."

CHAPTER 93

"This is so not the way I thought this would go." Jillian waited as Tommy opened up the door to the main entrance to Living Word.

"I told you to let me get everything set up"—Tommy held the door for her—"and then you come. You're not supposed to be hanging with the groom right before the wedding anyway."

"I don't care about the tradition part," Jillian said. "I'm talking about the way we scrapped our plans and substituted this one—only two days ago. And I love that we did. But who would've thought?— don't forget to set the door so others can get in."

"Done," Tommy said. "And yeah, the *last* thing we would've thought was that a pandemic would shake up our wedding plans." He headed toward the elevator with her. "And who could've imagined a stay-at-home order? But I know one thing—if St. Louis is ordering me to stay home, I need that home to have you in it."

"Amen to that," Jillian said. "I guess I'm just pouting because we don't get a honeymoon. Right after the ceremony, we get to move our things into your house and spend our wedding night with a ton of boxes and all four of my kids—who, by the way, won't be going anywhere, ever."

"I don't care about the boxes or the kids that'll be there indefinitely." Tommy walked onto the elevator and pushed '4'. "I don't care that we'll all be quarantined at home for weeks." He pulled her close and put his arms around her. "Remember what I told you? As long as we're together . . ." He kissed her. "I'll be able to wake up to your face every morning. Baby, that's everything."

"It does something to me when you call me 'baby'." Jillian kissed him again. "That was the attitude adjustment I needed. With the original plan, the honeymoon came with a May wedding—two months away. But God willing, we'll be waking up together *tomorrow*." She walked off the elevator and moved toward the chapel. "Everyone should be getting here in about fifteen minutes, right?"

"Wait, hold it. I can't." Tommy tugged her to a stop. "I need to walk in front of you, 'cause you are *wearing* that jumpsuit. I gotta keep my mind right for about another thirty minutes."

"Ha," Jillian said. "I won't be wearing it for long, since I have to change into sweats after the wedding and start lugging boxes. And what about me having to look at you in that well-tailored suit?"

Tommy got to the chapel door and opened it for Jillian, and she walked in—and saw her kids with Faith, Reggie, and Zoe, Treva and Lance with Joy and Hope, and Pamela holding Wes. Two beautiful bouquets of flowers adorned the front along with several lit candles.

Jillian looked at Tommy. "How did you arrange all of this?"

"I love that you underestimate me."

"Oh, Jill, that white jumpsuit." Treva walked up, eyeing her.

Faith came at the same time. "Aunt Jilliiiaaan. You are not playing today."

"Has she ever looked this fly?" Treva said. "And I can say that because I've known you your whole life, the majority of which you've spent not caring how you look. Girl, turn around."

Jillian smiled as she did so. "Cinda picked it out for me."

"Okay, mystery solved," Treva said, chuckling. "The one shoulder action with the crepe fabric, and those shoes . . ." She shook her head and looked at Tommy. "I hope you positively reinforced all this."

"From the second I saw her," Tommy said. "And you left out the fact that she did her hair."

"Oh, you like?" Courtenay said, patting Jillian's up-do.

"I didn't know you had skills," Faith said, looking at her cousin. "That's such a pretty style."

"Y'all are talking about Jill," Pamela said, "but Tommy's in new territory too. When have we ever seen him in a suit?" She came closer, Wes in her arms. "You're looking handsome, second son."

Tommy smiled. "That's my Momma Pam."

"He's been positively reinforced as well," Jillian said.

"Here's my two cents," Reggie said, taking out his phone. "We'll never see this again from either of them, so get lots of pics." He started snapping.

"Mom." Sophia came over, looking at her phone. "I've been going back and forth with Noah. The rest of his tour got postponed. Can you believe that?"

"I can definitely believe it, given the state of things," Jillian said. "I bet he's bummed about it, though."

"Really bummed," Sophia said. "He thought he'd be traveling the world, and he'll be home like the rest of us."

"You two interested in getting married today or what?" Lance called from up front.

"Yeah, somewhat," Tommy said.

"Then let's do this," Lance said. "Everybody, let's go ahead and take a seat."

Jillian and Tommy walked to the front and stood before Lance, flanked by the flowers and candles.

Lance took the microphone. "So clearly, this isn't your typical wedding ceremony," he said. "We're informal today, surrounded by family—and only family, given the current guidelines. As you know, the pandemic caused Tommy and Jillian to have to change their wedding plans, so this is impromptu. But also, it's not a first marriage for either of them. So they told me, 'Let's just keep it short and sweet. All we need are the vows.'"

"Well," Reggie said, sounding like an old preacher.

Jillian and Tommy looked at each other, wondering what was up.

"The problem is," Lance said, "*because* it's only family, we felt free to usurp your wishes." He gave an unapologetic smile. "We wanted to do something special. So before you say your vows, anyone who wants to speak will share what this occasion means to him or her. And I'll go ahead and start."

Tommy took Jillian's hand as they turned more toward Lance.

"As a pastor," Lance said, "I can't help but get involved with a lot of people's lives on a lot of levels. But when I can, I try to stay out of personal relationships because it gets too messy. So I've never said this to either of you." He paused, looking from one to the other. "This is a union that's close to my heart."

Jillian wondered if anybody had tissues. She could already tell she would need them.

"Tommy, you're my right hand. Period." Lance focused on him. "You've been that for years. You're always there, doing what needs to be done, and it doesn't even make sense half the time. I don't deserve your loyalty and commitment. I don't deserve the love or the service. You just *give* it, as unto the Lord. And yeah, I helped bring you into the faith and discipled you, but that's been the case with many people. This is a bond that only Christ could bring about. If you were Mom's *actual* son"—he smiled a little—"you couldn't be any more my brother."

Tommy's grip on Jillian's hand tightened.

"So after all that you've been to me," Lance continued, "it tore me up to see you going through. Yes, I'd talk to you about it. Yes, I prayed. But I could see you getting swallowed by the hurt and the pain. I kept saying, 'Lord, only You can help him. Please *help* him.' And I started noticing something—the Lord using Jill in your life." He glanced at her. "I had heard about this long-ago friendship, but now I was seeing it firsthand. She could reach you in ways nobody else could. It's like the two of you have your own language."

Tommy looked over at Jillian, his eyes glistening.

"And Jill," Lance said, "I shouldn't have been surprised because you did the same for Treva. She told me about her years growing up with daily rejection and pain, when she literally had no one—except you. You could reach her when she didn't want to be reached. You and Treva . . . had your own language." His voice filled with emotion. "Your testimony is that you didn't know the Lord back then, but His hand was on you, Jill. Treva wouldn't have survived without you." He blew out a breath, swiping a tear. "And His hand has been on you in Tommy's life."

Treva moved forward, slipping tissues into each of their hands and leaving a pack on the first pew.

"I didn't want to get emotional." Lance took a moment, wiping his eyes. "Over the past year, I've prayed a lot for you both, given everything you've had to deal with individually. And more recently, I began praying that fear wouldn't rob you of experiencing oneness in Christ through marriage, if that was the Lord's will. Standing here with you now—Jill, my sister, and Tommy, my brother—minutes away from pronouncing you husband and wife . . . I can't even describe the feeling." He brought the tissue to his eyes. "I love you both, and I know the Lord is with you. And Tommy, you already know—as long as you cling . . ."

Jillian hugged Lance as the tears fell. Tommy hugged him next, lingering as they exchanged words that only the two of them heard.

"That was supposed to be short," Lance said. "So I apologize— that's all we have time for." He smiled. "Who wants to go next?" He looked at the hands. "David."

"I don't know about you two, but this is the part *I've* been waiting for." Lance smiled as he looked at them. "I now pronounce you husband and wife. Tommy, you may kiss your bride."

Jillian's heart palpitated as Tommy took her into his arms and kissed her. She held onto him, feeling the emotion as everyone cheered.

"Family," Lance said, smiling, "I now present to you, Mr. and Mrs. Thomas Everett Porter."

Cheers echoed in the chapel again, and since they were few in number, the mingling and congratulations were instantaneous.

Treva was the first to hug her sister. "I know we're not in Maryland, and this wasn't the ceremony you thought you'd have. But it couldn't have been more beautiful. I've never been so moved at a wedding."

"I cried the whole time," Jillian said. "I wish we had thought to get someone to record it."

"I thought you might want it." Reggie lifted his phone and pressed play. They could hear the portion where Pamela was speaking.

"Ahhh," Jillian said, smiling. "Thank you, Reg."

Jillian and Tommy spent a few moments with each family member, thanking them. Every one of them had spoken words of encouragement and blessing during the ceremony.

Once they were done, Jillian turned to Tommy. "We need to get out of here and get the moving underway. The ceremony went longer than we anticipated."

Tommy looked at her. "Girl, you aren't moving a thing today."

"Huh?" Jillian said. "Why would we wait? Are you saying the kids and I *aren't* staying at your house tonight? I thought we—"

"Jill," Tommy said. "You know how we labeled everything to designate what was going now and what could wait? That was for the movers."

"What movers?"

"The movers I hired," Tommy said. "I got a local company that's already on it as far as safety protocols. And Cedric said he'd oversee everything. It's probably done by now."

"I can't believe you," Jillian said.

"You actually thought you were about to change out of that jumpsuit?" Tommy said. "To lug boxes?"

"So we're heading back to your house then?" Jillian said.

Tommy took her hand and moved to where the kids were. "Listen up, guys, here's the plan. We're heading to the house. All of your boxes should be there by now. Your beds and all of that got moved too. So you can start unpacking and getting your rooms together so you can sleep comfortably tonight."

"Mom," Courtenay said, "do I really have to share a room with Sophie? Now that I'm home for the rest of the semester, that's just not gonna work."

"Agreed," Sophia said. "I won't be able to FaceTime in private."

"You two will have to make it work," Jillian said. "Everybody will be inconvenienced on some level. We're in a pandemic."

"Yeah," Faith said. "We thought we'd be out of the house by the time Tommy and Aunt Jillian got married, but it happened two months early."

"We 'bout to be *deep* over there," Reggie said. "Maybe we can get our own show, like the Walton's."

"But this plan today just isn't right," David said. "We all talked about what this wedding means to us, and there's no celebration whatsoever?"

"There will most certainly be a celebration," Tommy said. "But given the circumstances, it'll be a private one." He put an arm around Jillian. "Just the two of us."

Jillian looked at him. "What are we doing?"

"Meanwhile," Tommy said, looking at the others, "Reg, I'll give you money to order some pizzas tonight. Maybe you guys can watch movies or something."

Trevor smiled. "Yes!"

"Okay, let's start moving out." Tommy blew out the candles. "Momma Pam, Treva, do you want to take one of these bouquets to your house? Reg, you can grab the other one."

"I'd love to," Treva said.

Chatter swelled as the group of them walked out and waited for elevators.

"Hey," Jillian said, taking Tommy's hand, "we're not going home?"

"Only to pack a bag."

"To go where?"

"Patience, Mrs. Porter."

~

"I can't believe I didn't think of this." Jillian walked into the B and B with Tommy. "Like, really? It should've been my *first* thought as a place to get away."

"It was Stephanie's idea," Tommy said, locking the door. "She wanted to be a blessing after the way you blessed her with all your help."

"That's so sweet," Jillian said. "Let me see if she's in the kitchen so I can say hello."

"They're on the third floor," Tommy said. "Steph said they won't be thinking about us and for us not to think about them."

Jillian nodded with a chuckle. "I have no objections." She looked at him, still by the door. "Sooo are we going upstairs?"

"I'm following you," Tommy said. "And not because you know the way. Just because I can."

"Are you flirting with me, Mr. Porter?" Jillian headed upstairs.

"All day. 'Cause you look *good*." Tommy came behind her with the bags.

"What if I wanted to follow you?" Jillian said. "I love how you look in those jeans."

"All the things we never knew," Tommy said. "And one more thing. Steph said they won't be booking guests any time soon, and to consider the room ours whenever we want a getaway."

"Okay, wow," Jillian said. "That's an offer we won't be refusing." She paused on the second floor landing. "Which room?"

"Faithful & True," Tommy said.

Jillian opened the door, walked in, and completely stopped. "This part wasn't Stephanie," she said. "Tommy." She turned to him, speechless.

"Steph did have to light the candles," Tommy said. "I texted her when we pulled up."

Jillian continued inside, and Tommy put the bags down as she explored the room. Rose petals were everywhere—on the floor, strewn across the bed, on the nightstand, the side table, and even on the windowsill. But it wasn't the petals themselves that captured her. It was the colors—red, white, yellow, and—she picked one from the bed—"Are these *black* petals?"

"Those are black rose petals," Tommy said.

"Oh, Tommy . . . How did you even have time to think this through?"

"We couldn't travel to the University of Maryland," Tommy said, "so I brought some Maryland to you."

Jillian moved closer to the bed, where candlesticks of varying height lined the top of the headboard. Candles flickered on the nightstand and side table as well.

"It's so warm and cozy," Jillian said, checking out the fireplace, already ablaze with candles and petals on the mantel.

She saw light flickering from the bathroom and followed it. "Oh my gosh," she mumbled. The four rose petal colors had been strewn across the floor, the countertop and a whirlpool tub filled with water. Smaller candles lined the floor and countertop as well, and red, yellow, white, and black towels were stacked on a wicker basket stand.

Music filled the suite now and Tommy hugged her from behind as she took it all in. "I love what these colors represent," he said. "Four years of connection, laughter, and sharing. Four years of creating our own language. Four years of friendship." He kissed her cheek. "And somehow, in Christ, we've got all that times a thousand."

"I'll never forget this, Tommy. This is so beautiful." Jillian closed her eyes and swayed slowly with her back against him. "And I should've known you'd bring music."

"It's not a vibe without it."

"You're trying to spoil me, playing Luther first."

He nibbled her ear lobe. "You got points for keeping the jumpsuit on."

Jillian angled her head as he kissed her neck. "And how long am I supposed to keep it on?"

"Oh, it's losing its appeal real fast," he said, turning her around.

Tommy kissed her softly, then kissed her again, going deeper. Jillian wrapped her arms—

The shrill sound of a ringtone pierced through the music.

Jillian groaned. "I thought I turned it off." She resumed the kiss as it rang several times, stopped, and started up again. "I'd better get it."

She walked into the bedroom and got the phone from her bag. "Soph, is something wrong?"

"Mom, looking at the rooms today, David and Trevor's room seems a little bigger, and Courtenay and I are trying to get them to switch, but they're talking about it's too late"—

"Mom," David said, "were we not here yesterday, looking at the rooms? Courtenay and Soph got to pick the one they wanted, and they chose the lower level. Now they're trying to change it"—

"Give me my phone, David"—

"Sophia," Jillian said, "you and Courtenay got first choice, and you chose the lower level. It's done. I don't know why you're trying to switch anyway. You'll have a lot more of your coveted privacy down there."

Sophia sighed. "Fine."

"And listen, I'm silencing my phone," Jillian said. "I'm reminding you and Courtenay of what you love to remind me—you're eighteen and twenty. You can certainly handle things while I'm gone. And whatever you can't handle, Faith and Reggie are there."

"Okay, sorry, Mom," Sophia said. "I know you're lightweight on a honeymoon."

"Love you, Soph."

"Love you too, Mom."

Jillian hung up, silenced her phone, and looked at Tommy with a sigh. "Remember you said you didn't care about the kids who'd be there forever? I don't know if you fully understood."

"I have a lot to learn, for sure," Tommy said. "But I'm excited about having a house full. That's a vision I had for my life, and I'd given up hope that it would ever happen."

"Well, buckle up," Jillian said. "Because with all of us confined together for the next who-knows-how-long, it's about to be—" She paused as "Voyage to Atlantis" came on, her eyes folding to a close. "That sounds so good right now."

Tommy took her hand and led her to the middle of the bedroom floor. Enclosing her in his arms, he swayed with her to the sound of the electric guitar, and Jillian felt everything tingle inside.

"We've never danced like this," she said.

"I want to hold you every day. Just like this. To this song." Tommy spoke softly in her ear. "This moment is taking this song to a whole 'nother level for me."

"It can't go any higher." Jillian's head rested against him. "It was already your number one. But I have to say . . . This is taking it to number one for me."

Tommy pulled back just to show his surprise. "All the times you *refused* to move Luther from your number one—*and* number two —spot?"

"You know I love my Luther," Jillian said. "And you just played both of my Luther faves. But hearing this in this setting, in your arms . . . it's hitting different."

"I feel like the night is complete then." Tommy spread his hands, backing up. "I'll just take the win and—"

"Boy, get back here." Jillian pulled him close and kissed him, feeling another tingle as his arms brought her even closer.

"Wait a sec," she said.

"Really?"

"These bobby pins are driving me nuts."

Jillian reached inside the up-do and pulled out one after another as her hair tumbled down. Tommy resumed the kiss, taking it deeper as his fingers ran through her hair. Jillian let the pins fall to the floor, lost in his touch, the music, the feel of their bodies swaying to the rhythm.

"Jill."

"Mmm-hmm," she said, kissing him still.

"I am now sick of the jumpsuit."

Jillian chuckled softly. "What should we do about that?"

Tommy lifted her in his arms and laid her on a bed of petals. He joined her, taking a moment to gaze into her eyes. "Baby, I love you so much."

Jillian returned the gaze, relishing his brown eyes. "I love you too, baby."

He traced her brow with his finger. "Are you really my wife?"

She kissed him. "I am really your wife."

"I need to hear that one line again."

"What line?"

"Till death do us part."

"Till death do us part," Jillian said, entwining her fingers with his. "And we've got a bonus—the friendship is forever."

"I love that." Tommy slipped the fabric from her shoulder. "But I'm not in friendship mode tonight."

"You're not?" She kissed him, her hands engaging the muscles in his back.

"Nah. I'm in countdown mode." He found the zipper. "This jumpsuit needs to be a distant memory in 5 . . . 4 . . . 3 . . ."

CHAPTER 94

*I*n a dimly lit sanctuary Sunday morning, Tommy stood on a riser checking the camera setup with its associated cables, making sure it was ready for the livestream. They typically had cameras filming the sermon from multiple angles, the footage then edited and uploaded to YouTube. Today they'd have one camera hitting Lance straight on.

They'd had several meetings throughout the week, a designated team weighing how the service would proceed. Given St. Louis's mandates as well as rapidly shifting warnings and protocols, they'd decided to pare down to bare essentials. This meant, though they were divided, that they wouldn't include the praise team, at least for now. It also meant that Tommy would become central to the media team. He'd always had a hand in tech and media matters at the church, given his experience with live broadcasts through the years. But now, given the shutdown, his responsibilities had shifted. He would oversee the broadcast of Living Word's service each week.

Tommy headed back to the media room. *Lord, You know we didn't have much time to prepare for today. But thank You that the power is not in the setup. It's in Your word that goes forth. I pray Lance ministers with power from on high and reaches people who have never heard the gospel preached.*

He opened the livestream software on the computer and double-checked the settings, then took a look at the interface because if they had any issues with sound—

"Hey, you're here?" Lance said, walking in. "I feel bad that you had to come in, man, not even twenty-four hours into your honeymoon."

"It is what it is," Tommy said. "This is far from a typical Sunday. Anyway, I had to be here. You don't know what you're doing."

"Solomon is coming, though, right?" Lance said.

"Yeah, but he's never done a livestream," Tommy said. "Remember we did a handful of these at Living Hope?"

"We sure did," Lance said. "And you handled the tech side."

Tommy double-checked the interface. "Solomon should be here shortly. We need to do a quick run through with you and check sound, lighting, positioning of the podium, all that. Remember— you've got one camera. You can't be all over the platform."

Lance nodded, looking through the media room window into the sanctuary. "We've never been here, Tommy. The sanctuary could be empty for weeks, maybe months. Whole city on lockdown starting tomorrow, except for essential services."

"And you'll be right here, God willing," Tommy said, "preaching this word every week, faithful to your calling."

"No," Lance said. "*We'll* be right here." He turned and looked at him. "I thank God we can ride this out together."

Tommy nodded. "Always, man."

Lance checked a notification on his phone. "Mom says—'I want to pray with my sons before you all go live. Call and put me on speaker.'"

"She's got a whole new prayer ministry," Tommy said. "Everybody who watches the broadcast will be covered." He took a seat. "You might as well call now while we've got a minute. Don't be leaving Mom waiting."

"Oh, now it's just straight 'Mom'?" Lance said. "You make the call then."

Tommy smiled, taking out his phone. "I got her on speed dial."

READING GROUP GUIDE

1. In Lance's cling sermon, he spoke to the tendency to view romantic relationships as the "ultimate situation" in life. He said there is no "ultimate situation" apart from Christ, and that Jesus *is* our ultimate situation. Whether you're single or married, do you view your relationship with Christ as your ultimate situation? If not, how could you begin to see your relationship with Jesus as the ultimate relationship in your life? What does it look like when you view Jesus as your ultimate situation?

2. Lindell said that intimacy with God wasn't something he'd thought about. Stephanie said it sounds good in theory, but do you ever really get there? Do you long for intimacy with God? Do you take steps toward a lifestyle of intimacy with God? If so, what does that look like in your life?

3. In John 15:14, Jesus said, "You are My friends if you do what I command you." In the first cling challenge, Tommy became more intentional about talking to Jesus like a friend. Also, he asked Jesus to redeem those moments when he's alone, so that he could spend more of them talking to Jesus. We saw other characters talking to the Lord as well. What

about you? Do you talk to Jesus as a friend? Do you share your day with Him—your reactions, emotions, questions, concerns, and joys? How do you build that friendship?

4. At one point, Stephanie was on fire for God and believing His promises, so much so that she helped her sister-in-law Kelli believe. But over time, the trials of life caused her faith to waver, especially in believing that all things are possible with God. Have you had seasons in which your level of faith was higher than in others? Have you had particularly hard seasons that caused you to doubt God's promises? How did you respond? Did you run to the Lord and His word to build your faith back up? Did you cry out for the Lord to increase your faith and help your unbelief?

5. Tommy said that people act as if marriage is the default status in the kingdom, as if something is wrong if you're not aiming for it. Likewise, when Trey expressed to his mother that marriage wasn't for him, she told him he would grow out of it. In your own circles, do you think singleness is viewed as the "second-class" status in the kingdom? Do you view singleness as a worthy calling? If you are in a season of singleness, do you embrace the truth of the Scriptures, that this is a time in which you can be specially devoted to the Lord? (1 Corinthians 7)

6. Pamela was a prayer warrior, but she couldn't see that she'd allowed fear to govern in certain areas of her life. Is fear an issue in any area of your life? Have you been seeking the Lord about it? As they did in the Cling study, are you willing to deal with it, no matter how hard it may be? Talk about how you can cling to the Lord and His word with respect to your fear(s), so you can be free of it.

7. In the Cling study, Tommy said our relationship with God can't thrive if it's one-sided—that is, if He knows us intimately but we don't know much about Him. He spoke of the importance of knowing God through His word, so we can cling to Him more tightly. Do you spend time getting to

know the Lord through His word? Do you look forward to that time with Him?

8. Jesse spoke of experiencing the sweetness of the Lord's presence as he woke up earlier to spend time with Him. He called it *"our* time" and said he puts his phone away. He also said the Lord speaks to him in a special way during that time. Do you delight in the Lord and His presence? Do you block out time such that it belongs to you and Jesus alone? How have you seen the Lord respond as you delight in Him in this way?

9. Stephanie and Jillian put everything on the altar in prayer, desiring to cling to God and His will alone. Are you willing to pray such a prayer? Do you trust God enough to cling to Him and surrender your will? If you're not quite there, are you willing to pray for grace to get there?

10. Jesus tells us that we will have tribulation in this world (John 16:33). James tells us that we will encounter trials (James 1:2-3). Tommy endured one of the most difficult trials of his life, but he learned this: *"I can overcome, be perfected from, all the trials that come, You can help me run—as long as I cling."* Have you learned to cling to God in the trials of life? Have you seen His faithfulness in helping you to run? Share your testimony of how clinging to the Lord helped you overcome a particular trial or hardship.

ABOUT THE AUTHOR

KIM CASH TATE is the author of several books, including *Cling: Choosing a Lifestyle of Intimacy with God* and the *Promises of God* series. She has created and written a scripted web series called *Cling The Series*, in which she played a leading role. In addition, Kim wrote and performed the songs on the *Cling Soundtrack (Seasons 1 & 2)*. One of those songs, "If I Didn't Have You," spent more than 30 weeks on the Billboard Gospel charts. She and her husband Bill have two young adult children.

Connect with Kim:

YouTube.com/kimcashtate
Instagram.com/kimcashtate
Facebook.com/kimcashtate
Twitter.com/kimcashtate
kimcashtate.com

Made in the USA
Middletown, DE
25 April 2021